# Shining Through

# Magic Hour

*BY THE SAME AUTHOR*

*Novels*

Compromising Positions

Close Relations

Almost Paradise

*Screenplays*

Compromising Positions

Hello Again

# Shining Through

# Magic Hour

---

Susan Isaacs

Diamond Books
An Imprint of HarperCollins*Publishers*
77–85 Fulham Palace Road,
Hammersmith, London W6 8JB

This Diamond Books Omnibus edition first published 1994



ISBN 0261 66273 2
Printed and bound in Great Britain by
BPC Hazell Books Ltd
A member of
The British Printing Company Ltd

# *Shining Through*

In memory of Gloria Safier
She *lived*.

# *Acknowledgments*

I sought help from the people listed below; they gave it freely and cheerfully. I appreciate their generosity:

Arnold Abramowitz, Consuelo Saah Baehr, Jonathan Dolger, Sheldon Elsen, Janet and Robert Fiske, Phyllis and Milton Freeman, Helen Isaacs, Inga Joseph, Rita Kashner, T. Barry Kingham, Edith and Herbert Mendelsohn, Otto Obermaier, Frank Perry, Mary Rooney, Angelica Rosa, Cynthia Scott, Jeff Stolow, Hilma Wolitzer, Hon. Inzer B. Wyatt, Susan Zises, and the staff of the Port Washington (New York) Public Library.

My assistant, AnneMarie Palmer, deserves commendation not only for her loyalty and good humor but also for the formidable amount of work she did. Tim Guzley was a great help with research and translations.

Owen Laster more than lived up to his celebrated reputation. He is a talented agent, and a wise, congenial and kind man as well.

Larry Ashmead, my editor, offered me reassurance, guidance, sound criticism and a lot of great jokes. As usual, he was wonderful.

In addition to their warmth and support, my children, Andrew and Betsy Abramowitz, gave me valuable editorial comments. They also, on occasion, pulled me away from my word processor. I thank them for their impatience, as well as for their patience, their love and the pleasure of their company.

And after four novels, two screenplays and twenty years of marriage, Elkan Abramowitz continues to hold on to his title: Best Person in the World.

# *Chapter One*

In 1940, when I was thirty-one and an old maid, while the whole world waited for war, I fell in love with John Berringer.

An office crush. Big deal. Since the invention of the steno pad, a day hasn't gone by without some secretary glancing up from her Pitman squiggles and suddenly realizing that the man who was mumbling '. . . and therefore, pursuant to the above . . .' was the one man in her life who could ever bring her joy.

So there I was, a cliché with a number 2 yellow pencil: a working girl from Queens who'd lost her heart to the pride of the Ivy League.

And to make matters worse, John Berringer bore absolutely no resemblance to the typical Wall Street international lawyer, the kind whose gray face was two shades paler than his suit. Sure, a girl could wind up losing her heart to one of those dreary men. There's nothing quieter than an old maid's bedroom, and in that black stiffness it's so easy to create magic: A lawyer, with the profile of a toad – Abracadabra! – is transformed into an Adonis, pulsating with passion under his pinstripes.

But John didn't need any of that midnight magic to turn him gorgeous. The big joke in the law firm was how could I *not* have a mad crush on him. 'You've got to be made of iron, Linda,' one of the girls said at lunch, 'not to go nuts for those blue eyes. They're blue like—' Someone at the far end of the table called out, Twilight! And someone else chimed in, No, like a clear lake . . . but with a funny kind of depth, like on a cloudy day. John Berringer made poets out of stenographers. Someone else piped up, Come *on* . . . blue like pansies, and Gladys Slade, my best friend, called out from the head of the lunch table, 'How can anybody even *think* of the word "pansy" in the same sentence with "Mr Berringer" in it?" Everyone giggled.

In private, Gladys said, 'Listen, Linda, don't kid a kidder. I'm the first person to understand your not wanting to make a public announcement, but even if you didn't care about looks, think about brains. I mean, you're always reading the papers and wanting to talk about – oh, God, you know – English naval power. Or French politics. So aren't you attracted to someone brilliant like him? I bet he loves all that boring stuff.'

'It's not boring. Three quarters of the world is—'

'He's *so* charming,' she cut me off. 'Like a blond Cary Grant.'

'Gladys,' I explained, 'when you sit across the desk from this guy day in and day out, you realize he's *always* charming. It kind of wafts up from him, like B.O. Don't you get it? It doesn't mean anything. And his looks . . . Yeah, he's handsome, but what's behind it?'

'That's for you to find out,' Gladys ho-ho-hoed.

'I've got to tell you,' I said, 'there's something deep-down unappealing about a man who knows he's stunning and uses it. You know, like it's six-fifteen and you're so tired all you want is to suck your thumb, but he has forty-seven letters he still wants to dictate. So he flashes that five-thousand-watt smile and that's supposed to brighten up your life and make you want to go on. But see, a guy who pulls that sort of thing isn't . . .'

'Isn't what?'

'Isn't masculine.'

'Oh, come off it!'

'I'm serious, Gladys. And he's *much* too blond. Girls are fair. Guys should be dark. And with those big blue eyes. It's like some artist made him up to illustrate "Cinderella." Can't you just see him, with green stockings and those bubble shorts, holding a glass slipper?'

'I can see him *with* green stockings . . . and *without* green stockings.' This was a very racy remark from Gladys, whose idea of wild sex was Fred Astaire loosening his tie.

'He's Prince Charming,' I said. 'Who needs it? I've got to stay late when he asks me, even if he looked like a pile of you-know-what. It's my job. But he thinks: Ha! I've charmed her. I've got her where I've got *all* the girls, in the palm of my hand.' I looked Gladys straight in the eye. 'You know why he doesn't do a thing for me? Because he's a woman's man. Not a real man.'

Naturally, I was lying through my teeth. But I kept my secret love a secret. I would not let myself (as his secretary) be honorary president of the John Berringer Fan Club. What I felt for John wasn't meant to be shared with the girls. It was precious, and different.

Because even way back then, I felt *I* was different.

But was I (am I?) really different in any way from all the women from Brooklyn and Queens and the Bronx who trekked up the stairs from the subway every morning and got lost in the dark canyons, the gloomy buildings that loomed over Wall Street? Well, I'm not in Queens anymore. I'm certainly not a secretary. I'm not the girl I was.

But how did I get all the way here from there?

Because when America finally did go to war, the other subway secretaries fought Hitler by saving their bacon grease in tin cans and putting makeup on their legs instead of silk stockings. My fight, though, was different – perilous, real. I wound up in the middle of the Nazi hellhole. Me, Linda Voss.

So what I did during the war: Was it my fate? Was it courage? Or was it inevitable? Did I finally realize that all those people in Europe could be me, so that I *had* to be responsible? Or did I just take so many small, stupid steps that I slipped over the edge, into an abyss where I had to either do – or die? Would any girl in my shoes have done the same?

Now they say I'm a hero. But who are the heroes, anyway? The brave? Or the terrified ordinary?

I still don't know. The only thing I do know is that when I start going over all that happened, the first thing that pops into my mind is not one of those major moments, which proves: Hey, that Linda! *So* special. I had more than enough of those major moments. If you saw them on a movie poster – PASSION! BETRAYAL! WAR!

DEATH! LOVE! – you'd assume you were getting one hell of a double feature.

But when I look back, it's funny: What I remember first is just a regular day – the last before my life slowly began to change.

At home that morning, I put the old, dented coffeepot on to perk and looked out the window. Nothing unusual: a dull white January sky, like a bleached-out sheet. The attached houses of Ridgewood, six in a row, were as lifeless as cardboard cutouts: no hyacinths popping up, no maple trees turning red, no kids on roller skates. My down-the-street neighbor's cocker spaniel, Champ, came and did his business on a Christmas tree that had ben lying on the curb all week; then he trotted off, leaving drippy tinsel and a yellow stain on the dingy snow.

At work, the view of Manhattan from the forty-sixth floor wasn't what you'd call thrilling, either: not at all that exquisite jagged line of skyscrapers you see in those turn-me-upside-down-and-I-snow paperweights. I glanced out at the narrow streets and overpowering buildings. New York looked gray, tired of itself.

In the office, the radiator clanged, reheating the air it had already overheated. My face flushed hot and red. My lips were so chapped it would have hurt if I smiled. And my sweater had fuzz balls.

But who cared? John Berringer, the man I loved, was there. He sat at his desk. Naturally, he didn't bother to look up.

'Are you positive you gave me the Kunstadt contracts?' he asked. I stood up, put down my pad and pencil, walked around his desk and stood by his chair. His hair gleamed gold and soft under the light of his desk lamp. I imagined touching it.

Was this one of those magic moments they're always singing about on the radio? Did I somehow *know?* No. But still, looking back, that ordinary day in January 1940 is lit so brightly that I can see everything about it: even the streaks of bronze and platinum that shot through John's beautiful fair hair.

'The contracts are right here, Mr Berringer.' I tapped the pile of papers with my finger, and it slid back the quarter inch into his line of vision.

'Oh. Thanks.' He paused, then looked up and smiled. 'What would I do without you?' Probably get up, go to the men's room, then come back, pick up the telephone and call the employment agency for another bilingual secretary. 'You're the best there is, Miss Voss. You know that, don't you?'

I thought to myself: This guy is so full of it that it pours out in an endless, effortless stream. I knew that what he was saying meant absolutely nothing to him. But guess what? I still believed it.

He picked up the contracts and, of course, forgot me. That was the end of my excuse to stand close to him. I went back to my seat and picked up my pad.

I can see myself sitting there, like in a spotlight. Pretty. Really pretty of you bothered to look close, but if you didn't – a secretary.

But in one way maybe I actually was different: I wasn't just some girl worshiping her boss from afar, cherishing the very impossibleness of her dream. See, I was a true democrat; I honestly felt I deserved John.

He may have known the difference between an ode and a sonnet, but I had no doubt, even then, that I was as good as he was. If it hadn't been for a few twists of fate, you could have seen our engagement announcement and my picture (with pearls) in the *New York Times*. And the reason you didn't was just a few not-so-giant twists.

Twist one: John's father's family had made it out of Germany three or four generations before my father's family did. And so the Berringers had plenty of time to drop their lederhosen and lose their accents. To become real Americans.

Twist two: John Berringer did not seem to know I was alive. Well, in a way he did. I mean, he wouldn't have allowed a dead secretary to hang around his office. But although he was always charming – with the wide smile that showed both rows of teeth (perfect and white, but with one slightly crooked front tooth, to prove he was human, flawed) and the wink that said: This is our private joke, Linda – what he offered me was really no more than he gave the bookkeeper or the shoeshine boy: reflexive enchantment. I wasn't really real to him in the way, say, lawyers were; I was less than a person but more than a typewriter.

And I don't know if this was a twist or not, but John was all that Americans are supposed to be (Protestant), and I was only half. My mother's family, the Johnstons, had been Americans – Brooklyn-Americans – for a hundred and fifty years. But my other half happened to be Jewish. Granted, John didn't seem like the prejudiced type, but how many people are there in the world who jump for joy over a Jew? Not that he, or anyone else in the office, knew. I wasn't an idiot. Wall Street law firms didn't hire Jewish secretaries (to say nothing of lawyers), so since I didn't look it, why volunteer? Besides, no one in my family had anything at all to do with being Jewish. So the couple of times people said, Um, what kind of a name is Voss? I'd look them right in the eye and tell them the truth: It's German. Well, it was.

Oh, and finally, twist three or four (depending on how you count): There was a Mrs John Berringer.

But still, I knew I deserved him.

If I'd gone to college, we could have had brilliant conversations.

If my great-great-grandfather Ludwig – or whatever his name was – had come to Manhattan around 1800 instead of hanging around a Berlin butcher shop flicking chickens, John would be getting me my coat instead of vice versa.

If only John knew what I really was inside, he would love me. I was positive. He would want to kiss me exactly the way I wanted to be kissed. He would get up, walk around to my chair, pull me up and hold me so tight against him that I would feel the itch of his worsted trousers through my skirt. Oh, Linda, he'd practically moan, and before I had time to say, Mr Berringer! and try to push him away so he wouldn't think I was cheap, his hands would be all over my—

Enough! I fought to keep those thoughts out of the office.

I was almost always hysterically busy, and I couldn't allow myself to do what I really wanted to do: retreat into a world without houses or trees, without anything except me and John, a world of desire. But to tell the truth, taking dictation in two languages, typing and filing tons of paper kept me from creating ten thousand different sizzling scenes of our coming together. When you've got an inch-thick contract to type in German, and it's seven o'clock at night and your boss wants it by seven-thirty, it doesn't help to imagine his muscular, hairy thigh rubbing between yours. For real lust, you need leisure.

And another thing. I was usually too nervous around John to relax enough to let those thoughts rise up: nervous just being so near to him, nervous that I'd make some stupid slip of the tongue that would let him know the score. I could actually goof and call him John. Oh, God, less than a month before, I was saying, I want to wish you a Merry Christmas, Mr Berringer, and I couldn't believe it, but I almost said, I want to kiss you a Merry Christmas. Every time I thought of that I got the shivers.

He said, 'I want those letters to Frankfurt to get out today. I know it's asking a lot . . .'

'Oh, it's no problem, Mr Berringer.'

He started to dictate again. His hands, holding the contract, shone in the circle of light made by the fancy modern desk lamp his wife had picked out. The lamp was long and skinny, like Alice in Wonderland's neck, but with a bulb instead of a head at the end.

I sat up straighter. If nervousness wasn't enough to keep steamy thoughts away, his cold, modern office could; it was the talk of the law firm. But because of who his wife was, the talk was very respectful: Oh, what sublime taste! She'd picked out everything for him. Black furniture so shiny, every time you lifted a pencil it looked as though another hand, trapped inside the desk, was doing the same thing. Ultra-ultramodern design. His carpet and chairs were somewhere between brown and gray, the color of new sidewalks. The walls were such a bright white that even if you worked forty-eight hours straight, you couldn't doze off.

Like the office she'd designed, Nan Berringer had no soft edges: no lace around her neck. I'd only seen her twice, but both times she'd worn those severely plain, fantastically expensive dresses classy fashion magazines call simple. But if that makes her sound hard, she wasn't. Even if you're like Nan, aristocratic and intellectual, it's hard to be hard at twenty-one. And besides, she was terrific-looking.

John stopped dictating and cleared his throat. 'I have to be away from the office this afternoon. And probably tomorrow as well.'

He sounded a little stiff, but that was because he was still talking German; sometimes when he finished dictating in it, he'd forget he was still speaking it. 'I hope you will have time to finish all the work I have given you.' Was his accent great! Before law school he'd spent three years at the universities in Cologne and Heidelberg. He spoke the language as if he'd been fraternity brothers with Goethe.

My accent was nowhere near so hotsy-totsy. It was pure *berlinerisch*, courtesy of my grandmother. People always say that *berlinerisch* is to German what cockney is to English. For all I know, they could be right; I never met a cockney. 'Is there anything special you'd like me to do?'

'No. Nothing special,' John answered. What did I expect him to say? Take off your clothes? 'I know I've given you too much.' When he smiled his eyes crinkled, so you couldn't see their glorious dark blue, but the smile made his face glow; it made you feel you had your own sun to warm you.

I popped back into English, where I sounded as well-bred as I had in German (that is to say, as far from being a Vanderbilt as a human being can get), but in which I felt much more comfortable. 'Really, that's okay, Mr Berringer. I'll try to get everything done by the end of the week.'

Fat chance. We'd stopped being swamped six months earlier. Now we were drowning. The great thing about being one of the top Wall Street firms is you have the top clients: the biggest corporations and banks in the world. The bad thing is that before they pay you, you have to do work for them. Since John's work was representing their interests in Europe, they all wanted ninety-seven times more work done than had ever been done before in the course of legal history.

Half of them said, Get us (and our holdings) out of Germany. Now. The other half said, Hey, look at what those Nazis are spending! It costs a fortune to conquer Europe. Get us a piece of it. Now.

'It would be great if you could catch up,' he said in English. 'Oh, I forgot. Mr Leland wants to borrow you this afternoon. He has a letter to go to Germany. Very simple. You can translate it yourself and send it off. Could you fit that in – without hating me forever?'

'Yes, Mr Berringer.'

'And still be caught up by Friday?'

'Sure.'

'Wonderful!' He looked up at me. 'Miss Voss . . .'

He stopped for a second, maybe to think what else he wanted. I didn't care. I'd wait. While his mind was someplace else, I could study him. His mouth was open, just a little. What a mouth! Beautiful, not one of those thin, mean men's mouths that look like an appendix scar. Full, but not too full. He'd be on top of me, roughing up my face with his, but then he'd bring his mouth over mine and—

'Miss Voss.'

'Yes, sir?'

'Thanks. You can go back to your desk now.'

My dream world was like all those European countries in the papers: Poland, Czechoslovakia, Albania. One minute beautiful. The next, destroyed.

Listen, the Voice of Reason would probably butt in here, what you're talking about isn't love. It's a crush: a common enough occurrence, *n'est-ce pas?* (The Voice of Reason sounds a lot like the executive secretaries, Vassar girls who work for the senior partners.) A working girl from Ridgewood, Queens . . . bright enough for what she is, but a suitable match for John Berringer, Esq., *magna cum laude*, Columbia College, editor in chief of the *Columbia Law Review?* How *marrrvelously* droll. (You get stuck in a booth in the ladies' room a few times when the Vassar girls come in to powder their noses and you get to be an expert on how Voices of Reason talk.) *Delightfully* piquant. And a trifle touching too, this secretary's dreams of 'love' with a married man.

Well, it may have been droll, but as I said to myself, over and over: Hey, this is love! Although not at first sight. I'd seen him for nearly ten years in the firm's international department, from the time he was out of law school.

We'd talked about John even then. He was ridiculously handsome, I told the girls, like a young movie star playing the Big Man on Campus role in one of those *Cubby Cooper Goes to College*-type movies. He was meant to be fifteen feet tall and black-and-white; he was too good to be real. I remember he'd worn white shirts so starched they could carry a life of their own. He'd shared a secretary with three of the other young lawyers. When he had to write a letter in German, he dictated it to himself.

Way back then, I was twenty-one years old and a secretary to one of the middle-level partners, P. Louis Tracy. You'd think there was something a little wrong with a guy who answers his phone, 'Good ahfternoon. P. Louis Tracy.' There was: not his head, though; his heart. Nine years later, on the Fourth of July, 1939, P. Louis Tracy joined his wife at the bar of their country club after playing eighteen holes and dropped dead over his Rob Roy.

Even before P. Louis Tracy played his last hole, John had been made a partner – the only other member of the firm really fluent in German. Back then, the fact that he was about thirty times smarter than P. Lou hadn't been a secret around Blair, VanderGraff and Wadley. But since, despite his brains, he was also about thirty years younger, he hadn't been considered one of the important international partners. But suddenly he was; less than a week after July 4, John inherited P. Lou's office, cases, percentage of the profits – and me.

At first I looked at John and thought: Another pretty face. In fact, the prettiest. I can live with that. It definitely beats working for a guy with four chins. Okay, he dictates like a snail, but at least he gets it right – doesn't make me retype fifty thousand times. John Berringer was going to be a good boss. But fall for him? Not me. Even though he was supposed to have a brilliant legal mind, all I could see was the gleam of the surface: eyes, hair, teeth. John shone – for everybody: Hello. You're wonderful. I'm gorgeous. Life is grand.

But late one January afternoon, when the sky outside looked like a thick blackvelvet ribbon, I glanced across his desk and realized he was *beautiful*. Deep-down beautiful – and more.

Let's face it. He was hot. Beneath his gloss, under his charm, he had it. *It*. John Berringer was one of those men on fire. It took a while for me to feel that heat beneath the cool, impersonal brightness. But that afternoon, just watching his thumb flick the pages of a memorandum of law (dumb, but true), I suddenly *knew*.

Unfortunately, from the way he flew out of the office the second he finished work, it was obvious Mrs John Berringer knew too. Knew, and was waiting, because she loved everything he had to offer.

On the last normal day, Hitler sent endless cables to his generals, Mussolini had several recorded temper tantrums, Neville Chamberlain took a long, silent walk, and the secretaries of Blair, Vander-Graff and Wadley ate lunch. After all, this was America.

Like just about every other day, the partners strolled out to their clubs around twelve-thirty. At twelve-forty, making sure the elevators had time to empty out so the partners couldn't see their stampede, the young lawyers – the associates – made a mad dash for their restaurants. Five minutes later, the Vassar girls tippytoed off to their tearoom, where they met other Vassar girls from other law firms, probably to talk about what they were always talking about, like what Schubert had been played at last night's symphony concert and who the *really* top-drawer Princeton men were.

Exactly two second after they left, the regular secretaries raced to the conference room – ten or twelve of us, with lunch bags, at that giant rectangular table in that giant wood-paneled room. It was like eating inside a mahogany tree. Suddenly it was as if somebody yelled, *On your mark . . . Get set . . .* But instead of a gunshot, one enormous crinkle – the noise of ten or twelve sandwiches being ripped out of waxed paper.

'Why I even bother to mention this, girls, is beyond me,' Gladys Slade began, her voice slightly muffled by Spam on white, 'but Mrs Avenel called *four* times this morning!' Gladys put on her haughty, high-class voice: ' "Gladys, my deah, *do* hate to disturb you, but *would* you get my husband on the line for one *tiny* second." ' Gladys shook her head. 'She probably wanted his permission to flush.' Her boss's wife called at least ten times a day. We nodded in sympathy because our mouths were full, and huddled in our sweaters.

It was always cold in the room. We had to keep the windows open so the lawyers wouldn't sniff out secretary-lunch smells and know we were eating in there.

Gladys was Queen of Lunch. Better, actually. Gladys Slade – with beginning-to-gray brown hair cut into what was meant to be a neat Dutchboy but frizzed into crazed curlicues when the humidity was more than five per cent, with hazel eyes a little too small and a little too close together – looked absolutely ordinary. Well, except for her nostrils: They were so immense she could have hidden two salamis up her nose. But she was a born leader.

Her being forty didn't hurt, either. Gladys had been at the law firm longer than any other secretary, twenty-two years, and no one knew more about what was going on at Blair, VanderGraff and Wadley than she did. Someone – Shakespeare, George Washington – once said, Knowledge is power. She'd seen it all: Mr Blair becoming under secretary of the Treasury, Mr VanderGraff going bald, Mr Wadley dying of a stroke while waiting for the elevator. She hadn't actually seen him die – no one had – but she was one of the first afterward, while he was still purple. Gladys knew everything. And not just the big stuff. She knew who was doing what to whom, and probably how, when and where, but Gladys being Gladys, she never let on about the really sizzling stuff. She probably tuned it out; all Gladys thought about were clothes and hairdos and innuendos, not bodies. For her, life did not actually exist below the neck or under the vest.

But for good old-style gossip, she was better than anyone. My dears, she would begin, like we were whispering in a corner at a society cocktail party, did I tell you who the widow Carpenter brought with her to the reading of the late Mister's will? Her 'financial adviser'! With a pompadour! I thought Mr Avenel would have a stroke, because she insisted . . .

Since I was Gladys's closest friend, she turned to me first. 'What about Mr B, Linda?' It was just a regular lunch question. No one in the office, including Gladys, had a clue about what I felt for John. 'Anything new?'

'Who has time for anything new?' I answered. 'We're going crazy trying to keep up with Europe.'

'What's with Europe?' Wilma Gerhardt called from down the table. Her voice was so horribly nasal that every time she opened her mouth it was like listening to a bad vaudevillian attempting a Brooklyn accent. God knows no one else from that borough ever made you cringe like that at the wrongness of the sound, worse than the *eeeeek* of chalk on a blackboard. But she was saved from total awfulness by a single grace: her looks. Wilma was a knockout. 'You going to Gay Paree or something, Linda?' She patted her dazzling dark hair; she was the only girl in the office who wore an upsweep every single day. Luckily for her, she had plenty of time for hairdos. Her typewriter was untouched by human hands.

'What's with Europe?' I repeated. I had to lean past Helen Rogers – who as usual was dribbling onto the shelf made by her bust (this time the shelf was dotted with little yellow dabs of egg salad) – and past Anita Beane, who was nineteen, dewy and engaged. 'Wilma, you ever read a newspaper?'

Gladys interrupted: 'Linda, you're not going to give us your Growing Nazi Shadow speech, are you?'

'I'm just asking Wilma a simple question.'

Wilma gave me a simple answer. 'Why should I read a newspaper? The ink gets all over your hands!' For a second, Wilma was so thrilled by her brilliant, witty comeback that she forgot she was with the girls and actually broke into an acutely adorable giggle. It was a technique, like her eyelash-battering, she wouldn't ordinarily have wasted on women. She saved her talents for men, and they were talents not sneezed at; they'd helped her get her a job eight or nine years earlier, in the pit of the depression, while lots of inky-fingered readers of the *New York Times* and the *Herald Tribune* were stretching their hands high above their heads and taking swan dives off skyscrapers.

'Haven't you ever heard of Adolf Hitler?' I demanded.

'So is Mr Berringer dictating letters to him?' Under the Brooklyn accent, her voice had a nasty edge. She could be tolerant of homely girls like Rose Guthrie in Trusts and Estates, who looked like Winston Churchill (or, more accurately, Winston Churchill's bulldog), but anyone who had a chance of attracting a man's attention – like me – was a threat.

I'd always been intrigued by Wilma. Her entire life was dedicated to men and to getting them. She made no pretense that she cared about who the mayor was, or what Gladys thought of *Gone With the Wind*. She never looked beyond her own cleavage. Did she choose to be that way? Or did it come naturally? Was her selfishness just self-protection, a by-product of hard times?

Sometimes I wished I could be like her, absolutely contentedly selfish, not having to smile, not being forced to listen to Helen Rogers go into her umpteenth recounting of her Uncle Gus's brother-in-law's funeral, where they'd botched up the makeup on the late lamented, and it formed globules under the heat of the lights, so it looked as if the guy in the satin-lined box was sweating. Helen would recount: 'His wife *screamed*, "Mickey! Mickey! You're hot!"And they had to grab her because she fished out her hankie and was going to—'

Wilma had turned to Helen one day and snapped, mean and hard, 'Hey, shut up with that vomity funeral crap, would ya?' And Helen had. What would it feel like, being free to say something like that?

Gladys's theory was that Wilma could say anything she wanted to; all she had to do was show up at the office. Her job, her life, would always be safe. Why? Because she had someone to protect her. See, she and her boss were friendly.

I agreed. Very friendly. Only for a very special kind of friend would an influential partner in a major law firm sneak in early in the morning to do his own typing. (Helen had once come in early and caught him typing a letter on the firm letterhead with two fingers, *very* slowly.) You got to figure, I'd told Gladys, that Mr Post was catching the 5:37 A.M. from Garden City just to catch up on his correspondence. He was no spring chicken, either. Another few months of the ebony-haired Wilma by night and the 5:37 by day, and we'd be chipping in for a wreath and writing letters: Dear

Mrs Post, I'm only a secretary at Blair, VanderGraff, but I was so sorry to hear about Mr Post's sudden demise. His late hours were a measure of his devotion . . .'

'What does Mr Berringer write?' Wilma kept going. ' "Dear Adolf: How are you? I am fine." '

She would have babbled on, but Gladys turned to her: 'Can it, Wilma.'

That's all Gladys said, but it worked. Even Wilma showed deference to Gladys. She mumbled, 'You can it,' but it wasn't a challenge; her words had no heart. She just took a vicious bite of what actually looked like a steak sandwich (old Mr Post kept her in protein) and chewed ostentatiously, as if to say, *I* got something to bite into, not like you girls with your crappy cream cheese.

Gladys turned back to me. 'Anything new?' she asked once more. 'I am *desperate* for gossip, Linda.'

'Well, nothing scintillating,' I began. 'Mrs Berringer called late yesterday. Didn't even want to speak to him. Just left a message that she was having cocktails with her museum committee and wouldn't be home for supper.'

'Dinner, Linda,' Gladys corrected. 'Where's your class? Ditch-diggers eat supper. Attorneys dine.'

'Okay, she wouldn't be home to dine.'

Very daintily, Helen Rogers picked her egg salad droppings off her bosom as she asked, 'You think the lovebirds had a fight? Her just leaving messages, I mean.'

'All married couples fight,' Gladys pronounced.

I noticed Anita Beane flashing a fast look down the table to Fay Landon. They were the only engaged girls, and the look said, Would you listen to these old maids pretending to be marriage experts? But naturally, being nineteen and twenty-one and not complete fools, they didn't challenge Gladys. What did they have to gain? By June, they'd be married, and free from Blair, VanderGraff forever.

'Mrs Berringer went to Smith College. Right, Linda?' Gladys asked me. I nodded and took a bite of my meat loaf sandwich, which would more accurately be described as a bread-crumb loaf sandwich, the price of meat being what it was. 'Smith College sounds *so* average,' Gladys explained to the group, 'but it's *the* poshest. Every year, they have one or two graduates who become duchesses or . . . earl's wives or . . . Anyway, it's *much* better than Vassar. Now describe Mrs Berringer, Linda.' Gladys was bossy, but she was fun. Well, not a bundle of laughs herself, but at least she was able to find fun for us – in the lives of lawyers. 'Every single miniscule detail,' she added. 'Give us the works.'

Everyone leaned forward. There were a lot of reasons why everyone in the room was interested – no, fascinated – with Mrs John Berringer.

All that attention on me – and on that tender topic – made me a little nervous. I had to put my sandwich down; I was squeezing it so hard, pretty soon I'd have a fistful of mush. Questions would arise: What's with Linda? She was talking about Mr Berringer and she squished her sandwich . . . Oh!

'You girls know what I know,' I said, fast. 'And what I know is that Mrs B must really be something. Mr Berringer would do *anything* to make her happy.' Everyone nodded. They loved it. 'He spent *six hundred dollars* on some oil painting she fell in love with at an art gallery. He gave me a certified check, sent me over to this art gallery, to some skinny guy with one of those nipped-in-waist suits, and the guy there says, "Oh, for Mrs Berringer. So young, but such a discerning eye." '

When I went to the gallery that day, all I could think was John was buying her a birthday present that cost half what I earned every year. And he was taking her to dinner besides. I knew; I'd made the reservations.

Helen Rogers said, 'Six hundred dollars for a picture! Can you beat that?'

'For *art*,' I said.

'Was it pretty?'

'How should I know?' I answered. 'Did I go to Smith College? It was modern. Mostly red squiggles with a little black – like old chopped meat.'

'Linda,' Gladys said, 'at least *pretend* you have some taste.'

'For that much money I'd get emerald earrings,' Wilma said. She massaged the lobe of her ear. I had a feeling Mr Post was going to buy her a present in the near future. 'Not the dangle kind. You can't wear those during the day. Just give me big, fat emeralds that go right smack on your ear.'

'I'd take a mouton jacket,' someone else called out. 'And with the change . . .'

Anita Beane twisted her engagement ring round and round and said, 'I'd buy a house for me and Herbie.'

'I hate to say it, Anita,' Gladys said, 'but you can't buy a house for six hundred dollars.' She was tired of hearing about Herbie, who worked as an assistant in a beauty parlour in Washington Heights and had another year to go before he could be called Mr Herbert. 'You'll have to move in with his parents. But you'll save up.'

Then Gladys opened her thermos of coffee with the pads of her fingers. It was the ladylike way, but there'd also been an article – 'How to Avoid Nail Tragedy' – in the *Mirror* the day before. She took her time pouring, and that was a signal for all the others: free-play time. Ten or twelve soprano voices started squeaking at once.

But over all of them I heard Gladys, talking in a voice just meant for me: 'I don't know, Linda. Sometimes when a man does too much for his wife, she gets to not appreciating him. Sometimes . . .' Gladys deliberately drowned her voice in coffee. Then she turned – fast – to Winnie Curtis, at the farther seat down the table, and called out: 'Doesn't Mr Nugent look like Ronald Colman with pockmarks?'

Edward Leland's face looked wrong. But he was so close to being normal-looking, you were dying to get up close and examine precisely how his face was. But of course, you didn't get anywhere near Edward Leland. He was the most senior of the senior partners.

He was a genuine war hero too. In 1917, he'd taken his rifle, crawled on his belly through a forest in France, and mowed down a platoon of German soldiers. He'd saved his men. He might have gone on, gotten more Germans, or gotten killed, but he crawled over a mine. His face and his shoulder had been blown up.

There were so many rumors in the office about how many

operations he'd had to get put back together, it was impossible to ever know the truth. The only thing we did know was that half his face was flatter than the other half, as though one or two pieces were still missing. Someone swore he had lots of little scars, but I couldn't see any. What I could see – what nobody could miss – was that the left half of his face was paralyzed. It didn't move; it didn't show expression. He was very scary.

As the cold afternoon light slanted through the big window behind his desk, Mr Leland's heavy black brows, like twin awnings, cast shadows; you couldn't see what was in his eyes, although I had no doubt it was strictly cold, hard business. I was on loan because he had a letter to send to Germany. I'd been on loan before, but never to Edward Leland.

Despite his position, he was not where he was because of his age; he was actually younger than most of the senior partners, in his early fifties. But whatever he had that the rest of them lacked – intelligence, cunning, courage, personality: who knew? – had made him extraordinarily powerful. The strings he pulled were tied not only to the law firm but to government. Anytime a New Dealer decided to talk to a Republican, guess whose phone rang? And did he ever bring in business!

I stood across the room from him, my back flat against the door. His secretary, Katherine from Vassar, had told me to go in, but not how far. His desk seemed half a city block away.

'Come in,' he called. I began. The trek along his rug seemed forever. Each time I looked at Mr Leland, he appeared just as far away; the rug was an eternal Persian stretch of dark red and blue. And the worst of it was not making my way across that vast space but knowing he was watching me. He made me a nervous wreck.

At last I made it to his desk and stood before him. My left ankle wobbled, and I had a hideous picture of my leg giving way, and me crashing to the floor and trying to lift myself up by holding on to the edge of his desk, but instead pulling down his blotter and inkstand. 'I've forgotten your name,' he said, interrupting my nightmare.

'Linda Voss.' I was amazed I still had a voice.

I made myself look straight at him. There were only two things right about his looks: his chin – tough, squared off – and his nose, an ordinary nose, although inappropriately upturned for such a man, daring to suggest that he'd once been a cute little boy.

'Linda Voss. That's right.' He paused. I snuck a fast peek around. Actually, his office wasn't as big as I'd thought – nowhere near what you'd expect from such a big shot. To be equal to Edward Leland's clout, though, the room would have had to be the size of Radio City Music Hall. But it was medium-sized, with the kind of seedy leather furniture you see in *The Adventures of Sherlock Holmes* – lots of cracked old leather chairs with fat feet, and scratched tables. That was the point, of course, the rattiness of it. If he'd gotten nice new slipcovers, everybody would have thought he was an upstart.

'Please sit down,' he said. No big deal, right? But just go into some lawyers' offices to take a letter and they keep you standing for half an hour. Even if you fainted on the floor, they'd just keep dictating, as if they came out of the Gestapo, not Yale Law School. Mr Leland not only said, 'Please sit down,' he said, 'Please sit down, Miss Voss.'

Look, I knew he knew I wasn't one of the executive secretaries, but he treated me as if I was. For someone like that, I'd take dictation till my fingers fell off. Because even though he was scary, you knew he was decent.

Okay, the real truth? The decency, but mainly because Edward Leland was John Berringer's father-in-law. And Gladys, who'd filled in a few months before when Kat from Vas was out with whooping cough, had told me about a picture of John and Nan – their wedding portrait – Mr Leland kept on his desk. As I flipped open the pages of my pad, I noticed an oval silver frame angled so that if I leaned forward a little, I could get a glimpse. So I leaned forward.

Nuts. In the frame was a picture of an old-fashioned looking young woman. She was pretty, with hair that reached her shoulders and curled in little commas over the lace of her dress. Her neck was long, what they call swanlike, and she wore a locket. The picture must have been taken years and years ago . . . and then I realized. It was Mr Leland's late wife. Very late. She'd died from some terrible liver disease when Nan was two, nineteen years before.

But where were John and Nan? I was dying to see the wedding gown. I'd imagined it as something airy and beautiful, like chiffon or tulle – the stuff gowns in fairy tales are made of. But then I thought, no, nothing airy for Nan. She'd wear satin, with a tight bodice and bell skirt, and everyone in church would whisper, Ooh, look how tiny her waist is!

'Dear Herr, uh, Doktor Uhl,' Mr Leland began. 'Herr Doktor? You'll do all that for me, Miss Voss? Keep the "herrs" and the "doktors" straight?'

'Yes, sir,' I said. 'It's easy. Lawyers are always "Herr Doktor." '

He leaned toward me. It looked casual enough, but when Edward Leland was leaning in your direction, it didn't feel casual. You were too nervous to begin with because he was so important, and then you were extra nervous because you didn't want him to catch you staring at how *still* half his face was, and, even worse, you were afraid he'd know you were trying not to let on how you couldn't stop looking at him—

'Were you born in the United States?' he asked.

I started to take it down in shorthand until I realized he was asking me a question. 'Yes,' I said, a little too loud.

I knew why he was asking that; people at work, hearing that I was a bilingual secretary, often spent months waiting for me to slip and say, *Guten Morgen* . . . oops, good morning, or – if they were real anti-German – to goof and, instead of a friendly wave, give a fast *Heil Hitler!* At least, Mr Leland had the sense to realize that the English you learn in German schools is not spoken with a Brooklyn-Queens accent.

'Were your parents born here too?'

'Yes. My father's parents came from Germany. Berlin. My grandmother lived with us.'

'And it was she who taught you German?'

Gladys would have swooned with pleasure over the way he said 'And it was *she*.' She'd say, See, Linda, class will out. Mr Leland wasn't even tempted to say, 'And it was her'; you could tell.

'Yes, she and my father and I' – I made sure I said *I* – 'all spoke it at home, and I took it in high school too. That's where I learned to write it, and learned the grammar. Well, whatever grammar I know.'

'But you practiced it with her?'

'It wasn't really practice, Mr Leland. She never learned English. She never had to. See, we lived in Ridgewood – that's in Queens – and there are loads of Germans . . .'

God, was I ever running off at the mouth! I was mortified. But Mr Leland smiled, a nice half smile. At least I didn't feel like a prize imbecile, even though I knew that he knew I was feeling funny about talking so much. I managed a small smile back. I mean, you just don't sit there and give a powerhouse like Edward Leland a big, fat grin.

'My clients have just completed reviewing the most recent versions of the proposed contracts for your clients' acquisitions of the specified industrial components,' Mr Leland began suddenly, 'and it would appear that with the exception of two points, all matters have been settled.'

Nan Berringer hadn't gotten her looks from her father. I realized, as I tried not to peek over at the picture again, that Nan resembled her mother: good-looking in a clean way. Even though they were Society, the Leland ladies didn't look like the sleek, snooty Merle Oberon type. But still, you could tell they were for real, with far more than passably pretty faces. And then there was their background; it added an extra glow, like candlelight. If I'd been born rich, I wondered, would I have been in the same league as the Leland ladies?

'We have considered at great length your requirements for assurances of the delivery date . . .' Mr Leland's voice was so deep that there were moments when it made you shake inside; it was almost a growl.

'My client obviously cannot assume the risk of commitment for dates of delivery at Port of Bremerhaven.'

Boy, I thought, comparing myself to Nan Leland Berringer! Still, it was interesting to think about what a couple of millions could do for a girl.

'Inasmuch as both of the above points have been previously

discussed at some length and you had indicated that your clients would probably have to agree . . .'

Unlike ninety-nine point nine percent of all lawyers, Edward Leland did not lean back and close his eyes while he dictated. Instead, he looked straight at you. Not *at* you, but it wasn't off into space, either. So you couldn't stare at him. And you couldn't give the Life Saver you were hiding a fast suck during pauses; I had a puddle of lime Life Saver juice under my tongue.

But in one pause, he seemed to be looking away, thinking about something else, so I took the opportunity to really check over his desk. Maybe John and Nan's wedding picture was just a teeny one, and I'd missed it. But it wasn't there. I felt so sad, as if I'd just had a loss.

'Miss Voss.'

'Oh, sorry, Mr Leland.'

'. . . We are assuming that all terms have been met and appropriate contracts including purchase orders will be forwarded within several days for execution by Volkswerke A.G.,' he went on. 'On behalf of both my clients and myself, I would like to thank you for your courtesy and efficiency in helping to bring this negotiation . . .'

My pencil was going fifty miles an hour; I could have gotten the Billy Rose Stenography Prize for 1940. Because I *knew* Mr Leland had definitely been onto exactly what it was I'd been looking for on his desk – and hadn't found. You don't get to be Edward Leland, talking to presidents of Chase Bank and Ford Motor and the United States, for nothing. So I wrote like mad, which nudged him into dictating faster.

But Edward Leland wasn't in business to miss a trick. I think he knew what my sudden speed was about. And not only did he know what I'd been looking for, but he probably even knew why I'd been looking.

My hands got so wet my pencil almost slipped, but I kept on writing. Yes, he knew. But he wasn't going to make a federal case of it. Why should he? He saved his federal cases for when he had dinner with his dear old chums, the justices of the Supreme Court of the United States.

But just for a second, Mr Leland looked me straight in the eye.

A kindly look on that messed-up face. A little sad for me. And then he just kept talking.

As we left the office that day, I waved a copy of the *World-Telegram* in front of Gladys's face. 'Look at this. You think Hitler's playing games? He's just given Göring total control of the whole German war industry.'

Gladys said, 'Quiet! I have *real* news. You're going to die when you hear it. And not a fast heart attack. A slow, painful, hysterical death.'

'Oh, sure,' I said, positive it was going to be some gossip about Mr Hastings in Litigation.

Gladys clutched her coat around her. A little dramatic. Although it was January, with that cold dampness that makes your toes ache, there wasn't even a snowflake swirling under the street light, much less the blizzard she seemed about to brave. But that was the wonderful thing about Gladys's theatricality. How many old maids are there who can watch life from behind a typewriter and find passion, thrills and chills in a law office? Me, you say? No. I didn't just want to watch. I wanted to *have*. Gladys didn't. She savored it all, but from a distance. 'When you hear this, you're going to say, "Take me to the hospital. I'm having a stroke from shock." '

'Gladys, tell me!'

'When you were in Mr Leland's office today . . .' She smiled for a moment. I knew what she was doing: remembering when she had started at Blair, VanderGraff, when Mr Leland had gone from being a loving husband to being a young widower with a small child. *That* had been great drama. 'Right after his wife died,' she said, 'Mr Leland turned gray. His hair, I mean.' She paused. 'What do you think he looked like when he was young? Before *it* happened with the land mine.'

'I don't know. Forget Mr Leland. Tell me: What's the big secret?'

'How was Mr Leland today?' Gladys insisted.

'The usual. He wanted to gossip about Carole Lombard and Clark Gable and—'

'Come on. Didn't he seem at all funny?'

'Yeah, Gladys. He told me three jokes. *Very* dirty. About filthy things you never even heard of.'

'Linda, listen!' Gladys slowed down, but the crowd wanted to get home. It forced us faster along the street, toward the subway. 'Mr Berringer is Mr Leland's son-in-law, right? Well, you may think you know all there is to know, but hold your horses!'

It was what they say happens in an awful accident: Time slows down. Not slow motion, but in the terrible moment before the awfulness, you're more alive than you've ever been before. Everything matters. I felt my scalp tighten. I could smell the soggy wool of Gladys's tweed. Coal soot made my eyes water. The wind whooshed down the street, and a flyaway page of the *Post* slapped against a lamppost.

'I'm holding my horses,' I said, cool, a regular cucumber. Like, what could there possibly be about Mr Berringer that would surprise me for more than a tenth of a second? Like, come on, Gladys, let's get this over with so we can get on to something *big*.

'How long have they been married?' Gladys demanded.

'Mr Berringer and Nan Leland?'

'Oh, don't be cute. Tell me. Two, three years?' I nodded. 'Well, that was enough for the young Mrs B!' Gladys proclaimed.

You'd think I'd have dropped dead right there on Rector Street. But all I said was, 'Oh, Gladys!'

Gladys was stunned – and peered – at my disinterest. 'Linda, this is a *fact*.'

'Har-har-har,' I answered. Look, I wanted to say, if there was anything going on with John Berringer, wouldn't I be the first to pick it up? But I didn't trust my voice enough.

'I have proof,' Gladys said.

'What? A mysterious stranger's fingerprints on Nan Berringer's you-know-what's?'

'Would you please get your mind out of the gutter and *think*. What would be final proof?' Gladys was having fun. This was nothing more to her than office drama – but the most supreme, the richest, the juiciest.

'I give up.'

'Why are you giving up so easily?'

The crowd swept us on, a great force that stopped at nothing, down the gritty stairs to the subway, past the overhead 'To Brooklyn and Queens' sign, past a giant Nestlé's Cocoa ad. I felt out of control. Halfway down, my foot skidded on the cellophane from a pack of cigarettes, and if I hadn't grabbed the banister I would have gone crashing down. My body was finally comprehending what my mind had learned.

'Linda, are you okay?' Gladys asked.

'Fine.' I swallowed, although all that made me do was realize how sick I felt. 'So,' I managed, 'is this what you were talking about at lunch? About a wife not appreciating?'

'Linda, don't you realize . . .?'

'No. I really don't. Listen, it's some ridiculous rumor. I'd know if there was anything with anything.'

'For your information, it just so happens I was slumming today.' That means she was hanging around Marian Mulligan's desk. 'Who does Marian work for?'

'Mr Wilson.'

'Mr Wilson who does *matrimonials*.' Oh, God, I thought, oh God! I managed to shrug. 'Guess who Mr Wilson was writing to?'

'A sob sister. "Dear Penelope Potts, I am a creepy attorney with so much hair hanging out of my nose people think it's a mustache and—" '

'Linda, listen! Nan Berringer is going to Reno! Mr Wilson was writing to a Nevada divorce lawyer, giving him *all* the details of who gets what.' Somehow I had gotten down the flight of stairs and was on the platform, waiting for the train. 'Do you believe me now?' I nodded. 'Are you shocked? Linda, are you shocked?'

She would have been heartbroken if I wasn't, and, of course, I was. So I gave her something for her trouble. 'Yeah, Gladys, I'm shocked.'

'Good. I mean, you should be.' The subway roared through the tunnel into the station and screeched to a stop. As the doors opened and we pushed our way on, she said, 'You should *see* the list of what she's getting. Stocks. Bonds. And much more. One hundred and fifty-seven pieces of sterling-silver flatware. With all their friends and family who shop at Tiffany, you'd think they'd have more, but . . .'

Dear God. John was going to be free. My dreams were dangerous.

# *Chapter Two*

'Linda, honey, put on some rouge, stick you boobies in his face, and bingo! He'll be kissing your feet.' My mother was great at advice to the lovelorn. 'What are you waiting for? Mistletoe? *Now's* the time to grab Mr Whosis. That John guy you work for.'

'Why would John give me the time of day?' Why would any normal, rational human being take me and John Berringer seriously, even for two seconds? The answer: They wouldn't. They'd say, Snap out of it, Linda! But this was my mother, and the normal and rational categories were not the places you'd go looking for her.

'Angel, if he wanted some rich Manhattan snot-nose, Mrs John wouldn't be in Reno, Las Vegas.'

'Forget it, Mom,' I said, 'I'm living in a dream world. Men like him don't marry girls like me.'

Instead of saying, Hey, what about Cinderella and the prince? My mother merely sighed; she was too drunk to give me a fight. Then she lowered her still-gorgeous eyes and gazed passionately at her plate. An outsider would have thought she'd fallen in love with her salmon croquette.

Last night's booze still sloshed inside her. She looked the way she usually looked on any typical winter Wednesday night – or any night: half drunk, half hung over. She didn't even make a stab at her salmon, but then, my mother hardly ate anything. I worried about her; gin and ginger ale wasn't carrots and peas. The booze drowned not only her beauty – and my mother had been so incredibly lovely – but her health. Her clear white skin, with its faint glimmering of pink – like a seashell – had turned yellow. Then the tiny crisscross lines on her face deepened until, under the glare of the light that hung over the table, her skin resembled those terrible pictures of the Okies' dry, cracked land, desperate for rain.

She'd bought that light herself, soon after she'd gotten married. It dangled from a once-white wire; the bulb was half covered with a glass shade painted with pink, blue and purple bunnies. Cute, silly, meant for a frilly boudoir – like my mother. The light didn't belong in the kitchen, and neither did she. It was a useless room as far as she was concerned. She couldn't cook and she wouldn't eat.

Even if she'd been starving, my mother wouldn't have picked up a fork. Eating interfered with drinking. Two spoons of mashed potatoes could soak up a shot of gin, and my mother liked to get sloshed as fast as possible. That she held off till I got home from work, so we could have dinner together, was proof of her love. She needed a drink so badly; she had d.t.'s nearly every night: not near-convulsions, but gentle, feminine d.t.'s. Pale, trembling hands. She kept them in her lap, hoping, I guess, that I wouldn't see them and get upset. She honestly tried. Though she was no prize as a mother and she knew it, she loved me as much as she could.

But she wouldn't eat to save her life – not even for me. Eating smudged lipstick, and, even plastered, my mother managed enough self-control to keep her makeup perfect. Well, almost perfect: I noticed she'd drawn one of her eyebrows into a higher arch than the other, so it looked as if she had doubts about everything I said.

Suddenly, she sat straight up and smoothed the front of the pink duster she was wearing over her dress to protect it from the dinner she wouldn't touch. She'd remembered we were having a conversation. 'Linda, dollface, why do you keep thinking Wall Street lawyers are different? Sweetie, men are all alike. There's only one thing that makes them happy. You know that. You wanna hook this John? Clue him in you're ready to . . . I'm not shocking you, am I? You're over twenty-one.'

'By ten years, Mom.'

'Men aren't like girls. They *need* it. He'd probably give his right arm to have your company tonight. Unless you think the reason Mrs Whosis took a walk was because he has a chippy on the side.'

'No, he's not that type.' That was my worst fear: Nan getting a divorce because John was in love with someone else.

'Sweetie, they're *all* that type.'

'Why don't you try the croquette? Just a bite. It's not bad.'

'I bet it's great! You're a wonderful cook, lovie. But I'm just not hungry tonight. Now listen to me about men. I *know* what puts a smile on their face.'

I (obviously) didn't. Maybe my mother was right. After all, Betty Johnston Voss had been born to please men. She was beautiful. Huge, limpid brown eyes instead of the predictable blue. Blond hair so soft that it looked like the froth on top of an ice cream soda, and if that wasn't enough (and it wasn't), the world's deepest dimples. My father had pulled a fast one, beating out the competition by eloping with her the day she turned sixteen. I'd been born nine months later.

'Now's your chance, Linda. I know you're more like your father than like me. Real smart, listening to the news, reading the papers. You could get yourself a lawyer if you weren't – well, you know – such a stick. Get your hair out of that old-lady bun. Wear red lipstick. Give him a little thigh.'

'Mom, that's not law firm etiquette.'

'Baby doll, you use your brain. So what's wrong with using your legs too?' My mother smiled encouragingly, then belched. 'I wouldn't tell you this if you was a kid, but now . . . Listen, if he wants a virgin – you'll pardon my French – he's gonna find a young one, so you might as well . . . What the heck. Live a little.'

It was so hard being a brainless ex-beauty. There she sat – in a chair upholstered in faded red oilcloth at a creaky old kitchen table – behind a wall of makeup, forty-seven years old. She'd started boozing soon after she'd lost my father, when she suddenly realized it was impossible to be a child bride when you were no longer a child – and when the groom was kaput. A bride was all she'd ever been or wanted to be.

When I didn't want to scream at her for stealing food money for her boozing or for throwing up in her bed or – once – for carrying on with three men in a car parked right in front of the house, my mother broke my heart.

'Don't be afraid of a little fun, Linda,' she went on. Her eyes were made up to look wide and girlish, and she'd painted her moth into a young pink kiss.

My mother was the youngest and prettiest of five sisters. Her father, a subway maintenance man, had died of a heart attack when she was six or seven, and her mother had kept the family going by taking in boarders, and from a few things my mother had said ('Mama had her favorite boarder, and Lucille had *hers*, and Meg *hers*, a trolley motorman with a peg leg, and . . .'), I guessed they'd managed to supplement the family budget a little above and beyond the rent money. They'd had to. My mother's father's family – the Johnstons – hadn't helped out at all after he'd died. The Johnstons weren't a close-knit group, although for some peculiar reason they could always be counted on to show up in droves for a funeral. As far as I knew, my mother's mother's family – she thought their name was Dunstan or Duncan – were all dead, although there might be a cousin in California.

My mother gave her hair a tender, loving pat, checking to see if it was still fluffy. 'Let loose. Like I do. Live a little!'

Six nights a week my mother let loose. She traipsed from bar to bar along the Brooklyn-Queens border. Nearly every night she wound up with the first man who gave her the eye. Usually she was home before dawn, but sometimes she didn't show up for days at a time.

'Why don't you give old John baby a try? You two got a lot in common, working together on law stuff, talking German. How many girls speak it? I'm not talking about those Kraut piggies with earmuff braids. Your father could've had a million of them, those fatties. It would have made his old lady happy, but he wanted an all-American girl, not some frow-line. But I admit, I used to think it was so nice, your father saying sweet nothings to me in German – when we were alone, if you get me. Not that I got what he meant, but it was *so* Continental.'

That my mother could have spent almost thirty years living in a German-speaking house never caring enough to even learn the meaning of the word *ja* explains what she was like. That her mother-in-law, my Grandma Olga, could have come to America in

1884 and spent fifty-four years in Brooklyn and Queens – until she died in 1938 – refusing to understand a simple *yes* explains what she was like too. My mother at least had an excuse. Like many born beauties, she had been allowed to concentrate on her own loveliness; skills like speaking foreign languages, scouring bathtubs and shopping for groceries were things she could get other people to do for her. My Grandma Olga, on the other hand, would not learn English because it was a waste of time; she'd truly believed it was only a matter of a year or two before she'd go back to Berlin in a fur coat. And when she no longer believed that – that America was the land of opportunity – she refused to listen to its language.

My mother rested her elbow on the table. It creaked. The table had been Olga's choice: plain wood, straight legs; cheap but serviceable. She'd bought it in the late 1880s or early '90s, after she'd come to America. Throughout the house, her no-nonsense chairs sat stiffly beside my mother's flamingo-and-palm-tree wallpaper; her white iron bedsteads were covered with spreads that my mother picked, with flower, kitten and bird designs in every single pastel shade ever invented by man.

'Lookit, Linda,' my mother said, as I brought the dishes over to the sink. 'I got an idea to help you loosen up. Make believe you're me! Come on, don't laugh. It'll work. Flirt with that John a little, call him big boy in German. Play your cards right and before you know it, no more typing for you. He'll set you up real nice someplace.'

'Mom, I don't want to be set up.'

I went back to the table, swept off a couple of crumbs and put the ketchup in the icebox. It was just as well my mother didn't even try to help anymore. Dishes flew out of her hands, then crash-landed on the floor. And her idea of an interesting use for leftovers was to dump everything into the garbage. I went back to the sink and wrapped her salmon croquette in waxed paper. Her dinner was almost always my next lunch.

'So maybe he'll set you up legit. What's the matter, you never heard of a boss marrying a secretary?'

'I've heard about it, but . . .'

'Listen, for the time being get what you can out of him. A good time, satin nightgowns. Some girls get diamond watches, even. And then who knows? Maybe a wedding ring.' For a second, a mist came over her eyes. She blinked it away before it could ruin her mascara, but when she spoke again, the mist was in her voice. 'Maybe he'll be your Herman, honey!'

Was my father something! To hear his name – Herman Ernst Voss – you'd think: Big deal, another Heinie. But would you have been wrong! My father was a real American. Tall and strong. And smart.

Right from the start, my father was good in *everything*; sports, math, history. And so all-American he could have been Andy Hardy's taller, handsomer big brother. If he hadn't quit high school to get a job, he could have gotten a scholarship to any college; that's what the principal told him. But he had to.

His father, Otto, had died of influenza when my father was little. Otto had been a butcher, but he never got to own his own shop. When he went, all Olga had was a little insurance; it was enough to cover the casket, but not the hearse or the hole in the ground. Some German-Jewish charity paid for that, although they wouldn't have been too thrilled if they'd heard Otto Voss's claim to fame had been his pork patties.

For the next eight or nine years, my Grandma Olga went back to the work she'd done in Berlin as a girl. She got a job in a button plant in Brooklyn, operating the press that made the holes in the buttons.

She worked till she couldn't. Her arthritis got so bad she could hardly lift her pocketbook, much less heavy machinery. So my father had to leave school and support her.

But my father. When he left school, he told his mother, 'I'm not going to get stuck making sausages the rest of my life. This is temporary.' By the time he was eighteen, though, my father was the master sausagemaker of Ridgewood, a prince among butchers, and he was making the wages of a man twice his age. And he seemed content. He was always having fun, something Olga (being German) was slightly suspicious of.

Fun was something that happened on Sunday afternoons. If you came from Berlin, sure, you were much more lighthearted than the average potato-dumpling German, but you were not exactly a fluff-headed fool. You knew real fun was for the people who could afford it: business tycoons who kept cabaret singers as mistresses; barons who threw huge post-boar-hunt bashes. It was the job of the rich to have fun. The *berlinerisch*-speaking lower and middle classes were supposed to be the happy masses. But it's an effort to be a happy mass, and Olga couldn't manage it a lot of the time. She was too busy trying to figure out why she'd been born poor and plain and Jewish – why life had shoved her into three slots she wouldn't have chosen for herself – to let loose and go whoopee. Olga had wanted to be a grand German lady, and she never even came close. And so while she kept her solid *berlinerisch* ability to laugh at the guys at the top, she couldn't laugh at herself too well; she had never realized a single one of her lovely dreams. That was no laughing matter.

But my father was an American. And was he a popular, *happy* American! Olga used to say it was a blessing they couldn't afford a telephone, because it would never have stopped ringing; as it was, there was a parade of girls past the house every summer night. He was so handsome it didn't matter that he was a Jew. He was a catch for any girl. Olga said it a little wistfully, because any girl would have been better than what he got; my mother was not exactly what Olga had in mind as daughter-in-law material.

But my father wasn't having anything to do with the local Helgas; he wanted a girl as red, white and blue as he was, and sure enough, he found one. He was twenty-three years old, keeping company with a girl named Annabel Johnston. Could you get more American than that? It seemed so, because to both families' amazement, my father dropped twenty-year-old Annabel and eloped with her sixteen-year-old sister. Her name was Betty. My mother. The all-American girl – dumb blonde variety.

Truly dumb. Smart dumb blondes marry sugar daddies with limousines and fat cigars. But my mother was the real McCoy: absolutely magnificent, genuinely dim; she picked a guy who worked ten hours a day in a two-bit sausage plant, who came complete with a live-in mother who didn't speak English. And smart dumb blondes keep their figure; my mother got pregnant with me a couple of weeks after the wedding.

But big deal: they were crazy for each other. When I was a kid, my mother would leave Olga and me with the dishes and lead my father toward the bedroom. He wouldn't look back, but my mother would give us a wave. 'Nighty night,' she'd call. 'We're so-o-o sleepy.' Even then, when I didn't understand. I knew.

It wasn't just in the bedroom, either. They were more in love than Romeo and Juliet. When the Depression came and the meat business got bad and my father got laid off for almost a year when his plant closed, a lot of beauties would have taken a hike. Not my mother. She loved having him around the house, and even though for a while there things got very bad – to keep us going, we had to take scraps from a butcher my father knew who was still working – she was blissfully happy. (To be fair, my mother only looked at the pictures in the Sunday paper, and since we couldn't even afford the paper in those days, she probably didn't realize there was a Depression on.)

There was only one thing my mother couldn't give my father: companionship. But that was okay. All she had to be was his 'little girl.' That was enough. That was wonderful, in fact. His mother had been smart and hardworking, but so German. Finally he had someone who wasn't ambitious for him; he had a dumb, happy American, not an ambitious immigrant. If it wasn't for *her*, Olga told him, you'd own a string of butcher shops by now. My father grinned at his mother and said, Who needs butcher shops? I have my family. What he meant was, I have my little girl.

And so what if my mother couldn't give him companionship? For conversation, he had the guys at work. And then he had me. Since 'little girl' was taken, he called me his pal.

'Hey, pal, I'm gonna take you to the plant Saturday. Show you what a real, prime pork belly looks like.' Boy, did we have great times! Going places, or just talking. 'What are you, a parrot? Don't tell me what the radio says. Tell me what *you* think.' Naturally, we had our moments. If I was fresh, he wouldn't take any guff from me. 'Shape up, Linda!' he'd snap, and a couple of times he gave me the back of his hand.

But most of the times was wonderful. Just walking to the hardware store with him to pick up a bunch of penny nails, I'd be so proud. All the other girls' fathers looked like fathers. Mine was tall and lean, with strong, manly features. He looked special, like someone famous who was just passing through the neighborhood.

We talked about everything – movies, baseball, politics. He was a dodger fan and a Democrat. 'Pal, there's only one group in the world richer and rottener than the Yankees – Republicans. They don't care about anything but holding on to everything they got. They don't give a damn about the little guy, and don't ever let anyone con you into believing different.' He told me all about sausage casings, and I told him all kinds of dopey things about the kids in my class and, later, about the people at work. We talked about everything in the world – except two things: ragtime music, which he loved, which I didn't get . . . ragtime music, and my mother.

My mother did nothing except stay beautiful; at thirty, she still acted like the sixteen-year-old my father had eloped with. She listened to the Victrola, visited her girlfriends (they gave each other manicures) and went to the city, to the fancy department stores, to try on clothes. So my grandmother got down on her arthritic knees and scrubbed the floors. She did laundry, she cooked. Naturally, I worked alongside her. I guess I figured housework was something that skipped a generation. But once I finished high school and went to business, I wasn't much of a help. My grandmother was really the housewife in her son's home – which I guess made my mother, the dumb blonde, the kept woman.

Olga was smart. (My father didn't get his brains at Woolworth's.) She read every German-language newspaper and magazine she could get her hands on, kept up a correspondence with a couple of old relatives in Berlin. And so she was at least as well informed about what was going on in the world as the average US senator.

By the mid-thirties, Olga and I started having fights about Hitler. She called him the Austrian, and she said he was an embarrassment. *An embarrassment?* I fumed at her. We stood on opposite sides of the table, stretching strudel dough. 'An embarrassment is when you spill soup on the tablecloth. He's passing laws saying Jews can't be citizens. They have to have a "J" on their identity cards.' She eased the dough, coaxed it, into a paper-thin sheet. She was a great German cook. Her strudel technique was not only graceful, it was flawless. 'You're the perfect German,' I went on. 'But not in their eyes. Don't just read what they say. *Believe* it. You're not one of them. They'd make you go around with a "J." They hate you.'

She looked away and murmured: 'And you also. You're half . . .'

I lowered the dough so I could look her right in the eye. 'I know. You know what they call my parents' marriage? *Rassenschande.*' Race defilement. I didn't rub it in by pointing out that her son would be considered the defiler and that his dopey wife would be viewed as Miss Aryan Purity. 'You call all that an "embarrassment"?'

My poor, smart, sweet, hardworking grandma . . . stuck in a foreign country she didn't understand, hated in her homeland, living with a birdbrained American daughter-in-law who, if she thought about Olga at all, considered her an old foreign thing attached to a mop.

I tried to talk to my father about it. I tried to tell him how hard it must be for Olga; she couldn't say a bad word about my mother to him because she was afraid he would get so angry he'd ask her to leave. And where would she go? But my father didn't want to hear about it. Listen, pal, your grandma's a good sport and she *likes* to keep busy. Anyway, if she had a gripe, wouldn't she tell me?

I tried to say, Hey, Dad, Mom will pick up a dust rag and spend a half hour admiring the fabric and then forget to dust. He wouldn't listen. I'd try again. She'll put down the dust rag, wander over to a mirror. She'll make a little face; she wasn't perfect. So she'll drift into the bathroom for repairs. Makeup. Eyebrow tweezing. He didn't want to hear any of it.

Whenever I started on him, my father would just shrug or stick his head back into the paper or smile. Love isn't blind. It's deaf. He wouldn't hear me. And he couldn't hear the weariness in his mother's voice, or the sadness. But he was all ears for his Betty, his little girl. The minute she warbled, 'Herm, honey,' he'd leave me in the middle of a sentence and rush down the hall to their room.

When I started working and got to listen to some of the lawyers, I realized my father was as smart as any of them. What he lacked was education – and ambition. But they lacked something my father had: a honeymoon waiting when they got home. They worked till all hours on Wall street, but in Ridgewood when the clock struck six, my father could have been sorting a new truckload of meat, getting his pay or talking to his boss. It didn't matter. He took off and ran home.

In 1933, when he was forty-six, he died when a fire caused by a sparking electric meat saw blazed out of control in one of the refrigeration rooms. The funny thing was, it happened about two minutes to six. Just a hundred and twenty seconds later, he would have been safe, rushing through the streets of Queens, back home to his little girl.

I know, I know. It may not have been a breeze to be the sole support of an arthritic grandmother and a lush mother, but it's no old-maid guarantee, either. Some smart girl could have landed a guy who'd buy a house with a couple of back bedrooms.

So why wasn't I married? Was I a prune-face, a blimp? Did my breath wilt celery? Did my small talk send guys into comas? No. What went wrong, I guess, was that I waited too long. I was looking for someone to love.

In senior year of high school, when the rest of the girls were grabbing up anything with hair under its arms, I said, Uh-uh, not me. I can do better. I was smart enough, and pretty.

While I didn't inherit my mother's true beauty, at least I had her fair hair and her eyes: big and brown. Depending on the light, they made men think I was either sad or intelligent or romantic. And I'd wound up with my father's good, solid German bones: definite cheeks, strong mouth. It wasn't a gorgeous face. People didn't pass me in the street and go Ooh! But if a guy looked twice, he might say, Hey, not bad.

So while I wasn't whistle-bait, I looked pretty nice in a dress and heels. And without; sometimes after a bath I stood on top of the toilet seat and angled the medicine cabinet mirror so I could see myself. It looked okay to me. From the front, anyway. I couldn't really see the back. So except for guys who insisted on a girl with a chest like two footballs, I could do fine. Then how come I didn't?

Nineteen, twenty, twenty-one, I was doing okay. There was always someone for Saturday nights; there even was a proposal. Willy Bauer was a bookkeeper for Con Ed and going to Brooklyn College at night to become a accountant. He had a friendly face – like the men in chewing gum ads – and there was nothing wrong with him. But at twenty, that wasn't enough, so I said no.

I had a half proposal too. Michael Donnelly, who was a steamfitter, asked me to marry him after knowing him three weeks. It was half a proposal because there were strings attached; our children would have to be raised as Catholics. Michael said 'Catlicks,' and that probably had more to do with my saying no than any worries about my future kids in a confessional. In any case, our romance happened so fast I never actually learned what a steamfitter was.

And then came twenty-two, twenty-three and twenty-four. Suddenly the phone got quiet. All of Queens, to say nothing of the other four boroughs, was married. And the few guys who weren't, the bachelors and the widowers, either had the brains or faces of cockroaches or were old enough for my Grandma Olga.

Sure, I could have kept busy with someone at the firm; in the history of the world, it is not unknown for lawyers and secretaries to be buddy-buddy. There was always some corporate partner from New Canaan who wanted to grab a couple of laughs (etc.) before grabbing the 8.38. They didn't tempt me, though, those lawyers whose wallets bulged with pictures of their kids. But even if my tongue had been hanging down to my knees for one of them, I would have said no. I was supporting Olga and my mother. Getting mixed up with a married man could mean a lot more than lonely Christmases. It could mean a pink slip when the fun stopped, and you'd have to be a complete fool to take such a risk during the Depression. The world was full of fast typists. So no married lawyers. And no unmarried ones, because what did they need me for?

It was then, right before my twenty-fifth birthday, that I suddenly realized I'd missed my chance. I was so lonely. All my friends were married, and I was the old maid. I had reached the age when guys say, So what's wrong with her she's not married?

Well, she waited for someone wonderful to come along, and he never did.

George Armbruster walked back into my life when I was twenty-eight. As George said: 'Hey, twenty-eight's a lot older than the last time I saw you. But you still got a pretty face.' Then he gave me the once-over. 'I bet the rest of you's not bad, either.'

By Ridgewood standards, George was a very eligible bachelor. he was an electrician who'd moved somewhere on Long Island but who had his own shop on Metropolitan Avenue and his mother had just died. What could be more perfect? We'd gone to the same high school, and one Saturday when I was at the grocery store communicating with a slab of Swiss cheese, he came up beside me. I said hello. Despite a hairline that had inched backward, the face was familiar; he was one of a pack of boys in my English or civics class – the sort of boys who laugh sneaky har-har-hars, and until you see who they're laughing at, you're always afraid it's you. But he was alone now, and seemed okay enough. He said, I forgot your name. Linda Voss. Yeah, that's right. George Armbruster. You were at Grover Cleveland, right?

He came calling every night. Olga had been thrilled. Holding down a decent job in 1937. So what if he was Lutheran. He was very attentive. And okay, no one would every say, 'Hiya, handsome' to him but good looks don't pay the rent.

Even right after he shaved, George's beard looked dark, like the bully in comics. That wasn't so bad, but he had eyes, nose and a mouth just slightly less appealing than everyone else's; there was not a single thing about him to go Ooh, how nice! No great eyelashes or broad shoulders or even interesting ears. And while he claimed he was five eight, I was just under five five, and you could have drawn a straight line over our heads.

I said to myself, Well, it takes time to get to warm up to some people. What do I have but time? My front door didn't have dents from eligible bachelors pounding on it.

Besides, George wasn't awful. In fact, he was slender and even graceful, like Leslie Howard from the neck down if he'd been an electrician. And he traveled in style. No subway: George had private transportation, his own truck. On the door was painted 'Armbruster Electricals,' and just below that, an arm with a grapefruit-sized muscle.

Every night, rain, shine or sleet, there was George at the door. Olga beamed and my mother actually risked her makeup to smile when George came for me and said Hiya.

Hiya, he said that first night, as we walked down the wooden stairs from the front porch onto the street. Howya doing?

Fine. I was a nervous wreck. I had a whole list of subjects to talk about, courtesy of the girls at the office. If he was going to be the strong, silent type, I would have to keep the conversation ball rolling all by myself. But conversation wasn't necessary. George talked all the time.

'Wanna come see my shop? Hey, I got this new job in Glendale. I'm telling you, one more day and the place woulda been on fire. Never saw wiring like that in my life. I turned on my flashlight and thought, Jee-sus, this looks like a plate of Italian spaghetti. And the fuse box! Lemme tell you, it . . .'

Maybe I'd watched too many movies. Maybe I was a romantic sap. But maybe I'd been alone too long. This was obviously the way men and women talked, and I'd better get used to it.

We arrived at his shop, that first night and every other night for the three months we went together. Oh, boy – went together. Well, what else should I call it?

'So that George is coming around a lot,' my mother observed. 'Guess it's serious, huh?' My mother, who generally went off drinking before George came to the door, passed him now and then on her way out, when she was still sober, so she remembered him. After the second time, she pulled me aside and said, 'He certainly is . . . well . . . You know how they talk about good things in small packages. Not that he's *that* small. Having a good time with him?' Another time she giggled and started humming 'Here Comes the Bride.'

My Grandma Olga had the time of her life, telling the butcher, the grandson of the man my Grandpa Otto used to work for: Linda and George Armbruster are keeping company. The butcher said, Oh; he hooked up my refrigerator. Every morning at breakfast, Olga demanded, 'Tell me about last night.'

Well, I'd say, we had coffee with some friends of his. We went to a movie. The one I saw last week, but I sure didn't tell him that. Olga would nod, smile. We went dancing at the Trylon Terrace. We went to Coney island and went on the rides. We went to the city, to a restaurant that had candles on the table. He's a real gentleman. Olga agreed. She could see that; George always got me home by nine the latest.

But none of that was true. That first night and every night . . . three guesses. We never really needed the truck because we never went anywhere except to his shop. In the back was a couch with an itchy green afghan his mother had finished crocheting the month before she died.

'Come on,' he said, and started to unbutton his shirt.

'George!' I couldn't believe what he wanted me to do, and boy, did I ever let him know it.

'Come *on*,' he insisted. I shook my head no. 'Hey, Linda, you're so pretty. I wanna see a pretty figure to match that face.'

He turned on a light bulb hanging from an old electrical cord. And I let him see.

Me, who had never let a boy in high school do more than kiss me good night, and after high school, not much more. I let George take off all my clothes in that dim, flickering light. He was trying to unhook my brassiere, and I was looking at the light bulb and thinking: Some lousy electrician, some rotten connection. Me, who had the guts to tell one of the senior partners in the first law firm I'd worked for, Listen, Mr McCallister, I'm not that kind of girl. Well, I was.

For a little more than twelve weeks, I let George Armbruster do anything he wanted on a couch that smelled like it had gotten rained on two years before and never really dried. Not that George's anything was such a big deal. I thought: This is what people make such a big to-do about?

What went on between men and women seemed like Thanksgiving turkey: Everyone always says, 'Great!' even though it's invariably dry and disappointing.

And then one night he stopped coming around. George has a real bad cold, I told my mother. He called me at work, still has a fever, I said to Olga. George is getting better, but he has a big job in Brooklyn. I kept it up for nearly two weeks.

I stopped because one night I came home from work and Olga pulled me aside and said, 'The butcher took me to the back room, with the sink.'

'What?' I figured, Oh, God, now we're in for it. It's bad enough with three fourths of the neighbors. Now the butcher's going on about my mother's being a drunk. Maybe she took off her panties again.

'He feels bad about you.'

'About *me?* The butcher?'

'About you and that George Armbruster.'

'What about George Armbruster?'

Olga kept her head down. She chopped an onion. She muttered, 'About that he's married.'

'Married?'

'Ten years.' She chopped. 'Right after school. He got married then. When everybody else did.'

Olga died the next year. Her heart gave out. So many times in those two years since she'd been gone, I'd thought: Maybe she would have managed to hang on if she'd just had George Armbruster to believe in. She could have been alive, believing in me and George, except for that damn big-mouth butcher.

Instead, she left me alone with the mop and my mother.

# *Chapter Three*

John Berringer could hardly bear the loss of his wife. He looked terrible, and boy, did that make me feel good. Dark gray circles appeared under his eyes, and their glorious deep blue glint died. His glow faded. It's not that he wasn't still gorgeous, but he was now gorgeous and in pain; you could see it. His skin was chalky. His lips were almost white. And you know what I thought, watching him suffering? Wonderful.

I know I sound like a monster, but I really wasn't that bad. I think I was just hoping that as John got closer to the end of his rope, he'd need someone to grab on to. And who better than me? There I was, only four feet away, in my good white blouse with the soft, floppy bow at the neck.

He rubbed his face. 'We have about another hour,' he said. 'Can you manage?'

'Yes, Mr Berringer.'

It was after seven, dark, silent. Nothing is deader than Wall Street at night and – sure, corny – it was as if we were the only two people left in the world. He'd loosened his tie a little, so I got a bonus: a couple of extra inches of neck, the smooth part, where he didn't have to shave. I would have loved to kiss him right there. I smiled; if I was the only girl left in the world, maybe he'd let me.

He saw me smiling. *So* embarrassing. I couldn't decide whether to pass it off as a cooperative smile or, because it may have looked something more than cooperative, to make up a boyfriend: Sorry, Mr Berringer, just thinking about, um, Joseph. Everyone calls him Big Joe. We're kind of engaged to be engaged, and . . .

'All right,' he said, 'let's get to work.' I could have taken out my teeth and strung them on a necklace in a permanent grin; he wouldn't have noticed. 'We still have the Hayn matter and . . .' His voice faded. For a second, he looked at the papers spread out all over his desk. He looked more than sad; he looked desperate, as if he knew his mind was somewhere in the room and his job was to find it.

That's how I knew what bad shape he was in. John's mind was always under control, whirring away like a perfect machine – even when all the other lawyers were sitting around looking like some lower, dopey form of animal life.

'We have Grunberg to take care of' I said, trying to help him. 'And we're a little behind on the Schaaf matter too.' He looked at me. His shadowed eyes looked empty, like the eyeholes in the tragedy mask at the Roxy.

The work! It was too much. I felt as lousy as he looked. We came in before seven every morning and stayed late just trying to stop the clients' fright from turning into panic. It wasn't easy. There was no one terrible event that March 1940, but each night the world grew worse. Turn on the radio, pick up a paper, and the only names on earth seemed to be Hitler and Mussolini. One evil, one deranged, and they grew huge, thriving as Europe sickened. And as their blight spread, the clients wouldn't leave us alone. Those beady little corporation eyes that had been gleaming at the thought of the rich fascist war machine the month before were suddenly blinky, nervous; now all they wanted was to see their way out: Can you tell us what the situation is? What they really wanted to know was: Will everything be all right? And their only hope was that John Berringer – brilliant, calm, masterful – would tell them, Don't worry. What they all wanted to hear was, Everything's going to be just fine.

They probably would have paid him double to hear it, but he wouldn't have taken their money. He was too ethical. He was the best kind of international lawyer. He didn't just come up with a solid contract. He had the patience and the brains to explain to his big corporate clients how the German system worked. He didn't just speak its language. He understood its laws, it ways of doing business, its people. But every day John was making transatlantic calls that didn't get through. He was writing letters to people who no longer answered. Then he had to go back to the clients and say the words nobody wants to hear from a lawyer: I can't help you.

'Mr Berringer?' I said softly. He jumped, as though I'd just come into the room and yelled Boo! 'If you have a lot of preparation, I could come in real early tomorrow and we could finish the dictation then.' Maybe I was no diplomat, but it was better than saying, Hey, listen, you'd better get a good night's sleep or you're gonna find yourself on a funny farm.

If a man has some pleasure in one half of his life – home, work – he can usually take pretty much what the other half has to dish out. But in those weeks, what did he have? Hysterical bankers weeping on his desk in the office – and a lot of extra closet space at home. No wonder he looked like Boris Karloff's first cousin.

And he just sat there, helpless. This had never been a helpless man. His face tilted upward, as if he was looking past me, at the door beyond. Oh, how I could have kissed that neck, slipped my hand under the shirt and rubbed his shoulders, his chest.

'Mr Berringer?' I whispered. Nothing. He'd forgotten he was handsome. He didn't remember he was charming. He closed his eyes and exhaled a sigh, not even trying to cover up how loud it was. He simply didn't know what he was doing. 'About six tomorrow morning,' I said. Nothing. 'Six, Mr Berringer?'

'Six,' he repeated but I wasn't sure if he got me.

'In the morning.'

'Of course,' he said at last. 'Of course, Miss Voss.'

Gladys smiled, but to me, Friday night did not signal freedom or fun. All it meant was the beginning of two days of being overwhelmed by the ordinary, two days without John to make my life come alive. So what the hell: I took a gulp of my whiskey sour, but since I'd spent lunch hour filing, the alcohol went straight north. Not that it made me silly. I didn't leap up on the cocktail table and begin a soft-shoe routine. The liquor just made the sides of my head sensitive; I was suddenly aware of the weight of my ears. It was the kind of feeling that signaled: You should be home.

So why was I sitting in the Blue Elephant, a cocktail lounge for third-rate lawyers and washed-up stockbrokers, a place so dark you couldn't see the last guy's greasy lip-prints on your glass, even though you just knew they were there? To get whatever highly sensitive, top-secret information Gladys Slade had picked up on John or Nan or Mr Leland. And also to keep her company.

The old company Gladys had at home was a radio and the *Reader's Digest*. A couple of times I'd been up to the third-floor room she rented in an area of Brooklyn with no name, south of Greenpoint. The wallpaper was so old the roses had turned brown. Even on Christmas, her landlady never once said, Come on, have cup of eggnog with my family; Gladys had to mail her rent check because the family that lived in the rest of the house wanted 'privacy.'

Both her parents had died of TB by the time she was twelve, and she had no brothers or sisters, no cousins, even. All she had were the girls at work.

I can't say life with a mother who giggles in the bushes was anything *Good Housekeeping* would recommend, but still, it was family. She'd lost track of all her sisters except for Annabel, who had married a sailor and lived on a navy base and sent birthday cards. And there were still Johnstons left in Brooklyn. We got asked to all their funerals and – until my mother had started showing up drunk – to an occasional Thanksgiving or Christmas dinner. And I had a neighborhood. I knew Ridgewood's fruit and vegetable man, the dentist and the corsetiere. And on summer nights when we all sat out on our stoops, I knew everybody's business, and they knew mine.

But after Gladys's parents died, she'd been pushed off on a cousin, who died right away, as if to say, The *nerve* of such an imposition. So Gladys lived at the Sarah Stewart MacDougal Home for Girls, run by some cheap Presbyterians, until she was eighteen. They found her the first of her furnished rooms the day she found her first (and only) job – at Blair, VanderGraff and Wadley.

Still, seeing her at the office, you'd never feel sorry for her. The law firm was all she had, but she made it hers.

Gladys took a long but ladylike slurp of her second whiskey sour. 'Do you think Mr Berringer is behaving' – she paused, and then found her word – 'normally?'

'Normal for a lawyer who's so tired he's two minutes away from dropping dead.' But there was something funny in her question, a tightness in her voice that even the loudness of her slurp wouldn't ease. 'Why?' I asked. She shrugged. 'You know something I don't know, Gladys? I can't believe it. We've been sitting here for twenty minutes.'

'Well, I know one thing.'

'What's that?'

'I know you're in love with Mr Berringer!'

My stomach flopped over; for a second, I thought I was going to give back my drink. But I just swallowed and said, 'You talk about behaving normally? *You're* the one who's nuts.' I tried to kid myself: Gladys is a great kidder. But Gladys was genuinely upset and very serious. She held her head high; her flared nostrils looked like two dark tunnels cut into a mountain. 'When did you come up with such a crazy idea? Hey, and anyway, if I was gone on someone, wouldn't I tell you, of all people?'

'I always would have thought so, Linda. We're best friends.'

Boy, was she ever on the alert. Her eyes were like two thumbtacks, trying to pin me to the wall. The possibility of me, Mr Berringer, a secret crush: It was the stuff Gladys's dreams were made of. And if I did anything – sip my drink, twirl my beads – it would give me away. So I sat frozen. But there was a terrible silence. I could hear the bartender squeezing out the sponge, moving a glass, cleaning up a spill. Then I made myself smile. I said, 'Okay, you're right, Gladys. Mr Berringer really swept me off my feet. I'm madly in love. It was his smile that got me. You know, the smile he only gives to seven million people every day. So deeply personal. So very, very private.' But Gladys didn't let down her guard. 'Oh, come on. He's not a human being. He's a charm machine. You don't think—'

'All I know is, you say you're drowning in work, but you have time to run around the office, talking to this one, that one—'

'So what? Since when do you stay stapled to your desk?'

'All of a sudden you're best friends with Marian Mulligan, and you're asking her so many questions even she's getting suspicious. If *she* gets suspicious . . . And you never even told me you were talking to her.'

'Gladys, I'm sorry. I've been crazy with work, and this is the first choice—'

She cut me off. 'How come you have time to talk to that moron Marian?'

'Because I'm *very* curious. Okay? I admit it. I'm curious about Mr Berringer, and her boss is handling part of the separation agreement. And Mr Berringer's *my* boss . . . How many bosses do you know whose wives leave them?'

'You're buttering up Marian, and then you're stopping off at Wilma's and Helen's, asking all kinds of questions, like you were Mr and Mrs North.' She almost had tears in her eyes. With the other girls she was queen, but I was her *friend*. 'I would have gone with you to ask.'

'Gladys, what's the big deal?'

She banged her glass on the table. 'Linda, the big deal is, all you do is talk about him. Someone says, Gee, there's a great glove sale at Ohrbach's, and you say, Oh, Mr Berringer, *he* wears gloves. Oh, and by the way, Mrs B, when she walked out on him . . . do you happen to know what color gloves she was wearing when she left?'

'Gladys, what's with you? I didn't talk to you about Mr Berringer for a couple of days, so it's a major felony?'

'I just don't want you to make a fool of yourself. If any of the partners get wind of it . . .'

What was she trying to pull? I thought. And then I realized: She wasn't only desperate for gossip; she was scared that if I'd fallen for John, I'd want to cherish him alone. I'd float up to the clouds, abandon her. Gladys wanted to keep me, and keep my crush for just the two of us. A Sunday special.

And part of me wanted to be kept. What a relief it would be, to talk about John, to have someone – a sober someone, my best friend – to take pleasure in all I'd gathered. Let me tell you about the veins in his hands, Gladys, about the way holds the phone. But then what would I be? Just another girl with a cheap pash for her boss.

It burst out of me: 'Listen, Gladys. There's a big, fat difference between worrying about someone – someone you have a lot of respect for – and going nuts over them. It so happens I *like* Mr Berringer. Okay? He's a wonderful, decent man. And—'

'Linda, calm down.'

'No. I mean, how would you feel if I accused you of holding back on me?'

'I didn't mean—'

Don't back down, I said to myself. 'Gladys, I'm a human being. He's someone I see five days a week, and sure, I'm sorry Mrs Berringer took a powder. More than sorry. Sad. But I'll confess something. I'm nosy. So sue me. I asked a couple of questions. You know damn well that if Mr Avenel's wife packed her bags, you'd bring in the bloodhounds, and don't tell me different. I think you owe me an apology.'

I waited. When she spoke, I could hardly hear her voice. 'I'm sorry, Linda.'

'It's okay.'

I thought: What's the percentage in turning to mush under a little pressure? Like that British boob who gave away Czechoslovakia. The only time you back down is when you're dead.

Gladys lifted her glass. 'Thanks.'

I gave one of those conspiratorial winks that you see in the movies but never in real life, but we'd just had a very dramatic situation and, sure enough, Gladys not only fell for it but winked back.

I said softly, 'A girl in my position can't be too careful. If I got tipsy . . .' I paused. 'Who knows? I could start babbling my secret. About my grand *passione* for my darling, precious John.'

Then I laughed, and my friend Gladys joined me.

I couldn't believe it!

I'd been trying to pick up the tiny little strings of eraser stuck way down between the typewriter keys with the tip of my pinkie, and there I was with my finger in my mouth, rewetting it, and who should walk by and stare at me but Nan Berringer.

Was I shocked! I thought she was in Reno! I started to say, 'Good morning, Mrs Berringer,' but I was so nervous I hadn't taken the finger out of my mouth. And she was in such a hurry all she must have heard was 'Goo—' By the time I pulled out my finger and got to 'morning,' she was past my desk, the heels of her expensive black suede shoes making shappy sounds on the brown tile floor of the corridor where the secretaries sat.

She'd swept right by John's closed office door, so she hadn't come to fling herself into his arms and say either, I forgive you, John, or, My dearest, my love, I'm so deeply sorry. No, she just kept going, and fast. Still, in that second when she passed, I got a chance to see her like never before.

God, was she pretty! I could see why John loved her. Her skin was so flawless it looked as if it was made out of the stuff that covers pearls. She wasn't actually beautiful, but what made Nan Leland Berringer a knockout was that everything was wonderful. Wonderful, nice eyes. Same with the nose and mouth. Her hair may have been a nonbreathtaking brown, but somehow it was a richer color than anyone else's. It was styled in a perfect pageboy: longer than her chin, shorter than her shoulders, and unbelievably shiny, as though she'd been given sole access to the world's best shampoo. If God had worked in a beauty parlor, He would have said, Okay, *this* is what hair is supposed to look like.

Naturally, her figure was as superb as the rest of her. Lovely, but not lovely like the figures of other lovely women. Nan was about my height but built on a finer, smaller scale. Not skinny; just petite enough to make a guy feel she'd been custom-made.

Her clothes were like gift wrapping for her specialness. Her gray dress was superior to anyone else's gray – the softest color, and the fabric so fine it looked like someone had taken a steamroller and flattened out a couple of yards of wool. It was absolutely plain; this dress didn't even have a button you could see. Still, it was beautiful.

On top it was politely tight; the skirt flared. The dress said, Look at the classy narrow shoulders and the delicate waist, and if you've got an extra five seconds, take a gander at the regal posture. You could see why John loved her.

It wasn't only the way she looked. It was Nan herself. She wasn't just a pretty twenty-one-year-old matron. Oh, sure, she was that, but she was more. Smart. It didn't only show in her eyes, like with most people. Everything about Nan was smart: the size steps she took, the way she carried her purse. Smart in a way I would never be. If I could have been anything in the world, I would have been Nan Leland Berringer.

And I thought: God, what a loss. How he must miss her.

Then I got up and trailed her.

I was definitely no intellectual, but I wasn't the class dunce, either. I figured if anyone caught me tippytoeing ten feet behind Mrs Berringer, they'd think John had sent me to spy on her, and that wouldn't be so terrific for either him or me.

So I snuck into the supply closet and came out with a couple of boxes of typing paper, enough pencils to last till 1947 and two bottles of ink; then I didn't even waste my time looking where Nan had gone. Instead, I sauntered by Gladys's desk. There's that old joke about the three major means of communications: telephone, telegraph, tell a woman. The comedian had probably worked at Blair, VanderGraff and knew Gladys.

She was on the edge of her chair, talking a mile a minute to Lenore Stevenson, the bookkeeper, who everyone called Lenny, and I don't think it was just a nickname. Lenny looked like a man in a skirt. A big man, and she had a pair of hands that would have looked great on a Giants pitcher, plus a cigarette voice that came pretty close to being as deep as Mr Leland's.

'Lin-*da*,' Gladys said, 'come here.'

'Yeah,' Lenny echoed, 'come here.' She was huge, but strong – not fat: a rhinoceros, but a gentle one. She was shy – she ate lunch alone with her ledgers, never with us in the conference room – and she hardly talked, except to Gladys, who she practically worshiped. But Lenny had a good heart and was always doing sweet things, like slipping me my pay envelope Thursday night instead of Friday morning.

I rested my supplies on Gladys's desk. 'I can't talk. I got to go and kill myself, because that's the only way I won't die from overwork.' I sighed, putting a little quaver in it – 'Boy oh boy' – and picked up my stuff.

'You must stay,' Gladys said, in her Queen of England voice.

'I "must" stay? You going to pull out a silver teapot and pour?'

'Stay, Linda,' Lenny said.

'I can't.'

Gladys added, 'We'll make it worth your while.'

Lenny nodded and crossed her arms. Gladys swiveled her head around, looking for lurkers; when it came to gossip, she trusted no one. Then she nodded at Lenny, like Go ahead.

'I was down by Mr Leland's office—' Bookkeepers could go where secretaries fear to tread.

'And guess who just happened to dance into Mr L's office?' Gladys butted in.

'The Rockettes,' I said.

'Linda, be serious,' Gladys hissed.

'Okay, I'm serious.'

'Mrs Berringer! Gladys said.

'Mr Leland's daughter,' Lenny added.

'Thanks, Len.'

'Yeah, sure, right,' Lenny rumbled. 'Anyway, guess what she told her father?'

'They invited you in to join them? You got an engraved invitation?'

'Aw, Linda, you're a card!'

'How come you got to listen in, Lenny?'

'She didn't get the door closed fast enough.'

'What did she say?' I demanded. Ever since my drink with Gladys, I stopped pretending I wasn't curious; I'd come to realize that when you're trying hard to be something you're not, people think you're phonier than you are.

Lenny raised her eyebrows and looked upward, like the secret was between her and Him . . . and Gladys too, because the next second, Lenny looked straight at her. And Gladys was almost jumping out of her chair, like she had taken a double dose of Castoria. 'Tell her,' Gladys bubbled. 'It's okay. Go *on*, Len.'

'Awright.' Lenny made circles with her shoulders, like she was getting ready to throw her world-famous fastball. 'Mrs Berringer walked in there and said, "Daddy, I won't wait another day. I'm going to Reno *tonight*." '

'Tell her what happened next,' Gladys ordered.

'Mr Leland said, "Close the door, Nan." ' Lenny could add and subtract like a genius but sometimes seemed a little slow at general thinking.

'*No.* After that,' Gladys said.

'Oh. See, Mrs Berringer came back to close the door, but the second she was doing it, you could still hear her. And you know what she said? "I don't care what you say. I'm going to marry Quentin!" '

# *Chapter Four*

The window behind Edward Leland's desk was open, and the year's first warm breeze floated in; even Wall Street smelled sweet. But in that office on the forty sixth floor, there wasn't a trace of spring softness.

Mr Leland stared as I stood near the door of his office. Not a man's stare – no *Look at those legs!* – but a cold look, searching for something, and the worst of it was, I had no idea what he was after. Without thinking, I brought my pencil up to my mouth; when you're scared, there's nothing like a good, hard chew on a pencil for fast relief. But the way Mr Leland's eyes were boring through me, he would have known the depth of the teeth holes. I lowered it.

Some men undress you with their eyes. Edward Leland did worse. He looked inside you. Sure, I knew he couldn't actually read my mind, but still, I would have felt a lot safer if that dark stare had been meant to burn through my yellow sweater, my gray skirt, to observe my most private of privates – instead of my mind.

'Sit down, Miss Voss,' he said from behind his desk. Somewhere outside, a bird flying over the southern tip of Manhattan, not knowing it didn't belong in the corridors of power, tweeted. For that second, the half of Edward Leland's face that could move softened. Then it went back to its usual hardness, and I looked away.

His office was filled with the mess of an organized man: manila file folders in precise stacks on two cushions of the couch, a couple of cartons under the window. The glass doors of his bookshelves were open, and the gaps where books had been pulled looked like knocked-out teeth. The books themselves were piled on a corner of his desk. An open travel case – a big, black one, like a giant doctor's bag – rested on a brown leather wing chair near the wall. I gave a fast peek as I passed. The white of underwear. Shoes. A heavy sweater – beautiful, like Sonja Henie's ice-skating partner would wear.

I sat in another leather chair, right across the desk from Mr Leland, opened my pad, flipped to a clean page and looked up, ready. But Mr Leland wasn't. He wasn't ready to do anything except stare. This time it was not to examine my mind but to send a message, to let me know that he knew I had taken inventory of his travel bag. I shifted a little but the leather seat was so slippery I nearly slid off. I thought about landing on the floor – splat – on my backside, my skirt flying up, and then felt my face flush. Edward Leland saw that; in fact, he seemed to see everything. He probably knew I was crazy about the sweater in his bag. (It was dark blue, with white starry snowflakes.)

'I suppose you're curious about why I asked you to stop in, Miss Voss.' What answer did he want? Yes? No? I thought about it so long that when I finally decided Yes, it was too late to say it.

Edward Leland sat motionless, framed by the high back of his chair, never moving his eyes from me. He was like a scientist examining a new specimen: Note how these secretaries react under pressure. Their eyes dart around the room. Oh, and observe, they chew their bottom lip. I took a deep breath. I forced myself to sit as still as he was. Then, suddenly, as if there had been no silence, he went on. 'You know, I've been out of the office quite a lot lately.' I nodded. 'Do you have any idea where I've been?' I don't know how I knew, but I knew this was not a moment to play dumb.

I told him what the girls were saying at lunch. 'I heard you were in Washington.'

'I see. Well, what are people saying I'm doing in Washington?' he inquired. Get me out of here, I thought. Never once moving his shadow eyes from my face, he asked, 'Am I making you uncomfortable?'

No, I said to myself, this is my idea of a truly swell time. But out popped: 'A little.'

'I don't mean to, but I like to know what's being bruited about the office.' His eyes were darker than brown. They were black disks; there didn't seem to be any difference in color between the irises and the pupils. 'Now, what am I supposed to be doing in Washington?'

'No one really knows, sir.'

'No theories?'

His voice was low and so growly; that's what made his questions scary. This great, important voice, this voice that accomplished whatever it wanted – it was being used on me. Oh, God, I was starting to sweat: down the back of my neck, then in front, dribbling from under my brassiere to my belly button.

That was the moment he picked to smile at me. It was a wide smile, kind, the sort lawyers never give out, except maybe to their best clients. Like his voice, his smile was a weapon an effective one, all the more because it was off center in that damaged face. But it lit him up. It made him the most wonderful person in the world. I found myself flooded with happiness. Life was good – and Edward Leland was letting up on me.

'No hunches about what I've been up to, Miss Voss?' Okay, so he wasn't letting up.

'I guess you're doing something for your clients, Mr Leland.' His smile stopped. He turned a paper clip over and over, waiting, patient. He knew he'd get what he wanted. 'Is there anything else, sir?'

'What kind of something, Miss Voss?'

'Mr Leland, I'm sorry . . .'

He leaned toward me. The light reflected off his black eyes; they looked unnaturally bright. 'Come now. You seem to be a bright girl. There's a war going on in Europe. What would a lawyer want in Washington?'

It didn't take a genius. Anybody who had enough intelligence to know how to turn on the radio could figure that one out. 'I guess it would help your clients if you knew the government's plans. Like for instance, how much aid we're going to be giving to England. If it's a lot, they could make a lot of money.' I should have said 'profit.' Rich people don't like the word 'money.'

But it didn't seem to bother Mr Leland. 'Very good,' he said. 'Any other ideas?'

I swallowed hard. My throat hurt. He was playing a game. No, he was giving me a test, and for the life of me, I didn't know whether it would be better to pass or to fail. But I gave it the old college (or, in my case, high school) try. 'You could be, well, a person who feels we shouldn't get mixed up over there and you're trying to make sure we don't.' In other words, an America Firster, an isolationist bastard. If he kept asking questions, sooner or later (sooner) he'd figure out my politics; they would not put a song in the heart of a Republican. But how could I stop his examination? Bash him with my steno pad? Run?

'I'm an isolationist? An intriguing theory, but I'm quite open about my interventionists leanings. But I find this interesting. I like to know what people are thinking and sometimes' – he picked up a gold and black fountain pen and rotated it between his palms – 'I get rather out of touch. Tell me more.' My throat closed tighter. I hated his cold, upper-class 'rather.' He put down the pen. 'Go on, Miss Voss.'

It burst out: 'Maybe you're doing some kind of spy stuff for the government.' I tried to laugh at my crazy imagination (and prayed he would join me), but I couldn't even begin to push my face muscles into a laugh. You know why? I believed it was true. Sure, I just tossed off the remark, but I must have been thinking it, deep down, for a long time. This guy across the desk from me who's always taking trips could be doing *anything*. And something dangerous seemed more like Edward Leland than something just clever.

Then suddenly I thought: This isn't fair, calling me in here, pressuring me, forcing me to talk. He could ask me anything he wanted, and if he didn't like my answer, or didn't like me, there went my twenty-five bucks a week. There went my life.

'This isn't fair,' he said. 'I've been cross-examining you and haven't given you a clue to why I asked you to drop in.'

How do you figure someone like him? I saw a man who could almost read minds, who made trips to Washington the way I made trips to the five-and-dime. But I also saw something more than a powerhouse New York lawyer. I'd seen a few of those. He was different.

It showed in Edward Leland's fascinating face. For some reason, it was a face every big shot in the country was drawn to look into. And every little shot: I had to force myself not to stare at him.

Although Edward Leland's voice was tough – gravelly, low – and although the word around the office was that he'd grown up poor, on a Vermont farm, talking to cows, 'You're quite perceptive. I am doing a bit of work for the government.' A bit of work. 'Although certainly not your "spy stuff." '

Certainly not, my behind, I thought. 'Yes, sir,' I said.

'The thing of it is, what with the situation in Europe, I need someone who can do some secretarial work – in German. Not a great deal. Nowhere near the sort of thing I'd want to hire someone for.'

'If there's anything I can do, Mr Leland . . .' That was the best I could come up with. No secretarial course at Grover Cleveland High School had offered Good Manners in Potential Espionage situations.

'I've taken the liberty of checking your personnel file and making a few enquiries,' Mr Leland went on. 'Do you know why?'

God, if the law business ever went bust, this guy could make a fortune playing Twenty Questions. Then I started talking fast, because I didn't want him to read *that* thought. 'If you're doing stuff for the government, then you probably don't want someone taking dictation who has a secret crush on some German general.'

'Who's your favorite German general?' he asked suddenly. For that second he seemed playful, almost young. I guess he was relieved I hadn't gotten up and goose-stepped yet; so far, I was okay.

'You mean who do I hate most?' He nodded. 'Right now, I guess Kaupitsch.'

Wow, he stopped being lighthearted real fast; I'd pushed the magic button. But it was weird; it didn't take a Yale lawyer to know about Kaupitsch, the Nazi bum running the invasion of Denmark; his name was plastered on page one of every newspaper in the city. 'I see you're up-to-date on the invasion,' Mr Leland said, not sounding too thrilled about it.

Not up-to-date like I bet you're up-to-date. Would I love to have said that. 'I read the *Daily News*, Mr Leland,' was what I said instead.

And then, boom! My mind went straight to that sweater in his valise, that heavy snowflake sweater on a warm April day. I bet it wasn't so warm in Denmark. But then I thought: Nah. How could he be going any place near an invasion? He could go down to Washington and read spy reports, but—

'This is how it stands, Miss Voss. Your file looks fine. The next step, because this does involve the government – in the most peripheral way – is to have one of the agencies check into your background.'

'You mean like the FBI?'

He just kept going. 'I have some papers for you to fill out. The usual information: name, school, previous employers. But before you do, I think we should make certain' – I got another smile from him, a little smaller this time, not real; a smooth lawyer smile, like the ones John gave out – 'that you don't mind having your life under, shall we say, scrutiny. Do you understand?'

'You want to make sure my favorite uncle isn't in the SS.'

'Exactly. I'd like to know a bit about your family.'

'Well, my mother's side is all English, I think. But not English English: American.' He picked up a pencil and jotted something down. I could have saved him the trouble, taken it in shorthand and given it back, word for word. 'My father's family is one-hundred-percent German, but dead. And even when they weren't – dead, I mean – they weren't Nazis or anything.' I could have said, Hey, listen, there's nothing to worry about: they're Jews, and cleared up the whole thing. Cleared it up so much I might lose my job. So I just went on. 'My father worked in a sausage plant. He was a foreman. But you know, the Depression . . .' There was something about Edward Leland that made you keep talking. If I didn't watch myself I would give him my life story, from my first spoonful of Pablum to my father's religion to my being madly in love with his (for another couple of weeks) son-in-law. 'My grandfather died when my dad was little – back in the 1890s, I guess.

And my grandmother worked in a button factory until my dad got his first job.'

'She's the one you spoke of so fondly, the one who taught you German?'

'Yes.' So that's why he'd been so interested back in February.

'Any other family, friends?'

'My mother has four sisters, but the only one we keep in touch with lives in Seattle now. And we have some cousins in Brooklyn – Oh, you mean my father's side. Just a couple of old relatives in Germany – Berlin – that my grandma used to write to.'

'Do you know their names?'

What he was asking was, Are they Nazis? 'I can't remember their names. But they're probably in their late seventies by now. They were two old ladies, sisters. I think one was called Liesl.'

'What was her first name?'

'Liesl's a first name, Mr Leland.' These guys thought everything female should be Mary or Babs. 'I don't know her last name. Anyway, they could be dead by now. I think they were around my grandmother's age, and she'd be seventy-nine.'

'Do you have any friends, relatives or neighbors who've expressed sympathy with Hitler or his policies?'

'Mr Leland, the only people who really like the Nazis are some of the ones who came over in the last ten, twenty years. They're still German. But people in Ridgewood are loyal Americans.'

'I'm sure they are.' It was weird; for a second we just eyed each other, both of us knowing that his gentlemanly 'I'm sure they are' was full of bull. And in the next second, both of us decided to forget it. We looked away.

'All right,' Mr Leland said. 'I think that's all.' He pushed the forms towards me. 'Naturally, you understand that what we've discussed here goes no farther.'

'Yes, Mr Leland.'

'*No one* sees these forms. Should there come a time when you do work for me, that work is to be completely confidential.'

I folded the papers carefully and stuck them in my steno pad and wondered: Does this mean I won't be working for John anymore? I clutched the pad so tight the wire top cut into my hand. Does this mean that with Nan in Reno, John might be leaving the firm and they had to find something else for me, that—

'I'll only need you now and then. Naturally, you'll continue to work for Mr Berringer,' Mr Leland said. 'Do you find the arrangement satisfactory, Miss Voss?'

'Yes, sir.'

He stared at me again. 'Well, I look forward to working with you, Miss Voss.'

'Thank you, Mr Leland. Will that be all?'

'For now.'

By eight o'clock that night, I was overtired the way a little kid gets: clumsy, and so irritable I felt on the verge of tears. My whole body was so weary, so limp, that if I didn't watch myself, I'd flop forward and crack my head on my typewriter; I could see the blood dripping onto the semicolon and the *L*. And what made working late even harder was thinking about my mother home alone, all made up, with no one to tell her how beautiful she looked before she went out into the night.

But I perked up fast, and it didn't take a gallon of coffee. John came out of his office, stood by my desk and picked up the letters I'd typed. He signed them fast. 'I spoke with Mr Leland late this afternoon,' he said. I stopped what I was doing, which was licking an envelope, and remembered just in time to put it down, or I would have wound up with an envelope dangling from my tongue. All day I'd been worrying about what to do if Mr Leland had work for me. Since I wasn't allowed to talk about it, I couldn't say, Pardon me, Mr Berringer, I have to stop what I'm doing for you and go to Mr Leland's office and take a spy letter. And I couldn't excuse myself to go to the ladies' room and saunter back an hour and a half later. 'He mentioned he'd given you some forms,' John added.

'Forms?' Mr Leland had ordered me to stay mum. What could I say? Sure, I've got this mile-long FBI form to fill out. Want me to show it to you?

John smiled, nodded and gave me one of his special winks.

'You're right, of course. You have no idea whether my interest . . .' His hand rested on my typewriter: long-fingered, elegant – but not too elegant. 'Good thinking, Miss Voss. I'll ask Mr Leland to let you know I'm all right.' I was mesmerized by his hand. 'You'll find' – his voice dropped to almost a whisper, but a whisper full of pride – 'that I'm working very closely with Mr Leland' – he pulled back his hand, slipped it into his pocket – 'on this matter.'

I wanted to believe in John completely. I wanted to think there was nothing he did that wasn't absolutely perfect. But I couldn't. If some guy's daughter had turned my life upside down, I wouldn't be bragging about working very closely with him.

And as far as Mr Leland went, if a son-in-law didn't have what it took to hold on to my daughter, I wouldn't be sipping brandy with him and saying, Well, old bean, how do we best contain the growing Fascist peril?

And look at Nan. Twenty-one years old, a genuine intellectual, a girl everyone said, if she'd been a man, would have gone as far as her husband, or even her father. A brain, but she runs into her father's office blabbing away about Quentin when even a chimpanzee would have had the sense to close the door.

I couldn't figure them. They didn't act like real people – or even movie people. They acted as if they had secret rules no one else was in on. Stick John and Mr Leland in a closed room where normal guys would throttle each other, and what happened? They got cordial. They worked 'very closely.' Put Nan Leland Berringer in a public place, under pressure, where you'd think: Well, here it is, Stiff Upper Lip Time, and what do you get? A Smith College genius jabbering so loud about marrying number two – while she still had number one – that you could hear her in Hoboken.

I could sort of understand John: not his pride, but at least his unwillingness to tell a man like his father-in-law to go soak his head. The one I really didn't get was Edward Leland. For all his expensive suits and good grammar, he was a guy *nobody* would want to cross. And what does he say to his only child? 'Close the door, Nan.' Okay, no one knew what went on after, but everyone could see she got exactly what her little heart desired: a first-class compartment on the next train to Reno.

Sure, Nan was probably a handful, but couldn't her father – a real tough customer, who handled handfuls for a living – couldn't he say: Listen, sister, you were so crazy about this guy you couldn't wait till college let out in June to marry him, so what are you doing? Throwing him over in less than three years? Come on. Give him a chance. Go home, have a couple of kids. And if I hear one more word about this Quentin, you'll get a good, swift kick in the pants.

That's what my father would have said.

The worst thing about being a secretary is the little chairs. They're very low, so when you boss comes over to your desk, that first instant you turn to him – guess what you're staring at. Not that you could see anything, because in the entire history of the Association of the Bar of the City of New York there has never been one single pair of revealing trousers.

John came out of his office again. He was so near, reaching across me to put down a bill of lading. 'You'll see this gets to Mr Withey first thing in the morning,' he said.

'First thing,' I said from my chair.

He was so close his arm brushed against my shoulder, and that second my guard must have been down, because all of a sudden, wham! Desire that started deep, low down, then exploded, destroying my sense. My face got feverish. I was dizzy. I tried to get control, to slow my breathing so it didn't give me away; I concentrated on a piece of carbon paper. I held it up to the light, pretending to check if it was still any good. That let me turn away from him, because it wasn't just the heat of my own face I was feeling. He was close enough that I could tell some of that heat was coming from him.

But it wasn't me who was heating John up. I felt it anyway, the rising temperature of a man in desperate need of a woman, a man dying to rush out of the office, leave the day behind him. He shifted from one foot to the other, ready – more than ready – to break out into the night.

'Is there anything else, Mr Berringer?'

'Excuse me?' He was distracted. It wasn't fatigue.

'Anything else tonight?'

'No. I'll be going now.'

Where to? Back to his apartment? To eat dinner alone? To get into bed, to lie on sheets he hadn't changed since she'd left a month before, to breathe deep, trying to pick up the dying scent of her perfume?

Or to go to someone else? A lady, another Nan, who would ease him, massage his neck with cool, smart fingers? Or to some tramp, as hot and ready as he was?

'See you in the morning, Mr Berringer. Have a good – '

But he was halfway down the hall. He didn't even take his briefcase.

Whoever made the modern furniture in John's office was a great craftsman. In the darkened room, lit only by the hall light, his black desk had such a gorgeous, deep glow it looked alive. I sat in his chair and swiveled back and forth. No one was left in the whole law firm, not even the cleaning lady. In the silence, I pushed aside all the other women I'd imagined John with and thought about him alone in his apartment. I pictured him throwing aside his jacket, loosening his tie, unbuttoning his shirt, feeling the soft night air on his chest. Standing there, in a foyer or living room as dark as his office. Alone, in the quiet, aching to be touched. Just like me.

I stroked the desk's silky wood, ran my fingers over the smooth corners. Beautifully made.

Strong too. There was no way you could get the locked lower-right-hand drawer open without a key. Not that I would have done anything funny with a hairpin, but with most drawers, you don't need burglary tools: one good fingernail and sharp yank would do the trick.

I sat up straighter; I would never jimmy open a drawer. Then I felt under the blotter and the base of the desk lamp. Nuts. Nothing. Not in the unlocked drawers, either. But in the end I found it, inside the flap of his leather calendar: his desk key.

Talk about good craftsmanship: The key opened the lock without even the tiniest click, and the drawer slid out as if I'd whistled and it couldn't wait to come to me. I felt around. Just one thick manila envelope.

I got up and locked his door. If you know you're doing something you should be ashamed of, you should either stop or do it thoroughly; there's not such thing as semi-sin.

Then I came back and switched on John's desk lamp. The envelope was one of Blair, VanderGraff and Wadley's. It had nothing written on it. I eased open the metal clasp, spilled everything out onto the desk, memorized the mess, then arranged it all into a perfect pile. I may have been a sneak, but no one could say I wasn't a great secretary.

Then I looked through it. It was all hers. John had collected enough mementos to open a Nan Leland Berringer museum. Except it would have been a pretty pathetic museum: love tokens of a wife in love with someone else.

I started with the two letters. the first must have been written right when they began:

> Dear John, On Sunday, I told you I am congenitally incapable of being coy. Therefore, I will not try to subvert you with feminine wiles, nor will I have some mutual acquaintance drop my name before you at frequent intervals. I will merely say I want very much to see you when I get back to New York, right after my exams.
>
> Yes, I realize this is awkward for you, that you did not intend an afternoon's conversation, a mild flirtation, to be taken so seriously. Your womanly ideal is not an eighteen-year-old college freshman. And yet . . . And yet, I know you were drawn to me as I was to you.
>
> You see, John, I told you I could not be coy.
>
> You said I must be getting the rush from the Amherst boys.

I don't know if it is a rush. I do know I have no interest in boys. I want a man of brilliance and sensitivity. A man like you.

I cannot begin to tell you how much our conversation in the gazebo meant to me, to have someone who not only cares deeply for the things I care about, but who can express himself with such insight and profundity. I want very much to talk again. I feel we have a great deal to say to each other.

I told you I was not coy. What I did not tell you was that I am relentless. If you don't call me, I will call you.

My best,

She signed it 'N.' I thought: That's how they get rich, saving money on ink. And then I thought: I can't believe an eighteen-year-old girl would have the guts to write that kind of letter. And even more, I can't believe she had John Berringer alone in a gazebo and walked out in a tizzy over his profundity. Profundity? But there it was, in black and white.

The second letter was signed 'N' too:

Darling I can't tell you how sorry I am. It was my fault. I should never have gone to the hotel with you and let things get that far. I know you're not some adolescent, that you are used to having anything you want from a woman and that your needs are a man's needs.

I put the letter down on the desk. This was the worst thing I'd ever done. It was like being the lowest – a Peeping Tom.

But, John, when it happens, it has to be right. It has to be done (please, oh, please, don't think I'm being pretentious) in a state of grace. I love you. I adore you. And if you insist, I will do anything you want to prove I am indeed yours. But I beg you, don't insist until, well, until it is truly the time.

Forever,

I held the envelope up to the light. The postmark was February 19, eleven days before they got married.

I put it down and thought of what I'd done with George Armbruster. If I hadn't come so cheap, if I'd played my cards right and said, Uh-uh, nothing doing without a state of grace, Georgie – who knows? He could have introduced me to his bachelor brother the next day, saying, This here is a fine, upright girl. I could have had a house, two kids, a dinette set.

The life before me was more interesting than my own. I went back to the pile on the desk. Ticket stubs. A book by Goethe, *Divan of East and West*, which I'd heard was pretty hot stuff. It was from her; in it she'd written, 'To mein Liebe, From N.' To my love. She may have been a genius, but N could have used a couple of German lessons; if she was going to use 'love' like that, it should have been *Für meine einzige Liebe* or maybe *mein Geliebter.* John would know that, but what could he say? My darling, 'mein Liebe' is stinko German. Your usage definitely isn't anything to write home about. But he couldn't say anything to Nan anymore. So he kept the book, the letters – all of it – because it was the closest he could get to her. In the late afternoons, when he said, No calls, Miss Voss, he was probably sitting there fingering the ticket stubs or rereading the Goethe.

There was a concert program from Carnegie Hall. The orchestra must have been rotten, because all over the page that told about Bach's B Minor Mass there were scribbles. 'Putrid!' 'The tempo!' and 'Will it ever end?' in Nan's handwriting. 'I love you' in his. There were a couple of clippings from the society page: their engagement and wedding announcements. I got a few new pieces of information: a list of bridesmaids with expensive names – 'The Misses Floria Wyatt, Honore Delafield, Dorothea and Alice Brinton, Eleanor Randel and Victoria Courtney.' I thought: I bet me and Honore Delafield could be great buddies. Hi, Honore. Linda, sweetie! Hi! I found out Nan's real name was Anne and that the late Mrs Edward Leland's name was Caroline Bell and that she was President Theodore Roosevelt's cousin. I learned that John was the son of the late Mr and Mrs Charles Berringer of Port Washington, New York.

I was so taken up with these new Berringers, wondering who they were and when they'd died, that I didn't notice the picture until my elbow rested on something slick. It was a small, glossy snapshot of Nan and John. They were lying together on a hammock, their arms and legs so tangled up they looked like one person. She wore shorts and a pullover. He wore cotton slacks. No shirt. Nan's head rested on his shoulder and her hand, with its wedding ring, seemed to have been caught by the camera, as it caressed his bare chest. They weren't talking profundity in that hammock. What they had was what I would have died for.

God, was John beautiful! Nothing I'd imagined being under his suit was as good as what was in that little picture. His body was so perfect it almost didn't seem real. It looked as sleek and as hard as the modern furniture Nan loved. No wonder she hadn't been able to keep her hand to herself.

I took a deep breath. I put everything back into the envelope. Well, I thought, and let out a high half laugh, that was a good night's work.

Then I turned off the lamp, sat in the black room and started to cry.

# *Chapter Five*

The sun sparkled, and the surface of the dark water of Sheepshead Bay glittered as if someone had tossed in a handful of diamonds. Gladys Slade, wearing a middy blouse that would have looked great on a kid in third-grade assembly, stood with her hand shielding her eyes. But she did it so dramatically she could have been Admiral of the Fleet, saluting all the ships at sea. 'Mr Leland used to have a summer house right on the water. In Connecticut.' She spoke a little too loud, as if to be heard over the crash of the waves, except there weren't any waves – only the relaxed slapping of the water against the wooden piles of the pier. 'He sold it when Nan went off to boarding school, right before the Crash. I hear he made a pret-ty penny.' Gladys could take any subject – water, *The Private Lives of Elizabeth and Essex*, pickled watermelon rinds – and tie it up to the law firm.

I sighed. My best friend. But to tell the truth, Gladys was one of the unspoken minuses of being an old maid. Forget about your face shriveling into a prune, about not having children, about having to support yourself; the real bad news was that you got stuck with other old maids for friends. I know that sounds hard-hearted, but frankly, 99.99999 percent of them were walking around ringless not because of a receding chin or a polka-dot complexion but because of some tragic flaw in the personality department – no humor, or too much, or they were whiny or pathetically eager to please. All my friends from high school, bright, lively girls, had gotten grabbed up, and right from the start they were too busy keeping their husbands captivated to have any spare nights for girls like me: the Unfortunate Unmarried. And so, sure, maybe I did spend most of my time longing for John, but part of that yearning was pure: a prayer for someone to talk to who had something to say.

Gladys continued to squint out at the bay. A slight breeze ruffled her bangs, and she clapped them tight against her forehead as if her head had been hit by a hurricane. 'So anyway, he had this house on the water,' she went on. 'And then his wife dies. Well! Linda, there were *days* at a time when he didn't show up at work. He didn't even call in or anything. You know what he did? He'd leave little Nan with her nanny – isn't that funny? Nan, nanny – and drive up to Connecticut and take out his sailboat and just sail for four or five days, *all alone*. Not that anyone ever said anything.' She looked away from the bay, right at me. 'They wouldn't have dared. I mean, even way back then, Mr Leland had that way about him, and being a war hero and all that, he could pretty much do what he wanted. But you know what the most fascinating thing is? He chose classiness. It was what he automatically wanted, even in grief. I mean, sailing is *very* stylish.'

'Why does going out in a sailboat make him classy? Is puking on a starboard or whatever it's called an upper-class mourning practice?'

'You just talk like that to get attention,' Gladys said. ' "Puking." And sex things.'

'Never in the same sentence.'

'I'm serious, Linda. And if you don't mind, while I'm on the subject of your talking: You kept forcing everybody at lunch Friday to listen while you went on about the war, like you were a man or a college professor and it was really interesting. You've got to stop it. I mean, name me one single person in the law firm – not counting lawyers – who wants to hear about troop movements. I'll bet you anything the lawyers don't even care.'

I looked across the dazzling sunlit water. 'Listen to me, Gladys. Don't you understand that it's not just Europe – or Asia? It's the whole world. It's *you*.'

'Stop it.'

'I'm telling you, France will be next.'

'Here it comes: Linda Voss with her ever-popular "The Big, Bad Nazis" song and dance.'

'Gladys, don't you get what people are letting Hitler do to them? They're giving up because they're terrified – of a bully. What do they think he's going to do next? Send them roses? No, he's going to hit them again, harder and harder.'

Unlike Gladys, the part of the world that read beyond the society news and the comics was actually surprised. That was what was so hard for me to believe: that all the military geniuses and hotshot politicians couldn't have figured out what was going to happen.

In Brooklyn it was a beautiful spring Sunday. People were smiling as if they didn't have a care in the world. But the Germans were on the march again. Holland was gone, Belgium was going.

'You always expect the worst from them' Gladys said.

'They always do the worst.'

'But you're German, Linda.'

'I am not.'

'I don't mean you go around drinking beer from those funny glasses. It's just that . . . you are *very* interested in whatever they do.'

'Aren't you?'

'Not the way you are. I mean, grabbing everybody's newspaper, reading *battle* reports.' She looked at me accusingly. 'Anita was talking about her bridesmaids' gifts, and you started going on about the Maginot Line.'

The Sunday crowds filled the sidewalks. Teenage boys spilled onto the piers. They'd taken off their shirts, ignoring the slight spring chill, and rolled them into pillows and stretched out on the wood boards. Their chests, white from winter, rose and fell with each relaxed breath. But before long, a dark, leather-skinned boat captain yelled, 'Hey, get outta here!' And the kids got up, put on their shirts and shuffled off, mumbling, 'In your hat and over your ears, bud.' But they were a good-natured bunch.

'Gladys, listen to me. If those boys lived in the countries their families came from, they'd be carrying rifles.' Then I added: 'Or they'd be dead.'

Gladys started to stroll again. I gave up and went along. Everyone in the city wanted to be outside on a day like this. They all seemed to have grabbed a trolley and come to Sheepshead Bay to stare at the water and inhale the sharp salt air. For a nickel, it was like traveling to another country. Gladys and I weaved in and out of the crowd. Finally, we found an empty bench. I sat and put my head way back and let the sun warm my cheeks.

Gladys and I spent every Sunday together; I wasn't sure whether to feel grateful or doomed. It had started a couple of months after my Grandma Olga died. Suddenly, I had a long day with no company; Saturday was Binge Night for my mother, so Sundays she could barely manage to stagger to the bathroom, much less walk around the block. I'd said to Gladys one Friday in the office, Maybe if you're free Sunday, if you want to go to a movie or something . . . I was nervous she'd think I was overstepping the bounds of what was a nice office friendship, but she said, Well, I have nothing special this Sunday, as if every other Sunday for the next two years was booked up.

So we went to a movie and then out for a club sandwich, and while I was trying to decide whether to wait three or six months before asking again, Gladys said, Do you want to go for a ride on the Staten Island ferry next Sunday?

After all those years with the whole world married, I had someone to do things with. A friend. We went all over the city, mainly to movies, but sometimes to the zoo, the botanical gardens, a couple of times even to a museum.

She was my best friend, my only one, but all we ever had on those Sundays was more lunch conversation – although with hideously elaborate detail. Did you know Mr Nugent was Phi Beta Kappa? You never saw his key? Or: Helen Rogers says Margaret on the switchboard says the widow Mr Leland is keeping company with is a Mrs Carter. Or Mrs Carver. Last year he was seeing Mrs Lambert Jones. The divorcée, but it wasn't her fault. Did I tell you about her? See, her husband fell in love with her son's cello teacher. Anyway, Mrs Jones – the first one; she's not supposed to be musical and the husband *loved* music – she has practically a mansion on Fifth Avenue and . . .

Gladys was ecstatic to have all Sunday – an entire day uninterrupted by work – to talk about the office. Blair, VanderGraff and Wadley: that was the extent of her life. And I never asked for anything deeper from her, because I'd poked around and discovered her passion for the law firm was her sole passion. She liked the movies only to the degree that Gary Cooper in *Sergeant York* reminded her of Mr Leland.

'If you're so American,' Gladys suddenly said to me, 'why did you bring German magazines to the office? And how come you know more about what's happening over there than Roosevelt?'

'If I know more than Roosevelt, then we're all going to be goose-stepping a year from now.' I turned and looked at her. 'Listen, don't you understand what's going on over there?'

'I read the *Mirror* and the *Journal-American*.'

'So?'

'So I still can't see why you get so . . .' She paused to find a word. 'Upset.'

'Upset? Did the *Mirror* or the *Journal* happen to mention what those Nazi shit-heads did to Holland?'

'Linda!'

We both sat back and stared out at the bay; she wouldn't look at me. The boats at the piers right in front of us – *Little Muriel* and *Star of Brooklyn* – bobbed on the gentle, lapping water. The Nazis were bombing Belgium, mopping up in Holland – murdering the few good men they hadn't already slaughtered – and Gladys was reeling from shock because I'd called them shit-heads.

I couldn't understand people. Gladys, the other girls at work, my neighbors. Why weren't they angrier? I got hot under the collar just thinking about the excuses people had been making since the year before: Oh, Hitler had some good reasons for going into Czechoslovakia.

Come on. If you're a German dictator with a problem, you throw a few chancellors together in a room and you figure something out. You don't go rolling in with panzer divisions.

If you have a beef with someone, do you sent in the Luftwaffe with a couple of tons of bombs, the way he did to Rotterdam, that son of a bitch?

'Do you really think he'll go into France?' Gladys finally asked.

Her voice a little softer; maybe I was too hard on her. She was no dope, but she didn't want any part of what was happening over there, so she'd simply put it out of her mind. Now, though, American were beginning to get troubled. Frightened, even. I could hear it – that tremor of fear, that Oh, no, I could get *hurt* – in Glady's voice. But why wasn't she – why weren't all of them – angry, like me?

'Of course he'll go into France,' I said. 'And all we can hope is that the French are tougher and smarter than I think they are.'

'What if he beats them?'

'Gladys, what do you think?'

'I don't know.'

'England.'

'No. Come *on*.'

Gladys got up and walked over to an ice cream cart. It was an old white icebox on two bicycle wheels, covered with decals of ice cream pops, cones, and sundaes in every gorgeous color possible. Usually, though, all the carts ever had was vanilla, so soft that by the time it got scooped into the cone and handed over to you, it was mush that flowed over your hand and down your arm.

What if I could *really* talk to John. I'd say, You know, two years ago, right around this time of year, I was sitting on a park bench in Ridgewood with my Grandma Olga. Such a smart lady, but she was still saying, 'Hitler and his people. Trash.'

John would believe me. He'd know that when Hitler came into power, most of the German-speaking people in America, like Olga, viewed him as if he were some slobby fifth cousin who shows up at Christmas diner, shoots off his mouth, and then drools into the *Berliner Scholsspunsch*; he wouldn't be around long. But he was, and none of those smart German-speakers could explain it or understand it. So they said, Oh well, what's the real harm in it? When I'd explained the harm to Olga in 1935 she didn't believe me. That day in 1938 in the park she'd said, 'You'll see, he'll calm down, now that everyone takes him seriously.' I answered sharply: 'No he won't. And you-know-who he especially won't calm down about.'

Olga didn't say anything, dismissing my reminder; she may have been a Jew, but she wasn't a *Jew.* Finally she said: 'But even if you're right, Linda, what can we do?'

What can we do? That kind of thinking would make John as crazy as it made me. We'd agree that what got us more than anything else was the effect of that maniac on *everyone*, not just on an old German lady. On big, strong, smart men. Listen to any of his speeches – not the few sentences before the radio switched over to the commentator and the Jell-O commercial – and just *hear* the German under the voice of the translator. I would turn to John and say, Listen, you know he's out of his mind with his rantings about Siegfried and a whole bunch of stupid Germanic gods – what's he talking about? And his carrying on about inferior races. What was *he?* John would answer: The lowest of the low. He'd understand.

All you had to do was look at Hitler and you saw it – a flat, mean peasant face. But right from the beginning, all these big, strong, smart men fell apart the minute he challenged them. Old von Hindenburg, the cream of the crop, the best Germany had to offer: What does he do? He says, Here, Herr Hitler, take Germany. It's yours. Take whatever you want.

And before Hindenburg bellied up, all you had to do was read the paper to realize what Hitler and his group were: garbage. The worst kind of garbage, because they weren't just out-of-control animals or petty criminals. They were twisted, and so filled with hate that one or two nights' rampage wasn't enough to wear them out. *Nothing* would ever be enough for them, and I knew it and anyone with half a brain knew it, and what I wanted to know was *why*, damn it. Look at all the best men in Germany, the best men all over the world, and tell my why their guts turned to calf's-foot jelly over the Nazis – over garbage.

If men can't be men, who do they expect to be brave? Women?

John would say, Don't worry. There are men like me . . . We'll take care of it.

Gladys came back empty-handed from the ice cream Wagon. 'They were out of strawberry,' she said.

'Too bad.' Maybe I'd sounded too sarcastic. Why should I be mad at Gladys because she wasn't mad at Hitler? Neither one of us had a life so full of wonderful moments that we could afford to throw away a perfect Sunday where passersby might smile at us, where a strange man might tip his hat. We needed whatever pleasure we could find – including strawberry. 'You want to look for a candy store or something?'

'No.' She sat down beside me. 'I don't want to give up the bench.' She waited for a second and asked her inevitable next question: 'Anything new with Mr B?'

'Nothing.'

'He hasn't said *anything?*'

'Not a peep.'

'No' – she gave me a significant stare – 'signs?'

'Not even a twitch. But you know beneath all those Charlie Charming smiles he's not the most emotional guy in the world.'

'Linda, do you honestly think he *cares* she's gone?'

'He's got to care. I mean, forget the marriage stuff – you know, man and wife. Who does he have to talk to?'

Gladys nodded. And then I thought, Who do *I* have to talk to? Not about Mr Leland's dead wife or Mr Avenel's unfortunately live one, but about the world. If I could actually talk to John, not just imagine conversations . . . He knows so much. We could discuss –

'Oh, look! There's another cart down there, past the big boat,' Gladys said. 'You want anything?' I shook my head. 'Let me see if they have strawberry. I'll be right back.'

Gladys hurried off to the right. From the left, a group of day fishermen in mashed-down sports hats clomped by, carrying their catch on strings; the flounders, still wet, dribbled along the sidewalk. Then one of the men opened his mouth wide and held up his string of fish over it and – while the others gave off loud, manly ho-ho-hos – let the fish water drip down his throat.

I wanted so much to *talk*, to be able to ask John why – forgetting Germany for a minute – why all the little countries and England and France could say, Okay, Adolf, old buddy, it's all yours. What was wrong with them? Were they terrified by a couple of torchlight parades? By rifles? Did Franklin Delano Roosevelt go belly-up to the Ku Klux Klan? No! So why did they just give in to the Nazis?

Gladys was coming back with a broad smile and a strawberry ice cream cone. Her Sunday was a success. We'd talk about John and Nan and the mysterious Quentin. We'd look out at the water some more, then close our eyes and once again put back our heads for a few minutes. When we'd open our eyes, the sky would be a gorgeous blue.

Whenever I thought of Europe, I imagined its skies clouded and dismal, like just before a storm. But it had to be spring there too.

Then I thought about Gladys and her ice cream cone, the fishermen, and all the people strolling along Sheepshead Bay in their flowered dresses and seersucker slacks. And what I was really dying to ask John – because he would know, he would care – was, Are we any different? Would we have the guts? Or will it turn dark here too?

But talking to him, kissing him . . . Forget it. It still was all a dream.

# *Chapter Six*

The file room had Blair, VanderGraff and Wadley's records starting from 1916, and the air was sour, as if some major case – the 1927 General Motors litigation – had sprouted mold years before. But although it smelled, at least it was private – at the end of a long, narrow tiled hallway, so you could hear the tap of footsteps ten yards off. And you had the absolute peace of mind of knowing the footsteps were made by a secretary. Guaranteed: Since the signing of the Magna Carta, no lawyer has ever retrieved his own files.

I waited, alone, peering up at the shelves sagging under the weight of old cartons of dead cases. Then Gladys slipped in and, three seconds later, Lenny Stevenson. Lenny came in on an angle; she really wasn't that huge, but her mental picture of her own bigness ruled her whole life. And while it was true that no one would ever slip and call her dainty, she wasn't King Kong. Still, she maneuvered as if anticipating the doorway would not be wide enough to hold her. 'Hiya,' she said quickly. She wasn't much for elaborate greetings. Then she gave Gladys an am-I-supposed-to-talk look.

'I'll tell her,' Gladys said. Lenny sighed with relief at getting off the social-chitchat hook, a sound that in the funnies is written 'Whew!' Meanwhile, Gladys patted her hair and blotted her lips together, as if cameras were about to roll and capture this earth-shaking announcement. 'Linda, we found out who Quentin is!'

'Oh, come on!'

Gladys made a big dramatic deal of cleaning the clip-onto-the-nose glasses she wore for close work; they hung from a rust-colored ribbon around her neck. 'We did some detecting,' she said finally. She tapped Lenny gently on the arm. 'Go ahead, Lenore. Tell her.'

'Uh,' Lenny began. She paused. She swallowed. 'Um . . . you know Dahlmaier Brothers?' Lenny asked. 'The investment banking firm?'

'We represent them,' Gladys informed me.

'I know.'

'Anyway, Lenny went on, they had a question about our billing. I was looking at their letter and saying, 'Those financiers can't even add; no wonder there was a Depression – when all of a sudden something catches my eye. Guess what?'

'What?' I asked.

'On the top of the stationery, on the left-hand side, there were all these names. Nicholas Dahlmaier, Reynolds Dahlmaier – '

'Quentin Dahlmaier,' I said.

'You knew!' Lenny exclaimed. She wasn't really dumb; she just didn't understand people. I think her size as well as her lack of any quality that might be called feminine had made her pull away from the world of women and men; she wasn't fish and wasn't fowl, so she hid in her ledgers, so much so that she couldn't even join in the easy give-and-take of everyday talk. When you said, Hi, Lenny, how are you? you could actually see her think before she answered.

'Go on, Lenny,' Gladys urged.

'Wait a second,' I interrupted. 'Quentin's not the most common name in the world, but there's got to be more than one in the entire borough of Manhattan. It's probably – '

'Linda, would you please?' Gladys demanded grandly, like she was Bette Davis in a very-great-lady role. Then she nodded – graciously – at Lenny, a do-go-on nod.

So Lenny went on. 'Anyway, I saw this name, Quentin, and I figured what do I got to lose? So I called up the bookkeeper over there to explain the billing – and I got chatty with her.'

'I told her to,' Gladys explained to me.

You'd think Lenny would have been insulted, with Gladys coming right out and saying she was running the show. But Lenny wasn't. She was gazing down at Gladys's plain, big-nostriled, I-know-everything face with so much respect it was almost adoration. Lenny could have been a nun (a king-sized nun) staring at a little statue of the Virgin Mary.

'Right,' Lenny agreed. 'I said everything that Gladys told me. I said to the bookkeeper, Gee, the name Quentin Dahlmaier is *so* familiar. Where do I know it from? Was he in the paper or something? And she says to me, Well, there was a story about him in the *Times* or the *Trib* when he gave all that money to the Philharmonic. So I told her, Yeah, that must be it, the Philharmonic. And then *she* says to *me*, What did I think about his picture, wasn't he distinguished-looking? And so I said, You know, it's hard to tell from a newspaper picture.'

'Good work, Len,' I said.

Lenny grinned. She had too much of everything; her smile was so vast it looked as if she had sixty-four teeth.

'She said he's very good-looking for an older man, so I asked her how old he was, and she said she thinks about forty – '

'Then that can't be him,' I interrupted, 'because Nan's just twenty-one and – '

This time I was interrupted, by Gladys. 'Mr Berringer's what? Thirty-four, thirty-five?'

'Thirty-five,' I said.

'So? What's five more years to a girl like that? Go ahead, Lenny.

'Anyway, she said he's filthy rich – all the Dahlmaiers are filthy rich – and that he had a winter house in Palm Beach and a summer house in Southampton on Long Island, but – '

'Listen to this "but," ' Gladys said breathlessly.

'He's planning on going away the *whole* summer. The bookkeeper said usually he just goes to Europe for one month – to Monte Carlo for two weeks and then either Ireland or Scotland, but now with the war – '

'Terrible how it louses up people's vacations,' I said. Gladys actually nodded, so I went on: 'But listen, just because he's taking an extra month off doesn't mean he's going on a honeymoon. I bet you it turns out he's married.'

'Well, you bet wrong, because he's *divorced*,' Gladys said.

Lenny added, 'She told me, Mr Quentin's divorced, you know, I said, Oh, yeah, I'd heard about it.'

'Just because he's divorced . . .' I protested. This all fit my dream world so well, it was so perfect – from the debonair name Quentin all the way to the Palm Beach house, which I just knew had to be cream with a red tile roof – I couldn't believe it. 'Rich people's marriages break up all the time. They have nothing else to do and they're bored, so a divorce is like going to the most emotional movie in the world – except it's starring them.'

Gladys rolled her eyes the way the comedians used to do in vaudeville skits when they got stuck with a real dumb hopeless case. 'Tell her what else, Len.'

'See, I was kidding around with this bookkeeper about this Quentin Dahlmaier being a catch – '

'And guess what?' Gladys interrupted.

'The bookkeeper said, Not anymore he's not. At least she doesn't think so. There's all sorts of talk around Dahlmaier Brothers that Mr Quentin is getting married, and his secretary told her – the bookkeeper – that he's on the phone two or three hours a day with a lady in Reno, but even his secretary doesn't know her name because Mr Quentin told her, "Just get me connected and I'll take care of the rest." Like he didn't want anyone, even his private secretary, to know the lady's name. So anyway, I said, Gee, did the secretary happen to say where the lady's staying in Reno? I got a cousin in Reno.'

'Good work, Len!' I said. 'Did she know where?'

Lenny grinned. 'The Bar None Ranch!'

'Now do you want to hear what *I* found out?' Gladys demanded.

I smiled. The two of them weren't exactly Mata Hari, but they weren't bad. 'Sure.'

'I went over to Marian Mulligan's desk to borrow her staple remover and said, Oh, by the way, when you sent all the papers to Mrs Berringer in Reno, do you happen to remember the address? My cousin's boss has a sister who's going to get a divorce. And believe me, Marian didn't have to look it up.'

'The Bar None Ranch,' I said.

'How many almost-divorced ladies establishing residency in

Nevada at the Bar None Ranch in Reno are going to marry men named Quentin?'

'What do you think, Linda?' Lenny asked.

'*Great* detective work!' I rested my elbow on a dusty carton. 'God, Quentin Dahlmaier.'

'And *Mrs* Quentin Dahlmaier,' Gladys added.

I smiled again, an even bigger one. If Nan was going to change her mind, she had a week and a half. And with good old filthy-rich, Philharmonic-loving Quentin on the phone with her two or three hours a day, she probably wouldn't want to.

It finally happened about two weeks later, in, of all places, the Blue Elephant, the bar all the secretaries went to. Any decent place with that name would have had lots of pudgy blue elephants pasted up on the wall, or girl and boy elephants on the ladies' and men's rooms, or blue swizzle sticks. But all the Blue Elephant had was an elephant painted on the mirror over the bar, and a pretty crummy painting too; most of the elephant's rear end had flaked off – probably into the bourbon.

Not that it bothered the drinkers at the bar. Though it was a Tuesday night, all the stools were filled. Despite the dark, I could get a pretty good idea of them from my table. Sad silhouettes: middle-aged associates never tapped for partner, brokers so down on their luck they couldn't even find a potential customer to buy a drink for.

The rest of the Blue Elephant, the cocktail lounge, was where the law firm secretaries went to sit in peace and quiet. The drinks weren't too expensive, and you didn't have to put up with who-do-think-you-are-coming-here stares, like in the fancier places. Also, the guys at the Blue Elephant bar were serious drinkers, almost always too far gone to think about girls, much less make a pass.

'Another?' the waiter asked.

I still had three quarters of my sloe gin fizz. I'd ordered it because what the heck, it was June, and I couldn't think of any other summery drink, but it was so sweet, like a lime rickey, that it coated your whole mouth and made you want to run out screaming for a toothbrush. 'No, thanks. I'll wait for my friend to get here.' He gave me a look, as if he had a mile-long line of parched boozers begging for my table, even though over half the tables were empty, but I didn't give in, so he walked away.

It was twenty after six, and it looked like Gladys was a lost cause. After lunch she'd said, Remember Pat Keyes with the club-foot, who used to work for Mr VanderGraff, Jr.? I just found out her sister Marie is a keypunch operator at Dahlmaier Brothers. I'll give her a call and see what else I can learn about Mr Quentin. Meet me for a drink after work, okay? Gladys's eyebrows had gone up and down. I think she was trying to look sophisticated, but she looked more like Groucho Marx.

But when I went to pick her up, Gladys was sitting at her desk, tapping her foot, waiting for Mr Avenel to reword a clause. She said, 'He's *still* on the phone with Madame, so if I'm not at the Elephant by six, don't hang around.

I gave up and paid the bill. Whatever goods Gladys had gotten on Quentin would have to wait for tomorrow, because she didn't have a phone in the room she rented, and the owners of the house she lived in wouldn't take calls for her.

Still, I could be patient. If the information I'd pried out of Marian Mulligan that morning was right, Nan had left Reno and was probably with Mr Quentin Dahlmaier – three days into their honeymoon. I tried to picture old Quentin, but all I could come up with was the standard rich guy: gray at the temples, tan from Palm Beach and Southampton, thin – like Basil Rathbone – with a smoking jacket. He and Nan would be taking glasses of champagne from a silver tray the butler was holding. It was like a hundred movies – all second features – I'd seen. Sublime honeymoon, Nan, darling. And we'll have the entire summer together too. Gad, how we shall frolic!

I passed the bar. Out of the corner of my eye, I noticed one of the men swing around and get up. I felt, more than I saw, that he was heading toward me, and not too steady either. No big deal, I figured: This one's so pie-eyed he'll probably be using his nose for a pillow by the time I'm out of the door. So I just kept going.

Not fast enough. Just as I reached the door, a hand tightened around my arm. Before I could say anything, the man pushed me against the wall of the tiny vestibule. His Scotch breath was humid on my face as he said, 'Hello.' Not letting me go. But what could happen to me in a public place? Still my heart started pounding as if it was trying to bang its way out of my chest. The man wouldn't loosen his grip, and it was tight. I pulled, trying to free my arm and get away. But he moved in closer, using his entire body to pin me to the wall.

'Listen, you creep . . .' I began, and real loud, too. Nothing happened for a second, but then he backed off, tripping a little over his own feet, and mine. But he still held on to my arm. I tried to tear it out of his grasp. 'Let *go*.' I put a you-watch-it-Buster glint in my eye. It faded fast.

'I just wanted to say hello,' John Berringer said softly. 'I'm all alone. I have no one to talk to.' Even in the near dark, I could see his eyes mist over. 'Do you know what happened to me?' Even though his voice was soft, his question was for the whole world.

He was drunk. Not falling-down, but his words were a sad slur: Know wha' 'appena me? 'I'm sorry,' I said, and eased my arm out of his grasp. That very second, my heart started up again. Boom! He'd actually been touching me!

Then he started to sway so slowly that only someone who'd lived with a drunk would realize that any second he'd be crashing onto the floor.

'Hey,' I said, grabbing his shoulders, bracing him.

We were so close then. In the red light from the exit sign over the doorway, his face was flushed, steamy. Strands of hair lay wet on his forehead. 'Are you okay, Mr Berringer?' He didn't answer. 'Mr Berringer?' Oh, this was going to be great the next morning, when I had to look him straight in the eye. 'Would you like me to get you a cab?' I asked him.

I didn't wait for an answer. I started to slip past him. But then he moved fast, for a drunk. He blocked my path and gave me the beginnings of a smile – as if he wasn't quite in control of his gorgeousness and wasn't sure what effect the smile would have. I tried to smile back. But there wasn't time. Suddenly, he slammed me against the wall.

'Please, Mr Berringer.'

He pressed himself so hard against me I could feel something I never thought I'd feel in my whole life. 'I'm all alone,' he whispered, and started rubbing against me. 'Don't push me away.'

This had to stop, I thought, but when I opened my mouth I didn't say it. All I could think of was the feel of him, of his legs touching mine. If anyone walked by . . . I wanted to warn him, but there were no words. I tried. I looked up.

His mouth came down and right away I was kissing him back. And suddenly that kiss became all there was in the world. It went on and on.

We couldn't stop; we could go on forever. Both of us began to let out noises that weren't even words. And I lost all awareness of time, of reason, certainly of common sense. All I wanted was more of John.

I swear to God I would have done it right there, in that public vestibule, standing up. He grabbed my hair, yanked my head back so it hurt, and kissed me even harder. He was so drunk. He pushed against me so hard I could hardly breath anymore. That's when I started to fight him, just to get some air.

'Don't leave me,' he said. But then he backed off a fraction of an inch. 'Come on, you want it as much as I do.'

Oh, I did. 'Yes.' I put my arms around him and drew his face near. I rubbed my cheek up and down against his, then slowly brought my mouth back to his again.

But this time his kiss was gentle, brushing, barely touching – teasing. I tried to pull him back into the embrace we'd been in before, but he wouldn't be pulled. I thrust out my bottom to get his attention again, but he stepped back. 'All right,' he said. Still drunk, but I knew him enough to know his mind had started working again. Dear God, I thought, don't end it yet. Just a little more. He reached behind him, unfastened my arms from around his neck and placed them at my sides.

'I ought to be getting home,' I whispered. It was hard to talk. My mouth was raw from kissing. But also, I did not want to cry.

'No,' he said. 'You'll come with me.' Then he got behind me and pushed me out the door.

The electric chair probably hurts a lot, and so must being flogged, but for plain, ordinary agony, you can't beat embarrassed silence.

In the taxi, John gave the driver his address, then settled back into the seat like he was alone, with a lot to think about. His head tilted back, his eyes were half closed. It was a perfect profile, and each time we drove past a street light, his hair shone.

He didn't touch me. By the second red light, I wanted to jump out; I didn't want to see the expression of horror – Oh, no! – on his face when he sobered up and realized what he'd done.

I did try to relax, sit back. At least I could enjoy the ride. I'd only been in a cab once: to go to the hospital to identify what was left of my father. People from Ridgewood who took taxis sat in the driver's seat. I tried very hard; I looked out the window as we drove up Fifth Avenue, attempting to look rich and bored with being in a cab, but I couldn't concentrate. I kept turning around to get another look at John. I couldn't get enough of him.

A couple of times I almost spoke up: It sure is muggy out, and then, It's getting late and you look tired, so why don't I . . . You know how they say words get stuck in your throat? Mine never got that far. I was mesmerized by John's upstretched neck, still glossy with sweat, the fullness of his mouth. There was nothing I could say. Silence filled the cab like smoke.

The driver must have sniffed something, because he kept sneaking looks in his rearview mirror. At the same time, I could see his bald head and his reflected pale eyes. At one point, he seemed about to turn around and open his mouth – maybe with a breezy: Hey, by any chance you Dodger fans? – but he must have sensed something, because he quickly shifted gears and sped on.

'Do you know about my wife?' John boomed out so suddenly the driver and I both almost jumped out of our skins. 'Do you know she's gone? Do you?'

I nodded.

'Do you know why she left?' His voice wasn't just loud, it was out of control, almost shouting. 'I asked you a question. Do you know why she left?' I shook my head. 'She said she needed something more.' He looked at me suddenly, straight in the eye. I couldn't meet his glance. I turned away. The cabdriver was watching everything in the rearview mirror. A great show, and the tickets were free.

'Shhh,' I said to John. I didn't say it as much as breathe it: to soothe him without angering him. He didn't hear me.

'What she meant was, she needed *someone* more.'

'The driver,' I mumbled.

'What?'

'The driver,' I repeated, this time in German.

Drunk, but not that drunk. He switched languages. 'She found a man who could give her more. Whatever more is. Do you know what more is?'

'No.'

The driver was so beside himself he hardly had his eyes on the street anymore. 'I don't know what it is either,' John went on. I met the driver's eyes in the mirror. He turned his away fast, but still, the suspicion was there; here was a guy who probably watched as many British movies as I did. Nazi swine! His eyes said. Secret agents! In his cab! 'All I know,' John continued, his voice softer in his educated German, 'is that three days ago my wife got married. That's illogical, isn't it? If she's my wife, how could she have gotten married? Therefore, either she is not married or not my wife.' His eyes filled up, and he wiped them with the back of his hand. 'My wife,' he whispered.

At light, the driver turned around and very slowly, as if he wanted to make himself understood to foreigners (and foreigners up to no good), asked, 'Sev-en-ty fifth between what and what?'

John was about to continue; I really don't think he heard. 'Um', I said, 'the driver. He wants to know what streets you live between.'

'Park and Lex,' he said, back in English.

The driver gave us one last once-over before he turned back. I knew what he was thinking. I could hear the lines from the movie of his life story, *The Isidore Pincus Story*, playing in his head: 'Their

English was exceptionally good, Mr President, and that aroused my suspicions as much as . . .'

Silence filled the cab again, but this time John's eyes were open. On me. Not looking into my face for understanding. Looking south.

'That's a nice dress,' he said softly.

'Thank you.'

He lifted the hem and rubbed the material between his thumb and index finger. 'Very nice.' A rayon dress for $6.95 isn't very nice.

But by the time I got out another than you, his hand had slipped beneath the dress. I watched it slide up under the fabric, snaking along my leg. The driver stretched his neck. I lifted my hand to push John's away, but he spoke again in German. 'Kiss me.' I kissed him lightly on the cheek. 'Not like that.' I kissed him on the mouth. When I glanced over, the cabdriver was watching the Nazi spies pretending to be lovers. Then I turned away and forgot him as I kissed John again.

His hand inched higher. His fingers slipped under the top of my stocking and started massaging the inside of my thigh. How did he know how good that felt? His other hand circled me and pulled me close. 'Don't stop kissing me,' he murmured. 'Please.' I didn't. I couldn't.

The taxi screeched to a standstill. My head banged against the window. And as we started to straighten up, we heard the driver. In a voice even louder than John's had been, he announced: 'Achtung! Ve haff arrived!'

John hurried me through the apartment, so even though he flipped on a couple of lights, the only room I really saw was the bedroom. He was going so fast I got scared. I tried to calm myself by saying, Okay, you're thirty-one years old, and even though you're no Jezebel, you're no tender flower of innocence, either. What did you expect, a guided tour? On your right, Miss Voss, is an ultramodern couch. And over here on the piano is my wedding picture. Please, come into the kitchen so I can show you where I keep the can opener.

He pulled off his jacket and tossed it on to a chair. I waited for him to hang it up; he was so neat in the office he never even left a fingerprint. But no, he pulled off his tie. By the time it landed on top of the jacket, he was already unbuttoning his shirt. Oh, God, I thought, he's going to take off all his clothes!

I looked around the room. Nan's work. A double bed that looked like a mattress floating on air. A couple of expensive boxes – night tables – and a chair made of the same shiny wood as his desk in the office. A big, ugly painting above the bed, modern art – thick green smears, like someone had gone nuts with a can of peas. Not a dresser in sight, but a wall of doors, so maybe they kept their underwear and hankies and . . . Out of the corner of my eye, I saw his shirt drifting down onto the pile of clothes on the chair.

I started to study my shoes, but a second later, I knew his undershirt was off. I was about to look up, but that second I heard the sound of a zipper. I turned around and faced the door.

What was I going to do? Run into the closet? My heart raced.

'Aren't you going to turn around?' he asked me.

I shook my head. The hall outside the bedroom was a dark rectangle framed by the door. He came up behind me, put his arms around me and drew me against him. I could feel his nakedness along my whole back. For a minute I stiffened, but then my eyes started to close. I leaned back against him, almost drowsy. Then I opened my eyes and looked down. His arms were bare, strong, beautiful. The veins in his hands ran up his forearms. One arm hooked around my waist. The other held my shoulder, and his thumb moved back and forth in a slow massage. I took his hand from my waist and cupped it over my breast.

He didn't need much more, and neither did I. He spun me around, and the instant before he kissed me, I saw him. I whispered, 'Oh, my.' It was as if he'd been carved instead of born.

'Do you like me?' he asked, and he wasn't asking if I thought he was a nice guy.

'Yes.'

'Let me see you, then.'

'I can't.'

'Come on, Linda.'

I almost fainted, him calling me Linda for the first time ever, and so handsome he was beyond handsome; he was beautiful. And while I was concentrating on not getting the shakes, he put his arms around me.

I raised my head for another kiss, and he gave me one, but his real business was unbuttoning the back of my dress. I kept kissing him, though, concentrating on him, on his smell of Scotch and sweat, the manliest smell, letting myself get so intoxicated from it that I hardly felt my dress dropping to the floor, my slip being pulled over my head. Suddenly it seemed the most natural thing, getting rid of all those tight clothes.

He took off my brassiere and touched me till I was dizzy. Then he dropped to his knees and unhooked my garters. My fingers played with his hair. He put his arms around me, pressing his cheek to my midriff before he stood up again and kissed me.

'Take off the rest,' he ordered.

I pulled off my girdle, my underpants, my stockings. He watched. When I was as naked as he was, he pulled me to him again. I was thirty-one years old, and this was the first time I was alive.

Then he led me to the bed. He yanked away the covers and pushed me down.

'Do you know how beautiful you are?' he asked as he lay down beside me. Tell me how beautiful, I thought.

Then I remembered something I'd heard: When men were drunk, something happened to them in the bedroom. But I was too shaky to remember. It took longer? Shorter? They couldn't do it at all? They could, and better?

John could. Better. He ran his fingers from my neck down to my stomach, and below. Then he kissed me, his lips following the same path as his hand. 'So beautiful.' He wasn't talking about my face. He worked his way up again, 'Linda.' I was so beside myself that when we started to kiss again I had tears in my eyes. 'I always thought you must be something,' he said, 'but not like this.'

He'd thought of me before! I wanted to think about that, savor it, but when two bodies are that close and that hot, brains stop. There were no more words.

Magic. That's what happened between John and me. From his

first kiss I knew all my imaginings were right. And I knew he'd brought me home because, in that ugly little bar, drunk, lonely, tired, his defenses down, he'd somehow understood there was magic too.

But neither of us realized how powerful the magic was until it happened. It was as if everything else we had done in our lives wasn't worth a thing. *This* was what each of us had been created for, to be half of something greater than any other two people in the world.

In that messed-up, sweaty bed, John Berringer and Linda Voss became a miracle.

# *Chapter Seven*

They never touched this one in Business Etiquette. Not one teacher at Grover Cleveland ever told us: After you do everything in the book with your employer, including some things you'd heard about but didn't believe people really did, the correct behavior is to – how best to put it, girls? – get up, put on your girdle and say, Will that be all, sir?

So I was at a loss, and it's terrible to be at a loss and naked. Just minutes before, the two of us had been the perfect pair. And now, the perfect mistake. Lying beside John, no longer touching, but still close enough to feel the heat rising from his skin, I agonized, trying to think of something to say that wouldn't make him groan to himself, How the hell am I going to get out of this nightmare?

But as it turned out, all my agonizing was wasted; John's breathing grew slow, low, slower, and then very loud. He hadn't been going crazy over how to ditch me; he'd fallen into a drunken sleep.

At least I know all about that. What he was to international commercial law, I was to boozers. And John was a doozy: stretched out flat on his back, one arm hanging limp over the edge of the mattress while the other gently cradled his pillow, his hand now and then moving as if he was still doing it, stroking the pillow or cupping a feather-filled corner.

Slowly, I slid off the bed and tippytoed over to my clothes. But no, I didn't have to be careful. I could have belted out 'The Star-Spangled Banner'; it would have taken a ton of TNT to blow John out of bed.

I got dressed slowly, as if he was watching me – arching my foot like a ballerina when I put on my stockings, then lifting my leg up real high. When I hooked my brassiere, I turned my back to him, but then I peeked over my shoulder: so coy. I said to myself, You must look like a soon-to-be has-been starlet in the back pages of *Photoplay*. But then I realized I was just copying any sexy gesture I could, because I'd never really felt that the part of me from the neck down was so . . . so useful. I touched – caressed, really – the skin on my shoulder and then turned around to look straight at John.

But then I couldn't stand to leave. What was there in Ridgewood – in all the rest of the world – that could beat this? I sat on the edge of the mattress, right beside him, like a wife. When I combed back his hair with my fingers, he didn't stir.

He was so wonderful to watch. Everything. The curlicues of hair on his stomach made little *c*'s and *o*'s. Finally he rolled away from me, over onto his side. His back was graceful, wide-shouldered, narrow-waisted and strong, as if he spent his days on parallel bars instead of practicing law. At last I stood, covered him with the sheet and left the room.

But when it came to leaving the apartment . . . Well, I couldn't. Not only did I want to know more about him; I wanted a detailed map of his life. I wanted every question answered. I moved around, poking into drawers and closets. I went through every room like a sleazy detective. Down on my knees to see if there was anything interesting under the pale living room couch. (Just a beige carpet.) I opened the linen closet, to check the color of the towels; beige again, with Nan's monogram in white. I even examined the dishes in the sink: white.

If John and Nan's apartment meant anything, it meant good taste was the opposite of what I liked. *Nothing* there had any color, not even the food; all that was in the refrigerator was a bottle of milk that smelled as if Nan had bought it right before she caught the 8:02 to Reno (to prevent John, starving to death a day or two later, from committing some atrocious crime, like bringing orange juice or red meat or green beans into the apartment).

Only the few paintings she'd left had color. There were four or five empty picture hooks. But you'd have to be a big smear fan to appreciate the art she'd left. Yellow globs and black brush strokes in the hall. In the living room, one with skinny blue lines, like a close-up of varicose veins.

Suddenly, I felt so tired. I turned my back on the blue lines and walked over to the window. I opened it a crack, leaned my forehead against the cool glass and looked down at the street. Silent, except for one 'Come on, stupid!' of a man walking his wife's toy poodle. Even from six stories up, you could see the rhinestone collar on the dog's neck. What kind of a man would let a woman make him walk a dog with a rhinestone collar?

My eyes closed. Oh, how I wanted to sleep. But one thing I knew: Either I got out right away and made the long subway trip back to Queens, or I'd be drawn back into the bedroom.

What got me going was the picture of John's horrified face as he woke in the morning – to me.

I left, and fast.

I invented whooping cough, imagined the mumps. I even created old Grossvater Oskar, who had a fatal heart attack, and – Listen, um, Mr Berringer, I'm real sorry – the funeral arrangements had been left to me. But in the end, I was at my desk the next morning. I waited. Nine, nine-fifteen, ten, ten forty-five. John hadn't called. He hadn't come in.

I'd once read in an article in the *Brooklyn Eagle* that when you're afraid, you're supposed to force yourself to think of the most awful thing. Then, whatever finally happens will be a breeze. But that turned out to be crummy advice. I thought of all the worst things – how could I help it? – and by eleven o'clock my stomach was killing me. It wasn't a normal bellyache, like after an iffy piece of Boston cream pie. This was agony, so that every breath, every involuntary movement, was like being ripped open by a knife.

One fourth of a sloe gin fizz was no excuse for what I'd done the night before. At least John was drunk. I hadn't considered the consequences for even two seconds and the consequences were frightening. I could get fired.

The pain was so bad. Just losing my job would be a picnic. I could get tossed out on my ear without a recommendation. Up and down the street, every employment agency saying, Sorry, Miss

Voss, but without a letter from your former employer . . . Going home to concoct some story for my mother, having to take charity handouts.

John could call me into his office, call me names. A guy's drunk and you don't even have the decency to push him off. Slut. (Or whatever happens could be better. Ha-ha. He could burst into the office with one of those long white boxes they put roses in and announce – real loud – Linda, I love you. Talk about daydreams. But at least my stomach felt soothed for that minute).

He finally came in, a few minutes after eleven. He nodded but didn't look at me, walked straight into his office and closed the door. I couldn't look at him either, but out of the corner of my eye I caught the shadow of his dark suit.

It was keep busy or go nuts. I said to myself, No matter how terrible the pain is, you've got to move. I made myself squat down and spent a half hour straightening out file folders in the bottom drawer that were already as straight as a company in Rommel's Seventh. That was the German in me: neat, precise. Like my Grandma Olga's icebox, where the cheese had marched behind the milk, where the carrots almost stood at attention and the chicken wings practically saluted.

But I hadn't been so German the night before. I don't know what I'd been, but the scratch marks I'd seen on his back were not made by a controlled person. But then, neither of us had been exactly under control. I had the marks his teeth made along the soft underpart of my arm. when I thought about them, they throbbed, like a pulse.

'Miss Voss.'

I hadn't heard the door open, but there he was, standing, waiting for me. I got up slowly. I walked into his office and closed the door, but then my heel caught on one of the tiny gray-brown nubs in the rug. It was a miracle I didn't fall splat on my face, although it took some fancy footwork – step, jump, step – not to go sprawling across his desk; for a second I must have looked like I was doing some dopey dance, trying to be cute. So when I sat down, I made my expression doubly serious, to show him this secretary was no silly, dancing fool. This was the ever-efficient Miss Voss.

He sat at his desk, hands clasped, looking at me, serious, lawyerly. Just let it be quick, I began to bargain silently. No 'I'm sure you comprehend what an awkward situation this is, Miss Voss, and much as I wish we might avoid . . .' Oh, God, my stomach.

'Do you have your pad?' he asked.

'What?'

'Your pad,' he said. 'I have a few letters, and then I have some calls to make.'

Nothing showed in his deep blue eyes. He worc the face of a man who had spent the night before at a Bar Association meeting instead of rolling around in his bed, naked, drunk, crazy.

'Is this a good time for you, Miss Voss?' A slight smile, about what he would give the guy at the newsstand, or a men's room attendant.

'Yes, Mr Berringer.'

I left to get my pad. So this was how he wanted it: It never happened. I could get all worked up and think about standing on a breadline, but in the real world, how many bilingual legal secretaries were there who took shorthand at one hundred twenty words a minute? In the real world, real men need real stenographers, so they pretend real things never happened.

But then I thought: Is it possible he could have forgotten? Could he have blacked out, blanked out, and not remembered what had gone on between us? I returned to his office, and even as I sat down he was saying, 'To Gunther Hoffmann. Do you have his address in the files?'

'Yes, Mr Berringer.'

He wanted to forget. Or he couldn't remember. I would never know which.

I turned a corner in the hall and ran smack into Edward Leland. 'Whoops!' It just slipped out, and when I said, 'I'm sorry,' I sounded too loud, too emotional. I lowered my head in embarrassment, but since he didn't move, I looked up again. He looked different, and for a second I couldn't figure out why. 'Excuse me, Mr Leland.' That sounded better, although he just stood there, looking through me with those black, spooky eyes. But then, before

I had time to become a basket case, I did a silent Aha! Mr Leland *was* different: darker, healthier-looking. If he was in a movie, he'd adjust his tie in a mirror and say, I *do* feel fit.

But what he actually said was: 'I'm glad I ran into you. Could you spare some time for me tomorrow, Miss Voss?'

'Yes, Mr Leland.'

He'd definitely been in the sun. His nose was peeling. It was easy to see his nose because he wasn't very tall. I realized I'd never seen him standing before and had assumed a giant was behind that desk. But he was only a few inches taller than I was. Big, though, with too-broad shoulders, as if his mother had snuck out on his father and had a fast one with a prizefighter.

The tops of his cheeks were peeling too. But when you looked harder, it wasn't the tan rich lawyers get sitting on one of their rich beaches. His skin was red beneath the brown – the kind of burn you get from wind as well as sun. That time I'd been in his office, looked in his valise at his heavy snowflake sweater and – crazily – imagined him on some spy mission in Scandinavia. Could it actually have happened? Could Edward Leland have –

He interrupted my thoughts. 'I'll need you for at least an – '

But then all of a sudden he just walked away. Like I hadn't been there, like he hadn't stopped to talk. He just strode down the hall toward his office, taking confident, there's-only-me-in-the-world, senior-partner steps. I turned around; then I saw what Mr Leland had heard. It was Mr Conklin, an associate who would never make partner because he wore bow ties. It was spooky that Mr Leland had *known* Mr Conklin was there; even when he'd been talking to me, acting as if he hadn't a care in the world, he'd been listening, not trusting.

Mr Conklin looked at me a little strangely: Why was a secretary standing alone in the middle of a corridor? And then I realized that was exactly what Mr Leland had wanted him to see: a secretary. A secretary. Big deal.

Late in the afternoon, John came back from a meeting in the conference room. As he walked past my desk, his jacket sleeve touched my shoulder. Naturally, I was as cool as a cucumber; I jumped so that I nearly ripped out the *Kapital* to *Kartoffel* page of my German-English dictionary. He murmured, 'In my office, please.'

This time I was all set with my pad. But John just put a small piece of paper, the kind torn out of a pocket diary, on the far edge of his desk near where I stood. I waited for some clue – a nod, a wink – but I got nothing. I didn't exactly rush to reach for the paper, but since he didn't yell, Hey, what do you think you're doing? I picked it up. It said: Hebel's 325 East 87th Street.

When I looked up, he said, 'Seven-thirty.' And when I looked back down at the paper, he added, 'That's all for now. Thanks.'

Unless you were a sauerkraut tycoon, there was no reason to like Hebel's. It was one of those phony gemütlichkeit places in Yorkville where waiters from Saxony ran around in Bavarian lederhosen. Their pale, fat thighs looked like bratwurst. Beside the cardboard Wiener schnitzel on the plates they were toting were balls of potato mixed with sauerkraut, sprinkled with caraway seeds; they looked like bombs made to Luftwaffe specifications.

Hebel's was a German restaurant strictly for Americans. It was always advertised in the papers, a place where some tourist from Indiana would say, 'Gee, Mary Lou, let's do something crazy and try this here Nazi food so we can tell the folks back home.

I sat alone at the table, ignoring the beer stein collection on the high shelf that ran around the restaurant. I made eyes, noses and mouths on the frosty outside of my water glass. John wasn't there, even though it was ten to eight. So that's when I started feeling sorry for myself again; if I'd had a hankie, I would have dabbed my eyes. I saw myself starring in a silent movie – the country girl led down the garden path by the city slicker: seduced, abandoned. There's be a close-up, I'd blink a couple of times, my mouth would form a big, sad 'O' and then the words would flash on the screen: Oh, the shame of it all!

That was so corny even I couldn't stand it. Anyway, if I still needed to be pathetic, I could feel sorry for myself all the way home. It was time to go. John – who in all the years I worked for him had never been more than forty seconds late for anything –

wasn't going to show. So naturally, just as I pushed back my chair and stood up, my head crashed into his chin.

'God, oh, I'm sorry,' I said. 'Are you okay?'

Yes,' he said, with much too much heartiness for someone who's just been clipped. 'Fine.'

Slowly, we both lowered ourselves into our chairs. 'Would you like a drink?' he asked.

I wasn't really ready to trust my voice, so I just shook my head. He moved his finger a tenth of an inch and a waiter leapt to the table, responding to John's handsomeness, his authority – his rightness – with menus and a wide lackey's smile.

The two of us got very busy for a few minutes examining the menus. You would have thought John was going over the toughest contract of his career, the way he was reading every word. I kept sneaking little looks at him. Hey, I wanted to ask, how come you were twenty minutes late? You left the office a half hour before I did. Where were you? He wasn't giving out anything, except, suddenly, a stare – right into my eyes. It made me nervous, but I could learn to live with it. His eyes, locked on mine, were something! Funny, but I never realized what beautiful eyelashes he had. They were light, but long, and they made thick shadows on his cheeks.

I tried to take in everything: the comb marks in his hair, the bulge of his knuckles. But then the waiter came, and John looked up.

'What would you like?' he asked me.

'Gee, well . . . I'm not . . . uh . . . Whatever you're having.' My shining hour.

I was so nervous I didn't even hear John order, but two minutes later the waiter brought out two plates of stew; it had probably been simmering since the day of von Hindenburg's funeral. The way it was heaped on the plate, this was the cook's last chance to get rid of it. They must have been shouting with glee in the kitchen.

The waiter opened a bottle of wine. I couldn't believe it! *Wine.*

I sipped (I once read in *Look*: 'Ann Harding delicately sips champagne by her swimming pool'), which was a plus, because so did he, because that was obviously what you were supposed to do. Both of us studied the mound of food in our plates with passionate concentration.

Don't think I didn't try to start a conversation. 'Have you been here before?' I asked.

'No,' he answered. He did give me one of his better smiles, but he wasn't talking.

That's when I remembered the advice the sob sisters give to girls. Never ask a question that has yes or no for an answer. Instead, ask him about his interests. I already knew two of his favorites. The law. And the interest he'd shown me the night before. Both of them were great icebreakers. What's your favorite international trade agreement? And how about: That thing with your tongue – did you ever try it on Nan?

John poured himself more wine.

Part of me wanted to stay with him forever. Another part was so sure it belonged in Queens, it was all I could do not to bolt and run like hell for the subway.

The awful thing at a time like that is you actually *feel* your eyes, your cheeks, the little valleys between your fingers. You're so miserable with your own wrongness, everything about you feels homely, clumsy. You're afraid to eat – not because of the lousy food, but because you know you'll dribble gravy down your chin. And the *worst* thing is to know it's more than just a matter of not being able to make light conversation. You have real questions you can never, ever ask:

Are you embarrassed? Are you ashamed?

Are you going to fire me? Or wait a few months – so I won't think it's because of what I did with you – and then fire me?

Now that you're not drunk . . . did you like it?

Did you really mean it when you said I was beautiful?

Are we going to do it again?

If we do, you don't want me to call you Mr Berringer. Do you? And I can't call you John. Should I just not call you anything?

Is this your way of saying thanks and goodbye? (My mother would say, No, Linda, dollface. A man of his caliber would give you at least perfume – and I *don't* mean just eau de cologne.)

But if this is the big kiss-off, I thought in that silence, then what about me? I know – as you often dictate – it is not germane to the matter at hand, but if these are our final moments, if I have nothing more to hope for, then how can I bear the rest of my life? If this gloppy stew now and, later, memoranda of law at some other firm and watching Hitler consume the world are my present and my future, then why—

It was weird, but just then, at my saddest, I began to feel lighter. Better. And of all reasons, because I remembered I was also working for the tan, scary Mr Leland. Spy stuff. It made me a little excited. I started wondering how Mr Leland would explain his new color to his friends. Mountain climbing, Chip. Bit of a windburn, Dick. Deep-sea fishing. Golf. Polo. Tennis, Bob. The rich have a million opportunities to change color.

'Linda.' I jumped, even though John's voice was so soft it barely made a sound. My imagination had been sneaking around, following Mr Leland to Denmark.

'Yes?'

'It's getting late. Let's move on.'

'Move on?' I repeated, not quite daring to get what he meant.

He didn't explain. One hand signaled the waiter for a check. The other hand moved under the table. Hidden by the cloth, it showed me specifically what he had in mind.

# *Chapter Eight*

All those nights I had been working – legitimately working – I had never really given a second thought to my mother. Sure, we weren't having dinner together anymore, but all dinner was for her was pushing a hamburger around her plate, giving it exercise; I ate, we talked.

So when my nights with John began, when I began coming home at what my Grandma Olga would have called a disgraceful hour, I didn't think it could make any difference. Work didn't end until eight or nine at night, and then we went to his apartment, and then . . . So what if I was getting home in the hour before dawn? My mother wouldn't know. She never toddled in before daylight. How could she possibly miss me? Ten o'clock, midnight or four-thirty; it was all the same to her.

And even if she had known, I wouldn't hear any motherly shrieks of dismay. She'd squeeze my hand, kiss me, encourage me: Linda, sweetie, stay overnight! Buy yourself a black brassiere and it'll pay off – in spades! He'll be taking you to a furrier by August!

But then one Saturday afternoon, I glanced at my mother and actually felt that shiver of recognition they write about in serious *Saturday Evening Post* short stories. My mother had become a sick old lady.

Not that she acted it. 'Baby doll,' she cooed, as we walked past the German bakery on Metropolitan Avenue, with its basket of shellpacked pumpernickels. We were walking arm-in-arm, like fifteen-year-old best friends. 'I can't *stand* the suspense anymore. So he gave you dinner, right?' I nodded, and then – fast – managed to grab her around the waist, just in time to stop her from falling.

There hadn't been a curb or a stray pebble; for the third time that day, she'd stumbled over nothing. 'Okay, dinner, which is very nice, *especially* with the wine. I mean, it's a real gent who orders wine. The small fries with a couple of bucks in their pocket are always shoutin', "Waiter, champagne." Not Johnny . . . What's his last name?' A car backfired.

'Berringer.'

'Oh, yeh, right. You know, I *like* B names. Anyway, Linda, lamb, what I want to ask you is this . . .'

She looked me right in the eye. The whites around her huge, gentle brown eyes were a dull yellow and shot through with red veins.

Despite her white summer dress, scoop-necked, sleeveless, splotched with its pattern of pink and purple daisies, there was nothing even remotely young about my mother anymore. Her skin had turned from luminous to waxy; it was sickness, not just a drunk's pallor. It was such an awful shock.

Of course, she didn't notice how I felt. She just babbled on. 'Did Johnny give you anything else?'

'Like a present?'

'Lin*da*, you know what I mean, and I do *not* mean a box of chocolate creams. Did he . . . did you do it?'

My mother's voice was not exactly well-modulated, and we were just passing Hugo's Dry Cleaners, where there was actually a line outside; half the neighborhood were bringing in their wool coats and blankets. 'Shhh!' I hissed. Ridgewood was mainly Germans, plus a little Irish, a little Polish. It liked a few steins at the beer garden, potluck suppers at church, and well-swept front stoops. It did not like public discussions about doing it.

'Don't "shhh" me. I wasn't talking *that* loud,' she whispered. Some whisper: more like a foghorn on an empty ocean.

Just then, a middle-aged couple with matching gray hair, carrying their itchy winter coats, passed by on their way to Hugo's. My mother ignored the woman, but wiggled her fingers – a cute little 'hi' gesture – and then winked at the man. Some wink. It was like she was an act at the Palace and wanted to make sure some guy in the last row, balcony, didn't miss it. Well, no one missed it. The man went absolutely white but kept on walking. His wife whined through her nose, 'Walter, who is that? *Walter.*'

I pulled her along. 'Walter?' I demanded.

'Gee, I thought his name was Arthur,' my mother said vaguely.

'Who is he?'

'He hangs out at Fritz's.'

'What does he do?'

'He could drink you and me under the table. Now listen, sweetie, you and Johnny. Are you and him making beautiful music together? Oh, don't give me a sour puss. It's not such a terrible question.'

'I know, Mom.'

'That's not an answer.' She wasn't *that* dumb a blonde.

It wasn't an answer, and why not give her one? She wouldn't be shocked by anything I could admit to. A woman who could not remember the name of a man she'd had sex with but could probably describe the color and texture of the upholstery of his Chevrolet – that was not a woman who would grasp at the thought of her thirty-one-year-old daughter lying on top of clean sheets underneath a lawyer between Park and Lexington avenues.

'We're getting along fine, Mom.'

'Tell me *exactly* what he looks like.'

All her attention was a little overwhelming. In my whole life, she had never shown so much interest before; but then, I'd never done anything so interesting. But here we were, a thirty-one-year-old legal secretary with pinned-back hair and sensible shoes, and a forty-seven-year-old drunk with brown age spots dotting her temples, gossiping about guys.

'He has blond hair, light, like ours, but not as full. You know, it's the kind that flops when he walks fast. And he has dark blue eyes. His nose is regular, but—'

'You already told me about his face. Come on, move south.' I was blushing, not believing we were having this conversation, walking past Steiner's Hardware with its window full of drill bits. 'Tell me what he's like downtown.'

'Well . . .' I paused for a second. 'Mom, he's wonderful.'

'No kidding! Oh, Lin, baby, that's terrific!' She reached out to put her arm around me and, with her left foot, stepped on the edge of her right sandal and tripped herself. I caught her as her knees buckled; we both pretended it hadn't happened. 'Is Johnny' – she gave me a girl-to-girl smile, happy, delighted for me – 'fun?'

'Well, you know, he's quiet. We don't talk all that much.'

'The quiet ones surprise you.' She raised her voice over the honks of cars and the rattle of trucks. 'All those words they don't say go straight you-know-where, if you get my drift. Am I right or am I right?' she demanded.

'You're right.'

'So?' she said, as the light turned green and we crossed the street. 'What do I gotta do? Get down on my hands and knees and beg you to talk?'

'After work, I've been going to his place.'

'And? Come on! Be fun!' I didn't know what to tell her: Hey, it's just great, Mom. We're having a swell time. Or the truth: Mom, you wouldn't believe what it's like with us. We can't wait for it, working all day, acting normal, being polite, and then finally, when we get to his apartment, almost tearing at each other. But all those in-between times, between the desk and the bed – good manners, a polite smile or two and . . . nothing.

'And,' I finally answered, 'I can't believe it's actually happening to me.'

'You're in love, sweetpea?'

'Yes.'

'And him?' Just then, she stumbled again, but before I could reach for her, she recovered on her own. 'It's nothing. Damn ankle straps.'

I tried to be gentle with her. 'You know, you're looking a tiny bit pale—'

'Lay off! I ran outta rouge.' She shut me up in a voice I hardly ever heard – hard, hoarse: the voice of a tough old broad.

I wasn't going to be shut up. 'Mom, *please.* Have you been feeling okay?'

She changed back to her cutesy voice. 'It depends on who's doing the feelin'.'

'Have you been eating?'

'Sure. The olive in the martini. My green vegetable.' Her oldest joke. 'Now stop changing the subject. How does Big John feel about Little Linda? Huh?'

'I think . . .' It wasn't just that she'd aged. Every trace of her beauty was gone. You looked at her sallow, sunken face and scrawny arms and legs, and if you hadn't known, you would never have realized Betty Voss had once been the ultimately desirable female, a soft-mouthed, hazy beauty with a halo of white-blond hair and huge, liquid eyes. You'd think she'd been a sad little wallflower who'd grown up into a pathetic, drab drunk.

'Don't be shy about telling me about Johnnie, lovie. I know the score when it comes to guys and gals.' She smiled. 'He's nuts for you, isn't he?'

'Yeah, Mom,' I said. 'He is. Absolutely nuts. He can't do enough for me.'

'Linda, it's about time you're getting what you deserve!'

Almost every girl in the office had some sort of outside interest. Gladys's, naturally, was Lives of Important Lawyers; her eyes took in the society page with such intensity it was a miracle the paper did not ignite. Lenny Stevenson was such a Giants fan that she actually lived in a rooming house eight blocks from the Polo Grounds. Wilma Gerhardt loved clothes (*expensive* clothes), and Marian Mulligan probably had every color nail polish ever produced during the entire history of Hazel Bishop – including Ripe Plum, a red so close to purple that her boss, Mr Wilson, asked her please not to wear it to the office anymore. (She took that as a compliment, deciding that her nail polish was too wildly exciting for a place of business; she claimed that when she wore it on weekends, she was besieged by passionate glances and had even had a couple of offers.)

So my particular interest, the war, was probably considered eccentric, but it was accepted. I bought the *News* each morning, but as the situation in Europe got hotter, so did my desire to know. By the end of the afternoon there would be a pile of *Suns*, *Journal-Americans*, *Posts*, *Tribunes*, *Mirrors*, *World-Telegrams*, and *Times*es, all donated by the girls themselves or recovered from their bosses' wastebaskets.

The girls could no more understand my need to read every version, every interpretation of what was going on than I could comprehend why anyone with half a brain could work herself up over Ripe Plum or the Giants, but they were willing enough to help me with my hobby, as long as I didn't bore them by talking about it. Oh, sure, they'd join in a fast discussion of the Dunkirk evacuation, like, Gee, all those little boats were really something. But if I did ask anything like, Was Dunkirk inevitable? all I'd get would be a couple of shrugs, a sigh, and then Gladys pointedly clearing her throat and demanding if anyone had heard that Mr Nugent was keeping company with a girl in New Jersey whose family raised something – either cranberries or chihuahuas.

One afternoon, after John and I had been together (I don't know what else to call it) for nearly three weeks, he glanced down at the stack of newspapers on my desk and asked, 'How come you save all those papers?'

'I read them,' I said.

'Oh,' he said. 'Good.' Then he smiled in his most automatic way and wandered back into his office. I wondered whether he realized how interested I was in what was happening in the world or whether he just assumed I liked to clip recipes for Ground Lamb Supreme.

By that time he'd learned I could cook. After our first endless, awful restaurant dinner, we'd given up on going out to eat. But because we worked so late, we had to come up with something; it's hard to sit in a taxicab gazing hungrily at each other while your stomachs make grumbling noises.

So the fourth or fifth time, John asked, 'Can you cook?'

'Well, nothing fancy, but I'm pretty good, especially with German dishes. My grandmother taught me to cook, and she was terrific. Did you ever try *Gefüllter Krautkopf*?' He shook his head, and it was pretty obvious he could live a rich, full life without ever trying my *Gefüllter Krautkopf*.

But the following Monday when we arrived at his apartment, I opened the refrigerator and instead of finding the slab of cheese and bottle of milk that we'd been grabbing, there were four lamb chops (four! lamb chops!), some potatoes and carrots.

'If you feel like cooking . . .' John said.

I practically leapt into the refrigerator at the chance to try something else to please him. I clattered about while he wandered into the living room to go through the briefcase he'd brought home with him.

I sliced perfect, tiny carrot circles. I boiled the potatoes and mashed them till they were absolutely lumpless. (I had to do it with a fork. Either Nan wasn't much in the potato department, or she had gotten the masher as part of her divorce settlement.) And the meat! I hadn't had a lamb chop since 1929, before the Depression. I broiled them. They were perfect.

And so every night when we got to his apartment, I cooked, he worked. We ate. And then . . . Dinner itself was the only real problem. When it came to the bedroom, real life with John was far better than my dreams. But the long conversations I'd imagined – with John guiding me into a deeper and richer understanding of the world, of Europe at war – still remained dreams. Give it time, I told myself. When it stops being so . . . wild, out of control, he'll give you a chance. And in fairness to John, he had twenty partners – worldly men – he could have stimulating conversations with. He wasn't starved for someone to talk to, the way I was.

One night in early June, right after Dunkirk, we sat over broiled chicken and rice with absolutely nothing to say, after he'd given me a congenial 'Nice rice.' It was late, after eleven, one of those nights when we'd been unable to keep away from the bedroom. After almost two hours there, I'd come out and cooked. But once off the wrinkled, sweaty sheets, he was tired and had nothing to offer me, not even an 'It certainly is getting muggy,' or an 'I love the way you looked in there a minute ago, standing and cooking.'

We sat at a table – dark wood, plain white linen place mats with Nan's white monogram, plain white dishes – in the dining room. I couldn't stand the silence, broken only by a clock ticking. It just burst out of me: 'What did you think of Churchill's speech?'

'What?'

I put my voice down real low and took on an English accent

' " . . . The New World, with all its power and might, steps forth to the rescue and the liberation of the Old." Did you like what he said?'

John looked a little taken aback, as if his chicken breast had spoken. 'Churchill's quite articulate,' he finally said. He smoothed the lapel of his beige bathrobe. It was the softest cotton, with light brown piping, so fine – and so neutral – I knew it had been a gift from Nan.

'I know he's articulate, but what I was talking about was, you know, the *meaning* of what he said.'

His eyebrows went up a little. 'The meaning?'

'Yeah, the meaning. Don't you think what he's saying is that it's inevitable that France is going to be beaten to a pulp and that all that's going to be left is England? Well, England and America.'

'It seems that way.' He gave me a warm smile and combed back the front of his hair with his fingers.

'I'm not saying that it's not a brilliant speech.' I went on: ' "We shall fight on the beaches . . . We shall never surrender." Nobody, not even FDR, speaks like him.'

John didn't say anything. For a minute I assumed he was being thoughtful. And then I realized: I was wearing his undershirt. The strap had fallen off my shoulder and he was staring at that. His mind, the mind everyone swore was so astute, so brilliant, so original, was not on Winston Churchill.

But I tried again. 'Come on. Listen to me for a second. What I'm wondering is, for all the good this speech is doing for English morale – and I bet it's doing a lot of good – don't you think it's a terrible message to be sending the French right now? Look, no one's saying there's any real hope, but don't you think—'

John stood, walked over, pulled me out of the chair. He eased the strap off the other shoulder. The undershirt slid down to the floor. 'Who wants to talk about politics?'

'I do.' I looked at his beautiful, intelligent face. 'Hey! I have an idea. Why don't you do something crazy, something you've never tried before? Talk to me for five minutes.'

'Come on, Linda. You know you're very intelligent.'

'Then talk to me, damn it. Listen to me.'

He started to kiss me – my eyes, my cheeks, my mouth. 'You listen to me,' he whispered. 'We'll talk about politics some other time. I promise. But right now . . . you're driving me out of my mind. You know that, don't you?' He pulled me down to the bare wood floor of the dining room. 'Let's do it again. Right here.' And I was ready.

More than ready. I tore at the sash of his bathrobe, wildly eager.

Maybe my mother was right. Maybe what I was getting was what I deserved.

# *Chapter Nine*

Snoring, my mother sounded like a huge, slow, rusty machine. That would have been half bad. What made it worse that she talked – yelled, actually – in her sleep. 'SWEETIE!' she roared, exploding the soft silence of the Sunday morning. '*Sweetie!*' Sometimes I thought she was dreaming about my father, but she could have been calling one of her barroom guys, whose names she could never remember.

'Sweetie!' reverberated throughout the neighborhood. It was too hot to close the window; if I did, my mother would wake up soaked with sweat, retching. I knew that from experience. 'Sweetie!' Whoever she was hollering at in her dream wasn't giving her the time of day.

I stretched my neck to look out the living room window from where I was sitting. Just my luck. Across the street, Buddy Knauer and his pregnant wife, Sally, who had gone to high school with me, were standing on the stoop of their two-family house, shaking their heads at my mother's howling. They were on their way to church. Their three dimply little girls came skipping out the door in their candy pink, daffodil and powder blue dresses, looking like Easter eggs. So Buddy and Sally just tsk-tsked at another 'Sweetie!' with Christian forbearance.

If it had been a Saturday, Buddy, a telephone company installer, would have yelled across the street, Shut up, you god-damn bitch! and Sally would have tried to hush him up and then later, tiptoed over and asked, in a voice like liquid sugar, Can't you do anything about your mother, Linda? I always wanted to ask her a question back: Can't you do anything about your idiot hairdo, Sally? Thirty-one years old – like me – and she still pinned back the sides of her hair with bows. Teeny orange bows that Sunday, like dead goldfish glued to the sides of her head.

You really got to know your neighbors in the summer, and it wasn't only from sitting on the stoop. Summer meant wide-open windows, and I could hear them all, just like they could hear my mother. Mrs Schwarz next door talked to her cat, Peaches, like they were best friends: What do you think, Peaches? Too low-cut? Think it'll cause a riot? On the other side, Jerry Morrissey practiced the 'Toreador Song' endlessly on his accordion, even after his mother begged him to stop. And the Herrmanns, who lived above their candy store on the corner, kept their radio tuned to a short-wave band that broadcast Hitler's speeches. They were a fat couple who obviously ate too many of their own Baby Ruths. Their mouths were usually stuffed; they hardly said anything, except *Danke* when you paid for your paper, although now and then a little chocolate dribbled out between their lips. But certainly no political opinions. So I never knew if the Herrmanns sat on their couch listening to Hitler with nougaty smiles or expressions of horror on their faces.

'Swee,' my mother called, quieter this time, but more hopeful. It was eleven in the morning, the second Sunday in July, but already it was a scorcher. I got off the couch, lay down on the living room rug and spread out the *Times*. I always splurged for it on Sundays. The carpet sweeper, unused, stood straight, soldier-like, prepared against the wall a few feet away. I ignored it – and the dusty furniture – as I studied maps and charts like a general about to wage his ultimate battle.

Over a month ago, in May, Germany had gone and done what I knew was inevitable: invaded France. The Nazi bastards had done it so easily, so quickly, that even I was stunned; the French military genius General Huntziger had probably been yawning in front of his mirror, pomading his hair or aligning his medals, when the German high command stuck the armistice papers under his nose to sign.

Soon after that, in June, Churchill proclaimed that the Battle of France was over. The Battle of Britain was about to begin. Let us . . . so bear ourselves,' he intoned over millions of radios, 'that, if the British Empire and its Commonwealth last for a thousand years, men will still say: "This was their finest hour." ' Boy, could that guy talk!

In her bedroom, my mother had had it with dreamy patience. She yelled, 'Sweetie, get over here!'

I thought: A thousand years. You've got to hand it to the Europeans. I mean, Roosevelt *maybe* is thinking beyond November, beyond his third term, all the way to the 1944 election. But a thousand years? That's for Reichs and Empires. In America, nobody really thinks much beyond next Tuesday.

The *Times* that morning was full of news about the Free French. General de Gaulle was already picking a fight with the British – although you wouldn't think he was in a position to be picky. But de Gaulle probably had his own thousand-year *État* on his mind and so wasn't about to worry about everyday niceties like politeness and gratitude to allies.

They all seemed so different from us. And that's what I was dying to ask John about: Why do Europeans have this sense – not just of history but of the future too? Are we missing something? Or are we the smart ones? John had gone to school in Germany for three years and was brilliant. He'd know.

I realized than that if I started mooning over John I'd go off into a fog. I didn't have time; I had to meet Gladys. I slid over a few inches and peered through the door, to the kitchen clock; it was five after eleven, and I was supposed to meet her at twelve. I was so late I couldn't believe it!

Gladys and I were going to walk on the Brighton Beach boardwalk so she wouldn't actually have to descend to the beach. She hated sand, and the bathing-suited crowd, so near to naked, seemed to make her nervous. We'd sit on a bench. She'd say something like what she said the week before: Mr B. must be coming out of his funk. He's not working till midnight anymore. Her voice would fall to a whisper, as if there were spies all around us: Helen Rogers saw him waiting for the elevator Wednesday night and it wouldn't come and he kept pushing thc button. *Very* impatient – Gladys would do her eyebrow lift – like he had someplace to go, if you get my drift. Linda, has he gotten any calls from people of the female persuasion? No, I'd say. Then *why*, she'd demand, is he acting like he has someone? She sensed I was holding something back. Linda, swear to God, no crush? No, Gladys. Well, Marian says she sees a gleam in your eye whenever – No!

How could I explain to Gladys, who didn't like to see bare arms and legs, what was making Mr B. crazy to get on that elevator? And so, just like the week before, she would finally give up, and we'd go for a hot dog, corn and a beer at Nathan's in Coney Island.

I did a fast top-dusting and raced the carpet sweeper around the room, banging it into couch legs; it was a good thing Olga was already dead, because if she'd seen what a sloppy housekeeper I'd become, she'd have wanted to die.

In the bathroom, I turned on the faucets. The plumbing belched, then water gushed into the tub. I was in a mad rush, but too sticky and dusty from housework not to bathe. I stepped in; the water was so cold around my ankles, it took a second to work up the courage to lower my body into it.

And just as the icy water shocked me, the phone did too. I vaulted out of the tub, grabbed a towel and ran. The only calls we usually got were about my mother's family – another dead Johnston – or wrong numbers. But Gladys had my number, and if she hadn't been feeling well, maybe she'd dragged herself to a phone booth . . . Not that I wished it on her, but I wasn't overjoyed at the thought of a stroll along the boardwalk, knowing that at three forty-five I was doomed to eat a hot dog and corn even if I was positively drooling for an ice cream sundae, and then to watch Gladys salting her corn with tiny little sprinkles and to hear her saying, with each shake, When (shake) do you (shake) think (shake) Mr Berringer (shake) will find himself (shake) some (shake) feminine (shake) consolation?

I answered, a little breathless, on the third ring. 'Hello.'

'Linda?'

I nodded, then managed to come up with a word to say into the phone. 'Yes.'

'John Berringer.'

'Oh. Hi. How are you?'

'Fine, thank you.' What did I expect: Read any good newspapers lately?

'Are you in the city?' I managed to ask.

'Yes.'

'I guess I just assumed you spent your weekends in the country or . . .' I'd pictured him as he looked in that picture locked in his desk drawer, in a hammock strung between two leafy old trees – but with no Nan curling around him.

'I'd like to see you,' he said at last.

I could tell by the deepness, the slowness of his voice that he was still in bed, lazy, sexy, probably stroking himself – and had just decided I could do it better. He was right.

'I'd like to see you too,' I said softly.

'Then why don't you come over?'

'When?'

'Now.'

John didn't say 'You look so pretty' or 'What a great idea, spending Sunday together.' What he did was grab my wrist and pull me into the apartment. 'I've been waiting,' he said.

'Oh, my God!' I whispered. Riding in on the subway, I'd pictured him in his Sunday best: tan slacks, a shirt – maybe stripped – opened two buttons' worth, sleeves rolled up. Instead, he gave me his real Sunday best; he was naked. In the dim light of the foyer, his chest and shoulders gleamed like a Greek statue in the Brooklyn Museum.

He pivoted slowly, not showing off – more like a fashion model displaying a priceless dress. 'You love looking at me, don't you?' he demanded. This was a new John, full of himself, his beauty. Away from the office, he could do what well-bred men do not: preen, strut, display. 'Don't you?'

'Yes.'

'I know. Tell me about it.'

'You're . . . you have a beautiful physique.'

'What do you like best?' I couldn't help it; my eyes shifted downward. 'I know that, Linda. What else?'

'All of you.'

He leaned against the wall, standing right in the narrow column of light thrown by the small ceiling fixture, and observed me impatiently. 'Be specific,' he insisted. 'Come on. My shoulders, my legs.' He did a complete – and astoundingly graceful – turn. 'My ass. Pick something and *talk*. You're always complaining we don't talk. Now I want to.'

'Your legs are wonderful.'

'*Tell* me about them.' He stepped close, reached around me and started to unzip my dress. He did it not like a man undressing a woman but in a neutral way, like a Gimbel's salesgirl. I put my arms around him, but he withdrew. 'Later. Talk now.'

What does a girl say when a guy wants to hear about his legs? It wasn't a topic I was naturally eloquent on. And worse, I sensed from his impatience that this game of Naked was one he'd played before, with someone else, someone with a bigger vocabulary – and a Smith College accent. 'I love the muscles in your thighs,' I said at last.

'Keep going,' he said.

But I couldn't. He pulled my dress over my head. I raised my arms so it wouldn't tear, praying there were no sweat circles after the sweltering subway ride into Manhattan.

It was my favorite dress, a cotton, the softest pink, the pink I'd always thought of when I heard 'peaches and cream.' Such a lovely, gentle color, but – as Gladys might say when she was in one of her uppity Margaret Dumont moods – a dress utterly inappropriate for the office. Its skirt was all right, full, but it fit much too tight on top. It had been on sale, and that had been my excuse for getting such an eye-popping dress. It had looked so sexy in the dressing room mirror, with its wide, deep V-neck, and I even remembered standing there and daydreaming about John staring at my bust. Then, after I'd bought it, I'd been too embarrassed to wear it anyplace. It was a she's-asking-for-it dress. But John hadn't even noticed it; he just pulled it off and dropped it onto the floor.

'I like . . . I love . . .' I couldn't be specific the way he wanted me to be specific.

'Don't be self-conscious.' He drew my slip over my head, then started to work on my girdle. 'You shouldn't wear these. You're so beautiful, so female. I hate seeing you constricted.' He let me step out of the girdle and pull off my stockings. 'Keep talking,' he urged. 'Say anything that comes to mind.'

'The hair on your legs is like red gold.'

'A simile!'

'Don't talk down to me.'

He moved in close, unhooked my bra and threw it on top of my dress. 'You have beautiful tits.'

'Stop.'

He put his hands under my breasts and pushed them up as high as they would go. 'I'm sorry. Beautiful breasts.'

'Please.'

'Please what? Do? Don't?'

'Don't say things like that.'

'But it's the truth. You have ravishing breasts. Impeccable breasts. The Platonic ideal of breasts.' He paused, smiled, then put his mouth to my ear; his words came out hot and damp. 'Someday, if you're a very good girl, I'll explain what "Platonic ideal" means.'

I stepped away from him. 'I know what it means.'

'You do? What?'

'Something to do with Plato.'

'*What* to do with Plato?'

I swallowed. 'I don't know.'

He pulled off my underpants. 'Of course you don't. That's your charm. Come on, don't give me that hurt look. You're too sensitive. I'm not talking down to you.' He smiled. 'I'm just grateful that when I'm with you I can relax, be myself. I don't have to parade my intellect.' He took my hand and put it on him. 'I just have to parade this.'

'But there's more to life than – '

'I know,' he said, as he pulled me to him. 'Oh, baby, I know.'

Later that afternoon he was talkative. Well, talkative for John. He went into the kitchen and brought back two glasses with ice, and an open can of orange juice. He put the can on the shiny black night table, then quickly lifted it off, as if someone had snapped, Don't! It will leave a ring.

Then, defiantly, he banged the can back onto the night table. Juice splashed out and made two puddles on the black surface. He put down the glasses and poured the orange juice. 'You're right, you know. There's more to life than . . . I haven't been giving you the attention you deserve.'

'Five minutes on the strength of the RAF would take care of it.'

'You're entitled to much more than five minutes – but you're too distracting.'

He smiled again, but it was just the mechanical movement of his mouth; his attention was on the night table. He rested the freezing glass on my stomach. I managed to grab it before it spilled. 'What are you thinking about?' I asked.

He stared at the glass of orange juice. At last, when the long silence became too heavy for him to bear, he murmured, 'There's a name for gin and orange juice. Everyone in Bucks County was drinking it last summer.' Just like that. He was giving me genuine chitchat. 'It's not a mimosa. That's champagne and orange juice.' He looked away from the glass on my stomach and out the open window. 'Nan loves mimosas.' I stared at him. Since the first night we were together in the taxicab, he had not mentioned her name.

'You still miss her?' But although it came out as a question, John knew I already knew the answer. He just shrugged and kept staring straight outside, as if watching Nan in a window in the building across the street.

He finally answered. 'Yes. Of course I still miss her.' His cheeks and lips moved slowly, almost stiffly, as if talking like this was so against his nature he had to force the words. 'I'm not going to pretend – '

'I know.'

'I can't give you what you want, Linda. I wish I could. You're a fine, decent girl. You deserve – '

'I'm happy with what I have.' But I was sure there could be more. All he needed was time. I mean, here we were having a conversation that a couple of days before I would have thought was impossible. I asked him, 'Have you spoken to her since she remarried?' John shook his head, but he didn't seem as if he wanted to break off the discussion. In fact, he poured himself an orange juice and sat on the edge of the bed beside me, waiting for the interview to continue. 'Were you surprised when she told you about' – I almost slipped and said Quentin – 'the other man?'

'Yes. No. I don't know.' He pushed me toward the middle of the bed and stretched out on his side in the space where I had been lying. He propped his head up on his hand. After he drained about two thirds of his glass, he said, 'Our separation . . . it was inevitable. If I'd been the least bit objective, I would have seen it. You see, you can't look at Nan from a conventional perspective.' He paused. 'I mean . . .' he began to explain.

And I thought: To hell with it. I've had it. 'You don't have to tell me what you mean. I can figure out the big words. Tell me.'

For a minute he looked as if he didn't want to, but the subject was irresistible. 'Nan is a law unto herself. It's not just that she's different from other women. It's that she's above them, beyond them.' He looked at me for the first time since Nan's name had been dropped into the conversation; his eyes were so bright, so alive, you could almost see the picture of her he had in his mind. 'Do you understand what I'm talking about?'

'You know, you never ask that question in the office. You assume I understand everything: words – ideas, even. Why would I suddenly turn into a moron when I leave Wall Street?' Exhaling slowly, he made a big deal of showing me how patient he was being. 'I happen to know exactly what you're talking about, and you want to know something? I think you're dead wrong. She's not above *anyone*.'

'Then I'm sorry, but you don't understand.' He turned over, away from me, so I got to look at his back. It was a magnificent back.

'Okay,' I said to it. 'She went to fancy schools, so in that way she's certainly above and beyond anyone you'd find punching a cash register at Woolworth's. But she's not God, not even close. Okay, so she's brilliant. Terrific. I'm a big fan of brilliance. And she's pretty – '

The back stiffened. 'Beautiful,' he muttered.

'Fine. But there have to be other brilliant, beautiful girls walking around. Who else goes to Smith College? Are they *all* above and beyond?'

'How do you know Nan went to Smith?'

'Does it take a Ph.D. to figure out why you're sending a check to the Smith Alumnae Fund? I answer your mail. I balance your checkbook. I'm your jewel of a secretary. Remember?' He turned, reached over and poured more juice. 'Is she really different? Was she born that way?' I honestly wanted to know. 'Or is it just how she's been brought up?'

'She's different.' He turned on his back. I couldn't help glancing down. I knew it; he was ready for me (or someone) again, but he was too involved with Nan to realize it. 'She has an extraordinary, analytical mind, almost a man's mind – even though she's the most feminine person I ever met.' Talking about her, John's voice was almost reverent, as if he was in church. 'But Nan's restless, terribly restless. All that brilliance, all that beauty . . . She was too much for Smith. Smith couldn't hold here. She had to have more.'

Oh, God! It sounded like an advertisement for a bad Mae West movie: *She had to have more!* But I just nodded.

'It was the same when we were married. There's something larger than life about her, even though she looks so incredibly delicate.'

'She had to have more?' I asked. John looked annoyed.

'Not in *that* way. Everything was fine.'

'As fine as with us?' I actually asked.

'No,' he said. 'Does that make you happy? Is that what you want to hear?' Then his voice got all misty again. 'She was my wife. But not a typical wife. There was nothing typical about her.' He paused, then abruptly announced: 'Fidelity is a middle-class virtue.'

'So every upper-class person commits adultery?'

'Conventional rules don't apply to Nan,' he said sharply.

I took a couple of sips of the juice. It was bitter, like drinking liquid tin. No wonder little Nannie preferred mimosas. I said, 'Conventional rules don't apply to Adolf, either.'

John gave me his first real smile. 'That's really not an apt comparison.'

'Why not? Everybody has to obey the rules.'

'That's too simplistic.'

'I don't think so. Because if you say Edward Leland's daughter or Edward Leland or Adolf Hitler has special rules, then why not Henry Morgenthau and Clark Gable? And who decides who gets special treatment? The person who wants special treatment? Me? You?'

'I admire your . . . sense of fair play, your democratic spirit. Really I do, Linda. But you have to understand, Nan is genuinely extraordinary: intellectually, emotionally – even socially.' He exhaled slowly. 'I could only satisfy her' – he got tongue-tied for a second – 'that way. And intellectually. Socially . . . her mother was related to a President, and her father, well, Edward is one of the most powerful men in the country. Nan spent her entire life in superior company. She went to the best schools, traveled abroad, had every possible cultural advantage.'

'What does culture have to do with it?'

'With what?'

'With cheating on your husband?'

'Please stop it.'

'Okay. I'm sorry.'

'Try to understand: Faithfulness is for people who don't have the money or the imagination for pleasure.'

'So how come you were faithful? What were you missing? Money? Or imagination?'

John pushed himself up and sat on the edge of the mattress. His back was toward me again. He put his glass down on the table. 'You really can't comprehend the situation.'

'Try me. In English or German. I'm versatile.'

'But you can't grasp the subtleties. You see, just because someone has graduated from an Ivy League college does not make him upper class.'

'What makes someone upper class? Money? Ancestors?'

'It's extremely complex.'

'So what are you saying – in the whole history of the world there's never been an upper-class wife who's behaved honorably? You know that's baloney.'

'I wasn't fun enough for her.'

'Fun? The new husband is fun? What does he do – Jack Benny imitations?'

'Look,' John said, 'I'm not witty, I'm not particularly urbane. What can I say to make you understand? I'm not one of them. I can't get drunk at the Plaza and take off my shoes and wade in the fountain and scream with laughter over Louisa Buchanan's tasteless wedding invitations.'

I sat up beside him. I took his hand, and he didn't pull it away. 'Is that what you do for fun when you're so brilliant you're beyond the rules? Get drunk in fountains and laugh screamingly about wedding invitations?'

John lowered his head. When he spoke, his voice was unnaturally slow, as if his throat had been numbed by the ice in the juice. He could barely form the words. 'I told you that you wouldn't get it.'

Did it bother me that I'd left Gladys Slade to broil on a hot boardwalk? I hardly gave it a thought. We'd once agreed, since she had no phone, that if I ever didn't show up, she'd wait one hour and then assume I'd had some emergency and wouldn't be able to make it.

I sat in the subway as it hurtled back into Queens, and I tried to think up a good excuse for Gladys. But I couldn't concentrate. I looked up at an ad for Prince Albert Crimp Cut Pipe Tobacco, with its picture of a boringly handsome middle-aged man who looked the way lawyers were supposed to but never did (except John, who looked better), and worked on feeling bad that I was behaving so rottenly to a friend. But the only thought that came to mind was that an hour in the sun would do Gladys good. Her skin was so white: not Scarlett O'Hara, southern magnolia white, but bloodless, like typing paper. Drenched in the dirty, humid night heat of the subway, I tried to feel guilty for not feeling guilty, but all I could think about was John.

Okay, even if we would never have a heart-to-heart about Rommel's strategy, weren't men supposed to sweet-talk their . . .? I couldn't figure out what I was to him. Definitely not his girlfriend.

And not his mistress; as far as I could see, letting John foot the bill for my lamb chop didn't constitute being a kept woman. Not his lover, either, because neither of us was Greenwich Village bohemian type who had lovers, and also because I knew he didn't love me; worse, I wasn't even sure if he liked me. Was sex with me *that* good that he would put up with someone he didn't care about just to get more?

Yes. It was that good. It was perfect.

But what about me? How long could I love a man who might never love me back? What kind of love is it that basically says, Sure, fine, I understand that you can't be seen walking down the street with someone like me.

On that stifling summer night, as the subway screeched under the East River, I said to myself, It doesn't matter. You will love John Berringer forever. And he may learn to love you someday. Search, look for small signs, anything is possible. But even if he never learns, your love for him – and nothing else – is the central fact of the rest of your life.

I ran into Gladys at the newsstand in the lobby of the office building the next morning when I bought my weekly roll of Life Savers. She was handing over a dime for a tin of violet breath mints.

I hadn't rehearsed my excuse, but I gave it everything I had. '*Gladys*, am I glad to see you! I'm so sorry about yesterday.' Then I noticed her tomato face. She looked absolutely awful. 'I feel *terrible*. I was all set to leave, but all of a sudden my mother got so dizzy . . .' Gladys's eyes, puffy from sunburn, narrowed, so I knew I had to shovel it on. 'She actually fainted! If I hadn't been there to catch her – '

Gladys simply did an about-face and marched toward the elevator.

'Look,' I said, rushing to her. 'I can't tell you how bad I feel, but that's why we made those emergency plans.'

'For an emergency!' she spit out.

'But I told you, my mother actually fainted.'

We reached the bank of elevators. There was one ready; the elevator attendant waved us in, and a moment later, half of Wall Street followed, pressing in, almost flattening us against the wall. Gladys stared straight ahead.

'What's wrong with you?' I asked softly.

Her eyes remained focused on the brass-grille door; she spoke between clenched teeth. 'It so happens I called your house yesterday, after I'd waited for *two hours* in the burning-hot sun. I spoke to your mother. And do you know what she said?' *Oh, no*, I thought. I kept quiet, hoping, I suppose, that silence was contagious. It wasn't. ' "Lin's not here, honey," ' Gladys mimicked. 'And so I said, "Well, Mrs Voss, we had an appointment, and I'm a little concerned about her, not that I want to worry you." And do you know what she said? "Listen, don't *you* worry, sweetie. Linda's probably kicking her heels up with her boyfriend. The one she's with every night. John Whatsisname. You know." ' Gladys turned and glared at me. ' "Her *boss*." '

Someone in the conference room had eaten a sardine sandwich, and even though a thick, hot breeze came through the opened window and ruffled the paper napkins, you felt you were trapped inside an airless sardine can. Everyone sat around the table going through the motions of eating her lunch, but this day there was no fun, no gossip. In fact, the room had gotten so quiet you could hear the squish of pits plopping from Marian Mulligan's watermelon chunks as she coaxed them out with her pointy Mango Orange fingernails.

Everybody knew something was up. Why else would Gladys Slade have pointedly taken her seat at the head of the conference table and then said – tittered, actually – to Verna Glover, a human slug with a personality one inch from dead, 'Verna, come sit next to me.' Then Gladys graciously offered Verna the seat that had been mine for the last seven or eight years.

Helen Rogers sat beside me, but then was afraid to look my way because then she'd have to either talk to, smile at or snub me. Instead, she picked nervously at the caraway seeds from the rye bread that dotted the white polka dots on her blue blouse. The chair on my other side was empty; the girls had caught on fast that something was wrong.

Gladys sat straight, like a school poster for good posture. She'd tucked a napkin over the front of her dress to protect it from the drippy peach she was eating; the white of the napkin against her sunburn made her face look maroon. For at least the tenth time I tried to catch her eye, and, for the tenth time, I got looked through; it was as if I was invisible and she was examining the light switch on the wall behind my head.

What was she *doing?* In all my life, I'd never felt such anger. What I'd done to Gladys was wrong, but we'd had all those years, all those Sundays. I didn't deserve being cast out like this, like I'd committed some horrifying crime. No one would look at me.

The room was completely stiff and still, like an old photograph, except for the tiny dust twinkles that danced in the lines of sunlight coming through the wooden slats of the venetian blinds. Breathing was hard.

Suddenly, Gladys turned to Anita Beane and said, in her most regal, pearly Queen of Lunch tones: 'You haven't spoken about your wedding plans in *days*. Tell me, have you chosen your tablecloth color yet?'

You could hear a great sigh of relief at the return to normalness: a chorus of ten or twelve voices exhaling together. And then, on and on, Gladys, Anita and the girls debated the pluses and minuses of daffodil versus golden-rod. But every once in a while, I'd get a look, a flash of wonder or curiosity – or downright antagonism.

And that's when I knew that if I didn't stop Gladys, I was finished. One by one, all afternoon, they'd float through the halls, slip over to her desk, ask, What's with Linda? and finally she'd say, I wish you hadn't asked, but you know me. I have to tell the truth. I called Linda's house Sunday and her mother said . . .

So right after lunch, when Gladys bolted for the door, I bolted too – and faster.

'Gladys,' I called loud enough for all the girls strolling back to their desks to hear, 'I know we talked about not sitting together all the time, but you know something? I kind of missed you.' I clutched her elbow as thought I wanted a quick arm-in-arm promenade with my best friend, and hurried her down the hall. From the relaxed murmur that rose behind us, I knew I'd subdued at least a couple of doubts.

'Let go of me!' Gladys tried to jerk away, squeezing her arms tight against her body as I rushed her along. Her elbow had red fingerprints where I'd grabbed it. 'I want nothing to do with you,' she spit out. 'Is that understood? You played me for a *fool*.'

'Please, let me explain – '

'You let me go on and on, all these months. Carrying on with him, pretending you didn't even *like* him, even when I said, "Oh, Linda, you *must* have a crush on him." And you said, "Oh, *no*, Gladys. I'd tell you. We're *such* good friends. But Mr Berringer is so boring, with his big blue eyes. He's *too* good-looking. Like a third-rate movie star." *That's* what you said. Oh, you must have felt *so* superior, you smug – '

'Please, let's sit down after work. I want to explain – '

'*Explain?*'

'Gladys, what else could I have done? I know you won't believe me, but I feel terrible. I've done you a great wrong, and I'm so sorry. I shouldn't have – '

'What does "shouldn't" mean to someone like you? You've been *doing it* with him!'

I couldn't help it. 'Oh, stuff it up your nose!' I blurted out. Was she ever the wrong person to say that to! 'Look, Gladys, standing you up yesterday *was* a rotten thing to do, okay? And not confiding in you was . . . maybe . . . was worse. But let me tell you, what I did doesn't compare to how you almost ruined me in there. Everyone was treating me like a leper. They're going to think – '

She cut me off. 'You must be so proud of how you deceived me. "I can't meet you for a drink, Gladys. Mr Berringer's rushing off." He was rushing off to you! "I'm sorry, but I have to work late." *Work*.' She rubbed out a fingerprint from the patent leather on her handbag. 'What kind of "work" do you do for him? Does he pay you overtime?'

'Is that what you want, Gladys? The details? Fine. You want me to give you a blow-by-blow description?'

'You are utterly revolting!'

'Listen!' My voice sounded far off, and strangely tough. 'I don't want to hear one more damn word from you. And if you ever pull anything like what you tried at lunch today – '

Gladys simply walked away. Well, why not? She was positive she had me. She could be mysteriously cold to me for a week or two, savor the attention and then . . . One word to Helen or Marian, and in ten minutes all the secretaries would be whispering. By three o'clock, enough hints would be dropped to enough bosses that the lawyers would start finding excuses to go past John's office, past my desk, to look me over, and then go laugh in the men's room. By four o'clock I'd be called in, maybe with John with a 'You stupid . . .' or even by one of the senior partners. Oh, my God, by Mr Leland: Under the circumstances, Miss Voss . . .

'Gladys!' I barked.

She stopped only because she hadn't expected to hear anything more from me. I caught up with her and walked along beside her. I smiled as Mr Ervine from Real Estate passed. We made way for him and he said, 'Hello, girls,' and kept walking.

'Gladys, listen to me, because if you don't you'll be sorry.'

'Don't you threaten me, you tramp.'

'You say one word, just one word to anybody – the secretaries, Lenny Stevenson, the janitor – and you're finished.'

'No,' she said. '*You're* the one who will be finished.' A nasty look, pretty close to a malicious smile, passed over her face. 'I really wasn't going to say anything in there, you know. But now you're threatening me, and I *do not* like threats.'

'I don't care what you like, Gladys. Just shut up and listen. I know that one word from you, and the whole office will know. And I guess that will give you satisfaction,'

'I'm not that small-minded.'

'It'll give you satisfaction,' I repeated, 'but it'll also get you fired.'

'Oh, comc on!'

'John is ready, willing and very able to do *anything* I ask him,' I said. 'I have him in the palm of my hand.' She blinked, then did it again and again, until it became a nervous tic. Blink, blink, blink.

She couldn't stop. 'Don't test me, Gladys. No more cold shoulder at lunch, or you'll find yourself out on the street. Do we understand each other?'

She blinked again.

'John loves me. Whatever makes me happy makes him happy.'

'All right,' Gladys said at last.

'So if you like your job . . .'

'I never had any intention of saying anything.'

And then she rushed away.

# *Chapter Ten*

September 7, 1940. The Battle of Britain was in its second month. On that afternoon, a Saturday, the German *Dreckenschweine* sent three hundred bombers and six hundred fighters to attack the London docks. And later that night, they sent in more bombers; dark orange fires burned along the banks of the Thames, lighting the night fliers' path toward their targets. But that was over there.

Here, between daylight and dark of that day, I sat on a green plaid couch finishing an article in an overthumbed *Good Housekeeping* from January. 'Hollywood has little trouble finding new and lovely girls to photograph – witness Dorothy Lamour, Rosemary Lane, Sigrid Gurie and the lush Hedy Lamarr, to mention only a few of today's raw recruits – but able actresses are not come by so easily.'

*Good Housekeeping* knew. 'You're a lousy actress, Linda.' Dr Guber shook his head wearily a few minutes later in his office.

'*Me?*' I asked, opening my eyes wide so I'd look honest and innocent, unlike lush Hedy Lamarr.

'Come off it, kiddo.' His desk chair creaked as he leaned forward. 'I've known you all your life.'

Dr Guber was so tall and thin you could see the stringy muscles where his arms dangled out of his short-sleeved white doctor coat. He was built like a cowboy but talked with a thick New York accent.

'I got a cancer and a rheumatic fever out there,' he went on. 'You think I'm gonna play *Let's Pretend* that it's your mother's specimen that killed the rabbit? Your mother drinks so much her uterus probably looks like a pickled corned beef.' Dr Guber pushed back his chair and stood up. He must have looked at me then, at the moment the smile I'd worked so hard on collapsed, because he came over to my chair and squeezed my shoulder. 'Come on. You're a big girl.' He paused. 'You must've had a clue.'

I must've. Even a supreme moron could add up what sex seven days a week plus two missed periods equals. It took high intelligence to have found new ways to keep avoiding reality the way I did. Every morning I woke up and ran to the bathroom, and when I didn't find my period, I'd think: Oh God, oh, no, please! But then I'd think: No. Calm down. It's nerves. You're getting yourself in such a stew you'll never get another period again. Relax!

But then, oh, I knew. Every afternoon the last month, I'd felt sick. Like I was going to give back my lunch when I leaned over a drawer in the filing cabinet. And smells. Mum deodorant: sickeningly sweet, like decaying corpses in detective stories. the roll of Life Savers in my purse stank, especially the purple ones. And I couldn't help it, but I kept thinking of food, maybe because I wasn't able to eat all that much, but I'd imagine a hamburger patty or split-pea soup, and wave of nausea would rise up in me.

I couldn't pretend anymore.

'Come on, Linda, let's go in the examining room,' Dr Guber said, in the too-calm voice people use with people about to get hysterical. 'Five, ten percent of the time, it's something else that kills the rabbit – a heart attack, or who the hell knows. Anyway, their little pink noses stop twitching and people get nutsy for nothing. You could be fine.'

His long legs took Texas-length strides, and I had to do double time down the narrow corridor. He opened the door to his examining room and stood back to let me go in first. The room had a black leatherette table in the center. He handed me a sheet and said, 'Just take off your bottom stuff and your shoes and get up on the table.' He turned away and whistled 'Daisy, Daisy, give me you answer true,' while I pulled off my pants and girdle and he pulled on a rubber glove. 'You ever had an internal?' he called out.

'No,' I said, and took off my shoes and stockings and stretched out on the cold paper that covered the table.

'Listen, it's nothing. Easy, just so long as you relax.' He turned back and started to pull the sheet first down and then up, as if he was a fussy housewife, so it covered even more than the vast areas I'd already covered with it. Then he began the examination, staring straight into my eyes. 'So how's your mother lately?' He pushed up with the gloved hand and, with the other, pressed down hard on my stomach.

'Fine,' I gasped.

'Fine, I don't want to talk about her, or Fine, she's quit boozing and is studying ancient Greek?'

He was pressing so hard. If I really was pregnant, he could squash the baby. 'She's still drinking.'

He switched on a floor lamp, then pulled over a stool and sat at the foot of the table. 'Too bad. She looked like hell last time she was in here.' He lifted the sheet and bent over. 'Such a beauty-ful girl. I remember when she first came in, years ago, pregnant with you.' All I could see were the tops of his ears.

'Am I?' I asked. In London, the air raid sirens were screaming. In Dr Guber's office in Ridgewood, it was still.

He looked up. 'Yeah, Linda. You're about two, two and a half months into it, I'd say.' Dr Guber swallowed his discomfort; his Adam's apple bobbled nervously in his long, scrawny neck. 'Sorry, honey.' His hands appeared from under the sheet. He stood up and pulled off the rubber glove. It made a squeaky sound; I shivered. Before I could think of a thing to say, he lowered his head and stared at my toes. 'Don't . . .' he began, 'Uh . . . I can't help you with this.' Five or ten possible sentences came into my mind, but they couldn't get from there to my mouth. The doctor moved his eyes and stared at his own feet. 'And don't go anywheres else, either. Don't listen to your girlfriends.' Did he think we sat in the Blair, VanderGraff and Wadley conference room chatting about getting rid of babies over our cheese sandwiches? 'These guys are dirty, filthy. You could die.'

'Oh,' I said. Neither of us knew what to say next.

'The fella . . .' he said at last. 'Is he married?' I shook my head, and Dr Guber broke out into a smile. 'Then you got nothing to worry about! Listen to me. He'll be surprised, yeah, sure. Maybe a little upset. You know bachelors. But then . . . he'll be thrilled.'

He pronounced it *trilled*. 'You mark my words, honey. Absolutely thrilled.'

The Monday after I went to Dr Guber, I was sitting at my desk, in the middle of a tidal wave of nausea that came from some wandering secretary's eau de cologne – and from my almost continual state of pure terror – when the phone rang. It was Mr Leland's secretary. 'Mr Leland has a bit of dictation for you. Would this be a convenient time?' Yes, especially if he'd like to see me throw up.

Lucky for me, Mr Leland wasn't wearing any deodorant or hair oil or talcum powder – anyway, none with a smell. I sat across from his desk and started to take down another one of his strange letters.

'Dear Felix,' he began. He was wearing a navy blue suit. A thick gold watch chain dangled from his vest, as if he was off to make a speech somewhere or attend a dressy funeral. 'I hope you had a grand summer. It's so refreshing, being close to the sea. I am enjoying the breezes, and the sight of birds diving into the water.'

He cleared his throat. I looked up from my pad. 'Is there a word in German for seagull?' he asked.

'Probably,' I said. 'Canary is *Kanarienvogel*.' God knows why, but I added, 'We had a canary when I was a little girl.'

'What happened to it?'

'The usual canary things. It sang a lot, ate a little birdseed, and died.'

The half of his mouth that seemed to work right smiled at me. We weren't exactly what you'd call great buddies, but at least I was a lot less terrified of him. Gradually, I'd noticed – from the way he treated his own secretary to the way he talked on the phone during calls he'd take while I was sitting in his office – that Edward Leland was, for all his importance, all right. Sure, if you crossed him he probably would do something very, very horrible back to you. But as long as you did your job, you were okay. More than okay, because he had a sense of humor: joking to secretaries, witty to lawyers, hysterically funny to clients. Well, why not? He was so high up in the world he could afford to laugh. He was far beyond having to worry about being taken seriously.

'No canaries in this letter. When you get back to your desk, find a seagull or a tern or some sort of ocean-type bird in your dictionary.' He paused and then added, 'If you can't find it, check with Mr Berringer.'

A new wake of sickness came over me at the mention of John's name. And to make it worse, not only did Mr Leland realize something was wrong; he had been waiting for it. He may even have tossed John's name out for curiosity, or a test, to see what it would do. It did a lot. For the first time in those five weeks of acute afternoon nausea, I felt I really was going to throw up. I lowered my head; it would be terrific, a bright addition to the dark colors in Mr Leland's Oriental rug.

'Are you all right, Miss Voss?' I could hear in his voice that he felt bad.

'I'm fine, thank you.' I raised my pencil – and then my head – so he could see I was ready to get going again.

But I must have looked pretty crummy, because he asked, 'Would you like a glass of water?'

'No, thanks. I'm okay.' He looked like he didn't agree. 'Really I am.'

So he began to dictate again. My dizziness didn't go away, but my stomach calmed down enough so that I felt assured Mr Leland wouldn't have to witness the reappearance of my ham and tomato sandwich.

'I spent the month of August sailing with my three sons,' he said. Of course, I knew he didn't have three sons (just one beaut of a daughter). But this letter was no crazier than any of the others I'd taken in the past couple of months. 'Please send my fondest regards to Maria and the two little ones. I remain, Yours, Vincenzo. V-i-n-c-e-n-z-o.'

I couldn't help asking, 'Vincenzo?'

'That's Vincent in Italian.'

'I see,' I said.

'You do? Well, Miss Voss, tell me what you see.' It was always questions with Mr Leland, but working with him three or four hours a week, I'd learned that whether or not he liked my answers, he never held them against me personally. I was convinced the questions were completely impersonal, asked to get information or a reaction, not to test me – Linda Voss – in any way.

'My guess is the letters are some sort of code to someone in Germany.' No reaction. 'And maybe someone will be mailing this letter from Italy . . .' Annoyance. 'Because of the Vincenzo business.'

I typed the letters at an old Royal he kept in a closet in his office. I never typed envelopes for them. I never made carbons. When I gave Mr Leland the typed letter, I had to give him the steno pad I'd used. Each time I went to his office, I needed a brand-new pad. I never knew who mailed the letters or where they went.

'Any other deductions, Miss Voss?'

'I hope I'm not . . . I don't want to overstep my bounds.'

'Go on.'

'If this has anything to do with harbors or ships or aircraft carriers or E-boats or U-boats . . .' My stomach did a flop, but I clutched my pencil tight, as if grabbing on to a subway pole, and I got through that bump. 'What I'm saying is, the Germans aren't dopes. If this is a code, I hope it's about something . . .' I paused. 'Something not watery.' No reaction.

But I was starting to be able to read him a little. My father had always said I was really smart about people, and that if I didn't wear my heart on my sleeve about everything, I'd have made a good poker player because I could see past the faces people put on. And I think he'd been right. I bet most people wouldn't have noticed Mr Leland getting annoyed about a comment that the letter was going to be mailed from Italy. The change in his face was so small it wasn't really a change at all. And I also knew that whatever the code was, it was okay; it had nothing to do with anything watery.

What I was curious to ask him, and naturally I couldn't, was how come he used me as a measure of how good his secrets were. I guessed I was his Miss Everybody, his Jane Doe, his average American.

What I was also dying to ask him was what I should do about my whole life. He was so smart. He advised senators, judges.

Everyone said he even got calls from the White House. I need some advice, I could say – just like FDR would. See, I'm two months down, seven months to go, and how can I possibly tell John Berringer that I'm going to have his baby?

I told him by just telling him. I went straight from Edward Leland's leathery, lawyery office into John's immaculate modern one and said, 'I have to talk to you.'

He smiled and said, 'Later,' but did not look up from the letter of agreement he was marking with a red pencil. I didn't move. My reflection in his shiny desk must have annoyed him, because when he glanced up, he took a fast, deep breath and then quickly forced his face into its I'm-not-only-handsome-I'm-a-nice-guy expression: His head tilted a little to the right; the corners of his mouth turned up just enough to show that despite the chilly blond superiority of his looks, he was truly good-natured. But I knew him well enough to know that at this moment he wasn't – at least not toward me. Still, I was under the influence of Edward Leland's world, where men with damaged faces made terrible, secret decisions, a world where a fringe of thick lashes over sapphire eyes didn't count for a damn. It gave me courage.

So I spoke. 'I have to talk to you *now*.' Whatever was in my voice made him put down his pencil.

'This can't wait for tonight?'

'No.'

'Linda, I'm really under enormous pressure.'

'So am I.'

He cut me off. 'I'm sure you are.' He glanced down at the letter he was editing. 'I hate to be rude, but the longer you stand here, the longer it will take me to get this back to you to be retyped. Are you in the mood to be stuck here until ten, eleven o'clock? Because I'm not. I'd like to get home and . . .' He gave me a little smile. It meant goodbye.

I sat myself down in the small, ugly modern chair by the side of his desk; it looked like a tilted soup plate.

'Please, have a seat,' he said, really irritated now. 'make yourself comfortable.'

'I'm pregnant.'

'*What?*' But he heard me, because it was as if he switched gears. Now you could almost hear his mind whirring, as if he was starting up the most intricate argument against the toughest opponent of his career. 'Are you sure?' he demanded.

'Yes.'

'What makes you so certain?'

'I've missed two – '

'That doesn't necessarily mean anything,' he interrupted. He was talking fast. 'There could be any number of reasons for a skipped period.'

'Two periods,' I managed to say. To this day I can't figure out how I was able to keep such control. I sounded so composed I could almost have been a match for him. 'I missed two periods – please let me finish – so I had a rabbit test. It came out positive.' John's fair skin went from pale to white. 'And I went to the doctor to double check. And I am.'

'Didn't you use anything?' he finally asked.

'Use anything?'

'Use anything! A diaphragm.' I shook my head. 'Jesus Christ!'

'I wouldn't know where to get one.'

'From the same damned doctor who confirmed your pregnancy!'

'But he's been our family doctor for years.'

'So?'

'I couldn't go to him. I didn't want him to think I was . . .' My hands were in my lap, clasped so tight my fingers began to throb.

His hand turned into a fist, and he crashed it down on the desk. 'You did this purposely, didn't you? *Didn't you*, damn it!' He banged again, harder. 'The minute Nan left, you started planning – '

Then came one of those moments that kill drama. John's eyes turned dark with anger, I tried to shrivel up to invisibility in that disgusting chair . . . and the phone rang. Softly at his desk, but through the closed door I could hear it shrilling at mine. Automatically, I reached over, picked up the receiver and very calmly said, 'Mr Berringer's office.'

'Mr Waring calling for Mr Berringer,' a secretary at some other, more chaste law firm said. She sounded so efficient, so calm. No two missed periods for her.

'I'm sorry, Mr Berringer is out of the office at the moment.' John's eyes moved back and forth, as if he couldn't decide whether to be grateful or grab the phone from me. 'May I have him return Mr Waring's call tomorrow morning?' She said I could, and I hung up with a courteous 'Thank you.'

And then I turned to John. My voice was still secretary sweet. 'Let me just tell you one thing. I didn't lay any traps for you. If you happen to remember that first night, it was you, not me, who insisted on being friendly. I'm not a sneak, and I would *never*—'

'Fine. Wonderful. You're far beyond opportunistic intrigues. But somehow it never occurred to you in all these weeks that you might take precautions.'

'I guess not,' I answered. 'You're the smart one. Did it ever occur to you?'

There was silence that went on too long to be a moment of silence. At last he said, 'Please go now. I have work to finish. We can continue this discussion later.'

And then he picked up his red pencil, changed a colon to a semicolon. I returned to my desk.

When you're writing things down, no matter how detailed you try to be you always wind up leaving things out. So let me put in what I've left out. (You know what Dr Freud says, that you don't leave anything out by mistake? It had always sounded like a lot of Viennese *Schlag* to me, but who was I to say? I was the girl who left out a diaphragm.) Anyway, the details.

After our first time together, I'd stopped saying Mr Berringer, but I never called him John.

He never asked me anything about my family, or even if I had a family. Once I mentioned something about going home to Queens, and he said, 'Oh, I thought you lived in Brooklyn.'

He'd grown up on Long Island, in Port Washington. He told me his father had been in business out there. I asked what kind of business, and he'd said, 'Financial.' He didn't like to talk about his parents. They'd died in a car crash in 1929, when he was in his second year of law school, and I couldn't tell whether or not it still hurt him to even think about them or whether maybe there was something about them he didn't want to talk about.

I'd asked him, 'What church did your parents go to?'

'What?' he'd asked.

'What church did your parents go to?'

'Episcopal.' He was staring at me like I was nuts, because we had just finished – we were still breathing hard, still sweating, actually – and most people wouldn't dream of discussing church before they took a shower.

'Both of them?' I inquired.

'Yes.'

Another thing: He had been an only child.

Another: John was in demand. Two weeks after Nan left, the phone started ringing. It was this or that partner's wife, wanting him to meet this or that girl. How did I know? How do you think? Once, after John picked up in his office, I clicked the button fast, covered the mouthpiece, then eavesdropped. 'John, my dear, I have an absolute dream of a girl you must meet. Laura Steele. Of the Steeles.' John said he'd love to. Not yet, but very soon. 'You're not being naughty and seeing anyone else, are you, John?' the voice demanded. 'No,' he'd told her. 'No one.'

He called me back into his office about seven o'clock that same night. It wasn't dark yet, but the moon was out, full, risen so it was almost as high as John's head, and it had the soft, slightly yellowish shine of a giant ball of taffy. His office lamp wasn't on, so the room was illuminated by moonlight; it made the hard furniture – and John – seem more gentle.

His posture, though, was so straight, businesslike, that for a second I thought he was going to give me a letter of agreement to retype. But when I glanced down at his desk, I saw that he hadn't gotten any further than the semicolon he'd been working on three hours before.

'Sit down,' he said. With the moonlight pouring through the open window, his hair glowed, as if he had a halo. 'Let me be blunt, Linda. Are you willing to get rid of it?'

'The baby?' I whispered.

'Yes. I've learned of someone, a reputable physician. It can be done in a hospital in Puerto Rico. Very clean. And all on the up-and-up.'

Here was this shining man, and all I wanted to do was make him happy. But as I started to nod, to think the words 'Whatever you want,' I thought about my being pregnant in a way I hadn't before. Maybe not in a goo-gooish maternal-instinct way, imagining something soft and pink and smelling of Johnson's Baby Powder. But for the first time I comprehended that my awful afternoon sickness and the tight waistbands of my skirts were due to something more than a medical condition that was lousing up my life.

I can't say I wanted a baby. I didn't picture myself buying tiny, fluffy sweaters. It was only later that I thought it would have fair hair, like me and John, and wondered whether it would have his deep blue eyes or my brown.

'Please listen to me carefully,' he said. 'This is probably the most important decision you'll ever have to make in your life. I hope you'll make it . . .' His voice faded away, as if it wasn't worth the energy to go on.

'What?' I asked. 'Finish what you were going to say.'

'I hope your decision will be rational.'

'Do I look like a raving lunatic?'

'Linda, must you be so argumentative?'

'If I'm capable of being argumentative,' I said, 'then I'm obviously capable of being rational, so you can relax.' He never expected that from me; he stared, almost as if he was waiting for the ventriloquist who'd said that line to pop up behind my chair. 'And being so rational, I'd appreciate it if you were a little clearer.' I pulled my chair closer to his desk. 'What do *you* want me to do?'

'You know what I want.'

'Tell me.'

'I would like you to get rid of it. I want you not to use the fact of your getting pregnant as leverage.'

'Leverage?' I asked, but I knew exactly what he meant.

'To get me to' – he could hardly bring himself to spit out the words – 'marry you.'

'I don't expect you to do that.'

'What am I supposed to do if you decide not to get rid of it?'

'I don't know. It's not anything I've thought about.' I paused then, and I thought. It didn't take much time. 'You could give me some money so I could have it,' I said.

'So you don't want to . . . you won't consider even speaking with that doctor?'

'No. Please, now I'd like you to listen to me. No matter what you think, I'm not some cheap floozy trying to trap you.'

'I never meant to imply that, Linda.'

'And I'm not some dope who can't understand the pickle she's in . . . and you're in. So just hear me out.' I hated this, thinking on my feet or, more accurately, on my behind. But since I hadn't prepared myself, I had no choice. 'I guess I'll have to get out of here pretty soon, before I start getting noticeable, or it'll be bad for you. I'll need some money to live. No more than I'm getting now, twenty-five dollars a week. Well, money for a doctor too.

'I can't go away anywhere, because I have to take care of my mother. But since no one you know would ever put even his little toe in Ridgewood, there's nothing to worry about.' For him. For me, oh, God, it was going to be something going to the grocery with a belly the size of a watermelon. 'And I'm not going to do anything to embarrass you after I have it. You don't have to concern yourself. I'm not going to come in with some little bundle in a blanket and stand weeping by the elevator bank.'

John went absolutely green around the gills. 'You'd *keep* it?'

'I don't know.' I wanted to cry. 'It's a baby.'

He leaned toward me and rested his arms on his desk. 'I could arrange for someone to take care of your mother, so you could get away. And then, later, for a nice, quiet adoption.'

'As opposed to the usual noisy ones?'

He closed his eyes, as if he was silently counting up to ten for patience, but he only got to about four when he opened them. 'If we can agree to a certain sum,' he began calmly, 'a very generous sum, would you be willing to sign a document absolving me of any—'

'How could you be such a bastard?'

It wasn't exactly a knife to his heart. He just went on. 'Would you sign such a document?'

'Only if there was no generous sum involved.'

'Don't be foolhardy.'

'I can be anything I want to be. You're absolved.' And I stood up and walked out.

But before I got to the door, he was behind me. He put his hands on my shoulders, turned me around and kissed me. 'Linda,' he murmured.

I put my hands against his chest and pushed him away, hard. 'Go find yourself some debutante with a diaphragm,' I said. I clutched the doorknob, pulled, but he slammed the door and then stood against it, holding it shut.

'I'll marry you,' he said.

'No.'

'I'll marry you.'

'*No.* You don't love me. I don't even know if you like me. If I disappeared off the face of the earth tomorrow, you'd only notice when it came to take off your pants. And that wouldn't be any big deal. You know that. All you'd have to do is smile at somebody, and in five minutes you'd be having your needs taken care of.' Slowly, I lifted my head and looked into his eyes. 'But there's no one who can take care of you like I can.'

That night, for the first time, John asked me to sleep over at his apartment. Around midnight, when he went to the bathroom, I got up and smoothed out the sheet we had rumpled, then fluffed the pillows, shook out the quilted cotton comforter and turned it over, making sure Nan's [NLB] monogram was facing down. A few seconds later, when he returned smelling from tooth-powder, I was under the comforter, my eyes closed.

'Linda,' he said. I breathed in deeply. 'Come on. You didn't have time to fall asleep.' I opened my eyes. He slid under the cover and came up beside me. 'Listen to me. There is really no alternative, since you insist on . . . having it. We'll get married.'

'We have nothing in common,' I answered. 'Except sex, and we can't do that if we're invited out on one of the partners' boats for an afternoon.' He stared at me. I think it hadn't occurred to him until that instant that if I was going to be his wife, he might, occasionally, have to trot me out of the bedroom. 'Look, let's be honest with each other for once, because now we have to be. I know how thrilled you are every time I open my mouth to try and make conversation. How do you think your friends will feel? I would be an embarrassment to you.'

'Is that what you believe?'

'I don't know. But you believe it.'

'You don't know what I believe.'

'So tell me.'

Instead, he stared up at the ceiling. So I told him, my mother was a sick drunk, and I had to take care of her. He didn't seem either surprised or interested. But he said, 'I'll give you money for her, if that's what you want.'

'Look, a few hours ago you were ready to dump me—'

'That's not true. I was ready to be responsible—'

'Responsibility's one thing. Marriage is another. Am I what you want to some home to every night for the rest of your life?'

Instead of answering, he said, 'Shh,' turned, and pried apart my legs with his knee. We did it again.

At three in the morning, after we'd slept a couple of hours as far apart as the double bed would allow, we accidentally knocked together and woke up, startled to find each other. Quickly, we turned away and pretended to go back to sleep, but it didn't work. I could hear his shallow, nervous breathing, his swallows that were almost gulps. I sat up and touched the silky hair on the back of his head. 'Tell me why . . . why you're willing. Is it to get back at Nan, to show her how she destroyed your life, that you buried your troubles in your secretary – and knocked her up?'

'Stop it.'

'Is it to give her a slap in the face, to show her that what it *really* takes to satisfy you is a hot little item from Queens?'

'This conversation is completely inappropriate, so let's end it.' It was hard to hear, because he wasn't facing me; his words were muffled in the pillow.

'Is it that it's so good with me you can't give it up, even if you have to marry me and let me have your child?'

'Go back to sleep. You're upset. Worn out.' He sounded weary, not tired.

I tried to act lightheaded, the way classy people are supposed to in nasty situations. 'Think about your practice. Do you think marrying me is going to do wonders for your reputation for sound judgment? What are your foreign clients going to think, when they meet your pregnant dumpling with the *berlinerisch* accent?'

'Stop it' he snapped. He took a minute to compose himself. 'Linda, I'm responsible for this situation. I got you pregnant. And I want to do what's honorable.'

'*Why?* Because that's what gentlemen are supposed to do?'

'Yes.'

'But there is no love.'

'You love me.' He was so kind and so cold. 'Do you want to leave me, Linda? Or do you want me to marry you?'

Maybe when he feels it kicking, I thought. He'll put his hand on my stomach, and he'll look at me and all of a sudden . . . 'I want you to marry me.'

'All right, then.'

I put my arms around him and rested my head on his shoulder. He grabbed me tight, climbed on top of me, and so we did it again.

# *Chapter Eleven*

The high-ceilinged room in City Hall smelled of cigarettes ground out on the already dirty brown and tan tile floor. Couples pressed against a wood railing, waiting their turn to enter into matrimony. Not holy matrimony; this was the Municipal Building of the City of New York, and in the interest of peace in the Melting Pot – to say nothing of keeping the line moving – the clerks were not supposed to utter You-Know-Who's name.

It was only then that I realized how much I wanted to hear it; I imagined a deep, velvety voice intoning, *Dearly beloved, We are gathered here in the sight of Gawd* . . . If I'd had to put a face on that voice, I guess it would be the minister who was always burying Johnstons in Brooklyn. I didn't know his name or his denomination, but he looked like someone born to perform religious rites: white hair, a hawkish nose and ice blue eyes that appeared to look down at whoever was getting buried. But now and then he broke into a kind smile, which showed a couple of teeth missing on the side. The parsonage roof probably leaked too, poor guy.

Since I'd fallen for John, my daydreams had been detailed, but they'd almost always been about sex, not ceremonies. Still, my secret night dreams must have been traditional: being married by the Reverend Smith/Jones/Williams in a Christmas card church, a simple, pure-white building with a nice steeple. Out of respect to my Grandma Olga's memory, the reverend would just say 'God; whenever he came to His name, and not make a big deal about details like the Father, Son and Holy Spirit.

A little runt of a groom-to-be next to me was puffing like a titan of industry on a giant cigar, and his about-to-be bride was chomping on a wad of spearmint gum. To keep my stomach from flipping over, I turned my head toward John and inhaled the aroma of clean wool from the sleeve of his suit. I realized that I'd not only pictured the minister; I'd even imagined my dress. An old-fashioned handmade lace – a rosebud and rose design. Olga had brought a square of lace like that with her from Berlin: a handkerchief some rich cousin had given Olga's mother for her trousseau.

In the wedding dream I hadn't known I'd been dreaming, I'd be wearing a strand of pearls from somewhere and carrying a bouquet of white roses and the tiny white dot flowers whose name I didn't know, all tied up with long white ribbons. I'd have on a white leghorn hat with a white velvet band. I wouldn't wear a veil because it would be a day wedding.

And it was a day wedding: no moon. And no June. It was September 16, a Monday, and I was wearing a blue dress that had seen its best days in 1937, when I'd bought it at Ohrbach's End of Summer Sale, which they held in July. (Some tight-mouthed red-headed lady had tried to grab it from me as I took it off the rack, but I'd held on to it and marched majestically to the fitting room. It had been a little baggy, but the redhead was giving me the eye when I came out, so I'd bought it.) It wasn't baggy anymore.

I didn't look pregnant, but my waist was rapidly vanishing. Each night, in front of the full-length mirror in the small, square dressing alcove just outside John's bathroom. I saw my curves disappearing – except in the bosom department, where I was getting like Hedy Lamarr: lush.

So there I was in City Hall in a plain blue dress and black patent-leather heels, my hair pulled up, pinned tight in place. A working girl's outfit, but who knew that morning when I came to work that I'd be a bride by lunch?

John called me into his office a little after ten. 'I have a ten-thirty conference over at Two Wall Street. I'll meet you at eleven forty-five at the Municipal Building second floor, by the elevators. Put some papers in an envelope and say I called and asked you to bring them to me. Also, you have no idea when you'll be back, because one of the lawyers is from Germany and he may have some memoranda he wants to dictate.' My expression must have confirmed his estimate of my intelligence. 'Don't forget, the Municipal Building,' he said again. 'On Centre Street. I've arranged to have matters expedited. We can get the license and get married right away, without a waiting period. We can be finished by twelve-thirty.'

'You have a conference at one?'

'I thought we could go out to lunch afterwards, to celebrate.'

He gave me a small smile. I gave him one back, but halfway through it I realized John's smile was a brave, public one: chin up, noblesse whatever, courage under fire.

He'd probably offer a gracious toast at lunch.

The little man with a little toothbrush mustache came up beside John and, tiptoeing, led us past a line of clerks, who sat in cages like monkeys on high stools, and into his little glassed-in cubicle, so we wouldn't have to wait on line. That's where we filled out the application for a marriage license.

'Listen,' I said, 'I didn't know we'd be here today. I don't have my birth certificate or – '

'Shhh!' John said.

'But – '

'I will see to everything, miss,' the little man said. 'Just write down your vital statistics – ' His face reddened, his mustache twitched, and he glanced nervously at John, afraid he'd made some blot on my honor. 'Parents' names, date of birth, borough of birth,' he said quickly. 'You *were* born in New York City?' he asked, a little suspiciously, I thought, like maybe I'd snuck in from Minnesota and was trying to pull a fast one.

'In Queens,' I said.

He sighed, relieved. Then he turned to John. His manner turned too – embarrassingly eager to please. '*Delighted* to have been of help, Mr Berringer,' the man said. 'Any friend of Commissioner Tuttle . . .'

But whoever Commissioner Tuttle, puller of strings for Wall Street lawyers, was, he cut no ice in the room where you got married. We had to wait our turn along with about fifteen other couples. Only two of them looked really happy. Most of the others seemed like sad stories. There were several young girls – very young – with their slit-eyed parents and miserable-looking grooms-to-be; the grooms ranged in age from about sixteen to sixty-five; all those girls had bellies. A couple of couples looked as if they'd been keeping company since Calvin Coolidge was elected; they seemed tired of everything, especially each other. An elderly lady with a corsage and marcelled hair was less tired, but she was holding the hand of a too-pretty young man of no more than twenty-five.

But all these couples – the happy and the sad – stared at John. It was obvious he didn't belong. It wasn't just that he was wearing a suit – a few of the other men were – but it was the way the suit fit. And the way the shoulders under the suit were broad. Not broad like one of the men, a construction worker who'd rolled the sleeves of his blue shirt so high you could see his tattooed biceps. John's muscles didn't come from work; they came from playing sports in white uniforms.

His shining hair brightened that room. One of the other guys, an Irishman who had gotten a dark Jewish girl pregnant, had hair as fair as John's but it just didn't gleam.

So in the end, John wasn't stared at because of his clothes, or even his looks. He was simply apart from them, as though some fairy of Good Fortune had waved her wand over his baby carriage. Or, if he hadn't been born different, maybe he'd been initiated into some Ivy League secret society that transforms boys into privileged men.

Just as everybody there knew he was different, John knew it too. And he didn't want to be with . . . well, with people like me. He wanted out of that gritty, noisy, overlit, everyone-is-equal place in the worst way.

'Berringer!' a clerk yelled out.

We walked through an opening in the railing to a small arca where another clerk, a primly dressed man who looked like he sold caskets, checked our papers. He took a long time, so I pulled out my hairpins and shook my hair loose.

'Ready? John Wilson Berringer, do you take Linda Rose Voss to be your lawful wedded wife?'

No 'to love, honor and cherish'? I wondered.

'I do.' John said.

Apparently not.

'Do you, Linda Rose Voss, take John Wilson Berringer to be your lawful wedded husband?'

'I do,' I said. My voice sounded so normal.

'Ring?' the clerk said.

And just as I was thinking: He forgot, John took out a box. I stared as he opened it. Brown velvet, and inside, on white satin, there was a gold wedding band. Nice. Not insultingly thin.

'Thank you,' I whispered, as he slipped it on my finger. It fit. Well, maybe just a little loose.

'I now pronounce you man and wife.' The man waited, then he cleared his throat with a very fake 'Ahem!' We kissed so it would be over and the next couple could start their live together.

Then I looked into John's eyes. They were filled with tears.

'Mom.' I shook my mother gently. It was five in the afternoon of my wedding day. The air coming through the open windows had a crisp, almost sharp, bite. It was that short, false New York autumn that comes in September and blows away the heat of the summer for a few days. I was chilly in my blue dress. My mother's shoulder was cold, which was not surprising, since her blanket had fallen to the floor.

'Five more minutes,' she mumbled, and curled herself up into a shrimp shape.

'Mom, I have to talk to you.' I switched on the lamp on her night table. She'd bought a pair of these lamps when she and my father were first married; the base of the lamp was an extremely fat cherub – even as cherubs go – standing on grapes he somehow didn't crush; he wore a lampshade on his head. 'Mom, please wake up.'

She put the crook of her arm over her eyes and said, 'C'mon, Lin, baby. Don't be a pain.' She'd gotten so thin that in the lamplight I could see the faint outline of two bones in her forearm. 'Two more minutes.'

I sat on the edge of the bed. The pillowcase was soiled with her hair cream and, I guess, her droolings; it hadn't been changed since I'd changed it, the week before.

'Mom, I have to talk with you,' I said. I was trying not to get angry. I'd heard her come in around five-thirty that morning, and now I could see she'd slept in her dress. From the streaks of dirt at the bottom of the sheet, she hadn't even bothered to take off her shoes, although they'd fallen off during her sleep. One had dropped to the floor and another lay on what had been my father's side of the bed.

On the way down to the Municipal Building, I'd had a yen to splurge and take a cab to Queens, pick up my mother and bring her with me. Mom, put on your good navy dress with the white ruffle collar and come watch me get married! I'd say, and she'd leap out of bed, splash some water on her face and say, Oh, Linda, sweetie, you've made me so happy you wouldn't believe it!

'Go 'way,' she mumbled. 'I got a lousy hangover.'

'It's five o'clock, Mom. In the afternoon.' This didn't seem to make a big impression on her. 'I have some wonderful news for you.' Slowly, she lifted her arm away from her eyes and squinted at me. 'John and I got married today.'

She couldn't stop squinting, but she broke out into a huge smile. 'Oh, Lin! A lawyer!' She reached out, squeezed my hand and wriggled around as if to sit up, but didn't make much progress. Her hand was freezing. I picked up the blanket from the floor and put it around her, tucking it under her feet. Her big toe poked through a rip in her stocking. 'When did you do it?'

'Today.' I started to apologize. 'We decided at the last minute,' but since she didn't seem to notice she hadn't been invited, I stopped.

'Tell me *everything*. Did he get down on one knee and propose? That's what Herm did. It was my sixteenth birthday, and he got down on his knee and said, "Will you be my birthday girl for ever and ever?" Was your John romantic?'

What could I tell her? That at our wedding lunch, right after the waiter poured champagne and we lifted our glasses but didn't clink them because either John didn't want everybody in the restaurant to know we were celebrating or because clinking glasses was simply not done, or naïve or something, he'd told me to take off my ring before I got back to the office, since he hadn't decided how to 'present the situation.' Naturally, I'd be leaving in a week or two. 'No, make that closer to three. It's not going to be easy replacing you.' He smiled, for the waiter, returning with menus, as well as for me. After the waiter walked off, John added, 'You're a good secretary, Linda.'

'A great secretary.'

'And very modest.'

'That too.'

'It will take a few weeks to come up with someone even remotely suitable.'

'And you'll have to pay her more.'

'Probably.'

'So am I better at the typewriter or in bed?'

He put down his champagne glass. 'Come one,' he whispered, 'let's forget lunch. We can go back to the apartment and celebrate.' Not a chance. In fact, I told him, I had to take the rest of the afternoon off and get things set up for my mother. 'Your mother?' he murmured. He couldn't seem to remember I'd come from parents, not an employment agency.

So after lunch I'd gone home to Ridgewood and stopped in to talk to Dr Guber. He'd hugged me and said, 'Hey, I knew the guy would mary you! Now relax, be a wife. I know a nice old maid, a practical nurse, over in Bushwick. She'll live in and cook, clean, take care of your mother. Don't worry,' he'd soothed me. 'This girl's got the constitution of an ox. For fifteen bucks a week, she'll do everything. More than you could do, working all day.'

I put my hand on my mother's icy shoulder. 'Mom, listen to me. I gave a key to Dr Guber – '

'That old fart?'

'Mom, he's going to give it to a girl from Bushwick, who'll be coming in to clean and cook whatever you want and look after you.

I'll pay her, and I'm going to give you money every week. But you can't spend it all in one day.'

'Who, *me?*' my mother asked, and tried to wink, although it didn't work. Her cheek just twitched. 'So tell me, honeybunch, what's your name now?'

'Berringer,' I said.

'Write it down for me,' she said, 'so I can tell all my friends.'

I took a piece of paper and a pencil from my notebook and wrote 'Linda Berringer' for the first time, and added John's home phone number.

'Here's my phone number, Mom. And I'll call you every day. But if you need anything, you call me.'

'Listen, dollface, you did good.'

'Thanks, Mom.'

'You pregnant?' She gave me an inquisitive smile.

'Yes.'

'That's what I figured. Linda, lovie, you're one smart girl, hooking him before he could wiggle away to another rich one. I'm *so* proud of you.'

Then, before she went back to sleep, she gave me a big hug and a kiss.

It wasn't until a few minutes after six, fighting the end of the crowd rushing down, that I pushed my way up the subway stairs on my way back to the office. I was wondering if, being a lawyer's wife, I could have taken a taxi to see my mother. In John's neighborhood, I'd seen rich ladies in suits and alligator shoes who stood on the corner of Park Avenue and raised one finger, and cabs pulled over and screeched on their brakes and drivers smiled.

I was preoccupied, coming up and out of the subway, wondering how John would give me house money, whether I'd just find it under a pillow or if he'd hand me two or three or four twenties – whatever lawyers' wives get every other Friday, the day he got his check. And how was I supposed to know what it was for? I figured, okay, groceries, newspapers, a lipstick. Do lawyers' wives say, Darling, I need an extra forty for a sweet little peau de soie at

Tailored Woman? What if he forgot to give me anything? Was I supposed to remind him?

Anyway, I was almost at the top of the steps, slipping my wedding ring off and putting it in my pocketbook, thinking that it was going to be pretty embarrassing, but I was gong to have to ask John for a new winter coat because the old one not only was embarrassingly ratty, with an unsewable rip under the left arm, but wouldn't button over my belly when the time came, when – not more than two seconds after I'd gotten up to the street – I slammed into Gladys Slade.

'Excuse me,' she said. She was so busy being polite, she hadn't seen me.

Those were really her first words to me since we'd come to the understanding that she'd keep quiet. Of course, she included me in a 'How are you?' if I was coming through the door with a group of girls. To do anything else would be to call attention to the fact that I'd done something terrible that called for a boycott, and she was nervous enough about my 'power' over John that she kept herself under tight control. Any 'hello' or 'What's new?' was just in self-defense.

To tell the truth, the only reason I missed my friendship with Gladys was that on a lot of Sundays we went to the movies together; since I'd started seeing John seven days a week, I hadn't been to a single movie. I'd missed Fred Astaire and Eleanor Powell in *Broadway Melody* of 1940, and I was dying to see Laurence Olivier in *Rebecca*, even though Joan Fontaine was so whiny I always wished her leading man would smack her across the face and say, Shut up, you pain in the ass!

Gladys was huddled in her office sweater, which she'd worn home because of the chill. It was a too-loose cardigan, the color of Wheatena. Suddenly, I felt cold and massaged my empty ring finger with my thumb. 'How've you been, Gladys?'

She nodded, and I guess only because I didn't move out of the way, she said, 'You weren't at lunch today.'

'Mr Berringer' – I blushed – 'had a conference over at Two Wall. He wanted me there.'

'Well, I'm sure he was delighted to have you.'

'Look, Gladys, I'm not going to say anything corny, like "Let's be friends," but at least we could be civil to each other. We've known each other so long and . . . Why don't we go out for a drink, maybe early next week?'

'I can't see any point to it.'

'There is no point, really. Just to talk.' What I wanted to do, after John 'presented the situation' of our marriage, was to sit down and tell Glady's before she heard it from the office grapevine. I felt I owed her that. Or maybe deep down I just wanted someone to talk to. Funny, I had nobody now.

Gladys opened her pocketbook and made herself busy searching through her change purse to find a nickel for the subway. 'What you're obviously dying to talk about' – she spoke into her pocketbook – 'I don't want to know about.'

I should have felt angry, but all I could think of was how embarrassed . . . no, embarrassment was nothing compared to what Gladys was going to feel when she heard about me and John. Look, I wanted to reassure her, I'm never going to tell him how you talk about all the partners, especially not how you talked about him, how you went on and one about how gorgeous he was and said, 'Can you *imagine* what he must look like in tennis clothes?'

She found her nickel. I stepped aside. 'I'll let you go, then,' I said.

But she wasn't quite ready. 'I think I ought to warn you,' Gladys said, 'that your little interlude may be coming to an end.' She stopped. She waited for me to beg her to go on. I didn't. 'Mrs Avenel is having a dinner party Saturday for all the partners. She's hired a butler to pass around the hors d'oeuvres. Mr Berringer had been invited, and Mrs Avenel had arranged for a *very* eligible girl to be his dinner partner, but . . .'

Her long, dramatic pause was so overly long and dramatic that I finally lost patience. I knew she was out to hurt me again, and I couldn't be hurt. Well, not by her anyway. 'But what, Gladys?'

'He called Mrs Avenel this morning and told her' – she gave a long, supercilious sniff – 'he'd met someone and was *getting married!*'

I asked softly, 'Did he say if he was still going to the party?'

'Didn't you hear me?'

'I heard you. Is he going?'

'*Yes*, he's going.' Her tone turned into a sneer. 'With his fiancée.'

No, I was dying to say. With his wife.

Right after we'd finally turned out the lights, I'd asked John when I could wear my ring to the office. 'Oh,' he'd murmured. I waited. 'Whenever,' he finally said. 'When you went to your mother's, I spoke to Ed about our . . . and your leaving.' 'Did you tell him I was – '

'*No.*' He turned his pillow over and, before he went off to sleep, added. 'Stop worrying. He said it was fine with him.'

Well, it was the day after my wedding and it wasn't fine. I was standing in front of Mr Leland's desk because he hadn't asked me to sit down, and I was being yelled at by a man who was able to yell without raising his voice.

'Did it occur to you at any point, Mrs Berringer, that you had responsibilities to someone other than yourself?' Edward Leland was furious. 'Did you ever consider that apart from the damned nuisance of engaging another bilingual secretary, it usually takes a minimum of ten weeks to get someone security clearance for the sort of work you've been doing? You're cleared for secret work. Do you think we can pick some German-speaking stenographer off the streets of Yorkville and dictate our codes to her? It could take weeks, *months* even, to find someone whom we can even approach for an FBI check.

'You know how things are heating up here. You know that the volume of this . . . this sort of work has increased a hundred-fold. What am I supposed to do if I have a message to send tomorrow? Or three or four weeks from now?' I couldn't get an answer past the lump in my throat. 'Send it down to Washington for fifty idiot bureaucrats to pass from hand to hand before they translate?' His face darkened. 'Ask your husband to type it up?'

'Please, I'll be glad to – '

'To what, Mrs Berringer?'

'To do whatever I can.'

'You're a married woman.'

'No matter what your wedding night is like, you don't forget shorthand.' I couldn't believe I'd said that.

Neither could Mr Leland. 'I don't need clever retorts. I need a secretary with security clearance.'

'I'm sorry.

'I assumed – obviously wrongheadedly – that you realized that despite the seeming simplicity of the letters I've ben dictating, they serve a purpose.'

'Mr Leland,' I began. But then I started crying. Not just a few cute tears. Real, true weeping. I covered my face with my hands, and as I did, my pad and pencil dropped.

'For God's sake!' he said. And then he added, 'Oh, sit down.' I sat. 'Here.' He leaned forward and put his handkerchief right in front of me on the desk. I hated using it, because I thought: How am I going to get this back to him? but I used it anyway; my nose was running. Except for my sobbing, it was absolutely quiet, and I think I finally spoke only because I didn't want him to fill the silence by telling me to get a grip on myself or, worse, that he was sorry he'd upset me.

I took one last sniffler and looked up at him. 'Mr Leland, I'm sorry to be carrying on like this.' Nothing resembling an emotion showed on his face. 'I'd like to explain things.'

'That is not necessary, Mrs Berringer.'

'I think it is.'

'All right. Go on.'

'I know you think I'm inconsiderate, and you're right. I didn't consider it for a minute. You know why? I was in a pickle. I was carrying on with Mr Berringer – '

'This really isn't necessary.'

'I know, but please listen, anyway. I got pregnant, Mr Leland.' His black eyes widened, not because he was surprised; I'm sure he wasn't. He was surprised I was talking about it. 'I know it's something people don't discuss in polite company – but I'm not such polite company. Anyway, I'm sure you've already figured out Mr . . . that John didn't marry me for my money or my great mind. He married me because he had to.

'So you're right,' I went on. 'I was a wreck and I didn't think about anyone beyond myself. Well, I thought about my mother. She's a drunk and she's not in the best of health and I support her. But maybe you already know that from the FBI or whoever checked me.'

'Yes, I know about it,' he said softly.

'So all I can do is apologize and say this conversation is probably as uncomfortable for you as it is for me, but I want to set the record straight. Like you guys say, there were extenuating circumstances.'

'I understand.'

'But just because I got myself in trouble . . .'

'Go on.'

'It doesn't mean I can't work. Okay, maybe I can't come to the office during the day, but I could come in real early or real late. I don't want to louse you up. I know . . . well, I don't *know*, but I figure what you're doing is very important, so until you find someone else, I'd like to do whatever I can.'

'Thank you,' he said. 'I'm sure I'll be able to manage without you.'

That was it. Like the sergeants say in all the army movies: *Dismissed!* I picked up my pad and pencil from the floor and took that long, familiar walk across his office rug again. When I was halfway to the door, Edward Leland called out: 'Mrs Berringer.' I turned and faced him. His soft handkerchief was balled up in my fist.

'Yes, Mr Leland?'

'Whatever happens . . .' For the first time since I'd known him, he hesitated. 'You're all right. Don't ever sell yourself short.'

# *Chapter Twelve*

Henry and Florence Avenel lived somewhere in Westchester, in an important-looking white house with pillars that would have been perfect for Thomas Jefferson or Scarlett O'Hara but seemed a little much for a bulgy-eyed corporate lawyer who looked like a toad in a striped tie. So the house was grand, although a couple of steps down from palatial, but whoever the Avenels had bought it from had obviously gone bust – probably in '29 – and, before giving up the last of their mint julep dreams, had sold off most of the ole plantation. Just as you drove up and were about to go Ooh! you saw another, newer, smaller, semi-Tara on the left and an English Tudor squeezing in on the right. If someone in the Tudor had sneezed, it was so close – separated just be a border of trees shaped like lollipops – Florence Avenel might have said Gesundheit!

Mrs Avenel was not only polite; she was wildly enthusiastic. 'John!' she gushed, as we came through the door. 'This must be Linda! John, she's lovely! Beyond lovely! Like Jean Harlow brought back to life!' I bore as much resemblance to the movie star as she bore to Minnie Mouse: barely any, but enough to comment on if you were truly desperate for something to say. 'But she's *so* much finer-looking than Harlow, of course.' She had to say that, naturally. She wasn't going to risk telling her husband's partner that his new wife was a ringer for a world-famous platinum-blond slut. 'Congratulations, John!'

Then she beamed at me, not failing to take in my midsection, which, I'd made sure, was covered by the long boxy jacket of the black faille dinner suit I'd bought. (I'd known purple and low-cut were wrong, but was less sure what was right. So I'd come out of the kitchen after finishing the dinner dishes and asked John if I could have some money for a dress for the Avenels'. He'd gone to his wallet and handed me two fifty-dollar bills and said, Is this enough? The hundred dollars had made me mute, but I'd nodded yes, it was enough. The next day, I marched into Saks Fifth Avenue and looked around until I found the perfect salesgirl; she looked like one of the executive secretaries: a Vassar type with a tight mouth and a tighter behind. I told her: I'm going to a Saturday night diner party with a bunch of Wall Street lawyers. What've you got? She raised both eyebrows, but picked out the suit and a soft gray silk blouse to go with it, and told me, Wear pearl earrings. Ha, But I'd worn my hair down to cover my ears. When I walked out of the bedroom, all dressed and ready to go, John looked flabbergasted. Like Mrs Avenel, he'd probably been expecting red sequins and chewing gum. He was caught so off guard by my lack of bad taste that he mumbled. Oh. You look beautiful.)

Mrs Avenel at last spoke to me. 'My dear, Henry and I are so very, very happy for you.'

All those years, Gladys had actually been managing to mimic Mrs Avenel pretty well. 'My dee-ahr.' From the imitation, I'd always imagined an overpowering woman with a bust so commanding it could easily lead a battleship across the Atlantic. But Mrs Avenel was tiny, barely five feet tall, and so thin the bones on her chest stuck out, like a chicken's. She was wearing a floor-length bottle-green dress with a deep V neck and a sash, which looked more like an overdone bathrobe than a hostess gown.

She took my arm and led me across a hallway with a marble checkerboard floor, toward the living room. 'Now tell me, my dear, how long have the two of you been married?'

'Five days.'

'Ah! Five days! You must call me Florence.' She smiled up at me. I smiled back; it felt unnaturally broad – the smile you make standing in front of a bathroom mirror looking for food stuck between your back teeth.

But after a second, I realized she was no longer appraising me. Her eyes finally fixed on John, and now that she'd done what was proper with me, she could concentrate. Concentrate was putting it mildly. Little Flo was beaming at my husband with the intensity of a radio signal on top of the Empire State Building. Her gaze broadcast a powerful message: Wow! Wow! Wow!

And he, of course, was smiling back. Hey, I could have told her, that's the smile he gives to hatcheck girls and the building superintendent's wife. And to secretaries. Obviously to every female. That smile is his routine you-are-bewitching-and-you've-captivated-me-completely smile. It's pure reflex, like a jerking knee, and he does it to reduce you – and all of us – to jelly, so just in case he wants something from you, you're ready, available, thirsting to do whatever it is he wants. Come on, Florence, you're fifty years old, not very bright, eagle-beaked and chicken-breasted. Do you think he wants you?

She did. And so did they all. Florence led us into her living room, with its high ceiling, tall windows and long sofas, and every woman in the room fell into silence and gaped at my husband. Then John smiled, a general nice-to-see-you smile, but the women, obviously remembering previous, more personal smiles, like the one bestowed upon lucky Florence, all broke into joyous grins of gladness.

'Everyone!' Florence Avenel trilled. '*This* is Linda.'

It was only then that the women's eyes turned to me. And their husband's too. Seven or eight partners of Blair, VanderGraff and Wadley opened up the tight knot they'd been standing in by the fireplace, glanced over and smiled at me. Not the way John smiled, of course, but courteously enough. A couple of them waved. After all, I'd become a wife. Their faces were a blur, but then Mr Wilson lifted his cocktail glass in a toast. 'To the newlyweds!' he said, and suddenly glasses were raised and ten or fifteen cultivated voices were repeating: 'Nyoo-lyweds!'

And then there was silence as all those well-bred people, the toasting out of the way, just stared. For the men, seeing me in black faille, with makeup on and hair loose, was discomforting. It upset the normal balance of things, as if their barber had all of a sudden showed up at a partner's meeting in a three-piece suit and plunked himself down at the conference table and said, Hiya, guys.

The women gazed in cool assessment . . . well, maybe not so

cool. A couple of fast looks were flashed between two older women in print dresses, and a stunner of about forty, with ivory skin, gray-blond hair pulled tight into a chic chignon, and brilliant red lipstick, lowered her glance from my suit (which I guess was okay – to my shoes (which, from her quickly sucked-in cheeks, obviously weren't).

'Well,' boomed Mr Avenel as he came over. He pushed a martini into my hand with so much heartiness I nearly spilled it. 'How's the new bride?'

'Fine,' I said, and then everybody, relieved, began to talk again, lots of tight, buzzing conversations.

'Well, let me introduce you to the ladies.' He grabbed my free hand and pulled me across what I think was a Chinese rug – anyway, it was blue, with flowers – to the women. 'Claudia Boland, Mimi O'Connell, Sarah Weedcock, Lorraine Wilson . . .' He spoke so fast I had no way of knowing who was who, although I guessed Lorraine Wilson was the freckled one with a big jaw, because she was such a good match for Mr Wilson, who also had freckles and resembled a ventriloquist's dummy. 'Mary Shawcross, who's here with Ed Leland . . .' I hadn't seen him. I made myself not turn around to the pack of partners by the fireplace. Mary Shawcross smiled just enough to show teeth like perfect tiny white tiles. She was the elegant one, with the pale, pulled-back hair and red lipstick. More than elegant. Almost beautiful, with high cheekbones and sleepy, heavy-lidded eyes.

I took a gulp of the martini. 'Carrie Post,' Henry Avenel continued, and I came face-to-face with the woman whose husband was spending all his evenings with Wilma Gerhardt and paid for Wilma's manicures – to say nothing of her fox jacket and an endless supply of silk stockings. The pudgy, cheated-on Mrs Post summoned up her good manners and managed a 'Glad to meet you.' It took some summoning; this quiet, double-chinned woman had to work at being cordial because she *knew* – I just knew she knew – and the sight of a former secretary with a lawyer's wedding band on was, to say the least, painful.

'Oh,' Mr Avenel boomed on, 'let me not forget out Ginger Norris!' I turned, expecting to see a pug-nosed tennis player.

Instead, I saw a woman in her mid-fifties, who was a real pill; while all the others had managed a decent 'So pleased,' or even a plain 'hello,' Ginger just inclined her head, as if she was doing a Queen Mary imitation.

And then, right after the introductions, things went back to normal. Mimi spoke to Sarah, Lorraine spoke to Mary, and everyone spoke to everyone – except to me. All of a sudden, I was alone with my martini. And I realized then that all that momentary graciousness had been exactly that: a warmth that lasted about sixty seconds.

So I just stood there, the only one not being talked to, and the only one being watched. I sensed it. Quick, sideways glances. And if I'd wandered over to inspect the Avenel's framed flower pictures or toddled off to the bathroom, they would have known how I'd felt: frightened and alone – heart pounding – in enemy territory.

I took another long sip of my martini. I hated gin, and vermouth and an olive didn't help the situation. I glanced across the room and watched the men murmuring to each other. They stood around the fireplace, which was filled with a giant urn of yellow chrysanthemums. A deep, manly hum arose from them, an uninterrupted hum, as if they were having an endlessly fascinating conversation. John was sandwiched between Mr Norris and Mr O'Connell, and all three were nodding in absolute agreement. I took a step to the right and saw they were nodding at who I thought they'd be nodding at: Edward Leland. Mr Leland looked content, content with whatever he was saying, content with the way his high-powered partners hung on to his every syllable, and probably most content that after dinner was over, he'd be taking Mary Shawcross, her chignon, her exquisite cheekbones and her bright red lips home.

There was one good thing about the dinner itself – the hot rolls.

There was more than one bad thing. First, watching the crazily elaborate ceremony of carving the roast beef. A maid carried the roast into the dining room and slowed down as she passed Mrs Avenel, who gazed at it with so much pride you'd have thought it was her firstborn. Then the maid, with the heavy silver platter resting on both palms, continued down the length of the table, all the way over to Mr Avenel, and lowered it before him. He pushed back his chair and lifted up the fork and carving knife laid out before him, cut a slice and held it up on the fork. Some blood dribbled back into the platter, and he said, 'Voilà!' I looked away for a second; the martini – and maybe the pregnancy – had made me dizzy, and queasy.

As Mr Avenel began to carve in earnest, he breathed hard. His eyes bugged out even more than usual, and his face got all flushed and damp. He was nervous, anxious to do it just right, as if he was the high priest of some religion, finishing up a sacrifice to a bad-tempered god. As he labored, the maid ran up and down the table, handing out the meat. I couldn't stand the smell.

The next bad thing was watching John at the far end of the table, seated between Florence Avenel and Carrie Post, being charming, laughing at Florence's clever remark, which I knew couldn't be clever, admiring Carrie Post's locket and listening seriously as she told him about something like her gall bladder or her son in boarding school. It wasn't that I was jealous. It was that I realized, observing John from a distance, how he gave himself equally to everybody – or, more accurately, to nobody.

He didn't look down the table at me even once. Why should he? I only had one reason for being; all I could do for him at the Avenel's would be to embarrass him, and since I hadn't, he could forget me until we got home – or partway home, when he'd take his hand from the steering wheel, reach over and grab mine, and press it between his legs.

Another bad thing was sitting back and having to listen to a roomful of Republicans talk about the presidential campaign. Okay, Wendell Willkie wasn't the worst person in the world; he'd even started out a Democrat. But to hear these so-called smart lawyers go on and on about him, you'd think he was Jesus Christ.

They called him Wendell, as if he was one of theirs, and I suppose he was. Edward Leland, of all people, sitting on Florence Avenel's other side, who I'd thought had more brains than the rest of the table combined, referred to FDR with sarcasm, calling him 'our esteemed leader' and saying, 'The average American cannot comprehend that it's a tacit New Deal policy to encourage unemployment. Their bureaucrats have nothing to gain from a healthy private sector. What they want is a perpetual Depression, so they can keep their jobs.' I couldn't believe he was saying things like that. Of course, he was better than Henry Avenel, who called Roosevelt 'the cripple' and said Wilkie would 'kill him' on election day. I felt like taking his wife's potato soufflé or whatever it was and dumping it on his fat head.

And the last bad thing was that after the soggy apple pie, the men went someplace to have brandies and smoke cigars, and I was left in the living room on a club chair, while the other women gathered in tight twos and threes and admired each other's outfits and hairdos. Occasionally one of them would allow a glance to pass over me. There'd be a whisper and then a soft 'Shhh!' They didn't try very hard to hide their elbow nudgings; they barely muffled their giggles. And that was how I knew these ladies weren't ladies.

I wasn't going to fall apart. When the men came back, I made myself stay in that stupid chair; I'd be damned if those rich bitches would see me leap up and run to John.

So I sat there, staring out the night-blackened window, deliberately not watching John, although out of the corner of my eye I saw him swirl his brandy and nod at whatever Russell Weedcock was spouting off about. And just then, a man sat on the arm of my chair and said, 'Well, how are you enjoying yourself?' I didn't have to look up, although I did. I knew Edward Leland's voice.

'It's a pretty nice party.'

'You seem to be having a fine time,' he said coolly.

'Very fine.'

'Good!' he said in his deep voice, and everyone turned and stared. 'I noticed how enthralled you were with the political discussion at diner. No doubt you're a great fan of our Mr Willkie.'

'He has wonderful hair.'

'Oh, come on. You can give him more than that.'

'Okay. Other than FDR, he's the strongest supporter of the Democratic Party platform we have around.'

'Please,' he said, looking annoyed and disappointed, as if he'd overestimated my intelligence by five hundred percent.

'Look, Mr Leland – '

'Please, call me Ed.'

'Oh, God, I thought. As if this night wasn't hard enough. 'Willkie's a me-too candidate. He's for everything Roosevelt's for: the draft, aid to England – '

'Nonsense!' He shifted on the chair arm so he could look me right in the eye. I sensed, more than saw, the whole room watching us, trying to hear what we were saying. 'He made it quite clear he feels Roosevelt is courting a war – a war we're completely unprepared for.'

'Yeah? Well, it's a war we could have been prepared for if your isolationist Republican buddies, your big hero Lindbergh and Senator Vandenberg, hadn't been holding us back – and sending Hitler kissy-kissy, do-whatever-you-want signals.'

'You must know better than that. Wendell Willkie has always been a friend of European democracies.' I looked up and noticed a thin white scar running down the side of Edward Leland's face, from his temple all the way down to his jaw. 'He's not that sort of Republican.'

'There are a lot of dead Dutchmen and Poles and Czechs and Belgians saying, "You made us what we are today, O Party of Lincoln." '

He shook his head and began to smile. 'You certainly fight the fair fight, Mrs Berringer.'

'Why not fight the way I want to? What can you do?' I smiled. 'Fire me?' Then I looked straight into his eyes. 'Oh, and please, call me Linda.'

He let go and started to laugh. Really laugh. And everyone in that room turned and watched Edward Leland being amused, and suddenly, all of them, including my husband, were moving in, smiling at me.

John was pretty detached later that night. God forbid, he could have said, Well, that must have been a real strain for you, but you did just fine. Or even a casual, husbandly, What the hell was that potato glop? Instead, he whistled to himself on the way home, and not something nice, Rodgers-and-Harty, but a slow, creepy classical thing that sounded German, probably some Wagner stuff, a lament for Wotan or Kriemhild or one of those types.

'What did you think of tonight?' I finally asked, when he was sitting on the edge of the bed, pushing a shoe tree into his shoe.

'It was all right.'

'Did you have fun?'

'No.' He started on the other shoe. 'But these things aren't fun.'

'So why do you go?'

He stood, walked to his closet and slipped the shoes into their place in the lineup, between another pair of black ones, exactly like the ones he'd just taken off, and some cordovans. 'I go,' he said, as he took off his pants and folded them over the hanger, 'because it's part of my job. It's a professional obligation. Just like a Bar Association meeting or sending out Christmas cards to clients.' He took off his jacket. 'Did you order the Christmas cards?'

'Yes.'

'From Tiffany's?' He put the jacket on the hanger, buttoned it, and shook out the suit before returning it to its place among eight other dark, dark pinstripes.

'Yes.'

'Did you pick out the one I showed you, the one I sent' – the one *they* sent – 'last year? White with – '

'No. I picked out something with chartreuse polka dots and naked elves.'

He smiled. 'Sometimes you're very quick.'

'You could say smart.'

He moved close to me. I took off his tie. 'I'll consider it,' he said, and kissed me.

'I have some smart things to say about the party,' I managed to say between kisses. 'Want to hear them? Like about Roger Post. You know about him and – '

'Let's forget tonight,' he said, as he took off my suit jacket and then my blouse. And we did forget.

But the next morning, a warm, hazy Sunday, as he sat in the living room, surrounded by newspapers, it was clear he remembered. 'What were you talking to Ed Leland about?'

'Willkie.'

'Oh, Jesus! Did you say anything?' he demanded, his voice filled with something close to dread. 'Ed's a personal friend of Willkie's.'

'I didn't call him a creep or anything.'

John let the *Tribune* financial pages drop to the floor. 'What *did* you call him?'

'Hey, what are you so upset about? I didn't start anything. He . . .' – I made my voice very low – ' "Please call me Ed" . . . he asked *me* what I thought about the candidates.'

John made a small circle with his lips and exhaled very slowly. 'And so you told him. Leaving nothing out, I'm sure.'

'Well, if I call him up on election day and say, "He, Ed, I voted for FDR," I don't think he'll clutch his chest and fall down with a major heart attack from shock.'

I picked up the *Times* – the *London* one! After sex, and knowing that for the rest of my life I could look across the dinner table and see this extraordinary man, and (I hate to make myself look grasping, but I was, a little) being able to walk into Saks Fifth Avenue with a hundred bucks, the best thing about being Mrs John Berringer was that I could buy every single newspaper and magazine I wanted – even English and German ones – because he wanted them too. Still, I was like a kid given a giant spoon and absolute freedom in an ice cream parlor.

I started to read again. Even though you had to take everything in the British papers with a grain of salt because of wartime censorship and their need to keep up morale, it was pretty clear that the Battle of Britain wasn't going to be the fast triumph the Germans had thought it would be: a few bombs, then invasion. That Wednesday, the Royal Air Force had lost twelve planes. Not good, but the Luftwaffe had lost nineteen.'

'John, do you think if the German losses – '

He cut me off. 'Tell me what you said to Ed about Willkie.'

'For God's sake!'

'Linda, this is important.'

'Why?' He just crossed his arms. 'Okay. What I basically said was the best thing about Willkie was his hair, and he was a me-too candidate, and that his program was pretty much lifted from the Democrats' platform,' John's mouth tightened. He was across the room, so I couldn't tell if it was with annoyance or anger. 'Listen: Mr Leland – Ed's seen my FBI papers. He must know I'm a Democrat.'

'Christ.'

'It's not like I'm a Nazi or a prostitute. For God's sake my father was a sausagemaker who lost his job in the Depression. What am I supposed to do – be a cheerleader for Herbert Hoover?'

'You're supposed to have the sense not to alienate one of the most important men in the country.'

'Alienate him? he was having a good time talking to me.'

'He was being courteous.'

'No! He was being amused. Listen: He doesn't need another person to bend over backward not to offend him. The line's probably ten miles long.'

'I'm not suggesting you be a sycophant . . . someone given to false flattery. But there's absolutely no need to be so damned direct.'

'Why not? My pal Ed thinks I'm a breath of fresh air.'

John leaned forward. His hair fell into his eyes and he shook his head to get it off his forehead. 'Can't you begin to understand the awkwardness of the situation?'

'Yes.' He sat back. So I leaned forward. 'He's your former father-in-law.'

'That's right.'

'And he's probably heard an earful about you from Nan, and you, being a gentleman, of course, can't defend yourself. You can't tell him that his daughter's an immature, spoiled – '

'Enough! We're not talking about Nan.'

'Sure we are! When we're talking about Ed, we're talking about Nan. For God's sake, let's clear the air, John. Take an objective look at her. Forget her morals. Think about her character. She doesn't have any. She's a two-bit little sneak.'

He stood up and roared at me: 'Don't you *dare* talk about her!'

I found myself roaring back 'I am sick and tired of tippytoeing around every damn time the name of one of the Lelands comes up. She was an *adulteress.* Don't you get it? And for all her class, she didn't have the guts to come to you and say, "Listen: I've made a mistake marrying you." She betrayed you instead, and you talk about her like she was a saint!' John turned and stalked off toward the bedroom. I rushed after him, almost running to keep up. 'And Edward Leland . . .' I was breathing hard. 'You carry on like he's God himself. He's not. He's a *man.*'

John turned to me in the corridor just outside the bedroom. 'Edward Leland is everything I could ever hope to be.'

'Like honorable.'

'Yes.'

'And brave.'

'Yes.'

'How about scary-looking? Do you think if you took a land mine in the face he'd finally have respect for you? Why is this man so important to you?'

It took a long time before he was able to answer. 'It's not the sort of thing you'd understand.'

'Try me.'

'I care about excellence. Do you understand that? I care about decency, fair play.'

'So do I.' He shook his head, like saying, You don't get it. 'Listen: I have a great idea. If you're so crazy about decency, why not practice it on me?'

'Did it ever occur to you, Linda, that despite all the self-effacing noises you make, you are monumentally self-centered? We cannot have one discussion without your saying, "I want more! I *demand* more!" '

'John' I began, 'all I want is to be treated like – '

'Like Nan. I'm truly sorry, but I can't accommodate you. You aren't Nan. But I believe I am treating you decently and fairly. I'm trying, Linda. I'm doing the best I can.'

'But I want better. I know you're capable of so much more. If you'd only – '

'Please don't hold on to those kinds of hopes. This is not . . .

this is not a love match. It has nothing to do with you. It's me. I'm the one who can't . . . Linda, you can't get blood from a stone.'

# *Chapter Thirteen*

During the bleakest days of the Depression, in 1931, the sausage plant closed down for nearly a year, and my father had no job. My salary, fifteen dollars a week, was all we had, and so we'd alternate: one week food, coal, doctor bills; one week mortgage money. But by March it was clear we couldn't keep up the payments, and sure enough, a foreclosure notice came in the mail.

My father sat on the couch, his face in his hands, his shoulders heaving, the letter on the cushion beside him. I stood in the hallway, not knowing what to say, when my mother slipped past me, brushed the notice off the couch and sat down beside him.

'Bad news, Herm?'

'They're going to foreclose on the house, Betty.'

I don't think she understood what he meant, but she understood how he felt. She put her arms around him, spoke to him so gently I couldn't hear what she was saying, and then kissed him until he finally stopped crying.

She took his hand. 'Everything'll be fine, Herm.'

'Betty, honey – '

She turned his hand over and examined his palm. 'Ooh! I see *lots* of good things. Lookit here, how the line kinda turns right. You know what that means? Money!' My father laughed. 'No kidding. Money. A long trip. And a beaver coat. Ha-ha, go ahead and laugh. You'll see!'

My father kissed the top of her head, then her forehead, and when he took her in his arms, I'd walked away.

My mother had been quite a fortuneteller, though. Okay, no

beaver coat, no trip. But money: The plant reopened and my father went back to work.

I bet anything he never forgot how much she believed in him and in the luck of their marriage. And I never forgot what it was like to look at an ordinary, down-in-their-luck middle-aged couple and to be able to feel, across the room, the depth and power of true love.

So I knew what the real thing was, and I knew I didn't have it. But at least I had a lot: a handsome, educated husband, a spacious apartment not more than thirty-five steps from Park Avenue, all the newspapers I could read and all the sex I could desire. My husband didn't drink, gamble, beat me or womanize; he just didn't love me.

But by a little more than a month after we'd been married, in late October 1940, I'd come to understand that John couldn't really love anyone. Well, except for the Lelands, and maybe he didn't even love them. He idolized or idealized them. This may not have been an electrifying news flash to anyone else, but one chilly Thursday night, it came to me like a shock.

It was about ten-thirty. I'd snuck up in the office at seven. John's new secretary, Anna – an older woman with a thick German accent, a gray, chopped-up Dutchboy haircut and glowing, slightly demented blue eyes, so she looked as if she was suffering from a mild case of whatever Hitler had – was not a bad secretary.

'But she's so *slow*,' John said, almost as an apology. He sat on the edge of what once had been my desk.

'I don't mind. Honest.' I put my fingers back on the home line of the typewriter and peered at the steno pad. I'd begun transcribing the ton of letters he'd been dictating to me for the last three and a half hours. 'It gives me something to do.'

'Would you rather be doing this than . . .' He paused and shifted so he almost sat on Anna's pencil cup; I pulled it out from under him in time. '. . . than being a housewife?' Not counting the Are you, Do you, Can I questions he asked during sex, this was the most personal question he'd ever asked me.

'I'd rather be married to you.' He didn't look thrilled, but he didn't look unthrilled, either: just neutral, as if I'd stated the obvious and he was waiting for more. 'But it's sometimes a little – you know – boring. There's not much to do,' I went on, 'at least not till the baby comes. Especially if you've got my streak of German efficiency, you an get through the housework in – oh – an hour. Except on Tuesday, when I iron your shirts – and what's that, an extra thirty minutes? And how long does it take to make a pork chop presentable? I've got a *lot* of free time.'

'You don't like all that leisure?'

'No. I know it sounds ungrateful, but I'm becoming *too* well-informed. I mean, I know the exact route of the invasion of Rumania and what the German army ate for lunch on October 7. I practically know the color of Antonescu's socks.' (I also knew that on that same day, the Germans ordered all the Jews in occupied France to register with the authorities. For what? I'd asked myself. But I knew it wasn't a census to satisfy curiosity. The German military mind was purposeful; it didn't make casual inquiries.)

'Look, Linda,' John began. But then he stopped.

'What? Oh, come on. I know something's on your mind.'

'It's not a particularly good idea for you to be seen here.'

'I'm your wife. Make believe I came by to say hello, or to drop off a pot roast sandwich so you wouldn't be hungry.'

'I don't mean in the office itself. I mean here.' He patted the desk.

'You mean it would be bad for morale if someone saw me doing your secretary's work?' He nodded. 'But Anna's bad for *your* morale. She can't do it all.' He nodded again. 'Oh! Okay, I get it. You want me to say, "Poor John, you're under so much pressure. Why don't you bring a typewriter with a German keyboard *home*, so I can help you in all my free time?" '

'Yes.' He smiled a little. 'That's what I want you to say.'

'Okay. I've said it. but you know, it would have been easier if you'd just come out and asked me.'

John sighed and gazed up at the ceiling for a second, looking for patience. He found it. 'All right. Let's leave now. Take the pad, and then you can arrange for a typewriter tomorrow.' He seemed so pleased at having handed over the details of his life to a more efficient secretary that, as he was helping me on with my coat, he said, 'Let's go out for dinner. I know a little French place that stays open late.'

Everyone at the little French place knew John, although they clearly had not been expecting me. The headwaiter bowed, though, did the merest twiddle of his mustache and said, '*Bon soir, mademoiselle.*' To my real surprise, John corrected him: 'Madame Berringer.' Give the French credit: They fell apart in battle, but they're imperturbable when it comes to affairs of the heart – or lower down. 'Ah, Madame Berringer!' he said as he started to lead us to a table, and went into something fancy in French, which I assumed meant: Welcome to my humble abode, although, for all I knew, it could have meant: I see Monsieur Berringer knocked you up and had to marry you. He held out a chair for me. I prayed he wouldn't kiss my hand. He didn't.

He and John had a complicated French discussion then, and John turned to me. Apparently, it all boiled down to: Does Madame want chicken? I said, Sure, fine, and the man wriggled his mustache for a second and then left.

'I didn't know you could speak French,' I said.

'Not as well as German, but I can manage.'

'Anything else I don't know about you?' I watched him put his napkin on his lap and straighten out his silverware. 'I mean, anything you want to tell me.'

'Well, no other languages. I'd like to learn Italian someday.'

'Tell me about your parents.'

He peered around the restaurant. There was only one other couple, older. The woman was wearing a corsage. Then he studied a mural on the wall to his left. It was Paris, I guess, because it had the Eiffel Tower right smack in the middle. The whole thing was kind of murky, so it was either Paris at dusk or the mural needed a good cleaning. 'What about my parents?' he finally said.

'For starters, what were their names, what did your father do, did you have a happy childhood?'

'My father's name was Charles. My mother's was Julia.'

'So what were they like?' He shrugged. 'What does' – I imitated his shrug – 'mean. You don't know, or you're not talking?'

'I guess . . . it means I don't really know. Honestly, I'm not trying to keep anything from you. It's just that my parents were very quiet.'

'Did they ever say hi to you, or tell you to wear your galoshes?'

'Yes. Of course.'

'What did your father do?'

'He worked in a bank on Long Island. He was a vice-president, but not . . . it was just a title. If you sat in that particular chair for twenty-five years, they called you a vice-president, but he was essentially a glorified transfer clerk.'

'And your mother?'

'She stayed at home.'

'And did what? Scrubbed floors? Gave fancy tea parties?'

'Neither.' Another waiter came, opened a bottle of wine and poured some for John to taste. John nodded. The waiter finished pouring and then bowed, as if he was taking leave of Louis the Something. 'My mother's family was one of the first families in Port Washington,' John said. 'They settled there in the early seventeen hundreds.' I waited. 'They didn't have money, but they had a lot of . . . of pride.' He took several too-eager sips of wine.

It doesn't look like you think pride's a plus.'

'Well, in my mother's case . . . it's as if her pride, her snobbery about her background, was her one and only character trait. I remember once – I was nine or ten – I broke my wrist in gym. We were climbing ropes, and I fell. They called her from school and she took me to the doctor's. We were sitting there a *long* time. My wrist was getting more and more swollen.'

'It must have hurt like hell.'

'It did. And so finally I said, "Mother, could you ask how much longer it's going to be?' I mean, she was just sitting there, her hands clasped in her lap, looking straight ahead – not at me, not at my wrist, not even at a magazine. So she got up, and I heard her talking to the nurse or receptionist or whatever. I couldn't hear what she was saying, but all of a sudden she lost control. She raised her voice. Really raised it. "My family was living in this town while Dr Russo's family were still apes in Italy." '

'Oh, God.'

'I just kept staring at my wrist. My fingers were starting to swell too. And I kept thinking she didn't even flinch when she saw my wrist. She'd just spent an entire hour sitting next to me when I was in so much pain – and the only thing she could get worked up about was her lineage. A family tree, but so what? It was a tree that was completely undistinguished; the only thing to be said for it was that it was tenacious. It held on through the years – didn't die out.'

This was not the moment to clue him in that he didn't have to explain 'tenacious.' 'Did her tree cut any ice with your father?'

'I think so, when they first got married. He was from New Jersey somewhere, and came to Long Island to work in the bank. I got the impression he'd believed he was marrying into this great American family, a kind of Port Washington Adams clan. So they wound up being disappointed in each other. He never became a great financier; he stayed a bank clerk. The most interesting thing that ever happened to him was he got bald; I remember he used to touch the top of his head all the time, as if he couldn't believe his hair had gone. So he was a disappointment to her. And she wasn't the Junior League charmer he'd thought he was marrying. For all her airs, she wasn't invited *anywhere*. She had no personality to speak of, no . . .' His voice faded as he looked straight at me.

'No what?' He couldn't seem to come up with the word. 'No class?' I asked.

'I suppose that's it.'

'So she played gracious lady to an audience of none, and he pushed papers around.' He nodded. 'How did you turn out so good?' I saw his expression. 'Oh, come on! You know what I mean. So *well*. They must have been smart, terrific-looking.'

'Well, my father was handsome . . . in a bland, clerkish way.'

'Which one had the brains?'

'Neither of them, really.' He turned back to his wine.

'So what did you do for laughs as a kid?'

'Nothing special. I had friends to play ball with, but I never was, um, one of the boys. I was too serious for that. You see, I really liked school. More than liked it. I loved it. My mind came alive in high school.'

'Came *alive?*' Oh, come off it, I thought.

'You sound so contemptuous of education . . . like everyone I went to high school with.'

'And where are they now? you're going to say. Mopping floors. Punching tickets on the Long Island Rail Road. Right?'

He smiled and said, 'Right.' Then the waiter came with chicken pieces hanging around in a sauce with a lot of mushrooms and tiny onions. I tasted it.

'Hey,' I said, 'this is great! I thought all that stuff about French food was a lot of bull, but – '

'I'm glad you like it.' I could have been chewing on the tablecloth, for all he noticed; he was staring at the mural of Paris again and chewing his bottom lip. His parents obviously weren't his favorite subject.

'Your parents died in a car crash?'

'In '29. A couple of weeks after Black Tuesday.'

'How did their death hit you?' He shrugged. 'I know you didn't say "Whoopee!" But were you . . . shattered? stunned?'

'Well, obviously I hadn't expected it, but really, I was in law school, and I'd hardly seen them since I started Columbia. I used to spend Thanksgiving, Christmas with friends' families.'

'Your parents never said, "Hey, John, join us for candied yams"?'

'No,'

'Weren't they hurt that you didn't come home?'

'Hurt?' He looked so startled. I realized then that Mom and Pop Berringer weren't the type to pick up the phone and croon a chorus of 'Sonny Boy.' John refilled his wine glass, held it up to the light of the candle on the table and stared into its depths. That was obviously it for the Berringers.

So I moved on. 'Did you use to come here with Nan?'

'What?'

'Nan,' I repeated. 'Here.'

'Oh. Sometimes. We had five or six places we liked to go.'

'Did she ever cook?'

'Not usually. Well, she cooked selected things. She could make cheese toast and roast a duck and prepare a good salad dressing. Oh, and make the salad.'

'But you didn't have duck and salad every night. Or cheese toast.'

'No. But we liked to get out.'

'Don't get mad at me if I ask one question.' John's shoulders hunched up, as if he already was. 'Relax. It's not such an awful question.'

'Go ahead.'

'Did you have fun with her?'

'I . . . valued her beyond anything I can express.' He looked at me; his eyes began to take on the Nan Leland Berringer shine. 'I loved her.'

'Why?'

'Why did I love her? For her intellect – '

'Come on. You don't love someone for their *intellect*.'

'You do if they have one.'

I put down my fork. 'What's that supposed to be? A knife in my heart?' It was.

'I'm sorry. Really I am. It was a cruel, unnecessary remark.'

'So what else did you love about her?'

'Her beauty. Her elegance. Her taste. Her verbal facility. Her aesthetic sense. Do you know what "aesthetic" means?'

'Does it mean having a rich society mother who was Teddy Roosevelt's cousin?'

He actually laughed. Then he asked, 'How did you know about her mother?'

I wasn't going to tell him from spying in his drawer, rifling through his secret papers and finding his wedding announcement. 'Office gossip.' I took a piece of bread and buttered it 'So her mother had a *real* tree. And her father? How was Big Ed's tree?'

'He came from Vermont. His father owned a farm, but he died when Edward was young. They were very poor.

'But that's good, starting out in poverty, on a farm. It's pretty close to a manger. And look what he became! Edward the Noble: War hero. Adviser to Presidents. Legal genius.'

'Edward's not a legal genius, if you want to know.' John buttered a piece of bread. I would have given him mine. 'Believe it or not, I'm the better lawyer.'

'Then what makes him what he is? What makes all these smart men – you, everyone – think he's better? The best?'

'They recognize his special brilliance. Ed is a genius with people. And a genius at sizing things up, at manipulating *any* situation to his advantage.'

'And?' I asked.

'And . . .' He hesitated, then tried again. 'I don't know. He's just . . . never at a loss. And unlike . . . the rest of us, he always seems to do what's right.

Ha! I had it. I finally understood why John was so fascinated by Nan and Edward. What the Lelands had – and what John, what most people, didn't have – was fearlessness.

Fearlessness. Not that I thought Nan didn't ever get scared. Even if she wasn't frightened by thunderstorms or the idea of hell or vampire movies, she had to have let out a screech the first time she saw the cockroaches that were living in the cabinet under her ex-kitchen sink. But that was minor stuff; in the major leagues, the social world, Nan was so sure of her brains, her looks and her place that she didn't fear anyone. And being unafraid gave her the freedom to do whatever she wanted. She never worried that people wouldn't want to sit next to her at lunch. She knew her own worth, how high it was, so she was free – to chase after John, drop out of college, buy ugly modern art, walk out on her marriage, take on a new husband twice her age. I remembered her stride down the office corridor to her father's office; it had been so absolutely lacking in indecision. I'd never seen a woman walk like that, ever.

But my pal Ed's fearlessness was different from his daughter's – and far beyond hers. It had nothing at all to do with being confident that no matter what you did, any dinner party invitation you desired was, ipso facto, yours. What Edward Leland possessed was true courage.

Obviously physical courage: Crawling through a forest you know is mined, moving *toward* German fire because you calculate you have maybe a thirty percent chance of knocking out their cannon and saving your men . . . well, that's courage. It's a willingness to take risks and to accept consequences. And Edward Leland wasn't just some foolhardy kid. He'd been thirty years old – a volunteer, not a draftee – when he'd assessed the risk, taken it and had his face blown up.

But my guess was that as soon as Edward came to and understood what had happened to him, he'd taken charge. He'd said, Get me the best doctor, one of those plastic surgeons, the guy who takes the neatest stitches, and let him do what he can with this mess.

So while the results weren't ravishing, while he looked as if half his face was the distorted reflection in a fun-house mirror, he'd been courageous enough to say, Okay, I've got to spend the rest of my life not looking like Douglas Fairbanks. And he'd gone out and wooed a society beauty – and won her.

His courage lasted beyond the Great War. Here he was, in his early fifties, in 1940, going on mysterious missions that *had* to be dangerous. He was still willing to take risks, accept consequences. I wondered whether it was harder now, because his life was so soft and safe and successful: he had so much to lose. And I wondered whether it was harder because he *knew* how vulnerable he was. He knew it every morning, when he shaved his lifeless half face.

But it wasn't just Edward Leland's physical courage that made John so in awe of him. It was his ordinary, day-to-day courage. I'd seen enough of Edward Leland to understand he couldn't be cowed by anyone: not clients, Presidents, Nazis, or even elegant blondes with tight chignons.

He really interested me, and I'd tried to figure him out. I was dying to ask him, How could you not be scared? And I decided that knowing you're tougher and shrewder than most other guys is a definite plus. And the other plus was Edward's comprehension (a comprehension John lacked) that Edward Leland wasn't God. He could get hurt, and he knew it. So he'd look his opponent – a German soldier, a Ford Motor Company lawyer – right in the eye and say, Go ahead, you son of a bitch. I understand what you can do to me and I'm willing to take it – but you'd better be good and ready to take what I'm going to dish out to you.

I bet almost all of them backed off, because Edward Leland could dish out plenty.

Trick or treat. It was Wednesday, the night before Halloween. The stew was simmering, the table was set, and a little before seven I plopped down on the bed and turned on the radio. No treat. War as usual: the Italians and the Greeks at each other's throats in Albania, U-boats and British ships sinking each other in the Atlantic, the blitz continuing over England, Hitler trying to dazzle General Franco in the south of France, while farther north, the Vichy government passed laws, prohibiting Jews from public service and from anything much beyond menial jobs in industry, radio, newspapers and magazines.

The Vichy regime smelled like a rose compared to the German scum. In Germany, Jews were outlawed from going to public parks or to restaurants; they couldn't use public telephones, stay in railway or bus station waiting rooms or buy newspapers. Oh, and they couldn't go to 'Aryan' hairdressers. All those prohibitions were a little something extra, in case you missed being stomped to death by the Gestapo in the street, or deported to God knows where. I shook my head, remembering my Grandma Olga, how she'd despised America and pined for her beloved Berlin.

The news went off and an announcer was going on about razors. His voice was thick, rich, as if the inside of his throat was coated with melted marshmallows. 'Schick Injectors will make you like better the face that you like best.'

I reached over and turned off the radio, and all of a sudden I remembered the two cousins in Berlin Olga used to write to: Liesl and someone else. Oh, God, what had happened to them? I didn't have a single doubt that not being able to go to a beauty parlor wasn't the worst thing in the lives of those two old ladies. My cousins.

I stared at the closed venetian blind. If the Germans came over here, and won, what could happen to me? When the Reich Citizenship Law had come out, in November 1935, an amendment of 'the Law for the Protection of German Blood and German Honor,' I'd read it over and over in the *Trib.* A person with three Jewish grandparents was a Jew. I'd be what's called a *Mischling* – a mongrel – because two of my grandparents were Jews. From what I read then, there was a chance I wouldn't be considered a Jew because my father didn't belong to a temple, didn't do anything Jewish. I remembered wondering whether Grossvater Otto Voss had ever snuck off and hung out with rabbis. But now most of them were saying, Make it simple. Anyone with Jewish blood is a Jew. If I were in Germany, I'd be God-knows-where. All my Aryan Johnstonness wasn't worth a pfennig.

I switched on the lamp on the night table and wondered about John. I remembered all those warmhearted sermonettes on Sunday morning radio church shows about Christians shielding Jews from the Nazis. You got the picture of thousands of teeny-nosed people throwing their fair-skinned bodies over the big-nosed and saying, No! Never as long as I live! John would probably say, *I* didn't know she was Jewish. Oh, by the way, she's in the bedroom.

And then I got a terrible pain in my stomach. It was so sudden and violent that I could hardly make it out of bed. In the bathroom, I found myself staggering and tried to hold myself up by bracing my elbows on the sink. But I couldn't take the pain. I slid down on to the cold floor. And then I saw it, on the tiny octagonal tiles and out on the carpet in the bedroom: drops of blood.

Another pain, like the most excruciating period cramp, came over me, as if some horrible fist inside my stomach was squeezing my . . .

I knew then what was happening, of course. The cramp subsided. I clutched a towel beneath me, so I would bleed all over Nan's monogrammed terry cloth, not on the floor, and made it to the phone. Another cramp. That was the worst of it. Just when you might recover, the next pain grabbed you so hard it knocked the breath out of you again. No. That wasn't the worst of it. I picked up the phone and dialed John's office. The worst of it was I was going to lose the baby.

'Why do I feel this way?' I asked John. He sat on the edge of the hospital bed, tie dangling, unknotted, vest unbuttoned.

'They gave you something.' His suit was like a black hole in the spotless white room. 'For the pain. It makes you drowsy.'

The pillows were plump and smelled like fresh air. I turned my head away from him and closed my eyes. 'It hurt so much.'

'It was the womb. It contracted. The way it does during labor.'

'It was labor,' I said softly. He took my hand between his. 'It's over, isn't it?'

'Yes.' My whole body felt so heavy I couldn't roll my head back toward him; I was so drained I couldn't even manage that half-cough, half-whimper of heartache that starts up a good cry. 'The doctor said it was what they call inevitable. There was nothing they could do.'

'It was about four months old. Do they know if it was a girl or a boy?'

'Try to get some sleep,' he said.

I must have, because when I woke up, John was in a chair at the foot of the bed. Outside, the sun was rising. The sky over the East River was pink and gold. 'Where am I?'

'Lying-In Hospital.'

'That's where babies are born,' I said, and began to cry. My tears were quiet, not at all elaborate, but I drew up the starched sheet and used it as a handkerchief. 'Why did it happen?'

John came over and sat on the edge of the bed. He tugged the sheet out of my hand and gave me his handkerchief. 'They don't know. Probably because when things aren't right with the, um, the fetus, the body senses it and gets rid of it. It's better that way.'

'Oh, it's terrific.'

He smoothed the hair off my forehead. 'I'm sorry,' he whispered, and kissed the top of my head.

This tenderness was so awkward that for a minute neither of us could find anything to say. Finally I found something. 'Did you want it?'

It took him a moment, but he said, 'I don't know . . . It would have complicated our lives.'

'Babies aren't so complicated.'

'We would have had to move.' He'd picked up a lock of my hair, and he twirled it around his finger again and again. 'And you might have felt tied down.' he paused. 'Did you really want it?'

'I must have. I feel so empty now. Maybe it's just – I don't know – a physical feeling.'

'I'm sorry,' he said again.

I looked past him, around the huge, square room. Mine was the only bed in that stretch of blinding hospital whiteness. I eased myself up and looked out the window. Across the river, Queens was flat and colorless, even in the bright dawn. A barge drifted along so slowly you could hardly see it make any progress, like the hands on a clock.

'What are we going to do?' I asked him.

To his credit, he didn't say, About what? He said, very composed. 'nothing.'

'You married me so there wouldn't be a little Berringer bastard running up and down Wall Street calling, "Daddy! Daddy!" '

'Don't talk that way.' His voice was so comforting, as if he was singing a lullaby.

'You're being calm on purpose. You're afraid I'll lose control.'

'I want you to get some rest.'

'And then what?'

'You'll come home.'

'Oh, come on, John.'

'What do you think I'm going to do, Linda? Toss you aside?'

'Look, I don't mean to sound bitter. But you did what you did because there was a gun to your head. You had no choice. But the gun is gone now. You don't have to drag me around for the rest of your life. Come on. No one will think any less of you. They'll only think less of you if you *stay.* "He's with her out of choice. How unspeakably odd!" '

'You don't give me credit for having any character at all, do you?'

'I think you're an ethical lawyer. And you were decent to marry me.'

'And that's it?'

I started to cry again. 'I love you,' I said, and put my arms around him.

He held me tight against him and murmured, 'I know.'

# *Chapter Fourteen*

December was a miserable month, drab, bitter cold. And almost the whole world had fallen under Fascist control. Only England stood – alone. America was busy wrapping Christmas presents.

John reached up and pulled down a carton of Nan Leland Berringer's Christmas tree ornaments from the top shelf of his closet. 'Wait until you see how *ex*quisite these are!'

He knelt down, wiped the top of the carton off on the sleeve of the flannel shirt he was wearing, and then took out the decorations one by one and held them up so they caught the light. Well, I had to admit it; they were gorgeous. All glass. Big, small, clear, frosted, etched with angels, embellished with hair-thin silver designs. 'I don't want them,' I said.

'Linda, I appreciate how you feel, but you're being – '

'It's half my tree. If you want to put your ex-wife's stuff up on your half, that's fine with me.'

'Don't you think you're being a little unreasonable?' He was being tolerant.

No, I didn't think so. The apartment wasn't big enough for three people, but I couldn't get rid of Nan. I slept on her pillowcases, ate from her soup bowls, looked at her paintings. Now I was supposed to ooh and aah over her glass balls. What I really felt like doing was to take running jump, land smack in the middle of the carton and hear a loud, glorious, soul-satisfying crunch.

'What do you think I'm going to do? Go out and buy orange plaid reindeer?'

'Not at all. It's just that these ornaments happen to be very beautiful. It would be a shame not to use them.'

'Maybe what I would buy would be beautiful too.'

'I'm sure they would.' I wanted to say, Oh, come off it! 'But these were very expensive. Wouldn't it be foolish to go out and buy others?'

'I could learn to live with it.'

He smiled and lifted the carton. 'Come on. Let's get the tree up.'

Sure, I could have another big confrontation: You still love her. You can't let her go. You won't give me money for new towels because you want *pieces* of her in the house. And so forth. But how many times can you accuse your husband of desiring another woman when – if pushed – he'll willingly plead guilty? Did I really want to hear: 'Yes, I love Nan and I love her glass dingle-dangles that make crystal music'?

Next year, I said to myself, next August, I'm going to Tiffany's or Bergdorf Goodman or whatever is the ultimate glass-ball store and pick out –

The bell rang. 'Damn,' John said, and then added, 'You get it.'

I was wearing a yellow fleece bathrobe, and I hadn't combed my hair. 'You get it.'

'I have a carton,' he said.

'Put it down.'

'Damn it, Linda, just get the door.'

The bell rang again. John carried Nan's carton into the living room. I stomped, barefoot, into the entrance hall and yanked open the door. And standing there, right before me, homburg in one hand, the other poised to ring the bell, was Edward Leland.

'Merry Christmas, Linda.'

'Merry Christmas,' I managed to say back. I stuck my hands in my pockets so I wouldn't start patting down my messed-up hair.

'John!' Edward's deep voice was full of holiday warmth. I turned. John had come up behind me; the look on his face was astonished and overjoyed, as if Santa Claus had truly come down his chimney. 'Sorry to drop in on you unannounced, but your doorman seems to have been enjoying his eggnog. Nodded off, so I slipped by.'

'Please, come in,' John said. I bet his jaw was hanging open. 'We were just putting up the tree.' He turned to me. 'How about making us some coffee, dear?'

'Sure!' I said, like I couldn't wait to dash to the percolator. Actually, I needed a few seconds to get over the surprise of Edward's visit and the shock of my husband's calling me 'dear.' They moved off to the living room. I hung up Edward's coat, put away his hat and went into the kitchen.

Being two classy men, they spoke in what they'd call hushed tones, but I could hear almost all of it, except when I rattled the pot and banged a closet door to show how absorbed I was in being a hostess.

'Forgive me for the intrusion, John.'

'Not at all.'

'Obviously this is something best not discussed in the office.' Maybe it was going to be about Nan; my hand must have shaken, because a scoop of coffee was suddenly all over the sink. 'And I'd rather not use the phone.'

There was a slight pause, probably John nodding.

'I'll be as direct as I can,' Edward continued. 'Lend-Lease is going to pass.' In the press conference a few days before, FDR had put forth a plan that England could get all their war matériel from us now and pay for it later – in effect, a giveaway. I put the coffeepot on the stove and lit the gas. 'And Donovan's done a complete turnabout. He's all for it now.'

The Donovan Edward was talking about was William Donovan, a Wall Street lawyer from O'Brian, Hamlin, Donovan & Goodyear, who'd gone on to become head of the COI, the Office of Coordinator of Information, which was a typically overcomplicated, lawyery way of saying US espionage headquarters. Unlike Edward, who clearly preferred private meetings and secret missions, Donovan was a much more public man, a diplomat – or politician. He was known for being outgoing, congenial and very, very clever.

'Have you spoken with him recently?'

'I spent most of last week with him in London.' There was the silence of John nodding again; I could almost see him, awe-struck but managing to look merely respectful. I took out a fruitcake I'd baked, sliced it, and fanned out the pieces on one of Nan's white serving plates. 'He's finally come around to seeing how vital Britain's survival is.'

'If they're defeated,' John agreed, 'we're next on their list.'

'Very likely,' Edward replied. I opened a cabinet, took out a tray and arranged the cake, cups and saucers, plates, milk and sugar, spoons and forks. 'Don't forget, if Germany defeats England, they would have both the French *and* the English fleets at their command.' I folded three napkins. (Unfortunately, all our napkins had you-know-who's monogram. I'd once said to John, All I want is to buy *plain* napkins. I don't want my initials or anything. And John had said, It's foolish to throw out money. And *you're* the one who keeps calling attention to them. I never even notice them.) 'With a navy like that, Germany would strangle us in the Atlantic,' Edward was saying, 'and with Japan making nasty noises in the Pacific . . .'

What's the point of all this cordial, manly chitchat? I wondered. Why had Edward Leland dropped by? So far, the only semisecret thing he'd said was that he'd seen Donovan in London the week before. That information was slightly interesting, but I didn't think it would make a Nazi spy jump up and down and clap his hands.

I took the coffee off the stove and poured it into the white china pot. Once I brought everything in, I'd have to leave and go into the bedroom, and I probably wouldn't be able to hear much from in there. Nuts, I thought, as I walked into the living room.

'England is the key, you see,' Edward was saying. 'In more ways than one. British intelligence has several first-rate sources within the German foreign office and the Abwehr.' The Abwehr was the espionage and counterespionage service of the German General Staff. 'The Vatican has a couple of sources too. And Donovan has one. But – ' John cleared his throat as I came in. Edward fell silent. I put down the platter on the coffee table. I couldn't believe that Edward Leland, who could hear a fly climb up a wall in the Bronx, hadn't heard me walk into the room. And hadn't seen me. My bathrobe was not exactly the most subdued yellow ever invented.

Both men made a tremendous fuss over the fruitcake. I didn't know what to do next: Did I leave everything on the tray or was I supposed to do one of those sophisticated Mrs-Berringer-is-pouring routines? Neither of them leaned forward from his chair, so I quickly set everything out on the coffee table. Then I asked Edward: 'How do you take your coffee?' I tried not to sound like Miriam Hopkins.

'Cream and one sugar, please,' he said.

I lifted the top of the sugar bowl, but John put his hand over mine and said, 'It's all right, dear. I'll take care of it. I know you have more presents to wrap.'

I stood straight, but before I could go, Edward said, 'John, really. Her security clearance is better than yours.' He looked up at me. 'You haven't developed Nazi sympathies since you filled out those forms, have you, Linda?' I shook my head. 'Then please sit down and join us.' I waited for him to add, If it's all right with your husband. He didn't.

I sat across from them, on the beige couch, and went ahead and fixed his coffee, and, without being asked, John's. I served the fruitcake and tried not to stare at the men. The contrast was so powerful I had to force myself to turn away; I looked over at the naked Christmas tree.

Obviously, Edward was older than John, seventeen or eighteen years. But the age difference was just for starters: fair, dark; graceful, hulking; handsome, not; John's blue eyes glowed; Edward's black eyes glowered. I turned back to them. Edward held the cup and saucer in big, clumsy farmer hands; his fingers were too heavy to hold the cup handle properly, but – I couldn't help this thought – they'd be perfect for choking somebody on a dark night. John laid aside his cake; the hand that did it was elegant, long-fingered, pale and tantalizing.

Edward started talking again. 'I was telling John that Colonel Donovan of the COI' – he waited until I nodded that I knew what that was – 'has long had a source, a spy if you will, high in the German government. This source has provided us with some interesting information about the internal politics of the Reich, some of it quite valuable. And over the last year, both I and another associate of Bill's have spent a good deal of time renewing old business friendships and cementing relationships with individuals in high circles in Germany.' He smiled. 'My sources, fortunately, are fluent in English.' He leaned back. 'Last week, Bill asked me if I'd be willing to spend some time in Washington – a great deal of time, actually – organizing a unit within the COI to be called the Office of Commercial Analysis.' John began to nod, until Edward added, 'A meaningless name, obviously.'

'Then what kind of office is it?' I asked. 'If I'm not out of line.'

'It will be my job, and the job of my men, to corroborate what our sources are telling us, not only in Germany but throughout Europe. Much of it will be the simple checking of facts.'

'Not so simple, I'd guess,' John said.

'Not so simple is right,' Edward answered. He took a bite of fruitcake and smiled first at me, but then much more winningly at John. In fact, his attitude toward John's observation was so flattering I figured he had to be up to something. 'How do we learn the unknowable?' Edward asked. Then he answered himself: 'By gathering facts – from radio transmissions we can manage to decipher, from recent refugees, especially those from Germany, from resistance organizations within the occupied countries. Then we must put all the pieces of this terribly intricate puzzle into a picture that makes sense. It *has* to make sense. Not merely for the information itself, although that is important; you and I, John, have long agreed that our entrance into this war is inescapable, and we must know all we can. But there's a further need for our brilliant puzzle-solvers.'

This was too interesting. I couldn't *not* open my mouth. Anyway, Edward had invited me to join them. 'You want to make sure if what your high German sources are saying is the truth,' I said, 'or if they're' – I knew my Nazi spy movies – 'double agents.'

'Yes,' Edward murmured. 'Precisely.' Both of them looked surprised at my conclusion. John, of course, always looked astonished whenever I figured out anything more complicated than his checking account balance. But I was disappointed; somehow I'd expected better from Edward. 'And it goes without saying, John and that's why I asked Linda to join us – that I'd be very happy and relieved if you'd consider moving to Washington for a time . . . To be my foremost puzzle-solver.'

The girl and who took care of my mother had one of those Slavic names no one wants to bother to pronounce, Mrshklva or something, so she told everyone to call her Cookie. At about sixty, she wasn't a girl, and she wasn't such a cookie, either. She was short, with long, skinny arms and legs and a pudgy little body, and when she moved around fast – she was never slow – she looked like a monkey in a nurse's uniform.

Cookie hoisted my mother out of a taxi onto the Fifth Avenue sidewalk. It was a bright day, cold but without a hint of wind. 'She's not too bad, Missus,' she explained to me, as if my mother wasn't there, right beside her, but home in Queens. 'Except she's hiding gin somewheres.' My mother immediately became absorbed in getting a new slant to her hat. It was an old brown felt she'd had for years, with a wide brim and a crown that looked like a huge, upside-down soup pot. But when she moved it forward I realized she'd gone out (or had sent Cookie out and bought a holiday pin: a sprig of artificial holly, with slightly limp fabric leaves and berries of red beads. She was so absorbed in her hat she didn't notice the seventy-foot Rockefeller Center Christmas tree straight in front of her nose. 'I could smell the gin fumes when she came out of the bathroom this morning,' Cookie went on, 'fresh on her breath, and I searched high and low, even down the toilet, but it wasn't there.'

'Cookie smells like toilet water,' my mother announced loudly. '*Real* toilet water. Stinky!' In the cold air, her breath came out in a weak white puff. People on the street, walking toward the tree, pretended they had heard nothing more than distant carols.

'Shut up your mouth. It's Christmas,' Cookie said, but it was obvious she thought my mother was funny, and she might have cackled and gotten into a whole toilet tête-à-tête if I – the person who paid her – wasn't there.

'You shut up *your* mouth, stinkpot Bohunk.' My mother laughed, a very feeble laugh, because she didn't have the strength to do more. Her arm was draped around Cookie's shoulder; she could no longer stand by herself for any length of time. About a month after I'd gotten married, when I made one of my twice-a-week visits to Ridgewood, I'd been so frightened by how she looked –

closer to a skeleton than to a woman – that I called Dr Guber. He'd come to the house, checked my mother over and pulled me into the hallway, closing her door. He said, She's got cirrhosis of the liver. She's not just falling down because she's weak. In his gruff Brooklyn voice, he'd gone on: Linda, not good. She's got nervous system damage, jaundice, edema. She's a mess, kid. You gotta be able to see it yourself.

I could. And although I knew the answer, I finally asked him, Can you do anything? He'd answered, Not anything that would help. Is she going to die from it? I'd had to ask, and he's said, 'Yeah, kid. Six months, a year. What a waste. Such a beauty she was.'

Cookie had been standing beside me the whole time, listening to the doctor. She shook her head and said, Most of them get mean sooner or later, but she's such a *cute* drunk.

'Where's Johnny?' my mother called out, her volume higher than ever.

'He's over at the restaurant, checking if we can still have our reservation. You know you're over an hour late, Mom.' She gave me an innocent, Oh really? look and fluttered her eyelashes. I wondered if she'd be fluttering if she'd seen the look on John's face after sixty minutes of watching every taxi going up and down Fifth Avenue. I took her arm and, with Cookie on her other side, half led, half carried her toward the tree. She gawked at it, like all the tourists, but paid much more attention to the women's fur coats.

'Beautiful!' she said of a passing sheared raccoon. 'I'm dying to meet Johnny,' she went on. 'He better be as gorgeous as you say or I'll tell him, "Hey, my Linda's got taste up her – " '

'Cookie,' I interrupted, 'why don't you take a walk around the tree. I'll stay here with my mother.'

The minute Cookie slipped away, my mother grabbed my collar. 'A blue wool coat? You marry a filthy-rich guy and he gives you *cloth?*'

'Mom,' I said, as softly and as gently as I could, 'please be on your best behavior today. You know what I mean.'

She patted my hand. 'I know, honey. Gee, you look stunning.

You look terrific in blue. And you're wearing mascara, finally?' I nodded. 'So how're things?'

'Fine,' I said.

'How's the baby coming along?'

'Mom, I had a miscarriage. Over two months ago. I told you.'

'Oh, sweetie, I'm sorry, I swear to God, I forgot. You know, who wants to remember something like that?' She pushed back the sleeves of her coat – a too-vivid brown, purple and cream-color plaid I knew would make John's jaw go rigid – but the sleeves were too long and drooped over her hands again. I tried to make a cuff, but she pulled away. 'Cuffs are for old ladies,' she said. 'I had one, you know. A mis. You weren't even a year old when it happened. But the doctor did it – the mis – on purpose. We asked him to. You know what I mean?'

'Dr Guber?'

'Nah! He was chicken. A guy on Queens Boulevard. Twenty bucks he charged, but Herm said, "It's well worth it." Listen, I was just seventeen, and I already had you.' Her eyes filled with tears. I thought she was thinking about her lost baby. But then she said, 'I loved your father.' She swallowed, sniffled and then hollered: 'Merry Christmas, Herm!' A Negro family who'd been standing near us gave each other this-one's-a-lunatic looks and edged away. My mother reached out and put her cold hand in mine. 'You think he hears me?'

'I'm sure he does.'

'He wasn't all that crazy about Christmas, to tell you the truth. Him being a Jew.'

'Mom,' I said, 'don't mention anything about that to John.'

'Why not?'

'I just never got a chance to tell him. Not that it would matter.'

'You ashamed of your father?'

'No!'

'Jews are smart!'

'Shhh!'

'Where do you think you got your brains from? Me? Johnny wouldn't care. Anyway, you look like me, even though Herm didn't look like one, or I'll tell you, I wouldn't have married him. Not with those dark beards and greasy hair like they got.'

'Well, just don't say anything, okay?'

'Okay.'

'And – '

She cut me off. 'You gonna give me a list?'

'Please don't talk about him being a rich lawyer.'

She glanced at my coat again. 'Maybe he has a nice Christmas surprise when you get back home.' Actually, John had already given me my gift: a gold pin shaped like a butterfly, with two tiny rubies for eyes and emerald chips down its body. It was a little too large and a little too fancy: in other words, what he thought I'd appreciate.

Just then, John arrived. He was wearing his good navy suit with a red tie. His gray topcoat was open. His darker gray cashmere scarf was tossed around his neck with the perfect degree of casualness.

'Merry Christmas, Mrs Voss,' he said. I could see he was shocked at how sick she looked, to say nothing of his reaction to her coat.

'Merry Christmas!' My mother was genuinely impressed. John started to button his coat, as if to cover himself. 'Hey, relax.' He took a small step back. 'So you're my son-in-law. Well, my girl's *very* lucky.' She turned to me. 'He's some guy, Lin! You shouldn't let him go out for a walk by himself.'

Cookie, realizing mother-daughter time had ended, rushed over. 'Merry Christmas, sir!' she greeted John. Her voice was breathlessly girlish.

He seemed stunned to see this sudden servant who looked as if, any minute, like a chimpanzee, she might leap up and swing from branch to branch of the Rockefeller Center Christmas tree. 'Merry Christmas,' he mumbled. Then he looked at my mother, then at me. His eyes closed for an instant. When he opened them, he said, 'I took care of the maître d'. Why don't we walk over to the restaurant?'

After everything I'd told him about my mother, John's idea of a perfect Christmas probably would have been giving her a year at a sanitarium as a present. But he knew I wouldn't go for that, so when I started talking about what to do Christmas Day, he immediately suggested we bring her to the apartment, give her her presents (fast), have a (quick) dinner and say good night. If he could have managed to have her slipped in the back door and brought up in the freight elevator, he would have. Not that I could blame him; unfortunately, I'd told him the truth about her, including her tendency to fall on her face, call out to strange men and, to get my father's attention, shout to the heavens. I could see her making a megaphone of her hands and booming 'Herm, lover!' in front of our building, in front of the neighbors.

But I'd told him no dice, I wanted to treat my mother to Manhattan, take her to see the tree and then out for a dinner fancier than she'd ever had. I said, John, it's probably her last Christmas. He picked a large, well-known restaurant that catered to blue-haired ladies whose idea of Christmas dinner was three martinis and a stuffed tomato: a respectable, even stuffy place, but no one he knew – no graceful people – would ever go near it.

'Isn't he something?' my mother asked Cookie. 'Better than a lifeguard. High-class.'

I took my mother's arm to help her walk. John moved reluctantly to the other side.

'Don't worry,' my mother said to me, as she grabbed onto his arm. 'I won't say nothing to embarrass you, sweetpea.' She looked up at John. 'You gonna buy me a cocktail, Johnny?'

'Hey – ' Cookie called, from behind the three of us.

My mother didn't bother to look around. 'Big fat deal. It's Christmas.'

'Mom,' I said, trying to sound calm, 'you're not allowed to drink anymore. You know that.'

'Why not?'

'Because it ain't good for you,' Cookie blurted out. 'You know that, Missus.'

My mother stopped, so abruptly that Cookie banged into us. 'And *you* know and *you* know,' she blared out to me and Cookie, 'that I got six months, a year, tops. You don't think I listened in when Dr Creep came over?'

I couldn't move. I couldn't think how to answer her. Then I started to cry.

'Come on, Linny, your mascara'll run in front of Johnny, and you look so pretty.' I tried to absorb my mother's calm, collected knowledge of her doom. I peered into her eyes – outlined with seven or eight times the amount of mascara I had on, coated with pistachio-green eye shadow – when she leaned toward John. It was a jerky movement, and he had to catch her so she wouldn't fall. 'You'll take good care of my little girl?' she asked, still in his arms. 'Promise?'

I think he was touched. At least his voice had a catch in it. 'Yes,' he said quietly, 'I promise,' and stood her upright. Somehow, we got her to the restaurant.

'Wow!' she said, looking at the wood-paneled walls and the eight-arm brass chandeliers. 'Johnny, you sure can pick 'em!' She picked up a water glass and clinked her nails against it. 'Nice stuff.' Then she smiled at John. 'Well, cocktail time!' It was two-thirty. 'Come *on*. A big-money lawyer like you can afford a little gin. Order me a double, okay?' I made no move to stop him – I was too numb. How could my mother bear knowing? But I was also a little numb anticipating what her next move could be, once she'd had her double: making a pass at John; telling a few Jew jokes while winking at me broadly.

John called over the waiter, ordered us drinks and slipped away to the men's room. It could have been in Cleveland if you judged by how fast he took off. 'Oops,' my mother said, as soon as he was out of earshot. 'Sorry about the rich business, Linda, lamb.'

'That's okay, Mum.'

'I know I got a big mouth.' I didn't give her an argument. 'But listen, while he's gone . . .' I could see her trying to come up with her version of maternal wisdom. And she did. 'He's built like a dream! And he talks so cultured, Lin. He's really smart. You know, smart-smart. And *so-o-o* good-looking you could die.' Suddenly, her chirpy, life's-a-party tone fizzled out. She touched my chin with her fingertips. 'Baby, watch out for him.'

'What do you mean?'

'You know what I mean. Deep down, he's a rat.'

It took me a minute to find the words. 'What makes you think that?'

‘Oh, Lin, I know guys. He’s not good, like your father. And I can see it in *your* eyes, how he feels about you. Don’t tell me no.’ She took a deep, shaky breath. ‘Oh, Linda, I wish you could’ve found someone to love you.’

# *Chapter Fifteen*

North Africa, the Balkans, East Africa, Crete, Iraq, Yugoslavia. The black cloud grew bigger, more poisonous, but I remember waking from an afternoon nap in May 1941 – a few months after we moved to Washington – and, still in bed, looking through the sheer curtains at the red geraniums in the window box and thinking: My life is nice. Okay, almost.

At first, the best part of moving to Washington was putting all the New York furniture in storage; the sight of the movers carting off Nan's couch was – up to that point – the greatest moment of my marriage. The next-best part was renting a pretty furnished house in a neighbourhood not far from Washington Cathedral. John insisted the area was exclusive, but in spite of that, it felt comfortable to me; our block could have been plunked down in half a dozen spots in Brooklyn. The big difference was the rent (high) and the tranquility (total). The streets were absolutely silent. No one in Washington hung out their windows and waved or whistled hello when you walked down the street on your way to the fruit man's or the candy store – if there'd been a candy store, which there wasn't. People sat back on their private porches, not on their it's-okay-to-be-nosy stoops.

Maybe they'd decided life in Washington was too predictable to bother. What was there to look at? The men worked for the government and looked like lawyers, even if they weren't. The wives all seemed to have been born in Alabama. They said 'Ha' instead of 'Hi', and they never sat down unless they were sewing something. They needle-pointed pictures and piano bench covers and eyeglass cases; they repaired their mama's old lace tablecloths; they made quilts for their beds and everybody else's beds; they took endless hems up and down.

'Ha, Linna,' my across-the-street neighbor Lucy MacPharland said. She stood at my door with her sewing bag and a chocolate cake. At the beginning, I thought the cakes were welcome-to-the-block gifts, and they were, but later I realized that while it was okay to drop in unannounced, you never knocked on any door without at least a pound of baked goods.

'Hi,' I said. 'Come in.'

'Sure you're not busy?' she asked, as she pushed past me and walked down the hall into the kitchen. She set her cake on the table, where there already was a pecan pie. 'Katie-Lou was here?' The evidence was undeniable; Katie-Lou Wilcox edged her pie crust in overlapping scallops.

'This morning,' I said. I opened a drawer, got out the roll of waxed paper, and covered the evidence of Katie-Lou's visit. I put it in the refrigerator, next to Bessie Campbell's sticky buns.

Lucy elbowed me aside and snatched the percolator out of the dish drainer. 'Well, now,' she said, and then murmured, 'three, four,' as she measured coffee. 'Tell me every little thing that's occurred since I' – they all actually said 'Ah instead of 'I' – 'last saw you.'

'Let's see. What's happened since yesterday?' I murmured. 'Oh! I know! Cora Sue Young left' – I paused dramatically – 'for a visit to her mother.'

'No! She said she was visitin' her mama?'

'Rita Harwood saw her leave the house with a suitcase and get into a *car*.'

'Mah word, Linna!' She wasn't just whistling 'Dixie.'

What all the fuss meant was that one of our neighbors, whose husband was third man at the Argentinian desk at the State Department, had discovered a driving school instructor who had no interest in Argentina but a lot of interest in her. His parked Ford had caused comment long before Cora Sue confided in yet another neighbor, Rebecca Jean, that she was having an affair and was making plans to spend the weekend with her instructor – and not to practice shifting to second, either. She was using a visit to her mother in Opelika as an excuse, knowing (she disclosed to big-mouth Becky) that her husband was too involved in South American trade routes to even think about her, much less check up.

What all the fuss meant to me, personally, was that finally I was one of the girls. I was included. On the five blocks that made up Rosedale Avenue, the only person who cared that I hadn't gone to Mount Holyoke College, didn't play tennis and couldn't whistle *Das Lied von der Erde* by Gustav Mahler was my own husband.

Okay, so maybe it wasn't a social plus to be a Yankee. And I couldn't thread a needle. But I was a whiz in the kitchen; I could bake a cherry pie with the best of them, to say nothing of *Apfelkuchen* and *Schwarzwalder Kirschtorte*, and after all those years of lunches at the law firm, I could gossip like a champion.

The fact that I was a cultural minus didn't matter at all, since hardly any of the neighborhood wives had gone to college – and those who had didn't bring it up all the time, the way they did in New York. And while a lot of them seemed to come from wealthy families – Mama missed goin' to Paris in the spring for her clothes, what with the war on, and Daddah was always callin' on his brokah – my neighbors didn't act Wall Street Lawyers' Wives rich: clannish, heartless, indifferent to any hurt their coldness might cause anyone (me).

Strangely enough, for a person from Queens, I looked like my neighbors. I blended in with a group of pretty women who worked much harder at being pretty than I did; if we'd keep silent, you wouldn't have known I didn't come from where they had.

In Washington, I didn't feel *wrong*. In New York, all the other wives seemed to buy their shoes in a top-secret store; they put on their private-color-*you'll*-never-be-able-to-find-it lipstick in exactly the same way, as if they had a classified blueprint for thin lips in a drawer in their vanity table. In Washington, no one gave me a mean once-over; when Lucy, whose husband was an economist in the Treasury Department, said, 'Ah *adore* that blouse, Linna,' she wasn't being snide. It was the sort of blouse she'd buy, or Mama would run up on her Singer and send up from Tuscaloosa.

After three months, there wasn't any one of these women who I would have sworn would be my friend for life; it was still a little hard to distinguish them. Sure, I knew Lucy was vivacious and had a low, loud voice, and Katie-Lou was dreamy and always crocheting doilies, but I couldn't get far enough past the southern accents and hospitality to see which of them – if any – I really cared about.

But if they didn't matter so much individually, they mattered a lot as a group, because they were the only people in my life. I hardly ever saw John, although I often felt him, when at two or three in the morning he'd wake me, slipping underneath the covers, and come up beside me or on top of me. Unlike Bessie's husband, a colonel assigned to the War Department, John was not 'limp as an ol' dishrag, an' I do mean *limp*' after his eighteen-hour day. John's interest in me thrived in darkness. In those late nights, he wasn't just hot; sometimes he was tender, stroking my hair, curling round me and cradling me in his arms as he fell asleep.

The only fly in this warm, loving ointment was my tendency to – now and then – open my mouth and say things like 'How are you?' That blew it for him. 'Fine,' he'd answer, and get busy making the perfectly puffed pillow. 'A little tired.' And I'd say, 'Well, you have a right to be,' and he'd say, 'Hmm-hmmm,' in agreement as he'd shift away from me, just enough so we were no longer touching, and fall off to sleep.

One night, though, there was no chance for me to work up to being anonymous. John came home about eleven. I was in bed but still wide awake. It was an awful early-June night, hot and unbearably humid. The air was so thick it almost hurt to breathe. I'd thrown aside the thin patch-work blanket, but was half covered with the already read *Washington Times Herald* and *New York Times*. I held *Time* magazine against my chest and said, 'You're so early!' What did they do? Throw you out?'

John's white shirt clung to him and was sheer with his perspiration. 'No. I just had to get out of there. The place is a hell-hole.'

The COI's main officers were bad enough, but John and a French professor from Yale shared what sounded like a room not much larger than a stall in a men's room, in a mysterious subbasement in the State Department.

I got out of bed, cleared up my reading matter and said, 'I'll make you some lemonade.' I was juicing the lemons when he came into the kitchen and practically flopped into a chair. He'd taken off his shirt and pants, but looked too drained from the heat to do anything about his underwear, which was drenched. 'Are you sure you're okay, John?'

'I'm fine.' He watched as I added water and sugar and slammed the ice cube tray around to get the ice unstuck. 'I appreciate this,' he said, and took the glass and held it against his forehead before he guzzled it down.

'Not so fast,' I said in German. 'If you drink something cold too fast it will give you a headache.' I switched back to English. 'That's what my grandma used to tell me. That and' – I spoke German again – ' "Potato soup is good for a chest cold" and "If you sing at the table you'll get a crazy husband." '

'Did you sing at the table?' he asked in his impeccable German.

'Probably. Before I knew what could come of it.'

We always spoke English, so when he reached out, pulled me onto his lap and kissed the tip of my nose, I assumed it was the change in language that had loosened some screw and was making him so . . . I couldn't think of any word except affectionate. 'I want some more lemonade,' he said, 'but I don't want to let go of you. How do we arrange that?'

'I'll come right back.'

I made another glass of lemonade, and as I handed it to him, he pulled me back into his lap. 'Can you stand being so close to me?' he asked. 'I must smell like something that's just come out of a jungle.' That took me a second to figure out, because I'd never heard or seen the word before: *Dschungel.*

'Some wild jungle beast,' I said, but then I sat back and eyed him closely. 'No, some exhausted, pathetic, half-dead animal.' I took a paper napkin out of the holder and wiped his face.

'Thank you.'

'You're welcome.' I eased off his lap. Unfortunately, he didn't try to stop me. I guessed that was it for affection, so I shifted back to English. 'Why don't I run you a cool bath?'

'That would be nice,' he said.

I walked up the stairs, one of my favorite places in the house. A steep, old-fashioned staircase, it had a carpet runner of dark green, with big roses that were even darker green, almost black.

Everything in the house was unstylish and very old, but it didn't look down-at-the-heels. Thirty-eight Rosedale Avenue had an all-American classy shabbiness that said: I was furnished with quality materials in 1903, and I expect they will last for quite some time.

In the bathroom, the tiles were small black and white squares; some of them were cracked, but they gave the floor character. The big tub had claw feet, and its thick porcelain was chipped. I put in the plug and turned on the water, sitting on the edge of the tub, occasionally holding my fingers under the flow to make sure it wasn't too hot or too icy.

John came in, dropped his underwear and socks, and eased into the water with a soft 'Aaah.'

'Is that what they call a sigh of relief?' I asked. He smiled. I closed the lid of the toilet, sat down and watched him. He threw back his head, scooped up some water and poured it on his neck. It was the best sight in town – *much* more beautiful than the Washington Monument. 'Do you want me to wash your back? Like those Japanese women.'

'Geishas. No, thanks. Um, Linda . . .'

'What?'

'Ed Leland's back in Washington.'

'I know. I read about him. He was at the White House last week, the night Roosevelt made the national emergency proclamation.' The Germans had been sinking British boats much faster than the British – or we – could replace them, and FDR had issued a statement saying we had to strengthen our defenses 'to the extreme limit of our national power and authority.' What he was saying was: This is our next step toward war. I handed John a washcloth. 'The paper said everybody was pretty tense after Roosevelt spoke, so they had music. "Alexander's Ragtime." Irving Berlin was there. And Donovan.' I paused. 'Have you ever seen Ed Leland tense?'

John put the washcloth over his face. 'No.'

'*Intense*,' I said. 'That's what he is. Anyway, how is he? Has he been up to anything you're allowed to talk about?' I reached over and pulled away the washcloth.

'We went for a walk this afternoon,' John said.

'A walk? It was ninety-seven degrees.'

'I know, and it was a long walk.'

He lowered his entire head into the water. When he brought it up, his hair dribbled water down on to his shoulders. He gazed, seemingly fascinated, at a little stream running down his arm. 'Are you going to play Watch the Water? Or do you want to tell me about what Ed wants?'

'Why do you think he wants something?'

'Come on, John. What does he want?'

'He wants you,' John said, very, very seriously.

'As what? A human sacrifice?'

'Be serious.'

'Okay.'

'Aren't you going to ask *why* he wants you?' he said at last.

'I know why he wants me.'

John looked annoyed. 'Why?'

'He needs a bilingual secretary who can get top-secret clearance, and he probably needs one fast. Hey, don't look so disappointed I guessed.'

'I'm not.' His chin had sunk down almost to his knees. But then it perked up. 'Well, what's your inclination?' he asked.

I remembered being pulled into his lap downstairs, about how it felt to receive his affection, even though I now understood the reason for it. 'What's yours?'

'It wouldn't be a bad idea. It would take some pressure off Ed.' And make him indebted to John: Say, old boy, thanks for your wife. 'And I know I'm no prize, working these hours. It would give you a chance to get out a little more.' Into a ninety-eight-degree sub-subbasement in the Interior Department, or an elevator shaft in the Bureau of Mines. 'Do something for your country.'

'Oh, come off it!'

'Don't be so touchy.'

'I'm not touchy.'

'Come in the bathtub with me.'

'Are you trying to seduce me so I'll do anything you want?'

'Is seduction necessary?'

'No,' I said. 'I'll do anything you want.' And then I took off my nightgown and climbed in.

Two days later, at two-fifty in the afternoon, I stood inside the lobby of an office building on Massachusetts Avenue in one-hundred-and-two-degree heat, waiting for five minutes to pass so I could get in the elevator and arrive at Edward Leland's office precisely at three. The hundred and two degrees was the outside temperature, but there was nothing – not the smallest stirring of air – in that marble box of a lobby to convince me that inside was any cooler than the streets I'd just survived.

Still, the marble was so white it looked like the walls in some delicious, frosty waiting room just outside heaven. I leaned against it, but all I got was an icy jolt. I pulled away. My whole body felt disgusting: My skin was gummy and my slip clung to it like a revolting phantom in a horror movie.

I was watching my watch, trying to hypnotize it into moving faster so I could get upstairs, where I imagined Edward Leland sitting in an office with two fans: a small one he'd managed to requisition from the government and a huge one he'd gone out and bought himself. And suddenly there he was: Edward Leland.

'Hello,' he said. 'What are you doing down here?'

Like he didn't know. My bet was, this was a trick he pulled more than once, catching someone who had an appointment with him waiting, nervous, off guard. 'I'm waiting.'

'Why didn't you come upstairs?'

'Because I would have been early. I gave myself an extra ten minutes so I wouldn't be late, because if you're even part German, being late is a major felony, but being early isn't terrific, either. I spend half my life hanging out in lobbies or on street corners so I can be *precisely* on time. Does that answer your question?'

'Fully,' he said. 'Let's go for a walk.'

'A walk?'

'You don't want to walk?'

'Do you?'

'That's not what I asked, Linda,' he snapped.

I couldn't figure if he was grouchy from the weather or was giving me a hard time for fun. Or not for fun. For work. To see if I could take the heat. I didn't know if I wanted it. For the first time in my life, I was doing nothing except being female, and I was really liking it; I wasn't going to trade it in for a steno pad and a boss, scary enough to begin with, who was going to give me a hard time.

But why was he giving me such a rough time about going for a walk? Ha! It was another Edward Leland Test: How far would you go for him? How fearful of his power were you that you couldn't say, 'Listen, in all this heat I'd rather not'? How many miles would you trudge by his side? Because one look at Edward, with his tough face and tougher, massive build, and you'd know that he could – and would – walk forever.

'Okay,' I said. 'The answer is, I don't want to go for a walk because it's over a hundred degrees and the sidewalk feels like it's starting to melt and I even have a little headache, but if you insist on it I'll go because I'm the secretary and you're the lawyer.'

'Let's go upstairs,' he said.

His workroom was not some government-issue cubicle but an office in someone's law firm, larger than he had in New York but with the same lawyery leather and wood and Oriental rug, except this version was all brown and yellow and gold, with brocade drapes that were so beautiful you figured the Washington lawyer had given his wife the green light and a blank check.

There was no fan, but it was cooler than the lobby. Edward offered me a chair in a couch-chair-coffee table setup across the room from his desk. 'You're always two steps ahead of me, Linda,' he began. 'I suppose you know why I wanted to speak with you.' He sat across from me, on the couch.

'You need a secretary.'

'Yes.'

He stopped talking and just stared at me. Not stared, but probed. Then he eyes moved downward, and I thought: He wants to see if I'm pregnant. 'I'm not pregnant,' I announced. This time he did stare. 'Well, you were . . . you seemed to be looking . . .'

'I was *not*.'

'Okay, so I have an overactive imagination,' I said.

'I think you do.'

There was a long, uneasy silence. I'd overstepped the invisible, unknowable bounds. Finally I stood up. 'Listen: This isn't going to work.' He crossed his arms and glared up at me. 'I can't be a secretary anymore.'

He stood up too, slowly. 'I see.' Boy, was he cold. 'You've forgotten how to type.'

'No. I've forgotten how to be a sweet, obedient girl. I can't be what I was. I can't – '

'Sit down!' he barked at me. I sat. Then he did too. 'I really don't give a damn whether you're sweet or not. I'm not in the market for a subservient little creature who gets the vapors every time I raise my voice. I need someone efficient, someone with a brain, someone I can trust and someone who is fluent in German. Period. Do we understand each other?'

'Yes.'

'Fine.'

'Do you want to tell me about the job?'

'No.'

'I'll just show up one day and you'll have a typewriter and confetti? Like a surprise party?'

'Sarcasm doesn't become you, Linda.' Boy, did that remark make me feel lousy. And he knew it. 'You need some additional security clearance. It will take another few days.'

'They're already working on it?'

'I took the liberty of assuming you'd agree to help me.'

'Can you tell me what the hours will be?'

'Long.'

'Will I be working here?'

'Now and then.'

'Will I be working for anyone besides you?'

'Perhaps.'

I took a deep breath. 'Are you always going to act like this, or are you going to get nicer?'

For a minute he didn't react at all, but then suddenly he started to smile. 'I'm going to get nicer.'

'When?' I asked.

'Tomorrow. Friday. I can't say with any certainty.'

I stood up again 'Well, I'll look forward to it.'

'To what? An improvement in my disposition or to working with me?'

'Both,' I said.

'Good.' He got up, reached across the table and shook my hand. 'Welcome aboard, Linda.'

# *Chapter Sixteen*

I'd never thought my life could be so interesting, but working for Edward Leland, it was. To begin with, this wasn't any 'Take a letter to Herr Teufel re issuance of convertible debentures'; a girl can get just so enthusiastic about convertible debentures.

This was war: ugly, but real. I took down every word of a meeting at COI headquarters between Edward and a Herr Kaufmann, who'd once been a rich industrialist in Düsseldorf and was now a poor old Jew with a pitiful cough and an incredible, near-total recall of the location and layout of every machine-tool factory in Germany – at least as they were until 1936, when the Reich had seized everything he owned and then imprisoned him for 'crimes against the Fatherland.' (Herr Kaufmann had been lucky to have a cousin in St Louis who'd managed to move enough money into the pockets of enough German officials so that he'd been released and 'deported' in 1939.)

He and Edward pored over maps, while a simultaneous translator rendered English into German and vice versa, so the men could have an easy exchange. I sat in the corner, a quiet, conscientious, invisible stenographer, taking down the English version. I only spoke once, when I said, Excuse me, Mr Leland, could you repeat that, please.

When Herr Kaufmann and the translator left, Edward said, Poor old fellow. Still doesn't comprehend what hit him. Probably never will. And I changed the subject: The translator's no good. What do you mean? he demanded. So I told him: He's accurate when he's translating Kaufmann's information about factories in major cities. But listen, he'd have to be; anyone, even you, would have spotted it if he'd translated 'north Stuttgart' as 'west Frankfurt.' Even I would have . . . I mean, he thought I was just another dopey American stenographer who could hardly speak English, much less German.

Then I explained how the translator, precise about city manufacturing, had been way off when it came to the countryside. He doubled, tripled or, once, halved the number of kilometers of a factory from a town, and did the same with the capacity of a factory. Edward demanded, Are you *sure* they're not just careless errors? *No.* Listen: I may not have the biggest vocabulary, but I know German well enough – and have been typing contracts for industrial deals long enough – to know that *Dieselkraftstoff* isn't a small truck, it's diesel oil, and Kaufmann's next three or four sentences – about underground oil tanks and their storage volume – the translator just ignored. See, in the beginning he was testing you – making sure you had no knowledge of German. If you'd known anything beyond *auf Wiedersehen*, he wouldn't have taken that risk. Edward said, But it was rather clear I'm abysmally ignorant. I smiled and said, Yeah. Abysmally.

Edward said. We'll have to take care of him. Make him disappear? I breathed. For God's sake, Linda, you've got to stop going to the movies. So I asked, What else do you guys do with someone like him? You know he's bad, probably SD. (That was the *Sicherheitsdienst*, the Nazi Party's intelligence service.) Edward said, Well, since, um, forced disappearance strikes me as something of an overreaction, how about we stop using him as a translator? I said, That's *it*? No, Linda, that's not it. We'll turn him over to the FBI. Of course, he said, looking disgusted, they're the ones who recommended him in the first place.

We'd gone down to the car by then, to drop Edward off at the State Department to meet with John and to take me to the office he used. We talked about the rivalry between COI and the FBI, and then, because I asked, he told me what he thought about J. Edgar Hoover (brilliant bureaucrat, monumental ego), and then he asked me if I still had such an inordinate fondness for Roosevelt, and I said yes, I was crazier about him than ever, and added that if Willkie had won, he'd have folded under isolationist pressure –

that had been clear enough in the campaign – and instead of being in Washington, we'd all be at some lawyers' dinner party on Beekman Place, saying, Tsk-tsk, isn't it too bad about those nice little English schoolchildren being forced to say *Heil Hitler.* He told me I'd make a poor lawyer because I always overstated my case, and I told him I'd make a great one because I always picked the right side (like Roosevelt's), and what he called overstatement was actually a forceful presentation of the truth. The car stopped at State, and then, instead of saying goodbye, he smiled and said, See you in court, counselor.

Most of the times it was like that. Working for him was at least worthwhile and interesting, usually fascinating and sometimes fun. And always hard. He was the head of counterespionage for a country that believed that gentlemen do not open other people's mail: his responsibility was to seek out enemies pretending to be friends on behalf of a government that wasn't at war.

He was an honest man doing an under handed job in a deceitful world. He had to be more flexible, more alert, had to move faster than the enemy: the Germans, of course, and the American officials who didn't want a new intelligence service.

The car became Edward's main office; he said he didn't want to build an empire – a central organization with easy-to-spot telephones, secretaries, bookshelves and staplers. Empires, he said, are apt to be infiltrated or over-thrown. So he spread his people out, and we went from meeting to meeting, from his borrowed law office to government buildings to, now and then, the backs of stores, mansions in Virginia, or, once, a shack in rural Maryland.

One day we were in the car, a big old Packard he had somehow managed to seize for himself from the government. But this time it wasn't interesting or fascinating or fun.

Edward's voice had an edge – a sharp one: 'Don't tell me! There are actually limits to what Linda Voss – excuse me, Linda Berringer – can do?'

'Just one limit,' I replied lightly, trying to convince myself the edge wasn't there. A cold November rain streaked the windshield. Everything looked distorted, like when you try on someone's too-strong eyeglasses. 'One per secretary isn't so terrible.' I'd finally gotten up the courage to tell him I couldn't take dictation in the back seat of his car. 'I'm sorry, but it makes me carsick.'

'I find it hard to believe that we've been driving all over Washington for the past few months with you feeling ill.' He paused and leaned forward to his driver, a man named Pete with a deeply lined red neck, who always wore a Washington Senators baseball cap. I thought he'd say something like: Easy on the sharp turns and the brakes, Pete, with Mrs Berringer here, but instead he told him, 'While we're at COI, double back to my place. I forgot my evening clothes. They're in a black garment bag, probably still hanging on the door of the closet.'

'Yes, sir,' Pete said in a happy, snappy voice. He'd retired from the navy a few years before, and always seemed thrilled to be subjected to unreasonable demands. Edward would say Pete, would you mind picking me up at 3 A.M. I have to meet with someone in a coal mine a hundred miles into West Virginia, and Pete would declare, Yes, sir! With other lawyers and government officials, Edward commanded respect – usually mingled with a little awe and sometimes fear. With Pete, he commanded unqualified obedience – and probably love.

He sat back and peered at me. 'Why didn't you say anything sooner?' he demanded.

'I don't know,' I murmured.

'It's not as if you're a shrinking violet.'

'No. I mean, I'm not.'

'And I'm not some sort of ogre.' When I didn't respond instantly, he snapped. 'Well, am I?'

'No. But . . .'

'But what?'

'Sometimes . . . you're kind of . . .'

'Kind of what?'

'Formidable.'

Ninety-nine point nine percent of other formidable men would have said, Me? Formidable? Don't be ridiculous. Edward didn't go anywhere near the I'm-a-regular-guy routine. 'I really don't see what my being' – he shook his head in annoyance – 'formidable has to do with your unwillingness to tell me that the work I'm asking you to do is making you feel ill.'

I turned from him and stared out the window. People were huddled in raincoats and taking small, cautious steps, as if the sidewalk was icy. Pete, of course, sped along. 'I didn't want a . . . a minor problem of mine to interfere with you,' I explained, still gazing out, not wanting to face him. 'Anyway, it's not *that* bad.' It was.

'Then why mention it?'

I swiveled around and probably glared at him. 'I'll be damned if I know.' I flipped my pad back open and added, 'Go ahead. Dictate.'

'So you're going to grin and bear it after all?'

'Right.' He looked straight ahead, at the back of Pete's neck. 'Come on,' I said. 'I know you want to get out that memorandum on Pharaoh.' Pharaoh was the code name of the valet of the German ambassador to Spain. He'd approached a third secretary of the American Embassy in a café and offered to photograph documents. He didn't want any money; he claimed to be anti-Nazi, said that the Gestapo had arrested and then murdered his niece. No one, including Edward, had yet decided whether the valet was for real or a plant.

'The memorandum can wait,' Edward snapped.

'I told you I really don't mind – '

'Enough!' He reached over, swatted shut the cover of my steno pad and resumed staring at Pete's neck. The bad side of his face was toward me, so there was no expression I could read. But I could feel his anger.

I thought: If he only knew how miserable these fights – or whatever they are – make me feel, maybe he wouldn't start. They happened every few weeks, and I never knew precisely what I'd done to trigger him. The same kind of remark he'd normally be neutral about – or even amused by – would set him off. His temper would flare up for a minute, but then, even worse, he'd withdraw into cold, silent fury.

Once I'd gotten up my courage and touched his sleeve, about to say, Is it really what I said or is it that they cut the thirty thousand dollars from the cryptographic budget? but I never got my words out. *Leave me the hell alone*! His teeth were clenched, and if I hadn't heard his words I wouldn't have believed he'd said them; they were so harsh, and his rejection of me was complete, final.

I tried to tell myself at these times that he had terrible pressures on him, decisions to make that were truly life-and-death, and he had no one to blow up at. Was he going to call Nan in New York and fume? Was he going to blow up at John, at one of the other geniuses who were working for him? At Donovan? At the President? Was he going to start screaming at one of the society beauties he was always squiring around to wherever men need women?

Maybe he picked on me, I thought, because I was almost always available, and what the hell, for eighteen hundred bucks a year, Linda Berringer could take a little temper. Or maybe over time I was too great an irritant: I kept going a little too far, being too wise-guyish, too outspoken, too relaxed – even happy in his presence. I'd forgotten who I was.

For days after one of these blowups, I'd feel unbearably low. Going to work, facing Edward, wasn't the only struggle. Just getting out of bed was; I'd put my feet into my slippers and my throat would close up and I'd walk past John, who was busy getting dressed, with my head lowered, so he couldn't see that my eyes had filled up. And not breaking into tears during work was a monumental effort. We'd sit in the car a day or two later, everything seemingly friendly and jolly again. Edward would smile, say, Excuse me, and bury himself in a report. I'd gaze out the window and be overcome by sadness, which seemed stupid – even to me – because Edward, having blown off steam, seemed to have no recollection of the incident that still had the power to make me feel cold, alone, without hope.

Well, this definitely was one of those incidents. Pete drove around to the back entrance of COI headquarters – we never used the front – and Edward got out of the car. I slid across the seat to follow him upstairs, and he slammed the car door in my face. Then he hurried through the cold rain into the building.

Pete sat straight in the front seat, silent. He was Edward's man. I never knew what he listened to or what he thought.

'See you later, Pete,' I made myself say.

'Okay.'

So I took a deep breath, stuffed my pad and pencil into my pocketbook and got out of the car. The rain had turned to sleet, and it pelted my face and dripped down my neck. I stood there shivering. Then Pete pulled away, and the tires spun out a thick spray of dirty, icy water all over my stockings.

I had a choice then: to do what I wanted to do or what I ought to do. So I didn't stand there in the sleet and sob. I said, 'Oh, shit!' and kicked a puddle of freezing water with one of my new suede shoes. Okay, maybe I had tears in my eyes when I did it. But then I went back to work.

The Japanese bombed Pearl Harbor on December 7, 1941, a Sunday, and everybody in Washington kept asking everybody else: Where were you when you heard the news?

'Where were you when you heard the news?' Edward Leland's latest lady asked John. Her name was Felice Benedict, and someone at the part of Edward's house had whispered that her father was Granville Publications and her former husband was Benedict Aluminum, who was now married to Pendleton Timber's widow.

'Where were you?' John asked, smiling back at her, thereby avoiding either a lie or the truth, which was that we were doing it on the floor in the living room, with the New York Philharmonic on the radio as background music, when an announcer broke in, proclaiming: 'Ladies and gentlemen, the Japanese have bombed Pearl Harbor! I repeat . . .' For an instant we lay frozen in a position not appropriate for a momentous public event. Then, as we pulled apart, I said, Oh, my God, it's happening, and John said, I'd better get to the office and see what the cable traffic is. Where are my pants?

'I was at home – in Florida,' Felice answered. She stood close enough to John to get a good view. She appreciated quality; you could tell from her expensive perfume and the emerald on her right hand, so big it looked like half a broken beer bottle. 'I have a little place down in Palm Beach where I spend the winter. I was enjoying a peaceful Sunday . . . or so I thought.' But although she stood close to John, she stood closer to Edward. Whatever Edward had seemed to be what she wanted. Felice withdrew a cigarette from a gold case, and before she could flick her gold lighter, five men's matches and lighters rushed forward to meet at the cigarette's tip. She chose Edward's. 'I was listening to the Philharmonic broadcast – '

'So was I!' John cut in.

'Weren't you absolutely *jolted*?' she asked. He sure was, I thought.

'Stunned,' he agreed. A waiter in a white jacket put a round silver tray right by his hand, and John picked up a cheese straw. It was a December 12, the Friday night after Pearl Harbor, and we'd all been invited to Edward's house to celebrate going to war.

That sounds horrible, twisted even, but it wasn't. I think almost all of us where had felt that someday we'd have to fight to stop Hitler, stop the spread of his evil, and now, finally, we could. The day before, Germany and Italy had declared war on the United States, and Congress had responded with declarations of its own – and voted as well that American troops could be dispatched anywhere in the world.

The waiter, swiveled toward me and I took a cheese straw. I'd been wondering what dinner at Edward's would be like, since I couldn't exactly imagine him basting a leg of lamb. We'd been working at a killing pace all that day, and if John hadn't told me about the invitations the night before, I wouldn't have had a clue that Edward – who was keeping me and two other secretaries, borrowed from the Justice Department, busy – was hours away from having company. I kept waiting for him to tell me, Call my housekeeper and remind her to wash off the watercress – *something* to show he was aware he was having a gang over for a meal.

But when we got to his house, a beautiful old brick place that had to be the ultimate example of some sort of Great American Architecture, in, naturally, Georgetown, I saw that there had been no need to worry; it had all been taken care of. Cooks, waiters and a butler were busy creating perfection, and all it had probably taken was one phone call to some Rich Persons' Whims Agency. Dinner for ten at eight-thirty on Friday, Edward would have said, and they'd have said, *Of course*, Mr Leland. You can rely on us.

'And now the Italianos and the Nazis,' Felice said. She pronounced Nazis the way Winston Churchill did: Nazzies. 'All in one week! Did they declare war on us because they're friends of the Japs, Edward?'

'Yes, but I think there's probably more to it.'

'Oh, there's always more to everything with you.' She sent him a meaningful smile, then took a deep drag on her cigarette.

Felice Benedict sounded like all of Edward's women, with that slow, smoky upper-class voice. She looked like them too, in that she had a hairstyle that would remain unmoved in a hurricane, perfect, chiseled features and a posture that suggested a spine of steel. But she was older than the others – closer to fifty than forty – and flashier.

Not that Felice chomped on gum and had a skirt slit up to her thigh. But she had a big bust and a small waist and wore a figure-hugging bright green knit dress that flashed Go! She touched Edward as often as she could – smoothing back a supposed out-of-place hair, reaching into his vest pocket to look at his watch – and in case anyone didn't know what the score was, she'd said, My God, it's nippy! a half hour earlier and then added, I'll get my shawl. It's with my things, upstairs. Upstairs, of course, were probably a few guest rooms – and Edward's bedroom.

Well, no one really thought she'd come to Washington to stay at a hotel and visit the National Gallery, but Mrs Something Weekes, whose husband, Norman Weekes, was, despite some ridiculously confusing title, one of COI's top spy coordinators, had pursed her thin lips in disapproval as she'd watched Felice's bright green backside disappear up the stairs.

I have to admit that for that instant even I had felt my face get hot with embarrassment, because Felice drew arrows and flashed blinding lights around her private life. Where I came from, people didn't do that. (For that matter, where she came from they didn't, either.)

All the other women John and I had seen Edward with were so classy and fashionable they'd looked like beautiful heads plopped on top of Parisian dresses, with no human body inside. But despite her aristocratic accent, her emerald, her ropes of pearls and her little place in Palm Beach, which probably had fifty-six rooms and was right on the ocean, Felice was more than just a well-dressed set of cheekbones; she let you know she was female – and doing female-male things with Edward.

John had once told me that Edward was quite a ladies' man. I'd said, You're kidding! No, John went on, he always has someone. He spoke carefully, analytically, as if he was dealing with a fascinating legal concept instead of Edward Leland's sex life. You see, he explained, by the time, um, Ed's wife died (the 'um' was because he was on the verge of saying 'Nan's mother'), he'd established himself as, well, as quite important, both socially and professionally. He was therefore *extremely* eligible. And aside from his obvious credentials, he has a way with women. I must have made a face, because John added, Sophisticated women. So all along, he continued, Ed's been inundated – he's had more women than he knew what to do with. All wealthy, intelligent, pleasant, pretty, chic. And because the supply was so abundant, his demand seemed to diminish. Do you understand? Someone perfectly suitable was always available for . . . whatever he was interested in at the moment. He had no particular need for anyone permanent.

But what about love? I asked. He must have been so lonely after his wife died. And he was young. Didn't he want someone?

He had the law, John declared. You have the law, I said. It never got in your way. John sighed: Ed had responsibilities to Nan. Come on, I interrupted again, don't tell me he couldn't find time to get married because he was so busy making chocolate pudding and tying Nan's little shoelaces. Great men, John humphed, don't concern themselves with conventional domestic matters.

But it looked to me as if Felice was looking for something nice and conventional, and I wished her well. She had a nicer nature than the others. For instance, she didn't ignore me. She'd actually talked to me. 'Tell me, Linda, were you listening to the Philharmonic too?'

'Well, I was in the room, but I'm not the music lover John is. I was probably reading the paper or something.'

'Your favorite boss' – she took Edward's hand – 'was in New York, you know.' I nodded. 'Listening to the New York I-think-the-Giants playing football with people from Brooklyn. Can you imagine? But the announcement didn't come as a shock, because he'd already gotten a call from Donovan and Roosevelt over an hour earlier.' Edward stood there, his hand in hers, looking amused and, I thought, a little charmed at her name-dropping. 'He was on the telephone after that, but kept the football game on for God-knows-what reason. Probably to listen to all those masculine grunts of agony. So coarse, but that's what men like, don't you think?'

'Maybe I just wanted to hear the news when it came over the radio,' Edward suggested.

Felice gave him an aren't-you-clever smile. Then she took my arm, said, 'Girl talk,' to Edward, and led me over to the couch. She sat right beside me and took a deep breath, as if getting ready to give a prepared speech. She delivered it fast: 'Linda, dear, Edward has such respect for you. I *know* you're his right hand.' I knew she wanted something, and it wasn't to give me a prize as Washington Secretary of the Year. I felt a little ill at ease, but it must have been harder for her; she rubbed her cigarette case between her palms as if it would warm her hands. 'I hate to intrude on – oh, Linda, you know – the relationship between a private secretary and her employer.' She was so nervous, swallowing too often, fiddling with her cigarette case, crossing and recrossing his legs, that for a minute I thought I'd gotten her wrong. Maybe what she was after was government secrets. But then, one look at her, chewing off her dark lipstick, and I knew she wasn't working for Germany or Italy or Japan. Her long fingernails, the exact same color as her lips, tapped out a nervous rhythm on the gold case. 'You know what they say,' she murmured. 'A man has no secrets from his valet. But we're so modern nowadays, it should be: no secrets from his secretary.' She eyed my wedding ring. 'Oh, not that you're just a secretary.'

'Felice,' I broke in, 'I really don't – '

'I'm not going to ask you about the others. If there are others.' Her voice had a tiny question mark at the end, but I pretended not to hear it. 'I was just curious if he ever – oh, you know – ever mentioned me.'

I shouldn't have looked up that second, because my sixth sense was poking me in the ribs, telling me that Edward was looking right at me. But naturally I did, and there he was, carrying on a deep and serious conversation with Norman Weekes, getting a fresh drink from the waiter – and still managing to take in everything going on between Felice and me.

'I'm not asking *details*,' Felice said softly. 'That wouldn't be right.'

Edward was giving us one of his unreadable stares, but I knew him well enough to read it anyway. He was something less than delighted at Felice's 'girl talk' with me. If I could read between the lines, if said: 'Keep your mouth shut. But what was I going to tell her? That the most personal Edward ever got with me was when he'd climb into the car on a Monday and say: Did you have a nice weekend?

'Felice, I only know him in a business way. As his secretary – and as John's wife.'

'But surely he *must* have said something . . .'

I made a big deal of glancing over to Edward, but she was too intent on our conversation to pick up the hint. 'I'm asking because – you see – I've grown quite attached to him.' She put a beautifully manicured hand on mine; veins stood out, prominent and pale blue against the deep green of the emerald.

'I'm sure he's attached to you,' I said. I wanted to give her something because, well, she loved him.

'He's mentioned something?' She was so overjoyed.

'No.' her face fell. 'But you know Ed. He's . . . he plays things close to the vest.' She smiled and nodded. 'But he wouldn't have asked you here, with all this . . . this war fever, unless he wanted your company. I mean, it's a crazy, hectic time. He must feel so comfortable . . .'

I could hardly hear her. 'I'm afraid I presented myself as something of a *fait accompli*, my dear. You see, I turned up on his doorstep Tuesday evening. I'd just thought, well, with all this tumult, it would be such great fun to be at the center of things. I hoped he wouldn't be . . . irked. And he didn't seem to be.'

Just then I glanced up, and there was Edward standing before us. Irked. His hands were jammed into the pockets of his trousers, and his dark eyebrows were drawn together, shading his eyes; even though I couldn't see them, I knew they weren't twinkling. Still, as he held out his hand and pulled Felice up from the couch, his expression eased. The scowl passed. His eyes were warm. And I was willing to bet that the smile he gave her erased the memory of his displeasure in Felice's mind. If she'd thought he was mad at her, that outstretched hand and lit-up face made her think: Oh, no, he *adores* me.

Edward led Felice over to a former judge from Albany who'd joined the White House staff, an old political crony of FDR's who Edward had suddenly become great pals with when one of his budget requests got stomped on. The judge had something to do with loosening up executive-branch money, and although he was supposed to be an old shrewdie, it was clear it didn't occur to the judge that he was being used; Edward Leland was his true friend.

Both the judge and his wife were obviously thrilled to be at Edward's house. It was more real than the White House. An invitation to Edward Leland's wasn't a political courtesy; it all but said, You've arrived. Every time the wife walked past another piece of furniture, she'd give a fast stroke to the upholstery. When the waiter came over to ask what she'd like to drink, her elbow nudged her husband's side, as if to way, Wally, we're *here*.

I was just starting to get up, to walk over to John, who was stuck with witchy Mrs Weekes, when Norman Weekes sat down beside me. Too close, naturally. 'Linda,' he said. I waited, but that was all for a while. He said my name as if it was a code with a very deep meaning.

'How are you?'

'Now I'm fine,' he answered. His thigh wasn't touching mine, but it was close.

I suddenly realized that it was his conversation with Norman Weekes that had made Edward cross the room with such a glowering expression. I understood, as I edged away from Norman's thigh, closer to the arm of the couch, that it wasn't girl talk that had caused Edward's eyebrows to come together in anger. Felice wasn't the problem. At most, Edward might be irritated by the notion of the lady who showed up on his doorstep for secrets. Okay, and a little annoyed with me, because even from across the room he's spotted that I was reassuring her, and maybe he didn't want her to feel so comfortable, so free to just 'show up.'

So it wasn't the rich, eager and willing divorcée. It was Norman Weekes, a banker who had moved through Germany in the twenties and the thirties as smoothly as he moved through upper-class Boston, where he'd been born and raised. Norman, Edward's esteemed colleague at COI, obviously made Edward *furious*; he didn't make me exactly delighted, either.

'You look quite delicious tonight, my dear,' Norman said. 'Good enough to eat.' John told me Norman was related to all sorts of Boston names: Cabots, Lowells. I wondered if he'd inherited his yellow teeth from them – too say nothing of his tendency to dribble spit out of the side of his mouth. Norman leaned in closer and asked, 'Can I take a bite out of you?' His breath smelled like a stale onion roll. 'Just a little bite.'

I laughed, pretending it was all a joke, that he wasn't a repulsive old lecher, but a delightful predinner companion. He didn't join me, though, not even with a chuckle. But he did shift about a tenth of an inch away from me, so I sensed my laughter had succeeded in pulling his fuse. Good.

Norman Weeks was in his early sixties. He had thin white hair, except for wisps – like cotton cosmetic puffs – over his ears. Still, he seemed to see himself as irresistible, and the three or four times we'd met, he always made a beeline for me, on the theory, I guess, that if I was already married to a magnificent-looking man, I might have room in my life for another. Also, he was enough of a wise Washington operator to want to get as much as he could on a colleague, and a colleague's secretary was a first-rate source. That he got absolutely zero in either department didn't stop him.

'How are things over in your office?' I asked. He was staring at my legs. In my eagerness to pull away from him, the skirt of my dress had ridden up above my knees; I wanted to tug it down, but

I wouldn't give him the satisfaction. 'This must have been a hectic week.'

'Ghastly,' he said. 'I wish I had a girl like you to help me out. Edward's a lucky man.' I smiled. Across the room, Edward was charming the judge; his arm was around Felice's waist. But he turned and saw Norman Weekes drooling over my legs. 'Of course, your husband's a luckier man, if you know what I mean. Tell me, is John happy, working for Ed?'

'Yes. Very happy.'

'Not a bit awkward, all this incestuous business. Oh, come, my angel. Don't give me those big, innocent brown eyes of yours. Incest. Your John was married to Ed's girl . . . what's her name?'

'Nan.'

'And now you're working day and night for your husband's former father-in-law. Tell me, isn't it a bit much? Don't you wish you could have your husband all to yourself . . . cut those old family ties? Hmmm, Linda?'

I didn't know why Edward detested Norman Weekes so much; I was just able to sense him seething whenever Norman called or his name was mentioned, or now, across the room, watching Norman breathe into my ear.

But I knew why I hated Norman Weekes. He was a snake. Not some dumb, slithery thing that bites, but a smart one. His genius was finding people's weaknesses and playing on them. I'd heard he'd recruited agents through flattery, appeals to patriotism, bribery and, when all else failed, blackmail. But all else rarely failed, because Norman was such a skilful serpent. 'Linda, lovely Linda,' he said, 'you deserve a husband who's hundred percent.'

'I have one. Thank you.'

'Counterespionage is dreadfully tedious. Isn't he bored with working for Ed?'

'You know John can't discuss what he does with me . . . or anyone.'

'Of course not. But really, my love, you should encourage him to break his ties to Father Edward. He'd have much more independence – working with me. I need someone like him, and believe me, dear Linda, with me . . . how best to put it? John could be the man he will never be with Edward Leland.'

'Mr Weekes, I don't see any point in – '

'And furthermore,' Norman went on, 'it would be in *your* best interest to get your handsome husband away from the, um, House of Leland, shall we say. My dear, the word is seeping out that my dear old friend Quentin's pretty little wife is somewhat discontent. Yes, isn't that surprising? Young Nan is rumored to be on some quiet island in the Caribbean right now. 'Thinking things over,' as they say.' Norman took my hand in his; his skin was horribly dry, like something dead for a long time. He spoke so softly his voice was hardly louder than a hiss. 'Rumor has it the sweet thing may just decide to visit wise old Père Edward, to get some fatherly advice. Who knows, she may stay in Washington for some time. It's *so* exciting here.' He squeezed my hand tight. 'I know you're listening, my dear, even though you don't like what I'm saying. But do your best to persuade John. I promise you, if we have any . . . sweet young visitors to our beloved capital, I'll see to it that John has to make an urgent trip out of town. For as long as is necessary.' He turned my hand over and scraped the nail of his index finger across my palm. 'And when the cat's away,' he said in his high-class Boston accent, 'the mice can have a most stimulating time. Do consider that possibility, dear Linda. You look like a girl who can appreciate . . . stimulation.'

So what was I supposed to do – say to John, Want to hear some terrific gossip about Nan Leland Berringer Dahlmaier? That was the last thing in the world I wanted him to hear.

My husband had never stopped loving his first wife. On good nights, when John didn't roll over and sleep right at the edge of the mattress, when he stayed in the middle of the bed with his arm slung over me in his sleep, his hand resting on my shoulder, or, once, on my cheek, like a night-long caress, I'd think: Okay, so Nan will always be his ideal woman. Big deal. It's not her as a person John loves; it's the idea of her. When he talks about her, he talks about her mind: her passion for music and art; her misery at having to go through the debutante ritual (as if Edward held a carving knife to her throat and said, Have a tea dance or die). And he thinks she's beautiful, because she almost is, with her pale, flawless features and delicate, small-boned body.

On good nights I'd think that sure, maybe every day with me wasn't New Year's Eve, but he never really had fun with Nan. He never mentioned long walks or picnics – or grabbing her the minute he got home and doing it standing up.

As for Nan, my guess was that John's big attraction for her (besides whatever culture he had that made her intellect squeal with pleasure) was exactly what made me crazy about him: his beauty; his quiet seriousness, so you were always dying to know what he was thinking, because you were never sure of where you stood; his powerful appeal to all women, so by picking you he had somehow shown the world – and you – how special you were; and, finally, his real gift: his ability as a lover. But in that department, even though he would never go into it (Linda, this is *not* a subject for discussion), I knew Nan never set him on fire. He adored her, and it must have given him enormous reassurance to know he had such a hold over her, but . . . Okay, so maybe I was reading between the lines, but I was good at that, and I *knew* Nan wasn't woman enough for him. And I knew I was.

But on bad nights, I knew Nan was everything John wanted and loved in the world. He loved her nanny; her father's town house on Washington Square, where she grew up; her romantically-dead-at-an-early-age rich. Theodore Roosevelt cousin of a mother; her dancing lessons, her harp lessons, her boarding school; her summers in Europe, her winter vacations skiing in Vermont; and her horse, Daisy, who died in a stable in Central Park when both Nan and the horse was fifteen. John loved how Nan's eyes would fill up whenever she spoke about Daisy. And he loved – worshiped – her father.

To have been taken up into that family was the acceptance John had always dreamed of. He'd been allowed to be one of them; it was too bad wives take on husbands' names, because he would have loved nothing more than to be John Leland. But then Nan got rid of him. It must have been like an angel being tossed out of heaven, doomed to live in the workaday world after knowing paradise.

So I wouldn't talk to John about Nan. And I couldn't tell any of my forty-seven Alabama neighbors, who I hardly ever saw anymore with my crazy work hours and who anyway didn't know my husband had been married before and, besides, wouldn't say anything more than 'Ah do declare!' and then run out and give the forty-six the big news bulletin. And I couldn't tell my mother, because even though I wrote every day, I doubt if she looked at or even listened to Cookie read my letters. I called her once a week, but her voice was so faded, so thin, that even if she had the strength to concentrate on what I was saying, I didn't have the heart to tell her: Mom, maybe you were right about John.

And I couldn't tell Edward. Listen, Ed, did you hear about my husband's ex-wife? The sweet petunia may be on the loose again. You got any of that famous Edward Leland wisdom for me? Any ideas about whether this little intellectual flower is going to come for a comforting visit to her daddy and screw up my life? Huh, Ed?

'Linda,' Edward said to me. It was the Monday morning after his dinner, and Pete was driving up over a narrow, hilly, icy road somewhere in Virginia horse country at sixty miles an hour. 'I need a breath of fresh air.' I was about to crank down the window when he added, 'Pete, pull over for a minute.' The Packard skidded to a stop. Edward opened the door and said, Come on.'

I followed him, and we walked for a few minutes in silence. Then he turned right, on to a dirt road. After another few minutes, he stopped and leaned against a white fence. I buttoned the top of my coat and fished my gloves out of my pocket. I had no idea how long I'd be breathing fresh air.

God knows Edward needed some. Since Pearl Harbor, his job had become a horror. Before December 7, he had been head of counterspionage for all of Europe, to make sure that the agents who were feeding us information were really ours – and to make sure their information was accurate, that someone, somewhere, in

German intelligence hadn't discovered that a diplomat or a prostitute or a chauffeur was a spy and was allowing him to pass us misleading information.

But now Donovan and the President wanted more. Edward would continue to oversee Europe, but he'd also have to take on the United States. That was the FBI's job, of course, but the three men had agreed a little extra coverage couldn't hurt.

Meanwhile, Norman Weekes and ten men just like him signed up agents – lawyers, writers, college professors – free-lance agents living in America and coming out of the woodwork to offer us wonderful secrets, agents for desk work, like John, and agents, spies, to be slipped into whatever dark cracks we could find in enemy territory. Edward would have to make sure they were what they claimed: good Americans, or dedicated anti-Fascists.

I blew on my hands and glanced up at him. He had deep circles under his eyes. He'd nicked himself shaving in three or four places on his bad side, where he had no feeling. I'd never seen him look tired before.

'Tell me about Friday night.' He spoke so suddenly I jumped.

'Oh. It was . . .' I tried to think of one of those appropriate words, like grand, or divine, and I did, but they sounded jerky, so I said, '. . . a terrific party. Your house is beautiful. Felice was very nice.' I couldn't believe I was standing right near a horse field in December telling him what a great host he'd been, but if that's what he wanted . . . 'And the dinner – '

'Oh, stop it!' he snapped. 'Do you think I'm fishing for compliments?'

'How am I supposed to know what you're fishing for? I thought I'd give compliments a try.' I turned up my collar.

'Are you cold?'

'I'm okay.'

'Tell me what Norman Weekes said to you.'

'Oh, God!' I said. 'Please.'

'I'm not talking about his . . . advances toward you. It's obvious he finds you . . . whatever.'

'He makes me want to throw up!' I suddenly said. Edward

examined the painted wood of the fence. 'I apologize,' I said. 'That just slipped out.'

'Understandable,' he muttered. 'He makes me want to throw up too.' I stared at him. 'Norman Weekes is a foul human being. Now that we have that established, please go on.'

So I told him. I told him about Norman's saying how lucky he was to have me as a secretary. Naturally, Edward didn't say, Well, at least Norman's right about one thing. He just waited for me to continue. 'Look,' I said, 'this isn't my favorite kind of conversation.'

'I'm sorry, Linda. I have to know what he said.' He waited. And he knew how to wait, until you became so uneasy with the silence that you'd do anything to stop it.

'He wants John to come and work for him.'

'Goddamn it! All right. What precisely did he say about John's leaving me to work for him? Don't waste any time, Linda. I know when you're . . . when someone's holding back on me.' I gazed out at the field. 'As you know, I have a very full schedule today. Don't make it more difficult.'

'You're being unfair,' I blurted out. But I didn't take it back. 'I told you what's important.'

'It's all important.'

'Some of it's personal stuff.'

'I want to hear it.

'Why?'

'Because Norman Weekes would like nothing better than to destroy me.' He glanced at me and said, 'You look cold. Let's walk.' He chose the direction: farther down the dirt road. 'I suppose you'd like an explanation.'

'Only if you want to give me one.' I took a deep breath of cold air. 'Don't you know I'd take anything you said on faith?'

'I appreciate that.' He walked fast, and I had to hurry along the road to keep up with him. Finally he spoke. 'For years, Norman's been doing business with a banker in Munich. A conservative, a Catholic and, according to Norman, a man contemptuous of the Nazis. And yet this man has been close to the government – through his contacts at Krupp, United Steel, I. G. Farben. In late '39, he met Norman in Switzerland with a briefcase full of documents – page after page of statistics on industrial production. He swore to Norman he was a good German, a good Catholic, and precisely because of this he was morally obliged to take a stand against Hitler's regime. He told Norman: I know you have friends in Washington. Please see that these fall into the right hands.'

I stopped for a second to take off my shoe and shake out some gravel. 'The statistics – were they important?'

'If they were accurate, they were an invaluable picture of German industry – and from that, we could derive quite a clear idea of their military strength. And so, throughout '39 and '40, we accepted these figures – and passed them on to the British. And Bill Donovan asked Norman to come to Washington and do more of the same.'

'But he wants to *destroy* you. So you must have found out that his statistics . . .?'

'I did my homework. To this day I don't know what made me do it. A hunch. And through the years I've come to trust my hunches. I had John and an economist compare this banker's information with data we'd gotten from different sources. Linda, none of it jibed. The figures were grossly understated. The Germans were far stronger than we had been led to believe.'

'Did you go to Norman?'

'Not right away. I did some checking on this man from Munich – nothing terribly difficult; the sort of investigation someone in Norman's position ought to have done.'

'But he hadn't.'

'No. He was so damned sure of this friend of his, this honorable, refined, old-money banker. When I finally brought my findings to him, he told me, "Ed, please. The fellow's wife's a von Schleicher, for Chrissake." ' He stopped and turned to me. 'How was my accent on von Schleicher?'

'Terrible,' I told him. 'As usual.' I paused. 'What finally happened?'

'Ultimately, Norman did himself in with his own arrogance. He went to Donovan and issued an ultimatum: Either Ed Leland goes or I do. Well, the next day the three of us got together for a drink. Bill was being congenial, trying to minimize our differences;

Norman was saying his honor was at stake and that his source was a Catholic. He looked right at Bill when he said it.'

'Real subtle.'

'Yes. And then I did what I'd come prepared to do: I handed Bill my documentation and said, "Forget the statistics. Look at the pictures.'

'You got pictures?'

'Yes. Some photos of Norman's friend with *his* good friends: high Nazi officials – including Göring.'

I tucked my hands under my armpits to keep them warm, but it wasn't just the weather. 'Where did you get the pictures, Ed?'

'Linda, everyone remarks what a bright girl my secretary is. So you tell me: Where did I get the pictures?'

'You had someone go into the man's office or house – '

'Very good. His house.'

'And they stole – '

'I prefer to say appropriated.'

'How did Donovan react when he saw them?' I asked.

'Gracefully. The we-all-have-our-bad-days approach.'

'But Weekes must have looked like something less than a bargain.'

'Considerably less. Bill had relied on Norman, on his judgement, and it was faulty – in the extreme. And we simply cannot afford that. Look, you've seen how we've had to operate. Until last week, when we declared war, we were the most rudimentary operation. We had no great network of agents, no committees to assess intelligence. All we had was a few men. Norman Weekes was one of them. Still is. But no longer, shall we say, the force he once was.'

'You're right,' I said. 'He does want to destroy you.'

'Yes. But look on the bright side. If he succeeds, you'll have time to read or go to the dressmaker or whatever it is working for me keeps you from doing.'

I didn't smile. 'The scary thing about Norman Weekes is that he's very smart, but he's not intelligent. Do you know what I mean?'

'Yes. I'll tell you what it is. He sees small pieces with . . . well, amazingly acute vision. But he has no sense of the big picture –

or even that there is one.' He paused. 'Now, Linda . . . will you tell me what he said about John?'

'I'll tell you because you have to know what this guy is doing, what knife he's going to stick in your back.'

'Thank you.'

'But I hate doing it. I want you to know that.'

'I understand.'

'He said counterespionage was boring, and that John would be better off with him. Not just because of the boring part. Because . . . he said . . . John can't be the man he could be if he's . . . working for you.'

Edward's voice was much colder than the frigid air. 'The implication being that I somehow . . . what?'

'Take away John's independence. He looks up to you too much to be his own man.'

'And?'

'And . . . the family business. That maybe it's – you know – awkward for me because John was married to your daughter.'

'What else?'

'That's it.'

'No. There's more. You and he were talking a long time.'

And that's where I decided to stop. I wouldn't tell him, Hey, Norman tells me someone besides Santa Claus may be coming to town. 'That's all.'

He turned abruptly and we hurried back along the long dirt road to the main road, and the car. We didn't have anything else to say. But when we reached the car, Edward stood at the rear of the car and put his foot on the bumper. 'You know, I used to close my eyes at night, and in two minutes I'd be sound asleep. Now . . . sometimes I'm up for hours. It's not just the business about Norman. The whole damned COI is filling up with men like him, men who are still playing Cowboys and Indians. Norman says, Trust my blood brother . . . and look what happens.

'Last August, he had a boy, fresh out of college in Maine. French-speaking parents. He sent him into occupied France, someplace outside Paris where a German official kept a mistress. He tells the boy – a good-looking youngster – to seduce the mistress and get all he can on the German. It was an idiot plan . . . created by Norman but approved with great enthusiasm by two of our top men. Well, the boy was caught the first day. Caught and killed. And Norman says, "At least we tried. You can't make an omelet without breaking a few eggs." '

I wished I could have taken his hand and held it. 'I'm sorry.'

'I meet with men like myself, men who should know better, and they're hatching half-baked schemes. Playing games. I like games. I'm good at them. Golf, bridge, chess . . . But these games they're playing use people as pawns. I sit at a conference table and hear things that make me sick, and when I object, I'm told, Ed, old man, you've lost your nerve.' He looked at me and suddenly aimed his finger at my heart. 'Bang! You're dead! Cowboys and Indians. That's how these lawyers and bankers and businessmen are going to win the war. With clever strategies. Games. Bang! But when the Germans and Japs go bang . . .'

'You really are dead,' I murmured. He nodded. 'But the other men in COI . . . some of them are like you, aren't they?'

'Some of them are.' He stared straight and motioned me to the car door. Before he opened it, he said, 'I don't know if we'll ever make the omelet, but we're going to have dozens – hundreds of dozens – of broken eggs before this war is over. Linda, it's going to be a mess.'

# *Chapter Seventeen*

John had a new office, but that was only to be expected. He was now running the counterspionage operation in Germany and France – the part that could be run from behind a desk in Washington. Technically, of course, the entire world was still the Edward Leland Show, but Edward was busy flying around, not only looking for concealed enemies but also trying to calm down a close-to-beserk J. Edgar Hoover and his pet politicians, who were convinced that anytime anyone from COI breathed in the United States, he was stealing the oxygen, the life, out of the FBI.

The American flag behind John's desk, with its thick pole topped by a gold eagle, the long view of the Capitol dome from his window, and his executive secretary, who was fluent in French as well as German, showed just how far John had come. Okay, the office was only slightly larger than an orange crate, but it had a carpet. And while his secretary was a strange, bent-over woman with coarse, shoulder-length brown hair, who resembled a grizzly bear, she did have a Phi Beta Kappa key from Barnard College.

'Edith,' John said to her, 'this is my wife . . .' He paused for a fraction of a second. Normally, as wife, I'd be introduced to a secretary as 'Mrs Berringer.' But since Edward had flown off for three weeks of mysterious meetings in secret places, I'd been sent over to work for John. '. . . Linda Berringer,' John said, leaving it up to Edith what to call me.

'I am pleased to meet you, Mrs Berringer.' Actually, she said 'Frau Berringer.' John was going to spend the morning interviewing refugees from German, and we were warming up our German.

The refugees were key pieces of the puzzle Edward's unit was trying to put together. The more information we had – on everything from changes in train schedules to the extent of the flour shortage in eastern Germany – the better we were able to get a picture of how their war effort was going and, just as important, to check if our sources were giving us accurate accounts.

'I'm glad to meet you, Edith. And please, call me Linda.' Her small, too-wide-spaced eyes fluttered a little when she heard my accent. She spoke the same educated *hoch Deutsch* John did.

'Edith,' John said, 'would you be good enough to take down the preliminary background information for Herr Doktor Schwerin? Also, you might want to offer him some coffee.' Edith nodded, did an about-face and walked out the door, to the anteroom where John's visitors waited. Walked is maybe too normal a word for what Edith did. Her legs were heavy, short and strangely far apart, so her progress was more like an animal's lope. If she'd growled or scratched the scalp under her thick hair instead of saying, 'Yes, Mr Berringer,' it wouldn't have seemed out of character.

'Poor girl,' I said, after she shut the door. 'To look like that. I wonder if she's ever had a boyfriend. I mean, do you think some guy can see beyond her homeliness?' John shrugged. Edith's love life was obviously not an item on his agenda. 'Is she a nice person?'

'I don't know. She's all right, I suppose.'

'Is she madly in love with you, John?'

He let himself go enough to smile for a moment. 'Probably.' He was behind his battleship of a desk; it took up three quarters of the room. I left the straight-backed chair I'd been in and went to sit on the edge of his desk. He motioned me to come over further and pulled me onto his lap. I rested my head against his shoulder. He massaged the back of my neck, then slid his hand down the back of my blouse and stroked my skin. 'Edward's let you sit in on all his meetings with Schwerin?' he asked.

'Yes, he needs me there. Schwerin doesn't speak a word of English. What could he do? Play charades? Can you see Edward pantomiming "panzer divisions"?'

'Your hair smells nice. I wish you'd wear it loose.'

'It doesn't look right at work.'

'I guess not.' John kissed me.

The more Edward trusted me, the more attentive – and affectionate – John because. 'Schwerin's not one of these refugees you should get all teary-eyed about,' I murmured into the woolly lapel of his navy chalk-stripe suit. 'He's a two-bit Berlin lawyer who happened to be at the right place at the right time – and did the wrong thing. He got involved in some sleazy black market stuff – selling silk that was going to be used for parachutes to a company that made ladies' panties. He's lucky he got out.'

John's deep-blue eyes blazed at me with such intensity they seemed to be lit from within; he was madly, passionately in love with my inside information. At first, John could barely believe that I was allowed to sit in while Edward made phone calls to Donovan. Or that, riding around in the Packard, Edward would analyze the differences between the French and Dutch resistance movements – or tell me about the love affair between Wendell Willkie and the book review editor of the *New York Herald Tribune*. John had gaped when I told him: The Democrats got hold of some of Willkie's letters to her! 'Dolly notes,' they were calling them, and they were actually going to release them, except the Republicans found out that Wallace, FDR's running mate, was tied in with some weird Russian mystic and had written some crazy religious-nut letters. John had asked, He *tells* you all this? Or do you overhear it? He tells me, I'd answered. You know, when we're driving around, or sometimes when it's slow, like when we're waiting around for a transatlantic call.

For a while, John couldn't accept that Edward actually talked to me. I think he tried to come up with excuses for these lapses: Maybe Edward was thinking out loud, or perhaps he was tired. But finally John's awe won out; Edward was so perfect, so sound in his judgment, that if he talked to me, I was – for whatever reason – obviously worth talking to.

What I never told John about were what I called the private talks. About a week after Edward told me of his concern over the COI boys in three-piece suits playing Cowboys and Indians, we'd slowly drifted into conversations I knew we never could have had with anyone else. In my case, the need for someone to talk to was obvious; no one, least of all my husband, showed any inclination to listen to all the things I wanted to say. And in Edward's case, I guessed it was that he had a lot on his mind – too much – and needed more than an ear; he had to have a mouth that would stay shut.

So what began on that dirt road in Virginia kept going. The next talk had taken place about nine o'clock one night in the middle of December. Edward, not looking up from a letter he was proofreading, told me he was going to have a late dinner and a brandy with Donovan in an hour; Pete would drive me home. I said fine. But a minute later, as I was collecting his day's mess of paper clips, which were scattered all over his desk and on the floor around his chair, I suddenly squeezed all the paper clips tight in my hand. Their metal edges made painful little pinholes in my palm; my mouth went dry. But I stood up from the rug and asked him, Why do you think all the wives in the law firm hate me so much?

Scared as I was, I somehow knew that he wouldn't think I was going too far in asking that question, or that I was a jerk for thinking such thoughts. And I was right. He got out of his chair, went over to the antique cabinet where he kept a couple of bottles of liquor for visitors (and a bottle of schnapps for hysterical refugees), took out two glasses and inquired: Scotch all right for you?

Yes, I said, and he poured me enough to anesthetize a patient for a twelve-hour operation. He poured himself a lot less.

They don't hate you, he told me.

Well, they give a pretty good imitation of it, I replied.

It's that you're not one of them. Then he said, Sit, and pointed to the wing chair where he usually sat when he talked to other lawyers. He sat on the couch, put his drink down on the coffee table and leaned toward me. Linda, they've created a nice, neat little world for themselves, where everyone speaks the same language, knows their place, where wives are wives and secretaries arc –

Less than human.

I thought he'd disagree, but all he said was, Well, perhaps not quite as high on the evolutionary scale.

But why are they so rotten to me? You know what they do every single time? They say, 'Oh, hello-o-o, Linda, dear,' and then ignore me for the rest of whatever dinner party we're at, and let me tell you, lawyers have too many damn dinner parties. If they're so classy, why aren't they nice to me? You know, like they are to their cooks? 'Dear old Martha. She's one of the family.'

Are you going to drink that Scotch or look at it? he demanded. I took a sip. All right, he went on, the reason they can afford to be nice to dear old Martha is that she probably *is* old and rather plain, and even if she's not, she doesn't marry an attorney and want to join them for lunch and matinees.

I never wanted that!

I'm talking in generalities, Linda.

Maybe talk in specifics. I didn't go to Radcliffe.

Specifically, you frighten them. You lured one of the most eligible lawyers in Manhattan –

Oh, stop it! They all know what kind of a lure it was, and I'll bet anything they spent weeks gossiping about how noble he was to marry me. And I'll bet you double they all knew I had a miscarriage and he wound up stuck with me.

He said quietly, You're very hard on yourself.

I said, You know how everyone admires you, calls you tough-minded, a realist? He nodded. Okay, I'm a realist too. I understand my own situation.

He took a long drink. Do you want to know why they don't like you? Let me be direct. You have blond hair, a nice figure – and a bit of a Brooklyn accent.

Queens, I whispered.

You attract their men. You are precisely what they fear when their husbands call and say, 'I'm working late tonight, dear.' And there's more. Shall I go on?

Yes.

You're intelligent and you've got, well, let's call it guts. Deep down, they recognize you're as good as they are. This nice, pleasant world they've created is really a rather fragile one, dependent on the illusion of their superiority. And, Linda, you walked into the Avenels' living room that night and, very simply, they sensed their world starting to crack a little around the edges. So they did what they had to do to save themselves – and their illusions. They forced you to remain outside.

I must have drunk too much; all of a sudden I wanted to laugh. I asked, Will they ever accept me? Like in thirty-five years?

Edward's deep voice had been so soft I could hardly hear him: How hard are you willing to try to emulate them? Are you willing to bend? Break? How much do you want to become what they are?

I don't.

Then, Linda, when this war is over, and if we are all still here, free, alive . . .

Then what?

Then you'll live happily ever after with your husband and, I'm certain, your children . . . except for a series of obligatory dinner parties where you'll be ogled by doddering attorneys and snubbed by their wives. Does that answer your question?

So there I sat in my husband's lap, cradled in his arms – somewhat happily, although not in Cinderella post-glass slipper ecstasy. Maybe it was because I'd learned that John was not affectionate by nature. Sex, sure. But as for cuddling, only for cause, as the lawyers say. What he wanted from me, at that moment as he kissed my forehead, was the inside scoop on the low-life Berlin lawyer Herr Doktor Schwerin.

John, of course, was no male Mata Hari, seducing state secrets out of me. He had as much right to know what I knew as he did. Of course, he was too much the gentleman to ask directly. But I'd discovered he liked to hear what was going on so he could test his theories, his conclusions: to see if they jibed with Edward's. 'This Schwerin's not important for himself,' John observed.

'No. Just for being able to corroborate Sunflower's information.'

Sunflower was Edward's best source inside Germany. He was head of one of the country's biggest mining firms, a brilliant financial planner, a manager, and a man who, right from the beginning, had hated Hitler and all he stood for. He was one of the German industrialists who were great believers in boosting their economy through *amerikanisches Geschäft*, doing business with America, and he'd gotten to know Edward in the late 1920s. By 1933, when the Nazis came to power, he had started keeping Edward informed about the ties between business and Hitler's government.

Once the Germans went on the march across Europe, the relationship between these two men became less casual. They would meet every few months in Paris and, after Paris fell, in Switzerland. Through his family, Sunflower had ties to upper levels of the military. Through his business, he spoke with other industrialists. And finally, the treasurer of his company was a fanatical Nazi – and a boastful one. The man was proud of his stature in the Party, and he'd brag about his coffees with Himmler, his dinners with Göring and, most of all, his frequent lunches with his old school pal Karl Hanke, the Gauleiter of Silesia. Hanke was a powerful man in the Third Reich – a friend of Mrs Goebbels, who was the patron of Albert Speer, Hitler's favourite architect. And because Sunflower was so charming, so interested, his treasurer gave him elaborate reports on the smallest details of Nazi high society. And these details eventually found their way back to Edward.

Sunflower's only liability was his honesty. He was discreet in his office, but for years, among friends, he'd made no bones about how much he hated the Nazis, about how they were duping not only the German man in the street but the upper classes, and how they would bring the country to ruin. Because he was so successful – and wellborn – most people ignored Sunflower's rumblings, or passed him off as an eccentric, foolish for speaking his mind, but harmless. Edward, though, was always afraid that someday, someone in government would catch on to Sunflower; at worst they would kill him, and at best, feed him false information to pass on.

'So far,' John asked, 'Edward seems satisfied? Schwerin's information dovetails with Sunflower's?'

'Yes,' I said. 'So far.'

'Did Edward say anything else?'

'No, nothing else.'

Not about Schwerin. Actually, he told me a lot else. And there

who earns his living by being, well, articulate. Calculating. Rational. And I was struck dumb by a seventeen-year-old girl. She wore a black velvet ribbon around her neck.

What was she like? I asked.

High-spirited. Good-natured. Edward smiled to himself. This was 1918, he said, and she appeared a very proper young lady, and she *was* proper, but . . . she had a great sense of fun. And enormous energy and determination. I got her permission to ask her father for her hand – we did that sort of thing in those days – and her parents were quite taken aback. Not that they didn't like me, but I came from a rather undistinguished background and I'd only known Caroline a week and a half when I proposed.

A week and a half? I repeated.

Well, I knew it was right. And so did she. But for all my persuasive abilities, it was she who convinced her parents to let us get married right away. She was very strongwilled.

She must have been very smart, I said.

He turned his inkwell around and around, as if he was thinking of his wife's intelligence for the first time and needed to concentrate. Finally he said, I honestly don't know how smart she was. Most of the time, we'd just talk about everyday things. Who I spoke to in the office. What I ate for lunch. Did I like potted palms . . .

That second, if Edward had been almost any other man in the world, he would not have had the self-control to keep his eyes from welling up; the potted palms had obviously reminded him of something terribly tender he hadn't thought about for years.

But he just went on. If she wasn't a great thinker, he said, at least she was bright enough, and lively. And very, very kind. He looked straight at me. She died three years later. Cancer of the liver.

That stinks, I said.

Yes, it does.

Do you think about her a lot?

Not so much anymore. But at first, all the time. Do you know the strange part? I think back to Caroline now and I really can't remember . . . the texture of our life together. What I have are very clear memories of certain events, the moments I recalled over and over right after she died. But after a while, the memories themselves – a hike we took in the Adirondacks, the night Nan was born, a pink hat with a plume she bought for Easter and I'd laughed at – the specific memories became the reality. That's when I knew that I'd truly lost her.

I said softly, I guess in a way you mourned her twice.

Yes. First her death and then . . . her spirit. I can say: Caroline was lively. But I say it more than feel it. I hate . . . Edward's voice got very quiet. I hate it.

You never found anyone else?

Caroline made me happy. That much I do recall – vividly. And no one else ever did.

I worked for John from January 1942, when Edward left, until April, when he came back to Washington. He might have stayed away longer, in 'San Francisco,' as the cables said but that I knew was London, or at a so-called army base, Camp Brady. The wires would read: 'Farmer [that was Edward's code name] and Matthew in San Francisco Stop Farmer on to Camp Brady to check tractors Stop.'

I went ice cold the day I read that wire, because what it really said was that Edward had gone into German-occupied Poland. No one, not John or any of the other men who worked for Edward, knew the entire code, so for all they knew, Camp Brady could have been some dirty, sweltering army facility in Mississippi or a swank officers' club in Los Angeles.

Of course, they sensed he was somewhere important. Dangerous. But all those lawyers and corporation men and Yale professors had modelled themselves on Edward. They were little Lelands, not only courageous but casual, so they didn't go cold with fear. They murmured, Wonder when Ed'll be back, or, Funny, you'd think Ed would've sent a postcard from Camp Brady: 'Having a wonderful time. Wish you were here.' Chuckle, chuckle. A couple of million Nazis couldn't scare the little Lelands.

I remember coming home very late one night in March with

John, both of us taking tiny, cautious steps up the iced-over front stairs of our house. It was old snow, with specks of coal soot frozen solid since February, when René Villiard of the Free French had come to Washington, and John was so busy meeting with him (and I was so busy typing up transcripts of his meetings the day before with German refugees) that we didn't get home before midnight. But almost every day had been like that. By the weekend, by the time we bought a shovel, the ice was rock hard, too hard to make a dent in, and so it stayed.

John and I zigzagged our way up the steps, finding small patches of stair safely unfrozen. We skidded across the small wood porch with its snowed-on glider. As I opened my change purse to get to my key, John asked, 'Do you know where Camp Brady is?'

'You mean where Edward is? Yes.'

'I just wondered if you knew. Don't tell me.'

I opened the front door, and a blast of dry, overheated air hit me. 'Why can't I tell you?' I asked as I switched on the light and walked into the house.

He followed me, closed the door behind us and said, 'Shhh!'

'What do you think, some Nazi secret agent has been hiding under the bed all winter, waiting to hear me whisper classified secrets to you?'

I opened the closet and reached for a hanger. John leaned against the wall, and in a voice too casual to be his, said, 'Really, Linda, it's of absolutely no consequence. If Ed wanted me to know, he would have told me.'

It was his little-Leland, fake-Edward voice that got me upset. Whenever any of the guys in counterespionage wanted to show how brave and noble they were, they put on that voice, and no matter where they came from – Long Island like John, or Ames, Iowa, or Charleston, South Carolina, they pitched their voices low and talked slo-o-ow, the way Edward did, even down to the trace of the Vermont accent, like when they talked about the Republican Party.

It didn't get me angry when all the Yale guys talked as though they'd spent their golden boyhoods pitching hay on some New England farm. Half of the COI (which had just changed its name to OSS, Office of Strategic Services, probably because someone's uncle had the contract for government stationery), maybe even three quarters, had graduated from Yale, including Edward Leland, and if he was their ideal of what a Yale man should sound like, it was okay with me. But it was another thing to hear my husband, whose only connection to Yale had probably been a football game they'd played against Columbia in 1925 and he'd gone to. What bothered me about John's fake nonchalance, his false I-can-go-face-to-face-with-Adolf attitude, was that it showed him – like all of them – to be exactly the opposite of what he was trying to be: brave.

Talk about Cowboys and Indians. It wasn't just that they were playing games with people's lives; it was that they saw themselves as heroes. They put on Edward's hat and became the marshal who moseys into a dangerous town with his trusty six-shooter and gets rid of the no-good varmints.

Edward *was* the sort of man who thrived on going eyeball to eyeball with no-good varmints. But John was a thinker, a legal scholar, a born puzzle-solver. Why couldn't he be happy being what he was? What he was was so impressive.

I put my coat away, gave John a hanger, and asked, 'Is it okay if I just make eggs tonight?'

'With toast.' His voice was muffled by the coats in the closet. 'Not too dark.'

What I wanted from my husband was not a lot of talk about honor and valor, but a display of it right where we were, at home in Washington, DC. I wanted him to be what he was, to be *real*. Let him just say to me, Hey, I'm dying to know where Ed is. Tell me, and I swear to God I won't say a word to anyone.

And I didn't want to see him in a warm kitchen, eating scrambled eggs and buttered toast and pretending to be light-hearted after a grueling, eighteen-hour day. He had all the Yale men and even the guys from Ohio State and City College who had somehow managed to sneak in – they all acted easy, relaxed, as if nothing fazed them.

Listen, I wanted to tell my husband, you're an extraordinary man. You're doing important, exhausting work, work you should be proud of. *I'm* proud of you. Don't pretend to be someone else.

I want you here, John. I want you safe. Do you think I could stand it if you disappeared for months, like Edward? Do you think I want you to have his crazy, rigid sense of honor, so that you won't endanger anyone else by sending them to meet what's left of the Polish underground, and you insist on going in yourself? And most of all, do you think I want a man who deep down cares so little about what happens to him that he has no fear?

'You look exhausted,' I said to him, as he came into the kitchen.

He shut his eyes and shook his head, as if to deny his fatigue. 'It's nothing I can't bear,' he said. But he pronounced the word *bayah*, as if he'd spent his summers in northeastern Vermont. Come *on*! He'd been caddying at the Sands Point Golf Club. 'Linda, you have to understand. I have to bear it. This is war.'

No, *this* was war. At the end of June, Norman Weekes called a conference in his office. Six of his men and John and Edward sat at one end of an interminably long table with fat feet and a deep red-brown shine so rich it looked like it had been stolen from the White House dining room.

Norman's secretary, a man in his late forties wearing a light brown suit so crumpled it resembled a paper bag, sat next to me; our rickety, government-issue chairs were placed against the wall. We both took down every word that was said. I considered myself something of a short-hand whiz, but he was faster, and determined to prove it to me. He obviously knew I was there because my boss didn't trust his minutes of the meeting, but he was a prissy man, full of stenographic pride, and didn't get that I was there because of OSDS politics; he viewed the meeting not as a critical discussion of our Berlin espionage network but as some fight-to-the-death shorthand contest.

Norman rested his elbows on the table, made a tepee with his hands, rested his chin on the tips of his fingers and contemplated Edward. 'Shall I begin?' he asked.

'It's your meeting,' Edward responded.

'Very well. We are here to discuss Alfred Eckert. A second-rate little dress designer in Berlin, although quite popular with the wives of high-ranking SS officials, women not generally revered for their chic.' Norman's men looked amused. Once he saw they were – and my guess is that besides a Harvard degree (his unit was the big exception to the Yale rule), finding Norman Weekes amusing was part of the job – Norman glanced toward Edward.

But Edward's expression was absolutely blank, almost scarily empty, as though he'd vacated his own premises. I had never heard of Alfred Eckert, and I couldn't tell if Edward had or not. Norman waited, a little uneasily, for some expression to appear on Edward's deadpan face. When it didn't, he quickly turned away and looked to John, who was sitting with his back to me. Still, I didn't need to see John's face. I could read his back; he was edgy, anxious even.

'Well, whatever our Mr Eckert's weaknesses in couture,' Norman continued, 'he was a first-rate agent.'

John said, ' "Was"?'

'Yes. Unfortunately, he died.' Norman turned to one of his men. 'Martin, can you bring us up to date on the situation?'

Martin looked like the rest of Norman's grey-suited, striped-tied men, except he had rimless eyeglasses that kept sliding down his nose. 'We're in a bit of a bind,' he said, his Boston voice so nasal he sounded as if he had a clothespin on his nose. If there were little Lelands in counterespionage, there were miniature Weekeses in espionage, German division. 'You see, whatever Alfred's motives were for working for us – they were always a bit unclear, and alas, now we shall never discern them – we do know he was fervently anti-Nazi. Since '38. Until then, he was just . . . what he appeared to be. With suspiciously thin, arched eyebrows, I might add.'

'For Christ's sake!' Edward broke in. Martin jerked up in his chair, as if he'd gotten a violent shock. 'Do you think I have time to listen to talk about eyebrow arches? He turned to John. 'What did this fellow do for us?'

'I believe he worked for *us*, Ed,' Norman interrupted.

'I meant us, the United States of America, Norman.' He looked back at John. 'Do you know what his role was?'

'He began by passing gossip he picked up from the wives of Party officials. That was during '38 and the beginning of '39.'

'Who was his contact?' Edward asked.

John was direct: 'I don't know. I've only been following his work for the last eight months.'

So Edward looked back to Martin, who was still upset after Edward's last words to him; he fidgeted around in his chair as if he had a sore behind. 'How did he pass on his information to us?'

'A florist. A friend of his who did all the flowers for the American ambassador's wife. Very efficient. We'd often get it out the same day we received it, by diplomatic pouch.'

The secretary sitting next to me was scrawling away at top speed, glancing over now and then to my pad, just to make sure I was behind him. I always was. Unlike him, though, I was consumed by what was being discussed. But he just wrote on; the nine men in the room could have been discussing a Securities and Exchange Commission regulation or comparing apple cobbler recipes.

'And what happened in '39 to change this fellow's status?' Edward demanded.

'I'd gotten wind of him,' Norman said. 'That he was quite an asset. So on my next trip to Berlin, I brought my wife along. She was a brick. Loathed his dresses, of course, but went through fitting after fitting at our hotel.' Norman added, 'Didn't want to arouse unnecessary suspicions, so I had him carry away a pile of pinned-up dresses. Actually bought the damned things. Priced like they came from Paris. My wife gave them to the maid. The ugliest colors and – '

'What did you talk to him about, Norman?' Edward asked impatiently. 'Hemlines?'

Norman pretended Edward was joking and chuckled. Then all his men chuckled too. 'Obviously I recruited him.'

'As?'

'As an agent. You see, I saw war coming, saw we didn't have much time left in Berlin – wouldn't be able to rely on the florist and the old diplomatic pouch – and needed more than "society" gossip. We needed specific intelligence, and we needed it fast. That's where our friend Alfred came in. He had friends in high, fashionable places. He had a car, all the gas ration coupons he could possibly desire, and was welcome everyplace, be it a villa near the Grunewald or a disreputable nightclub where what was left of the city's demimonde gathered. And most important of all, he had the wife of one of the most powerful foreign office officials as his confidante; she considered him her closest friend – her only friend – and he was always welcome in her quite splendid home . . . a home confiscated, I understand, from a wealthy Jewish mercantile family.'

Edward nodded to Norman, then turned to John. 'Alfred Eckert was reliable?'

'Yes,' said John. 'As good as they come. He was able to glean an enormous amount of information from this official's house.'

'I see. And now we have lost our gleaner.'

'Yes,' Norman responded.

'Any candidates for the job?'

'None. You know what it's like there, Ed. You can't slip a refugee into the home of a foreign office official, a man who is a prominent Nazi to boot; the danger of his being recognized is, well, enormous. And you can't expect to pass off a Yale German major.' No, I thought. Even someone like me, an ordinary person with a working-class accent; if I worked as this guy's file clerk or as one of his wife's maids, even, I probably couldn't pass. No matter how much a person knows – and I knew a lot about Berlin and its ways – it would still be a foreign city. To a German major from Yale, it would be another planet. 'And who over there is going to take the chance? A clandestine meeting in a private house, perhaps. A word whispered in passing in a men's room. But who would risk going into this man's house, sneaking into his study, searching through his papers? No one is that brave.'

'Your little dressmaker was,' Edward said.

'Ah, yes,' Norman agreed. 'But he's dead now.'

'Assassinated, I assume?'

'Yes.' Norman lifted up his yellow legal pad and his pen from the table before him. All six of his men pushed back their chairs, ready to leap up the instant Norman rose. 'Well, I thought it was important to pass this on to you and John, Ed. It puts us in somewhat of a pickle. We'll all have to give it some thought.' He stood, and his six men sprung to their feet. His secretary closed his steno pad with an embarrassingly loud slap.

But Edward remained seated, and so did John. Edward said, 'One moment, please, Norman.' I took it down. The other secretary was in agony, not knowing whether taking down Edward's words would be viewed as his job or as an act of betrayal. He peered around, then finally, with one of those overdramatic silent movie gestures, clutched his pad passionately against his chest. 'This recruit of yours worked for us in one capacity or another for four years. Is that correct?'

'Yes.'

'He had powerful friends, people willing to vouch for him? Other fashionable women married to influential men. Perhaps a highly placed deviate or two.' Norman said nothing. 'Am I correct in that assumption?'

'Yes.'

'No untoward incidents before this? No hairbreadth escapes?'

'None.'

'And yet suddenly he is assassinated.'

'Yes.'

'Obviously not by our man, the one who replaced the florist, who passed Eckert's information on to us.' He inclined his head toward John. 'That is code name Cactus, correct?' John said it was. Cactus was a German citizen, a surgeon, whose mother had been American and who had a brother, also a surgeon, in Ohio. 'And we've cleared Cactus?'

'We've checked him over and over. He does eye surgery in Berlin, and every month he flies to Switzerland, to a clinic he owns. He operates there for a day or two, buys medical supplies unavailable in Germany and returns. We know he's clean, and even better, they are convinced he is.'

Edward turned back to Norman. 'Let's move on, then, shall we? Was your man held incommunicado for a while? Tortured?'

'I don't believe so.'

'That isn't the usual pattern, is it? They must have been afraid that he was a threat to them.'

'Possibly.'

'And – I'm just thinking out loud now, Norman – they weren't afraid of us. Once they had him in custody, he couldn't give us any more. But perhaps they were fearful that his friends in high places could help him get free, or just manage to speak to him. What information could he pass on to them that was so threatening?

'I haven't the foggiest.'

'Could it be, Norman, that he suspected – or suddenly discovered – that one of the people in his own secret circle, perhaps one of the few he trusted, a seemingly devoted anti-Nazi, is a traitor? And the traitor had to silence him? Could that be why he was killed?'

'It's your theory, Ed.'

'But it is safe to assume that the manner of his murder was rather swift and brutal?'

'I gather it was,' Norman said coldly.

'You talk about my theory. But tell me, have *you* given any thought at all to the possibility that your network may not be inviolate?'

'I resent your tone.'

'And I resent your passing this off as just another nasty little wartime mess. You listen to me, Norman. Both of us have been around a long, long time. And both of us know there *has* to be a double agent operating in your network. And if I can hazard a guess, you realized it the moment you heard of Mr Eckert's sudden death.' Norman's six men looked away or cleared their throats. 'Someone found out your dressmaker was onto them. And so they quickly passed the word and – no more messenger service.' Edward paused. 'Do you have any idea who the rotten apple is?'

'No,' Norman said.

'Not even a guess?'

'Not even a guess.'

I couldn't get Alfred Ecker out of my mind. All that afternoon, while John sat in Edward's office, I sat in the little vestibule right outside, trying not to hear them. 'Calamity.' 'Disaster.' 'Catastrophe.' 'Terrible blow.'

The strange thing was, normally my ears would have been positively throbbing in an attempt to absorb every syllable. This wasn't just an Ivy League war; it was Grover Cleveland High School's too. I was always right in there, having to know what was going on. Over the months working for Edward, I'd mastered homing in on the low pitch of his voice, so – nearly all the time – I could hear his end of telephone conversations even if I was busy typing away. And when his door was closed for a meeting, I'd file; I'd learned to save up my *S* through *Z* correspondence, and at those times, squatting to insert letters in the bottom-drawer folders, I could listen in on at least seventy-five percent of what was being said.

But that afternoon I just wanted silence, so I could reflect on Alfred. Because right away, I was on a first-name basis with him. And I could *see* him: tall, with too-thin eyebrows, probably plucked; blond, marcelled hair; and a fairyish, fussbudgety walk – like Edward Everett Horton in *The Gay Divorcee*.

Sure, I knew it was all in my mind. For all I knew, he could have been short and fat and resembled a fire hydrant. But his picture came to me over the ocean, and even if it wasn't accurate, it was real. I could see him riding through Berlin in his dark green roadster, wasting gasoline. He kept an alligator or a crocodile – whichever was better – briefcase on the seat beside him, with some sketches of evening gowns and his pincushion.

God knows I'd heard enough about Berlin from Olga. And I'd stood before enough open maps of the city, seen enough photographs, while refugees pointed out this Gestapo house to Edward, that armory, that new pipeline. I knew the streets, the neighborhoods, and I could see Alfred being admitted to the villa of the important foreign office official, kissing the lady of the house on the cheek, standing by a window in her dressing room, letting out or taking in some darts under her bosom, then, later, sipping tea with her. Her husband would come in and be delighted to see Alfred: such a delightful, amusing fellow, always welcome. Then the official would go to his study, and then – somehow – Alfred would figure out a way to get in.

And I saw him parking his roadster, getting out for his twice-a-week walk in the Grunewald, the forest on the edge of Berlin, humming some tune about champagne. He'd pass a chestnut tree with a knothole in it, and he'd keep strolling along so casually that even someone spying on him would probably have missed seeing him slip the message inside the hole, to be picked up the following day by someone Alfred would never meet. Then, still humming, he'd return to his car and put the nosegay of wild-flowers he'd picked on his walk on top of the dashboard.

Alfred wouldn't be as fascinated with me as I was with him. In fact, he probably wouldn't give a girl like me two minutes. I didn't hold it against him, though. I wasn't his type; I would never go Ooh! over a bolt of silk shantung – although he might be a little intrigued with me when he saw John, because that would make me special. If he met me, he'd probably say, Delighted, although he wouldn't be. I spoke with the accent he'd been trying to hide since he was fourteen.

Still, Alfred meant so much to me. It was as if I *knew* him. Somehow, I felt for him in a way that I'd never felt for all the refugees we'd interviewed; all the Jews – shoe store owners, movie directors, bus drivers, labor union organizers, even a butcher, like my father and grandfather – and all the others who had to get out: Catholic priests, Communists, intellectuals, financiers, journalists.

All that day I'd put Alfred in different places, driving along Unter den Linden, walking along the beach, the Strandbad Wannsee. I'd dress him in different outfits and watch him puffing out sleeves and being a spy.

It wasn't until I was in bed late that night that I realized my newfound friend, the man who had become so alive to me so fast, who was doing the work I admired most in the world was dead. Murdered.

# *Chapter Eighteen*

The Fourth of July fell on a Saturday, and for the first time since we'd been married, we actually took a vacation. It was just for the weekend, to the Eastern Shore of Maryland, but at least I got John to take me somewhere. I wasn't exactly subtle, either. I called him at his office on the third and said, 'Hey, you owe me a honeymoon.'

'Hmm?' he said. He was probably reading a report.

'John, can't we get out of town this weekend?'

He muttered, 'I think Ed said he wanted to work straight through.'

'But I don't. Please. Don't you think I'm entitled to two days?'

And he actually sounded a little guilty when he answered, 'Yes. All right. I'll try to figure out something.'

We stayed at a country inn that was decorated in Early Duck. There were carved ducks – decoys – on every mantel. There were duck doorstops, duck designs on curtains and wallpaper. The innkeeper, who must have been in his eighties, had ducks on his tie, to say nothing of duck designs on every plate, soup bowl, cup and saucer. From our room, we could see over the treetops, to Chesapeake Bay.

'I see a lot of fishing boats,' I said Sunday evening, as we were getting dressed after a last time in a too-soft bed that was probably stuffed with duck feathers.

'Any ducks?' John asked.

'No. Not a single one.'

'I haven't, either. But I think I heard some quacking in the middle of the night.'

'It was probably me, talking in my sleep. The atmosphere gets to you after a while.'

He smiled, then came over and put his arms around me. He was so sweet that weekend that at first I thought he might have got me confused with someone else. But then I thought: Getting out of the office has done wonders for both of us. We took ferry rides, ate every form of oyster and crab known to man, went for long walks, and even talked. I told him all about Sheepshead Bay in Brooklyn, and he told me all about Long Island Sound and how Port Washington, where he'd grown up, had once been called Cow Neck. Okay, so it wasn't 'My darling Linda, I love you madly.' But it was still time together. And it wasn't like weekends at home, when he was editing a brief or reading the paper or listening to Mozart with his eyes closed. I had his full attention, even with my clothes on, and on Saturday night, when we saw *The Pride of the Yankees*, with Gary Cooper and Teresa Wright, we held hands, and he gave me his handkerchief before I even thought to ask for it.

So that Monday afternoon, when John unexpectedly walked into the anteroom outside Edward's office, where I worked, I was still so full of honeymoonish happiness that it didn't occur to me to wonder why he was there. It was just a pleasure to see him. After two days in the sun, his skin had a bronze glow. His fair, silky hair was streaked with pale platinum. He came over, sat on the edge of my desk and took my hand between his. I mumbled something like, 'Ed's over at the War Department,' even though I sensed, with a sudden flush of joy, that he'd come to see me.

'Linda.' His voice was gentle: not caressing, but compassionate. And that minute I understood he'd come to see me for a reason. Something was wrong. 'I had a call from New York.' He squeezed my hand. 'Your mother's nurse . . .'

'My mother?' I asked. It was a real question. I'd spoken to her right before we'd gone off to Maryland. Her voice had been so feeble it shook. She wouldn't let go of the idea that I was still pregnant, but she'd joked about being too young to be a grandmother, and told me to get smart with John and have him buy me a mink stole in the summer, when furriers are desperate for customers and you can pick up a good buy.

John squeezed my hand harder. 'I'm sorry.'

'She died?'

'Yes. In her sleep. The nurse – '

'Cookie.'

'Cookie thought it would be better if I broke the news to you.'

I sat back in my chair; it squeaked. 'I've got to get this thing oiled.' I said to myself, My mother is dead. It made sense, but it didn't mean anything. 'What do I do now?' I asked him.

'I'll take you home so you can pack.'

'Where did they take . . . where is my mother?'

'The doctor arranged for her to be brought to a funeral home, Linda.' John's voice was so sympathetic that for a second I wanted to say, Oh, come off it! It's not like someone died or anything. 'Did she go to a church where she'd want the minister . . .' I nodded. 'We ought to call before we leave, to give him some time.'

'I forget the guy's name. But all the Johnstons get buried in Brooklyn.' I swivelled around in my chair, but it started squeaking again, so I sat still. 'Did you know my mother's maiden name was Johnston? They all have brown eyes – and they're very good-looking. A little short. I guess I never told you about them.' I thought: 'You never asked. 'The men work on the subways. Maintenance men, conductors, but one cousin was a motorman. They looked up to him like he'd gone to Harvard. 'Jim's a motorman!'

Again he said, 'I'm sorry, Linda.'

'It's okay. They're not such a close family, and they're kind of dumb, but they always show up for funerals. I'll have to call one of them.' That's when I started to shake. My whole body started to shiver as if I'd climbed out of a hot bath into a cold room. I hugged myself and rubbed my arms to try and control it, but it only got worse. 'I can't remember any phone numbers,' I said. My voice sounded screechy. 'Do you know where my address book is? The little one, with the alphabet tabs?'

He helped me up and led me towards the door, one hand around my waist, the other steering me by my elbow. 'We'll find it when we get home.' He was so soothing.

I jerked my elbow out of his grasp, went back to my desk and started piling up the folders I'd been working on. John came up beside me, as if to stop me, but I snapped, 'Classified documents. I have to put them in the safe.'

'Of course.'

'You don't have to say "Of course." I'm not going to get hysterical!' I wasn't hysterical, but I was trembling so hard by then that I could barely stand, much less walk. I grabbed up the papers and tried to cross the room. I banged into the safe. 'Oh, damn it, John.'

'It's all right,' he said, his voice patient, tolerant. 'I'll take care of everything.'

And he did. Well, for the next three days, because, as he explained, he couldn't stay away from Washington that long, but he got me home, packed, called Edward to explain I'd be gone, eased me into a cab to Union Station, where – despite the mobs of soldiers and sailors pushing to the ticket windows – he got us a private compartment on the next train to New York. He would even have been willing to talk to me the whole trip. How are you holding up? he'd asked, sitting back, obviously prepared for four hours of hearing the answer, but I'd said, 'Okay, I guess,' and then I fell asleep. When I woke up, the train was in Newark, New Jersey.

In New York, in a hotel that overlooked Central Park, he spoke to the minister again, arranged for a burial service Wednesday morning, and then asked me, very gently, if I wanted to see my mother. When I said yes, he didn't even blink; he took me in a taxi to Hannemann's Funeral Home in Ridgewood.

I gazed down at my mother. The heavy funeral parlor makeup job, with its crimson bow lips and bright rouged cheeks, did nothing to disguise the fact that she had died a sick, wasted woman. Other than the dress Cookie had picked out for her – one of my mother's typical choices, a ridiculous pink gingham pinafore suitable for a fourteen-year-old – there was no sign that this old woman had been a beautiful, sweet-natured, not-too-bright goodtime girl. Her blond hair had turned a dingy white.

She lay in a coffin that had obviously been her son-in-law's choice: a dark, costly wood, but with simple brass handles and plain white satin lining. A casket for a proper citizen; she would have chosen something decorated with gold cherubs and lined in lilac velveteen. And if it had been up to my mother, the coffin would have been covered with a blanket of flowers more appropriate for the winner of the Kentucky Derby. John had chosen a perfect wreath of white flowers that looked like it had been made up by the Leland family florist and probably had been. I didn't ask.

John stood right beside me the entire time, waiting, I guess, for a moan of despair or a shriek of anguish to break out of me, so he could do something – hold me in his arms, lead me away and say, There, there. Once he glanced down at me and said, You're very pale; he may have been expecting a swoon or a faint. But I just stood straight and still, and thought about my mother and father and Olga – and for some reason about Alfred Eckert too. And I asked myself, Who do I really have in the world who loves me?

At last I said, I'm ready, and John led me outside, but not before Mr Hannemann, Jr., came rushing out of his office to hold the door open for us. His voice was thick with respect and courtesy: *So* sorry for your loss, Mrs Berringer. If we can serve you in any other way, I *do* hope you'll call on us. He made it so much worse for me, because his was the tone people in Ridgewood took with important people, and all of a sudden I felt even lonelier. I'd lost the last of my family. I'd become a rich lawyer's wife in expensive shoes, an outsider.

The taxi was waiting outside, meter running, and I asked John, Do you want to see our house? And he said, I really would like to, but we have to get back to Manhattan. You need a dress for the funeral, and I have to go over your mother's papers. I stared at him and he explained, I called Russ Weedcock at the firm and had him send over one of the secretaries to get your mother's papers together. I asked, Which secretary? and he shrugged, with a what-does-it-matter offhandedness. I looked down at my twenty-five dollar black-and-white spectator pumps, which I now knew should only be worn between Decoration Day and Labor Day, and I thought: Where do I belong?

When we got back to the city, John said, I think you should rest.

I'll have Saks send over a few things to the hotel so you don't have to deal with salespeople.

You're being so nice, I said. John, thank you. I appreciate everything you're doing. You're really a wonderful husband. He said, Please . . . Don't be embarrassed, I told him.

John put through a long-distance call to my Aunt Annabel in Seattle. The Johnstons were a little vague about family ties. Forget Christmas cards; my mother had completely lost touch with three of her four sisters. I got on the phone; Aunt Annabel, this is Linda. Betty's daughter. She started crying, and for a minute I thought she'd heard. Then she told me her husband, a navy man, had been killed in June, at Midway. She said, He was on the *Yorktown*, Linda. You hear about it? She cried some more and said her older boy was 4-F, but the younger one was a midshipman on the USS *Saratoga*. His name's Lester, she said, and then, without taking a breath, she asked, Did Betty die? Yes, I told her. She told me she was sorry and to send her love to everybody when I saw them at the funeral.

That night we had room service. Um, John said, your mother didn't leave a will. I answered, Estate planning was never her strong point. He went on: Her only assets were the house and a very small bank account. I looked up from my steak: You thought you were marrying an heiress? No, he said. I just wanted to keep you informed . . . as your attorney. Actually, I've asked Russ to handle whatever has to be handled. Is that all right with you? I told him sure, it was fine.

The bad part of being a working girl – and an old maid – is that you learn to do things for yourself, so when a husband finally comes along, you forget to be fluttery and helpless. This was the first time John had really done anything for me.

When we got into bed I said, You're so good at everything. He said, You don't have to if you don't want to, and then I realized he thought I was talking about sex. I pressed up against him. No, I want to, I said. But hold me for a while first. He put his arms around me, but since neither of us was wearing anything, it took much less than a while. He climbed on top of me and I ran my fingers down his back, over his behind and then lower. Oh, Jesus, he groaned. You do it to me every time. Linda, I can't take it. I moved my hand away and let my fingers drift down the backs of his thighs.

Want me to stop? I asked.

No. Oh, Christ, do it some more.

I love you.

Do it more.

Okay. 'Do it more' wasn't French for 'I love you.' But that night I went to sleep with more hope than I'd ever had since my marriage. John had been so tender, so decent. Not just since my mother died; even the biggest crumb in the world can manage to act appropriately for a couple of days when there's a death in the family. But he'd been so wonderful during the weekend in Maryland.

As I fell asleep, I only wished the change in John had happened one week sooner, so I would have had time to call my mother and say, Hey, Mom. You were wrong about him. He's really a good man. And I think he's learning to love me.

' "I am the resurrection and the life: he that believeth in me, yea, though he were dead, yet shall he live." '

The Reverend Bradley Norris of Brooklyn, the burier of Johnstons, had a voice that sounded like Cecil B. De Mille's in a coming attraction for *The Sign of the Cross*: resounding, important, slightly British. But he was a very old man, probably close to eighty, and pretty frail. And poor. His black suit was so worn it had a silver shine. He kept squinting in the blinding July sunlight and losing his place in the prayerbook.

' "The Lord giveth, and the Lord taketh away. Even as it hath pleased the Lord, so cometh . . . so cometh . . ." '

One of the cousins – I think her name was Etta – shouted out, ' " . . . so cometh things to pass"!'

I flashed her an angry look, but the Reverend Norris was either one of the genuinely meek or he was too old for outrage. He just brought the prayerbook up closer to his nose and continued, ' "Blessed be the name of the Lord." '

It was hot in that Brooklyn cemetery. The grass around the

tombstones had large, parched patches, and a lot of the earth dug up around my mother's grave was dry. I couldn't make myself look down into the grave, even though we were standing pretty near the edge.

John had his arm around my shoulder, both for comfort and for support, but I didn't feel I was going to lose control. I looked out at the cousins – more than twenty had come – and even though they were my family, I hardly knew half their names. They were a group of strangers who knew 'The Order for the Burial of the Dead' the way I knew 'The Star-Spangled Banner.' I felt like an outsider at a ceremony for a member of a club I didn't belong to.

And yet the weird thing was, when I looked out over that cluster of Johnstons, I knew I was in the club. I could see my mother's features in so many faces – a couple of them as beautiful as hers had once been. And I even saw variations of myself there: my hair on Ralph, Agatha and a boy of about seventeen; my exact eyes – the precise shade of brown and even the straight lashes that I bet were also immune to an eyelash curler – on a former Johnston who'd introduced herself as Lorna, although in her Brooklyn accent, a hundred times thicker than mine, which John had to control himself from shuddering from, it sounded more like Lawww-na.

The minister droned on: ' "Man that is born of a woman hath but a short time to live. He cometh up and is cut down like a flower . . ." '

John whispered, 'How are you doing?'

'Fine.' But I pressed against him even more. The relatives had obviously heard about John, and it was just as obvious by the way they were gaping at everything from the part in his hair to his perfectly polished shoes that they were awed, except for one of them, whose name I didn't catch. She'd taken him aside while we were waiting for the Reverend Norris and asked him if he would sue her dry cleaner for her because he'd ruined her husband's overcoat. John told her he was sorry, but he was in Washington now and wasn't practicing law in New York. Don't worry, she said, I'll *pay* you, and when he told her he couldn't, she looked disgusted.

' "In the midst of life we be in death." ' I thought: Come on. In

Brooklyn? But then I thought: In Berlin. ' "Of whom may we seek for succor but thee, Oh Lord, which for our sins justly art displeased." ' Alfred, I said to myself, this funeral's for you too. I bet you didn't have one. And so, as the minister went on, I translated a few sentences into German in my head for Alfred. ' " . . . ashes to ashes, dust to dust, in sure and certain hope of resurrection to eternal life . . ." ' I thought, still in German: Alfred, I hope it's not only eternal; I hope it's beautiful and elegant, the way you like it. ' "Death, where is thy sting? Hell, where is thy victory?" '

The Reverend Norris intoned: ' "Lord have mercy on us." ' I thought again about my mother and hoped that for her, heaven would be a rose-covered honeymoon cottage where my father would be waiting. And for my Grandma Olga – But at that very instant the minister proclaimed, ' "Christ have mercy on us." ' I said Whoops! to myself, put Olga off, and instead said silently, 'Bye, Mom. At last, the Reverend Norris said, ' "Lord have mercy upon us," ' again.

But I guess I'd already mourned Olga and my father enough, because instead of giving them their turn, I thought about the men and women and even little kids who'd been shot and burned and bombed in the lousy, goddamn war. Slaughtered. And that's when I wept. O Lord, I thought, have mercy on us.

John asked, Are you sure you'll be all right? The limousine he'd hired for the funeral pulled up in front of my mother's house. His eyes widened for a second, but then he composed his face into a bland expression, as if this was the sort of house he saw all the time. Through his eyes I suddenly saw the sagging roof and the tape on the windows where they'd cracked, and that's when I realized we had been poor.

I inched forward to the car door, but the damp black silk of my dress stuck to the back seat. He went on: Linda, I hate leaving you like this, but I have to get back to Washington. He kissed me softly on the eyes, and the driver slid out silently to get my suitcase from the trunk.

I tried to sound reassuring. Don't worry. I'll be fine. What I really wanted was for him to say, 'Oh, the hell with the OSS!' and stay with me. John kissed my fingers. I'll call you every night, he said, and if it gets to be too much, let me know. I'll come back. But I just gave him a final kiss goodbye, got out of the car and watched it as it pulled away, like a big, black yacht, and eased down the street toward Manhattan and Penn Station.

I thought I'd just sit in the kitchen and stare out the window at the Knauers' elm tree that afternoon, but instead I took off my heels and went to work on my mother's room. After six hours, all I could salvage from the mess of her life was her wedding ring, a gold bracelet, a picture of her and my father on the boardwalk in Atlantic City, and the silliest of her dresses – a slinky purple thing with two giant roses of the same fabric sewed onto each bust.

In one of my mother's galoshes I found an empty pint of gin; there was lipstick around the neck of the bottle.

Her medicine cabinet was worse than her closet. Aspirin and Bromo Seltzer were hidden behind lipsticks, tins of rouge, boxes of powder and eye shadows. An open cake of mascara had dried and crumbled years before, so a fine layer of black powder covered everything.

John called around ten. He was in the office. Everything's all right, he reported. Just the usual catastrophes. Are you managing, Linda? I'm fine, I assured him, and he asked, Would you forgive me if I cut you short now? I have hours of work here. I said of course, and we kissed each other goodnight on the phone.

The next day, I worked and I waited. The real estate man came, looked over the house and said he thought I could get two thousand dollars for it. Try for three, I said. Look, Mrs . . . he said dubiously. He was a slick man in a suit too dapper for Queens and an Errol Flynn mustache. I gave him Russell Weedcock's name and telephone number and said to him, My attorney. He'll be handling the negotiations and the closing for me.

After he left, I went into the living room. I realized that for all the years I'd lived in that house, my vision had conveniently blurred. Now I saw how bedraggled everything was. The brown wool on the couch and the chairs had worn away completely in spots. White upholstery stuffing sprouted in little bumps on the seats and arms. One of the lamps was cracked, another chipped, and the lampshades themselves were threadbare and had brown burn marks from too-strong light bulbs. The little end tables I'd remembered as being pretty weren't pretty at all; they were so flimsy that they shook if you put anything as heavy as a glass of water on their surfaces.

I turned away and went to the kitchen. It was in order – sparkling clean, in fact. Since my mother never ate, Cookie only had to cook for herself, but she'd cleaned, after a fashion; the faucets glittered like just-polished silver, although the corners of the floor were probably not meant to be noticed. Cookie had also bought: The pantry was crammed with row after row of canned candied yams, fruit cocktail, liver paste spread, and there were five large boxes of White Rose tea. I was fixing my lunch, cold candied yams and iced tea, when the doorbell rang.

'Coming!'

I wiped my hands on the white cotton butcher apron I was wearing, one my father had brought home from the plant, and hurried to the front door. It wasn't the gas meter reader. It was Gladys Slade.

'I . . . I hope you don't mind,' she said. She held out a manila envelope. 'Your mother's deed. Um, Mr Weedcock says it's in order. He was going to send Mildred Treacher, a new girl, but I said . . . well, I said I'd come because—' She was overheated, nervous, her too-white face wet with perspiration, like a glistening hard-boiled egg; her dress, her best, a green faille with a white lace collar, was meant for a Christmas dinner, not an errand on a blistering July afternoon.

'Come in, Gladys.' I held the door opened wide.

'Oh, no. I don't want to intrude – but I want to say – I am sorry for your loss.' Her speech was so jerky that I knew she'd memorized it, but she was so fidgety it was obvious she'd forgotten two or three sentences.

I took her by the arm and pulled her inside. 'Hey, stop talking to me like I'm Mrs Berringer. I'm Linda. Sit down.' Hesitantly, as if waiting for me to bark, What do you think you're doing? she inched into the living room. 'How are you?' I asked.

'Fine.'

'Want some iced tea?'

'No, thank you.' She was inspecting the room: the tables, chairs, curtains. 'It's a nice house. Very homey.' I guess I had become accustomed to living in John's world, because for a second I thought she was being sarcastic. But then I remembered her single rented room up two steep flights of stairs in a stranger's house. Gladys was gazing up, above the couch, at a picture of a field of red and pink tulips with a windmill in the background. It was framed, but without glass. In tiny letters on the lower right it said: Compliments of Roscoe & Schmidt Meat Packers 1908 Chicago. It had been a wedding gift from my father's boss. 'That's a beautiful picture.'

'Thanks.' If John had seen it, he'd have smiled, a compassionate it's-so-pathetically-predictably-tasteless smile, full of pity and superiority. But Gladys was drawn to it as if it was the Garden of Eden. 'Sit down, Gladys.'

'I don't want to interrupt.'

'Please. There's nothing to interrupt.' She sat stiffly, as I figured she would, on the edge of the couch. She'd come to see what I'd become, and probably also to find out if I'd given up the secrets of lunch, if I'd sat at parties with lawyers, regaling them with tales of their star-struck (lawyer-struck) secretaries. But seeing me in my high-priced black dress under the butcher's apron, my silk stockings, my expensive haircut, my wedding ring, she couldn't ask. 'How have you been, Gladys?'

'Fine.' She clasped her hands tight over her patent-leather pocketbook.

'How are all the girls?'

'Fine.'

'Lenny?'

'Fine.' She looked away from me, up at the tulips.

'Marian?'

'Fine.'

'Wilma?' She shrugged. 'Oh, come on, Gladys. I've never said a word about anything. You can tell me what's going on.' She glanced around, as if still expecting to be encircled by cops, ready to arrest her if she opened her mouth. 'I can see it in your face. There's some news about Wilma! How can you possibly hold back on me?'

It took her a minute, but finally she breathed: 'Fired!'

'She was fired? No! By Mr Post?'

'None other than. Actually . . . I *knew* it was going to happen.'

'How?' I sat down beside her. I was dying to hear everything, and she knew it.

'Well, all of a sudden he started going home at six on the dot.'

'You think Mrs Post gave him an ultimatum?'

'No.'

'No?'

'Wilma did!'

'You're kidding!'

'No. After she saw what happened to you . . . You know. Getting married. At lunch one day, we were talking about you . . .' She lowered her head.

'Listen, it's okay. If I was there, I'd talk about me too.'

Gladys, unthinking, put her hand on mine. 'So Wilma says, real sure of herself, "Who says lightning don't strike twice in the same place? There could be other bosses who find certain other secretaries definite marriage material." Anyway, two days later, Mr Post is rushing out at six, with his briefcase packed. And by the end of the next week . . . Well, at least he got her another job. At Dahlmaier Brothers, the investment – Oh! You know about them.'

'I say a little prayer of thanks to Quentin Dahlmaier every night. Hey, remember when Lenny found out about him? God, that seems a hundred years ago.'

'Linda?'

'What?'

'I'm sorry. I mean about how things wound up with us.'

'I'm sorry too, Gladys.' There was a silence that was comfortable for a couple of seconds, but it stretched out too long. I could feel her yearning to ask: 'What's it like? Being married. Being married to *him*. Going to lawyer parties. Being rich. Is it everything we always dreamed about? But I realized I didn't have any answers, not for her, not for me. So instead I asked, 'What about Anita Beane? Did she and Herbie get married?'

Gladys sat up straight. 'You mean you didn't hear?'

'No! What happened? Tell me.'

And she did, for two hours.

When we finally said goodbye, we both had tears in our eyes. And she had the picture of the tulip field tucked under her arm.

Late that afternoon, I went into Olga's room. I'd gone through it soon after she died, but now, while I waited for the janitor from the Lutheran House for the Aged on the other side of Ridgewood to come and pick up the furniture (the Salvation Army had turned me down when I'd described what I wanted to give them, but the Lutherans were clearly having a bad year), I went into my grandmother's room again.

There was nothing except her narrow, stripped-down bed, an armchair and a nightstand. For some reason, I opened the two small doors under the drawer of the stand. It looked empty, but I felt around and discovered a pile of papers neatly tied with string. They turned out to be about a hundred different recipes Olga had clipped from her favorite German newspaper. *Salat von Geräuchertem Aal*, smoked eel salad; *Zwetschgenknödel*, plum dumplings – she'd taught me to make them. I groped some more and found another pile. Letters, all yellowed, some so old they were falling apart, all written in the thin, spidery penmanship that was taught to girls in German schools. I realized they must have been from Olga's cousins in Berlin. They'd probably been corresponding since she left Germany with my grandfather, in the late 1880s. But then I looked closely. One of the letters wasn't a letter but a folded piece of parchment. I opened it up carefully and saw it was written in foreign letters that I was sure were Hebrew. I couldn't get a clue to what it was, but I folded it back with the letters and put everything in my suitcase.

It's so sad I can't even cry, I told John that night when he called. There's nothing left of my old life. I'm sorry, he said.

Friday was a bad day. There was nothing to do but call Con Edison and Brooklyn Union Gas and Russell Weedcock, and then wait for all of them to call me back. That night John said, When do you think you'll be home? I'm not used to being without you. I told him that I'd probably have to stay through Monday or Tuesday, because Russell had papers for me to sign and I had to have an extra key made to give to the real estate man. I miss you so much, I told him. Linda, he answered, I know it's not easy, but get all the ends tied up, so you don't have to go back. Listen: I have an idea. Call me when you're ready to leave, let me know what train you'll be on, and I'll pick you up at the station. If you can get in about six or seven, I could come right from the office . . . and then we'll go out to a restaurant. I don't want you having to cook on your first night back.

That night, in my old bed, I yearned for John. The desire was as strong and powerful as it had been two and a half years earlier, when I'd been his old-maid secretary. But the difference was that now I knew what I was missing.

So at six o'clock the next morning, I slipped my key and a note under the door of the real estate office, took a subway to Penn Station and then a train back to Washington. I got home in time for lunch, but I knew John would be at work. Still, I figured I'd have time for a nice long bath, and then I could go to his office. Surprise him. I did.

# *Chapter Nineteen*

John wasn't at his office. As I came through the front door, I heard classical music playing full blast. I put down my suitcase, smiled and walked into the living room. There was John stretched out on the couch. And in his arms was Nan Leland Berringer Dahlmaier.

'Oh, God!' They pulled apart. John sat up straight, stared at me for less than a second and then hung his head. I kept staring at him, wanting him to meet my eyes again. I couldn't make myself look at Nan, but I sensed her inching across the couch, toward the safety of its big arm. But my mind wasn't on her. More than anything, I wanted to see John's face, but all I could see was his hair. 'What can I say?' he breathed.

'You're really a wonderful guy, John,' I said. What a clear voice! I felt cool then, or at least in control. But a moment later, anger came upon me so suddenly and with such force that it was as if I was being attacked by a gang of toughs, kicked, punched. I could hardly breathe; I kept trying to gasp for air, but every time I did, my throat made a high-pitched squeal, like the cry of a helpless baby animal.

He'd abandoned me at the very moment when I most needed a friend. He'd betrayed me. Toyed with me that weekend in Maryland. I had been stupid enough to believe that his tenderness, his kindness, had risen out of love. Well, I thought, I guess it did. Love for Nan.

I turned to her then. She was scrunched up in a corner of the couch, clutching the arm. Her head was lowered too, but in terror, quivering, as if expecting that any second I'd pull a gun or rush over and start to pummel her. 'Oh, stop it!' I said. She looked up.

I thought to myself: All she inherited is good bones. Not her father's guts, not her mother's spirit. Her face was ashen – a close match to her perfectly cut beige linen dress. I couldn't think of anything else to do, so I jerked my thumb toward the door and said to her, 'Out!'

John lifted up his head. 'Please,' he said. 'Don't be angry with Nan. It's all my fault.'

'No,' Nan interrupted. 'It's my fault.' She had her father's eyes, and though they weren't as black or as brooding, they were compelling – bright and dark at the same time. 'I know I can't ask your forgiveness, Linda . . . May I call you Linda?' I just glared. That shut her up for a minute, but then she said, 'The last thing I want in this world – and I know I speak for John too – is to hurt you. This entire situation—'

'I want you to leave now,' I told her. Somehow I was polite. Like in the movies, when you say: Madam, would you please remove your hat. '*Now.*'

'Please. Hear me out. I know all three of us are in a state of shock, but personally, I feel a . . . a moral imperative—'

The politeness evaporated. I bellowed, 'You're pushing your luck!' I took a step toward her, around the coffee table, which had their two cups and saucers and the morning papers spread on it. My shin smashed into the table, but I didn't feel a thing. The dishes rattled hysterically. Then I took another step.

And Nan Leland Etc. Etc. was out the front door in five seconds flat.

For me, there were no tears, no screaming, no enraged slamming of doors. As for John, he just sat there. I stared down at the cups; there was just enough left in them to reveal that she, too, took her coffee black.

'I'm sorry,' he finally said.

'Sorry about what? Being caught? Or betraying me?'

'Both, I suppose,' he said softly.

'Sorry that you didn't go chasing after her when she ran out the door? You want to run down to the corner? She didn't have a chance to call a taxi.'

For a second, he shifted and glanced out the front window. But then he looked back at me. 'Could you sit down? We have to talk.'

I sat in the rocking chair that was across from him. I waited, but he just looked at the rug. 'You asked me to sit down. You said we have to talk.' John didn't say a word. 'Look, you're trying to come up with a brilliant presentation of the facts in your case. Forget it. You don't have a case. You're a cheat and a liar and a first-class son of a bitch. Those are the facts.'

He looked up. 'I won't argue with you.'

'When did it start?'

'In May. She came to Washington the end of May. But it wasn't what you think.'

'Come on. I bet it was. She came to visit Daddy and cry about Quentin, but maybe Daddy got a little impatient with her. And so she called you because she needed a friend. A sympathetic friend. Neither of you had any intention whatsoever of letting it go any further than that.' All of a sudden, I reached out and swept the cups and saucers off the table and onto the rug. A cup hit the table leg and the handle broke off. John pretended nothing had happened. 'How am I doing, John? Did I guess right?'

'I suppose . . .' he said, staring at the handle. 'If you want to look at it superficially.'

'How am I supposed to look at adultery? Deeply?'

'What I mean is, it's not as simple as you make it out to be.'

'So tell me, what is it? Go ahead, be profound, if that makes you happy. But I want you to try and understand one thing – something you've never understood before.'

'What?'

'I'm as smart as you are. Probably smarter. So don't try handing me a line of bull about poor motherless Nan or about two intellects that beat as one. I just want to know what happened. Who, what, where and when.' I kicked a saucer away from my shoe. 'I don't care about why.'

'We had drinks a couple of times.' He rubbed his hands together as if he was warming them over a fire. 'She just talked about her marriage.'

'Which one?'

'Please, Linda. She was unhappy with Quentin right from the beginning. He treated her like . . . like some . . . some object he'd purchased for his collection.'

'That must be some prize collection.'

'You're not making it easy for me.'

'I've made it very easy for you. Keep going. When did you start playing house?'

'Do you have to put it that way?'

'What would you rather have? A word starting with *f*?' My heart was racing, and once again, I couldn't get enough air.

'Ed went up to New York for a weekend the first week of June. I stayed with her. Is that what you want to hear?'

'But you came home every night.'

'Yes.'

'And you never stopped . . . You were having sex with her and with me?'

'Yes.'

'Why?' He didn't answer. 'Okay, I'm asking. *Why*?'

'Because I didn't want you to suspect.'

'So you did it to me out of kindness?'

'No.' He stopped rubbing his hands and began to wring them. 'I didn't want to . . . to give up everything I had with you.'

'Which is what?'

'Sex.'

'Sex and what else?' He didn't answer. My heart, which had been pounding much too fast, suddenly skipped a beat. I thought: Wouldn't it be funny if I had a heart attack and died? But I made myself go on. 'What else do you have with me besides sex that you don't want to give up?'

'Nothing.' He swallowed. 'I'm sorry, but you seem to want the truth.'

'Yes.' The truth, I'd been positive, as we held hands over a bowl of oyster stew in Maryland, and later that same evening when he lit the hurricane lamp in our room so we could watch each other's pleasure by candlelight, the truth was that he was falling in love with me. I could have sworn I'd seen it even in that dim, flickering light.

If my heart hadn't been thudding against my chest and if I hadn't been breathing deeper and deeper until I was dizzy, fighting for air, I would have thought I was dead. Because I felt nothing. Absolute emptiness. I said, 'So what happens now?'

'I don't know.'

'Do you move out? Do I move out? You're the lawyer. What's the next step?' I couldn't believe part of me was still able to talk. 'Do I hire a private detective? Or do I just go upstairs and find Nan's nightie on the bed and bring it into court?' He looked toward the stairs. I waved an imaginary frilly thing in the air. 'Here's Exhibit A, Your Honor.' I thought he was going to faint; I felt a little better. 'Come on, John. How do we get divorced? You must have talked to her about' – I deepened my voice – 'the Future. She must be waiting. She's not hanging around Washington all summer because she's crazy about humidity.'

'She's waiting.'

'For what?'

'For me to come to a decision.'

I broke out into a loud laugh. Who could help it? 'You've been stringing *her* along?'

'It's not a matter of stringing anyone along.'

'Sure it is. You're playing with her. You're getting back at her for leaving you. "Nan," ' I imitated him, ' "you left me. Did you truly believe your unmitigated insensitivity to be without consequences?" How's that?'

'Not bad.'

'Tell me what to do, John. Do I go to a lawyer?'

'Only if you want to divorce me.'

'And what do you want?'

'I don't know. I love Nan. I've never stopped loving her. I know how that must hurt—'

'It's wonderful how you're both so worried about hurting me. Look, just tell me what you want, for God's sake. Do you want to marry her again?'

'Part of me does.'

'Which part? The top part?' He put his hands in his lap. 'But the bottom part still's got the itch for me. Is that it?'

'I suppose so.'

'It's that good with me?'

'I think . . . that's fairly obvious.'

'Is it that bad with her?'

'Linda, I won't discuss that.'

'That wouldn't be honorable.'

'That's right.'

'And you're a man of honor.' He turned and peered out the window. 'Now listen to me. I'm a fool for you. We both know that. But I'm not a complete fool. I won't wait around while you resolve the conflict between your top and your bottom halves. If you really love her, then marry her.' I smiled. 'She's what – twenty-three? And she'll be Nan Leland Berringer Dahlmaier Berringer. I can't wait to see her notepaper when she's thirty.'

'Oh,' John said. 'Do you think she'd leave me again?'

'What do *you* think?'

'I don't know.' He took a deep breath. 'But I do know I'm not . . . quite ready to leave you.'

'Why not? For twenty bucks, you can get someone to do whatever I do, and you won't have to take them to dinner parties.'

'It's not just sex.'

'Two minutes ago you said it was.'

'I feel a moral obligation to you.'

'It's canceled. And listen: I know half the reason you're even thinking of staying is that you're worried you'd look bad – a heel, or a patsy for Nan. But don't worry. Just tell them I was this grasping, conniving bitch who broke up your marriage and that when you didn't give me a mink and a diamond tiara I ran off with a cardsharp from Canarsie. You know what the beauty of it is? All your friends will believe it!'

'Linda, stop.' He gave me one of the tender looks he'd given me on the shores of the Chesapeake, and in the cemetery in Brooklyn. 'I know you love me.'

'So? What does that mean? Did it stop you from going to bed

with Nan? From telling her you loved her? Did my loving you ever once get you to look at me like I'm a human being who has meaning outside the bedroom . . . who has dignity, goddamn it!' I stood up. 'You make love to her. You *talk* to her.' I started to get a picture in my mind, John and Nan, afterward, draped with sheets, conversing, smiling, nodding at each other's astuteness. In my imagination, the bed was so vast it went on into infinity. 'Where did you do it?' I demanded.

'I don't think it's an appropriate—'

'Here?'

'Just these past few days. Two or three times in a hotel. But usually in her father's house.'

'Oh, that's terrific. I'm breaking my back working for her old man till nine, ten, every night so you can have plenty of time for hot stuff in Georgetown.' Suddenly, I felt horribly sick, as if I was going to start to heave and heave and not be able to stop. 'Was Ed in on this?' I managed to say. John didn't answer. 'Damn it, was he keeping me there nights so you and his little girl—'

'No! Of course not. But he knew, naturally.'

'Oh, naturally.'

'Linda, he's a man of the world. He suspected early on—'

'He's known since when? Late May?'

'I don't know. Since early June, anyway. He made it clear to Nan then that he disapproved. More than disapproved. And last week, he asked her to leave his house, practically ordered her to go back to her . . .'

'Her husband.'

'Yes. The . . . situation has soured my relationship with him. More than soured it. Destroyed it, I think.' If John had looked uncomfortable and unhappy before, he looked miserable now. There was a catch in his voice when he talked about Edward, almost like tears in his throat. 'Not that he's said anything to me. But it's obvious he thinks it's all . . . unseemly. He's very distant to me.'

'Do you think she'll listen to her father, go back to Quentin?'

'Only if I . . .'

I finished his sentence. 'If you don't want her back.'

'Yes.'

'Well, you have a week to decide.'

'A week? It's my *life* you're talking about.'

'Listen to me. If you walk out on me, do you know what you'll have? A wife – and you don't even have to buy new monogrammed pillowcases. A profession. Friends with country houses and sailboats. A roof over your head. A place in the world.'

'Linda, there would be alimony.'

'John, alimony is money. If you walk out on me, what else will I have?' He looked down, to his summer-white shoes. 'So do you think I'm going to sit around for six weeks or six months watching for hopeful little signs? Praying that maybe you'll find something of value in me? And do you think I'm going to be able to stand having you touch me when you get home late, not knowing if what you're doing to me is the same thing you did to her a half hour before?'

'I wouldn't—'

'You would. You have. Okay, you're a stylish kind of guy. You probably took a shower in between. But there's not going to be any more in betweens. It's her or me. Choose.'

He chose me. He chose me because two days later, Nan chartered a plane and went back to Quentin. I asked myself, did she do it because the whole episode was so tawdry and not to her taste, or because she'd had her fun playing off one husband against the other, or because she'd had enough passion for the time being and wanted to go back to a man with three houses, a dozen servants and a seat on the board of trustees of the New York Philharmonic?

It was pretty easy to figure she hadn't flown back to Southampton, Long Island, because she was afraid John would choose me. Even in her panic she hadn't lost her wits, and I guessed that huddling in that corner of the couch, she'd still been able to appraise me – and to determine there wasn't anything much beyond my face value.

Listen, I said to him the night she left. Even if she's gone for good, you're not stuck with me. It's like what they say in car advertisements: Now's the perfect time to trade me in for a new model. Or just unload me.

Linda, please don't talk like that. We're married.

We've been married for two years, I said. What if she changes her mind again? What if she wants you back?

It's over, he assured me. His voice was quiet, firm, sincere. Well, at least he had the sense not to swear on his honor.

I didn't go back to work until the following Monday. Officially, I was in mourning. Unofficially, I was sad about my mother and, even more, depressed that I was alone, with no more family. I didn't count the Johnstons, because they appeared so infrequently, and only in black. And when I read the letters I'd found in Olga's room and brought back to Washington with me, I knew I'd probably never see the writers. They were two sisters, Liesl and Hannah Weiss. They'd never married. They lived in the same apartment in Berlin and wrote interminably long, misspelled, ungrammatical letters about events like Cousin Manfred's wedding to one of the Geist girls, with unending descriptions of the bride's dress and how chewy the hen was.

The correspondence had probably lasted over thirty-five years, and in that time, Liesl complained about the weather a lot, and Hannah about her teeth – eventually, her dentures. But in none of the letters was there any clue that they were Jews, and no indication that Hitler's coming to power had any effect on their lives – except for one sentence. In Hannah's last letter, postmarked February 23, 1937, she wrote: 'As you can imagine, our life is not so happy as it once was.'

I knew it wasn't. On Sunday night, John glanced up from a report he was reading. Listen to this, he said. After the end of the year, Jews won't be permitted to own pets anymore; they'll have to turn them in to dog pounds, and they'll be destroyed because they're tainted by Jewish blood. I couldn't speak. John didn't notice. He just went on: There's no limit to this insanity. I mean, I can understand someone not wanting to live next door to them, but this . . . And to kill *dogs*. He shook his head. Then he went back to the report and asked me to make him a glass of iced tea.

And also unofficially, I didn't go back to work because I didn't want to face Edward. That whole week I kept waking up three or four times during the night. I'd relive walking in on John and Nan, and think about all the clever or brutal things I could have said. Eventually, I'd fall back asleep. But when I thought of Edward's knowing about the two of them practically from the beginning – and how all that time I'd been talking to him so privately, giving over my life – then I'd be up, shivering in the Washington heat, for the rest of the night.

I knew, unofficially, that he'd talked to me in a way he'd never talked to anyone else – about Caroline, and about other things: How he felt like such a hick when he first went to Yale and no one wanted to bother with him, and how he had to force himself to stay and not run away, back to the farm. And how when he was recuperating in the hospital after all the operations on his face and shoulder, he couldn't understand why he didn't hear from his kid sister; he wrote and wrote, but it wasn't until he got home that his mother told him she'd died from polio a year before. He said he'd felt deceived in the cruelest way; someone who hadn't wanted to hurt him had caused him the greatest pain.

Well, old buddy, I wanted to tell him now, I know just what you mean. Because in this whole world, you were the closest I had to a friend – and you deceived me in the cruelest way.

'Linda,' Edward said. He stood, walked around his desk and came up beside me. He put his hand on my shoulder. 'I was so sorry to hear about your mother.'

I pulled myself back, so his hand dropped off. 'Thank you.' I thought: For a whole month you knew, and you didn't give me a clue. You could have said, I've been pretty busy lately, with Nan in town. Or if you're telling me the whole damn story of your life, forget your economics professor who took you into the bosom of his family and gave you warmth and sherry in New Haven, and instead drop me a hint that your daughter and Husband II may have had a bit of a tiff. That's all it would have taken, Ed, my friend.

'It must have been a double blow,' he said. 'She was the last of your immediate family, wasn't she?'

'I really don't feel like talking about it.'

'All right. I understand.'

He did, a second later. All of a sudden, we had one of our flashes of tacit understanding. We were looking at each other, and just like that, he stiffened. He knew that I knew – not only about John and Nan but about his knowledge of the whole business. The whole affair. Then Edward did what I never thought I'd see him do: He averted his eyes. Suddenly, a telephone message on the edge of his desk became overwhelmingly important. He picked it up and studied it as if it was a new cryptographic code he was just getting familiar with.

'Excuse me,' I said. 'I've got to get to work. That girl you had sitting in for me left about three days' worth of dictation to transcribe, and her shorthand's a mess.'

He put the piece of paper back down. 'Linda,' he began. Then his voice fell, and I had to strain to hear him. 'I don't know what to say, but I want to say something. I—'

'Thanks for your condolences.' And then I walked out of the room.

I became an efficient machine. For days I followed Edward to meetings, took dictation, answered phones, typed, translated. The line of refugees streaming on, offering up information, grew longer and longer. The anteroom where I worked was packed with people on folding chairs, chalky-faced people who never looked right into anyone's eyes – not mine, not each other's. They studied the floor, or their shoes.

When Edward was ready for the next one, I'd say, 'Frau Schluter [or: Herr Abendroth], please follow me.' And they'd shuffle inside, staring down at the floor like it was a treacherous path that might crack open, engulf them and then smash shut, crushing them so they couldn't even shriek for help before they were obliterated forever. For every one of them, I'd think: Poor lady, Poor guy, as I steered them over to the couch. Because Edward would never just question them, seeking out whatever intelligence he needed; he always wanted to know what had happened to them. So when I translated their unbearably sad stories, I'd think: Terrible. But it was the automatic pity of a machine. Tsk-tsk. Next. Tsk-tsk.

But then, a week after I went back to work, I led Werner Liedtke into Edward's office. He'd worked for the electric utility in Berlin, dispatching meter readers all over the city: an ordinary man, but one who might confirm or challenge the information we'd been getting on power generating plants all over northern Germany.

'Would you like some coffee?' Edward asked him. Herr Liedtke, who had come into Philadelphia two days before on a boat full of refugees, didn't speak any English, so I translated as I took notes.

'No, thank you,' he said. 'No coffee.' He gazed down at his shoes. New shoes, American, maybe a little too wide for him.

'The government of the United States appreciates your co-operation in coming here today. We know it must be difficult to talk about what you have just left, but we need all the details, all the facts, we can get.'

'Thank you, sir,' Herr Liedtke mumbled.

'And it is urgent that we get whatever information we can on power generation as soon as possible, before conditions change.'

'Yes, sir.'

'Did you come here alone?'

'Yes. Alone.'

'Do you have any family still in Germany?'

'My family . . . My brothers. A sister.'

'Are you Jewish?'

'Oh, no. Not me.' He pulled back his feet and hunched over, as if trying to make himself smaller, less of a target. 'My wife. She was a Jew. They took her in 1940. May 18. Gestapo came to the apartment and said, "Ruth Liedtke?" and she said "Yes." '

'And they took her then?' Edward asked softly.

'Yes.'

'You never saw her again?'

'No.'

I thought to myself: How many of these pathetic stories did Edward want to hear? 'Did you have any children?' he asked.

'A boy.'

'What is his name?' Herr Liedtke shook his head. 'I'm sorry,' Edward said. 'I won't ask you any more—'

I was translating almost simultaneously, and so we were both interrupted when Herr Liedtke said, 'Jurgen. His name was Jurgen,' he said to his new American shoes.

'I see,' Edward said.

'No. He was not taken when they took my wife. After that . . . nothing happened. I waited, but a long time passed and I knew . . . I thought: Jurgen is safe. He was allowed to go to school. No questions were asked. He was a good boy. Twelve, he was. He'd been a little fat, but he was growing, you know, so he grew more lean, except his face was round.'

'He sounds very nice,' Edward said. 'A fine boy.'

'Yes. A fine boy.' The father shook his head. His hair was gray. He had a bald spot the size of a silver dollar. 'There was a roundup of Jews the last week of June. I didn't fear very much. But suddenly they were at the door, banging on it, kicking with their boots, terrible noise, and they ask for Jurgen and I show them the boy and say, "Look, he is no . . ." And I show them his papers. "See?" I said. There were two of them. They each took an arm and dragged Jurgen out, down four flights of stairs. I ran after, and all the time he was screaming, "Father!" And they dragged him over to a small bus and tried to put him on and I ran to him and he was screaming and they told him to shut up and get on, but still he was screaming. "Father!" '

Herr Liedtke spoke in a monotone, and I tried to translate like that, but I called out 'Father!' too loud.

Herr Liedtke said ' "Father!" ' again, quietly, but his hands stretched out, involuntarily, reaching for his son. 'A soldier came down off the bus. Not Gestapo. An ordinary soldier with a rifle. A rifle with a bayonet. And Jurgen struggled with the men holding him, trying to break away, and all the time screaming for me, and I ran toward him, but before I could get there . . .' He lifted up his head and looked into Edward's eyes. 'The soldier – just a regular soldier – he drove the bayonet into Jurgen's throat. To silence him.' Herr Liedtke touched his Adam's apple with his index finger. 'There was blood, so much of it, and his mouth said

"Father," but he could not speak. And he could not . . . he could not die yet. He was in agony. Oh, his eyes. My boy's eyes, crying for me to help him, then looking down . . . at the thing in his throat. He didn't believe . . . He kept waiting for me to help him.' Herr Liedtke's eyes were dry.

I turned in my chair, so I could look out the window, hide my face. Edward said, 'Linda?'

'I'm fine,' I said. I could see that nice, fat-faced boy, howling in terror, making no sound. My shoulders jerked. A shudder. A convulsion. A machine breaking down.

'Try to keep going, if you can,' Edward said to me.

'Yes,' I said. 'I can.'

Herr Liedtke's voice remained flat. 'The soldier pulled out his bayonet. The blood then. He was almost gone. I was nearly beside him as he started to fall. But they would not give me . . . my Jurgen. They hauled him onto the bus, had the driver shut the door so he wouldn't tumble out. They drove away.' He shrugged. 'And that was the end of it.'

Two weeks later, at the beginning of August, on a day so cool and pleasant and, therefore, so abnormal for Washington that it was almost suspect, part of some sinister Axis plot, Norman Weeks came to Edward's office to discuss the OSS's crisis in Berlin. He had not given up a single member of his usual company of six; they trooped behind him in twos, like obedient first graders.

The ill-will level was lower than it had been at the earlier meeting. The two groups of men seemed to realize that since Donovan did not have the time to fire Norman Weekes (and perhaps also to realize that Norman's Boston bank gave its New York business to Donovan's law firm), they were doomed to work with each other. They were gathered in the couch and chairs around the coffee table, which was covered with legal pads, pens, coffee cups, water glasses and ashtrays. Everyone was determinedly congenial.

Well, except for Edward and John. They sat beside each other, but the relaxed give-and-take between colleagues had been replaced by strain. Bad strain. John's head was drawn down, his shoulders up, as if he half expected any minute to be yelled at.

Maybe he thought he had it coming. Three nights before, he'd slipped out of bed. It was two-thirty. I'd murmured – fake-murmured, since I'd woken up startled and full of dread – What's the matter? and he'd said, Shh, go back to sleep. I'm just going downstairs for a glass of milk. When he'd been gone for a minute, I'd tiptoed to the head of the stairs. There were no sounds at all. But then I heard him hang up the phone. I went back to bed and pretended to be asleep. All of a sudden, I knew what the word 'heartsick' meant.

The next night, John called home a little before eleven. We have a bad situation at one of the safe houses. I'll be late, Linda. He came home at three. His hair was perfect, just combed. I knew. I *knew*. It's Nan, isn't it? She's back. No, he said. I swear.

Whenever Edward spoke to John, he turned toward him but never quite looked at him.

'Norman,' Edward said, 'we've gone over your list of candidates for the, um, position vacated by Alfred Eckert. We've read your evaluations, had a look at their security clearance reports where they existed and done some preliminary investigating on our own. Shall we take them one at a time?'

'It's your meeting, Ed,' Norman said. They both smiled, hiding their loathing of each other pretty well.

I sat about two feet away from Edward. We were both facing Norman, who'd obviously just been to the barber, and a bad one; his one claim to distinction, his white hair, had been cropped close to his head, so he looked less like a Boston big shot and more like some old man who'd somehow been captured and sent away for basic training. Throughout the meeting, his hand kept drifting up to where his tufted sideburns used to be. He felt vulnerable.

Edward opened the first of three folders on his lap. From where I sat, it looked as if John had a couple more. I couldn't stand to look at him. He was so beautiful. The night before, he'd called and said he had to conduct an interrogation. He'd called again around midnight. This is going very slowly, he said. I said, Why can't you be man enough to tell the truth? Would you stop your nagging!

he'd snapped. Then I heard his deep intake of breath. All right, he said, I'm with Nan. Then he added quickly, But we're just talking. They must have had a lot to say. He didn't come home at all.

'Klaus-Dieter Fischer,' Edward said, 'Age, twenty-seven. Born in Leipzig. Moved to Berlin in 1925, at age ten. Father taught history at a *Gymnasium* – the German equivalent of a high school – and was also a Communist, something of a rabble-rouser. Father lost his job in '33, arrested in '34, presumed dead. Klaus-Dieter took up the cause, handed out pamphlets, escaped to Czechoslovakia in '35, just before he was about to be arrested. Escaped again to England in July '39, again by the skin of his teeth. Has worked at odd jobs – grocery clerk, waiter – but lives for the party. Made overtures to British intelligence, but they turned him down because of his political leanings.' Edward closed the folder. 'We should decline too. His loyalty is highly suspect.'

'He's willing to go in wherever we want him,' Norman said. 'And I've spent time with him. He is a Communist, but a realist too. Not at all the raving ideologue.'

'Is it likely he'd wave *Das Kapital* in your face?' Edward demanded. Everyone chuckled. 'He wants the job, Norman. And from what we can gather, he wants it badly – so he can pass information back to the Russians.'

'They *are* our ally, after all,' Norman protested, although without much conviction. A moment later, he waved his hand and said, 'Next.'

'Hugo Dreyer. Age, fifty-two. Born, raised and currently living in Berlin. Secretary to an officer of I. G. Farben, has been passing information to us for years through Sunflower.'

'He's really ideal,' Norman said. 'Right in place. And willing.'

'Excuse me,' John broke in. 'He's out of the picture. He had a stroke three weeks ago. He's incapacitated.'

'I see,' Norman said. He flashed a look of such malice at one of his men that if I'd been that guy, I would have had a stroke myself. Then Norman turned back to John, gracious, amicable. 'Any more surprises?'

John smiled. For a man who had been up all night, John still had unlimited energy to charm. The entire espionage unit smiled back. Even Norman bared his yellow teeth. 'No surprises I know of, Norman. Unless Ed . . .'

Edward alone remained uncharmed. John's smile faded. Edward simply shook his head. 'No surprises. Well, perhaps, in that for once I'm not going to give you an argument, Norman.' He lifted the last folder on his pile. 'Peter Fuhrmann. I don't have to go through his credentials. He's done some remarkable work for Special Operations in Hamburg. He appears clean as a whistle. I think he's your man, Norman.'

'Well, I have a surprise for you,' Norman said. 'Peter wants out. Out of Hamburg. Out of intelligence entirely. He's pleading exhaustion, and his contact seems to agree – says he's on the edge of a nervous breakdown. Sorry to have to put you to all this work. We just received the message this morning.'

'Quite all right,' Edward said. Norman nodded, and everyone in the room muttered. 'Too damn bad' or something like it. 'All right.' Edward glanced at John, but it was an icy glance, and he didn't say his name. 'You checked on the last two fellows. Please report.'

'Hans Kuhn. Age, thirty-nine. A lawyer. Born in Cincinnati of German parents, moved back to Dresden when he was eighteen.' John adjusted and readjusted his tie in a nervous, almost desperate manner. Edward's coldness had thrown him completely. 'He's a single practitioner in Berlin, and from time to time has passed information on to us through Alfred Eckert. We've done what checking we could, with refugees, lawyers who practiced in Berlin, and from everything we can gather, he's no good.'

'No good in what way?' Norman asked, almost off-handedly.

'Rumors he's looted escrow accounts, stolen from widows and orphans. That sort of thing. Womanizer. One person claimed to have seen him drunk and disorderly.'

'Sounds like one of your partners, Ed,' Norman chortled.

'Sounds like quite a few of them,' Edward responded.

There was subdued male laughter. Everything was still pleasant.

'The last name on the list is Erich Erdmann.' Norman's face brightened; I could see this was his man. 'Forty years old. Born in Munich. Professor of Romance languages at the university in

Munich until 1935. Jewish. Came to the US in '36. Taught at Tufts until this year, when he came to work for the OSS . . . Foreign Nationalities unit.'

'He wants to go back in,' Norman said. 'He's cultured, good-looking. According to Rex' – Rex was Norman's highest-placed spy, a career man who had worked in the foreign office since before the First World War but had had little contact with Alfred's important Nazi official – 'someone sophisticated like Erdmann would appeal to the foreign office fellow. And he's open to any suggestion we have.'

'That's the drawback, as far as I'm concerned,' Edward said. 'All this Erdmann wants is to make trouble for the Germans. It's certainly a commendable goal, but he's too intent on revenge. I'd send him in with a demolition team in a minute – if we could slip in a team and they needed a professor of Romance languages with them. But he's seething with anger, Norman. You can't send someone like that on a mission that requires infinite patience and self-control.'

'I think he could control himself if he's willing to keep his eye on the ultimate objective,' Norman said. 'And I know he's more than willing.'

'But he'll be in there alone,' Edward said. 'He'll have no one to get him to shape up when he starts losing his sense of balance. Look, whoever takes Alfred Eckert's place is going to have to walk on an invisible tightrope. We know there's a traitor in the resistance movement. People will be suspicious. We'll have to ease him in with extraordinary canniness. And only one person – as yet to be determined – will know his true identity. Then, gradually, he'll have to make a place for himself. It's an operation that calls for great subtlety, and this Erich Erdmann, for all his academic attainments, is about as subtle as a bull in a china shop.'

'But we're *desperate*,' Norman interrupted. 'Goddamn it, Ed, you keep shooting down almost every candidate we come up with.'

'Then come up with better candidates,' Edward replied. The congeniality was evaporating fast.

'Erich's a courageous man. I tell you, he would rise to the occasion.'

'He'll fall flat on his face. He can't even sit through an interview with me without banging his fist on the table every thirty seconds for punctuation. The man has no command over his emotions. It's not that I blame him. Believe me, I understand his rage. I applaud it.'

'He doesn't look Jewish,' Norman said. 'He'd fit right in.'

'I don't care if he looks like the archbishop of Canterbury. He's an accident going someplace to happen, and I'm not going to let it happen in Berlin. I'm against him. I vote no.'

'Ed—'

'I'll go to the mat with you on this one, Norman.'

The veins in Norman's neck and temples started to bulge. His face got so red it was almost purple. He tried to yell, but he was so infuriated he choked on his words. 'You're doing this deliberately!'

'Don't be ridiculous. This isn't a plot to foil you. But I won't allow any more suicide missions. I won't send a man to a meaningless, unnecessary death.'

'I need an agent! You find one for me, then goddamn it to hell! *You* find me a man we can slip in, someone with the brains and guts to knock on a Nazi's door and invite himself in.'

There was silence. John, wearily, closed his eyes. And all of a sudden, I found myself asking: 'Hey, how about me?'

# *Chapter Twenty*

'This isn't foolish!' Edward's fist crashed down on a table. 'This is insane! What's gotten into you?'

Two days after I'd suggested going into Germany, Edward had directed Pete, his driver, to forget his instructions to take us to a meeting at the Research and Analysis unit. Drop us at my place, he directed, and wait. I slid out of the car, not even bothering to take my pad and pencil, and strolled up the walk to his house.

I knew Edward; he was going to play gracious host, offer me a drink, and then, with great subtlety, try to talk me out of the idea. But the minute he closed the door, he'd yelled, 'You idiot!' That's when I realized that the only reason he'd brought me to his peaceful Georgetown home was that he needed a place where he could scream his head off.

'If it's all so insane, then how come Norman's whole espionage unit's for it?'

'Are you some kind of imbecile?' I had no idea such a low voice could be so terrifyingly loud. 'What the hell is wrong with you? Don't you know by now that all he wants is another player for his game?'

I was stunned – and frightened – by his outburst. But I knew if I started quaking in front of Edward, the closest I'd get to Berlin was a map. So I banged my fist, hard, against his living room wall. 'You have no damn right to shout at me like this,' I yelled back.

Besides, I'd had it with him. He'd sat in that meeting two days earlier letting Norman and his men and even John debate my going into Berlin. Well, John had said, her *berlinerisch* is not flawless. Not an American accent, but it's not . . . quite on the mark. But close enough? one of Norman's men had queried. And John had admitted he couldn't be sure. Edward had sat rigid and wordless, and no one except me had noticed how spooky his silence was.

'The thing that's *really* getting you is that you know I can do it,' I went on, 'and you don't want me to because of your dumb feud with Norman Weekes. And because it would be too much trouble to find a new secretary.'

'I have no patience for asinine remarks!'

'Would you please listen to me! I know the network, the codes, the whole operation. And I'm not some Tufts College professor with a crazy grudge. I'm an ordinary person. And give me three days with one of your refugees who speaks the *berlinerisch* dialect, and no one will ever know I'm not Frau Schmidt from around the corner.'

Edward stalked away from me, across the room toward the mantel. Suddenly he spun around, took three fast steps and was beside me. Before I even realized what was happening, I saw he had a fireplace poker in his hand. He drew it up fast, like a fencer; it was an inch from my throat. 'Are you crazy?' I breathed, staring down at it.

'Come on. This is Berlin,' he said. 'You can manage anything.' I turned my back on him, walked away and sat down in a big blue club chair. '*Now* do you understand that you can't begin to manage something like this?'

I looked up at him. 'I just managed it. You didn't poke out my jugular with that thing.'

'For God's sake!' he said, and hurled the poker to the floor. It bounced from the fancy old rug and clanged onto the dark wood floor. Then Edward began to pace. His hands were stuffed deep in his pockets. He wouldn't look at me.

'I know what's going to come next,' I said. 'You're going to take your hands out of your pockets and come over here, sit down, and try to talk me out of it. You're going to be very understanding and patient.'

Edward pulled his hands out of his pockets and took a seat not far away, in a club chair that matched mine. 'Linda,' he said understandingly, patiently. 'You haven't thought this through.'

'I have.'

'No, you haven't. Don't you realize that your life means nothing to a man like Norman Weekes? He's just using you for his own purposes.'

'Let me clue you in on what I've learned in the last couple of years. People like Norman Weekes – people like you – *always* use people like me. Why else bother having lower classes? You use us to work for you, to clean up your messes, to fight your wars. You use us to listen to your secrets, so you can say: "What? *Me* a tough, unfeeling bastard? No! I'm a deep, fine, compassionate human being. If you don't believe me, just ask my secretary." '

He rubbed his watch chain between his thumb and index finger. 'Is that what you think of me, Linda?'

'Pretty close.'

'It's a shame you didn't say anything. I wouldn't have wasted your time. It would have been easier just giving you a five-dollar raise in exchange for your promise to vouch for my compassion.'

We sat there, half facing each other, not speaking. It was a terrible, long time. Finally I said, 'There's really no point in sitting around here.' I started to get up, but then Edward stopped me.

His voice, subdued, almost hypnotic, was what got to me. 'There's a beautiful simplicity in all this. What you're looking for is precisely what Norman is offering: a suicide mission.' I sat back in the chair. 'You feel your life is . . . is unrewarding.' Edward paused. 'You've lost your mother. And your husband . . .' His voice trailed off.

'My husband has been having a flaming affair with your daughter.'

'Yes.'

'So you think I want to go into Berlin, go undercover, because I really want to kill myself, but I'm too chicken to do it, so I'll get some pig in the Gestapo to do it for me? Why when you do it is it heroic, and when I want to do the same thing it's suicidal?'

'You're distraught.'

'You didn't answer my question.' But all he did was give me one of his kindly looks, his hard eyes softening, his head tilted a little to the side: the kind of look he gave all the sad victims of the war.

And the lousy part of it was, it wasn't a phony look. His pity for me was real. 'I walked in on them,' I told him. He stiffened. 'No, not like that. It was when I got back from New York, from my mother's funeral. Oh, they were in each other's arms, but they were dressed to the nines and listening to classical music.' He reached over and tried to take my hand, but I jerked it away, into my lap. 'You really must be proud of her.'

'You know I'm not.'

'I don't know anything. All I know are the stories you decide to tell me.' He drew his watch from his pocket and stared at the case, but didn't open it. 'It's getting late,' I said. 'I really want to get out of here.'

Edward spoke as if he hadn't heard me. 'Nan's my child. I love her. That doesn't mean I approve of what she's doing. It doesn't mean I understand her.' He slipped his watch back into its little pocket and looked at me. 'That's a sad admission for a father to have to make, but even so, I have an obligation—'

'You know, you're all sensational at throwing around words like "obligation," "honor," "moral imperative." Go ahead, if it makes you happy. You can carry on about your integrity, your profound humanity, until you're blue in the face. I just don't want any part of it. I want *out* of your world.' I got up and stood in front of his chair. 'Send me to Berlin.'

Edward rose. He wasn't all that much taller than I was, so we were almost eye to eye. His voice was very calm. 'Don't throw away your life on John Berringer. He's not worth it. He has good looks and a good mind. But that's all he has. His character isn't worth two cents.'

'You know what the problem is? I've seen you at work too often. You're shocking me back to my senses with a brutal dose of honesty; you always have pretty good results with that technique.'

Edward broke away then and walked over to a cart that had whiskey and glasses on it. 'Would you like a drink?' I shook my head, and he poured himself one. 'I've been drinking too damn much lately. I wake up nearly every morning feeling . . . not right.'

I thought: What does he want – another heart-to-heart? 'So don't drink so much,' I said.

'Thank you. I'm touched by your concern.'

'You want my concern? Maybe you should drop the brutal-honesty business. John could wind up being your son-in-law again.'

'I would hope not.'

'You ought to thank me for taking him off your hands. Well, temporarily. I don't have what it takes for the long run, for chitchat in the drawing room. But for the short run, I'm great upstairs.'

'Don't denigrate yourself.'

'Hey, I'm not. I'll give you my other credentials. I'm smart. Imaginative. And you were the one who said I have guts. If you'll just listen to me, I'll tell you *exactly* how I can get into Berlin. I figured the whole thing out.'

'You're not going. You're not going to destroy yourself – and possibly put into jeopardy what few shreds of resistance are left.'

'I'm better than any name on that list, and you damn well know it!'

'You're staying here.'

'*Please*. Don't you understand? This is my war. I want to fight it. I belong there.'

Edward took a long drink. 'You don't belong there.'

'Why not?'

'For one thing, you're a Jew.'

I stared at him. 'What are you talking about?'

'Please. I saw your FBI report two years ago. Why do you think you were cleared so damned fast?'

'I'm not a Jew,' I said. He gave me one of those cool, neutral upper-class glances that still say, Yeah, sure. So I added, 'My father was, but he never did anything Jewish in his life . . . whatever it is they do.'

'If you were to go into Berlin, if they were to find you out – and believe me, they inevitably would – do you know what they would do to you?'

'Yes. And they'd do it to me, anyway – Jew, half Jew, no Jew at all.'

'They'd do it worse to you.'

'Come on! You think I'm going to walk into Germany with a big yellow star on an armband?'

'If they captured you, do you think it would take them more than ten minutes to find out everything they could possibly want to know?'

Without thinking, I reached out and took his drink. It was only after the whiskey radiated through me that I realized what I'd done. 'Excuse me,' I said, handing him back the glass. I took a minute to collect myself. 'To answer your question, if I saw myself sitting under a naked light bulb in an interrogation cell, I wouldn't be making this pitch. Okay? And if you'd let me tell you what I have in mind—'

'Sit down, please.' Edward motioned to the couch. We sat on opposite ends; his drink sat between us on the table. He cleared his throat. 'If you read the editorials, listen to Buy Bonds speeches, it's very fashionable these days to call Hitler's regime hellish. "The hell that is Nazi Germany," and so forth.

'Yeah? So?'

'Listen to me, Linda. It *is* hell. More than you can comprehend. It is absolute evil.' He held out the glass to me. I didn't take it, so he did. 'I'm going to tell you something only about ten people in the government know. Some . . . shocking news has come out of Switzerland, through Sunflower; he learned it from that disgusting little Nazi who's treasurer of his company, Himmler's friend.' He fell silent, as if he didn't want to continue.

'What? What's going on?'

'They're killing the Jews.'

'I know they are.'

'No. You don't know. They've started something new. Gas chambers. They expect to exterminate three to four million – did you hear that number? – three to four million European Jews in the next two years. More, if they can build fast enough and maintain their supply of prussic acid. Men, women, children. They want to annihilate the Jews completely.' He hesitated, and then added quietly, 'Your family, Linda. Your people.'

How do you react to something like that? I sat on that sumptuous couch in that rich, civilized house in Georgetown and I was numb. Not unfeeling numb, but as if everything inside me had frozen.

My only sensation was thousands . . . millions of tiny prickles of horror along my skin and scalp. 'Why?'

'There is no answer.'

I thought about the two old ladies, Liesl and Hannah. 'I have to go there,' I said.

'You can't stop them.'

'But I can do *something*. I can help. I can be one bullet, maybe one bomb. I can make a difference.'

'You can't. You'd be one more dead Jew.'

'Don't talk to me like that!'

'Linda, my dear, I am going over to the telephone. I am calling Norman Weekes and telling him to scrap immediately any plans he has involving you. I am going to stop this preposterous scheme *now.* If you don't have the brains or the desire to stay alive, I'll have to see to it for you.'

I don't know how I got through the rest of that day. Edward made his phone call, finished his drink in silence and poured another. I walked out and waited in the car, staring straight ahead, at the back of Pete's baseball cap. Edward came out a half hour later and acted as though nothing the least unusual had happened.

At five o'clock, he went off to a meeting at the White House, saying, 'I should be back by seven-thirty or eight.' Just like that. At six, I put a flawlessly typed note on his desk.

Dear Mr Leland:
This is to inform you that I am hereby submitting my resignation from the position of your secretary; the resignation is effective as of the close of business today.

Thank you for your consideration and courtesy.

Very truly yours,
Linda V. Berringer

Then I walked out of Edward Leland's office for good.

When I thought about it – and I now had plenty of time to think

– the idea of my going underground and surfacing in Berlin seemed right.

Sure, when I thought: Hey, I want to be a *spy*, the actual word would make me feel all fluttery. Worse than that: agitated. I'd pace from room to room, grab a sponge and wipe around the faucets for the twenty-seventh time, open the refrigerator and check if the peaches were too soft since I'd last looked, fifteen minutes before. *Spy.* Inspecting the bathroom to make sure we hadn't run out of toilet paper, I could almost hear the creepy music they play in movies when the secret agent walks down a cobblestone street and fog swirls around his feet.

But when I'd said to Edward, This is my war, I'd meant it. Okay, it was just something I'd blurted out because I was so unhappy, so frustrated, but there's value in misery. It's a test. When you're so oppressed and depressed by your life, you can cave in and show the world you're the sucker they've always thought you were, or you can finally come out fighting and say: Listen, you bastards, this is unfair; I won't put up with it. I'm entitled to . . . And whammo! Out pops what you really want. Out pops the truth. And the truth was I wanted to fight just as much as every eighteen-year-old boy who'd up and enlisted the day after Pearl Harbor.

Why not? I was as American as apple pie. Okay, the way I talked, no one would say, Wow, you must be from Nebraska! But there's apple pie in New York too. A little more mushed up, a little spicier, but still apple pie.

There can be more than one truth, though. I was all-American, but not all American. I'd grown up in a house with two women, where English was the language of dopiness and German the tongue of whatever intelligent thought there was. It was my mother's 'Linda, angel, what would *you* call this nail polish – coral or salmon?' versus Olga's 'Do you think the Dawes Plan will really help the German economy?'

Okay, there was my father too. He was most like me in that he spoke English and German with almost equal ease, but although he was smart, the fact that he was fluent in a foreign tongue meant zero to him. He could have been speaking Pig Latin for all he cared about Germany. He could talk about the Dodgers or Herbert

Hoover or his chance of getting a raise down at the sausage plant in either language, but his life was purely American.

But maybe because my parents were so busy with each other, they didn't have a lot of time for me. So I'd listened a lot to my Grandma Olga, who'd reminisce when she was waxing the floor or stuffing cabbage leaves or cutting out a corn plaster. The old country was her life, and I guess in a way it became mine; I'd always been fascinated with Germany – and especially Berlin – because she made it sound like fairy-tale place, the Enchanted Kingdom. The longer she stayed in America, the greener the German countryside became, the more graceful the boulevards of Berlin, the more glamorous and cultivated and merry its inhabitants. Maybe that's why when Hitler rose to power, she thought of him as a disagreeable quirk of history; he was a blot on her dream of perfection, and she figured it was only a matter of time before the neatest people in the world cleaned up their blot.

But as far back as 1923, when I first heard about him and his NSDAP party, I knew he was dangerous. I was a girl raised on fairy tales – not Cowboys and Indians – and so I'd learned there was more to life than good guys and bad guys. In every enchanted kingdom, there are monsters. When I heard Hitler's speeches, his combination of hysteria, hatred, pride and vengeance all tied up into a package with the gaudy ribbon of Germanic myth, I knew that here was one doozy of a monster.

And just as Cinderella and the fairy godmother had always struck a chord in me, I knew Hitler and his gods would strike a chord in the German people. Oh, they would snicker at his accent and maybe cringe at his rantings, but deep down they'd say, *Ach!* He knows *just* what I feel!

I guess I was too true-blue an American to ever really have confidence in the basic goodness of foreigners.

And so Hitler's rise didn't stun me. Actually, neither did Pearl Harbor. Did it surprise me? Sure. I never thought the Japanese could fool us *so* bad.

But although I followed the fighting in the Pacific conscientiously, it wasn't my war. My war wasn't the good guys against the bad guys. My war was against the monsters.

And damn it, I was finally ready to fight.

Edward left Washington the last week of August for, as usual, places unknown. I knew he'd been planning the trip, but just to make sure, I called this new secretary and made up a story about his promising to leave me a letter of recommendation before he went away. She said, Oh, dear, he must have forgotten. And I snuck in, And he won't be back for what – two, three weeks? More like four, I'm sorry to say, was her answer. Boy, did she have a big, dangerous mouth, giving out information like that. But I knew the coast was clear.

I hardly saw John. He'd called me late on the night after he hadn't come home, six hours after the meeting where I'd volunteered to go into Berlin. I waited for him to say, How could you humiliate me in front of all those people by interrupting, by pushing yourself where you *know* you don't belong? Or: How could you suggest anything so stupid? What he actually said was, 'I have to be honest with you. Nan and I still haven't resolved matters. I don't know when I'll be home.' I didn't even feel like crying. I wrapped the phone wire around my finger, tight, and said to him, 'Do you think it matters?'

I made up a bed for myself in the second bedroom. John didn't notice, because he didn't come home for two days. I was in the kitchen when he walked in. You here for a clean shirt before you go back to talking? I asked. I was peeling a carrot and didn't bother to look at him. Linda, he said, I know how hard this has been on you. But it will be resolved. Soon. I swear. He came up behind me and just rested himself against me. But in a minute he was rubbing and pushing me hard against the sink. His arms went around me. I need you, he exhaled into my ear. How long do you have? I asked. I'm going to stay the whole night, he replied. Oh, God, I have to have you. I peeled a long curl of carrot peel into the sink. No more, I said. Did you hear me? Get off me! Come on, he insisted, you have to have it as much as I do.

But I didn't! I couldn't believe it. I turned around. He was just another pretty face. It took me a second to catch my breath. Was this another loss? There I was, right on the verge of crying, but a second later, I found myself staring at the sink drain, trying to fight off a giggle. He was trying his Tragic Eyes routine, where dark blue eyes mist over, open wide, gaze at me; he was going to break my heart with his beautiful damp eyes, show me his infinite pain, his suffering. Except now I realized he could do it at the drop of a hat. I realized I'd seen Tragic Eyes about four hundred and seventy-seven times. I glanced up. Well, I told him, if it's true – if I have to have it – I'll have to get it someplace else.

At first I thought it would be smart to give Norman Weekes just what he wanted – a throaty, promising voice and an even more promising dress – so he'd give me what I wanted. But in the end I put on brown oxfords, an old gabardine skirt and a white cotton blouse that showed nothing more than how well it was ironed. I wore no makeup. I pulled back my hair into a loosely pinned mess that could barely be called a bun.

'Oh,' Norman said, as he lifted his behind from his desk chair when I walked in. I could see whatever his desire for me had been evaporating; it was a wonderful sight. 'Please, sit down.'

I came right to the point. 'Look at me. Do you think anyone in the foreign office would look twice?'

His eyebrows did one of those Aha! movements. 'Edward has said "Absolutely not," you know.'

'I know.'

'And your husband?'

'John has never said no.'

Norman cocked his head; his mouth hung open a bit. He was obviously dying to hear more about me and John. All of a sudden, I felt queasy, thinking: Oh, God, people *know* about John and me . . . and Nan. The whole OSS may know, and when everyone came up to me after I got back after my mother's funeral, offering sympathy, they were really—

Norman demanded, 'I really must know. How would he feel if

you put – let me be perfectly forthright about this – if you put yourself in, well, a rather perilous situation?'

'How does a wife feel when her husband goes off to war? She doesn't want it, but she understands.'

'I see.' A bubble of saliva formed on the side of his mouth and then burst.

'And I'm sure you also see, because it's your job to see, well, everything, that things aren't so great right now between me and my husband. If I went off, it wouldn't be like you were tearing apart the perfect marriage. I think John could probably learn to adjust to my absence.'

'I rather assumed . . . some distance . . . from his lack of . . . objections when we contemplated the possibility of your working for us at that meeting. But I didn't want to be presumptuous.'

He was waiting for more, a dose of scandal he could murmur about at his club. He'd light a cigar and say, Leland's secretary, Berringer's wife, told me . . . But I just said, 'Let me be straight with you. I know I'm your best shot. Your only shot.'

He grinned. With all that money, you'd think he could have afforded a decent toothbrush. 'That may be true, but we have that lit-tle problem with Mr Leland.'

I gave him a bigger, whiter, grin. 'But Mr Leland is out of town – probably out of the country – for four weeks.'

'I can't.' His office was bare in that old-money, New England way, but his desk was a mess. He tried to put down his elbow so he could make a platform with his hand to rest his chin on, but he had to shove over a stack of bound top-secret reports to find the room. The reports looked unread. His desk was like him: an important, repulsive mess. 'Forgive me for being profane, but if you went into Berlin, there would be hell to pay when Ed returned.'

'I flashed a you're-so-damnably-attractive smile and managed not to gag. 'What's a little hell to a man like you? And . . . please, I want to be honest with you.'

'Oh, do.'

'I know you and Edward Leland are . . . well, at odds. I want you to understand I feel a great loyalty to him. Not only as my former employer but as the man who's really been my husband's . . .

patron.' Wow, was that a great word. 'But I also know he's not right all the time. He's a human being. He makes mistakes.' Norman nodded. 'Lots of mistakes.'

'Yes,' he said. His upper lip curled into something just under a sneer. I'd been right. I'd sensed that puffing myself up as Miss Espionage 1942 wouldn't get to Norman Weekes the way a betrayal of Edward would. You've been right all along: That would be my unwritten message, aimed directly at Norman Weekes's limitless vanity. He's been wrong. You're strong. He's soft, muddleheaded. Norman would love the message and, hopefully, the messenger.

'Edward Leland is a very decent man, the way he cares about people. But he's—' I stopped cold. 'Please. No matter what happens, I hope this conversation—'

He cut me off with an impassioned. 'Of course. Never to be repeated.' He leaned forward, expectant, thrilled.

I made myself as comfortable as I could in that small, stiff wooden chair. 'He's too cautious. Look, I know what I want to do is dangerous. I wouldn't be worthy of the job if I didn't have that much sense. But just because it's dangerous doesn't mean it's nor worth doing.'

'You're a smart girl. But Ed would go running to Donovan and . . .'

'You've, um, disagreed with Edward Leland and – let's be honest – has Colonel Donovan ever handed you your walking papers?' Norman gave a small, self-satisfied, yellow smile. 'Please,' I urged, 'don't say no.' I offered him a little bit of husky voice so he'd pay attention, but not so much as to distract him. 'Say maybe. Give me a week at Assessment School. You know they won't let me go if I'm not fit. But if I am, you'll have your man . . .' We both smiled. 'Your man in Berlin. And I promise you, it'll be worth it.'

The next five weeks were the hardest I'd ever lived through, and the worst of it was that all along, everybody's expression said: You think *this* is bad? Wait.

My name was Lina Thiele. On Monday, the last day of August, 1942, I entered the OSS's Assessment School. The hunched-over man who let me in had a frighteningly flabby face with near-shoulder-length jowls. He looked like the doorkeeper in a Dracula movie. For a second I thought he was part of the process of terrifying recruits, but he just called out, 'Judy!' His jowls jiggled, and a girl about five years younger than me, with a lot of frothy Maureen O'Sullivan hair, came into the hall and said, 'Follow me, please.'

We walked down a steep flight of gray cement steps to the basement, and she led me into a curtained cubicle and said, 'Please take off all of your clothing except your underwear.' As I got undressed, she took my clothes and folded them.

Finally, when I was standing in my underpants and brassiere, she pulled a scissors out of the pocket of her skirt. I forced myself not to flinch, and reasoned: The United States of America is not going to stab you. This girl is here to test you. And so, even though all the light in the room seemed to be shining on the silvery point of that scissors, I made myself stand motionless, all calm and collected. And Judy said, 'I have to cut out any name tags or laundry marks on your underwear.'

'Oh. There aren't any. But there may be labels from the department store. Do you want to . . .'

'No,' Judy said. She really had very little interest in me. She kept squinting into a small, splintered triangle of mirror that was hung on the wall, obviously deeply involved with her eyebrows. 'When . . . whenever . . . if you go, they'll give you stuff from . . . wherever.' She licked her pinkie and wiped off the penciled end of her left eyebrow. She turned to me. 'How does that look?'

'Better,' I said. 'Terrific.' Oh, boy, I thought, the OSS in action.

'Good. Now, these are the rules. *Nobody* gets to know your real name. I'm going to take your clothes and your shoes and your pocketbook with me when I go out. You know, your whole identity.'

'I'm supposed to walk around in my underwear?'

Judy rolled her eyes and said, 'Oh, geez! I forgot. Wait here.' And she slipped out from behind the curtain and a few minutes later came back with clothes. Some clothes! Men's army fatigues and a pair of boots so heavy I had to use both hands to lift them. They'd probably been designed for combat conditions in Antarctica.

Then Judy led me upstairs – which was some trick in itself with the two-ton boots – and out a back door. The next thing I knew, I was in the back of an army-green, canvas-covered truck, with four men dressed in the same outfit I was wearing. None of them spoke, and, like me, not a single one of them looked like an American GI.

My advantage was, having worked for Edward so long, I had a fair idea of how the OSS operated. In fact, once we bumped onto a hilly road ten minutes into Virginia, I knew exactly where we were headed. I'd been down that same road in the Packard; it led to an estate in Fairfax, with acres of open field surrounded by a thick forest, and, in the middle, an old white mansion dripping with honeysuckle charm. But if I remembered right, the interior smelled as though the mildew had been in flower inside the walls since the founding of the Confederacy.

I remembered right. We were herded in through the front door and stood under a giant brass chandelier. The hallway itself was so wide and high it seemed more like the main aisle of a giant church. It ran the length of the mansion; at the far end were two glass doors that opened up on a sloping green lawn.

We never got there. We heard a theatrical 'Ahem' and glanced up. A man with a red face and a golf shirt was walking down the stairs very slowly. He would have looked like he was making believe he was a bride, except that instead of gazing straight ahead, he was looking down, scrutinizing us. This threw one of the four men I'd driven out with; he turned his eyes away from the red-faced man and started to smile nervously at all of us, as if we were his pals and would back him up. Then he wiped his palms – obviously sweating – on his fatigues.

When Red-Face reached us, he said, 'I'm Mr Jones.' That seemed to be the limit of his conversational skills. He just stood there and eyed the five of us. Not a word was said for at least ten minutes, and when you're standing around in army boots in a southern mansion on a hot day with someone you know isn't really named Mr Jones staring at you, that's a long time. The guy with the sweaty palms finally broke the silence by asking if there was a men's room. The sound of a voice was so unexpected that another one of the men flinched. 'Down the hall, second left, first door on your right,' Mr Jones said. As the man headed off, I thought: He's not going to make it. And I probably wouldn't put my money on the flincher, either, I decided.

'Lady and gentlemen,' Mr Jones said, when the nervous guy finally got back. 'Welcome. And now, down to business. A few rules. You are never to deviate from your cover story. Never. You'll see a friendly face, and he'll say to you, "Is that an Oklahoma accent I hear?" and just as you say, "Why, it sure is!" you'll be out on your butt.

'Now, most of you have foreign covers. Stick to the story we've invented, but unless we direct you to do otherwise, speak English. Not all of us can speak Hungarian or Japanese or what have you, so you'll save that for later, for the specialists.'

'Let me warn you that our purpose here is to get rid of you. You'll be under almost constant surveillance. We want to make you break your cover. We want to be there when you forget you're supposed to be a waiter and start talking like the truckdriver you really are. We're going to test you. We're looking for sweat. We're sniffing out weakness. *Your* weakness.'

It wasn't that I didn't take it seriously. I did. But I also knew that it was a kind of game – a rough one, but with one basic rule for winning: Don't show you're scared.

But the end of the first hour, I knew the easiest way to hide your fear was to keep your mouth shut except when asked a direct question. And there were plenty. I had intelligence tests and psychological tests every day. 'What does this inkblot look like to you?' they asked. I told the psychologists that it looked like a butterfly, and when he said, 'Look again and tell me what else you see,' I told him I saw a couple of big vases between the wings and the body. 'Is that *all?* he demanded. He was a small, mousy man, and he seemed unsatisfied. I told him, yeah, that was all.

There were physical tests, and not just someone with a tongue depressor and a stethoscope. After the first examination, I had to run for fifteen minutes. I thought I would drop dead, but I managed to do it. Then, after the doctor took my pulse, he told me to do ten push-ups. I stopped after three. 'More!' he ordered. I told him I couldn't. 'I said *more!*' I stood up, looked him straight in the eye and said, I can't. The next day, another doctor took me to a chinning bar and told me to do as many pull-ups as I could. I couldn't even do one. 'Christ,' he said, really disgusted, 'just look at you. You sit behind a desk all day and you've got no muscle tone.' I told him I didn't sit behind a desk. I was a housewife. 'What does your husband do?' I was a widow, I said. My husband had died the year before, in June, on the Eastern Front. 'Your husband's a German soldier?' Yes. 'Where was he killed?' Somewhere near Gorodischche. He waited, but I kept quiet. 'What was his name?' Johannes. 'Johannes what?' Thiele. 'I thought that was *your* name.' It is. My married name. 'What was your maiden name?' Fritsch.

Then he smiled at me. 'Look, I don't like doing this. I'm really a nice guy.' He put out his hand. 'My name's Richard Peterson.' He was Hollywood handsome. Maybe he was the inhouse tempter for potential female agents, or maybe they'd brought him in special for me – my security clearance revealing a weakness for gorgeous guys. 'But I want you to call me Dick, okay? By the way, I'm from Tampa. Before all this hullabaloo, I had a nice practice down there. Internal medicine.' He shook my hand, holding it, naturally, a little too long. 'Now I want to know everything about you.' My name is Lina Thiele, I said. 'Aw, come on, honey.' I didn't respond. Someone should have told him that 'Aw' and 'honey' didn't necessarily work on New York girls. He smiled. I didn't. He gave me a nasty look. 'Why the hell can't you do even one pull-up, Lina?' I don't know, I told him. 'You're soft,' he shouted. 'I'll tell you right now, you're not going to make it. You're no good. You're too weak.' I just stood there. 'Get out of here,' he said at last.

It was all a game. They'd said it would be hard, and it was, but not in the way they meant. I wasn't that scared by a bunch of Americans playing tough guys. Well, sometimes a little scared. But working for Edward, I'd seen the victims of the real thing, and I knew there was a world of difference. What made it so hard was, first of all, the fatigue. For a week, they kept you going day and night with tests, with jobs designed to frustrate you, exhaust you, make you sit down and cry.

One afternoon they led us to the bank of a stream and gave three of us a bunch of boards, a pulley and a rope, then handed us a rock about the size of someone's head. 'This is a very delicate communications device. You have to get it across the stream without jarring it or getting it wet.'

The boards were too short to go across the stream. One of the men kept trying to lasso a tree on the far bank with the rope, so he could Tarzan his way across. The other guy and I tried to get him to help us, but he wouldn't, so the two of us worked on making a bridge by overlapping the boards. We had ten minutes. All the time, the three OSS men with us were hollering, 'Come on!' 'Time's running out!' 'Hey, you, lady. Don't you know what a pulley is?' I didn't. 'Your time's almost up!' They started counting down: 'Sixty seconds, fifty-nine . . .' At forty, I took the rock, lifted it over my head, told the guy who wasn't playing with the rope to try and stay right beside me, and walked into the stream. It was cold, but I made myself go slow, so I wouldn't slip. Soon though the water came up to my neck. You jerk! I thought. Why didn't you let the guy carry the damn rock? I hadn't realized it was so deep, and I called out to the guy, who was a little behind me, Hey, catch up! I can't swim, so get ready to grab this thing. Just then the OSS men on the bank called out, 'Nine! Eight!' Talk about tripping up: The guy stumbled. I heard his splash, but I kept picking my way over the slick, moss-covered stones on the bottom of the stream. I didn't look back. On 'Three!' I got to the other side. I was gasping, freezing and wanted to curse – shriek out filthy things to the OSS pigs, but since I couldn't catch my breath, I didn't have to practice any self-control. A minute later, one of them shouted, 'Come back, Linda.' I stood up and managed to call out, My name's Lina. Then I stepped back into the icy water.

They took us for a hike in the woods. My teeth were chattering, my arms were still shaking from the tension of holding the rock over my head. My boots were filled with cold water and made disgusting squishy sounds at every step. The hike went on for three hours; there was no time to change my clothes until right before dinner. I was too worn out to eat. After dinner, they sent me to a lady psychologist. 'How are you bearing up? It must be so hard.' She had soft-looking, manicured hands and was wearing a beautiful gold cuff bracelet. Her voice was so sweet, so decent. 'Are you chilled? Would you like to borrow a sweater?' I said, I'm fine.

But exhausted as I was each night, I could hardly fall asleep. I kept thinking too much. I'd called John at his office and told him I was going back to New York for a few weeks, to stay at my mother's and put pressure on the real estate agent. I added, I had the phone disconnected, so if you want to reach me . . . He said, with great seriousness, I'll talk to you when you get back. I said, If you want a divorce, you can tell me now. I won't drop dead from shock. Linda, he said, please don't make every conversation we have a confrontation. It's not helping, you know.

So I said, John, I'm not going to New York. They're sending me to Assessment School.

For Berlin? he breathed.

Yes.

How did you get Ed to go along?

I guess Norman must have convinced him, I lied.

Well, he said, I don't know what to say. So I waited. Sooner or later he'd have to say something. And he did: Um, if you're planning on going in, maybe we should sit down first and, you know, talk things over.

You don't want me to go?

Linda, I can't make that kind of decision for you. It's your life that would be at stake.

And then I realized his talking things over meant: Hey, sweetie, if you're going to die in Berlin, let's be divorced so I don't have to wait seven years – or whatever it was – in legal limbo before I can marry Nan. If you're buried under forty tons of rubble or have a bullet in your head, I could be terribly inconvenienced.

I understand, I said.

Good, he said. We'll sit down and talk soon.

But what really kept me awake was the lie I'd told Norman Weekes. I'd said Edward was too cautious, but my unspoken words were: He's weak. You're brave, Norman. You're not some lily-livered lawyer who worries about the sanctity of life. You have the guts to send men out to their death.

I'd conned a weak man to get around a brave and strong one. I'd manipulated Norman to do what I'd wanted, and I'd turned my back on Edward Leland. Okay, he'd turned out to be a real crumb who'd sat back and let his daughter take over my husband and didn't have the decency – the decency that comes with friendship – to give me a clue that could save my marriage, save everything I had. But I'd betrayed him far worse. I'd denied all his advice, all his wisdom and, even more, all the good things he stood for. I'd gone over to his enemy to join the game of Cowboys and Indians.

It was early September then, getting cold at night in the countryside, and they'd only given us a thin, and not very clean, army blanket. Probably another test to see if we were strong enough not to beg for a goose-down quilt. Maybe Edward was right, I thought, as I tucked the blanket under my feet. Maybe I am on some crazy suicide mission. Or maybe my heart is in the right place, but there'll be a bullet in it two days after I get to Berlin. If I get to Berlin at all.

I got one step closer. I passed the Stress Interview, I sat on a stool in a dark room with a spotlight glaring in my eyes. Three or four men screamed questions at me in German. Someone threw water in my face. Down the hallway, I heard a woman shrieking as if she was in agony.

I passed. Easily. The Stress Interview was so close to my nightmares that I'd already lived through it a dozen times. 'You've failed this test,' one of them taunted me at the end, his voice full of contempt. I sat still. I knew that had to be part of the test too. And I was right. The next day, they sent me to OSS Training School.

The training school they sent me to to was a compound of drab cinder-block buildings in West Virginia, the sort of place that probably once housed exploited coal miners, or reform school girls.

The whole area was bleak. The ground was mostly gray gravel, and even the small patches of grass looked scraggly and unhealthy. There were no trees, and by afternoon you felt weak. There was no Indian summer here; just dusty heat and a glare that made your eyes burn.

Everything was dry and half dead, except for inside the cinder-block buildings. Even after the hottest days, they were so damp at night that when I woke up from the few hours' sleep I managed to get, my knees and neck and shoulders would ache, like a stiff old arthritic lady's.

I hadn't planned on being the kind of spy who crawls around with a grenade between her teeth. I didn't need this place. But go tell that to the OSS. Whether your cover was going to be third kitchen assistant, grinding out spaghetti for Mussolini's mistress, or a dockworker in Le Havre, you had to take the Course.

They put me into a class in close combat and gutter fighting – a subject I'd never anticipated studying in my days at Grover Cleveland High School. The instructor was a huge Marine with a head shaped like a canned ham. I thought he'd hate me, because when it came to giving a knee in the groin or a sideswipe to the Adam's apple, I was his least able and least enthusiastic pupil. But at the end he took me aside and said, 'Honey, you stink. So listen good. If you're ever in a hand-to-hand situation, you got one choice. Stick your thumb in the guy's eye. If you can't get your thumb, use another finger. Go *squoosh*.' The best that could be said for the class was that it was the last physical effort I had to make.

If you couldn't crunch the skulls of four Gestapo guys with your bare hands, at least they expected you to be able to shoot them. 'This weapon is the Walther P-38. It is the standard *Wehrmacht* pistol, *und* it replaced the Luger in 1938.' From his posture to the way he clipped off his native Bavarian accent, it was clear that our gun teacher (although we weren't allowed to call the thing a gun) had spent most of his life in the German military. Four of us – me, an Italian guy from New York, and two college types with eyeglasses – stood on the firing range, holding our guns – pistols – while the teacher said, 'You vil note the signal pin in the rear of the slide, vich vill enable you to both see *und* feel that there is a cartridge in the chamber.' He was all business. He didn't even bother with the usual false name: no 'Call me Hans.' And when I asked him a question about the safety catch in German, he gave me a dirty look, almost a hate-filled look, and answered me in English. When he taught us to dismantle the P-38, put it back together, and repair it by utilizing parts from other disabled weapons, there was no encouragement, no criticism, no nothing. Just *Ja* or No.

That was the worst of the Training School. There was no camaraderie, no sense that you were working together with people for a cause, no high-spirited feeling of We're gonna beat these bastards. No one had a name, not even a cover identity. It was a finger pointed, and someone said, 'You.'

'You,' they'd say, and shove the camera into your hand as they were teaching you to photograph secret documents. 'You,' they'd bark, 'who do you want to blow up – yourself or the Krauts?' when they taught us to handle explosives. I tried to explain to a man in a shirt and tie who seemed to be the administrator that no one had any plans for me to be blowing up bridges or derailing trains, that it was too funny to even think about; he just turned around and walked away.

What I hated about the place was that it was so un-American. Every once in a while at Assessment School there'd been a friendly 'Come on, stop complaining. We've all been through it' from the OSS men, or at least a couple of minutes of kidding around with the other recruits. But West Virginia was cold and hard and dead; it felt like Germany. Some nights, especially at the beginning, when I was all black and blue and upset – shaken up – from the close-combat class, I tried to cheer myself by saying, Maybe they're really smart to make this place such a lousy, miserable hole. It'll get rid of the rah-rah types, the ones who see war as a giant Coney Island, with shooting ranges and rockets and parachute jumps as part of the fun.

But other nights . . . like after the Scare House, where I'd been sent up a dark flight of stairs with my pistol and heard footsteps behind me, and threatening German voices off so low I couldn't make out where they were or what they were saying, and then all of a sudden out popped a thing – a scarecrow in an SS uniform – and I had to turn fast and fire, and then, seconds later, at a door at the top of the stairs, I heard loud, guttural voices, and I had to reload, release the safety catch, kick open the door, then fire again . . . those nights I wondered what good all this was doing me. If I had to depend on my ability to reassemble a Walther P-38 or derail a train, I wasn't going to get out of Berlin alive. I was so cold and so scared and, I guess worst of all, so lonely in this school with no names that I started to think: What am I doing here? Am I crazy? All the brilliant and devious plans I'd made for Berlin, all the clever reasons I'd found for them to send me in, didn't make much sense after a day spent learning where to hide steel wool in a truck's engine.

But the wheel I'd put myself on was spinning too fast for me to stop it, and all I could do was hang on desperately to one of the spokes.

After Training School was over, they drove me up to Baltimore. And as we passed Washington, I thought: This is crazy. I'm just going to tell them, 'Stop the car! Let me out!' I laughed to myself. But by that time we were almost out of Washington, and I realized that my silent laugh hadn't been high-spirited; it had been hysterical.

In Baltimore, I spent a week living with an old couple in the second floor of a white-stooped brownstone in a slum. They called me Lina and I was told to call them Mr and Mrs Pohl, which was pretty much like calling them Mr and Mrs Smith. The Pohls' only purpose was to drown me, smother me and choke me with *berlinerisch*. For fourteen to sixteen hours a day, the old bald man or his scrawny, washed-out wife carried on endless conversations with me and corrected my accent.

In the *berlinerisch* dialect, *g* is pronounced like the English *y* (or the German *i*), so that *ganz gut*, the phrase for 'okay,' sounds like *ynaz yoot*. I managed 'okay' okay, but after all those years of working for and living with John, sometimes I would slip and say something terrible like *gestern ist er gekommen*, 'he came yesterday,' using the correct (but forbidden) hard *g*'s. Or I'd use the High German *Ich*, with its guttural sound, instead of the *berlinerisch Ik*, for the word

'I'. Whenever I made a mistake, the old woman would put her hand to her forehead and make a grunting sound, as if my terribleness had given her a migraine attack. Mr Pohl would just exhale and tell me to do it again.

I kept waiting for the good old Berlin sense of humor to break out of these two old people, but either they'd never had it or whatever drove them out of Germany had killed forever their ability to laugh. So for seven endless days I sat at the oilcloth-covered kitchen table in their ugly apartment, learning to speak *berlinerisch*, not as I had from my Grandma Olga, with a comfortable 1880s ease, but with a 1940s lower-class seriousness. I did learn some happy Berlin expressions: *dufte* for 'nice' or 'great'; *klamauk*, a word for loud fun or a juicy scandal. But they were drilled into me the way an unfeeling dentist would drill a tooth: without letup or a smile, and with no diverting chitchat.

Mrs Pohl had apparently cooked the day before I arrived. It was a big stew, and we ate the grayish, stringy meat at one o'clock every single afternoon. At night, there would be cheese and some pickled cucumbers, and twice, an apple for dessert. And they would never let up: Is the meat good? Obviously, they weren't interested in the truth. What they wanted was a complete sentence, so I'd say, Yes, I am really enjoying the stew. How do you make it? Does it have a lot of onions? What seasoning do you use?

Neither of them ever smiled at me, and I couldn't figure out whether they were just two miserable people or whether the OSS, in one of its typical budget-cutting sprees, had gypped them out of half the money it had originally promised, and they were taking it out on me.

Then at last another car, a Packard, like the one Edward used, pulled up in front of the house. It drove me not back to Washington, as I'd expected, hoped, but to a military airport outside Baltimore.

The driver said, 'Inside those doors. Ladies' room on the second floor.' When I went in, a woman with a Scandinavian accent was waiting for me; she was very tall, with brown hair down to her shoulders and long, thin arms dangling from her sleeveless dress.

She said, 'Go into the stall and give me all your clothes, please,' and handed me new ones over the top of the door. Old ones, actually, probably straight off the backs of German refugees: a German brassiere, which was about as graceful as a sling, German cotton stockings, German shoes that made my army boots look stylish, and a German dress. When I came out, she handed me a German valise, which contained a few more items like the ones I was now wearing. 'Well,' she said. 'Good luck.' Oh, God, I thought, I should get to a phone and make some calls. I'm leaving from *here*. I have to say goodbye.

But I just asked, 'Where am I going?'

'To New York.'

'And from there?' I figured the best I'd get from her was something like: I don't know, or: I'm not supposed to talk about that.

But she put her mouth to my ear and said, 'Troop ship. England.'

'And then?' I whispered.

'And then, to the place where you belong.'

# *Chapter Twenty-One*

'Say as little as possible,' Konrad Friedrichs muttered. We walked out of the small white building onto a runway in the Lisbon airport, toward the biggest plane I'd ever seen. 'Your accent is not what it should be.'

'Do I sound American?' I asked. I had to hustle to keep up with him. He was tall, over six feet, and took long, determined strides. Although he must have been at least sixty, he held himself as if someone had just yelled: *Achtung*!

'No. You sound odd, as if you had a rare type of speech impediment.' I was about to chuckle, when I realized nothing Herr Friedrichs said was intended to be humorous. 'That is why you have been sent in as a menial. If there are any questions about your pronunciation, people will assume you are slow-witted.'

It's a measure of how dazed I was that I had even considered the possibility of chuckling. I'd been across the ocean on a troop ship where I had to lock myself in a tiny stateroom and have my meals left on trays outside my door so no one could see me. After that came three days in a metal hut with the rain beating down on it at an Army Air Forces base in England, where the head OSS guy, who looked like Al Capone, tried to convince me that no one they'd sent over had ever refused to go to parachute school and that, don't worry, when the time came no one would force me to jump if I didn't want to. I said so. I remembered Edward being angry once about the number of agents killed making blind jumps into enemy territory. It wasn't so much that they were getting shot; it was that the partisans couldn't get their lights to where they were supposed to be half the time, so the OSS agents wound up impaled on trees, or drowned, or just plain pulverized.

After three days of being screamed at for being a coward, they sent me to a rooming house outside London, where I studied maps and memorized a safe address where I could go only in a life-or-death situation, although they admitted – after I asked them – that the Gestapo's track record being what it was, 'safe' was maybe a slight exaggeration. Then I learned my peril code. If I was captured and forced to send a message, I was to use the word 'simply' in it. Like if there was a noose around my neck and a gun in my mouth, I should write: Don't worry. I'm simply fine, or: The weather is simply lovely. Not that they would come and save me; they'd just know not to believe anything in the message.

They changed my name to Lina Albrecht. They told me I had to wear my hair in braids and pin them up; it was apparently the last word in Aryan elegance. They gave me my false identity papers and flew me from the air force base to beautiful, balmy, neutral Lisbon.

'What if someone asks me a direct question?' I asked Konrad as we hurried toward the plane. 'Should I talk?'

'Obviously.'

'But this is not the time for idle chatter,' I observed. To put it mildly. About twenty feet ahead of us was the giant German plane, a Messerschmitt with six propellers – complete with an Iron Cross insignia on its side and a swastika on its tail. And talk about *Achtung*: A *Luftwaffe* officer, probably the pilot, whose posture made Herr Friedrichs look like a sloucher, stood at the bottom of the stairs, waiting for us.

There was a reason for this courtesy; Konrad Friedrichs was no slouch. He'd been working in the German foreign office since 1907, and was their ranking expert on Spain and Portugal. He was also a fervent anti-Nazi and Norman Weekes's most highly placed spy. Until he sat beside me in the waiting room in the airport, all I'd known was that code name Rex – Norman's famous Rex – would find me. In a voice just loud enough for the people nearest us to hear, he said, My dear Lina. I am pleased you have decided to return with me. Then he put his head close to mine and said,

Konrad Friedrichs. Foreign office. You know you are coming back to Berlin as my cook? I nodded. Smile at me, he ordered. I smiled. He went on: It is possible that people will assume you are also my mistress. Do nothing to discourage this supposition.

We were almost at the plane. 'Keep your eyes down,' he whispered; they were. 'No friendly glances. No hellos. You are a servant.'

The pilot clicked his heels together and gave the stiff *Heil Hitler* salute as we reached the plane. A terrible chill went up my back. I'd seen that gesture so often in newsreels that it seemed like part of a movie: something unreal, accompanied by popcorn. But now it was happening. Herr Friedrichs saluted back and, I sensed, held his breath for a moment. But I had been trained. The salute was not meant for me. Like an obedient German, I did precisely what was expected of me: held back, let my employer precede me up the stairs and followed, head down, suitcase in hand.

And then we were in the air, flying over Portugal, Spain and France, on our way to Germany.

Konrad Friedrich's house was pretty much what you'd expect of a high German official who'd been working in Berlin for thirty-five years and never married. But it took me two days to realize that. For the first forty-eight hours, I baked a cake, prepared his two favourite dinners, veal cutlets, *Naturschnitzel*, one night and codfish – the world's most disgusting food – the next. Somehow I managed to act in such a way that neither Herr Friedrichs nor his housekeeper noticed I was hysterical. But I was. As I grated a potato, I heard bombs dropping no more than a few miles away. All I wanted to do was crouch in a corner and cover my head with my arms and scream. Scream. Instead, I grated.

The house was a modest one of brick in the Wilmersdorf area, about ten minutes from the foreign office. It wasn't modest in an I'm-just-a-civil-servant way. It was on a pretty tree-shaded street with a lot of other small, well-kept houses. In a time of shortages and austerity – of wooden and cloth shoes instead of leather, when the bakers sold only day-old bread, to discourage demand for anything fresh and appealing – all the houses here had window boxes freshly planted with orange fall flowers. It was pretty obvious that this was a neighbourhood for the privileged. Privileged but not prime; Goebbels didn't live around the corner.

My room was in the basement. To say it was small makes it sound wildly luxurious. The furnishings were a cotton rug (which back in Ridgewood would have been called a substandard bath mat) and a bed – a mattress on a wood frame. There was a strip of window, painted black, just under the low ceiling. It didn't open. It was a very poor room, but my room at home had been poor. Still, a least there'd been a lace doily on my night table, and a calendar with a picture of a girl with long hair on a windswept moor. This room, though, was so empty it was mean, as if someone had deliberately stripped it. The first night, I'd gone out of the room to see if maybe there was a chest of drawers outside that I'd missed, but all I found was the coal chute, when I banged my head on it.

If I'd gone out ten minutes later, I would have banged my head on Konrad Friedrichs. It must have been right around midnight. All of a sudden, the door to my room opened and there he was, in pajamas, slippers and a bathrobe. No one had even suggested that this would be part of the job.

In fact, it wasn't. I saw that right away, when I watched him reddening at my expression. He closed the door behind him. 'This means nothing,' he said. His voice was lower than a whisper; it was more like a whoosh of air. 'My housekeeper is old, deaf, but I must maintain a fiction – in case. Therefore, to knock on your door would be inappropriate.'

'I'm a domestic, so you can just walk right in?' I couldn't believe this guy.

'I am not interested in your egalitarian sensibilities. Now, shall we get on with it?'

I motioned for him to sit near the foot of the bed. I sat near the head, or what I'd decided was the head; there was no pillow. 'Where does the housekeeper sleep?' I asked.

'On the other side of the furnace, the far side of the basement.'

'She has no idea . . . what I am?'

'No!'

'Does anybody – '

'Please, you are not to interrupt. I will tell you all you need to know. If inadvertently I leave something out, you may ask a question before I leave.' He blew what I guess was a speck of dust off the lapel of his bathrobe. 'As you may know, I have permitted you to stay in my house only because Herr Forest' – Forest was Norman Weekes's code name – 'put undue pressure on me.' His thin lips drew so right together that they became invisible; only the deep, resentful vertical lines that were etched into his upper lip remained. 'A man in my position is entitled to better treatment. I am idealist *and* a good German. For years I have passed information to Herr Forest in the hope that his . . . your people would wake up to the danger. I have risked my life in doing so, and what does he do in return? He gives me you to take care of, someone so unschooled that she is not fit to enter a house through the front door. You, who are to replace a clever, sophisticated, native-born German.'

'I was their only choice.'

'That is painfully clear. And so what can happen? They send in an amateur, she gets caught, and I – who for years have been above suspicion – am suspect. It is wrong!'

What was I going to do? Argue with him? 'You're right. It is wrong. Terrible. Outrageous.'

He only seethed on. 'The situation – seeing that you are placed in a certain official's household – compels me to associate with . . . with resistance types I would prefer to shun entirely. Do I make myself clear?'

'Yes,' I said. 'You only pass information to Herr Forest. What goes on among . . . these people in Berlin is of no interest to you.'

'That is correct. They plot over caviar. They care nothing about the Fatherland, only about their own circumstances. The degree to which they believe that that man will bring us to utter ruin is the degree to which they oppose him.'

His bearing never relaxed, not even when he sat on that terrible mattress, with what had to be a spring poking his behind. Back home, I thought, only a person with a chest full of medals, a mahogany desk at the War Department and an office full of visitors would sit like that. I remembered walking through the War Department with Edward one day and glancing into an open office, with just that kind of officer: upright, his left side just slightly lower than his right from the weight of his medals. A real stiff, right? The guy suddenly noticed me and blew me a kiss. I'd kept going, and Edward had asked, What are you smiling about? Oh, nothing, I'd answered.

But then I caught myself. Forget back home. In Training School, they warned us: Think only of the present. The future, when it is of immediate concern. Never the past: The past will devastate you. And when you think, think in the language of the country you have been sent to. Speaking it is not enough. To survive, you must *be* Czech or French or Hungarian. Or German.

I sat there in that impoverished little room trying to be fair, to admire Konrad Friedrichs, not detest him. If someone spends his whole life agonizing about the fate of his fatherland instead of what movie to see over the weekend or if he'll ever fall in love or grow bald or get to visit Florida, he's not going to develop a rollicking sense of humor.

And he had to be frightened, doing what he was doing – living in this Nazi hell he hated, spying for the United States – all those years. And he had to be bitter too; I'd clearly been shoved down his throat. Instead of being treated as a treasure by Norman Weekes, Rex was being exploited. The OSS was treating him the way they would routinely treat some two-bit adventurer in an ascot who hangs around the resistance for thrills, not like the paragon of virtues – honor, bravery – that he was.

'You will continue to work in my kitchen as you have been working for the next four days. On that day, Saturday, I will suggest to my housekeeper that she deserves a vacation. I will give what, to her, is a great deal of money and a train ticket so that she can visit her family in Würzburg for three or four weeks. She will think to herself that I am a foolish old man to take up with someone like you, but of course, she will not say anything. She will go.'

The section of the mattress I was sitting on was incredibly lumpy. I edged back and tucked one of my legs under me. Herr Friedrich's nostrils flared wide and then closed, and you didn't have to be his best friend to figure out this was a sign of intense displeasure.

'You will please,' he ordered, 'sit still like a proper German and not move about out of control as if . . . you are listening to jazz music. Now, once my housekeeper is gone, your training will begin. You are, as they claimed, a good cook . . . for those with a taste for the cuisine of common people. But where you are going . . . you must be taught to cook and serve in a more elegant manner.'

His house wasn't exactly the sort of place where you'd find footmen slinging caviar at guests in white tie and tails. But if Rex wanted elegance . . . I smiled and said, 'I'll be happy to try and learn whatever you like. I realize I'm not a professional cook and – '

'Do not interrupt! In three to four weeks you must learn to be an accomplished chef. That was the best cover they could find, because it suits Herr Forest's purpose perfectly. The plan is to get you into my colleague's household.' Rex's mouth turned down in disgust at the thought of the kind of person who had risen to become his colleague in the foreign office. 'You are to be *in* the household but not *of* it. You know our language, but you do not know our ways. So it is best that you be hidden away in the kitchen.

'Now, this colleague is a peacock who fancies himself a man of the world, a gourmet. His chef will have an accident in the next week or two.' He saw I was going to interrupt again, and he cut me off. 'I am assured it will not be a fatal – or even terribly serious – accident. Two weeks after that, a very respected person will mention what a glorious meal was served at my house and offer to help this official secure your services.'

'What if the chef wants his job back after the accident?'

'Be assured we have considered that possibility. While he is recuperating, he will be offered another position, at a far greater salary.'

'What's the name of the official I'll be working for?' I knew, naturally. Norman Weekes had given me his name. But I wanted to see how far Herr Friedrichs, Rex, would trust a fellow spy.

'Quiet!' Not very far. 'You will know what you need to know at the proper time. It serves no purpose for you to possess this information now. So I will continue, and you will stop asking questions. This official for whom you will work had been chosen because he is known to bring papers – top-secret papers – from his office to his home to work on.'

'I know. They told me – '

'Silence! This practice of his is, of course, forbidden. But those who know of his habit are in no position to suggest that he stop it.

'As far as I am concerned, there is only one redeeming aspect to this . . . this sanctuary *cum* cooking school I have been forced to run. The person they have chosen to teach you the fine points is someone I know, someone from the Abwehr. This individual comes from one of the oldest and finest families in Germany, and is the only member of the resistance . . . whom I consider a true patriot.'

He stood up very slowly. At first I thought it was his age, but then I realized he was being careful that the bed didn't creak. 'This individual will be risking everything to help you and your countrymen.' His nostrils flared again, and you could see more than his anger as he spoke of Americans; you could see his contempt. 'Your imprudent, arrogant "freedom-lovers." ' He put his hand on the door handle. 'Now listen to me! You must not compromise this individual. You are to keep quiet about your background, your destination, your mission. You must do nothing – *nothing* – to endanger . . .' He paused, took a deep breath and regained his composure. 'You will be taught what is elegant, what is correct, by one who is . . . flawless. Be silent. Be obedient. And be grateful!'

The past will devastate you, they'd said. So what was I supposed to think about, those first few nights in that cell in Herr Friedrichs's basement? The graciousness of my host? The warmth of his housekeeper? When I heard him say 'my housekeeper.' I pictured a lovable, pudgy old family retainer with a white apron, someone who'd have tea with me before she went off on her vacation and tell me where she kept the towels. Or someone with a quiet smile, who would nod, listening to you, as she peeled an apple in one long strip – like my Grandma Olga.

But Frau Gerlach could have posed for the witch in *Hansel and Gretel*; she had claw hands, and the bottom of her face looked more like an elbow than a chin. She had so many warts that you couldn't help counting them. Her personality matched her looks. She hissed '*Hure*' – whore – at me a couple of times and wouldn't eat anything I cooked. She kept a crock of cheese in the refrigerator, and when she came in to eat, she shooed me out with insane waves of her hands, as if she was getting rid of a rodent.

When I turned out the lamp, my room with its painted window – cheaper than a blackout curtain – fell into complete darkness. But even if I'd wanted to, I couldn't have slept. Airplanes droned above the house, and my stomach squeezed into a hard knot. Then came the muffled blast of distant bombing and, closer, the demented siren of police cars. And, because my window was level with the street, the sound of feet. The second night, somebody stopped right outside, and I lay in the blackness in absolute panic, saying to myself, They're just lighting a cigarette or they have a pebble in their shoe or . . . I can't stand this. I can't take another second.

So, I thought about America – and I thought about it in English. Like a sick baby who gets a warm bottle, I wasn't helped, but I was comforted. I thought about growing up in Ridgewood, where the Irish kids used to call the German kids 'Heinies' and make fun of German last names: 'Nudelfludel!' They'd howl with laughter. 'Von Stupelpoop!' And we'd feel so superior that we never even called them dumb micks. Sure, it was prejudice, but from where I sat (lay) it seemed innocent. You got it out of your system, and sooner or later you got over the fear, the strangeness; the Irish and the German kids grew up and joined the same building-trades union, sometimes became friends or even got married.

I came up with all sorts of pictures I didn't even know I had filed away: How a horse-drawn truck came rattling up Fresh Pond Road in the summer with watermelons. Getting off the subway at Seneca Avenue after work on December nights, looking down from the el platform and seeing everybody's Christmas lights. Going to my graduation from Grover Cleveland, walking slow because my mother was wearing four-inch heels, and how Olga stopped three or four times to adjust my cap and the tassel. 'A scholar!' she said to my father, and the funny thing was, even though I said, 'Grandma, it's just high school,' I knew she really meant it.

Naturally, I thought about John. I played 'If it's 3 A.M. in Berlin, what time is it in Washington?' It didn't matter, because whatever hour it was, in my mind he was always with Nan. I envisioned him at his desk, on the phone with her, or at the house, listening to music with her in his arms, the way I'd found them, or up in the bedroom; she'd run her fingers over her old monogram on the pillowcases and the top hem of the sheet, then run her finger over his lips and say, Oh, John, being with you like this is so wholly, unequivocally right. And he'd probably do something like kiss her hand and quote some poem they both knew in French. And she'd say, *Mais oui, mon amour.* But then she'd hesitate: We're in limbo, my darling. I hope you realize that. I can't believe . . . She just disappeared?

In a manner of speaking, he'd say.

Do you know where she is?

I can't . . .

Oh, I know you can't tell me. You're right not to. But how long do we have to live like this, sneaking, pretending? Oh, John this *has* to be resolved. When will she come back?

And he'd say, I don't know, my beloved. Maybe six months from now. Maybe never.

That Saturday, Frau Gerlach, warts and all, left for Würzburg. An hour later, my teacher, the individual from one of Germany's oldest and finest families, walked into the kitchen carrying a mesh shopping bag filled with groceries. She wore a burgundy skirt and a cashmere sweater set that was such a pale pink it was almost white. She held out her hand and said, 'Margarete von Eberstein.' I'd been up to my elbows in herring, so I quickly wiped my right hand on my apron, held it out and explained, 'Herring.' It was only when she started to laugh that I added, 'Lina Albrecht.'

She pulled off her cardigan, tossed it on to a chair, pushed up the sleeves of her pullover and demanded, 'How is old Konrad treating you?' Margarete possessed two qualities that I hadn't seen in any of the hundreds of Germans I'd met in the past two years: vitality and humor. She wasn't beautiful, or even pretty. And despite the 'von,' her bones were no more aristocratic than mine were. But she had dazzling blue-gray eyes and a wonderful smile. 'Is he as condescending as ever?'

'Pretty much,' I admitted.

'I know he is a . . . special friend of yours, perhaps, so forgive me, but he is such a dreadful snob. He adores me without qualification. It's so tedious.' Margarete's energy was a little overwhelming. As she spoke, she whirled around the kitchen, grabbing a crock of vinegar from the shelf, a paring knife from a drawer. She plunged her hand into the sack of flour, rubbed a bit of it between her fingers and made a face at the texture. 'Nothing has been good since those bastards came in – in '33.'

'Don't you think you should be a little more careful?'

'Why? Will you turn me in?' before I could answer, she said, 'Lina, if you and I and our friends are going to succeed, we must be very, very careful. But there are occasional moments when there is nothing to fear, and we must take advantage of them, *glory* in them, because they allow us the chance to be what we truly are: human beings.' She took an apple from a basket, quickly cored it, sliced it, and gave me half. 'Now let's talk about German cuisine. Meat and potatoes. All over Europe they think of it as banal. Leaden. Greasy. Olive oil for the Italians, peanut oil for the French, butter for the English, and for the Germans – bacon grease.'

'Don't forget lard.'

'No, we mustn't forget lard. Lovely, light, delicious lard. But what I want to show you is fine German cooking, the sort you must be doing to please the person for whom you will be working.' I wanted to say something, but I was chewing a piece of apple. Margarete held up her hand. 'No names,' she warned, but then she flashed her fabulous smile. 'No descriptions, either. Don't tell me, "The man I'm working for is a bald dwarf who lunches with Rommel's wife every other Thursday." The less we know about each other's . . . activities, the safer we will be.' She reached into her shopping bag and pulled out a large package wrapped in white butcher paper. 'Today, we are going to roast veal and prepare sauerkraut – but sauerkraut in champagne sauce.' She pulled out a small bottle. I glanced at it: French champagne.

'Aren't you a little nervous about walking down the street with champagne and half a calf?' I asked. 'The penalties for dealing in black market goods – '

'Lina,' she said, unwrapping the meat, 'I am a trusted employee of the Abwehr. My father's family has been eating fine veal since before the Hundred Years' War. And my mother, who is very beautiful and very charming, was a great success. She's retired now, but in the late twenties and thirties she was a favorite of our Führer, and his affection for her has never diminished. Should I feel afraid?'

'No,' I answered her. 'I guess you should feel pretty good.'

Margarete turned to me. Her hand came out of the shopping bag, and she was holding a bunch of parsley as if it was a delicate bouquet. 'I will feel very good,' she said quietly, 'when every single goddamned Nazi is dead.'

All the men on the streets of Berlin were in uniform. Those few who weren't were either doomed or people to be afraid of; you knew instinctively to avoid both. The women were more like me, in dreary coats of *Zellwolle*, a fake material that from a distance looked like wool but up close looked like a scouring pad. It did nothing to keep you warm.

Now and then, one of the wives or mistresses of men in power would glide by, wrapped in a cloud of French perfume and yards of fur; the invasions of France and Scandinavia had done wonders for the women of the powerful. In London I'd heard that Goebbels was trying to get them to play down their privilege; he'd even put an end to their morning horseback rides in the Tiergarten, the park in the center of Berlin. He didn't want the masses to be resentful. Ha. One look at Maragerete's cashmere sweater collection and her fox coat and her gold earrings in those days of standing on line for an hour and a half just to buy a turnip should have caused a riot of resentment. But either the Nazis' women were the German equivalent of movie stars – they lived sumptuous lives on everybody's behalf – or people were too terrified to show their resentment.

I was perpetually terrified, but who – even the most innocent –

would not be? The second time I left Herr Friedrichs's house, I'd seen three Gestapo men beating up a middle-aged man outside a bakery. The man's head was in the gutter, his body on the sidewalk; one of them stamped his boot down, again and again, on the man's stomach, and his head jerked with every blow. The other two just said, 'Move along,' to the people on the street, mechanically, because not a single person stopped or even slowed down. Maybe no one was innocent.

I'd finally gone outside, seven days after I arrived in Berlin. All my papers were in order – my passport, my work book and my ration card. The OSS may have sent men parachuting in the dark and going splat onto concrete highways, but everyone said they were great with documents. I hoped so. Herr Friedrichs had looked at all three of them, as well as the card I didn't have to carry, my *Ahnenpass*, my ancestry passport, which proved Lina Albrecht's Aryan descent. All he said was, Adequate. They had to be more than adequate, because there could be an identity check anywhere, anytime. It was all up to the discretion – and the mood – of the Gestapo.

The picture on my passport had been taken in England. It showed me in three-quarters profile, so if you looked close, you could really get a good idea of how stupid-looking the braids were and how washed out I looked without any makeup. Or maybe I'd just gone pale that day because right before they took the photographs, they put my right and left index fingerprints on the card. I remember I'd gotten that numb feeling again when I saw the partially filled out passport and pictured that if it had been made out to Linda Voss instead of Lina Albrecht, there would be a giant 'J' stamped on the left side.

But dead Jews don't need identity cards. One of the OSS men in the boardinghouse in London had mentioned, quite casually, that there were still about forty thousand Jews in Berlin, but then he'd added, No. Wait a second. Probably a lot less by now. They're in the middle of another roundup. More deportations and the usual deaths. I'd asked, What do you mean, usual? And he'd answered, Suicides. The ones from Eastern Europe don't know what's going to happen to them. The ones in Berlin are starting to understand.

I had to go to the fish store that first day. And even though I traced and retraced the seven blocks on the map and in my mind, the walk never seemed to end. Good German that Lina was, she kept her eyes down and minded her own business, but I worried that something in my stride, something in the way I carried my pocketbook, something in the way I looked at a traffic signal, would give away that I was an American.

My heart pounded so hard I could hear it inside my ears. I was going to meet my contact. Once I became a chef, I'd be giving all my information to the fish man. Now I was just going to introduce myself, to say, 'Good morning. I hope the walleyed pike is not as bony as it was last Thursday.'

I tried to ease the banging of my heart by telling myself that the OSS had chosen a reliable and cautious member of the resistance for me to report to, and the chances of a Gestapo agent hiding under the halibut were small. But as I waited to cross the street, I froze. I knew that whether I waited one second or twenty minutes, I could not take another step forward, and that inevitably, shamefully, I'd lose control and go running back to Rex's – giving away my hysteria, my foreignness, my guilt just by the mere fact of running.

But then Edward Leland stopped me. I stood there on that corner and said to myself, Edward had gone to ground in Denmark and in Poland and in Czechoslovakia and in Rumania, and he can't even speak the language. Does his heart ever beat like this? Does he ever want to turn and run?

And then I realized how well I'd gotten to know the man I'd worked for, because suddenly I understood that yes, something in him probably wanted to run back to whatever seaport he'd entered in Poland, screaming his head off. I crossed the street and asked myself, Why didn't he run? What made him keep going?

I couldn't figure out the answer, but it was as if Edward was standing next to me. I could hear his voice, deep, sure, soothing: Do it *now*, I could suddenly hear him say. Think about it later.

So I just wrapped my ugly brown *Zellwolle* coat tighter around me and walked fast, so Rolf Vogel, fishmonger, would not run out of walleyed pike before I got to the store.

# *Chapter Twenty-Two*

'There's an old *berlinerisch* expression,' I said. ' "*Eine jute jebratene Jans* is *eine jute Jabe Jottes.*" ' That was one of the nine hundred forty-two sayings that the Pohls, the awful old couple in Baltimore, had taught me.

Margarete von Eberstein, the sleeves of her red silk blouse rolled up, was showing me how to stuff the neck of a goose with a forcemeat of ground liver, pork and herbs. ' "A good roast goose is a good gift to God," ' she repeated, smiling, as she tried out my accent. She put the neck into my hands and remarked, 'Here. The good gift of God needs more stuffing.'

By the end of my third week in Berlin, Margarete had come to the house at least ten different times, both on weekends and after work at the Abwehr, where she was a translator. I almost laughed when she told me that: She could get along all right in French and Italian, she explained, but her specialty was English. Here we were, becoming friends, and I had to fight all my instincts and suppress the urge to turn to her and say – in English: Squishing all this slimy stuff into a goose neck is one of the most disgusting things I've ever had to do!

After all the hours I'd spent with Margarete, I could predict her reaction. Her mouth would drop and she'd stare at me, and then all of a sudden she'd burst into laughter. Not that ho-ho-ho, typical overjolly German guffaw, but the sort of laugh that's described in books as musical.

The odds on our ever becoming friends were about as great as my becoming great buddies with one of Nan's Smith College socialites: nil, or pretty close to it. But just as politics makes strange bedfellows, war makes peculiar friendships. We were thrown together by a single common denominator: We both hated Nazism. Of course, so did Herr Friedrichs, and that certainly didn't make him my pal. But Magarete and I discovered that we had a lot in common. Not that I shared her love of literature or her passion for cooking; how much did I have to say to a woman who got all flushed with pleasure at the mention of wild mushrooms? And if she'd known about it, she definitely wouldn't have shared my appreciation or obsession or whatever it was with the movies; I'd have been willing to bet that if someone had shown her a picture of Cary Grant, she would have had absolutely no idea who he was.

But what we did share, I guess, was a hatred of grimness. Right from that first Saturday afternoon, we'd sensed a quality in each other: fun.

What bothered me was that the more fun we had together, the less fun – if you can call it that – I was having perpetuating all the lies of my cover story. She believed I was Lina Albrecht, who was twenty-eight years old and the daughter of a Berlin butcher and a housewife (both dead), who had married a man twenty-two years older, a man who worked as majordomo in the household of an Austrian playboy who lived in Portugal, and that my husband had died of a kidney disease eighteen months before.

I'd hinted that the playboy had allowed me to stay on in his house, as his cook. Margarete got the impression (and getting this impression across was as much a part of my cover story as the part I actually spoke about) that the playboy had kept me around for more than my *Eintopf.* And she got the impression that just as the playboy was tiring of me, along came his cousin, Konrad Friedrichs, who saw in me not only what his cousin did, but also a truly new face . . . and someone he could use for his own political purposes.

Margarete trussed the goose once, and then had me do it. It took me six tries, and in comparison to hers, my results looked pathetic. 'What a mess!' I said.

'Lina . . .' she began.

'What?'

'What do you think of people who intrude upon the most private part of your life?' Margarete asked.

I lifted the goose and put it into the roaster. 'What do you want to know?' I responded.

'Are you in love with Konrad?'

'No.'

'Good.'

'Why is it good? Because elderly foreign office officials don't marry young – well, sort of young – household employees?'

'That's part of the reason,' she said. 'But also . . . I would feel better if I knew that what you are doing . . . you are doing out of deep conviction. Because if you do it out of love, Lina, if you go wherever you are going to please a man, then you surely won't survive. It takes a hard edge. I think – no, I *know* I have it. I don't know if you do. You seem so sweet so vulnerable. Losing your husband . . .'

As Margarete spoke, I immediately thought of John, but I forced that picture out of my mind and replaced it with the makebelieve Johannes Albrecht. Outside London, at the rooming house, the OSS people had shown me photographs of a man in his early fifties, heavyset, with a hard, bulldog face, and said, This is your late husband. You can't do better? I'd demanded. Come on, they'd said, and kept me up till three one morning telling them details about my 'marriage.' I told them everything, how 'Johannes' liked his socks folded, not rolled, and how indifferent he had become about sex after the first year of our nine-year marriage.

'Do you miss your husband?' she asked.

'No.' I smiled a little and added, 'Sorry.'

'Was he bad to you? Did he beat you?'

'Margarete, your view of reality is not exactly realistic. Ordinary, working-class husbands do not routinely get drunk and beat their wives.'

'They obviously lack a sense of the grand gesture. I am disappointed.'

'I'll disappoint you some more. Ordinary wives do not automatically have twenty children and commit suicide by drowning themselves in a vat of cabbage.'

'I never thought that.' She cocked her head to the side. 'But it is a magnificent image. I almost wish it were true. Not so anyone would actually suffer. But it's so magnificently German: so prosaic, so stoic. Now tell me, why don't you miss him? Did you ever love him?'

'No. I was fond of him, in the beginning. But at that time in my life, I had no one else to be fond of. I was an only child, and my father had died when I was ten, and then, when I was seventeen, my mother died. And two months later there was Johannes, on his holiday, visiting his brother, who lived in our building. Now that I think about it, he was probably looking for a wife. I guess he was tired of . . . the sort of women he could meet in Lisbon.'

'Prostitutes?'

'I suppose so.'

'Did you like living in Lisbon?'

'No.' I put the goose into the oven. Margarete had preheated it. 'We lived in a villa by the sea. It sounds very romantic, but it was just isolated. And Johannes didn't let me go anyplace alone.'

'Was he jealous?'

'No. There was too much work to be done. Polishing silver, dusting books, keeping inventory of linen. He didn't trust the local girls to do it, and now that he had a wife, he was free of those chores. I suppose he thought if I caught the morning bus to Lisbon and spent a lovely, interesting day, that I'd want to go the next day, and the next.'

'Do you speak Portuguese?'

'No. The man whose house we lived in – '

'The Austrian?'

'Yes. He only wanted German spoken in the house. Why he was so insistent upon that when it had been his choice to move out of Austria and into Portugal I'll never know.'

'So you've never been in love, Lina?'

'Well . . .' I remembered the OSS photos of the mythical Austrian playboy. A face that could have been on the cover of a Propaganda Ministry leaflet on 'The Greatness of the Aryan.' Except for the jutting chin, the man in the picture had looked uncomfortably like John.

'Oh! You were in love with the Austrian!' Her eyes brightened.

'Margarete, my life isn't a fairy tale. I knew it wasn't . . . mutual.

And I knew it would only be for a short time, and that there wouldn't be a happily ever after.'

'Was it worth it?'

'I guess so. I mean, I'm not like you. I don't have many opportunities to meet wealthy, educated, exciting men.'

'He was very exciting?'

I looked her straight in the eye. 'Yes. Exciting where it mattered most.'

'Oh, my!' Margarete breathed. She took the knives, spoons and plates we'd been using and took them over to the sink. Suddenly she wheeled around. 'Everyone thinks I'm a woman of the world, but I've never had anything like that.'

'You'll have it,' I said.

'I don't know. I've walked around the garden, so to speak, many, many times. And all I've met is . . . many boring men. Boring where it mattered most.'

'I don't think . . . excitement happens that often. It's chemistry. I really believe that. You can be fond of someone. Like at the beginning, I was awfully fond of Johannes. Good, steady old Johannes. But even if I'd loved him . . . when we were together, well. there just wasn't any chemistry.'

'Did you love this playboy?'

'No. He . . . he didn't have a very good character, and I think you have to admire a man to really love him. He was very rich, but he never worked a day in his life. He existed only to enjoy what he was born with.'

'He sounds like my father.'

'Oh, I didn't mean . . .'

'No,' she said thoughtfully. 'That's all right. My father wasn't . . . isn't a playboy. He's quite faithful to my mother, although the reverse, I believe, is not the case. But he's a man who rides and hunts and enjoys the fruits of his wealth, his inherited wealth, and who – ' She broke off.

'What?'

'My father will do anything and everything to preserve the status quo. In 1932, there was a group of noblemen, the DAG, who endorsed Hitler. My father was one of its leaders. Hitler is anti-

Communist, he said, and the National Socialists stand for a Germany that we all stand for. What he meant was a Germany where the aristocracy will be treated like proper aristocrats.'

'When did he become disillusioned?' I asked.

'He didn't. If Hitler doesn't turn on you, he can be a loyal and generous friend.' Her face grew somber. 'The Baron von Eberstein has prospered.'

'What about your mother?'

'You must be joking, Lina. My mother is an actress. Hitler was her admirer. He thought her brilliant. Do you think she could find anything sinister or immoral in such a man – or in the movement he led? No. To the contrary. My mother finds Hitler, finds Nazism, "brilliant" also.'

'Then how did you come to where you are?'

'I suppose because my parents ignored me. So I was free to look at their lives, look at their choices, and then form my own opinions.'

The baron, through luck and his ties to the Nazis, had managed to keep hold of his money and his land. There were moments, when Margarete described her father sauntering out of the woods after a morning's hunting, his black rifle slung over his shoulder, that he sounded like a handsome, romantic and exciting figure: a baron but, in his daughter's eyes, something of a prince. A remote prince, though, and a prince who brought a lot of brutal, loud-mouth peasants back to the castle with him.

Margerete's mother visited her husband's estate at Christmas, Easter and for a month in the summer, but she kept her own house in Berlin. She was one of the great actresses of her day, and she performed not only in German but in English and French as well. Goethe, Shakespeare, Molière. She could do them all. That she'd had a daughter was a fact she frequently forgot. Margarete said her mother came home the summer she was ten and kept calling her 'Pretty girl,' as if she'd forgotten her name. Margarete said, She could memorize all of *Faust* and *Antony and Cleopatra*, but she couldn't quite remember whether I was Margarete or Margot.

So Margarete retreated to the kitchen. When she spoke about her childhood, and about the warmth and patience of the family's chef and his wife, who assisted him, you could see – in her stories about getting lost while picking white asparagus or her early disasters in learning to eviscerate a hen – not only the girl who became the laughing, high-spirited Berlin sophisticate, but also the sad child who, despite her high and comfortable niche in society, had grown up feeling that there was no place she could really feel at home. Her father would be off hunting or decanting wine for Nazis, her mother would be off emoting, and even the kindly chef and his wife – the second their work was done – would rush off to their own two children.

Sometimes, she said, she'd stay in the kitchen after all the help – the menservants and the kitchenmaids – went to bed. I'd sleep there, she told me. It was the warmest place in the house. Warm not in degrees, but in . . . Do you understand? I said yes, I did.

'Lina, I have to tell you something.' I glanced up from the *Preiselbeeren*, the German equivalent of cranberry sauce, I had just started. 'I have a lover.' I had barely begun to smile when she added, 'I hate him.'

'Who is he?'

She was wearing a long white wool skirt – real wool – and she rubbed her hands up and down the front of it, discoloring it with the residue of goose grease that had been on her hands. 'No one knows.' She sounded edgy.

I understood. 'I won't ask, then.'

'Except the people in the . . . movement. They know. When I mentioned this man's interest in me' – she was talking unnaturally fast – 'they wanted me to . . . they encouraged it.' Suddenly her blue-gray eyes turned a shadow color and filled with tears. 'He is a colonel. On Hitler's personal staff.'

'I see,' I said.

'No you don't. He is fifty-four years old and he is fat as' – she lifted her head and looked at the oven – 'an overstuffed goose. With fat little fingers and fat thighs and breasts – like a sagging woman.' She came back to the table, lowered herself into a chair and wiped her eyes with a kitchen towel. 'Oh, God, I hate it.'

'Then don't do it, Margerete.'

'I have to.'

'No. There's a limit. Tell them you can't.'

She made herself smile and lifted her chin. High. Aristocratic. 'Oh, but, Lina, the information I get from those fat lips. He sneaks away from his sow of a wife and I prepare Königsberger Klopse and what takes me an hour to make he sucks in less than a minute. But then, before we go . . . inside, he sits back and burps and tells me about his day. In the time it takes him to digest, I get intelligence that sometimes saves lives. You tell me. Should I give him up?'

My eyes suddenly got wet with the tears that had been in hers a moment before. 'I don't know,' I whispered.

'Oh, Lina, I know there is something better than this. I only pray I live long enough to enjoy five minutes of it.'

If it had been up to Konrad Friedrichs, I would have visited the fish store every day. Practice! Practice! Practice!

But Herr Friedrichs was a spy only in that he gleaned information from the foreign office, flew to Lisbon on legitimate Third Reich business and, while he was there, brought in a suit to a dry cleaner, with the data written in code and folded and slipped into a minuscule slit in the cuff of his trousers. The dry cleaner would bring the suit to the back of the store, to a waiting OSS operative, and for Herr Friedrichs, that would be the end of it.

Unlike Margarete and Rolf Vogel, fishmonger, Konrad Friedrichs was always aloof; he worked alone. The idea of an organized German resistance cooperating on an American intelligence operation was too horrible for him to even contemplate. But he trusted Margarete. Not because she was trusted by Norman Weekes and not because of her bravery and skill, but because, despite her parents' fascist views, she came from a great family who for centuries had stood for the best Germany had to offer. When Norman stuck me on Herr Friedrichs, it was Margarete, his only contact in the resistance, who calmed him down, and Margarete who promised to make sure I indeed became the great cook the OSS claimed I was.

But Margarete had to be insulated from knowledge, protected from my operation, so it came down to me and Herr Friedrichs working together. The two of us were not born to sing a duet.

Konrad Friedrichs did everything from bathing to spying on a rigid, unvarying schedule. But as Margarete or Rolf could have told him, you can't have an obvious schedule when you're out in the field. So even though it caused a number of major nostril flare-ups, I told him I would not go to Rolf's every day to Practice! Practice! Practice! Practice!

'Listen to me. No human being can eat that much herring,' I told him, when he made one of his slippered trips to my room. 'If I go there that often, that regularly, someone in his store is going to think it's curious. I'm a cook working for a highly placed individual in the foreign office – *you* – and they know you have allowances ordinary citizens don't have. You could eat veal seven days a week for breakfast, lunch and dinner if you wanted to. So why is your cook hanging around the fishmonger's?'

'You're like all of them. "Secret agents." Enamored of cleverness. Disdainful of hard work.'

'If somehow the Gestapo gets onto Rolf, if he's being watched, don't you think they're going to notice me?'

'Your execution of the transfer of information must be flawless *before* you leave here and enter the household of . . . where you are going. You must – '

'Practice!' I said. 'Don't worry.'

' "Don't worry"! The vanity, the naïveté in that expression. I have been doing . . . what I have been doing for years. You . . . For all I know, they picked you out from . . . from a burlesque line. Your only credential is that you obviously grew up in a household that included a low-class individual from Berlin.'

'My grandmother was German. Whatever her social class, she was a refined woman. She would never make offensive remarks about other people's families.'

He stuck out his chest and took a deep, aggrieved breath. Very huffy. 'You think I am arrogant, pompous. That is not the case.' Boy did this guy need a mirror! 'I am not denigrating your grandmother. I am merely trying to emphasize the fact that you come to this occupation as a novice.'

'You may be right, but there was only one person in the whole world who could take the job, and that was me. I have the willingness and I have the guts. And what I lack in training I make up for in common sense.'

'Your common sense! You will soon be dead, or wish you were, and it will be worse, *worse*' – his voice rose to a panicked squeal – 'worse for me. You are my doom!'

I could sympathize with his terror. But I was really getting fed up with his contempt for me. 'Do you think I would risk my own life and the lives of other people if I felt I wasn't prepared?'

'You do not know what the word "prepared" means!'

I got up and opened my door, which wasn't easy because the room was so small I had to practically climb over Herr Friedrichs's knees. 'Please leave my room.'

He stood tall. 'It is *my* room. My house.'

'Well,' I said, 'our conversation is over. You can either leave or throw me out. Which would you prefer?'

Maybe I should have been more understanding about his predicament, but the truth was I was so preoccupied by my own near hysteria, I didn't have patience for his.

On the plane to Lisbon, the OSS had given me a pocket-book with a tiny compartment in the bottom that opened when you pressed against a hinge. They said, 'When you get to Rolf's store, have a sack full of heavy vegetables, cans, what have you. When he waits on you, he'll have to help you set down your packages, and in that maneuver he'll brush against your pocketbook. That's how he'll extract your information. He'll pull out the paper you write everything on from the hidden compartment in your pocketbook. Don't worry. This is guaranteed: No one will see what he's doing. He's a real pro. He knows how to trigger the mechanism; he's used this kind of transfer technique before. You just have to look burdened down so he can get close enough to help you. Relax. It's a piece of cake.

Except the piece of cake didn't work. On three separate visits to the fish store, Rolf couldn't get the bottom of my pocketbook open. Okay, we were just practicing, and all he would have pulled out was a small piece of black paper. But when the real time came, the paper – even with the tiny writing I'd mastered, with letters the size of commas – had to get out of Berlin. And he was the first step in its journey.

If anyone could have made that hinge work, it would have been Rolf Vogel. He was a man about my age, with thinning red hair, pasty skin, pale freckles and one arm. He'd lost the other in a motorcycle accident when he was young. But while that handicap kept him out of the army, it didn't keep him from boning fish with amazing dexterity or lifting a wooden crate of iced fish that must have weighed pretty close to what he did.

And he wasn't a nervous wreck like Herr Friedrichs. Rolf was so calm he even soothed me. I didn't know the reasons for his willingness to put his life on the line when ninety-nine point nine percent of his countrymen cringed and cowered and *Sieg Heil*ed till the cows came home, but whatever the reasons, they were deeply felt. And because he knew how great the danger to him was, and was willing to accept it, he wasn't going to fall apart. Rolf Vogel didn't sweat. He didn't bite his nails. In fact, he behaved pretty much the way I imagined Edward Leland would have. Matter-of-fact. If it's cold, toss a wool sweater with starry snowflakes into your travel bag before you slip into Denmark. If you know you're going into occupied Poland, just say, Well, see you in a few weeks, Linda, and simply walk out the door. Casual. In control.

And after the third failed attempt at making a transfer, he just said, 'Perhaps you would like to see the trout today.' He guided me toward the rear of the store. We were still in sight, but it was safer. 'What do you think of them?' he asked, looking at the fish. His hand rested on a stack of wrapping paper. He seemed to be saying silently, maybe we can work a transfer with this paper. I sniffed. I didn't like the idea; it was too open. 'They are quite fresh,' he assured me. I sniffed again: Lina Albrecht, the perfectionist. 'I like to see for myself.'

'Please go ahead,' he said, as if this was nothing new to him. At least a quarter of his customers were pains in the neck.

I lifted trout after trout, and stared into their dead eyes. Boy, were they ugly when you took the time to look at them. And resentful, with those little pursed mouths. But I had to come up with something. And then I cleared my throat. Rolf watched. I poked at a trout's mouth. It opened, and I stuck my finger down its throat or gullet or whatever it was. Well, whatever it was was large enough for a small piece of paper. Rolf barely tilted his head, but I knew he was nodding his understanding.

'I don't like these. Let me see the halibut,' I said.

'Certainly,' Rolf said. '*Certainly.*'

On my last night at Konrad Freidrichs's, I arranged my body in its usual position: twisted right, left and sideways to avoid the jabbing mattress springs. On an earlier night, I'd tried something extra: putting my right arm over my head, my shoulder covering one ear and my hand the other, so I couldn't hear the sounds of the bombing and the antiaircraft fire. But after a minute the silence wasn't golden; I had to be awake to hear the wrong set of footsteps, or a voice asking for me.

On that last night, I lay awake, brooding over Herr Friedrichs. I couldn't stand him, but in the end, I realized how much he'd done for me: bringing me in from Lisbon, allowing a member of the resistance to train me in his own house, hiding me, and most of all, nagging me all the time, shaking his head in disgust at my low-class stupidity, forcing me to be more frightened – and, I realized, more cautious and suspicious – than I might otherwise have been.

Two days earlier, I'd done what in England I'd been ordered to do: taken the subway all the way to Alexanderplatz, to test my ability to get around Berlin and to pass myself off as a working-class Berliner. Oh, had I been proud! I left early in the morning, and when I got to Alexanderplatz station, people were still leaving the safety of the underground; there had been an air raid the night before. I joined the crowd climbing up the stairs.

A good lesson. This was Berlin, not New York. Not a single person shoved, jostled, elbowed or thrust himself ahead of anyone else. I forced myself to walk at the measured pace of the crowd, not to try and beat it; I kept my head down, although it was as much to avoid the mass exhalation of the morning breath of people who'd slept underground as to mind my own Teutonic business.

Up on the street, the lines were already forming in front of the stores. Women held on to their pocketbooks, with their passports and ration books, more tightly than they did to their children. The people were poorer here, and at first I felt secure. I looked more like one of them, a housewife. When I walked into the fancier stores near Herr Friedrichs's, I really didn't belong. Shopkeepers eyed my knit hat, my shoes, and then realized: Of course! I was someone's servant.

I stood on a line for almost two hours. War showed on faces. People looked haggard, gray, exhausted by the effort to get through even this, the beginning of their day. That's when I realized I wasn't one of them, and I knew they realized it too. What set me apart was that I was healthy. My skin was clear; there was still a sheen to my hair. And most of all, I wasn't gaunt. Okay, I wasn't stout by anyone's standards, but I was an American: solid, comfortable, at peace. And I'd had four weeks at Herr Friedrichs's cooking with Margarete, where – despite my nervous stomach – I'd tasted a little of this, a little of that, and though I was too overanxious and overwrought to actually eat, I hadn't lost any weight. My figure appeared less like an ordinary German's and more like an upper-class Abwehr translator's: full, well-treated.

I examined those faces in the line; they all shared the same quality: They looked out at you but they didn't see you. Well, that's not quite right. Sure, they saw me, saw my suspicious vitality, but they didn't give me a funny look: no New York 'Hey, what's with her?' or even a cool, calm, collected German-style once-over, like Olga used to give me if I went off to school in a dress that she had decided was wrong.

It was not dead eyes; the women on line had dead brains behind the eyes. They had made themselves stop thinking, so no random, renegade expression could pass over their faces: not a tic or a blink that could be challenged.

The fear I felt from being just that little bit different diminished somewhat when I realized these women weren't going to call out: Hey, look at this one! She's *wrong*! If I was, they knew the authorities would find me. They would not turn me in, because they were as afraid as I was of making any kind of scene in which they would call attention to themselves.

It was cold, and my feet throbbed as I stood there in the early December cold. I thought: Would people from Queens and Brooklyn ever be like this? Could they ever be made so scared that their insides died? I didn't know. But then I looked down to the street corner from where I was standing in line and saw workers on their way to offices, stores and factories.

Not a single one of them put a foot off the curb when the light was red. New York was a city of jaywalkers, of parkers at fire hydrants. Would a cabdriver's unwritten license to say to a cop, 'Up yours, buddy,' protect a nation from Hitler and his Brownshirts? Could a Hitler arise in a nation where the average citizen never thought twice about exceeding the speed limit?

To be fair, though, when you see your neighbors being rounded up and taken away and their houses and furniture and even their canned tomatoes snatched up by Party favorites, and you never see your neighbors again . . . well, it doesn't encourage a big mouth and an anti-fascist sneer.

But to continue to be fair, Hitler and FDR had come into office within months of each other in 1933. Okay, conditions were much worse in Germany; they not only had a depression, they had the heavy burden of the First World War on them. But they picked a wild-eyed, booted, hate-spewing monster who screeched to them by torch-light: You are the Master Race! And we picked a cripple with gusto and gallantry, who sat by a homey, crackling fire and urged us to have courage, to have patience, to have decency and to have hope.

I finally got into the store; it had once sold a combination of housewares and hardware, but now there was nothing even resembling the cast-iron skillet I'd thought of buying. Its inventory consisted of two items: soup bowls and potato peelers. I left with a potato peeler, but at least the store owner had not detected anything strange in my accent; I was almost positive of that. And it hadn't bothered him that I was strangely robust; when he gave me my change, he said, Here, Fraülein, and then grinned at me. I put my head down so he'd think I was blushing, slipped the potato peeler into my pocketbook and left.

I'm doing okay, I thought, and though I didn't skip down the street and whistle, I felt far more confident than when I'd left Herr Friedrichs's that morning. I was almost at the station when I saw that a side street had been cordoned off. Police. Gestapo. I didn't look. I calmed myself by thinking it was an area that had been hit the night before. Even though the bombings were getting worse, the authorities kept trying to prevent people from coming face-to-face with terrible devastation – rubble and the awful empty craters left after the attacks – especially in residential neighborhoods.

A bombing, I thought. A face of life. And then I felt a hand on my arm. I looked up. Gestapo. A face that would have been nice-looking if it hadn't been so enraptured by its own ability to terrify. 'Show me your passport,' he ordered.

It took me a second to open the clasp, and my pocketbook jingled as I struggled. I prayed, Dear God, don't let that hinge work now. I handed him my passport. He examined it, and then he came up close. How had I given myself away? 'Is your name Lina Albrecht?'

'Yes.'

Had someone been watching Konrad Friedrichs all along? Was that it?

'Your age?'

'Twenty-eight years.' He had a thick pompadour, kept high off his forehead with hair tonic.

'Place of birth?'

'Berlin.' Oh, God – or Oh, Olga, Oh, Mr and Mrs Pohl – let him buy my accent.

Was the identity check one of those random ones they'd warned me about? I was just walking too slow for his taste, or too fast. He didn't like my looks. He liked my looks, like the shopkeeper who'd grinned. He stared at my passport, then at me, over and over and over. Was he trying to paralyze me so that when he finally proclaimed, You are *not* from Berlin! Your accent is foreign! all I'd be able to do would be incline my head in agreement.

'What are you doing?'

'I was shopping.'

'Shopping?' His eyes narrowed with skepticism, and he shook his head, as if I'd told him an outrageously unbelievable lie. 'What have you been shopping for?'

I started to rummage through my pocketbook, too frantically, I thought. Slow down. Find the potato peeler to show him. He yanked the pocketbook away from me. 'A potato peeler,' I said. 'That's what I was shopping for.'

Just as I uttered the words, he pulled out the peeler. 'You are from Wilmersdorf,' he said. 'What are you doing in this area?' He pronounced every word precisely, separately, slowly, prolonging the threat. And oh, did it work! I was so scared, and he was electrified by my fear. He moved in on me, pressing his face against mine, a horrible cheek-to-cheek. Looking sideways, I could see the almost invisible dots on his skin where he'd shaved. 'Well? Why are you in Alexanderplatz?'

'I heard the store here had potato peelers. The kind with the rounded top.'

'What?'

'So you can scoop out the eyes,' I whispered.

'And for that you came all the way from Wilmersdorf?'

'Oh, yes. I'm a cook. Please, my work passport is in there.' He jerked himself up, away from me, and groped through my pocketbook; he threw my handkerchief on the sidewalk. 'I work for Herr Konrad Friedrichs, of the foreign office.'

He pulled out my work passport and scrutinized it as if positive that any minute he'd discovered something I could be guilty of. A gust of wind came and blew away my handkerchief. He held the work passport up, so the sun could shine through it. I took a fast glance as he examined my papers. His face was in profile; he had a thick plug of yellow wax in his ear.

Suddenly he shoved the pocketbook back into my hands and slapped my identification on top of it. 'All right,' he said. 'Get going. And no more loitering.'

'Yes. I won't. Thank you.'

I walked down the street, clutching all the papers that registered me as a citizen of the Reich – allowing me to work and live – tight against my chest. When I turned the corner I walked faster, but then slowed myself down. Easy. Put your pocketbook in order. Here in Germany, kiddo, neatness counts.

On that last night in the basement cell of Konrad Friedrichs's house, I forced my mind to travel, to get back where it could be at ease for a few hours, to go home.

I thought about how my mother, who used her tweezers the way a carpenter uses his hammer, had worked on her beauty, but after my father was killed in that fire, before she actually started boozing, she was never able to get the seams of her stockings straight. The first sign she was falling apart. She'd come out of her bedroom and call, How're my seams, Linda, lamb? and after a couple of times when she'd gotten so upset she'd cried, I learned to say, Straight as an arrow, Mom.

And then my mind drifted into Manhattan, and I thought about having lunch in the conference room of Blair, VanderGraff and Wadley, with Gladys Slade controlling the gossip with the same thoroughness (but more seriousness) that Roosevelt would insist on in running a cabinet meeting. When I thought how the small talk about Mrs Avenel's pushiness and Mr Post's carrying on with Wilma Gerhardt and Mr Nugent's vague resemblance to Ronald Colman had once been the high point of my days, and how lying awake and inventing moments with Mr Berringer – who in my imagination I dared to call John – had been the crowning glory of my nights, I realized what had become of me. Well, not what had become of me, because I really didn't know, but at least that from where I had started to where I had wound up had been one hell of a trip.

And there was no return ticket. That night – and every night I was in Berlin – I had some bad moments. To be honest, bad half hours, bad hours. Lying in my bed, my motor racing, I wasn't able to concentrate on anything but one thought: I'm *stuck*. Caught. What border could I run to and say: Hey, let me across! I don't belong here! I'm from Queens! What person could I throw my arms around and cry: Oh, God, I want to go home! Help me!

I made myself get control. I thought about John. It wasn't easy. Not because it brought me any pain, but all I could conjure up as I lay in that miserable excuse for a bed was an image: his handsome face, his remarkable body. Images. John coming out of the shower. John's face when he glanced up from editing a brief, or looming over mine during sex. John with me in his arms. John with Nan in his arms.

Hey, I thought, no matter what's happened, this guy is still your husband. That didn't help. Trying to feel something for John was like forcing myself to fall in love with air. I couldn't. I felt no passion, no anger, no longing, no loss. Right before I finally fell asleep, I thought: The only thing I really feel is curiosity; simple curiosity. I mean, how can you love someone and feel absolutely, explicitly, indubitably nothing?

# *Chapter Twenty-Three*

If he'd lived in the United States, the best a guy like Horst Drescher could have done for himself would probably have been to own a small business – one renting wheelchairs and artificial legs, or manufacturing paper party favors – and been vice-president of the Lions Club; he'd never make president, because most of the members would think anyone who would wear a satin vest was a jerk and unfit for the highest office. He would live in the suburbs, because city life would be too much for his nervous-wreck wife, Hedwig, but since he fancied himself so urbane, he wouldn't want to be too far away from concert halls, the theater and expensive restaurants.

That's what he would have been in America. In Nazi Germany, Horst Drescher, at age twenty-seven, was one of the most fortunate men in the foreign office. The army couldn't go near him; he'd been born blind in one eye, and his feet pointed out so far it looked like he was doing a Donald Duck imitation whenever he walked. So he was fortunate. And powerful. Not because of the work he did, although he was chief of the British Section and worked at least twelve hours a day. And not because of his skills in diplomacy and language: anyone in the foreign service, from janitor to ambassador, could see through his so-called subtlety in two seconds flat. And the two times I overheard him speaking English to someone on the phone, it was so incredibly, stiffly German-accented that he sounded like a kid from Queens in a game of soldiers who got stuck with playing the Nazi.

But that's what he was, the Nazi. His fanatical party loyalty was the reason he had risen so high in that huge gray building on

Wilhemstrasse. That, and the fact that for one week Hitler had gone on a rampage, calling for 'young men, new blood' in government. He got what he deserved: Horst.

In the same year that *Mein Kampf* was first published, 1925, when Horst Drescher was ten years old, he joined the *Deutsches Jungvolk*, the junior version of Hitler Youth, and he had been a true-blue believer ever since. He wasn't loyal for any personal gain. He believed in Hitler and in what he stood for: the Master Race. What kind of ten-year-old boy wants to spend his time glorying in Aryan superiority instead of throwing a ball? According to the OSS report, little Horst Drescher. 'He is a passionate believer in Hitler's racial theories, and apparently believes himself to be an example of all that is noble, manly and cultured.' The report went on to say that Horst also embraced all the other Nazi notions: *Lebensraum*, anti-Semitism, *Führerprinzip* – everything, the whole ball of *Weltanschauung*.

Well, almost. Adolf the Ethical was a vegetarian. Horst Drescher would eat anything that didn't get up and walk off his plate – as long as it was washed down with a big glass of pilsener and a little glass of schnapps.

But when I started working for him at his beautiful stone villa in the Dahlem neighborhood, I didn't know that. All I knew was what the OSS knew, and their information had come from Alfred Eckert, who had most likely dashed off something like 'A callow youth who fancies old-fashioned German food, and a lot of it!' to pad out a too-short report. Some pencil-pusher at OSS naturally put a giant asterisk on that one. 'Drescher, Horst: Born 1915 in Magdeburg. *Weakness – German cooking!!!' The OSS had passed on the word to Konrad Friedrichs. And when in desperation he'd gone to Margarete von Eberstein and, without naming names, described the person whose house I was supposed to slip into – and how impossible the task seemed – Margarete had declared, I can help.

Sure, but on my second night at the Drescher', I loused up the pheasants. Else, the downstairs maid, who did the serving, came charging in from the dining room. 'You must hurry! They're waiting for the next course!' I looked at her, a little surprised. They must have inhaled the appetizer.

I opened the oven. 'Oh, my God!' I had been warming the roasting pan and the vegetables on low heat, but when I'd put in the birds, I'd obviously forgotten to turn up the oven. Else sidled over and we both stared at four barely cooked pheasants; they looked like they had been hanging around a hot kitchen instead of actually roasting.

'What are you going to do?' she squeaked.

'Hide them,' I said. They looked more wounded than dead; red juice was oozing our of the cavity. 'And pray.' I grabbed the pot of white sauce I'd planned to use on the carrots and poured it over the pheasants. It covered them like a heavy sheet. Then I decorated the platter with all the greens, lemon slices and capers I could grab, thrust the platter into Else's hand and said, 'When you walk through that door, smile. And *don't* be afraid.' Since she had a brain capacity equal to one of the pheasants', she did what she was told, unquestioningly, and marched toward the dining room with a wide and empty smile on her face.

As the door swung open, I got a glimpse of Horst's back, and the profiles of his wife, Hedwig, and his dinner guest, a somewhat older man, with a nose so upturned and flat that it looked like a pig's snout; the man had been Horst's beloved *Deutches Jungvolk* leader and was now the chief Party functionary in Saxony.

'How are we doing in England?' the man was asking Horst.

'Very well, Bruno,' Horst replied.

'But they are bombing us more and more.'

'Desperation, Bruno.' And the door swung shut.

I got busy, trying not to think about how Horst would react to the pheasant disaster. I spooned about a cup of butter over the carrots. Then I did the same with the potatoes and, as an afterthought, tossed in some dried dill that hung from the ceiling, which Else said had come from France. By the time the Germans get through, I decided, the only thing that'll be left in France will be the French.

Else came back for the vegetables. Her fair-skinned face was all flushed with pleasure. Good old Bruno had probably pinched her behind. I asked her, 'What kind of a mood does Herr Drescher seem to be in?'

'He wanted more bread.' Brilliant. Some master race. She toddled out with the vegetables.

No screams of dismay had arisen over the gloppy, white-coated revolting mess I'd sent out on a silver platter. I calmed myself by saying that even if the meal was the worst thing in Horst Drescher's life, he wouldn't fire me. His former chef had been hit by a car on his way to the butcher shop and had two broken legs. And I had come so highly recommended . . . by Konrad Friedrichs, of all people.

Originally, the OSS had hoped Herr Friedrichs could find someone else willing to sing the praises of my cooking, but, already frightened, he was firm: I will *not* enlist anyone else into this foolhardy operation!

Konrad Friedrichs's office was on the same floor as Horst's, and so, on a Monday, he'd said, Well, on Friday I am off to Lisbon for two weeks. Then on Thursday, having spent most of the past few days listening to foreign office gossip, he called Horst and said, I hear your chef has met with an accident. Most unfortunate . . . but perhaps fortuitous. I have a cook – nice, quiet Berlin woman, a widow – and I've been wondering what to do with her. I travel too much. Don't really need her. She's quite capable. If you're interested . . .

I arrived at the Drescher's villa on Saturday morning. It was a graceful stone house, set behind an ornate iron fence, on a cobblestone street. They had lived there for nearly a year; before that, it had belonged to a Jewish family who had owned a department store. They had 'emigrated,' which meant they'd been rounded up and sent somewhere east. Probably Poland or Czechoslovakia. No one talked about it. Their house, from attic to basement, including the beds, clothespins, sterling silver, couches and extra light bulbs, now belonged to the Dreschers.

According to the OSS report, Horst loved what had become his. Alfred was quoted: 'He will pass through a room and stroke the wood of his breakfront. He will discuss the value of his antique Meissen porcelain.' And I could just see him lifting a sugar bowl up to the light, peering at it with his one good eye, a small smile crossing his bland face. Horst looked even younger than his twenty-seven years. His face was still blotchy – although in the morning the pimples were beige with dabs of Hedwig's heavy foundation makeup. He was round-shouldered, and had a small, almost girlish build – except for his bloated, satin-vested belly. He was not the sort who got his Aryan kicks hiking in the Schwarzwald.

But if he was young, he had the tastes of an old man: beer, politics, food, culture. Not women. The report said: 'He seems immune to the charms of women other than his wife . . . and our sources indicate he may be immune to hers as well. The couple have been married for five years and have no children.'

His main love was his work. Too bad for Germany. According to the briefing Konrad Friedrichs gave me just before I left, Horst was of almost no use in the foreign office because he had no ability to analyze intelligence or plan strategy. But he knew every single minuscule fact there was to know about his area, Great Britain. No report, magazine clipping, aerial photograph or coded message escaped his eye.

The problem was, once he absorbed all this data, he had no idea what to do with it. Sure, if you asked him the square footage of Windsor Castle he could tell you, and he knew the name, address and telephone number of every German agent in England, Scotland and Wales. He could choke you on facts; he just couldn't think.

Still, all this information took time to digest, but so did dinner. Horst took great pleasure in returning to his graceful house, eating an elaborate meal and then going into his study to read over his reports. On the nights when he went to the opera or the ballet or the theater, where he sat in a box reserved for the highest officials, he would return and pore over his papers until two in the morning.

These nights of the lively arts were the best nights for snooping. That's what my friend Alfred had related to the OSS. Alfred, designer for the Nazi elite, had always managed to drop in to help his client Hedwig get ready – a very intricate process. Horst would come home, put his papers in his study, lock the room, have a lighter-than-usual supper – alone, because Hedwig and Alfred were probably doing up her corset – then rush upstairs and change into his tuxedo. He'd come down later, wait and pace, until, finally, Alfred would escort an overwrought Hedwig downstairs. She'd plead a headache, a terrible period, a congested chest. Horst would look to Alfred for help. Alfred would reassure her: 'My dear, look at you! I've made you beautiful. You will *dazzle* them! Go, now. Go.' The first few times, he'd picked up his case and left with the Dreschers. But then Horst, the gracious host, the man who knew that in Alfred he had found someone who could truly appreciate all his fine objects, said, 'Please, stay. Have a bite to eat. And drink, if you like. I have different glasses for red and white wine. No need to rush.'

Horst was deeply grateful for the help Alfred was giving him. He really needed help. Hedwig was definitely not an asset to his career – although that had been why he'd married her. Her father had been with Hitler since the early days in Munich, and although he was too old to hold a permanent position in government, he was a trusted – and therefore powerful – friend. But he died six months after the wedding, sticking Horst with a woman no other man, even the most politically ambitious, had been willing to take. Hedwig Drescher was lumpy, with hair so thin you could see her scalp, and tree-trunk legs. She was twelve years older than her husband.

She tried to disguise the age difference with heavy, masklike makeup and bright-colored dresses, but she knew the attempt was a lost cause. She was the clumsy, chunky daughter of a dumb, jovial Munich policeman. She had nothing to recommend her, not even her father's joviality; she just had his dumbness. No one wanted her around, least of all her husband, and yet as a proper wife she had to accompany him on his social and cultural outings.

But at least Alfred, with his charming patter and inspirational speeches, had been able to lift her out of her near-constant state of nervous tension and get her out with her husband. The OSS report had quoted Alfred: 'She gets hysterical because she wants to please him and can't, and so she makes herself ill. She loves him, poor cow.'

Else rushed back into the kitchen, breathless. 'The master says, "My compliments to the new cook. A fine partridge." '

Partridge? I thought. It's pheasant. But then I knew that at least I was safe in the kitchen.

The poor cow seemed to have her period three weeks out of the month. That's what Dagmar, the chambermaid, told me. 'All the time cramps. But the cramps, I think they are in the head, not in the . . .' She used some word I'd never heard of, but I nodded my understanding.

The assassination of Alfred Eckert was almost as much a disaster for Horst as it had been for the OSS. Now there wasn't anyone who could rally Hedwig for a night out with the Nazis, and in the next few weeks, past Christmas and into the new year, 1943, I could see his pasty face getting crimson every time he came home from work, passed the parlor and saw Hedwig curled up on a chaise, squeezing a hot-water bottle against her stomach.

Not that I saw too much. I shopped in the mornings, chopped and mixed all afternoon, and cooked into the night. After that, I climbed the back stairs to my room, a cubicle not much bigger than what I'd had at Konrad Friedrichs's. (Although at least the former owners had furnished it cheerfully: a bed with an old headboard that had a bouquet of roses painted on it, a wide strip of what – probably a hundred years before – had been a nice flowered rug, and a wood chest.)

I kept away from the Dreschers as much as possible. Once, Horst barged into the kitchen. He was giving his guest, von Ribbentrop's personal assistant, the grand tour of the house. I was juicing a lemon and stared at Horst, and then at the guest, a man so buck-toothed it looked as if he was eating his own lip. 'Carry on, cook,' Horst said, with a grand wave of his hand. The two of them inspected the stove and the icebox as if they knew what they were looking at. As they swept out, Horst called: 'And don't forget! More of those potato croquettes!'

Other than that, I managed to avoid anything more than a chance 'Good evening, sir' meeting in the hallway. But I couldn't stay away from Hedwig, because she was always around, clutching hot-water bottles or ice packs, reclining in a series of robes that I bet were Alfred-designed: long, beltless, all in shades of blue – aquamarine, sapphire, royal blue – with V necks, created to hide her formlessness and to bring out her small but decidedly blue eyes.

Her suffering room, the parlor, was right opposite Horst's study. Even if he went out at night and I was positive Else and Dagmar were asleep, I couldn't try to jimmy the lock when she was lying on the chaise – giving off occasional moans – with a full view of the study door.

How long, I worried, could I visit Rolf and stick messages into fishes' mouths, saying, Sorry. Can't get into study. Wife always lying in parlor opposite. Will try again.

I got embarrassed thinking about what Norman Weekes must be saying, as he and his Harvard crew rolled their eyes in hopelessness and honked, Well, what *can* one expect when one recruits such a relentless plebeian. But I got genuinely upset at the thought of Edward. On one hand, I knew my sneaking past him, collaborating with his adversary the minute he left the country, going against everything we both knew he believed in, would make him hate me. On the other hand, I still hoped for his admiration. For some reason, I wanted him to think – even if it was way in the back of his mind – that Linda was doing a decent job. She'd even picked up a few tricks from him, the champion spy.

So one night when Hedwig was sprawled out on the chaise in a turquoise robe and impenetrable makeup, having missed a Wagnerian opera because she wept and said she had the flu, I stood at the open parlor door and said, 'Madam, it would please me if you would allow me to make you some tea with honey. It would help your throat.'

'*No.* I don't like tea.' Nasty. Pouty. Unable to get her mouth to form a 'thank you.' And she had an awful whine. She was really worse than a cow. I had increased admiration for Alfred, that he hadn't lost control and plunged his pinking shears into her heart.

'Milk with honey, then?' I suggested. She hesitated. 'And perhaps a biscuit?'

'I'll try,' she sighed.

Two minutes later, I came rushing back with a tray. 'Madam, if I may suggest . . .'

'What?'

'It might help your chest if I put a bit of brandy in the milk.' If I'd taken even an eyedropperful of his beloved schnapps, Horst would have known in a minute. But there was a dust-covered case of brandy in the basement, and my guess was he'd forgotten it was there. 'Just a touch.'

'Whatever,' she murmured.

'Would you like to have it down here?' And then I tossed off what I hoped sounded like a casual suggestion. 'Or up in your room?'

'Well . . .' she said, gazing out of the room, probably overwhelmed by the thought of stairs.

'I could help you upstairs, Madam, and then come down and reheat the milk to the proper temperature.'

She held out her hand for me to help her, like Greta Garbo dying in *Camille*.

Twenty minutes later, Hedwig had enough brandy in her to make her sleep until the following afternoon. And I went down and knelt before the locked study door.

Horst guarded his key to the study as if it would open up the gates to heaven. Still, I solved the locked-door problem easily enough, even though jiggling the handle, a hairpin and a larding needle didn't work. I figured there *had* to be an extra key. In any well-run house, the wife isn't going to let her husband walk off with the only key in his pocket and not be able to let the maid get into his study to wax and dust and vacuum. I leaned against the locked door and asked myself, Where would a good housewife, where would my Grandma Olga, put the extra key?

It wasn't in the silver chest, my first choice, and it wasn't underneath the record player in the parlor. But finally I found it upstairs in the linen closet, under a pile of heavy damask tablecloths. Big ones, for when the table was opened to seat twenty. For their holidays. I touched the tablecloths; they were so rich. And I couldn't help thinking how little in common that nameless family of Jews had with my family of Jews. It was like comparing apples and oranges . . . or me and – I almost laughed thinking about it – somebody like Edward Leland. I closed the closet door slowly, and as I was easing my way down the hall – a weird, ice-skating motion they taught us in Training School, which was less apt to make a board squeak than tiptoeing – I thought about apples and oranges. Both fruit. So maybe Edward Leland and I . . . the tablecloth family and my family . . . In a world of barbarians, the light of simple human decency is so overwhelming, so blinding, that you no longer see things like old silver and Yale and fancy accents.

I stopped thinking and went down the stairs. They taught us stairs too: Sit on the top step, brace yourself with your hands and then gently, slowly, lower your backside. If someone catches you, the instructor had said, grunt with pain and hold on to your ankle and accept any offer of help. Don't forget to limp.

Recalling it now, it all sounds easy, almost mechanical. But finding the key, getting in the study, was the easy part. That first night, I just stood beside the desk and examined the heavy cardboard envelope of papers, not daring to touch it.

I had to be careful. I didn't know if Horst's suspicions had been aroused by Alfred Eckert's death. Did he know – did anyone – that Alfred was spying on him? Deep down, I was almost positive that the traitor in the resistance had found out only that Alfred was a spy – but not where he was spying – and had passed the word on. Because if the traitor had known, if the Gestapo had known, that Horst was the subject of Alfred's snooping, that he had been bringing home top-secret papers and leaving them while he went to hear Brunhilde hit a high note, he wouldn't be in the foreign office, or in Berlin; he'd probably be dead or, as everybody liked to say, 'East.' But I had to be certain.

I switched on the flashlight that I'd taken from the kitchen and held it over the envelope, looking for telltale hairs, dustings of powder – any of the tricks Horst might employ to make sure his papers weren't being tampered with. Nothing.

It was lying face-down, the flap unsealed. Then I studied his briefcase. Ordinary black leather. No special locks, no small explosive devices set to blow off a busybody's hands. It looked safe. All I had to do was put on a pair of thin cotton gloves, skim through the files and copy down anything that looked important: names, addresses, statistics or lists of any sort. Get whatever you can, Norman Weekes had told me the last time I saw him. This fellow brings home prime information at least once a week. Alfred had been given a miniature camera to photograph the documents, but since I was going to be living in the house, they'd decided not to risk it.

I switched off the flashlight. Now came the part that would always be the most dangerous: getting out. What if Hedwig was a secret drinker, and after all my cleverness, the triple slug of brandy I'd poured into her milk hadn't knocked her out but perked her up? What if she had toddled downstairs and resumed her place on the chaise? And what if Dagmar had sneaked down to grab the last cherry tart, or Else, to steal a lemon to lighten her hair?

I waited as I had been taught to wait, counting, so I would be forced to remain in place for five minutes. A slow, agonizing count to three hundred, all the while listening for a hiccup or a footstep – any sound at all. Linda Voss Berringer, secret agent.

I got that old familiar pain in my gut, sudden, stabbing, but worse than it had ever been. Still, I kept counting. When I got up to ninety-seven, the pain became so excruciating that I had to clutch my arms around myself, hold myself tight, as I doubled over.

And then it was time. Inch by inch, I forced myself to straighten up. Slowly, I opened the door. No one was there. I took a long, shaky, deep breath and thought: Two months in Berlin, and I haven't been able to get even the tiniest, most inconsequential fact.

But then I thought: Look at the bright side. I wasn't dead. And the key would always be in the linen closet.

I missed seeing Margarete. My day off was every other Sunday, and sometimes we managed to see each other for an hour or two, but we had to keep out of each other's lives. Even if she'd been allowed to know where I was staying, she couldn't have gone knocking at Horst's front door, wrapped in cashmere and fur, tied up with gold jewelry, and demanded, in her elite voice, Where is my good friend Lina?

And what was I going to do? Drop in when she was visiting her cousin Countess von Dorzeck or her old pal Prince Wolfgang zu Sayn-Graetz, wave my apron over my head and holler, Hiya! I'm Margarete's buddy. Or better yet, join her at her apartment for a midnight dinner with her lover, the gross, bloated Nazi. Just for the fun of it, to see if a member of Hitler's inner circle could spot an American spy.

So we met at odd places: at a workmen's café for a beer, in a bookstore not far from Alexanderplatz that was always filled with the bohemian types the Nazis hadn't gotten to yet. In late March, when it was getting warmer, we'd go to the zoo, or the Spandau Citadel – a beautiful old fortress, complete with a tower that Rapunzel could have let down her hair from. Spandau was just far enough away from the center of Berlin that it seemed like another country. A fairy-tale country. We sat near a lake and watched people paddling around in rowboats.

Then we walked into the woods. It was so quiet. Peaceful. Safe. Still, Margarete whispered. 'You know, there was terrible fighting right there during the Napoleonic Wars.' She pointed through the trees at the high brick walls of the fortress.

I grinned. 'Of course I know that.'

She didn't grin. 'I worry about you all the time. You're so naturally . . . lighthearted. You don't comprehend the danger, the bestiality of these people.'

I leaned against a tree. It was covered with tight, pale green buds. 'I may not know too much about what Napoleon did, but believe me, I know just how evil these people are. Why else would I be doing what I'm doing? Because I don't like their uniforms?' Margarete put her spring coat on the ground; it looked new, a light yellow, the color of pineapple. She sat on it and motioned for me to join her. 'You are really crazy,' I said. 'It must cost a fortune, and you're going to get grass stains all over it.'

'I like grass stains. Now, please, tell me how it is going with you.' She smiled; she had faint dimples. 'Just generalities, as usual.

No details.' She slipped off a shoe and massaged her arch. 'You know, this is all so dreadful, this having to protect each other from . . . from knowledge. Here we are, friends, but we can't even discuss the most boring, ordinary occurrences in our daily lives. I mean, instead of just saying "the colonel" whenever I talk about the pig, I would like to be able to say his name. And I know when you tell me about what you're doing, about where you are, you'd like to tell me . . . well, not their names, but what they are like and the degree of danger you are in and just . . . the feeling of what it's like for you.'

'The feeling is, this great man I'm working for still hasn't gotten over his acne and – '

'No!' She held up her hand, like a traffic policeman. 'No descriptions! Don't trust me, Lina. Don't trust anyone.' She took my hand for a minute. 'I'm really being selfish, you see. If you relax with me, I will relax with you. And that sort of comfort is a terrible menace. Don't you see, if I, if you, if any of us gets into trouble, we can't be in a position where we know too much, because we might be forced to reveal it.' She let go of my hand, picked up a stone and brushed the dirt off it with her thumb. 'I think we all have an inflated idea about our own valor. "*I* can stand up to torture. *I* would never break down." That's the worst kind of arrogance, because when we think that, we're not only committing the sin of pride, we are putting our friends' lives in peril.' She looked over at me. 'Am I babbling on too much?'

'No. Of course not.'

'If there can be any benefit from Nazism for me, it has been discovering friendship. Those of us who . . . who oppose have learned to cherish – almost worship – our friends and colleagues. Especially someone like me. I'd led such a pampered life, and my so-called friends were just as spoiled and narrow as I was. One of the things I value about my friendship with you, Lina, is that we're so different – and we're so much alike. Women who play a man's game. But you come from a part of Berlin I may have passed through, but I never really saw. Now, in the middle of all this inhumanity, you – and all the others' – she threw the rock hard and it ricocheted off a small tree – 'have taught me what it really means to be a human being.'

'What are you thinking about?' I asked.

'What do you mean?' she demanded.

'I mean, you always seem so calm. But you threw that rock like it was a weapon. Who were you trying to kill?'

'Them,' she said, with more feeling than she'd ever shown. 'I'm so angry because . . . it has become personal. Oh, yes, you know that eventually one of your friends in the movement – usually the most courageous – is going to be discovered. But when it's a *dear* friend, it's more than just an inevitable sadness. It's more than an acceptable risk of war. It's losing part of your life.'

'They got some of your friends?'

Margarete nodded. 'Yes. And among them, my dearest friend. Oh, you should have known him. What a joyous man he was!' And I thought: Oh, God, I know exactly who you're talking about. 'His name was Alfred, and he was a couturier. Not a particularly brilliant one, just all right. His success had little to do with his gowns and a great deal to do with his being extraordinary company. Lina, he was so witty, so full of silly gossip and great compassion. And energy! He went *everywhere*, all over the city, and people adored him, trusted him. And he was brilliantly successful because no one suspected. No one would have believed that this homosexual who'd managed to escape the pink triangle because of his connections, this faggot who put his hair in pin curls every night and wore a hairnet, could possibly really be a traitor.'

'Do you have any idea how he was found out?'

'Yes! He loved everyone in the movement. And he trusted too many of us. "Oh, I'm going here tonight, with that big-mouth fool So-and-so." Or: "Our friends sent me a new camera! *So* tiny!" I took him aside so many times and begged him to be discreet. I said, "Darling, stupid Alfred, don't you understand they are always trying to infiltrate the movement? What if they succeed? Do you think a traitor will give you a gold swastika for Christmas?" '

Margarete's voice cracked as she added, 'He was my trusting and beloved friend.' Once again she took my hand; she held it very tight. 'Listen to me. Alfred had a talent for spying – and a genius for living. But he believed so much in the righteousness of his cause that he couldn't comprehend that anything – or anyone – bad could be attached to it. And so look what happened to him. He prattled away once too often. He was given up, betrayed . . . by one of his own, one of his *friends*. Because – and this I will tell you – we know it *has* to have been a betrayal. So please, don't become too comfortable. Because either one of us could die in just the blink of an eye . . . or very slowly and horribly. Be my friend, but don't trust me. Don't trust *anyone*.'

Don't trust Rolf? Fine. I stayed cautious until the end of April. I'd visit his store, trek across the sawdust-covered floor and examine the fish like Field Marshal Rommel inspecting his troops. Finally I'd say: This one, and the one above it. No, wait. Give me that one instead.

Rolf would take the fish to a counter in the back, clean it, scale it, and somehow, with his one hand, take the paper I'd hidden and slip it away somewhere. I watched him once or twice; I never spotted a thing.

I wasn't sure how much all the intelligence I was giving him was worth. Well, I did know the OSS would get somebody hopping on security when I copied down a list, sent to the German foreign office by the army high command, of all the American aircraft on a base near Weymouth in England. And I knew they would be delirious with joy when one time the Gestapo stapled a handwritten note to their report from one of their agents, code name Elefant, a high official in the British Home Office. In the note, Elefant wrote: 'If you have any questions, do *not* call me at office. It is an intolerable and dangerous intrusion! Call me at home.' And then the dope gave his home phone number!

But most of the documents Horst brought home were obviously catalogs of British or American troop movements, page after page of statistics, directories of names and what I guessed were either triumphs of cryptographic genius or expense accounting by German agents in Great Britain. Shepherd's pie: 3 shillings.

Then one day I finally got word from home. Just before Easter,

Rolf was wrapping the trout I was buying. It was a lot of trout, even if it was only the appetizer; Horst was planning a dinner for twelve and carrying on as if it was the resurrection: a fish course with a cream sauce! no fowl! do not buy meat! I am endeavoring to obtain a spring lamb!

'You always choose the best fish,' Rolf said.

I gave him an I-bet-you-say-that-to-all-the-girls look, but I said, 'Thank you.'

'Your employer must be very happy with you.' For a second it didn't hit me. I thought he'd meant Horst. And then I realized: It was a message.

'I hope he is,' I said. 'He is a fine man. I am honored to work for him.'

Don't trust anyone. But at the end of February, there had been a mass roundup of the remaining Jews in Berlin. The SS called it *Fabrik Aktion*. Operation Factory. Everybody knew about it. Nobody spoke about it. Well, no ordinary people. But Horst did. After four or five pilseners, I heard him through the door, booming at his dinner guest, a Waffen SS general: I hear Goebbels is pleased with the roundup of the Jews. The general responded through a mouthful of potatoes: Not so pleased. We estimate there are still four thousand we have not picked up.

The last week of April, I couldn't stand it. I had to know about my family. I had to trust Rolf. I slipped a note into a haddock. 'My friend, if you read these papers and not just pass them on, could you find out for me what has happened to two old ladies, Jews, Liesl and Hannah Weiss, who live, or used to live, on Klarrenstrasse (I do not know the number). If you tell me to try the codfish, I will know you were not able to find out any information. Please, do not put yourself in any danger. This is merely a matter of curiosity.' I signed it: 'Your friend.'

In the next two weeks, I went to Rolf 's store three times. There was no signal at all from him. And then, on a beautiful day in May when even the inside of the fish store smelled good, he told me to have a look at the turbot. While I was inspecting them, he came up beside me. I glanced at him. He picked up two of the smaller fish and said, 'No good.' I understood. I watched as he carried them over to a large trash can on the other side of the store and, one at a time, tossed them into the garbage.

# *Chapter Twenty-Four*

Bombs scared me as much as the Gestapo. Maybe more, because at least with the Germans I had a chance to use whatever wits I had to save my own life. But when the Russians, and then the RAF Bomber Command, flew over Berlin and dropped a thousand tons of bombs in one day, being clever didn't help. Cowering in an air raid shelter was about all I could do.

The bombing began to grow in fierceness in the winter I first came to Berlin, 1942–43, but most of it was in the eastern part of the city, near the airport, and farther north, aimed at the tank and munitions factories. Of course I heard it. At night I'd lie in bed on the top floor of the villa in Dahlem and hear – even feel – low booms; if I'd been in my bed in Ridgewood, I could have convinced myself it was a Mack truck backfiring just across the borough line in Bushwick.

By the time I left Konrad Friedrichs, I'd learned to sleep through the attacks. Now and then, I'd wake up startled, my forehead and neck all sweaty, at the sound of the 'all clear' whistle, but that wasn't exactly a shocking occurrence; sweet dreams didn't come in Germany. Still, throughout that winter, a person – like a Hedwig – could live in luxurious suburban safety and only have to put up with a little disturbing background noise . . . and the strange red haze that hovered over the city each sunrise.

Not that Hedwig ever saw a sunrise after the milk, honey and touch of brandy – a touch big enough to knock out a hippopotamus – I brought upstairs to her every night. She forgot about her periods completely; now she just whined all the time about her violent headaches. A terrible thing to do to a fellow human being, right? Making some miserable, wretched wreck of a woman drunk every night. Maybe turning her into an alcoholic. Wasn't it awful? Actually, it didn't bother me one bit.

So Hedwig slept through the winter air raids, and the spring ones too. While the SS and the police were executing *Fabrik Aktion*, rounding up Jews – maybe my two cousins with the quivering, spidery handwriting – and shipping them east, she snored.

All that spring, I kept remembering what Edward had said about Germany being hell. I wanted so much to talk to him about it, tell him he was right, that hell wasn't just here in Berlin, with its red sky. This was only headquarters. Hell was where the gas chambers were, with prussic acid filling the lungs of silly old ladies who complained about their dentures. And the tiny lungs of babies.

I wondered if the Germans had been as efficient as they'd hoped to be with their construction. Probably. You couldn't get a goddamn cast-iron skillet in the whole city of Berlin, but boy, were they productive when it came to murdering Jews.

*Judenrein*. I'd heard it six or seven times from the dining room. Jew-free. The ideal, purified German state that Horst with his satin vests and pimples dreamed of: a perfect Reich for perfect Aryans like him and Hedwig.

The bombing stayed normal all summer. Well, if you lose electricity, gas and water for weeks at a time, life isn't normal. But at the villa, where the water truck pulled up to the curb, special door-to-door Nazi VIP service, where Horst came home with boxes of candles every night, life was tolerable.

Of course, Hedwig kept whining: Cold potato salad and sausage *again?* War is heck, Hedwig.

I walked through Berlin. There were no cordoned-off streets anymore with Gestapo and Wehrmacht guards making sure you didn't see the holes where houses used to be. You can't hide half a city. Buildings were blasted to rubble, dust. Now and then you'd come upon just a wall standing, looking like the pictures you see of movie scenery in *Life* – real fronts of Wild West bars or candy stores, but from the side, flat and false.

I tried not to think of home. New York – rude, pushy, funny: 'Huh, lady? Whadaya want?' Even Washington – clean, serious, courtly: 'May I help you, ma'am?' Quit it, I told myself. Don't think of life when you're in the land of the dead.

Outside Rolf 's fish store, spread-out newspapers were held down by bricks. (Bricks made great paperweights, and the city had mountains of paperweights.) You were supposed to wipe your shoes on the usual phonied-up casualty lists or the radio listings, to get the shards of window glass out of the soles before you went inside. Who could blame them? The city was made of glass. The farther east you walked on Kurfürstendamm, the less you could ignore the crunch-crunch of glass under your feet; the sidewalk became a dazzling, rough, crackling-loud pathway.

You'd tread carefully, farther on, and you'd meet up with dazed strangers, who kept pointing: I live in that apartment over there – four rooms. Except they were pointing at air. People wore bandages, eye patches, slings, casts. It was horrible. People wandered around in the early morning, still bleeding from the night before.

Did I feel sorry for them? You've got to be paralyzed not to feel some pity for an old man who's standing and crying by a pile of rubble, and you see a pair of legs sticking out from under all the pulverized mortar and bricks. His wife's legs, covered with heavy elastic stockings, the kind to help with circulation problems; she probably hadn't had time to find her shoes. And you'd have to be numb not to feel for the bewildered little kids who kept calling for their dogs.

Every time I heard the unmistakable sound of an RAF Mosquito coming close – and you knew what was coming before the 'take cover' whistle blew – I'd rush with the crowds, breathless, panicked, to find the nearest bomb shelter. But at the same exact minute when my heart was thudding and my mouth was dry with terror, I wanted to yell, Get 'em! Get 'em! More! More! More!

So did I feel sorry for them? These people huddled around me in an underground station or the basement of a fruit store were the same people who screamed with pride when Hitler told them of their destiny. I'd heard their screams on the radio in Ridgewood, way back in the early thirties.

Or if they weren't the screamers, they were the voters: Cast your ballot for the man who'll show the Slav and Czech scum just what German power really is!

And if they weren't the voters, they were the watchers. They watched the torchlight parades. They watched the soldiers march, the tanks and cannons roll down the street, and they cheered. They watched their neighbors lose their right to vote, their businesses, their citizenship, their houses and their lives. Maybe they didn't cheer; maybe they said 'Too bad' when the Gestapo came to get Liesl and Hannah – but not too loud; someone might hear them.

They had welcomed the devil, or at least didn't say, Hey, get out of here, and he had set up business right smack in the middle of town. So let the good people of Berlin get a little taste of what hell was like. And the answer is no, I wasn't sorry.

I lost all sense of time. I was in Berlin forever. The bombing would just keep getting heavier until one day there would be nothing to bomb anymore. November 1943, a whole year after I arrived, was the last time I knew whether it was a Tuesday or a Friday. There were fires burning all the time in the city that month, immense fires; the British had bombed Berlin's supply of coal, and nearly all the fuel for winter was in flames. I'd come back to the villa and my hair would have patches of black: the huge pieces of soot that drifted down all over the city.

By December, or it may have been February 1944 . . . It was winter, anyway, and people were chopping down trees in the Grunewald to burn to keep from freezing. That's when I lost track of the month. But somewhere in that time, the villa was hit. I could hear it coming. Walking through the city, I'd learned to judge, just by the pitch of the whistle a bomb makes, about where it was going to land.

At ten at night, I heard the whistle. I threw off my blanket, ran into the hall and screamed for Else and Dagmar. Else bolted out of her room, and together we ran down to the next floor and banged on Hedwig's door. But the bomb exploded before I could even shout, Wake up, you imbecile.

We were thrown to the floor. It wasn't a direct hit, because we would have been dead. But close. Even as I heard the blast, I felt the violent change in the air pressure. Oh, dear God! My chest kept moving in and out, but I couldn't breathe. It was like my lungs had been yanked out.

And then it was over. Absolute quiet. We pulled ourselves up, to discover that no one in the house had been killed. Horst wasn't even home; he was at the Philharmonic, getting culture. Of all of us, Dagmar suffered the worst. She'd just made it out of her bedroom when the door of the bathroom down the hall was ripped off its hinges; it went flying past her, but it managed to break her shoulder, her arm and a couple of ribs.

Else and I, lying on our stomachs, hands over our heads, were cut by slivers of flying glass. Horrible, because later you could feel them under your skin, but you couldn't see them, much less get them out. And most of them were in my back, so every time I turned or bent over, I got forty or fifty stabs of pain.

What happened to Hedwig was that her antique clothes cabinet fell down and all her blue robes spilled down on the floor.

So it didn't matter one bit what month it was, because when you alternate between being resigned to death and trembling uncontrollably at the thought, it doesn't really matter if it's Friday, March 10, 1944, or not.

When I wasn't thinking about death, I was thinking about my job – both jobs. It was getting harder to find food, even for Horst, and I worried that he'd decide he didn't need me, that Hedwig could slice a *Kochwurst* as well as I could. So far, I'd gotten reprieve after reprieve; the gas line was reconnected, so the oven worked; then someone in the foreign office flew back from Paris and gave Horst veal. So much veal! He and his friends sucked up veal roasts and veal stews and veal fricassees for a couple of weeks.

On the days I thought my job was pretty safe, I worried about the villa. Forget being a cook. I was also a spy. What if they scored a direct hit and bombed Horst's study? Then he'd have to work nights at the foreign office, and I'd be stuck in a Nazi kitchen, up to my ears in *Gefüllter Fasan*.

One of those nights in '44, toward the end of winter, wrapped up in a blanket on the cold floor of the basement, waiting for a raid that never happened, I let go of the present and thought, for a second, about going home. I realized that as much as I ached to hear English and to be back in New York, I had no one to go back to. Somewhere at OSS Training School, in a small brown envelope in a metal cabinet, was my wedding ring. Suddenly, it hit me that I hadn't thought of John for weeks – maybe months. I knew then, for sure, that the ring was going to wind up in some other cabinet, in the Unclaimed Property Office. It would stay there forever. I didn't want it, not even as a souvenir to stick in the drawer next to my 1939 World's Fair official embroidered handkerchief.

So, I thought, here are my choices: I would die, courtesy of a British bomb or German prussic acid; Germany would win the war and I'd be stuck as a cook for the Dreschers the rest of my life; or the Allies would win, and somehow, even if it took years, I'd have a shot at getting *home*.

So what if there was no one to go home to? Even if I had to start my life all over again, slinging hash in a diner in Long Island City or working for some fat-mouth lawyer on Court Street in Brooklyn. I wanted to be back in New York more than anything else.

But I didn't want to think about it too much, to picture lying on the sand in Rockaway, or drinking a chocolate malted, or ever really – being now, at last, at age thirty-five, of sound mind – finding my one true love. Because if it came down to dying, unfulfilled dreams would make death hurt even more. I'd rather check out with a few bittersweet memories: of John, of at least not dying an old maid, and of having done a good turn for the red, white and blue. I had enough regrets, like not seeing my mother before she died. And not, all those years, ever having had the guts to say, Hey, you want to know what kind of a name Voss is? It's Jewish. I hadn't even had the courage to admit it to Edward, the one person who knew me better than anyone, and knew the truth.

Edward Leland was my biggest regret. I'd slammed the door on that one forever by not resolving our fight, and by leaving that cold, typed letter on his desk: I quit. Then, just to make sure there was nothing to go back to, I'd burned my one last bridge by sneaking behind his back to Norman Weekes. So there was no chance of regaining the best . . . what? Friendship? Association? The best connection I had ever had. But, I thought, life is full of regrets. And I'll take life any way I can get it.

Because, you see, deep down I knew we were going to win the war. It was on every face I saw in the street, in the snappiness of Rolf's walk as he crossed from one side of the fish store to the other, in the ever-more-downward slump of Horst's shoulders. Sure, Berliners picked themselves up and tried to put as many pieces together as they could, but there was none of that energy, none of that quiet spirit, none of that zest for life I'd heard in British voices over the radio in those days back in 1940, during the Battle of Britain. The Germans were losers – and they knew it.

Hedwig took to bed almost permanently in the early spring of 1944, and while that may sound as if it would have been a boon for me, it was really a disaster. I found myself in the exact position I'd been in when she was sniveling away in the parlor: exposed. From her bedroom, she had a panoramic view of the linen closet out in the hall. And I couldn't rely on her stupors: One minute she'd be snoring, an awful sound, as if she was being forced to gargle with some hideous-tasting mouthwash. And then, just as I put my hand on the door handle of the linen closet, she'd call, 'Lina! My milk!'

'I was coming to see if you were ready for it, Madam.'

'Well, I am.'

I couldn't take that chance night after night, so finally I decided to keep the key. It was a risk, but not the worst I'd ever taken; sneaking into Berlin was not what you'd call the act of a totally balanced person. Besides, I was almost positive the second key had passed from the Jewish family into the Drescher's possession unnoticed. Horst had never invited more than twelve people, so there was no need for anyone to even breathe near those huge tablecloths. I couldn't see Horst saying, Gee, Hedwig, let's invite twenty people for a Passover dinner.

Naturally, I couldn't walk around twirling the key on a chain. I had to make sure no one could ever associate the key with me, so

I prowled through the house, looking for a safe, accessible hiding place; I couldn't risk keeping it in my room or in the kitchen. Finally I found what I needed.

There was a tree right by the side door of the house – a door everyone used except for formal occasions – and on it there was a branch barely above eye level. It had a small indentation in its upper side, like a little wood saucer. I could slip out the side door anytime; it was the way to get to the shed where they kept the garbage. I made it a point to always lift the small kitchen garbage pail up, away from me, as if to keep it from dripping. Plopping the key into its tree saucer was a comparative cinch.

Did I ever need easy access to that key! The German foreign office was buzzing about an invasion of France by the Allies. There was no doubt that it would happen; the only questions were when and where. So I took to sneaking into Horst's office every night, because it was clear that the invasion would be launched from England, Horst's territory. Going into his study was like entering a gold mine: There were reports of troop concentrations in England, of a feud between the British and the Free French; there were analyses of General Eisenhower's character and intelligence, and a pile of incompatible accounts on when the invasion would take place, accompanied by maps and by weather and tidal charts.

Even reading the material the way I did – at three in the morning, while Horst slept upstairs; with a quick glance just to figure out what was worth writing home about; and then trying to write those teeny letters wearing cotton gloves and by flashlight – I knew: Not only were their agents in disagreement, but their meteorologists were at each other's throats. But the OSS could make something out of all the facts and figures, because they knew which information was accurate; the more stuff I could give them, the more they would know about what the Germans suspected.

As for where the invasion was going to take place – well, it seemed to me the Allies had succeeded in baffling the Germans. There were three prime areas Horst's agents in England kept swearing would be *the* spot: Pas-de-Calais, Normandy, and running a distant third, Seine-Maritime. I'd creep up to bed by three-thirty and listen to the bombs and the anti-aircraft fire, and I'd try to conjure up a map of France, but even though I was positive I once knew which area was which, the only thing I could remember was that all three were north, across the Channel from England.

Mornings, I trudged toward Rolf's, stepping over bricks and twisted metal, moving aside for the streams of people left homeless, who wandered around with their few possessions in soup kettles or, if they were lucky, baby carriages, and I prayed that the fish store hadn't been hit.

One morning, though it had survived still another night, Rolf said, 'Bad news,' when I walked in. Fortunately, before my mouth could drop open, he motioned me farther into the store, and I saw what he meant. There weren't any more than ten fish in sight. That's okay if you're a cook for a foreign office big shot who brings home loins of French lamb and Polish hams, but it's not okay if you're a spy and there isn't a goldfish with a mouth for a message. 'Not even a mackerel can get through.'

'Too bad,' I said. As usual, I was holding my tiny piece of paper between my index and middle fingers. I always took it from a slit in my coat sleeve just before I walked into the store.

Rolf looked dejected. His head was down, and even his arm hung limp. But then I realized his index finger was pointing to the floor; he'd managed to steer me to the side of the counter where he cleaned and scaled, so our feet couldn't be seen by the two other workers in the shop. I dropped the paper on the floor. 'But come back as soon as you can,' he said. I noticed his shoe had moved a fraction of an inch and had kicked the paper under the counter. 'They say there's some nice herring coming in.'

'I'll try,' I said.

'Good.' He guided me back toward the door. 'The more you come, the better your chance of getting a nice piece of fish. It may be a bother, but I'm sure your employer will appreciate your efforts.'

So the OSS wanted the intelligence as fast as I could give it to them. And a week later, I knew I had something big.

It was a translation of a report from one of Horst's agents in England, but when I shifted the paper to copy it better, I realized there was another paper stapled to it: the original report, in English. From the old fold lines and the way it was curled up, it had obviously been rolled and pushed into a small space: a bullet casing, or even a pen.

> I have settled into the town of Lydd, and ensconced myself at the local pub, so much so that the Americans take me for one of the locals. One of them, a Captain Grayson, is a member of the liaison group between Eisenhower and Montgomery. Quiet chap. Quite the loner. He reads a good deal of poetry. I made his acquaintance after several nights of observing him reading from the works of Walt Whitman, the American poet.
>
> 'Ah,' I said, 'to think in this godforsaken spot there is someone else who cherishes *Leaves of Grass.*' He was stunned that the English knew of Whitman (!), but was rather thrilled. I used my cover story, and there is no doubt he believes that I am a (if not *the*) Royal Army expert on heavy artillery. I had 'a bit much' to drink and told him all about the Gun Mark 3.
>
> Last night I got him talking about French poets, particularly Verlaine. One thing led to another, and my dear Captain Grayson, responding to my passionate Francophilia, told me *the invasion will take place on the beaches of Normandy and that the talk of Pas-de-Calais is a ruse!* I made light of it, saying it was too painfully logical and therefore highly unlikely. I have invited him to dine with me Thursday, when I will show him my library and allow him to convince me that Normandy is the place.

I copied the English word for word, put back the envelope, flap side up, then stood at the door for the longest five minutes I'd endured since I'd started poking around in Horst's study. Someone *had* to stop this Grayson guy. Or encourage him; if he was a plant, Horst's agent in England believed he was telling the truth. And by the list of names at the end of the translation, enough people in the foreign office, SS, Army General Staff and Abwehr were getting copies to show that the Germans took him seriously. If 'Grayson' was OSS, he should keep piling it on.

I had to get to Rolf's, but the more I thought, the more I realized going the next day would be risky; I'd just been there and bought two carp. No one, not even someone like me, with unlimited ration coupons, could be in such dire need of fish as to come back the next day. My orders were clear: Come often, but every day is too often. I didn't want to risk arousing suspicions. I would wait one more day.

My mistake.

It was late afternoon, and I was in the kitchen seeding a cucumber, when Hedwig screamed. It was such a departure from her usual whine that it tore through the house, all the way down to the kitchen. By the time I raced up the stairs to the second floor, Else and Dagmar were already there. Hedwig stood in the dark, wood-paneled hallway in her aqua robe; it had a milk dribble down the right breast. Her hands were clenched tight on the open linen closet door.

All Dagmar could do was say, 'I didn't know there was a key, Madam,' over and over. But even if Dagmar had wanted to help Hedwig, she couldn't; Else had thrown her arms around the chambermaid in terror and was squeezing the air out of her, like a wrestler. And Hedwig herself was in such a woe-is-me state that, finally, all she could do was shriek again.

The three of them looked like one of those stuffed wild animal tableaux at the Museum of Natural History; they were absolutely incapable of freeing themselves from their ridiculous positions. I would have laughed, except that what was happening was so perilous and I was on the brink of hysteria myself. My voice quavered so much I was terrified that it alone would give me away. 'What happened?' I asked. 'Is there anything I can do?'

The actual sound of someone speaking a full sentence seemed to jolt them all. Else let go of Dagmar and began to cry into her apron; Dagmar bent over to the pile of giant tablecloths, which were now on the floor, and, clearly for the second or third time, began to open each one wide and shake it; and Hedwig said, 'The key is missing!'

'Key?' I asked. I had to do four things at once: get control of myself, look more innocent and dumb than even Else, figure out how dangerous my situation was, and see if I could save myself. 'What key?'

'The key to my husband's study.'

I tried to look confused. 'It's always locked. Doesn't Herr Drescher carry the key?' If I was nearly hysterical, Hedwig was far out in front of me. She clenched at the door even tighter, her hands like claws, and screeched, 'He called from the office! He forgot some papers here and he must have them. He is upset. No; angry. *So* angry. He told me I would find an extra key under the pile of big tablecloths.' She took a huge gulp of air and then whispered: 'He said, "This is a top-secret key. Tell no one!" ' Her whisper was replaced by a loud wail.

Else grabbed onto me; it was like being hugged by King Kong. 'We'll all look for it, Madam,' I said, in the gentlest voice possible. I pulled out of Else's strangulation embrace and moved toward Hedwig. 'Let me help you into bed. You must rest. I'll get you some warm milk . . .' I managed to unhook her claws from the door '. . . and then the three of us will find your husband's key.'

She allowed herself to be led into her room. I sat her on the edge of the bed, knelt down and took off her slippers. 'Everything will be fine, Madam.'

When I stood up, I saw her hands were now covering her face; she was sobbing. 'Hurry,' she begged. 'He sounded . . . like a madman when I told him I couldn't find it. He said he'd phone again, to see if . . . but he didn't. Dear God, he's probably coming home. You *must* find it, before he gets here.'

'I will, Madam.' I shifted her bulky body into the bed.

In the five or six steps it took me to cross the room and close the door, I realized I had to get out before Horst came home, or I was finished. I was the newest member of the household staff, and for that reason alone I would be under the most suspicion. But all of us would be grilled, over and over, first by Horst, then, if he was stupid enough to let out the truth about his bringing papers home every night, by the professionals. They'd check our stories, our papers, our histories.

'She wants her milk,' I told them. 'I'll be right back.' I hurried down the hall. For a second, I glanced at the flight of stairs that led to the third floor and my room. I should go get my papers, I thought. A change of underwear. But I couldn't risk letting Else and Dagmar see me go up there; even they might start to wonder.

I hurried down the stairs, through the dining room and into the kitchen, so, if they were listening, they could hear the door swing shut. I hung up my apron, grabbed my brown coat off a hook, took some loose change and an apple, and ran out the side door.

I looked up at the tree branch. Let the key stay; I wouldn't be needing it, and besides, I had to run. Except I had no sense of where to run to. I only knew that it was no more than a fifteen-minute ride to the villa from the foreign office, and Horst wouldn't be telling his driver, Twice around the Tiergarten.

I climbed the small wall in back that separated Horst's property from the neighbor's. There were sharp pebbles embedded in the stone and gravel; they bit into my hands and tore at my stockings. Just as I reached the cobblestone sidewalk outside the neighbor's house, I heard the squeal of the brakes of a too-fast Mercedes-Benz stopping in front of Horst's. The car door opened. Then came a faint but distinct cry of panic: 'Hedwig!'

It was almost six in the evening. Rolf's store would probably be closed. I had been in Berlin for a year and a half – too long to gamble on going to the safe address I'd been given. So if I was going to survive, I had no choice but to jeopardize the life of my best friend. My only chance lay with Margarete; she knew the way the game was played. She could tell me what to do and, if necessary, galvanize the resistance into action. But as I stood in front of her apartment building, I wanted to cover my face and cry for what I was doing to her.

It all looked so secure, so protected, with its ornate wrought-iron door. Imposing stone urns stood on either side. They were filled with red geraniums and seemed oblivious to the war. And just my walking through the front door, showing my face, would endanger everything Margarete had.

There was one small chance. Horst might realize that his own life was in peril because he had housed a spy, and he'd kept my disappearance a secret. But I doubted it; it was too risky. He knew

Else or Dagmar might talk, especially if he begged or bribed them not to; that was the beauty of his Third Reich. Or it would have to occur to him that the Gestapo might catch up with me – maybe when I was performing some terrorist act – and under torture I might cry out: Horst Drescher! Sooner or later – probably sooner, maybe within hours – the photograph on the passport in my room would be copied and sent to every policeman and Gestapo agent in Berlin.

There was no doorman, but just to be safe, I walked around the huge stone building until I found the service entrance. There was an elevator inside, a cage. It was open. The operator was gone; he'd left his newspaper on his tiny half circle of a stool. But I walked past it, over to the door to the service stairs. It was locked.

I had no choice. I got into the elevator, slammed the gate shut after me and turned the operator's wooden handle to the right. The elevator jerked and then started slowly, *so* slowly, to creak upstairs. Finally it stopped. Margarete had once remarked that she lived on the top floor of her building; it was an endless cave of an apartment, she'd said, but it had a magnificent view of the Brandenburg Gate.

I stepped out of the elevator, into a small alcove. There was a large metal door, the back door to her apartment, and another to the staircase. I made sure the door to the stairs was open and took the elevator down three or four floors, where I left it. Then, heart in throat, I climbed all the way up again.

It was obvious Margarete's endless cave took up the entire floor of the building; besides the door to the stairs, there was only one other door in the service alcove: The area itself was all empty space, with nothing to hide behind. I crouched close to the door to the apartment and waited, knowing all the time that if anyone came up on the service elevator, I was dead.

You focus on crazy things at times like that. There I was, listening at a back door for a front door to open, my picture about to circulate all over Berlin, and I was thinking: Why did I have three cups of tea this afternoon? because I had to go to the bathroom. That's all I could concentrate on. Okay, so maybe I thought a little about the rumor of the Gestapo's latest persuasive technique: They smashed the joints of your fingers, one by one, with a hammer. And then I thought: Wouldn't it be funny if all of a sudden, after going untouched, this building gets an early-evening bomb, with me on the top floor. But in truth, those pictures of peril seemed like nothing compared to the strain on my bladder.

I must have been there nearly an hour when, through the metal door, I heard someone enter the apartment. I listened: There must have been rugs but, finally, wood floors, because there was the click of a woman's heels. The noise advanced. I tapped at the door. Nothing. I knocked. The footsteps stopped. I said to myself, Oh, God, let it be her, then I put my mouth to the door and called out, 'Margarete!'

The footsteps clicked closer. 'Who is it?'

'Lina.'

The door was opened a slit. 'It is you!' she whispered. 'Why . . .?'

'I'm sorry.'

'No. You must be . . . in terrible trouble. Come in.' She led me into a small vestibule between what must have been a maid's room and the kitchen.

'Do you have a bathroom?'

'Lina!' she said softly, smiling. 'If that's why you came here, I shall be extremely annoyed. All right, follow me.'

Some cave. We walked through hallways hung with framed paintings – a couple of old barons, and the kind of German still-life paintings of fruit bowls that somehow always have dead rabbits and candlesticks too.

There were crystal bottles of bath salts, perfumes and lotions all over her bathroom, as though it never occurred to Margarete that in the middle of the night she would hear a whistle and then her life would be reduced to shattered glass.

She took me into her kitchen and we sat together on some sort of fancy wooden bench she had along one wall of the huge room. 'Let me make you something. A nice omelet?'

I said, 'Please, I can't eat.'

'Nervous stomach again?'

'Nervous . . . everything. More than nervous. Oh, Margarete, I've done a terrible thing coming here. I've brought you into this whole mess. If I'm seen coming or leaving, everything, all this' – I waved in the direction of the hallway, with its rich gold-framed barons – 'won't do you any good.'

Margarete slipped off her shoes and tucked her feet under her. For a minute she didn't say anything. She studied her hands, fiddled with the heavy gold bracelets she wore, but didn't look at me. 'Lina, it is simple. If you had a choice, you wouldn't be here, so there is no reason for you to feel remorse. Now tell me what happened.'

I told her all about Horst, Hedwig and the key. All about my work. Every time I added another detail, I felt as if I was digging her grave a little deeper. So, for whatever it was worth, I didn't tell her about Captain Grayson and how urgent it was that I get that message through. If I couldn't save her, at least I could try to give her a little protection, allow her to have the luxury of a little ignorance.

Both of us might be captured and forced to talk. But despite what she had once told me about how members of the resistance movement committed the sin of pride by thinking: Oh, yeah, I can withstand the worst kind of torture, I felt that I could last longer than Margarete. She had extraordinary courage and nobility, but I was afraid that the nobility might be the thing to do her in. Even though she'd talked a lot about how much she hated her pampered childhood, she had still lived it. Okay, I wasn't raised on the toughest streets in New York, but no one had ever ironed my clothes or polished my chandeliers for me. I was older, and just a little bit tougher. Looking at her perfect white hands, with their opal and gold rings, her gleaming buffed nails, all of precisely the same length, I sensed that that small difference might be important.

And there was another difference: I was half German but completely American. Even after all this time, they were foreigners to me. And if it came down to me and the Gestapo, I really believed I could hate them – and withstand them – a little better than she could. They had murdered her dear friend Alfred. Well, they'd rounded up and slaughtered my family. My people.

Margarete finally looked me right in the eye. 'Is there anything else I should know?' she asked.

'No,' I said. 'You know everything now. How terrible does it look for me? Would it save time,' I demanded, trying to smile, 'if I just went straight to the Berlin police and gave myself up?'

She leaned over and adjusted a loose hairpin on one of my braids. 'It might save time, but it would be infinitely stupid. Now listen to me, my dear friend. I'm going to tell you exactly what to do.' She glanced at a big wall clock. It was almost seven-thirty. 'You have to get out of here. The pig is due here in an hour, and he might stay the night, so I can't offer you my most choice accommodations. The first thing you must do is get to this Rolf.' She paused. 'But his fish store is certainly closed by now.' I nodded. 'So you will get to him first thing in the morning. Now, is your hair in your passport photograph braided?'

'Yes.'

'All right. Let's hurry inside. You'll take down your hair and I'll give you something to put on – less domestic, more well-kept mistress. You'll spend tonight in the Friedrichstrasse underground. Get in the middle of the crowds. Stay in the middle but don't talk. Anything, even the tension in your voice, could give you away. I don't think you comprehend how frightened you are, Lina.'

'Oh, Margarete, I really think I do. I'm *terrified*.' She stood and led me back through the long hallway, into her bedroom. I took out my hairpins. She wrapped them in toilet tissue and buried them in a wastebasket that was full of cold-cream and make-up tissues. She handed me her brush. Silver. I brushed my hair and she said, 'Don't leave the underground too early – even though there are always a few people who get up and go around dawn. Wait a little later, for the main part of the crowd to leave, and go out with them, blend in. Now listen to this: Do not take the train from that station to Rolf's. No one does that. Everyone goes home, to see if they still have a home and to wash up. Take your time. Walk to the Französische Strasse station. You should plan on getting to Rolf's between seven-thirty and eight. Even if the store is still closed, he will be there; they go to market early.' I put down the brush. 'How is his fish?'

'Not bad,' I said, 'but probably not up to your standards.'

'Isn't it odd?' Margarete said. She looked in the mirror of the dressing table, picked up the brush and ran it through her long brown hair. 'All these years I've never even heard there was a fishmonger in the movement.'

'It's too bad you don't know him,' I said. 'There's something really admirable about him,' I said. 'I mean, I don't really know him. The only strong opinion I've ever heard him express is that it's wrong to cut the heads off fish. But I know, to me, he really represents everything good about Germany. Well, Rolf – and you.'

'Oh, don't flatter me. But him. Lina, there you have it: the greatness of the common man.'

'And the greatness of the uncommon woman.' And then I turned to her and said, 'Thank you, Margarete.'

# *Chapter Twenty-five*

I didn't dare risk sleep, so I sat up. All night long I felt the damp chill of the wall of the Friedrichstrasse underground through my coat. I couldn't risk taking it off and rolling it into a backrest of a pillow, as I'd done in the past; the report on Captain Grayson was slipped into the slit I'd made months before, in the lining of the cuff of the sleeve.

Lives could be saved or lost; I *had* to get the intelligence to Rolf. So I leaned against the clammy wall at night, listening to the slow, heavy night breathing of the crowd, just waiting to get free, and thinking about Captain Grayson. Either he was an OSS jewel – the world's supreme conveyer of disinformation – or one selfish, rotten, weak son of a bitch. Selling his country down the river. For literature! I smiled for a second, imagining the army recruiting Nan and all the other little cerebralettes into a special WAC battalion to take care of morale for guys like him: Oh, Captain, forget the three panzer divisions. Tell me about Verlaine's metaphors.

Seven-thirty or eight, Margarete had said. Your friend should be there by then.

I half closed my eyes and pictured Rolf's store: the sawdust-covered wood floors, the scrubbed counters, the orderly rows of fish on their beds of chopped-up ice. They were all laid out whenever I got there – usually around ten o'clock. But, I thought, by ten o'clock the ice was always partially melted. I remembered it clearly then; I was always careful to lean forward, not to step too close to the counters, because the freezing, fish-scented water would drip onto my shoes. I figured they must set out the ice about five-thirty, six in the morning.

I couldn't stand the waiting. And so, soon after the 'all clear' signal, just after daybreak and the end of the curfew, I copied the first of the early risers: I yawned, stretched my neck and made my way on cautious tiptoes among the still-sleeping mounds.

But when I got to Rolf's, a little after six, he wasn't there. No one was. The door was locked, the store dark. I walked to the corner. The old man who ran the newspaper kiosk, a man I'd seen a million times, glanced up at me, not so much suspiciously as curiously. I couldn't afford curiosity.

'I was told to get here early,' I said, to explain. 'To the fish store. They might have some haddock.'

'No haddock today,' the newsdealer said. 'The policeman told me.' Oh, God, I thought. 'The man who worked there was killed last night. The one-armed man.'

You're effing falling apart! an instructor at OSS Training School had roared at me one time. Don't give me any of that tender-maiden crap! No flutters! No fainting! This is war, girlie.

'The one-armed man?' I showed surprise. A little regret. 'How was he killed?'

'A bomb.'

'Oh.' All the energy I had left seemed to seep out of me. Was it horror? Relief that Rolf hadn't been caught? I felt so weak. The apple in my pocket that I'd taken from the Dreschers' weighed me down.

'His wife came first thing, the policeman told me. Before dawn. Took his knives, the kind fish people use, and some other things that were his. Said she didn't know if they would bother opening the store again.'

A *bomb?* I kept thinking. But what did I expect? A special RAF note engraved on each casing: Abstain from detonating in presence of friends.

'Did he own the store?'

'Yes.' He cut the cord on a pile of papers. 'You know, I never knew how he lost his arm. I couldn't ask. He was quiet, kept to himself.' He looked at me expectantly. 'Do you know?'

'No,' I said. 'I never . . .'

Out of the corner of my eye, I saw a man walking down the

street toward Rolf's. Maybe it was nothing more than my own dread that made the whole world seem menacing, but I felt something was wrong about him. He looked okay, not tight, cold Gestapo. But even from a distance, his raincoat looked too clean and well-pressed. Or it could have been that his walk was not quite brisk enough for a government worker getting an early start on his day.

Maybe Rolf had been carrying something on him when he was hit, and when they found his body, searched it . . .

'Well,' I said to the newsdealer. 'It is sad. He seemed like a nice man.'

'A good business, if you don't mind smelling like that all the time.'

'Yes,' I said. 'Goodbye.'

And then I turned the corner, out of sight of the man in the raincoat, and walked fast. Not too fast. Just the sharp pace that an energetic cook would take when she is on the trail of haddock.

I went to the zoo. There was no grass; the ground was black, and the air was absolutely still. It had been bombed a few weeks before. The cages had been so badly damaged that the police had had to shoot the animals, for fear they'd get loose and run wild in Berlin. Boy, had everyone gotten all weepy over that: Poor animals! The slaughter of the innocents! The Germans were so compassionate.

I sat on what was left of a bench. The jagged ends of the wooden slats were scorched; when you touched them, they broke off into cinders. I took the apple out of my pocket and bit into it. It's funny; when you read about people who know their time is up, they're always tasting or smelling something and going Ahh! at the beautiful sense experience they never noticed before. Don't believe what you read. My time looked like it was almost up, and what might be my last meal was an ordinary, unexceptional, mealy apple.

I put it back in my pocket. I couldn't eat. My nerves were shot, and so was my stomach. For almost two years I'd done almost nothing but sauté, roast and stew. I'd lived in the middle of abundance, and yet in all that time I hadn't been able to get down one entire meal. I'd tasted a little. I'd drunk tea. And on those nights when I didn't have to hide from bombs, I'd gone to bed with a hot-water bottle clutched to my aching belly. My clothes hung on me. My skin had turned ashen. Finally I looked as if I belonged in Berlin.

Oh, I was so tired. A couple of times I felt my head drop to my chest. I made myself sit straight, the way aristocrats do. Back at right angle to seat: like Margarete, or Nan. It was an awful, uncomfortable position for a regular person to have to stay in, but it made me breathe in deeper and kept me awake. Maybe that's why all those sleek upper-class girls had that special air about them; they just took in more oxygen. Then I wondered about what kind of jerk I was to be sitting there, on a fragment of a bombed bench, doomed in a doomed city, thinking about my not being classy. If Edward was sitting where I was, knowing the chances were pretty good he didn't have much more than a day or two to live, what would he be thinking about? Apples and stomachaches and rich girls? Concepts: good and evil; the nature of justice? Or something I never even dreamed about?

It was time to get moving. The news about Captain Grayson had to get to the OSS before he could meet that agent for a home-cooked dinner, a few poems, a couple of drinks and then a confidential chat – fascinating, old bean – about the invasion of good old La Belle France.

Except I didn't know what to do. Fifteen, twenty minutes passed. I was crazy to be staying in one spot like that. A policeman or a soldier could come along any minute and demand my papers. But I was unable to move because I couldn't think of where to move to.

Okay, I said to myself. Enough with the inaction. This is war, girlie. Make believe you're Edward Leland and you're stuck in enemy territory and you've got an urgent message you've got to get out. What do you do? You think? Who do I know? Who can I trust? All right: I know Margarete. Oh, and I know old laughing boy, Konrad Friedrichs, the guy with the million-dollar smile.

But stop. Think like Edward. Analyze. Who has a better chance of getting that message out?

At about seven-thirty that morning, I lay behind a hedge, flat on my stomach in the dirt, and, with my shoe in my hand, hammered at a window gently, until it cracked. Slowly, patiently, I picked out the pieces of glass so the frame was clean. Then I slithered down through the narrow basement window – into my old bedroom at Herr Konrad Friedrichs's.

My number two fear was that when I showed myself to Konrad Friedrichs, he'd have a heart attack and drop dead on the spot. But number one was his housekeeper, the Wicked Witch of the West, Frau Gerlach: Just my presence in the house would probably be enough to set her warts humming. So I stood with my ear against the door of my old cubicle, going through my familiar count to three hundred, listening for any sounds. A little after two hundred, I thought I heard footsteps moving across the room above me. That would be the pantry; she was getting out dishes to set the table for breakfast.

I climbed up to the first floor and put my ear against still another door. No sound. I opened it a crack and peered out. That always works terrifically in movies, because the hero can always see the villains having a meeting forty feet down the hall and around the corner. But the only thing I could see was a tiny strip of wall. So I slid out the door and, fast, looked to the right, to the kitchen. Nothing. For all I knew, she could leap out with a skillet in her hand and attack me, but she might just be sitting and having a cup of tea; I wasn't going to hang around and count to three hundred again. I rushed off to the left, to the narrow wooden staircase, and, throwing all my Training School techniques aside, ran right upstairs, straight into Konrad Friedrichs's bedroom.

He didn't have a heart attack, although he seemed to stop breathing for at least a full minute. He just gaped at me. I gaped back. He was standing beside a high chest of drawers, wearing a starched-collared shirt and a tie, but he didn't have on his trousers. He had old man's legs: white, knob-kneed, hairless. 'My God!' he said. I put my finger on my lips to signal him to keep quiet. 'How dare you!'

'I don't have time to listen to you now,' I told him softly. 'I'm only going to stay two or three minutes, and then I'm going to get out. No one will know I've been here. But listen to me. My contact, Rolf, is dead.'

Herr Friedrichs walked over to his high, old-fashioned bed and, unmindful that he was in white undershorts and black hose, sat down and shut his eyes. 'They killed him?' he asked.

'No. At least I'm pretty sure they didn't. It seems to have been a bomb. But they know about me.' He rolled his eyes, one of those weary, it-was-inevitable expressions. I got so mad! 'Look,' I said, 'for a year and a half I've been giving the OSS first-rate intelligence, so don't give me any of your speeches about foolhardy amateurs. *You* try living in the same house with a Nazi like Horst Drescher, sneaking into his locked study four, five, six, seven nights a week, and see how long you'd last.'

He said, 'You have made your point. Proceed.'

'I have a message that has to get out, and there's no Rolf anymore.' He started to shake his head. 'Listen, there's a German agent near an American army base in England. He's getting top-secret information about the Allied invasion of France.' Konrad Friedrichs's eyes widened. 'You've *got* to let them know.'

'I cannot. I have just returned from Lisbon and Madrid. I am unable – '

'You don't have any choice.'

'Don't threaten me!'

'Herr Friedrichs, I'm not threatening you. I'm trying to save lives – including yours. Horst Drescher is no analytical genius. We both know that. But he's no fool, either. In a day or two, maybe even today, he's going to realize who recommended me so highly.' He covered his face with his veiny old hands. 'You have to get out.'

'If I leave my country now, I might never come back.'

'If you don't leave now, you'll be dead. Please, you've got to understand how critical this situation is. For you. And for the Allies. Yes, you do have to leave, but is the Germany you're living in the Germany you want? If there's any chance of saving the country you love, it lies in its defeat.' I paused for a second, but he wouldn't stop hiding his face in his hands. 'Don't you want to stay alive so that when it's all over, you can come back and help your people, guide them, show them what's right?' Slowly, he lowered his hands to his lap. They were shaking. He was a man who did things by the book, and this time there was no book. He didn't know what to do. 'Is there any way you can get straight to the airport now and get transport out on an emergency basis? Please, think. Help me.'

'There might be.' His speech was halting. 'But it will be harder for you. I would have to speak to Margarete, to try and get you . . . perhaps some sort of diplomatic passport.'

'No! You have to get out this morning, before Horst realizes your connection to me.'

'But what about you?' Give him credit. He was a cranky, rigid Prussian snob, but he was also a man of honor. Whatever I was, I was his ally. He would therefore save my life.

I wouldn't let him. 'Thank you, but if I go with you, there's no chance of getting the message out.' I reached into the slit in the lining of my cuff and drew out the tiny slip of paper. I walked over and put it in his hand. 'There will be copies of my passport photo at every train station, airport and border crossing in Germany. We both know that.' For a long time, he didn't speak.

'What will you do?' he asked.

'Margarete's already helped me once. I think I'm going to have to go back. I hope she'll be able to help me again.'

'I hope so too,' he said. He showed no signs of moving; he just sat primly on the bed, the message clenched in his hand.

'Come on now, stand up. Finish getting dressed.' He looked down at his bare legs in shock. 'I'm afraid we don't have time for modesty now. As soon as you're ready, you'll have to go downstairs and keep your housekeeper busy so I can sneak out.'

I took him by the elbow and eased him off the bed. That was really all he needed. He marched to his closet, turned away from me, stepped into his trousers and began to button them. 'Poor, dear Frau Gerlach,' he murmured. 'What will I tell her?'

'*Nothing.*'

He spun around, all red-faced, huffy. 'She's utterly trustworthy.'

'I'm sure she is.' I wasn't sure at all. She'd probably sell him down the river for ten pfennigs. 'But it's her devotion to you that you have to worry about. She'll fear for your life. She might call a friend of yours, a colleague, to get help for you. Promise me you won't say anything to her.' He stood there, stubborn. I lost my temper. 'Damn it!' I whispered. 'You don't have time to be noble. Don't you want to live? Don't you want to give me at least a chance to survive? For God's sake, promise me.'

'You have my word,' he said at last.

A little more than sixty seconds later, I was back on the streets of Berlin.

I imagined Edward again. Think, he said. What is there besides your passport – with your photograph and fingerprints – that can be used to identify you? How would Horst describe you?

Well, he'd say I had blond hair –

Don't waste time, Linda. All that information is on your passport. What else?

One of the maids would remember I have a brown coat.

Lose it.

I took off my coat and draped it over my arm. It was warm for April. At least I thought it was April; the trees that still stood were covered with the hazy green of new leaves. I used my last two coins for a bus ride. I climbed to the upper deck, took a seat and put the coat beside me. A few minutes later, when I was sure no one was looking, I gave it a light push; it fell to my feet. The bus rumbled on for another couple of miles; then I walked downstairs and got off.

I spent the rest of the day waiting in lines. I'd asked the imaginary Edward, Where should I go? Margarete's at work.

Become invisible. There are two ways to do it it. Find a hiding place that you know is absolutely secure. Or blend in with a crowd.

So at around eight-thirty or nine that morning, I joined the long line of women in front of a bakery. 'Hot, isn't it?' the woman in front of me said. Her dress was gray, the color of a mouse, and it had small white spots all over it from being scrubbed too many times.

'Yes, very hot. And so early in the day.'

No one had conversations that lasted longer than that. Berliners were too exhausted after a night of bombing, too wrapped up in their own hardship, to want to chat. This was a line for stale bread, not for tickets to Radio City Music Hall.

So when suddenly I said, 'Oh, no!' the woman looked pained, as if I was going to try and burden her with my troubles. 'My pocketbook!' Her expression changed. I saw sympathy. And fear. She understood I had lost my money, my ration books and my passport: my whole German life.

'Calm yourself,' she said, and then stepped aside so I could hurry off.

I made my way from neighborhood to neighborhood all day. I stood in the longest lines I could find, waiting an hour or two, and then discovering my loss. The waiting was so miserable. I had the headache that comes from lack of sleep, and the empty, aching nauseousness that comes as you start to move from hunger toward starvation.

In the late afternoon, as the sun was beginning to lose its strength, I started to walk toward Margarete's apartment building. It must have been around six-thirty when I got there, because the streets were filled with people coming home from work. I knew my chances of slipping up the service elevator were just about zero, so I went through the front door. Again, no doorman, but there was a uniformed operator at the main elevator. He had gold-braided shoulder brushes and cap with a huge medallion. He looked like a veteran from a much better war.

'Yes?' he challenged me.

'I'm Lina, sir. Hugo, the Baron von Eberstein's estate manager . . . Hugo told me to – '

'Get in,' he said, and whisked me up to the top floor. As I got out, he said, 'Just ring the bell, Lina.'

'Thank you, sir.' And after he disappeared, that's what I did.

'I'm coming!' I heard Margarete say. Her heels made a rapid clack-clack. She'd been busy in the kitchen. I could smell onions being sautéed. The door opened. 'God in heaven!' It was as if someone had pulled a plug: All the color drained out of her face.

'Is he inside?' I whispered. 'The pig?'

'No.' She put her hand over her chest and took a deep breath.

'Come in.' She pulled me inside and shut the door. 'I can't believe you are here!'

'I'll go!'

'*No!* It's just . . . Oh, dear God, I have been crazy with worry about you.' She put her arms around me for a second and hugged me and then said, 'Come into the kitchen.'

We sat at a table draped in a lace cloth that went all the way to the floor. The cabinets were all glass, but the rest of the room was a rich, dark wood. 'Are you hungry?' she demanded. She had a kitchen towel tucked into the belt of her blue silk dress.

'Yes, but my stomach – '

She leapt up. 'I have some lovely calves' liver.'

'Margarete, please, just a piece of bread.' She hurried over to the bread box, took out a loaf of dark bread and sliced it. 'I can't stay here.'

'Why not?'

'You know why not.'

'Do you want beer?' I shook my head no. She put the bread on a plate and then went to the refrigerator and returned with cheese and a bottle of milk.

'My picture is probably all over the city by now.'

'It is,' she said gently. 'Everyone in . . . the movement who knows about you has been so frightened. What's happened? Tell me everything.' She gave me a glass for the milk. A goblet.

'Please, I need a few minutes. I haven't slept or eaten since – '

'Then you must take a rest! I'll put you into a nice, soft bed with an eiderdown – '

'No, thank you.' I put a small piece of cheese on the bread. Like the apple, this didn't have any taste. Still, it was food. So I just sat there, ate a few bites and sipped the milk in silence.

Margarete was comforting and discomforting at the same time. She'd smile or pat my hand, but then there were moments when her entire body tensed, as she tried to keep her jumpiness under control. I felt she would like nothing more than to run out of the room, away from me and the danger I'd brought.

'I won't come here ever again. You have my promise.'

'Lina, you are always welcome.'

'I'm here to ask for your help: yours and the movement's. If I can find someone who's willing to hide me, that would be more than I could rightfully expect.'

'But you would like something more.' She knew me so well.

'Yes,' I said. 'I wouldn't even have thought of it if Herr Friedrichs hadn't mentioned it.'

'Oh, how is he?'

'Out of Germany, I hope.'

'I see! You saw him?'

'Yes, early this morning. When he was thinking about how he could get me out of the country, he mentioned the possibility of calling you. Maybe, with all your connections . . . in the Abwehr, all the people your family must know, even the pig . . . Margarete, is there some way you can get me out of Germany?'

She shook her head. It wasn't as much a denial as saying, I don't know. 'Lina, it would be so much easier for you to stay here. With all the bombings, we're becoming a nation of refugees. Give me a day. I can get new papers for you, decent ones.' Her face brightened. 'I know! We can cut your hair short and dress you up in my clothes. No one would know that the girl in the photograph with braids is the same person as the stylish young woman with the smart haircut!'

It was clear she was trying to sell me something, and although I knew I would probably have to buy it, I wasn't ready yet. 'Let me tell you why I have to leave Germany,' I said. 'I don't belong here.' Margarete waited. 'I'm sure you understand, being a translator, that there are some people who belong in a country – and some people who don't.'

'I'm sorry. I do not understand.'

And for the first time in the year and a half that felt like a lifetime, I spoke English. 'I don't belong in Germany because I'm an American, Margarete.' For a minute she didn't react at all. Then she began to laugh uncontrollably. But she wasn't having a good time. She was hysterical. 'Margarete. Stop it. *Please* calm down.' I banged my fist on the table. She jumped, and she stopped. 'Are you okay?' I asked.

'You speak English so well!' I began to laugh this time, and it was only a little bit of nerves. It was genuinely funny. And now that I was speaking English, I didn't know if I could ever speak German again.

'Of course I speak English well. It's my native language.'

'And your German?'

'My grandmother lived with us. She came from Berlin.'

'So you are German.'

'My father's parents were born in Germany.'

'Your mother's family?'

'Originally from England or Scotland.'

'OSS sent an *American* in here? *Why*?'

'Because there was nobody here who could do it. Margarete, come on. You know how efficient the Nazis are. Really, how many people are there in the resistance?'

'Very few,' she acknowledged. Suddenly, she asked, 'How is my English?'

'Excellent.'

The beginning of a smile lit up her face: the old Margarete. 'Could *I* get away with what you did?' She was playing her old game; she saw the danger, but she also saw the fun. 'Could I slip into Chicago or some other large city and pass myself off as an American?'

'No. You're a little too precise, too clipped. And your *w*'s . . . they're still . . . slightly German.' I grinned at her. 'We could work on them.'

'So my consummate Berlin friend is an American!'

'From New York. Hey, can you tell I have a New York accent?'

'No.' She was starting to get nervous again. She stood and paced the kitchen.

'Take it easy, Margarete.'

'That is rather difficult, Lina.'

'I know.'

She moved away from me and sat on a long carved wooden bench. 'You're not a recruit? You're OSS?' she inquired.

'I've been working for them on and off since 1940.'

'Did you do this sort of work for them before?'

'No. I was a secretary in New York and then in Washington. We moved down there before the war. Well, I mean before the US got into the war. Before Pearl Harbor.'

' "We"?'

'My husband's in the OSS also. He was a lawyer in one of those big firms on Wall Street.'

'What is his name?' She crossed her legs. Then she folded her arms and hugged them tight to her body.

'John.'

'Is your name really Lina?'

'Linda.'

'Linda,' she repeated. 'Linda.' Then suddenly she said, 'Oh, God, I need a drink. A brandy. Do you want one?' I shook my head. 'Excuse me, then. I'll be right back.' I smiled as she left the kitchen. Margarete sounded almost exactly like Marlene Dietrich. While she was gone, I let myself relax for a minute. It must have been because I was speaking English, but I remembered *Destry Rides Again*, and then I began to think how terrific it would be just to sit with a big bag of popcorn and stare up at a screen. I decided I wanted to watch something with Bette Davis. I thought: I bet she's come out with at least two movies since I've been away. I was really getting punchy, trying to remember if I'd read any story in the magazines where the reporter says, What are your future plans, Miss Davis? Then Margarete came back to the kitchen. She didn't have a brandy.

She had a gun.

'You will never know how sorry I am,' she said, in German.

'*What the hell are you doing?*' English.

'I think it should be obvious.'

And it was. 'You! You're the traitor in the resistance.'

'Is that what they call me?'

'You're the one who killed Alfred Eckert.'

'No! Alfred was my friend.'

'But you killed him, anyway.'

'No! Of course not.' I stared at her. 'Well, finally I had no choice but to report him. He was too talkative. Too trusting. I tried to protect him, Lina . . . Linda. I *try* to protect my friends. Truly I do. Most of them . . . It is easy. You yourself said it. We are quite efficient, and the so-called resistance is painfully ineffectual. I merely report what the amateurs are doing. Hardly anyone . . . gets hurt. We recognize they can do little harm, but we must keep track of them. You, however, were a danger, Lina. You were good. But still, I was going to save you. I swear I was. I loved you. I did. You were dear to me, special. You were everything I admired in the ordinary German. Hard-working. Smart. With a spare, simple beauty.' She shook her head in disbelief. 'You *look* so German.'

'So Aryan.'

'Yes.'

'You're really one of them, aren't you?'

'No more English.' She shook the gun at me, like a schoolteacher shaking her finger at a naughty student. 'German, please.'

'You believe all their crap,' I said, in English.

'I understand the American idiom. Do not disgrace yourself by using filthy language. Now, to answer your question, I happen to love the Fatherland. And I believe, as my family believes, that the Führer has saved Germany from – '

'I don't want to hear it, you Nazi bitch! Shut up!'

'I realize you are agitated, but you cannot speak to me like that! Now please get control of yourself. It is time to talk. What is your full name?'

'Lina Albrecht.'

'*Linda*, it should be obvious by now that I am in an unbearably difficult position. I will not hesitate to shoot. What is your full name, Linda?' She put the gun to my head.

'Lina Albrecht.'

'How can you possibly have any doubts about the seriousness of my purpose?'

'No,' I said. 'No doubts. But first tell me something. For old times' sake. Did you kill Rolf?'

The gun against my head made turning to see her impossible, but I could sense her pride. 'We picked him up within a half hour after you left last night. A mere half hour. He is probably dead by now.'

'Who is "we"? Your fat pig boyfriend?' She rubbed the muzzle of the gun against my scalp. Not a gun, I thought. A pistol. A Walther.

'He is not a pig! That was my cover story. His name is Franz Sommerfeld, and he is quite, quite handsome, actually.'

'Is that how you operate? Every time you feel forced to get rid of one of your dear friends, you just call up Franz and ask him to take care of things? He took care of Alfred, right?'

'Unfortunately, Alfred discovered I wasn't quite what I pretended to be. He was too much the man about town, saw me once too often with my . . . real friends. His suspicions grew. Apparently, he took to watching me from the little café across the street. He saw Franz. Leave it to dear old Alfred to notice a handsome man! And then he saw the two of us going out together. And after a few times, he realized that this' – her voice softened – 'beautiful man was the person I had been calling the pig. But Alfred's downfall was his romanticism, his belief in me. He couldn't believe that the disappearance of some of our . . . mutual friends had anything to do with his lovely, elegant Margarete – who wore his clothes with such chic. "You are having a silly infatuation," he told me. "Drop this man, and I won't tell anyone in the movement about him. Swear it, *ma chère Marguerite.*" But of course I couldn't trust him. He would have tattled on me. Alfred couldn't resist a juicy scandal.'

You know how people say, 'I almost threw up'? I almost did. I couldn't shake the sickness, the horror; when she talked about Alfred, her voice was filled with delight. He was still her darling, amusing friend.

But suddenly, all the charm went out of her voice. 'There is no more time. Move along.' She pressed the gun harder against my head, grabbed my shoulder and pushed me toward the door.

'You're not going to kill me here, are you?'

'Lina, you are so clever. So *terribly* clever.' The pressure of the gun made the whole right side of my face throb. 'I'm afraid that in the time it would take me to call Franz, and for him to send his men over, you might find a way to extricate yourself.' I stopped right where I was, about a foot from the kitchen door. 'Please,' she said, 'I don't want to do it in my kitchen.' Then she tilted her head – charming. 'You must think I'm terrible, saying that.'

'No. I think you're a wonderful person.'

'Listen to me. I am doing you a favor. Don't you dare smile! I *am* being kind.' She brought herself under control; her voice became subdued, soothing. 'You don't want them to get at you. We both knew it would be more than you could bear. With me it will be fast, merciful.' I turned my head a fraction of an inch; her eyes were actually moist.

'Please,' I said, 'I'm begging you.'

'Move, please.' With the gun at my head as a prod, she led me out of the kitchen and down the long, picture-covered hall.

'Are any of these portraits old von Ebersteins?' I asked.

'Do not attempt to ingratiate yourself. Be brave. Die like a German.'

But I didn't goose-step. I picked up my foot just a little higher than I had before. And then I smashed it down on her instep.

She screamed in pain, and in that second I grabbed her hand and bit it as hard as I could. It was a good bite, except her fingers didn't stiffen the way they said they would in Training School; they contracted.

Oh, God, my arm! Then the two of us became a mess of grappling arms, fingers, faces, all covered with my blood. Margarete jerked her hand away, to put the gun back against my head, but for an instant she stared at my teeth marks, and that's when I yanked at the barrel of the gun; it was burning hot from being fired, and slippery with my blood, and maybe that's why, the next thing I knew, it was mine.

I don't know how, but I managed to get a grip on it. And I put it against her head. 'Margarete, this is a Walther.'

'I know.' Her voice was a little higher than usual, but strong. She was being brave.

'The safety is already cocked. It will fire automatically now.'

'Are you going to kill me?' she asked.

'Yes.'

'Will you at least give me the final courtesy of a few quiet moments to compose myself and – '

'No.'

'Lina, let me just write a note to – '

'No.' I pressed my left arm against my waist; the pain was getting worse. Blood bubbled out of a small, black-rimmed hole and dripped on to her rug. I was getting dizzy. I jammed the gun harder against her head. Carefully, I inched around her until we were face to face. 'Who am I, Margarete?'

'Lina,' she whispered.

'No.'

'Linda.' This time she whimpered.

'I am Linda Voss. I am a Jew. Do you understand?'

'Yes.'

'Good.' And then I shot her brains out.

# *Chapter Twenty-six*

The linen napkin I put over the wound was like a sponge; soon it was soaked with blood. Slowly – I was so light-headed – I stepped back to the drawer in the breakfront in the hallway, tucked the gun under my chin, and with my good hand took out another napkin. A tourniquet: They'd shown us how in training school. We'd practiced on each other. Put it on that guy's thigh, they'd said, and so I put it on a Czech, and he'd looked away from me, embarrassed.

I glanced down. Blood had spilled out over my skirt. I was feeling faint now, and my knees started to wobble, my legs to flutter, as if I was doing some ridiculous 1920s dance. If a tourniquet can't be applied, they'd said . . . I lowered myself to one knee, then sat down. I tucked the gun into the waistband of my skirt, where I could reach it with my right hand; it had to be near.

Margarete's body was a few feet away. I'd put a napkin over her face.

Pressure. Apply direct pressure to the wound. An arrow of pain slashed down my arm and spread out through my fingers. I groaned so loud and so deep I scared myself. Keep up the pressure.

I fainted or fell asleep. I don't know how long I was out . . . not long, because from where I was, slumped against the wall, I could see the floor of a bedroom, and there was still a little daylight coming through the window. I dragged myself toward it. Just to get away, to give myself time.

If I heard the apartment door open, I would take out the gun and do to myself what I'd done to Margarete. I would not let them get me.

I crawled into the room. A large one. A bed with a footboard loomed in front of me, gigantic. If I could just lie in that bed . . . and drink a Coca-Cola from the bottle and listen to George Fisher from Hollywood on WOR . . . But I wasn't going to get home. I knew that. Until the end, though, I had to make it harder for them.

I looked around. Lace curtains, lace bedspread, a lace skirt on a vanity table covered with makeup and bottles of nail polish which reflected in a gold-framed mirror. Margarete's room. I pulled myself along the floor near her bed, toward her night table. I couldn't get up to see what was on it, so I took a deep breath and pushed. It crashed down to the floor. The neighbors, I thought. But if they missed two gunshots . . . There was a telephone. I put the receiver back on the hook. Then I went through the drawer in the table.

Earrings, maybe twenty pairs. Gold, gold, opals, garnets, diamonds. She'd tossed them all in. Hand lotion. A diaphragm and a tube of jelly. A leather-covered telephone book: dark red leather, with tiny flowers tooled in gold.

I had to make it harder. I picked up the phone and dialed a number from the phone book. Under S. Let it not be him, God. I really prayed. I rang just once. 'Colonel Sommerfeld.' But a woman's voice, thank God.

'Listen to me,' I whispered.

'I can't hear you.'

'Margarete von Eberstein.' This was it. No more *berlinerisch*. I put on the accent I'd heard but never spoken: John's, Herr Friedrichs's, Margarete's.

'I am sorry, it is difficult to . . .'

'Is the colonel . . .'

'He is not here, Miss.'

The bleeding had stopped. Maybe it had been some sort of release, because now the pain was unbearable. The whole inside of my arm was trying to shove its way out of the tiny bullet hole. . . . I wanted to howl. I covered the mouthpiece the best I could with my one hand, and a small, terrible sound came out.

'Miss?'

'I must send word to him.' I breathed into the phone. 'Urgent.

Lina is just inside. Good news. I have convinced her to take me to meet her contact. In Potsdam . . . Do you hear?'

'Yes. Miss. I will convey the message.'

'I will ring him tomorrow. As soon as I slip away from her. Do you understand?'

'Oh, yes. Shall I try – '

I hung up. I curled up on my side, closed my eyes. If the pig would believe what his secretary told him, I had eight, twelve hours. I opened my eyes and thought: Stay awake. You'll be dead a long time. It would be a shame to spend the rest of your life sleeping.

Maybe I should say some prayers. Or think of all the good things that have happened to me.

Or just think of one wonderful thing for eight hours. Every detail. Something to treasure, to take along with me. Remember the time . . .

A few minutes later, I passed out.

I woke up because cold water was spilling down my neck. I opened my eyes. Someone was pressing a glass to my mouth. Dear God. As I reached to my waistband, for the gun, I saw that the man bent down before me was Konrad Freidrichs. Oh, did I smile! Who cared if he'd never crack a smile back. Was I glad to see him!

'Drink,' he said.

'What time is it?'

'Sixteen hundred hours.' Four in the afternoon. The next day. 'Drink, please.' He angled the glass to help me, and some water dripped on to my blouse. 'Then you must tell me about Margarete. What horror is this? Such a beautiful – '

'We have to get out,' I told him.

Suddenly I realized! Konrad Friedrichs had understood the consequences of staying in Berlin; that's why he'd been willing to steal away, without even telling his beloved witch of a housekeeper. He'd known his choice was Lisbon – or death. So now, if he *was* in Berlin, it was because he felt safe. Oh God, he was one of them.

And then I was sure: I glanced beyond him. He was no friend.

In the doorway was a man in uniform. SS; high rank, from so far away; all I could really see were the boots, the trousers, the holster. But that's all I had to see. With what was left of my strength, which wasn't much, I shoved away the glass. The water spilled over Konrad Friedrichs, and as he gawked at his soaking-wet shirt and tie, I went for the Walther.

The boots rushed across the floor. I yanked the gun out of my waistband, raised it toward my head, and as I cocked the safety, the SS man grabbed my wrist. I screamed. I tried to bite him, but he twisted my arm. The gun fell into his hand.

'Linda.' The man knelt over me. He was going to take me away. '*Linda*, look at me.' English. I lifted up my head. And I saw Edward Leland.

I couldn't speak.

'Linda, are you all right?'

'What are you doing here?'

He lifted me so I was sitting up, resting against him. 'I thought I'd just drop by and say hello.'

I tried to laugh, but instead I started to cry.

He put his arms around me. 'It's all right. I've come to get you out.'

'It's too late.' He didn't answer. Instead, he stood and hauled me up.

Herr Friedrichs was sitting on the bed, staring at us, as if we were some terrible show he'd been dragged to. 'Did you go to Lisbon?' I asked him.

'I do not speak English,' he said in German.

I felt so woozy. I must have swayed for a second, because Edward grabbed me and held me up.

'What happened to poor Margarete?' Herr Friedrichs demanded.

'I'll tell you later,' I said to him. Then I switched to Edward, to English. 'Can we make it out of here?'

'We're going to damn well try. Can you walk?'

'Yes. I don't know how steady I'll be, but I can walk.'

'Tell Friedrichs to wait here, that I'm taking you to the bathroom to get you cleaned up.'

I stared at Edward. 'He doesn't speak English at all?'

'No. It's been quite a pleasure, travelling with your friend. Such a pleasant, relaxed fellow.'

'You were in Lisbon?'

'Yes. Come on now: Get a grip on yourself, Linda. Don't start crying again. We don't have time.'

I told Konrad Friedrichs to stay put, and Edward helped me out into the hall. I stopped short. Margarete's body was still there, the linen napkin over her face. Her hand, with its ornate gold ring and ruby nails, rested on her chest. Her fingers looked stiff. Edward tried to lead me away; I couldn't move.

'I killed her.'

'I assumed that. Let's go.'

'I can't.' I started to shake, seeing her there.

'You had a reason for killing her, didn't you?'

'Yes! She was the one. The traitor in the movement. And she was going to kill me.'

'Well, you did what you had to.' That didn't help. 'Do you want to stand here and wait for her friends to show up so you can tell them how abhorrent you find their political philosophy? Or are you a professional?'

'Sometimes I can't stand you.'

'I know. Let's move now, Linda.'

He took me into the bathroom, filled the sink with warm water and gently lowered my arm into it, to soak off the napkin. The water turned dark pink. I guess I turned green, because Edward began to talk. 'Two nights ago, we got word that your contact, Rolf, had been taken. I took the next plane out to England. When I got there, there was a message about Friedrichs. I flew to Lisbon right away.'

'Why?'

'Why do you think?'

'I don't know.'

'Look, this cloth isn't going to come of without some pulling. Shall I do it, or do you want to?' I reached into the water, pulled, and let out a scream of pain. Edward clapped a hand over my mouth and, with the other hand, lifted my arm out of the water, grabbed a towel and patted the area around the wound. 'It's infected,' he said, and he opened the medicine cabinet. No iodine. A lot more makeup. 'I can't read the German. Is there anything there with alcohol?' I pointed to a bottle of astringent.

As he uncapped the bottle, I said, 'You're going to tell me, "This is going to hurt, Linda. Be brave." '

'It's nice to see you haven't changed.'

'Just pour the whole thing over, fast.' It was so bad. I kept my teeth clenched together, and all that happened is I started crying again.

'I'm sorry I hurt you.'

'It's okay.'

'There's a train leaving at six tonight. We have to be on it, so we ought to put some speed on. Are you up to it?' I nodded. 'All right, let's wipe your eyes, and then you'll put on some make-up.'

'Are you kidding?' He reached inside his uniform pocket, pulled out a passport and held it up before me. A blonde, about thirty. Very pretty. Round face. Short hair with a wave that fell over her cheek. I looked at her name: Ingeborg Hintze. 'Ingeborg?' I said. '*I'm* supposed to look like that?'

'You've got three minutes.'

Edward left the bathroom, and with one hand and my mouth, I opened a box of mascara. I wet the brush, put on a few coats, then went on to rouge and lipstick. I looked into the mirror and then slumped against the sink. I looked lousy. No one would ever look at me and then say, Hi, Ingeborg.

Edward came back in less than three minutes. He was cutting a pillowcase into strips. 'You'd probably be better off without a bandage, but I don't want to risk your bleeding.'

'Ed, cut my hair.'

'*What?*'

'Look at that passport picture. Come on. We still have about forty seconds left.' So Edward Leland gave me a haircut. Not a good one, but at least I looked like I could be Ingeborg's plain, distant cousin. 'Why did you pick her?'

'Most blondes have blue eyes. This passport had brown. I wasn't in a position to be fussy.' He threw the hair down the toilet, flushed it, then put the makeup away.

'I didn't know you were such a neat person.'

'When her friends get here, should they find a display of cosmetics and evidence that a blond woman cut her hair short? Do you think that would make an interesting dispatch to send out to the army and the Gestapo?'

He bandaged my arm and led me into the hall again, past Margarete's body, back into her bedroom. Konrad Friedrichs was where we'd left him, sitting on the bed, looking exhausted, almost lifeless. Edward motioned him to leave; he didn't understand.

'Herr Friedrichs,' I said, 'please wait outside.'

'She is there. The beautiful – '

'The beautiful Nazi.' His mouth dropped. 'Please,' I said, even though I wasn't sure why Edward wanted him out. He couldn't understand English. He got up from the bed and slowly, like a man of eighty, shuffled out of the room.

'Take off your clothes,' Edward said. 'For God's sake, Linda. You're a bloody mess. You're going to be passed off as my mistress, and – '

'Again? Can't I cross a border as something else?'

'What the hell do you want to be? A goddamn cowgirl?' He stood in front of me and unbuttoned my skirt.

'I can manage.'

'We don't have time.'

'I can – '

'Do you think my goal in life is to see you in your underwear?' My skirt fell to the floor.

'Why are you being so rotten to me?' He took off my blouse. I wasn't wearing a slip, just an ugly German brassiere and pants. He turned away and went to Margarete's clothes cabinet and took out a black silk dress with long sleeves. 'It's too somber for this time of year,' I told him.

'This isn't a fashion show, for Christ's sake. If you start bleeding again, it won't show up on the black.' He held the dress so I could step into it, then eased the sleeve over my arm. 'You need some jewelry or something.'

'You said it wasn't a fashion show.'

'You don't want to look like you're going to a funeral. Where would she keep necklaces and things?'

My dress wasn't buttoned, but I walked away from him, to her bureau, and opened her top drawers. In the left one I found boxes. More earrings. Bracelets, probably more than fifty, beautiful, expensive ones, tossed into a box. Necklaces.

'I can't wear these.'

'What are you talking about?' He came over with a pair of black shoes. Heels, with a big grosgrain ribbon. He put them on the floor beside me.

'The jewelry has to be from her boyfriend. It's probably taken from . . . from people they sent away.'

Do you think the people who owned these things would begrudge you? Or do you think they'd want you to look like a proper concubine who's going over the border to Switzerland with her married SS boyfriend to have an abortion?'

'That's my cover?'

'Yes. If they call the clinic, they will be assured Ingeborg Hintze is coming in to take care of a female problem. Let's get going.' He grabbed my good arm and slipped on three or four bracelets. Then he handed me a heavy gold necklace. 'Friedrichs has a car downstairs. Oh, by the way, he has new papers. He's Werner Reinke now. He's going to put us on the train. Big send-off for the general and his floozy.'

'Why don't you just lay off!' I blurted out.

'Why don't you keep your mouth shut! Do you want the whole building to hear you yapping away in English?' He was pulling out underwear, stockings, sweaters. 'Go find a suitcase. Fast.' I stood there. 'Come *on*, Ingeborg. Move!'

Konrad Friedrichs sat in the front with the driver, a man in an army uniform who was so tall his hat touched the roof of the car. Friedrichs twisted around to speak to me. 'I will be putting you on the train, Lina. The conductor knows he will be taking care of a very important officer and his lady. He understands the general's disability and will not embarrass him.'

'What disability?'

'He is mute.' I turned and stared at Edward. I couldn't tell if he had arranged this chat in German or whether his mind was someplace else and he wasn't listening. Herr Friedrichs continued: 'When he came under fire in Russia last year, they shot him in the chest; the bullet lodged in his throat. If they ask questions, you will, of course, answer for him. He is General Manfred Steinhardt, First SS Panzer Corps. He replaced Dietrich and Peiper. Dietrich's now with the Sixth, and he is a close friend of General Steinhardt – '

'Isn't a general too high a rank? Won't they be suspicious?'

'They may, but there was no time to create papers for a colonel. He was quite insistent – perhaps that is too mild a word – about getting to you; you were in mortal danger, he was going in to get you, and that was that. I had the interpreter tell him that he could not manage alone, not knowing the language. I would accompany him.'

I didn't know what to say, but I figured Herr Friedrichs could live without a speech. 'Thank you.'

'You are welcome. Now I will see you onto the train. Then I will say goodbye.'

'Where are you going?'

'I am going to stay here.'

'Are you crazy? Herr Friedrichs, you're the one person in Berlin they want more than me. You've got to come with us, or – '

He held up his hand. Then, almost kindly, he asked, 'Don't you long for your America?'

'Yes. I long for it.'

'Then you will understand that I cannot endure being away from my country. I will stay. Your gentleman here has arranged sanctuary for me. I will do what I can to help others here to get rid of the pestilence and, later, to help begin anew. But if I die . . . I would rather go down in flames in Germany, for Germany, than live anyplace else.'

As we got to the train, an army officer saluted Edward. He saluted back and then handed over our papers and train tickets; we would not get them back until we reached the Swiss border. They would have sixteen hours to examine our papers, to discover us.

The officer opened my passport, looked at the photograph, then at me. 'I know,' I told him. 'I've lost some weight. All of us in Berlin have.'

He looked back down at the travel documents. 'You are going to the clinic in Basel?' I nodded. He glanced down at me; the clinic must be a popular one. Official Nazi policy did not discourage illegitimate children; the more Aryans to carry guns, the better. But apparently, upper-echelon officers, married officers, were allowed to make sure their mistresses kept their trim figures. The way the office had said 'the clinic' had a nasty, knowing edge.

Konrad Friedrichs, standing behind us, inched forward. He gave the officer a 'watch out' look. With reason. Edward looked displeased; he glared at the officer. It worked as well in Germany as it did in the United States. The officer turned pale, then quickly stepped back, allowing us to board the train. Edward took my arm. For the first time, I noticed he was wearing a white silk scarf around his neck, tucked into his general's uniform. A scarf to hide his mute, injured throat.

'Goodbye, General. Miss Hintze,' Herr Friedrichs said. He inclined his head, and then simply walked off, to disappear into Berlin.

Edward helped me up the stairs onto the train. On the door was an official SS notice, with the death's head insignia. It said: 'Reserved. Do not enter.' We entered. It was for us. He closed the door behind us.

The sleeper was large, but it was hard to see what it looked like. The blinds were drawn, and there was only one dim light on. I sat down on a couch. It was a hard, scratchy velvet.

Edward sat beside me and put his mouth to my ear. 'How are you?'

'Okay,' I whispered.

'In a lot of pain?' I nodded. 'I have some morphine with me, but if you can hold off, I'd like to wait until we're under way. They may have questions, and you'll have to answer . . . and I have to take my signal from the way you behave.' He was businesslike. Professional.

'I can wait.'

We sat in silence, listening to the activity outside on the platform. Then, without saying anything, he put his arm behind me and eased me down, so I was stretched out, my head in his lap. 'It will look good for the conductor and give you a chance to rest.'

'Thank you.'

'Every once in a while, saying something to me in German. "Are you all right, darling?" "Can I get you anything?" That sort of thing.' I nodded and closed my eyes. A minute later, he started to stroke my hair. 'I gave you a damned good haircut, Ingeborg.' I kept my eyes closed. He turned my face toward him. I looked up. 'Linda, I'm sorry.'

'Really? What for?'

'For the way I behaved before.'

'Actually, it felt like Old Home Week.'

'I was never that rough on you in Washington.'

'Want to bet?' He knew what I meant. Suddenly he became absorbed in studying the medals on his uniform. 'You know, you can be the coldest, most heartless . . . Sometimes, when I was working for you . . . Oh, never mind. It wasn't that often.'

'I'm sorry for all those times.'

The train jolted, then started to move. No toots, no whistles. It just eased out of the station, through the city.

'Would you like me to help you off with your jacket, darling?' I asked, out loud, in German. Then I whispered. 'Are you saying you're sorry because you think we won't make it?'

'Shhh. Relax.'

'What are our chances? Twenty-eighty? Sixty-forty?'

'I'd say about fifty-fifty. That's being objective. Subjectively, I wouldn't have come in if I didn't think I had a good chance of getting you out.'

'Or just getting me before the Gestapo did.'

'If that was all I could get, I would have settled for it.' The train picked up speed and we rushed through the countryside. 'Linda.'

'What?'

'It's been eighteen months of hell for me. Ever since I came back and found out you'd gone in, I've been . . . Quick! Say something in German!'

'I love it when you do that to my hair,' I said. As I was saying it, there was a knock on the door. I tried to grab Edward's hand, to squeeze it; I was so scared. But he just shook his head and put his hand on my shoulder. Possessively. 'Come in,' I called out.

The door opened, and there was a conductor in a white jacket. He bowed. 'General! Miss. I am Martin. I am at your service.' I lifted my head from Edward's lap, sat up slowly and curled up against him. He gave me an icy look that said, 'This is inappropriate behaviour. I expect more from my mistress! I pulled away. I lowered my head, ashamed. The conductor took it all in.

'General Steinhardt would like some brandy or aquavit,' I said. 'And some tea for me.'

'Will you be going to the dining car, Miss? Or may I bring you something? Bread, perhaps some cheese or cold cuts?'

I looked at Edward, expectantly. So he nodded. 'Some bread and cheese. The general is tired. He does not wish to be disturbed again.' Martin clicked his heels and closed the door.

'What was that all about?' Edward whispered.

'You don't wish to go to the dining car. He's bringing some stuff in for you. You don't wish to be disturbed.'

'Speak German again!'

'Should I have ordered coffee, darling?'

We sat silent for twenty minutes, until Martin returned with a tray on a cart and set it before us on the couch. After he left, Edward reached into his pocket and came out with two white pills; I poured some water and took one. 'I'll tell you if I need the other one. I don't want to get too fuzzy.'

'All right.'

'Edward . . .'

'Yes?'

'I'm sorry I did what I did. Sneaking behind your back to Norman Weekes the minute you left the country.'

'Are you really sorry?'

'I'm sorry about what I did to you.' I took a slice of cheese and made a sandwich. 'How mad were you?'

'Very. And terrified. I'd read the reports on the RAF attacks on Berlin and – ' His voice broke off. He ignored the brandy but took a piece of cheese. 'There wasn't one damned day that I didn't . . . fear for your life. Even after the intelligence you were getting started coming out. Especially then. I knew you were in that house all the time.'

'I was a cook. Did you know that?'

'Yes. Were you a good cook?'

'Of course I was a good cook, but that creep had no taste buds.' I took some more bread and cheese. 'Ed.'

'What?'

'I just want to tell you . . . I don't think there was ever a day I didn't think about you. Whenever I got scared, and that was almost all the time, or whenever I didn't know what to do, and *that* was almost all the time too, I'd ask myself. What would the great Edward Leland do?'

'If the great Edward Leland were living in Horst Drescher's house, stealing state secrets, being bombed every night, I think . . . I know he wouldn't have made it.'

'Sure you would have.'

He took my hand for a minute. 'I'm glad you thought about me, Linda.'

The train sped on.

I thought I was being professional, alert, but I woke up later and my head was in his lap again. 'How long did I sleep?'

'About three quarters of an hour.'

'Could I have the other pill?'

He leaned over, got some water and gave it to me. 'How bad is it?' I tried to sit up by myself. I needed his help.

'Bad.'

'Do you want a shot of brandy?'

'No thanks.' I touched the silk sleeve. At least it was dry. 'I'm not bleeding.'

'That's good. I wish I could do something more for you.'

'Ed. What if we make it out and they have to amputate my arm?'

'Stop it!'

'Rolf, my contact, only had one arm. You should have seen him clean fish. But who's going to want a one-armed typist?'

He smiled, then sat back. 'Are you planning to go back to work?'

'Can you think of a another way to earn a living?'

'Well, you're a wife.' I didn't say anything. 'You haven't asked me about John.'

'I guess that's because I'm not really interested in John.'

'He's your husband.'

'Not for much longer. Death or divorce, whichever comes first.'

'Linda . . .'

'Ed, in all those months in Berlin, when I was holed up in bomb shelters waiting to die, I thought about him, oh, maybe two or three times. But never: Oh, my dear beloved, how I yearn for you. Not even: Gee, I wish John was here to hold my hand.' I peeked through the blinds. It was dark outside. 'He didn't love me. You know that. And I didn't love him.'

'You gave a fine imitation of it.'

'Well, I loved what he was. His intelligence, his looks, his classiness. I thought: Here is what I should love. So I loved it. It was like I was reaching out for something beyond me, something better. But he wasn't better.'

'He's waiting for you in London.'

'He went with you to London?'

'Yes.'

'How come?'

'He knew . . . we all knew your life was on the line. You're our hero, you know. Heroine.'

'They must be hard up for heroes.'

'You know what you did. Living there all that time. And finally, giving up your chance to live so you could get the Grayson report to us. They confronted him, you know. He tried to commit suicide, but they caught him in time. Now he's feeding false information to the German agent – just slightly false, so everything he says becomes suspect and the Germans will decide he's a plant. Linda, what you did was so important, and so brave.'

'But I didn't do it out of bravery. I did it because I was stuck there, in Berlin, and it was my job. What else could I have done? Run? Where could I run to?'

'That's pretty much what happened to me in the last war. I was crawling on my belly, they started shooting, and I kept crawling. Where could I run to?'

'But you *are* a hero. You've gone in again and again, knowing how dangerous – '

'So did you.'

About an hour later, I said, 'I feel giddy. Not silly. I mean, the pills. I'm having a lot of pain, and I feel it, but it's like my mind is somewhere else, looking down at the pain. I had that same feeling when I was in the hospital, when I lost the baby.' Edward looked as if he wanted to say something, but then he just nodded. 'You know, John never came right out and said he didn't want it. He said it would have been inconvenient. We'd have to move. Good old honorable John.'

'Don't be so hard on him.'

'Why not?'

'Because he does the best he can with very little.'

'He's not much of a man, is he?'

'Linda, my guess is that if we make it to Bern – that's where we're headed, actually, not Basel – you'll recuperate for a week or so and take the first plane out to London, back to him. So let's stop the discussion right where it is. It's gone too far already.'

'I don't want him.'

'Whatever you say.'

'Well, I say that if he wants me now, it's because I'm the Sweetheart of OSS. All of a sudden I'm a hero. He can take me to dinner parties and not cringe over my accent. And you know what else I say? I say, if he was a man who wanted his wife, he'd have come and gotten me. He's fluent in German, for God's sake. But he left it to you.'

A timid knock. Martin. 'Forgive the intrusion. Shall I make up the bed, General? I don't wish to disturb you again, but . . .' I looked at Edward, as if asking what I should do, and then I told Martin to go ahead.

When he left, I asked Edward, 'When do we get to the border?'

'About ten tomorrow morning. Go to sleep.'

'I can't.'

'Go to sleep.'

I got into the bed. They gave the SS such soft sheets. 'Ed?'

'Yes.'

'How is your daughter?'

'Well, she's going to make me a grandfather.'

'From her . . .'

'Yes. She went back to him soon after you left. Well, back and forth. Nan seems to thrive on marital crises, and her husband puts up with them. She goes off to think things over and then comes back. The last couple of times, at least, her distress was genuine. She didn't run back to John. She had a lot to think about, and it seems that for the time being she'll stay with Quentin and be a wife and mother.'

'Well, congratulations, anyway.'

'Thank you.'

'How old are you?'

'Fifty-five.'

'I thought it would be about that.'

'Rapidly approaching fifty-six.'

'I hope you live to see your grandchild.'

'Linda, go to sleep.'

The awful thing was that right from where we were sitting, we could see the Swiss flag. But we were inside the German custom-house, with an army officer at an official desk, across from us. He had a thin face, like a hatchet. 'I am sorry, General Steinhardt, but we have been ordered to stop all women of the description of Miss Ingeborg Hintze.' Edward stared at him. The officer inched back in his chair, uneasy but not afraid. 'And if *you* will be so good,

General, could you please unwind your scarf so I might take a look at your wound.'

Edward just kept eyeing him. And with the officer eyeing me, I couldn't even move my finger to my neck as a signal. But just then, Edward sensed what was expected; he opened his collar. He kept the scarf tied, but slowly he unbuttoned three buttons and pulled open his uniform. As the officer tensed, his chair squeaked. Short, thick red scars covered Edward's chest and shoulder. A livid one, like a crater, was dug into the top of his chest; the surgeons who had put his face back together hadn't even tried with the rest of him.

The officer averted his eyes – not enough to seem unmanly, but enough so that he was looking just beyond Edward's shoulder. He was a deskman. Edward began to unwind his scarf.

The officer said, 'Please, that is not necessary, General Steinhardt. I hope you will accept my profound apologies.' Edward began buttoning his uniform, ignoring the man, which only made his apologies more profuse. 'It was simply that your not being able to speak . . . I – we – there was some concern that perhaps you were hiding a foreign accent.'

Beyond the small window, the Swiss flag fluttered in the breeze. A perfect spring day over there. 'Can we go now?' I asked.

'The general can go, Miss. I am afraid we must detain you.'

I got emotional. Well, I was. To see the flag, no more than a couple of hundred feet away . . . '*Please.* I have an appointment at the clinic in Basel. I must be there. Some . . . some surgery.'

'I am sure it can be postponed a day or two.'

'It's really very important, and the general has been kind enough to accompany me. I can't ask him – '

'I am afraid you will have to.' He reached under his blotter and offered me a sheet of paper. A handbill from the Gestapo. Attention! it said. And beneath it was Lina Albrecht's passport photo. I took it and handed it to Edward. He glanced at it, made a face – such a dreary little girl – and threw it back on the officer's desk.

'I regret to say, General, there is a certain vague resemblance.' He wasn't sure; the general, with his perfect papers, perfect uniform, perfect bearing and perfect scars, wouldn't . . . but any man can be duped. 'You, sir, are free to go, but I must phone my superiors and ask that they send an investigator to scrutinize Miss Hintze's documents.'

Edward nodded, as if he understood completely.

'May I see you out, General?'

It couldn't just end. I looked over at Edward and remembered when I thought it was all over for me at Margarete's apartment. I'd said to myself, Remember one wonderful thing. And what had comforted me, and then flooded me with pleasure, was the memory of sitting in the Packard beside Edward on an ordinary day, almost touching, having a long conversation comparing Churchill and Roosevelt, and his brilliant half smile when I'd said, 'Ha! Got you!' after he admitted the two men had a lot in common. I remembered his suit, the smell of starch on his white shirt, his hands resting on his briefcase, and I remembered not letting myself think about how I felt about him.

The officer shrugged his apologies to Edward. And Edward seemed to understand. He put his hands on the desk and pushed himself up from his chair. As he did, the officer leapt to attention. Edward smiled. The officer moved to go to the door, but Edward put a hand on the man's shoulder: Stop. The man's pale, thin face began to darken at this abuse of military etiquette. But suddenly the face brightened.

Sticking out from under the blotter was a souvenir from Edward: a thick wad of cash. As they used to say in Ridgewood, enough to choke a horse. Enough to buy a German officer, plus, I thought, some extra. The officer reached out for it and stuffed it into his pocket.

Then he picked up the handbill with my picture, crumpled it, and stuffed it in his other pocket. 'So many people pass over this border. Naturally, we are always besieged by papers such as these. The dull, bureaucratic mind at work.' The officer smiled. Edward turned toward the door. 'Please, allow me, General! Miss Hintze. If you will follow me, I will escort you to Switzerland.'

# *Chapter Twenty-seven*

My bed was like a crib, with high white railings on four sides. When the nuns in their white habits and their head coverings that looked like upside-down canoes came sweeping in to change my bandages or give me pills for the pain and the infection, they'd lower the side, go about their business and then raise it again. If I hadn't been so sick, I probably would have thought of it as a prison, but with my fever at a hundred and four for a few days, I was a baby again, and all those German-speaking nuns were like sugar-coated Grandma Olgas, straightening my blanket, feeling my forehead, making sure I was all right.

I wanted all the comfort I could get.

Edward came to visit me, and he brought me American presents: a Hershey bar, a Coke and, on the third day, an Eveready flashlight. He said the only other American object he could find was the American consul's Oldsmobile, and he couldn't fit it into the elevator.

I asked him how much it had cost to get me out of Germany. About twenty thousand dollars – in Swiss francs.

I know we talked now and then, but I don't remember what we said. The second afternoon, he brought in the head of the OSS in Bern, and they asked me all about Margarete. I guess I was speaking for a while, because finally Edward turned and said, 'Really, this is to much for her.' I hadn't thought it was, but I must have fallen right asleep, because I never saw them leave.

He came at night, and he'd sit in a chair next to the bed. When I'd wake up, he'd ask me how I was, and I'd say fine. I could have said a few things more, but what was I going to say? I love you? I love you now, and to make it worse, I probably loved you for ages and didn't even know it? Somewhere between New York and Washington, my awe turned into understanding and my respect into love? On the third night I asked, half hoping for something, 'Aren't you bored, sitting here?'

'Yes. Excruciatingly. If you go back to sleep, I can leave.'

On the fifth day, my fever was down. The doctor took off the heavy bandage and covered my wound with a gauze pad. I ate boiled eggs and toast for breakfast. And at ten o'clock, Edward Leland came to say goodbye.

'I'm going to Madrid later this afternoon. And then back to Washington.'

It had to happen. I knew it. I was prepared. 'Well, have a good trip. I'll see you in Washington or, more likely, New York.'

'Yes. I'll look forward to it.'

'Edward.'

'Yes?'

'You're really going?'

'You'll be fine. In a few days, you'll be out of here. Back to . . . wherever.'

'And you? You'll be back to wherever?'

'Yes.'

It still wasn't easy for me to move, because of the intravenous needle, but I edged over to the side of the bed and managed to grab a lever; the bedrail came crashing down. 'Sit down,' I said. He sat beside me, all dressed for the plane. Suit, striped tie, wing-tip shoes, a gray felt hat in his hands. 'Your Republican uniform.'

'Better than SS.'

'You look nice.'

'Thank you.'

'Very businesslike.' He rotated his hat on his lap. 'You want to get out of here, don't you? He didn't answer. 'Why? Why do you want to leave me?'

'Linda, I have to—'

'You love me, I know. I figured it out last night.'

He stood up. 'Please don't do this. There's no point—'

'I love you too.'

'No, you don't.' He sat down again and took my hand. 'Any feelings you have for me are just an outgrowth of our . . . adventure.'

'I've loved you at least since Washington. Maybe even in New York.'

'Linda, don't subject both of us to—'

'When did you start loving me?'

He lifted my hand and kissed my fingers. 'In New York, I suppose.'

'You suppose? Come on, Ed. We're having a crucial conversation.'

'In New York!' he boomed in his deepest, loudest voice. 'Is that better?'

'Yes.'

'There were at least twenty bright, German-speaking lawyers I could have asked to come to Washington and work for me. Why do you think I chose John Berringer? I came to your apartment that day, a Saturday or a Sunday, telling myself how stupid I was, that I should just get the hell out of town and forget about you. It was right before Christmas. You were wearing a yellow robe when you answered the door. A fluffy sort of thing, beautiful, and your hair was so soft . . . I desired you. And I desired your company.'

'Last night,' I said, 'lying here. I was thinking how much I want you. Not only that way. Every way. I wish you could take off that suit and just lie under the covers with me and hold me for a while. Wouldn't you like that? To feel each other—'

He got up. 'No!'

'No?'

'I think this should end now.'

'Edward, I love you. You love me.'

'I'm twenty years older than you are.'

'Big deal. Sit down.'

He sat, but stiffly, on the very edge of the bed. 'I want to tell you something,' he began. 'Something . . . humiliating, but I want you to understand. In Washington. It was one of those times I'd blown up at you: just being next to you in the car all day, joking about something, talking . . . and then the frustration of knowing you were going home. So I behaved badly. You left. I knew you were upset. I sat at my desk trying to understand myself: I don't attempt to captivate her and I can, on occasion, be captivating as hell. But instead, I don't even try. I alienate her. It's certainly not because of my belief in the sanctity of marriage, or at least not that marriage, because it's a sham. I push her away whenever she gets too close because I know she can never love me—'

'But I do.'

'—never love me as I love her. Passionately. Obsessively. That night, and several other nights . . . I called a man known in Washington. A procurer. I arranged for a room at a hotel and asked him to send me a woman. I described her. I described you. What he actually sent me was someone with bleached hair and an overripe figure, but I paid her twice what she expected, on the condition she didn't say a word. And in that dark room . . .' His eyes filled with tears. '. . . I pretended she was you. I made love to her and called her Linda. The next day, I said, Good morning, Linda, and gave you a list of telephone calls to place.'

I reached out for his hand and put it against my cheek. 'But now you can have me.'

'It won't work out.'

'Why not?'

'Because you can never feel about me the way I feel about you.'

'This is the first time in all the years I've known you that you've talked down to me. What's the matter? You think I don't feel passion for you? You think I'm not capable of the same deep, true love you're capable of feeling? Damn it, I want you!'

'I'm going to be a grandfather.'

'How about being a husband?'

'You need someone—'

'Why won't you marry me? Because you went to Yale and I went to Grover Cleveland?'

'Linda!'

'Because I'm a Jew? You're afraid to say to your partners, "Here's my wife, the lusty Jewess"?'

'You're a Jew now?'

'Yes. You called me that, and I said I wasn't, but I changed my mind in Germany. Listen, if I can love a Republican, you can love a Jew.'

'This is a ridiculous conversation.'

'Is it because of John, Nan, that whole business?'

'No!' But he was starting to smile. 'Although you must admit it might make for an awkward Thanksgiving dinner.'

'Just the first year.'

'And after that?'

'Nan, Quentin, the baby. You, me . . . and maybe the baby.'

He lifted up the cover and, wing-tips and all, got under the covers and pulled me close to him. 'The man is supposed to propose to the woman.'

'But he's not going to be able to if he's crazy and hysterical that she doesn't love him enough. So let her do it for him. Edward, will you—'

'Quiet! Things should be done properly. So I am going to make a short speech. My dearest Linda, you and I, we're two of a kind. I think . . . no, I truly believe we were made for each other. Will you marry me?'

'Oh, Edward! Yes!' And I kissed him. What a kiss!

'I love you.'

And God, what a man!

# *Magic Hour*

*To my best friend,*
*Susan Zises*

# *Acknowledgments*

I sought advice and information from the people listed below. All of them gave it freely and cheerfully. I want to thank Arlene Abramowitz, Janice Asher, Peter Corwith, Lawrence Goldman, Maddy Kahn, Susan Lawton, Neil Leinwohl, Tony Lepsis, Fr Thomas McCarthy, Bob Mitchell, Catherine and Robert Morvillo, Saundra and Herschel Saperstein, Cynthia Scott, Abby Singer, Dustin Beall Smith, N. T. Thayer, Sr, William Wexler, and Frank and Lisa Cronin Wohl.

A hug and a kiss to my great pal, Frank Perry, who taught me about making movies.

A salute to the police officers who answered my technical questions. Unlike Detective Stephen Brady, they were all straight shooters and gentlemen. I apologize if I twisted the facts to fit my fiction. Thanks to Detective-Lieutenant Eugene Dolan of the Nassau County Police, Captain William Kilfoyle and Officer Alan Paxton of the Port Washington (New York) Police, Lieutenant William P. Kiley and Captain John McElhone of the Suffolk County Police, and Sergeant William Crowley of the Southampton Town Police.

The staffs of The Hampton Library in Bridgehampton and the Port Washington (New York) Public Library were unfailingly courteous and helpful.

A special thank you to Paul Brennan, who was generous enough to share his memories of growing up in Bridgehampton with me.

My assistant, AnneMarie Palmer, deserves cheers, bouquets, standing ovations, and whatever else she might want for her hard work and grace under pressure.

Owen Laster, my agent, manages to be both hard-headed and kindhearted. He is truly a classic act.

Larry Ashmead is a great editor. All writers should be as lucky as I am.

My children, Andrew and Betsy Abramowitz, are no longer children. I thank them for their wise and perceptive editorial comments and, of course, for their love.

Finally, in case anyone is curious about who the best person in the world is, it is still my husband, Elkan Abramowitz.

# *Chapter One*

Seymour Ira Spencer of Manhattan and Southampton was a class act. Hey, the last thing you'd think was 'movie producer'. No herringbone gold chain rested on a bed of chest hair; there was no fat mouth, definitely no cigar. If you could have seen him, in his plain white terry-cloth bathrobe (which he was too well-bred to have monogrammed), standing on the tile deck of the pool of his beachfront estate, Sandy Court, sipping a glass of iced black-currant tea, talking softly into his portable phone, you'd have thought: *This* is what they mean when they say good taste.

I'll tell you how tasteful Sy Spencer was. He actually might have hung up, strolled inside and picked out a Marcel Proust book to reread. Except just then he got blasted by two bullets, one in his medulla, one in his left ventricle. He was dead before he hit the deck.

Too bad. It was a gorgeous August day. I remember. The sky was a blue so pure and powerful you almost couldn't look at it. Who could take that much beauty? Down at the beach, where Sy was, silver-white gulls soared, then dive-bombed into the ocean. The sand gleamed pale gold. Farther north, out beyond my back-yard, potato fields gave off a rich, dark-green light.

It was the kind of perfect Long Island day that makes the summer people say:'Darrr-ling [or *Ma chère* or Kiddo], this is *such* a glorious time out here. And do you know what's so pathetic? All the little social climbers are so busy being upwardly mobile that they never get to appreciate' – taking a deep breath, sensitive sniff of fresh air through their dilated nostrils – 'such breathtaking loveliness.'

Jesus, were they full of shit! But they were right. That day, the sun bathed the entire South Fork of Long Island in glorious light. It was like a divine payoff. For the last five years, one of the secretaries in Homicide had been bestowing the same benediction on me: 'Have a nice day, Detective Brady!' Well, God had finally come through. This was it.

For Sy Spencer, of course, this was not it. And to be perfectly honest, the day, wonderful as it was, wasn't so nice for me either. Nothing as dramatic as Sy's day. Definitely not so fatal. But the events of that sunny summer afternoon changed the ending of my story almost as much as they did Sy's.

I was home in the northwest corner of Bridgehampton, six miles east and five mile north of Sandy Court, in considerably less impressive circumstances. My house was a former migrant worker's shack. It had been renovated by a hysterically ambitious, pathetically untalented ponytailed Brooklyn Heights architect, who comprehended, too late, that the place would never be considered a Find. He had been forced to sell it cheap to one of the locals (me) because even the must gullible smoothie from New York would not buy a low-ceilinged, Thermopaned whitewashed hovel with a six-burner restaurant stove and aggressively cute fruits and flowers stenciled along the walls and floors, situated on a rutted, geographically undesirable road between the potato field and a stagnant pond.

Anyhow, somewhere around the time the bullet blasted through the base of Sy's skull, my life also blew up. Our two lives – kaboom! – were joined. Of course, I didn't know it. Unlike movies, life has no sound track; there was no ominous roll of drums. For me, it was still a nice day. A fantastic day. There I was, with my fiancée, Lynne Conway, lying on a blanket on the grass in my backyard, having moved outside from the bedroom for a little postcoital sun, conversation and iced tea. (I'd even thrown a couple of lemon circles into our glasses, to show that, okay, Lynne might have gone to Manhattanville College and known about fish forks, but I could still be a gracious host.)

Of course, if I had been truly gracious, we would have been stretched out on lounge chairs, but in the last few years I hadn't had time for amenities like towels without holes, much less outdoor furniture. So what? I knew all that would change in three months, when we got married. We'd have lounge chairs on a brick patio. A barbecue with a domed cover. Tuberous begonias. I would stop referring to the bacon-cheddar cheeseburgers I ate in the greasiest diners in Suffolk County as dinner; I would come home to poached salmon with parsleyed potatoes, fresh asparagus. I would, at age forty, be a newlywed.

I turned over onto my side. Lynne was so pretty. Dark-red hair, that Irish setter color. Peachy young skin. A perfect nose, slightly upturned, with two tiny indentations on the tip, as though God had made a fast realignment in the final seconds before her birth. She wore khaki shorts that revealed her fabulous long legs. It wasn't just her looks, though. Lynne was a lady.

She came from a good family . . . well, compared to mine. Her father was a retired navy cipher expert. His retirement seemed to consist of sitting in a club chair, his white-socked feet on an ottoman, reading right-wing magazines and getting enraged at Democrats.

Lynne's mother, Saint Babs of Annapolis, went to Mass every morning, where she probably prayed that the Lamb of God would strike me dead before I could marry her daughter. Babs Conway needlepointed all afternoon while she watched *The Young and the Restless* and *Geraldo*; she was eight years into her masterwork, a gigantic 'The Marys at the Sepulchre' throw pillow.

So there was Lynne: a nice Catholic girl. And a good woman. A beauty. Believe me. I knew precisely how lucky I was to have her. My life had not been what you'd call a charmed existence. Happiness was a blessing I'd doubted I deserved and never believed I would receive.

'For the honeymoon,' she said softly, adjusting the shoulder seam of my T-shirt, 'what would you think – this is just another option – if instead of Saint John we spent a week in London?'

'You want to snorkel in the Thames in late November?'

Lynne smiled, and the smile made her look even lovelier. She offered no wisecracks. No: Do you think I want to spend my honeymoon with some schmuck in flippers? What she said, without a trace of sarcasm, was: 'I think I get the point. Saint John.' I gazed in Lynne's fine brown eyes.

And then I stopped having a nice day.

Because there I was with a wonderful, kindhearted, titian-haired, honey-skinned woman, and all I was having was a nice day. I wasn't having fun.

This is nuts, I said to myself. I had to understand that Lynne was young. She didn't quite get me yet. To her, I was a man of the world. It was kind of sweet. Okay, I wished she'd loosen up just a little. I admitted it. I even admitted I was a little tense. I should have wanted a drink. But listen, I told myself, I *don't* want a drink. I'm doing fine.

Still, that was why, when Headquarters called fifteen minutes later and said, There's been a homicide reported in your neck of the woods, ha-ha, on Dune Road in Southampton – that's *the* high-rent district, right? – a movie producer, Somebody Spencer, was shot . . .

Jesus H. Christ, I said. Sy Spencer.

You know him?

I know about him. My brother's doing some work for him on the movie he's making out here.

Hey, is it true he won an Oscar a couple of years ago?

Yeah.

I bet I saw him! On TV, you know, one of those guys saying: I wanna thank my agent and my parents and my late cat, Fluff. Listen, it's your day off, but you're the only one who lives way the hell out in the Hamptons, and we just got called in on a mess in Sachem where some computer nerd got into a fight with his old man and strangled him and tried to hide him under the compost heap, so you could yet over and establish a presence? Keep the village police eager beavers from playing cops, sticking everything not nailed down into Baggies. You know how they can fuck up a crime scene. Thanks, pal.

. . . Well, I felt a certain gratitude towards Sy Spencer.

I walked Lynne out to her car and kissed her goodbye. 'Sorry, but this one sounds like it's going to totally screw up our weekend.'

She squeezed my hand and said, 'Come on. I'm an old pro by

now. I just feel awful about your brother's boss. What a shock!' Then she added, 'I love you, Steve.'

I thought: This woman is going to be a wonderful wife. A terrific mother. So I said, 'I love you too.'

A homicide would be a snap compared to this. Which shows you how much I knew.

The night was as beautiful as the day had been. But neither the moon that rose four hours later nor the floodlights from the Emergency Services truck shining on the crime scene could make cheerful what was, in fact, gruesome: a corpse.

Although a corpse in a spectacular setting. Sy Spencer's lifeless body sprawled facedown on his tile deck. These were no ordinary exorbitantly priced tiles; about one out of every five of the deep-blue squares was hand-painted with a different fish, all of them too fashionably thin and richly colored to truly exist in Long Island coastal waters. But as some New York exterior decorator probably explained to Sy, they combined an oceanic motif with tongue-in-cheek chic.

The pool itself was long, luminous aqua. In the cool night air, a mist, like a rectangular cloud, hovered over the water. Sy's graceful, sprawling gray-shingled house, built in the early twenties, in that lost era of huge families and happy servants, rose up three stories high behind the pool. If you turned the other way, you saw soft sand and the Atlantic.

'How's your beautiful bride-to-be?' Sergeant Ray Carbone asked me. We were standing right near Sy's head. Carbone wore a blue serge suit and Clark Kent glasses. With his small frame, potbelly and hunched-over back, he looked more like an overtaxed accountant than a disguised Superman.

'Still beautiful,' I said.

'She's a lot more than beautiful. Rita and I were talking about you two the other day. Lynne gives you just what you need. Stability. Stability's the name of the game.'

'For me, it has to be.'

'Don't think, I was talking about the drinking.'

'It's okay. You can talk about it.'

'As far as I'm concerned, that's history. Look, I know there's no such thing as a *recovered* alcoholic. You're always recover*ing* – for the rest of your life. But, Steve, you were classic emotionally labile.' Carbone, who had a master's in forensic science, was going for a second one, in psychology. 'You'd be Mr Nice Guy, and then you'd become so withdrawn – like no one was home inside – and then you'd start with the belligerence. But the past few years: what a difference! You're as solid as they come. Trust me. You don't have to worry.'

'No. I always have to worry.'

'Wrong. But you know what? Your not being complacent is a sign of wellness.' That's what happens to a guy after twenty-four credits at the State University at Stony Brook. 'Actually,' he went on, 'what I meant by stability was a fire in the hearth. Good company. A nice bowl of soup. We need something normal, healthy to come home to after what we have to look at.' Twenty-four credits couldn't entirely knock out Carbone's basic common sense.

A technician from ID elbowed his way past us, knelt down beside Sy, and slipped bags over the lifeless hands. (Paper bags. In movies, they use plastic. Scary when the camera moves in close, those lifeless hands wrapped like last week's Oscar Mayer pimento loaf. Very visual. But very phony: we never use them. Plastic traps moisture and screws up any chance of doing an FDR test, to see if the victim fired a weapon.)

'What did you find inside?' I asked Ray.

'Nothing. No signs of robbery, no violence. Sy had packed a carry-on bag to go to LA for some meetings. There was an unmade bed in the guest room. He could have taken a nap.' The button on Carbone's too-snug suit jacket popped open. Not counting his midsection, he was thin. But his clothes were always a size too small for his basketball of a belly. 'The cook was downstairs the whole time,' he continued. 'Nice lady. She gave me a bowl of clam chowder, the red kind. She's making something now for all the guys. All she heard was the shots. Nothing before that.'

'Nothing after?'

'No. She looked out the window, saw Sy, ran out to him, saw he was dead. The way his head was turned, she could see that one eye, open.' We both glanced down. The hood of Sy's bathrobe was pulled back far enough that you could see his quarter profile and a bit of his hair: short, tight gray curls, cut middle-aged-gladiator style. The one eye that was visible was wide open. Because of the position of his head, the eye stared downward, as though it had found a hideous flaw in one of the fancy fish tiles. 'She called the village police.'

'From the portable phone?'

'No. She said she knows not to touch anything near a murder victim. She went into the kitchen.'

'Okay, I thought, what kind of homicide do we have here? Not a heat-of-the-moment crime of passion, a murder arising out of jealousy or a family quarrel. And so far there was nothing to indicate a felony murder, a killing that occurs during the commission of another crime, like a burglary.

I knew I should hang on for forensic results – the autopsy report with photographs and videos, the toxicology and serology reports – but there I was, itching to figure out what kind of a guy/gal (I'm an equal-opportunity detective) the perpetrator was.

Well, it was easy to figure out that this killer wasn't some impulsive jerk who, in a moment of madness, grabbed a stake from the flower garden and turned Sy into a human shish kebab. No, this killer was extremely well organized, bright enough to plan the murder, bring his own weapon and take it away with him. His getaway had been slick too: completely uneventful. Judging from the lack of any physical evidence so far, he hadn't gotten rattled.

Another thing that struck me – from the first minute I saw Sy – was that although the killer had a brain, he had no heart. I always notice how the perpetrator treats the victim; it tells so much. This one didn't seem like a psychopath. I knew I'd have to wait for the autopsy, but it didn't seem like there would be mutilation – no sicko ritualistic marks, no deranged slashing. So he was heartless but no sadist; there was no need to terrify, no gun shoved in the victim's mouth or gut or genitals. Sy had been shot from a distance, from behind, impersonally.

But just as there were no indications of cruelty, there were no signs of decency either: no concern, no remorse. The killer had not covered Sy's face, or closed that awful, staring eye, or picked a flower and tossed it toward the body.

Of course, it could be a stranger murder, a nut case unknown to Sy. 'You hear about anybody else getting taken out this way?' I asked Carbone. I did my homework if I was in the mood; he always did his. If there was a serial killer operating within fifty thousand miles of Suffolk County, he'd have read about it. 'Rich people? Movie people? People shot from a distance?'

'I'll check with the FBI, but I don't think so. Unless this is number one.'

'We've got a cool cookie here,' I observed. 'An organized fucker.' We'd wait for the post-offense behavior, to see if it was a Son of Sam-type wacko who'd want to declare his genius to the police. 'Good shot too. Got to give him credit.'

'So what do you think the weapon was?'

'Low-gauge rifle?' I asked the ballistics guy, who was standing a couple of yards away, opening his case.

He nodded. 'Looks like a .22.'

Carbone muttered: 'Damn. That's not going to make our life easy.'

He was right. Here on the South Fork, .22s were a dime a dozen. Everybody had one; locals used them for target practice, small-varmint shooting. Or anything. If a farmer wanted to kill a pig, he'd get out his .22; my father had owned one.

'What background were you able to get on this Sy guy?' Carbone asked me.

'Fifty-three years old. Dartmouth College graduate. From a rich family – kosher provisions business. The ones with that commercial where they all sit around the kitchen table in crowns: "Bologna for the Royal Family!" But it sounds like he wasn't all that turned on by lunch meats. He wanted culture. He started a big poetry magazine, *Shower of Light*, about twelve years ago. Put a pile of money into it. But then he seemed to have decided that poetry wouldn't get him what he wanted.'

'What was that?'

'Who the hell knows? What do most guys want? Excitement.

Fame. Fortune. Superior ass. I mean, who would you rather hit on, a receptionist in a pastrami factory or a poet? Or a movie star?' Carbone the Thoughtful looked like he was actually beginning to contemplate the alternatives. 'Ray, the answer is: Movie star with giant boobs.'

'I don't like those big, big ones,' he said, thoughtfully.

'What do you like? A girl who looks like she's got two Hershey's Kisses glued on her chest?'

'No, but you see a young girl with giant ones, you figure that when she's thirty-five . . .' He shook his head in sadness.

'When she's thirty-five,' the ballistics guy interrupted, 'you trade her in for two seventeen-and-a-half-year-olds.' He chuckled at his own wit, then added: 'Move back a little, out of my way.'

'Anyway,' I continued, as we moved back, 'all along, Sy Spencer was pretty much a man-about-town, one of those people who pop up now and then in the gossip columns. No dirt: just some guy with major bucks who gave money to the right causes, went to all those jet-setty charity benefits. That seems to be where he met the movie types who have houses out here. And he got it into his head that he wanted to be a movie producer. Apparently, so do half the people in his world. But he got what he wanted.'

'You know, I've heard his name. Good movies, right?'

'No doubt about it. The guy had class.'

'So, Steve. Gut reaction.'

'It's going to be a media circus. Plus a major pain because we're dealing with hotshots who expect heavy-duty ass-kissing: "No, thanks, sir, I don't drink while I'm on duty," when they offer us the cheap-shit Seagram's they've been keeping from before they became famous. And – unless we get lucky in the next seventy-two hours and find someone in Sy's life stroking a warm .22 – it's going to be an absolute bitch to crack. Sy was the ultimate fast-track guy; he probably had fourteen Rolodexes, and those were just for personal friends.'

'Where would you start?'

'The movie he was producing, I guess. It's called *Starry Night*. They're shooting it over in East Hampton now.'

'No kidding! *Now*?'

Having spent my whole life being local color in what people called the Fashionable Hamptons, I was used to rubbing shoulders with celebrities. Well, not exactly rubbing. But from the time I was a kid, besides the regular rich and semi-rich summer people, there'd be famous models squeezing tomatoes at a farm stand, or TV anchormen picking out a toilet plunger in the hardware store in town – right next to you. We knew to pretend they were just plain people, but we also knew it was okay to ogle as they paid the cashier. Neither they nor we wanted them so plain as to be overlooked.

But Carbone came from the *plain* plain world, suburban Suffolk County, a world peopled by ex-third-generation Brooklynites – shoe salesmen and IRS auditors and junior high school social studies teachers – a world that, if plopped down outside downtown Indianapolis or Des Moines, would not seem an unnatural part of the landscape. 'East Hampton's only- what? – ten, twelve miles away,' he was saying. His eyes were lit by a starry sparkle. 'We may have to go over there to question some people on the movie set.' Carbone was normally so levelheaded, so thoughtful, you'd think he'd have been glitz-proof, but at the thought of Lights! Camera! Action! he was loosening his tie, unbuttoning the top button of his shirt. If there'd been a straw hat and cane, he'd have grabbed them and high-stepped over to East Hampton, belting out 'Hooray for Hollywood'. 'Who's starring?' he asked, much too casually.

'Lindsay Keefe and Nicholas Monteleone.'

'No kidding!' Then, fast, he switched back to his I'm-a-regular-guy mode. 'I always liked him,' he said. 'Reminds me of a young Gary Cooper. Good without being a goody-goody. And she's a good actress.' Carbone shook his head in sadness. 'But too left-wing for my taste.'

'With her body, do you care what her position on disarmament is?'

Suddenly it hit Carbone. 'Is Lindsay Keefe *here*?' he asked, his voice a little hushed with awe. 'In the house?'

'Upstairs, with her agent. You didn't hear her? He's trying to calm her down.'

'Can you believe it? I was *in* there, interviewing the cook. I didn't even know she was here, in the same house.'

'The agents brought her back from the set. Heavy-duty hysterics.' Carbone's eyebrows began drawing together in sympathy, so I added: 'Let's not forget she's an actress. Anyway, according to the agent, for the last six months Lindsay's been living with Sy. Here, and he has a duplex on Fifth Avenue. They're madly in love. Perfect relationship. Never a harsh word between them. Blah, blah, blah. The usual. Oh, and they were going to get married the minute the movie was finished.'

'You believe the agent?'

'He's not a slimeball. He's an older guy named Eddie Pomerantz. Late sixties, early seventies. You can't miss him. A color-coordinated hippo: pink polo shirt and forty-eight-waist pink madras slacks. He was the one Sy was on the phone with when he was killed. Claims they were discussing some minor problem about photo approval. A movie star gets to approve any picture before it's handed out to the press, and Pomerantz said someone on this movie slipped a shot of Lindsay drinking coffee with her hair up in curlers to *USA Today* and she started crying when it got published because it's detrimental to her career to be seen in hair curlers.' I shook my head. 'For this the guy gets ten percent. Anyway, Pomerantz said he head two shots over the phone.'

'You buy his story?' Carbone asked.

'I buy that he heard two shots. He sounded pretty definite on that. But he kept eating nuts like a fucking maniac. There was a giant bowl of nuts on the table in the library or den or whatever it's called, and he must have glommed two pounds of pistachios in five minutes. I was going to tell him not to eat potential evidence, but he was such a nervous wreck I didn't have the heart. He was upset about Sy, and *very* worried about his client.'

'Could it be normal professional concern?'

'Could be.'

'Listen, in this situation, concern would be an appropriate response. You know and I know and this Pomerantz must know that murder may mean publicity, but in the long run, being the mistress of a homicide victim isn't going to help anyone's career.' I nodded in agreement. 'What's the matter? Do you think he's afraid of something specific?'

'Couldn't tell. But we've got to consider if this business is in any way related to Lindsay Keefe. A jealous ex-boyfriend. Or some jealous ex-girlfriend of Sy's who got pissed off that Lindsay came into the picture.'

'And we have to find out if things were really that hunky-dory between Sy and Lindsay,' Carbone said.

'Yeah. Maybe Sy did something so terrible she felt she *had* to kill him.'

'Like what?'

'How should I know, Ray? Maybe he left dental floss with last night's corn on the cob on the sink. Who the hell knows what sets people off, makes them kill? Do you?'

'No.'

'Me neither. Maybe it was just something boring, like Sy was getting it on with the script girl.'

'You can't wait to start with the hypotheses, can you, Brady?'

'No. Now listen: someone on this movie besides Lindsay might have had a grudge. Or from some other movie. Or it could have been a cold-blooded hit. We've got to find out what kind of life Sy had – beyond his movie life. Did he gamble? Was he cooking the books? Into weird sex? Doing drugs?'

A video tech stepped in front of us and, walking around Sy's body, aimed his camera on the white robe. Then he zoomed in on the two small splotches: the one on the hood, where a bullet entered just above Sy's brain stem, and another by his left shoulder blade.

'You'd never think of a man like Sy as a victim of anything,' Carbone mused. 'He seems like the ultimate winner.'

'I know. Look at all this,' I said, glancing around the pool area.

White wood tubs overflowed with trailing ivy and deep-purple flowers that gave off a light, spicy scent: nothing too perfumy, nothing too obvious. The chaises lay back, deep, welcoming. Small stone tables were carved like diving fish. You'd put your drink on the tail. White umbrellas on bamboo poles stood tall, like giant parasols. Almost-invisible quadrophonic speakers peeked up from the velvet grass.

'Ray, I bet your wildest fantasy isn't as good as what Sy actually had. What was missing that any reasonable man could want?'

Carbone started mulling it over, probably thinking something like a cohesive family unit or Self-knowledge.

What I was thinking was: If Sy had stuck with kosher salamis and not had all his dreams come true, would he now be alive, dressing for dinner, buttoning a three-hundred-dollar sports shirt, or sticking his pinkie into the salad dressing to check whether his cook was using enough basil or chive or whatever this month's most fabulous herb was? Why, on this splendid summer night, was Seymour Ira Spencer, the Man Who Had Everything, playing host to a bunch of cops who were swabbing between his toes, tweezing fluff off his bathrobe and cracking Lindsay Keefe tit jokes over his dead body?

Look at a map. Long Island resembles a smiley but slightly demented whale. Its head – Brooklyn – butts against Manhattan, as if trying to get into some hot party for which it was deliberately excluded.

But unlike bubble-brained Brooklyn, the whale's body wants no part of the high life. Queens, Nassau and suburban Suffolk County just swim, eternally, in the bracing waters between the Atlantic and Long Island Sound, yearning to reach mainland America. See how the whale's hump arches up in longing? All it wants is to be part of the US of A, where life resembles a Coke commercial.

Okay, now check out the rest of Suffolk County, the whale's forked tail. The tail isn't swishing a salute to either Manhattan or Middle America. No, it's raised high to greet Connecticut and Rhode Island. The East End of Long Island is, really, the seventh New England state.

See? On the North Fork of the tail, there are Yankee-style farms, fishing fleets and a few intensely quaint colonial villages that lack only a hand-carved 'I am unspoiled' sign. And now look at the South Fork, my home. Our accents closer to Boston than the Bronx. Solid Anglo stock, augmented (most would say improved) by Indians, blacks, Germans, Irish, Poles and Others. More farms again. More cute towns. But unspoiled like the North Fork?

No, spoiled beyond comprehension.

For over a hundred years, artists and clods, geniuses and jerks, have been coming out here with their ways – and their money. To the Hamptons. 'We summer in the Homp-tons,' they say. Do they ever: in oh-so-social Southampton, don't-say-rich-say-comfortable Water Mill, bookish Bridgehampton, belligerently down-to-earth Sag Harbor, show-bizzy East Hampton, home-of-the-boring Amagansett (I think the last truly interesting person to live in Amagansett died in 1683) and I-am-one-with-the-sea Montauk.

This summer paradise isn't my South Fork, though; it belongs to men like Sy and to the legions of lesser New Yorkers who yearn to walk in his footprints in the sand. It is the Eden of the urbane: beach clubs, tennis clubs, yacht clubs, golf clubs; power breakfasts in the designated-chic local coffee shop, power softball games, power clam-bakes, power naps.

But along this narrow strip of trendy whale's tail, there are also hamlets called Tuckahoe and North Sea and Noyack and Deerfield. And there are people who neither know nor care that the copper beech is the Tree of Choice and the Japanese maple is Almost Out, or that duck is a passé poultry. There are people who are here not to vacation but to live lives: farmers, supermarket cashiers, dentists, welfare recipients, librarians, truckdrivers, short-order cooks, lawyers, housewives, carpenters, lobstermen, hospital orderlies. Oh, yes – and cops.

My name is Stephen Edward Brady. I was born in Southampton Hospital. A few days later, I went home with my mother to Brady Farm in Bridgehampton. It's still there. Not the farm, of course. My father sold everything but the farmhouse and two acres in 1955, a little more than a decade before the big land boom that would have made them rich, the only thing my mother had ever wanted to be.

I was born on May 17, 1949, to Kevin Francis Brady, farmer and (in the great South Fork tradition) drunk, and to Charlotte Easton (of the Sag Harbor Eastons) Brady, housewife and social climber. In 1951, my brother Easton was born.

I went to Sagaponack Elementary School, a one-room schoolhouse. (The summer people say: 'I love it! It's so *real.*' So okay, A for ambience. C – for education. B for freezing dampness that makes your fingers throb in the winter. And A+ for smells from decomposing rodents under the foundation in late spring.) Then I went to Bridgehampton High. And then the State University of New York at Albany.

It wasn't that I'd been such a saint in high school, but at least I'd known who I was and that I'd belonged. Sure, I was a bad boy in Bridgehampton – a little driving while intoxicated, a little breaking and entering. In my heart I knew it was a phase, that someday I would become a solid citizen, buy back my father's farm, sit on the school board.

But I picked the wrong generation, and the wrong genes. Up at Albany, I became just another whacked-out asshole with sideburns. I embraced my generation's holy trinity: sex, drugs, and rock and roll. I was a true believer. I screwed and drank and drugged along with Jim Morrison and Jimi Hendrix and Janis Joplin. I didn't die, though. I flunked out.

So I enlisted in the United States Army. Why? To this day, I have no idea. I can't re-create the boy I was, the boy could do something that dumb and self-destructive.

On my first day of basic, they clipped my hair with a machine that left it less than a quarter inch long. I remember standing at attention and having a five-foot-three Filipino drill sergeant reach up and grab those hairs between his thumb and index finger, pull at them, and scream up into my face, 'Fucking hippie!' All I wanted to do was go home. I knew I wasn't man enough to take it. Except I had to take it. In those eight weeks, the army's goal is to break you down, then build you up again into a machine that obeys all commands without thought or argument. Well, they broke me down. I cried myself to sleep every night. There I was, a big guy, a soldier, boo-hooing into my pillow so that no one, especially all the other crybabies, could hear me.

But I went off to war an infantryman, a master of the M79 grenade launcher. I fought for God and America and the honor of the Brady bunch. No. Actually, I just fought to stay alive. I fought even harder not to feel alive. Feeling dead was a major asset in

Vietnam. I moved on from hash and pot to smoking opium joints. And after about a month, skag.

Skag is heroin. Five or ten percent pure on the streets in the States. Ninety-six percent pure in Vietnam. No needles: cigarettes. You just had to inhale, so you weren't a junkie. We were all very clear on that. We were just a bunch of grunts sitting around smoking at night after a hard day's work in the jungle: a little patrolling, a little shooting, and then stacking up stinking dink corpses so we could get our body count and move on for more.

Skag was cheap: three bucks a hit. Skag was good for us grown-up GI Joes, better than pot, because pot makes time go very, very slow. Heroin lifts you out of your body, takes you out of time. It got me through those three hundred and sixty-five days in hell. No, I wasn't caught. If you had brains and a little foresight, you could get a buddy to pee for you and were home free. (Ha.) I was discharged, honorably.

I hadn't been doing skag every day. Just almost every day. I said to myself: You're not addicted. But when I landed back in the States after the eighteen-hour flight, I was sick – leg pains when we refueled in Guam, stomach cramps, the sweats in Hawaii. Terrible diarrhea the whole time, banging on the door of the airplane bathroom, doubled over, screaming at the top of my lungs: 'Please, oh God, let me in!

In San Francisco I had to buy heroin on the street. Three days, five hundred bucks. I couldn't handle a needle. The dealer had me wait in the basement of a burned-out grocery store; after the high started to wear off, I'd stand there shivering in the dark, my head twitching. I could smell the wet, charred wood and the decay, hear the deranged scurrying of rats. When there was a lull in his action, the dealer would clomp downstairs, hold a flashlight in his mouth and shoot me up. He had hunched shoulders and a thrust-forward turtle head, like Nixon. His damp, hot fingertips probed for a vein; there were crescents of green-black dirt under his nails. He told me: Don't expect me to keep doing this. This is a special introductory service.

It was that night I lucked out. I came up for air about two a.m. and ran right into a San Francisco PD street sweep. A big, mean-looking black cop grabbed me. He was about to pat me down when he took a second look and said, Army? I said, Yeah, and he said, You dumb piece of white shit, but instead of taking me in, he dropped me at one of those free clinics in Haight-Ashbury.

The clinic was run by a woman doctor. It took almost a week to get detoxed. Then I spent another two weeks in bed – with the woman doctor. Her name was Sharon. 'Positive reinforcement', she called it. Sharon panted a lot; I kept feeling her hot, moist spearmint Certs breath. She always gazed deep into my eyes the second it was over. Aren't I *marvelous*? her eyes demanded.

Marvelous? Somehow I was getting it up and, apparently, getting it off. But my dick could have been Novocained; I swear to God I felt nothing.

By the end of the second week, Sharon was after me to go back to College – in San Francisco. Hey! I could move in with her! What a fabulous idea! Together we could bang our brains out! Detox the toxed! Refinish the floors!

I did not leave my heart – or any other part of me – in San Francisco. I was back home for Christmas.

Two days of my mother and brother, and I moved out. I needed a job. One of my buddies from high school had joined the Southampton Town PD. No degree necessary. Decent pay. I applied, but there was a waiting list, so instead I joined the Suffolk County PD. I became Guardian of the Suburbs, Keeper of the Peace for the lawn-tenders and split-level dwellers.

I soon began showing my true Brady (as opposed to Easton) colors, popping a few beers a day. Then a six-pack. I was an alcoholic – not that I knew it – and an armed officer of the law. But hey, I was a terrific, ambitious cop. My job meant everything to me. In the beginning, I was even snowed by the dumb stuff: the uniform, the shield, the gun, the siren. Finally, I was part of something good. Law and order. With a little effort, I felt that my life, like Suffolk County, could be brought under control.

Mainly I worked. I spent my days off in Bridgehampton, picking up women and getting laid or watching the Yankees. (In an ideal world, it would have been both.) In eighteen years, I don't think I had a relationship that lasted longer than a month. I worked my way up to drinking two six-packs and half a fifth of booze a day. Scotch in winter, vodka in summer.

Like every other drunk, I was absolutely positive I wasn't a drunk. My mind was so sharp; I could give you every single start from Thruman Munson's entire career. And at work, when I was on a hard case, I could lay off booze completely. Hey, I had no problem.

By 1984 I was a detective sergeant in Homicide. I was working eighteen, twenty hours a day. I'd go on the wagon and stay on for a couple of months; then I'd slide off. But I was good at hiding my drinking.

Finally, not good enough. Fourteen years after I'd been an alcoholic, someone in the department noticed that what even my friends had been calling my short fuse might be a bad drinking problem when I got into a fight with some guy from Missing Persons in the parking lot at headquarters in Yaphank. I pulled my gun, aimed and shot out his side mirror. I have absolutely no memory of it. They told me I started up because this guy had parked over the line, too close to my car, an indigo '63 Jaguar, E-type. It could go from zero to fifty in 4.8 seconds. I loved my car.

My commanding officer, Captain Shea, suggested a vacation at South Oaks, the department's favored drying-out spot. Vacation: They took away my suitcase and searched it; they strip-searched me; they took away my razor.

I was so scared. No one else there was. This was the place to see and be seen. Anybody who's anybody is drying out, all the hip guys and gals in sweatpaints and slippers seemed to be saying. They all loved group; they loved to talk about their sodden daddies, their stinko moms. They couldn't wait to tell about waking up caked in their own vomit. They cried. They laughed. They hugged each other. They all seemed to think they were auditioning for the lead in their own TV bio-movie: *Debbie [or Marvin]: Portrait of a Long Island Alcoholic.*

I remember always being cold at South Oaks, and talking as little as I could get away with. But I thought all the time. I thought: My life is shit. All I have is work – death – my dick and TV. Listen, when you're sitting in a therapy session at a funnyfarm with seven substance abusers and a psychiatric social worker and you look back and realize that the highlight of the last decade of your life was getting cable so you could watch Sports Channel, you begin to realize you might be a little deficient in the humanity department.

I dried out at South Oaks. After I left, I stayed with AA. The department told me they wouldn't can me, but I would have to go back into uniform.

That was terrible. No, humiliating was what it was. Forget that I'd once been thrilled to be the boy in blue. Now I was a man. So what was I doing all dressed up like Mr Policeman for Halloween? Was I doomed to endless, mind-numbing cruising in a patrol car for the rest of my life?

I fought like hell for half a year to get back into Homicide. Besides the Yankees, my work – putting together the puzzle – was the only thing I really cared about in the world, the only thing that made me feel alive. I finally made it back in, mainly because Shea and Ray Carbone knew they needed me and went to bat for me. But I lost my rank of sergeant. I was clearly not a leader of men. Shea said, 'Bottom line, Brady. I don't give a rat's twat that alcoholism's a disease. That's your problem. If I hear you even walk within a mile of a bottle of anything, I'll bust your ass for good. Hear me?' Yeah, I said. Fair enough.

In January 1989, on my way home from an AA meeting, I met Lynne, age twenty-three, originally of Annapolis, Maryland, a teacher of learning-disabled kids at Holy Spirit Academy in Southampton, when I stopped to help her with a flat tire. Lynne was intelligent. Serious. Classy. Pretty. And competent: she really didn't need me to help her change the flat. And yes indeed, she was stable. On July 4, we got engaged.

There it is. *My Life*, by Stephen Edward Brady. Not precisely a sterling character. In fact, something of a not-so-good guy. Maybe even a bad guy. But a man who, like all men, holds within him the possibility of redemption. Right?

Anyway, my autobiography until that not-nice day when Sy Spencer was murdered and when I realized that – till death do us part – I would find peace and quiet and even happiness with Lynne.

But I might never have fun.

# *Chapter Two*

'Come *on*,' I urged the kid, hoping for an argument. 'Sy and Lindsay were the perfect couple.' Jesus, I wanted *life*. Believe me, I'd worked on enough homicides to know that the first interviews set the tone for the whole investigation. You had to charge up your sources; any passion – rage at the killer, outrage, grief, hostility to the police – was better than slack jaws and lead asses. I paced back and forth. 'Sy Spencer and Lindsay Keefe. A brilliant show-business couple: successful, in love, making a great movie.'

'No,' Gregory J. Canfield whispered. He had actually uttered a word. That meant he was metabolizing. But it was hard to tell; he was about as animated as the average homicide victim. Gregory was Sy's personal production assistant, hired through some work-study deal with NYU film school. Poor guy: not only was his personality bordering on inert, but he was a born creep. He was the world's skinniest human being, and his tight maroon T-shirt, which clung to his rib cage, and his wide-legged shorts with pleats didn't help. Also, he had those spooky blue-white, almost colorless eyes, eyes that belonged to some slime-bellied animal that crawled along the sticky, grape-soda-splattered floors of dark movie theatres. 'Uh, Mr Spencer and Ms Keefe – they weren't any Irving Thalberg and Norma Shearer.' I could hardly hear him.

In comparison, my voice sounded overly strong – like an announcer on a toilet-bowl-cleaner commercial. 'What are you saying? They weren't happy?'

'Maybe Lindsay Keefe told you something else, sir.' Gregory J. Canfield mumbled. That seemed as close to authoritative as he could get. 'But I think, you know, maybe they were headed for disaster.'

'What do you mean? Personal disaster?'

'Well, um, more with the film. Maybe the personal stuff would follow.' He bent down and ran his finger under a too-tight strap on his leg. He was wearing sandals, handmade things with leather thongs that crisscrossed up his stick legs.

'What was wrong with the movie?' I asked. But I'd lost him; his attention was riveted on Sy and the crime-scene crew. His eyes panned the activity and then bugged out for a close-up of a couple of ID apprentices who were unreeling a tape measure from the corner of the pool deck to the back of Sy's skull. Gregory's skin got a little green; he swayed: a potential fainter. 'Let's move,' I said, grabbing his shoulder and steering him away from the action, down toward the stillness of the dune heath. 'Talk to me. That's it. Concentrate. Now, what makes you think *Starry Night* was in trouble?'

'Uh, the dailies. What they used to call the rushes. They weren't . . . good.'

'Not good, or lousy?'

'Um, more than lousy. Actually, more than horrendous.'

His head had swiveled back to watch an ME tech swabbing Sy's nose with a giant Q-tip. I turned him around so he was facing the ocean and held my hands up on the sides of his face for a second, like blinders. 'Stop looking at all the cop crap, Gregory. You're a movie guy, not a Homicide guy. You'll just make yourself sick. Now tell me about *Starry Night*.'

'Lindsay was killing the film. You should have seen Sy's face after dailies: it went from disappointed to . . . traumatized.'

'What did he say?' I asked.

'Uh, well, you see, nothing. He was very – how can I put it? – reticent.'

'What do you mean? Reserved? Cold? Nasty?'

Gregory swallowed to clear his throat; his Adam's apple bobbled. 'No. He just didn't . . . didn't respond. It wasn't one of those comfortable Gregory Peck silences, you know? More brooding De Niro – if De Niro was playing an Ivy League type. Something was going on underneath, but you weren't sure what. Anyway, Sy's secretary was staying in his New York office, so my job was to always be there for him: place phone calls, keep lists of whatever he wanted people to do, run errands back and forth to the set that his personal assistant – the assistant producer – was too important to do. I was in the house a lot, sometimes in the same room. But he never said anything to me unless it was some specific request. Like get a glass of Evian; he liked it plain, no lemon. Or find out what kind of flowers the costume designer likes, because Lindsay had gotten pretty nasty over a red lace teddy. Sy wanted to smooth things over.'

'He never talked to you personally?'

'No. Just hello in the morning and goodbye when I left – if he wasn't on the phone.'

'Did you ever see him angry?' Gregory shook his head. 'Did you ever see him show any emotion at all?'

'Well, he'd laugh at someone's joke on the phone, that sort of thing. One time, when he was talking to someone who I guess was very important, he was doing William Powell. You know, roguish charm. But *nothing* else. Not while I was around, sir.'

'Sounds like he must have been rough to work for.'

'He was kind of like a combo William Hurt-Jack Nicholson. Classy-scary-cold. I think if you had some value to him he could be very nice. But I had absolutely no idea if he liked me or hated me.'

'But still, even though he didn't show emotions, you say you sensed he wasn't thrilled with the dailies?'

'Yes. The last couple of nights, he was white as a sheet after the lights came back on. He *had* to have known that Lindsay was running the film into the ground.'

'But do you know that for a fact?'

'No. I could just . . . intuit it.'

'Had Lindsay and Sy been fighting?'

'No direct confrontation. Not that I ever saw. But most of this week, the air was charged. I'm sure, with you being in Homicide, sir, you know better than most people that anger isn't always expressed verbally.'

'Yeah, I know that. But if you're trying to sell me a charged-air theory, you've got to give me some substantiation. Come on now. How angry was Sy? How angry was Lindsay? Angry enough to have pumped two bullets into him?'

Down near the beach, there was just enough light from Emergency Services for me to see Gregory's white skeleton arms start popping goose bumps. 'Please, Detective Brady, Ms Keefe may have been wrong for this particular role, but I have the greatest respect for her not only as a performer but as a human being. I'm sure someone of her intellectual stature and—'

'Can it, Gregory! This isn't NYU film school fucking seminar. Now, you'd been shooting the movie for three weeks. Isn't that early to know a picture's in trouble?'

'No. Everyone sensed it. You know how there's a feeling of intense community? Did you ever see *Day for Night*?'

'No. And don't tell me about movies or actors. Tell me about life.'

'On the set, the cast and crew were just going through the motions, talking about all the other movies they'd worked on. Not about this one.'

'But what about Lindsay Keefe? How could she stink? She's supposed to be one of the best actresses around, right?'

'She *is* a good actress. But her role calls for vulnerability under a brittle exterior. The *only* thing that came through in dailies was brittleness. And not sophisticated, Sigourney Weaver brittleness. Just hardness, shallowness. Very TV ministeries.'

'You personally saw these dailies?'

'Yes.'

'Well? Was she bad?'

'Yes, sir.'

'Did Sy express displeasure over her, either to her or to you or to anyone else?'

'Not . . . really. But he was so circumspect, you never had any idea what he was thinking unless he specifically told you.' Gregory hesitated. I couldn't tell if he was trying to come up with something – anything – to please me or whether he was honestly trying to remember something. But just then, Robby Kurz came sauntering down the lawn.

Detective Robert Kurz, shine, sleet, hail. Gunshot, strangling, knifing, poison. Man, woman, child. No matter what the conditions of a homicide were, Detective Robby lit up every crime scene with his big Howdy Doody smile, his endearing snub-nosed face and the bright white light of his enthusiasm.

'Yo, Steve!'

'Hi.' To get away from his relentless exuberance, I walked toward the beach, pretending I wanted to think. Naturally, Robby hurried after me.

Lucky for me, Robby was thirty. That provided some distance. I'd had almost ten years more on the force than he did. While he was still sitting in his patrol car, waiting for some commuter in Dix Hills to run a stop sign, I'd been the rising star of Homicide. In rank, having been busted, I was his equal. In fact, being lead detective, I was his superior.

He tried not to acknowledge it. Robby – despite the shiny bald spot he tried to hide by combing his hair sideways and spraying it into paralysis, despite his desperately-eager-to-cheat wife (Mrs Howdy Doody, with a silver heart dangling in her freckled cleavage) and, more important, despite his arrest record, which was, embarrassingly and unfortunately, almost triple his conviction record – had determined that he was the perfect cop. This notion filled him with pleasure; it was impossible to pass him in the john, on the stairs, at the coffee machine without getting a rapturous grin. Every morning he handed out bagels and crullers and Danish to the squad like the Pope bestowing blessings.

Robby stood beside me near the dune, one foot higher than the other, his body on an awkward slant. He was definitely not an outdoor guy; the security of Suffolk County-issue linoleum was vastly preferable to sand.

'What've you got?' I asked. I ran my hand over the spikes of some tall beach grass.

'Footprints on the grass near the house!' he enthused. 'From rubber thongs. The regular, cheap kind. Mitch from the lab says they're a man's size ten or eleven, although obviously' – Robby paused, probably so I could prepare myself for a blast of deductive brilliance – 'those kind of shoes can be worn by *anyone*. But if we can track them down—'

'Where exactly were the footprints?'

He pointed past the pool and the lawn, to the corner of the big porch that ran the entire length of the back of the house. I stretched my neck and squinted. A guy from the lab was straddling an area of grass right up against the house. He was just finishing photographing the footprints, getting ready to apply the dental stone we use for making molds of them.

At that particular corner, the crawl space, neatly covered in lattice, rose about five or six feet high, with the porch above it. From up on the dunes, not far from where we were standing, a hundred feet away, it would have been easy to spot a man with a rifle. But not from the house. Unless you were deliberately leaning over the porch rail, looking right down at the spot where lawn met lattice, someone with a .22 could probably crouch in the shadowy safety of the grand old house and you'd never see him.

'This could be *major* important!' Robby announced, nodding his head in agreement with himself. His sprayed hair didn't move.

But despite his excitement, I wasn't ready to have an orgasm over the footprints; good investigations shouldn't come too fast. I wanted to rule out all other possible explanations for the footprints before I wasted two days on a *major* thong hunt.

'See if you can get someone to check out the gardeners,' I said to Robby. 'Find out if any of them wore thongs. Also, take a look in Sy's closet. I didn't notice any in there when I did my walk-through, and I don't think he'd do anything like wear them, but this could have been the summer that guys like him decided K Mart was *très* amusing or some shit, and he'd have bought fifty pairs.' I thought for a second. 'Except maybe not a size ten or eleven. He was a little guy: little hands, little feet, probably little—'

I stopped before I even started. It was no fun being immature and dirty around Robby. His idea of humor was Polack knock-knock jokes. His concept of sex talk was to confide that he and

Freckled Cleavage had gone on a marriage encounter weekend. 'Anything else?' I asked him.

Robby grinned (boyishly) and fiddled with a cuff of his sports jacket, a shiny blue thing that had a half-belt stitched around the waist in back. He dressed as though he made an annual haberdashery pilgrimage to suburban Peoria. 'There were hairs. In one of the guest bedrooms, although there weren't any guests.'

'Were they all from Sy?'

'There was one pubic hair, probably his. Four head, someone leaning back against one of those wicker headboards. The hairs got caught.'

'Any with roots?' With the new DNA typing, you can get a genetic make on someone from any cell with a nucleus. But to test hair, you need the follicle cells that cling to the root, and although you can sometimes make do with one, it helps if you have a clump of ten or twelve hairs.

'Complete roots on two of the head hairs from the headboard. They were *not* Sy Spencer's hair, because they were black or very dark brown, and longish. He had short gray—'

'Yeah, I saw.'

I'd also gotten a fast look at Lindsay Keefe when her agent had half escorted, half hauled her out of the car, and she'd been what I'd remembered from movies. Blonde. In fact, the blondest.

'That's all you found?' I asked him.

'Come on,' he said. He was so goddamn chipper. 'You know how long it takes to get anything resembling an opinion from ID.'

'So while you were inside with Carbone you didn't happen to ask if there were any live-in people who might have had a quickie in the bedroom? Maids, valets – that kind of thing?'

'Relax. Where are you going? To a fire? I was just about to ask about servants, but I thought I'd fill you in first.' Robby paused. It had been three minutes since he'd displayed any disarming boyishness, so I got a lopsided smile. 'Look, we both know this is a major case, Steve. I want the brownie points on this one – and so should you. If we can close this neat and fast, it could mean *big things*.'

When you work with a bunch of cops, or any group of people, there are always some who are going to irritate you. Either with lousy character traits, like laziness, dishonesty, sloppiness, or just with irritating personal habits like teeth sucking, cuticle nibbling or superfluous grinning. But Robby wasn't awful. He wasn't hateful. Sometimes, like when he was talking sports, especially hockey, he could actually be interesting; nobody knew as much about the Islanders' offensive strategy as he did. And so what if behind all the smiles he was a self-righteous dick? I just steered clear of him.

But what I couldn't steer clear of was the fact that I thought he was a bad cop. And he thought he was Suffolk County's anointed Good Guy. Days, even weeks, before the assistant DAs felt they had a case, Robby would be pushing to arrest, because he *knew* who the bad guy was. and he was going to get him.

The smiles and the crullers he handed out to cops disappeared for suspects; most of his interrogations turned into finger-jabbing accusations. Sure, he could intimidate some kid into spilling his guts. But he'd alienate suspects other detectives had softened up, and instead of agreeing to a videotaped confession, they'd be screaming for a lawyer.

One time, my best friend on the squad, Marty McCormack, and I had a young guy whose new wife had disappeared. I knew – Christ, everybody knew – that he'd killed her and dumped the body. But how could we find out where? We played it as if this guy was the anguished husband; Marty kept him looking for his wife, thinking of possibilities where she could be. I kept him talking. One night, we stepped out for a bowl of chili and asked Robby just to come into the interrogation room and baby-sit. In the half hour we were gone, he came on tough. Hostile. Aggressive. He knew this was a bad guy. Who didn't? But he almost ruined it.

And I'd lost it when I found out, banging walls, calling him a stupid piece of shit in the squad room. 'You almost fucking blew it!' I yelled. He'd said, 'Just cut it out, Steve,' and even managed a boyish shake of the head that said: Jeez, that Brady and his darn ole temper.

It wasn't that I hated him. We were just oil/water, fish/fowl, day/night. And so without making a big deal over it, we'd pretty much arranged our lives – and our desks – so we stayed apart.

Until Sy.

'Steve Brady!' Marian Robertson, Sy's cook, exclaimed. Then she made a twirling motion with her index finger. Spin around, boy, it said. And, obediently, I turned around so she could get the three-hundred-sixty-degree picture. 'I can't say you don't look a day older than you did in high school,' she went on, 'though you are that same boy – but with a man's face. I said to myself the minute you walked in: "That's the boy who was shortstop on Mark's team," although I went blank on your name. I do see your brother. Easton Brady's your brother, right?' I nodded. 'Such a handsome boy. Could be a movie star himself.'

Mrs Robertson babbled away with the absolute self-confidence that came with the conviction that she was the South Fork's Most Unforgettable Character. In fact, I'd totally forgotten her until I walked into Sy's kitchen.

And what a kitchen – especially if you were a big eighteenth-century fan. Strings of garlic, wreaths of herbs, copper pots and straw baskets hung from the walls and the beams. An iron kettle hung in a six-foot-high brick fireplace; it was so gargantuan Sy could have played hide-and-seek in it.

Mrs Robertson turned away from me to finish cutting the crusts off the sandwiches she was making for the crime-scene crew and began arranging them in a perfect, intricate pile: some creamy-colored cheese on the bottom, pale-pink pâté next, and then dark smoked ham, so the platter looked like a spiffy architectural model of a ten-million-dollar beach house. 'Isn't this something?' she inquired. 'One of my specialties. Anyway, Steve, the minute you showed me your badge, of course I remembered hearing you had become a policeman, although as you may imagine, between you and I and a lamppost, you were pretty near the last boy at Bridge-hampton High I'd expect to see in uniform, so to speak.' She gave me a nose crinkle that (I think) meant: You may have a gun and a badge, but to me you're still a teeno with Clearasil dots. 'I see being a detective you can wear regular clothes. Rank does have its privileges, and that's nice, because you are looking fit.'

Marian Robertson looked the same as when she sat in the first row of the stands at every high school baseball game: dark-brown skin, short, with rounded features and a cute, pudgy body, as if, through interracial marriage, she was half sister to the Pillsbury Doughboy. The only change I could see was her hair; it looked like she'd slapped a gray wig on her head as a seventh-inning joke to give the Bridgies a laugh. Back in high school, she'd acted Unforgettable too, bringing cookies for 'you young fellows', handing each of us a chocolate-chip or a pecan sandy as we trotted off the field, calling out, There's more where that came from!

'Mrs Robertson, I know you gave your statement to Sergeant Carbone, but I have a couple more questions. What does the maid look like?'

'The maid? She's very plain.' Mrs Robertson opened one of the glass doors of the giant restaurant-style refrigerator, eyed the melons and took out an enormous beige ball that was probably a twenty-five-dollar, genetically engineered cantaloupe.

I glanced at my pad. 'There's only the maid, Rosa?'

'That's right.'

'Is she black, white, Hispan—'

'Portuguese.' Marian Robertson cut me off. 'Short, but taller than me. Maybe five foot two. You know, there used to be a song.' She cleared her throat: ' "Five foot two/Eyes of blue/But oh what those five two can do . . ." Oh, Lord! Steve, that I'm singing! I apologize. How it must look! But I've been working for Mr Spencer for fourteen summers, and it's so . . . Murdered!'

'Listen, you're upset. You have every right to be.' I paused. 'Were you very fond of him?'

'Well . . . fond enough. I mean, he was so polite. That's what everyone said: "Sy is *so* divinely polite. So courtly." You know how those Yorkers talk.' I nodded; all of us who were born here shared the knowledge that we were more decent and more down-to-earth than the slickers from New York City. When you really came down to it, we knew we were better human beings. 'Let me tell you, you can double the phoniness in spades for movie types. But Sy Spencer himself seemed to be genuine silk stockings – not at all flashy or fresh.'

'But did you like him?'

"Well . . . now that I think about it, I'm not sure. He was one cool cucumber.'

'Was he cold? Withdrawn?'

'No. Very toned down, but decent enough. Smiled a lot. Didn't laugh. Never treated me any different the first summer or the fourteenth. But it was like he had a script of how to act with a cook, and that was that. Teasing, like about how he was going to have to mortgage the house to pay for my chickens; I make a *very* rich chicken stock. But the same joke for fourteen years.

'And let's see. He was indeed polite: a compliment after every dinner party, and if he didn't like something, which was hardly ever, he wasn't rude. He'd just say, 'I am not entranced by chocolate-dipped fruit." ' She opened a plastic container and handed me a cookie. 'Viennese almond wafer.'

'Thank you. Getting back to the maid, Mrs Robertson. What does she look like?'

'Short, like I told you. Yellowish skin, but with pockmarks, poor baby.'

The cookie was good. I smiled. 'What color is her hair?'

'My, are you handsome when you smile! You should smile more often. It lights up your face like a Christmas tree.'

'Rosa's hair, Mrs Robertson?'

'Originally, only the good Lord and her mother know, although my guess is your basic brown. For all the time she's worked here' – she shook her head sadly – 'fire-engine red.'

'And you and Rosa were the only people who work here? I expected valets or chauffeurs or butlers.'

'No. He hired waiters and bartenders for dinners and parties. He had a driver in the city, but he took a helicopter out here and drove himself around in that Italian sports car of his.'

I held out my hand for another cookie. As she gave it to me, I asked: 'Who was in the guest bedroom today with Sy Spencer?'

'What?' She looked startled.

'Someone used the guest bedroom.'

'Besides Mr Spencer?'

'Yes.'

'Really? I have no idea, Steve. You know, he and Lindsay Keefe were living together. But they're in the master suite. What makes you think someone was in the guest bedroom?'

I took another bite of the cookie. 'Just some indications,' I answered. 'Did you hear anyone upstairs?'

'Only Mr Spencer. He was here all afternoon, packing to go to Los Angeles, on the phone. He had been supposed to leave this morning, but then he had to go over to the movie set, so I guess he was changing a few plans.'

'No one with him?'

'No.' She thought for an instant and then added: 'I mean, I won't cross my heart and hope to die, because to tell you the truth, you can count the times on one hand that I've been on the second floor of this house. But as far as I know, he was alone.'

'Where was Rosa?'

'She cleans and does a laundry every morning, then goes home for the afternoon . . . she has a little girl. Takes whatever ironing. She comes back about six, to tidy up from my cooking – scours pots, damp mops the floor, takes out trash, that sort of thing. Then she stays through dinner and does the dishes and sets the table for breakfast.'

'Mrs Robertson, I don't want to embarrass you, but in a police investigation we have to ask some pretty direct questions.'

'Go ahead.'

'Was there any indication that Mr Spencer had sexual relations in any other room beside the master bedroom?'

'I go home after dinner. So for all I know, he could be making hay in the sauna or in the screening room or in the wine cellar. All I can vouch for is not in my kitchen, because I would know in two seconds flat. *Nobody*, not the boss, not God himself, is allowed to mess with my kitchen. Got that, Steve?'

'Got it.'

'Good.'

Local cops – in this case the Southampton Village PD – secure the perimeter of a crime scene. One of them, a gangly kid my grandmother would have called a long drink of water, came into the tent on the far side of the pool where we were inhaling Marian Robertson's sandwiches. He called out: 'Is there a Steve Brady on duty tonight?' I put down my mug of coffee. 'A guy's out front. *Real* shook up about the murder. Says he's your brother.'

So I went over to Ray Carbone to tell him about Easton's connection to Sy, even though I had to interrupt Carbone while he was lifting up a triangle of sandwich and eyeing it suspiciously, clearly having deduced that it was, in fact, pâté. 'Can we talk outside for a minute?' I asked. He slid the sandwich back on the platter.

The green-and-white-striped tent we'd been in was a three-sided thing. I guess it was either for changing, if you were an exhibitionist, or for just lying out of the sun and wind. It was about ten feet away from the shallow end of the pool, a perfect distance for a police snack – far enough from the crime scene so that you wouldn't have to pretend Sy's body was a scatter rug while you were woofing down his food.

'Listen, Ray, my brother – his name is Easton – he's out front. He wants to see me.'

'Let him come back, take a look,' said Carbone. In the shadow of Sy Spencer's house, he'd suddenly become Long Island's most gracious host. He even did a be-my-guest sweep with his arm. Then he added: 'Easton?'

'Yeah.'

'What kind of a name is Easton?'

'My mother's from this Yank family up in Sag Harbor. It was her maiden name. They do things like that.'

'I thought you were Irish.'

'My father was Irish. About my brother—'

'What does he do?'

'A little bit of everything. Classy stuff.'

'Like what?'

'He sold Jaguars. I bought mine from him. Then he sold expensive real estate. Worked in a bunch of hot-shit boutiques around here.'

'Sounds as if he never settled into a defined role. How come?'

'I'm a borderline personality myself. How the hell should I know what's wrong with anybody else?' Over in the tent, the men were still swarming around the table laden with Sy's food. 'Ray, put a lid on the psychoanalysis for now. I want to get this over with it. It has to do with the case.'

'The case? Your brother?'

'Yeah. I mentioned the connection when Headquarters called, but I forgot to tell you. Easton was working for Sy. Listen, about three, four months ago he was out of a job: not exactly news. anyway, he heard about how Sy was going to be making a big part of *Starfry Night* in East Hampton, so he wangled an invitation to some jazzy charity party. To make a long story short, he got introduced to Sy and made a big pitch about how he'd been born and raised here and knew everybody and could be helpful. Sy liked him and hired him to be a kind of liaison with the locals – I guess to spread a little money around and keep things happy and get things ready for filming. He did so well that Sy kept him on for the movie.'

'Any problems?'

'No. It was really working out. That's the shitty thing; my brother finally seemed to have found something he was enthusiastic about, plus something he was actually good at. Sy had even made him one of thc assistant producers, with his name right up there. Not at the beginning, but at the end when you see all those names. Anyway, sooner or later someone will be taking his statement. I'm just letting you know about him because the department's so big on all that ethics crap.'

'Well, maybe let Robby take it.' I guess he saw my face. 'Steve, Robby's not a bad kid. Okay, too bright-eyed and bushy-tailed for your taste.'

'He has no balance.'

'He has enough, and if not, you'll make up for it. Robby is with you on this one. You'll see, it'll work out. He's really gung-ho. Anyway, it looks better if someone who isn't your closest friend takes care of your brother. But listen, I have no objection if you want to sit in the background. Quietly.' He paused. 'Is your brother, you know, a stable guy?'

'No. He's a demented twit who took a .22 and blew Sy Spencer away because Sy had become his mentor-father figure and Easton has such a low sense of worth that anyone who respected him and helped him self-actualize was ipso facto worthless and had to die.'

I'm not bad. Easton is handsome. Although we resemble each other, I look like an Irish cop and he looks like an Episcopalian lawyer. In other words, my brother is a WASPier, more refined version of me: his eyes a truer blue, his jaw more squared-off, his hair shinier, plus he actually is six feet. I'm just a shade under, which has always annoyed me because girls – women – always ask 'How tall are you?' and if I say six feet I feel like a fraud, but if I were to say five eleven and five eighths, I'd feel like a buffoon.

Easton was standing in the gravel driveway, not far from the stairs that led to the front door. He wasn't in one of his typical getups: a bright-colored blazer, or a pale-pastel sweater, looking more the leisured Southampton aristocrat than the real ones ever did. He was wearing a dark-gray suit with an impeccable paisley tie. His cordovan shoes, illuminated by the unobtrusive low beams that lit the circular driveway and entrance, were brighter than his face. Upset? Even in the dim light I could see he was very upset. skin waxy. Eyes red not so much from crying but, as I saw as I came up to him, from rubbing them, as if in disbelief.

'Hey, East,' I said. He jumped, 'You okay?'

'Sorry. Do you know what's so odd? Here I am, actually waiting for you, hoping you were here, but my mind was going in ten different directions at once, and just now, when I heard your voice, my first thought was: What the hell is Steve doing at Sy's house?'

'When did you hear about what happened?'

'When I got back from New York. I drove there today, to do some odds and ends for Sy, and when I got home, there was a call on my machine. From this perfectly awful film-school type who's his PA Production assistant. Something like: "Um, uh, you might wish to know that Mr Spencer was, like, murdered at his home." ' All of a sudden Easton stopped talking. He got the shakes. 'Damn. It's nippy,' he managed to say. Like my mother, Easton used words like 'nippy' instead of 'cold' or 'cool' or 'chilly', words to distinguish him from the proles. 'Oh, good God.' He rubbed his arms, but it didn't help. Then his teeth started to chatter, fast, like those stupid wind-up teeth in novelty stores.

'Did you speak to Sy today, East?'

'Last night.'

'Any indication of trouble?'

'No.'

'Had any threats been made against him that you know of?' He shook his head in answer – and in disbelief. 'Do you have any reason to think he was afraid of anything, or anyone?'

'No.'

'Any change at all in his behavior?'

He couldn't stop shaking. 'He was fine, I'm telling you.' For my brother, trembling was the absolutely perfect, tasteful way to fall apart, so proper. It didn't make any noise, and unlike sweating or barfing, you could have your breakdown and then go right on to a cocktail party without messing up your clothes and having to change.

'They can get your statement tomorrow. Why don't you go home? You look pretty shitty.'

'I don't even know why I'm here.' He glanced up at the house. 'Actually, I suppose I thought I should show up. In the back of my mind I was thinking: With all the chaos – police, God knows what else – maybe I can give Sy a hand. It's an insane reaction, but Steve, I have to tell you, this is such a shock. I mean, to get that message.'

'It must have been a real kick in the nuts.'

'It knocked the wind out of my sails. I can't believe it. Who in God's name would murder Sy?'

'Who do you think?'

'No one would want to kill him,' Easton announced. He was

positive. He stuck his hands in the pockets of his New York City fancy pants.

'The facts seem to indicate otherwise, don't they?'

'Probably a burglar.'

'No.'

'How do you know for sure?'

'What are you talking about? It's my job to know.'

'And you're never wrong, are you?'

As usual, after more than sixty seconds in each other's company, we were into our regular sibling routine – being irritated by each other. I decided this was one time I should be unirritated. More than that. He was my brother. He was genuinely upset; I should be gentle.

'There doesn't seem to be any evidence of a burglary attempt,' I said, as softly as I could.

'How was he killed?'

'Shot. From some distance. Most likely with something like a .22. It doesn't look like an impulsive act.' We had a long moment of silence. 'Listen, one of the other guys will interview you, probably tomorrow. Go on home.'

He shivered again. 'He was really good to me.'

'Yeah. Listen, I'm sorry. Oh, East, one more thing. Forget fights, threats. Did Sy give any indication that he was having problems with anybody?'

To give him credit, my brother really seemed to think about it. 'I've only been working with him for three and a half months. I can't set myself up as an expert. But from what I've seen, when you're producing a movie, you have problems with *everybody.* You're dealing with a cast and crew of a hundred prima donnas – and their agents, and their unions. And then you have the money-men, who always make life a living hell. A producer has to be tough-minded – and tough. And Sy was. He never backed off from a confrontation. He just kept going.' A small, affectionate smile passed over Easton's face for a second. 'Sy was like a steamroller. He wouldn't stop. You either moved or got crushed. At some point, just about everyone involved probably told him, or wanted to tell him: Drop dead.'

'Son of a bitch!' Carbone blew up in front of me and Robby Kurz. He was yelling about Eddie Pomerantz, Lindsay's agent, now safely on his way home, who, two minutes earlier, had informed him that Lindsay had taken a couple of Valium and was out like a light, but who then admitted, when Carbone started screaming at him, that she'd had four or five. Possibly six, although he wanted it clearly understood that his client was seriously not into drugs. Carbone explained to us: 'I had that doctor from the ME's office – the one with the Dumbo ears – go up to her room. He says she could be genuinely knocked out for more than eight hours. Passive-aggressive bitch.'

We sat in Sy's office, a room on the second floor that had probably been a kid's bedroom. You knew it was an office because there was a phone with so many buttons that it looked like it could launch a satellite, and a small computer. But that was it for modern stuff. The rest of the room looked like some fish-crazy English gentleman's study: there was a stuffed marlin on the wall, some washed-out paintings of salmon leaping out of the rapids, a bunch of gleaming, never-used rods, perfectly, casually arranged in a corner.

Carbone scanned his notepad. 'Now listen, no matter when we get out of here tonight or tomorrow morning, I want both of you back at ten to interview Lindsay Keefe. I'll probably be stuck in a meeting with Shea on how to handle this thing. This thing's bigger than *Newsday.* It's national. International. Now, Robby,' Carbone went on, 'before ten, get what you can from Steve's brother, Easton. Then meet Steve here, for Lindsay. After you're through with her, you work on Sy's business associates. First from this movie. Then start working back.

'Steve, you concentrate on all the nonbusiness-type movie people. Oh, and his women. Look into if he was currently involved with anyone besides Lindsay. And check his ex-wives. He had two of them. One lives in Bridgehampton, so maybe you can get to her before ten.' He glanced down to his pad. 'Bonnie Spencer.'

I shook my head. It sounded vaguely familiar, but I was sure it wasn't anyone I'd actually met.

'A movie writer.' He handed me a piece of paper with an address. 'You know where it is?'

'About two minutes from where I grew up.'

'The other ex lives somewhere in the city. She was the first, and we'll have a name and address on her by tomorrow. All right? We'll use Southampton village's squad room as a command post for the next day or two. I'll meet up with the two of you as soon as I can get out here tomorrow.' He stopped, looked right at me, and sighed. 'I think this is going to be it. The case where I find out that I'm too old for this kind of work.'

I stood in Sy's gym, talking to Lynne from his wall phone. All the not-fun stuff I'd been bugging myself about since the afternoon now seemed stupid. Engaged-guy nerves, a last-ditch defense of bachelorhood. Because, objectively, Lynne was so terrific.

One of the things that had always knocked me out about her was that she acted as though I had a normal, not-terribly-exciting job. I could be a manager of an Aamco transmission franchise. She deliberately did not focus on what I actually did. I understood why; homicide is the ultimate breakdown of law and order, and Lynne's whole life, as a teacher and as a person, was dedicated to being constructive. She was there to give someone a chance, not take it away. Murder wasn't exciting. It was sinful, and it was also outrageously unfair. In the deepest sense, killing wasn't nice.

Another thing: despite her career and her really astonishing competence, she was enough of a traditional female not to want to hear the details of a fatal beating, or how the scalp is peeled back from the skull during an autopsy. So she concentrated not on the subject of my work – the dead and how they got that way – but on the living.

So we were not chitchatting about the murder, other than the briefest summary of what had happened and where I was. Instead, we were talking people. We'd done thirty seconds on how Carbone managed to be an intrusive pain in the butt and a terrific guy at the same time, a minute and a half on why I couldn't stand Robby, and now we were on to my brother.

'Did you say anything like: "Gee, Easton, I'm sorry about Mr Spencer. I know how much you liked him and how important he was in your life"?'

'Don't bust my chops, Lynne.'

Except for the floor, the entire gym was mirrored. I was the only thing in the room that didn't gleam. Besides a stationary bike a treadmill and one of those stairclimbing things – all with glowing red or green digital displays – there was a bunch of Nautilus equipment. I stood up straighter; either Sy had a lot of vanity to work out in front of all those mirrors, or he needed tremendous incentive.

'Steve,' she said patiently, 'did you say anything at all to comfort your brother?'

'Yeah. I said I was sorry.'

'That's all?'

Just when I thought I looked okay in one mirror, I'd see my reflection in another. I pulled my shoulders back. I knew I didn't have a gut, but in the ceiling mirror I seemed to, so I sucked it in. 'Don't get on me about Easton now. I just called to say good night and I love you.'

'Well, good night and I love you too. It's just that I know how much you want a decent relationship with him. Wouldn't this be the perfect time to reach out?'

I told her I guessed it was, then we did the good night and I love you business again because I'd been on with her for almost five minutes and wanted to get back.

After we hung up, I lay down on the gray-carpeted floor and closed my eyes for about ten seconds, probably my total rest for the next forty-eight hours. I know it was sentimental – and probably inaccurate – to say Lynne had saved me, but I really felt she had. Sure, I'd been staying sober with AA. And since getting back into Homicide I was working better than I ever had before.

But by the time I met her, I was feeling scared. I was standing all alone, no crutches. No booze. No drugs at all. Two months after I got out of South Oaks, I got the flu. I sweated out a hundred-and-four-degree fever rather than risk becoming a Tylenol junkie. Hardly any women either: I had lost almost all desire. In the old days, almost anything that produced estrogen could get me going if I was in the mood to get going, but most of the time now I couldn't seem to find anybody who made me want to unbuckle my belt. And yeah, there was football – the Giants, who I liked a lot. But no Yankees: it was January. I was running at least five miles a day to stay in shape and get that chemical going in the brain; I forget the name of it, but at South Oaks they told us it was the body's natural narcotic and was okay. Running ten, twelve, sometimes fifteen miles on my days off, to get that high – and to exhaust myself because I was nervous about what I'd do with too much time and energy.

See, at the funny farm the shrink talked to me about what deep down I always knew – or, if I didn't know, sensed. That the drinking and the drugs and the womanizing were all pretty much the same thing, part of what he called my self-destructive pattern. Sure, I had been going for the high, but (a big but) the high hadn't been my real goal. What I'd really been searching for all that time was to feel nothing. Oblivion.

So there I was, finally, trying to turn my back on oblivion, to face the world, to take one day at a time.

But all that summer and fall, after those first heady years of sobriety, I started having nightmares: I was drinking again. I'd wake up from a dream about taking a bottle of icy, syrupy vodka out of the freezer, pouring it – almost against my will – and taking a deep, desperate sip. I'd feel panicked, sick to my stomach with despair. Because I knew how fragile my stability was. And I also knew I wasn't a resilient kid anymore. If I lost my grip again, I could fall into a bottomless pit, and I wouldn't have the strength or the courage to try and climb back out. I would be lost for good. I would die. Talk about oblivion.

And suddenly there was Lynne, standing by the trunk of her car, assembling the jack. She was cautious as I pulled over, but she looked me right in the eye and said, 'Thanks. I can handle it.' I showed her my shield and told her that was fine with me; I'd hang around and watch. I liked watching women changing tires.

She handed me the jack, and when I finished I took her out for a hamburger. All of a sudden, I found I was having a genuine, normal conversation. Not just talking to a woman to prove I wasn't only out to screw her. Real discussion. About the emotional problems kids with dyslexia can get. About whether a person's body language can make them more or less likely to be the victim of crime. About public schools versus Catholic schools. And about how I was an alcoholic.

And two weeks later, we went to bed. I lay there afterwards and thought: Oh my God! I'm having a *relationship*.

# *Chapter Three*

Bonnie Spencer's dog barked with joy: Hiya, hiya, wonderful to see ya! Its tail made giant circles of jubilation: Whoopee! We got company! It was a huge, happy thing, like a fat, black English sheepdog.

'Steve Brady,' I called out, and flipped open my ID.

Her dog interrupted its woofing only long enough to lick my hand and my shield: Hiya! Love ya! But Bonnie Spencer stood silent and motionless in her front doorway – and gaped. It was seven forty-five, the morning after her husband had been murdered. She obviously hadn't been expecting condolence calls; she was wearing turquoise second-skin biking shorts, a huge, shapeless faded pink cotton T-shirt and sweat socks. A pair of sneakers dangled from her hand, as if she'd been about to put them on for a run.

'I'm a detective with Suffolk County Homicide,' I added.

Her lips rounded as if she was going to say Oh!, but she didn't. She didn't do anything, not even glance at my ID. She simply gawked. 'Bonnie Spencer?' The dog poked her leg with its snout, as if to say: Come *on*, talk to the guy. But she didn't.

I put my ID away, stuck my hands into my pockets. Even though it was a warm, end-of-summer morning, the moist, leafy smell of fall was in the air. Bonnie Spencer didn't seem to want to look at me; instead, she seemed mesmerized by my car in her driveway. Listen, the '63 XKE is a truly great car, but when there's a detective from Homicide on your doorstep first thing in the morning, that should be the attention-grabber. 'Are you Bonnie Spencer?' I repeated.

She blinked, shaking off her daze. Her eyes brightened. 'Am I Bonnie Spencer?' She laughed. But then she did an awkward box step of embarrassment, probably sensing her manner wouldn't win any awards for Most Seemly Display of Wistful Sadness in a Situation in Which an Ex-Spouse Has Been Offed. She switched to subdued. 'Of course I'm Bonnie.' Then she added: 'Gee.'

Gee. Bonnie Spencer.

Okay, picture the ex-wife of a celebrated movie producer. What comes to mind? A cold, elegant bitch with tobacco-colored arms who wears jewelry to the beach. A stunner with pointy, polished nails that tap all the time, sending out the coded message: Fuck you; I'm dissatisfied.

But Bonnie Spencer didn't seem dissatisfied. And she definitely didn't come across as elegant, especially with that goof of a dog slobbering with happiness at her side. Looks? No glamour girl, not by a long shot. More like one of those girl-buddy types, tall – five eight or nine – broad-shouldered and clean, probably from some clean town where all the girls said 'Gee.' Nothing to write home about. Not much to look at. But the weird thing was, I couldn't take my eyes off her.

Her best feature was her hair, glossy and dark, pulled back into a ponytail. Other than that . . . well, okay features. Deep laugh lines around her eyes. She had the high, healthy color men have more often than women: that rosy brownness that comes to the naturally fair-skinned who spend a lot of time out of doors. In other words, Bonnie Spencer, sneakers in hand, looked like someone you never really got to know in high school: the big, strapping girl jock who gets over mourning the end of field hockey season by spending the winter stroking her lacrosse stick.

Except she was no girl – not anymore. The strong body and the shiny hair were deceptive. At first glance I had put her in her early thirties. But her neck was a little too lined, her lips a little too pale. She was in her late thirties, maybe even forty.

In relation to Sy she made absolutely no sense. To have seen the compact, richly robed, perfectly groomed Mr Spencer and his exquisite world of hand-painted pool tiles, and then to look at big, all-American Bonnie standing on the planked wood floor of a pretty but definitely not show-stopping old saltbox house . . . The question was not why Sy had dumped her, but how such a man had come to marry such a woman in the first place.

She was staring at me again. Her eyes were dark gray-blue, a deep, mysterious color for such a straightforward girl, the color of the ocean. I looked into them; that how-come-*you're*-here expression had returned.

'Ms Spencer?'

'Please,' she said, almost shyly. 'Bonnie.'

And then, once more, ka-boom, her mood changed. Suddenly she became friendly, easy. She gave me a smile. A great, generous smile. Perfect white teeth, except for a slightly crooked one in front, as though her parents had run out of money before the orthodonist had finished. Listen, it can make you happy to get a warm, uncomplicated smile like that. But why the hell was she smiling? Why the hell was her face lit up like that? What did she think I was going to do? Ask her to the senior prom?

'You've heard about your former husband, Seymour Spencer?'

'Oh, God,' she breathed. The smile vanished. Her eyebrows, the kind that slant up, like a bird's wing, drew together; they were eyebrows meant for a more delicate woman. 'It was on the ten o'clock news last night. One of those god-awful stories about famous people you don't know. Except it was about Sy.' For a minute, her expression reflected the normal disorientation of the average citizen confronted with murder: a flash of horror, then a fast flare-up of incomprehension. 'You probably hear this all the time, but I can't believe it.' Her voice was filled with fervent emotion. 'I'm *so* sorry.'

Too much emotion. Too goddamn fervent. Look, I'd been in Homicide a long time. Every working day of my life was spent with the distraught, the agitated, the grieving, the indifferent. And so I knew that something wasn't right about Bonnie Spencer. First of all, her 'I'm so sorry' was overly personal; it's hard to explain, but even the world's most extroverted person doesn't respond to a cop with that kind of familiarity.

And another thing: just standing there in the doorway, she kept changing her mood. Not in the usual way, like a dazed person trying to come to grips with a too-terrible reality, but as though she were searching for the perfect, appropriate emotion to show off to me.

How did I know all this? Any decent detective knows when to turn off his mind and tune in his gut. And my gut was saying: Something's going on with this woman.

So all of a sudden, instead of a routine interview with a dead hotshot's ex-wife to see if I could come up with any leads, I was on the alert.

'Would you like to come in?' she was asking.

'Thanks.'

It was a good-size, solid house, built for a farm family. I followed her – and the dog – into a roomy kitchen and, naturally, said 'Yeah, great' when she offered to make me coffee. (Saying yes to coffee during an investigation makes people feel you've accepted them; it makes them relax, open up. Unfortunately, half the time you wind up drinking stuff that tastes like lukewarm liquid shit, but in the long run it's probably worth it.)

She cleared the morning's papers – the *Times, Newsday*, the *Daily News* – all with their stories about Sy's murder, off the table. She must have gone out for them when the coffee shop opened, at six; they'd all been read. I tipped the chair back and sat quietly, the way I usually do. I wanted to see what Bonnie Spencer would reveal. But she turned away to put the water up to boil and measure out coffee, so for a few seconds the only thing she revealed was nice thighs – a little over-developed, but muscular, tight. Meanwhile, the dog puts its head on my lap and gazed up into my eyes – the soulful look a dumb girl who wants to be taken seriously would give in a bar.

Bonnie turned around. 'Moose,' she ordered, 'go to place!' She pointed toward one of those small, oval braided rugs. The dog ignored her. Bonnie shrugged, half to herself, half in apology: 'The dog has an IQ of a cockroach.' Then she opened a cabinet and took out a little white pitcher shaped like a cow. She was waiting for me to begin questioning her. I didn't. She asked: 'Did Sy . . .' She stopped and started over. 'The TV said he was shot.' I nodded. She held open the refrigerator with her hip while she poured milk into the pitcher. I glanced inside: no chilling white wine or goat cheese in there. God knows over the years I'd made it with enough summer women to recognize that, at least in the food department, Bonnie was not a typical New York woman. She was either on a budget, on a diet, or had given up all hope of visitors; she had a pint container of milk, whole wheat bread and a big, Saran-wrapped glass bowl that looked like she'd gotten overenthusiastic about broccoli. 'Was his death instantaneous?' Her voice was high, hopeful.

'We'll know more after the autopsy.' Just then, Moose gave a deep, lovelorn sigh and lay down at my feet. On my feet, actually.

'Everything I can think of to say is a cliché – but I hope he didn't suffer.'

'I hope not.'

'Well,' she said, 'I guess you weren't just cruising the neighbourhood and felt like a cup of coffee.'

'I guess not.' All of a sudden I realized I had seen her before. Probably at the post office, getting her mail.

'I guess you have some questions,' she said.

'Yes.'

But I didn't ask any. I got busy pretending to formulate a question while studying her cow pitcher. What I was actually doing was checking out if Bonnie had a body worth writing home about under that big T-shirt. Naturally, when I caught myself doing it, I got pissed because I'd always made it a point never to think about sex during work hours (which is generally a snap, homicide not being generally conducive to hard-ons), and also because wanting to know what was under her T-shirt made me feel ridiculous. If she were in a movie, she'd be the heroine's good-natured girlfriend, a tomboy with a heart of gold. But for someone who wasn't attractive, she was so attractive. Here I was, half hoping she'd need something on a high shelf. She'd have to stretch up her arms; her shirt would rise and I would get to see her ass. It made me feel like a louse. Since AA and especially since Lynne, I'd stopped my bad-boy crap, my automatic concentration on anything female, my reflexive coming on to almost every woman I met.

'Tell me about you and Sy Spencer,' I said quickly. 'How long were you married to him?'

'Three years – 1979 to 1982.' She poured the boiling water through the coffee filter. 'You don't take notes?'

'I think I can manage to remember 1979 to '82.' I'd forgotten to take out my pad. Suddenly it felt like a block of lead in my jacket pocket. 'Amicable divorce?'

'Even if it hadn't been, do you think I'd shoot him even years later?'

'I'm open to all possibilities.

'Well, I didn't shoot him.' Her manner was solemn, sincere, proper; if Bonnie Spencer's mouth was from the city, the rest of her had grown up in the nice non-New York hometown, wherever it was.

'Good. Now, do you want to answer my question? How was the divorce?'

'Amicable.'

'Fair settlement?'

'I got this house.'

'Just the house?'

'Yup.'

'Was their any litigation?'

'No. Both of us were just overflowing with amicability. "Bonnie, *please* take the alimony." "No, Sy, but thanks *so* much for thinking of me." '

'Why no alimony? He was rich.'

'I know. But back then, I didn't care about money. Oh, and I was in my wronged-woman phase: "Do you honestly think a monthly check will make up for the loss of a husband, Sy?" ' She shook her head. 'God, was I morally superior. You can imagine Sy – and his matrimonial lawyer. They must have been shouting "Hallelujah!" and jumping up and down and hugging each other.'

I didn't like this. At the same time I was being vigilant, trying to figure out just what was wrong with Bonnie Spencer – because I *knew* there was something wrong – I was finding there was something about her I really liked. Maybe I was just intoxicated by the homey atmosphere – being at the bright-polished wood table in the fresh-smelling country kitchen, watching a woman open a cupboard and think for a second before choosing from a bunch of mugs. Maybe it was that big hairy black mop, Moose, warming my feet. I could just feel myself letting go, my brain turning to mush. Bonnie put the cow pitcher and a sugar bowl down on the table and handed me a mug of coffee. The mug said 'I love' – the 'love' was one of those hearts – 'Seattle!' and had a cartoon of a smiley animal with funny-looking flippers.

'I know it's tacky,' she said. 'It was a choice between tacky and chipped.'

'You didn't get any alimony at all?' I tipped the pitcher. The milk came out of the cow's mouth. It was so dumb.

'I never dreamed I'd need it. See, when I met Sy, I was a hot screenwriter. My movie – *Cowgirl* – had just opened. It got great reviews, did decent business. And during the time we were married, I wrote five more screenplays. Three of them were in development.' She sat down across from me at the table. 'When you're a big success right off the bat, you assume it's going to go on forever.'

'It didn't?'

She shook her head. 'No. *Cowgirl* was my first and only movie. Nothing ever happened with any of the others. Anyhow, Sy offered to pay me alimony at least three times. But I wanted to show him I could be independent. And you know what? In the long run, it really was better this way.'

'Why did the marriage break up?' She was clearly not a New Yorker, because instead of giving me a socio-psycho-feminist analysis of the relationship, she clammed up. 'Come on,' I urged. 'I know this may seem like an invasion of your privacy, but someone's been murdered. I need a picture of this man's life – a complete picture.'

It took her a while, but finally she opened up. 'When we met in LA, Sy was trying to produce his first movie. I guess I was the important one – the toast of both coasts. Okay, the semi-toast. He loved coming along for the ride. He met a lot of people. You know, contacts.

'I don't want to make it sound as if he was using me. I think he truly thought I was . . . well, wonderful. And he was so smart and worldly that when he proposed I thought: Gee, if this man is in love with me, maybe I *am* wonderful. Anyway, pretty soon he made his first movie, and then his second. And let me tell you, Sy earned his success. He wasn't just another rich guy who wanted to get into the movie business to date actresses or impress his friends in Cleveland. He was a born producer.'

'What makes a born producer?'

Bonnie didn't have to think for much more than a second; she'd done her legwork on Sy a long time ago. 'He has to have a good story sense; Sy had a great one. And the ability to get people excited over his vision. And be a trendsetter. If everyone else was making heartwarming movies about farm families with lovable old grandpaws and alfalfa blights, Sy would make something stylized and science-fiction because he loved the script and believed it would make a great movie.'

'So he became a big producer. What happened to you?'

'Nothing much. I stopped needing an unlisted number.'

'You're not saying he dropped you when you stopped being a hot screenwriter?'

'Yup.'

Yup? 'Where are you from?' I asked.

'Ogden, Utah. Is Moose bothering you?'

'He's okay.'

'She. Can't you tell? She loves men. She drops me in two seconds flat for anything in pants. She's the town slut.' Real fast, Bonnie's doting dog-lover smile faded. She glanced away, up at the wall clock, but she wasn't interested in the time. I made a mental note to check on her reputation.

'How did Sy drop you?'

'How? Not too hard, considering how much he wanted out. He told me – very gently – he had been having an affair with someone. Some society lady, like his first wife, except this one didn't look like she ate oats and neighed. Anyway, he told me he was in love with her and it was causing him enormous pain to be hurting me, but that he would appreciate a divorce so he could marry her.'

'But he didn't marry her.'

'No, of course not. He just wanted out. He was having the affair anyway, so he used it. I guess he thought it would be easier for me if there was another woman; he knew I could accept love a lot better than him saying, "Hey, Bonnie, I hate taking you places because you're taller than me and a has-been." '

'And you weren't angry at this kind of treatment.'

'Of course I was angry! If you go back seven years, I bet you'd find twenty witnesses who heard me yelling: "I hope you die, you louse." But time passes. And the fact of the matter is, we wound up being friends.'

'When was the last time you saw him?'

'I'm not sure.' But she was! Damn it, I could feel it. She lifted her chin, examined a pot holder in a hook and pretended to think. 'A few days ago, I think. I dropped in on the set.'

'And before that?'

'Let's see . . . Oh, about a week before. He asked me to come over, to see his house.'

'Did you stay long?'

'No. He just gave me the fifty-cent tour.'

'How good friends were you?'

'Pretty good friends.'

'Did you spend a lot of time with him?'

'Not all that much.'

'Did he visit you here?'

'He dropped by once or twice. But we were mainly phone friends. He was my colleague, my collaborator. See, I hadn't written any screenplays for a few years, but last winter, when I gave it another shot, I sent it right off to Sy. I mean, I hadn't seen him since the divorce, but I knew he'd give me a fair reading. And he really like it!' She massaged her forehead. 'Oh, God almighty, I can't believe he's dead.'

'What about the script?'

'What? Oh, we were developing it together. It was a kind of female-buddy spy movie.'

'What exactly does "developing" mean?'

'It means working on a project – the script, the financing, trying to get a good director or a star involved. But Sy never moved on a project until he was satisfied with the script. And mine – it's called *A Sea Change* – wasn't quite in shape to be sent out. But he had a lot of suggestions. I was rewriting based on his suggestions.'

'And then he'd produce it?'

'Yup.'

'Was he paying you a lot?'

'Well . . . he wasn't actually paying me yet. But if I'd asked, he would have given me option money.'

'Why didn't you ask?'

'I guess the same reason I didn't want alimony. I didn't want to seem greedy. I know, that sounds stupid. No, it *is* stupid. But Sy always worried that people – women – were out for what they could get from him. I didn't want him to think that of me, either time. Anyway, I knew he'd be fair once we got rolling.'

'How do you support yourself? Family money?'

She laughed and looked around the kitchen. 'Does this look like family money?'

'You live in Bridgehampton all year round?' I was really surprised.

'Sure. Oh, I see; you thought this was my sincere little summer cottage where I go to get away from my forty-room Sutton Place triplex. No, this is it. I support myself by writing. I do the "Happy News" column for the *South Fork Sun*. I'm sure it's the high point of your week: weddings, babies, anniversaries. "Penny and Randy Rollins of Amagansett's famed Wee Tippee Inne celebrated their nineteenth anniversary with a gala extravaganza – featuring Penny's world-famous fish chowder!" And I write copy for mail-order catalogs. Stuff like "White swirls of rayon chiffon set aglow by luminescent faux-pearl buttons." '

'You didn't resent Sy, that you had to give up screenwriting, give up all that high living for something . . . less exciting?'

'Resent? A woman tends to resent a man who says, "I don't desire you anymore." ' She looked away, embarrassed. Then she went on: 'But that's on a personal level. Professionally, how could I resent him just because other people weren't hiring me as a screenwriter? That wasn't Sy's fault. Eight studios and fifty thousand independent producers rejected my scripts. They said they were sweet. Sweet is movie speak for insignificant. But in all those years I never doubted that Sy wished me well.'

'Did you ever talk about anything beyond this new project?'

'Sure. Look, I know his friends, his family.'

'Any brothers or sisters?'

'No. Just Sy. Both his parents died since the divorce. But he had aunts, uncles, lots of cousins. I knew them all; we went way back. When I met him, he was still publishing his poetry magazine and trying to get his first movie produced, and his office was still in the Spiegel Crown Kosher Provisions building.'

'Spiegel?'

'Spiegel was his name originally: Seymour Spiegel.' She shook her head. 'He changed it the summer before he went to Dartmouth. I never understood why. I mean, what did he think he would say at graduation? "These are my parents, Helen and Morton Spiegel. Their name used to be Spencer, but they Judaicized it." Or if he was going to change his name, why not go the whole route and call himself Bucky? I mean, Sy is not a quantum leap from Seymour.'

Just then, Bonnie got stopped by some memory of Sy. Her eyes opened too wide, the expression people use when they're trying not to cry. She stood up and got busy sponging off what looked like a clean stove.

And then it happened again: the imposition of self-control, followed by the conscious shifting of the gears of her personality. When she turned around, she was composed – but with just the appropriate degree of concern. 'Do you have any ideas about who killed him?' she asked. Sincere. Saddened. Full of sympathy. Full of crap.

'Do you?'

'No,' she said. For a woman her age, she looked like she had a great body. I tried to figure out where I'd seen her before. Maybe running. She had the slim, muscular legs of a runner.

'Think back over the last few weeks. Was Sy angry at anybody?'

She leaned against the kitchen counter and smiled. 'Everybody. When he was making a movie, anyone who gave him a hard time was an enemy. It was funny, because for all his charm he was aloof, and always in control. When we were married, we'd have fights where I'd yell, kick the refrigerator, and Sy would watch, like he was watching an actress doing an improvisation: Wife Losing Her Temper.

'But when he was producing – God, that was another story! Goodbye charm. And forget aloof. His money and his reputation were on the line. He never yelled – that wasn't his way – but he'd lace into people in this icy voice. It could really get scary – all that fury expressed in this absolutely cold manner. Let me tell you: he got his way.'

'Was he angry at anyone the last time you talked?'

'Lindsay, I guess.'

'But they were living together. They were supposed to be in love.'

'Well, I've got to tell you: the love part is debatable. But even if they had been, this is the movie business. An executive producer doesn't love an actress who's jeopardizing a twenty-million-dollar project. Sy told me the dailies were awful, which really surprised me because her success isn't just based on blatant beauty; she's a talented actress.'

'But you think Sy got disillusioned with her?'

'Sy had a gift for falling in and out of love pretty easily.'

'Let's put love aside. Was he annoyed with her? Angry?'

'Furious. He said she was just coasting – not putting any thought or energy into the role because it wasn't an "important film". That *really* ticked Sy off, because it was an article of faith with him that any movie that's true, that moves audiences – even a screwball comedy – is an important film. He believed in *Starry Night*. And Lindsay didn't. What made the problem even worse was that she had such an monumental ego that she couldn't see how flawed her performance was. And naturally, she wouldn't try to fix what she'd decided wasn't broken. Let me tell you, if he hadn't gotten killed, he would have made her life a living hell.'

'So he was ready to steamroll Lindsay?'

'Yup. And the director too.'

'What's his name?'

'Victor Santana.'

'Why was he mad at him?'

'Because Santana had gone gaga over Lindsay and couldn't or wouldn't get her to change.'

'Anyone else?'

'Oh, the usual hate list. The director of photography they'd hired – a French boy genius – was shooting too pastelly. The line producer was bellying up to NABET – the film technicians' union – too much. Sy was angry at *everyone*.'

'Okay, then who of the movie party was seriously angry at Sy?'

'I don't know. I'm not part of the *Starry Night* company.'

'How about Lindsay Keefe?'

'My guess is if you tell a critically acclaimed actress – a movie star – that her performance is putrid then, no matter how many little adjustments she makes, that the dailies are still awful . . . well, you figure it out. But even *I* wouldn't believe she'd shoot him because he criticized her work.'

'Who else?'

'I don't know.'

I looked her straight in the eye. 'He was your ex-husband. He could talk to you.'

'We didn't talk all that much.'

'You talked enough. What else was on his mind?'

'He never really said anything specific.'

'Tell me anyway.'

'Well, I just want you to know this is my interpretation of what he *didn't* say.'

'Go ahead.'

'This is a very expensive movie for an independent producer. I think maybe he was a little concerned that his backers were upset. The people who invested might have heard about trouble on the set, and they might have gotten anxious.'

'Who were they?'

'Specifically? Beats me. I think a couple of them may have been from his days in the kosher meat business.' She paused. 'You know there are some rough people in that industry.'

'Yeah, there's mob money in it.'

'From the little Sy said, though, these guys didn't sound like out-and-out goons. More like businessmen in suits and ties, except with five-pound gold ID bracelets.'

'Was that all? No one else with a grudge?'

'I'm pretty sure.' I waited while she thought. 'Nope,' she said at last. 'No one else. Definitely.'

I stood and faced her. She lowered her head so I was looking down at her dark, shiny hair. Her breathing became quick, shallow. I knew I was getting to her. Not just the cop: the man.

'Bonnie, you're smart, observant. Sweet too, and I mean that as a compliment.' She tried to look me in the eye – casual. But her face had flushed bright pink. 'You're not being straight. I get the feeling you're holding back, and that concerns me.'

'I'm not holding back anything.' Just for an instant her voice caught in her throat.

I moved in closer. 'You could help me solve a murder, Bonnie.'

'I can't. Honest. I've told you everything I know.'

'Listen, if things were going lousy with Sy Spencer's movie, with Lindsay, who could he confide in? Who knows the business? Who knows him? You.'

'Please. I've told you everything he told me.'

'I've got to tell you: something about you doesn't feel right. What are you hiding?' She turned her head away from me. 'Come on, do you want me to start thinking maybe you were involved?'

'Why would you think that?' She wasn't exactly scared, but she wasn't at ease either.

'Open up, Bonnie.' I stepped toward her. She inched backward until she was pressed against the sink. I moved in until we were almost touching. 'Tell me what you're *not* talking about. Be smart. Because if I start to think you were involved, I'll go after you – and I won't stop.'

I had a few minutes after Bonnie, so I drove down to the beach. I hadn't liked the way the interview had ended. A little official charm is one thing. That final minute, that simultaneous coming on to her and threatening her, was another. And I hadn't come on to her just for leverage; I'd really wanted to be close to her. I needed to clear my head.

Down at the beach, a stiff wind was whipping up the sand, blowing sharp, scratchy grains against my face and neck. Summer people were scuttling around, on the verge of hysteria. Nature was behaving badly. They closed their inside-out umbrellas, folded their chairs, picked up their coolers and rushed past me, back to their cars. There could be no grain of sand under gold spandex bikinis, or in eyes that had to be wide open for the next hostile takeover.

I took off my shoes, squatted down by the dunes near a patch of jointweed, pretty much out of the worst of the wind, and watched until all the New York bodies had run away.

Back in the late fifties, when I was a kid, people still slept on the beach, rightwhere I was, on hot summer nights. Grownups would pitch tents, but the rest of us would lug out the blanket rolls we'd learned to make in Boy Scouts. Sometimes we'd tell scary stories about the Cropsey Maniac or whisper dirty jokes, but by eleven, we'd fall silent and just lie on our backs, staring up at the night sky. The stars were so beautiful they shut us up.

I must have been about ten when I started sneaking out of the house one or two nights a week to sleep on the beach after the summer was over. I did it all year round, except for the winter months. Once the house was dark, I'd tiptoe down the steep back staircase and out the door, grab the blanket roll I kept in the toolshed behind the house, take my bike and race like hell for three quarters of a mile over the pitch-black road.

I don't know why I had to get out. Okay, even back then, my brother and I didn't exactly revel in each other's company; but our relationship was more mutual annoyance than animosity. At his worst, Easton was just a pain-in-the-ass prig who ironed his T-shirts.

My Mother? A lady. She didn't hit me or scream at me. She just didn't like me, and probably didn't love me. I was the mirror image of the drunk farmer who'd fucked her over and then taken off. Just being myself – dangling my legs over the arm of the couch while I read, whistling a tuneless few notes when I was doing something mindless like washing windows – pissed her off. She'd pass by, and there'd be just a sharp expulsion of air through her nose, an irate snort. When I was younger I'd ask, 'Hey, Ma, what's wrong?' Her answer would be 'nothing' in the form of a high-society chuckle – a throaty heh-heh of denial. Then she'd say, 'Steve, sweetheart, *please. Anything* but "Ma." Did I raise a hill-billy?' My mother always made me feel like a total shit.

I know. She didn't have it easy. The farm was gone, and so was my old man. There was no way near enough money to feed me and Easton, and keep us in jeans and sneakers, much less for her to lead the gracious-lady life she aspired to. So she got a job – at Saks Fifth Avenue in Southampton, selling expensive dresses to expensive women. And when she wasn't involving herself in rich lives by zipping up their dresses or stroking their embossed names on their charge cards, she was busting her chops doing scutz work for their charity groups. My mother would do *anything* – set up three hundred bridge chairs in the midday sun, lick one thousand envelope flaps until past midnight – to be allowed into their swan-necked, high cheekboned society.

I don't know where my mother got her obsession with the upper crust. Sure, her family was an old one in Sag Harbor, and to hear her you could practically see portraits of bearded Eastons in the brass-buttoned uniforms of whaling boat captains. But there were no portraits; I'd biked up to the Sag Harbor Library in eighth grade and learned there was absolutely no basis for ancestor worship. Early Eastons might have gone to sea, but they'd obviously been ordinary sailors: guys with bowlegs and black stumps for teeth. Her old man, who died before I was born, had sold tickets for a ferry company that had the Sag Harbor and New London, Connecticut, route.

Still, my mother was convinced, despite all hard evidence to the contrary, that she was a gentlewoman. She didn't give a damn about the local South Fork female elite, the wives of lawyers, doctors, successful farmers, or even the moneyed Yanks – maybe because they all knew who she was, or wasn't. No, she lived for Memorial Day, when her 'friends' opened up their summer houses out here. Even when we were kids, she'd sit at the supper table and talk about her New York 'friends.' Quality People.

Her friends, of course, were not her friends but her customers, summer women who came to the grand old houses, 'cottages' in Southampton – like the one Sy bought – for the summer. She'd go on and on about Mrs Oliver Sackett's hand-embroidered-in-England slips ('Divine, teeny stitches!'), or the thirty-one ('Norell! Mainbocher! Chanel!') dresses Mrs Quentin Dahlmaier had ordered from the main branch in New York, one for every night of the month of July.

Bottom line? My mother felt fucked every single day of her life because she didn't have a driver ('*Never* say "chauffeur"!' she warned Easton; 'it's *nouveau riche*') and a maid and a sable coat. She didn't even have a roof that didn't leak.

And I think that's why I got out from under her roof as often as I could. Sitting over a plate of her *spécialité de la maison*, macaroni and undiluted Campbell's Cheddar Cheese Soup (which, of course, she knew was not Quality, but which she announced was Great Fun), listening to her go on to Easton in her throaty voice – she was a heavy smoker and wound up sounding like Queen Elizabeth with laryngitis – Jesus. She'd talk about how Mrs Gabriel Walker ('one of the Bundy sisters, from Philadelphia') was mad for nubby linen, absolutely mad . . . Her conversation was directed to Easton, never to me. But then she knew and I knew that would be a waste of time.

I did not belong in that house. Like my old man, I was not Quality.

'Had Mr Spencer to the best of your knowledge received any threatening messages or phone calls?' Robby Kurz was asking Lindsay Keefe.

You could tell Robby had gotten up extra early to get spiffy. He'd arranged a yellow handkerchief in the breast pocket of his brown plaid jacket into points. The smell of his double dose of hairspray overpowered the scent arising from a huge bowl of white roses on the table in front of the couch he and I were sitting on.

'Of course there were no threats.' Lindsay exhaled, a sharp, pissed-off breath between pursed lips. She was trying very hard to be patient. 'What do you expect? That his killer went up to him and announced: "You're a dead man"? And there were no heavy-breather phone calls either.' For a woman in shock, Lindsay sounded clearheaded. In fact, completely self-possessed, not a hint of hysteria. The bat-shit, Valiumed, sensitive *artiste* her agent had described could have been some other person.

Even though I'd caught a glimpse of her the night before, in the back of my mind I must have been expecting a fifteen-foot-tall Goddess of Film, a gargantuan babe with enormous, glistening lips and colossal legs that could crush any man caught between them. But Lindsay, standing by the window, fingering the sheer white curtain, was of ordinary height, although so small-boned and petite (except for her world-famous tits) that she looked as if she'd been created solely to make men feel big, important. In her daintiness, she must have been a perfect match for Sy. Two exquisite pocket-size people: a separate species.

But Sy had been an ordinary-looking man. Lindsay Keefe's looks were extraordinary. No wonder she'd gone from doing Greek tragedies in little theaters in little midwestern cities to making avant-garde films in Europe to being an American movie star. Her features were beautiful. Okay, they didn't add up to perfection, but they came damn close. (Movie stars usually have one annoying flaw – a wen, a strawberry mark that you can't ignore, one defect that makes you wonder why they couldn't pop a few thou for a plastic surgeon. Lindsay had a black mole on her neck, at the spot where a guy's Adam's apple is. It was a thing you'd never think about on a regular person, but I couldn't keep my eyes off it.)

Her skin was the palest possible, the kind where you can almost picture the whole blood vessel network underneath. Her hair was some miraculous white-blonde, but with half silver, half gold overtones. And the eyes: pure black.

She'd gotten herself up all in white. A long, filmy skirt and a plain, schoolgirl blouse. The living room was all white also, like a stage set designed solely to flatter blondes. There were a lot of what I'm sure were antiques, but solid stuff: fat couches and chairs covered in different materials – but all whites too, various shades of it, so it became a kind of color.

'If you want to know the truth,' Lindsay went on, '*nothing* could scare Sy. He was a man in control, at the peak of his powers. Intellectually, emotionally, financially . . .' She stopped for a second. When she continued, it was with disgust, as though she'd caught us sniggering over the notion of Sy's 'powers'. She seemed exasperated with what she'd decided were our infantile, dirty cop minds. 'All right, I'll fill in the blank for you: at the peak of his powers sexually.'

Forget that her words were unfair, to say nothing of blunt, brusque and bordering on the stunningly snotty; it hardly mattered. Robby and I sat motionless as she spoke. Her voice had a deep, sensual undercurrent, a hypnotic hum. You wanted to hear whatever she had to say. She could be talking about Sy's death, or reciting erotic poetry, or reading the ingredients off a Kaopectate label. You couldn't resist being Lindsay Keefe's audience.

You wanted to applaud everything. Because besides the Face and the Voice, there was the Body. She had positioned herself perfectly in front of the window. With the curtains open, the late-morning light behind her was so strong you could practically see what she had for breakfast. Everything was lit up: her legs, the line of her bikini underpants stretched over her flat stomach, her hand-span waist – and most of all, the fact that she wasn't wearing a bra. Incredible: her boobs were flawless, the awesome ones that defy gravity and point north. And naturally, she stood slightly sideways, making sure the sunshine lit her up so you couldn't avoid seeing the pokes her nipples made as they pushed against the gauzy fabric of the tightly tucked-in blouse.

'Sy was a great success artistically *and* financially. You must know that this is not an industry where people wish each other well. But would someone murder him because his last film won the Gold Palm at Cannes and grossed ninety-two million? *Please.*'

Robby was nodding at everything Lindsay said, but it was nodding run amok. His head kept bobbing up and down, nonstop, like one of those jerky dolls with springs for necks you used to see in the backs of cars.

I wasn't nodding at all. Because, number one, although I might have been spellbound by the Voice, I still had enough brains to realize all we were getting from Lindsay were words. She was giving a brief (but wonderfully well lit) personal appearance that would satisfy two uncouth cops – without revealing anything.

And, number two, my nodding reflexes weren't working so well because I was genuinely stunned at Lindsay Keefe's absolute indifference to us. Hey, we hadn't dropped in to discuss delinquent parking tickets. You'd think, being an actress, she'd offer a few chest-heaving sobs, or at least sniffle. All she was doing, though, was going through the motions of an interview so she wouldn't get marked down as uncooperative – and keeping us titillated while she was at it, only because it would have been against her nature to be in the same room with a human dick and not titillate. But she totally didn't give a shit about what we thought about her. I'd never come across that before.

Homicide is not a common circumstance in most lives and, therefore, neither are homicide detectives. I'd always gotten *some* reaction: respect, hostility, obsequiousness, guardedness, guile, cooperation. Forget personal qualities: to anyone remotely connected to a murder, Robby and I were figures of authority, symbols of the Law. But not to Lindsay. To her, we were clowns in cheap sports jackets.

She lifted her hair out from under her collar, letting it fall over her shoulders. 'Is there anything else you want from me?' Lindsay demanded.

Robby tried to be cool. He didn't get anywhere. He started giving off a sour wet-wool smell; he was in a sweat of nerves and desire. 'Did Mr Spencer ever mention anyone from his past who might not wish him well?' he asked. Lindsay took a slow, deep breath, presumably to show us how she was trying to retain her composure so she could continue the ordeal of questioning. 'Miss Keefe?' To be fair, Robby's voice didn't quite squeak, but it wouldn't have won any prizes for resonance.

She left her position near the window and came and sat on a chair opposite us, her legs curled under her, her hands clasped in ladylike fashion in her lap. 'Look, I've given you all the help I can,' Lindsay said. 'I don't know anything more.'

That voice! It was one of those voices you read about in old detective stories, which girls with names like Velma have: rich, luscious, like warm cream. Except the funny thing was, for all her cream and translucent skin and superior tits and blonde hair and black mystery eyes, Lindsay Keefe wasn't knocking my socks off. Sure, if your taste ran to devastating blondes she wasn't bad. But on or off the job, I was never the kind of guy who gets off on contempt. Okay (to be fair), maybe this was Lindsay's tough act, to hide some vulnerability – or some real or imagined indiscretion she was afraid was incriminating. Or (not to be fair) maybe Lindsay was just an insolent, contemptuous, cold, emotionally defective twat.

'Well?' she asked. 'Any more questions?'

Robby wasn't completely star-struck, but he seemed to have forgotten momentarily, that he was the killer interrogator of the Suffolk County PD Homicide Squad and the beloved husband of Freckled Cleavage. He gulped. 'I think that about covers it for now,' he said.

'Fine,' she said, and stood. Robby stood too, although not without banging his shin on the white marble coffee table.

I stayed on the couch. 'Did Mr Spencer ever mention seeing any of his colleagues from his days in the kosher meat business?' Lindsay eyed me a little curiously. I hadn't said anything beyond a 'Hello' and an 'I'm sorry'; until now, I'd been letting Robby do the questioning. 'Why don't you sit down just for one more minute, Ms Keefe.' She sat, and then Robby did too. 'The meat business,' I prompted.

'No,' she answered. 'I'm almost positive he didn't see any of them. For him, that was another life. But let me say this, Detective . . . I forgot your name.'

'Steve Brady. Did any people he knew from the meat business invest in this movie, Ms Keefe?'

'Yes. One or two.'

'Do you know their names?'

'Just one. Mikey. Michael, I suppose.'

'Any last name?'

'I don't know it.'

'Did you ever hear of Mr Spencer meeting with this Mikey?' She shook her head. 'Having a phone conversation with him?'

'Sy made most of his calls from his study.'

'Right, but did you ever happen to be passing by and hear any call to this Mikey?'

'Actually, once. And I *was* passing by – not eavesdropping. Don't condescend to me.'

'Okay. What did you happen to hear, passing by?'

'Sy was reassuring this man that everything was going well.'

'Was Mikey worried that it wasn't going well?'

'No, of course not. It was one of those soothing, stroking, you're-so-important phone calls. Sy was a master of those.'

'No problems with *Starry Night*?' I asked. She shook her head, allowing a curl of her long platinum hair to fall in front of her shoulder. She started twirling it around her index finger; I assume my eyes were supposed to follow the little circles until I was mesmerized. But I couldn't stop watching the mole on her neck; it was so black it looked like an undeveloped third eye. 'Mr Spencer was pleased with how it was going?' I asked.

'Yes.'

'No problems with the director? Any of the actors?

'Nothing that wasn't routine.'

'He was happy with your performance?'

'Of course.' Emphatic. Clipped. 'Why do you ask?'

'Just trying to get the lay of the land,' I said.

'Let's be straight with each other, Detective Brady. I don't know what you've heard, but there's always on-set gossip about the star of a film. Sometimes it's more than petty nastiness. I'm sure there are people saying terrible things, like that I'm a tough bitch. That's because I'm serious – *passionately* serious – about my work. Or that my performance is somehow lacking. Or that my relationship with Sy was . . . well, one of mutual convenience. The truth is, yes, I am tough. But I also happen to be a vulnerable human being.'

'I'm sure you are.'

'And I loved Sy very, very much.'

'I understand.'

'I hope you also understand that Sy loved my work.' She bowed her head for an instant, a second of silence. Then she looked me right in the eye. 'And he loved me.'

'I don't doubt that for a minute,' I said, and thought about the long, dark hairs that had gotten caught on the headboard in the guest room.

'We were going to be married.'

I asked: 'What do you know about his ex-wives?'

'I haven't met either of them.'

'Did he ever talk about them?'

'Not very much. The first was named Felice. He married her right after college. She was getting her PhD at Columbia. Supposedly very brilliant. Came from a distinguished family. A great deal of money.'

'What happened?'

'Truthfully?'

'Please.'

'Bor-ing.'

'Did he have any contact with her recently?'

'No. I'm almost positive. They were divorced in the late sixties. She's remarried.'

'What about his second wife?' I asked.

'Bonnie. From out West someplace.'

'Do you know anything about that marriage?' Robby asked.

'A mismatch.' Lindsay placed the fingers of one hand in the palm of the other; they needed a rest, or else she was examining her nails. 'She's a writer. Well, she had one movie produced, and that's when Sy met her. I think he was enamoured of what he thought was a lively, unpretentious intelligence. All zip, and hero-worshipping quotes from Joseph Mankiewicz's screenplays. That appealed to him – for five minutes.'

'And then?' I asked.

'The truth? She had one movie in her. She was yesterday's news by the time they were married.'

'Do you know if he saw her at all?' Robby asked.

'No. Of course not. But she lives around here. When they split, she got their old summer place. Actually, though, Sy did hear from her a few months ago. She sent him some new script she'd written.'

I asked: 'Was he going to produce it?'

'God, no.'

I found myself swallowing hard. 'He told her no?'

'Of course. He told me he had to. Kindly, probably generously. But I'm sure very, very firmly. Oh, but wait a second. That's right. I'd forgotten. She came onto the set in East Hampton, *pursuing* him. I didn't see her, but she went and knocked on the door of his trailer. It was awful. But he said he told her in no uncertain terms: "Goodbye. Stay off the set of my film. And keep your screenplays to yourself." That may sound harsh, but he had no choice. This business is a magnet for all sorts of unstable people.'

'He knew her, though,' I said. 'She was his ex-wife. Did he think she was unstable?'

'No. As far as I know, he just thought she was a loser. But if Sy had given her the least bit of encouragement, she'd have been all over him: Love my screenplay. Love me. Do for me. Make me rich, famous. Make me a star. People like her are *desperate*. Sy had to get rid of her.'

# *Chapter Four*

The Homicide team meeting turned out to be six cops sitting around a blackboard shrugging shoulders. Robby hadn't been able to interview Easton because he'd been tracking down the kosher-meat guy, Mikey, who turned out to be Fat Mikey LoTriglio – a real sweetheart. Like the Spiegel-Spencers, Mikey's family had owned a major meat-processing plant, but he also had ties to another family – the Gambinos. He had a dandy record of arrests for extortion and aggravated assault – our kind of guy – but he'd never been convicted of anything.

Ray Carbone announced that all he'd been able to do, because he'd been busy calming down the higher-ups and helping write a press release, was find out that Sy's first wife's name was Felice Vanderventer and she lived on Park Avenue.

Our man at the autopsy, Hugo Schultz, the Sour Kraut, reported that not counting his death, Sy had been in great shape. No diseases. No traces of alcohol or drugs. His last meal seemed to have been bread and salad. There was evidence of recent ejaculation, probably post-salad. Oh, he'd been killed by the first bullet, which had gone through his head; the one that had gone through his heart was unnecessary: Target practice, Hugo said.

The other two guys listened and drank coffee. I briefed everyone on Bonnie's story on her screenplay versus the opposing Lindsay version – and how there was something not right about Bonnie, something that bothered me. Oh, and that Lindsay's claim of giving a stellar performance was countered by both Bonnie and Gregory J. and how I thought *Starry Night*, the twenty million dollars it was costing and, possibly, Lindsay's reputation might be headed for the crapper.

In other words, what I got from the meeting was not much. It was then that I thought about my movie man. Jeremy. Germy.

Jeremy Cottman, the most famous movie critic on TV, was my one rich and famous friend. Okay, so it wasn't exactly a big-ass buddy friendship. In fact, it had been over twenty years since I'd laid eyes on him.

Jeremy had been a Bridgehampton summer kid, the son of rich but not famous parents. His father had been a stockbroker whose only customer seems to have been himself. Mr Cottman played perpetual golf; his skin had the texture of a grilled cheese sandwich. Mrs Cottman, who called everyone 'cutie-pie,' had spent whole summers in a sunbonnet that tied under her chin, clutching a pair of clippers, pruning anything that didn't run away. Their house, a rambling white wood Victorian, overlooked Mecox Bay.

Rich kids like Jeremy played all summer: swimming in each other's pools, going to parties at each other's beach clubs, taking riding lessons in those puff-thigh pants. Kids like me worked. I started out scraping duck shit and sorting potatoes for the farmer who had bought our land. When I was twelve, I graduated to cleaning swimming pools, and later to caddying at one of the local golf clubs.

But in spite of work, summer had always been an enchanted time. It didn't get dark until late, so we'd grab a bite of supper and rush down to the ball field. We were in the four thousandth inning of a baseball game that had been going on since the summer after third grade: shirts and skins, our shirts getting progressively scruffier as the fifties gave way to the sixties, our skins darkening from the white, stick-out-ribbed chests of nine-year-olds to the broad, tanned, hairy torsos of high school seniors.

It was a strictly Bridgehampton game. Every once in a while, a summer kid would ride past – on an English racing bike. After a few nights of bypasses, he'd brake, knock down his kickstand and get really busy inspecting a tire. Usually we'd ignore him, as in:

This is one club you can't join, fuckface. But if he looked like a terrific jock, we'd be a little less exclusive. Sure, the kid would have to have the balls to grunt the opening 'hi.' But then, if he wasn't too well-dressed, we might ask him if he wanted to hit a few.

Jeremy (I was the one who started calling him Germy) made our team. He was an incredible power hitter, a so-so outfielder, and a cruel and funny mimic. He'd pick some movie star or a baseball player and have them say terrible things about one of the kids, so it was like being dumped on by Marilyn Monroe or Carl Yastrzemski (the greatest human being Bridgehampton had ever produced, even though he'd played for Boston).

I'd never met anyone like Germy Cottman. To be able to hit those line drives. To have discovered a way to say *whatever* was on his mind. God, how good that must feel! We became great summer friends, eventually trusting each other enough to share our most intimate sports fantasies. We were the best of buddies from about the time we were twelve until we went off to college.

Germy went to Brown. I went to Albany State. I looked for him that summer after freshman year, but his mother, clipping roses that were doing something to annoy her, said, Sorry, cutie-pie, Jeremy is in Bologna, learning Italian. I saw him around once or twice after that, but we didn't have much to say; by then, he was an intellectual, I was a druggie, and neither of us was playing ball anymore.

But every now and then Germy's name came up around town. I heard he was in graduate school in Chicago for something; he was working on a newspaper in Atlanta; he was working on a newspaper in Los Angeles; he was writing long movie reviews – film criticism, I suppose – for some high-minded magazine.

And then one night on TV: the Germ! I remember lying on my couch, pretty drunk but not totally gone, slugging down a beer, thumbing the remote control. There he was, swiveling back and forth in a big leather chair, legs crossed, telling us folks at home – in his familiar, clothespin-on-the-nose prep school nasality – why *Out of Africa* was such an overrated movie; then he did a brief, mean, but exceedingly accurate, imitation of Meryl Streep.

Germy was on the map. A celeb. And over the next couple of years, his show actually got better. He wasn't only negative. Sure, there were still his killer reviews and his snide imitations, but he stopped showing off his intellectual superiority and started displaying his real intelligence. He'd run a film clip in slow motion and explain exactly about how a certain shot was done, or describe precisely why So-and-so was a good editor, or a bad production designer. He knew the players too; he'd report how some internal fight at a studio affected a particular movie.

All America watched Germy: seven-thirty, Friday nights. And read about him too, in *People, Time, Newsweek*. I read he'd married the daughter of a famous 1940s director; that he had a house on a cliff overlooking the Pacific; that he'd moved back to New York; that he'd divorced his wife after fifteen years and married some very famous Broadway lighting designer – not that I'd ever heard of her. Around town there was the talk that his father had had a heart attack on the eighteenth hole and had died before they could get him back to the clubhouse and that his mother had died too, and Germy had inherited the house. But although I kept up with what he was doing, I hadn't spent any time with him since I'd played shortstop and he'd played outfield.

I felt a little nervous about calling him, but then I thought: I've got to give it a shot. It being a glorious, sunny Saturday afternoon, Germy could actually be a couple of miles away. He might be spending the day practicing a cruel Clint Eastwood imitation or banging the lighting designer or (I smiled to myself as I pulled into his driveway) sitting cross-legged on his bed the way he used to, working neat's-foot oil into his mitt.

A minute later, there he was at his front door, his hands braced against the frame, as if he were defending his house from some intruder who might push him aside and ransack his living room, or demand to know what Chevy Chase was really like. 'Yes?' Chilly, about to cross the border into absolute iciness.

'You don't recognize me, Germy?'

Then he did the Oh-my-God! I-don't-believe-it! bit, followed by our mutual finger-squishing handshake. It was for real. We were both pretty touched at seeing each other, although not comfortable enough to follow our natural inclination, which was to give each other one of those acceptable, non-homo, World Series hugs. 'Steve! Come in!'

I followed him through the front hall, toward the living room. It was like stepping back into 1959: the blue-and-white umbrella stand filled with tennis rackets, the dark, scratched-up old mirror in a carved wood frame. 'I can't believe it,' I said. 'It looks exactly the same. Any minute your little sister's going to come running in and spit at me.'

'That's right!' Germy said in his slow honk. 'I'd forgotten. She spent a whole summer spitting at you. She was madly in love.'

The Cottman house still had the we've-been-rich-forever shabbiness it had when we were kids: faded flower print cushions, threadbare rugs with flowers that skidded across wood floors, old wicker chairs. Out on the back terrace, there were flowers blooming in his mother's mossy clay pots, and the old, white-painted, wrought-iron chairs, chipped in the same places.

Like the house, Germy hadn't changed much. He was tall, about my height, but he hadn't outgrown his round-chinned baby face, with its button nose and wide-open eyes. Sure, his forehead was a little lined, his brown hair had a little gray, but in his horn-rimmed glasses and white tennis sweater, he looked more like a tall kid in a daddy costume than a full-fledged adult. He made a take-a-seat gesture. 'Can I get you anything? A cup of coffee?' Then he remembered. 'A beer?' I shook my head. 'Steve! God! Tell me about yourself. Where are you living? What do you do?'

Germy had much too much class to ask: What do you want? although it must have been in the back of his mind that maybe I was there for a handout, or with some obnoxious request: Can you get me an autographed picture of Goldie Hawn?

'I'm here, in Bridgehampton, north of Scuttle Hole – '

'Married, single div – ' He interrupted both me and himself with his own enthusiasm. 'I got married again last year!' He paused as if to give me time to prepare myself for something wonderful. 'To Faith Armstead!'

I nodded respectfully, as in: Oh, of course, I'm always dazzled by Faith Armstead's lighting. 'Congratulations.'

'She's stuck in a theater all day today. Can you believe it?' His second marriage was working; I could hear the pleasure as Germy pronounced his wife's name. And he seemed proud, almost awed by her dedication; she could have been the first wife since the dawn of history to work on a Saturday. 'Now, what about you?' he demanded.

'I never got married. I was pretty screwed up when I got back from Vietnam.'

'Vietnam,' Germy echoed.

'And then I got used to being single, being free. But I finally met a great girl. We're getting married Thanksgiving weekend.'

'You were in Vietnam,' he said softly. The new quietly moved reaction. After all those years of being Asian-baby butchers, we had somehow turned into national treasures. 'Did you see action?'

'No, you jerk-off. They needed a shortstop on the Saigon intramural team, so I spent the whole war on the ball field. Listen, I really want to catch up, but I'm actually here on business . . .' I saw his face fall a little, his round kid-cheeks flatten. 'Eat it, Je-re-my. You think I'm going to give you a life insurance pitch?'

'Well . . .' His embarrassment evaporated. 'No.' He became his real self, his caustic TV self. 'You look more like redwood decks, actually.'

'I'm a detective with Suffolk County Homicide.'

'*You*?'

'Yeah. Never thought I'd wind up on this side of the law, did you?'

'Homicide!' he said. 'Steve, that's exciting. Glamorous!'

'Yeah, well, the violence is fantastic, and I've always been crazy about decomposition.'

'Seriously, do you like what you do?'

'It stimulates my intellectual processes.'

'I said seriously.'

'Yeah, I like it. A lot. Now, do you know why I'm here?'

It took him less than a tenth of a second. 'Sy Spencer.'

'I need background, foreground, whatever you've got. Did you know him?'

He turned his chair so he was facing me; his back was to the bay. 'Slightly.'

'You didn't hang out with him?'

'No. He ran on that middle-aged fast track: a little old money, a *lot* of new money, and writers, restaurant owners, fashion designers. All those emaciated, face-lifted women and their beefy men.'

'Sy wasn't beefy. Five six, a hundred thirty-two pounds.'

'He was an exception.' Germy hesitated: 'Oh. You know how much he weighed from . . .?'

'Yeah. The autopsy. Listen, the guy was in fantastic shape. I should have his liver. If he hadn't backed up into those bullets, he'd have lived till a hundred. The thing is, Germy, I know more than I want to about all his organs. But I want to know about *him*. So I need you. Even if you weren't his best friend, you must know about him, about what he was doing.'

'Of course.'

'Okay, what do you know about *Starry Night*?'

'Gossip or substance?'

'Both. Substance first; get it over with.'

Germy took off his glasses and gave the earpiece a thoughtful chew. 'All right. I actually read an early draft of the script. It's an action-adventure-love story about a charming heel who marries a very rich woman for her money. Superficially she's the frosty, sophisticated sort – a "Hamptons" type, if you'll forgive me. She's overwhelmed by the heel's magnetism and sexuality. Well, to make a convoluted story short, his past – dealing a little cocaine – catches up with him, and some Colombian types kidnap his wife for reasons the script does not adequately make clear. The heel doesn't care at first. Then slowly he realizes he has fallen madly in love with the wife, and she . . . she's tied up in a basement in . . . I'm a little foggy here, but I think in Bogatá. Maybe Brooklyn. In any case, it dawns on her that he's more than a charming stud; he's the first true love of her life. He goes after her, she escapes, there's a gratuitous car chase, the bad guys seem about to win. But in the end they live happily ever after.'

I sat still for a minute, staring out at the shimmering golden reflection of the sun in the bay. 'Would a guy like me shell out six bucks to see it?'

'Hard to say, Steve. It's a film about breaking through your shell, discovering your humanity. The script has some of the best dialogue I've read in years. Genuinely witty. And some fine straight moments, before the kidnapping, when each starts to reveal himself to the other and then pulls back, as if they realize they're violating some unwritten Law of Superficiality of jet-set marriages. But it certainly doesn't cover any new ground. And as far as I can recall, the plot is pedestrian. But the characters are unusually well drawn for a postliterate script.' He slid his glasses back on. 'In case you don't know it, we are living in what is, essentially, a postliterate era.'

'Oh, I do know it. It's a tragedy I've got to live with every day of my life.'

'I knew you'd feel that way.'

We sat in comfortable silence for a minute. When you know someone since you've been kids, you have a kind of ESP. I could sense Germy, like me, relaxing, lifting up his face to feel the sun, and wanting – really, desperately wanting – to talk about all the amazing things that had happened to the Yankees since Steinbrenner.

But I had a your-guess-is-as-good-as-mine homicide hanging over my head, so I made myself stick to the subject. 'It sounds like maybe you have a qualm about the *Starry Night* script.'

'Well, it could make an exciting, stylish film. But it's all in the execution. Will the actors be credible? Will you believe in the possibility of a great love between Lindsay Keefe and Nicholas Monteleone? His appeal has always been more emotional than sexual. He's essentially a man's man; all his best movies have been about relationships between men – rodeo riders, Amazon explorers . . .' He grinned. 'Homicide cops. But the question about whether the movie will work goes beyond the two principals: Will the Colombians be offensively stereotypical Latino greasers or genuinely terrifying? How good a job will the director do on the action sequences? Will the big chase scene come off? Also, the real problem – the reason Sy didn't get studio financing – is that it was felt there is a limited audience for this type of vehicle: Cary Grant *cum* balls. It probably won't play to the under-twenty-fives. It's not moving enough to be another *The Way We Were*. And it's not a sizzler; even if Lindsay does bare her breasts once again, or decides it's time for a change and moons the camera, it won't help. First of all, audiences have seen her body too many times; there's a strong inclination to say: "Please, madam, keep your shirt on." In the script, the compelling sex is verbal, lighthearted man-woman word play, not sex play.' He leaned back and clasped his hands behind his head. 'Is that substantive enough?'

'Yeah. Now what about money? I've heard twenty big ones. Where does that kind of dough come from?'

'Private investors. Or banks who had faith in Sy's track record.'

'If you were a bank, what kind of faith would you have?'

Germy unclasped his hands, then crossed his arms over his chest. 'I'd invest – although not twenty million. That seems awfully high for a film that will be shot primarily out here and in Manhattan, even with all the lavish set decoration and costumes and an anxious director who's known for a lot of retakes. But forgetting dollars and cents, Sy's films were really good. Bankable. He believed in starting with a polished script. He'd go for the gifted actor over the big name. I always admired his movies.'

'Just admired? You ever love any of them?'

He took a minute to consider the question. 'No. I can't really explain it, but there was something a little smug about every picture he produced. Each one seemed to be saying: 'Aren't I sensitive? Provocative? Don't I have superb production values?' There was always intelligence and care, but never any real spirit. I suppose his films were like Sy himself.'

'From the little you knew him, what did he seem like?'

'Intelligent. Polished but not slick. And for the movie business, where hugging and kissing and screaming "Dahlink, you're a very great genius" is an institutional requirement, he was notable because he was so restrained. A gentleman.' Germy stopped short.

'What are you thinking about? Even if it seems totally irrelevant.'

'Well, Sy wasn't definable. He struck me as something of a chameleon. Man-about-town with men-about-town. Lover boy with women. Tough negotiator with the unions – a real dirty street fighter. And full of Jewish show-biz warmth with a couple of the old-time reporters, dropping Yiddish all over the place. The few times he and I talked, he was very professional – as if the only thing he lived for were discussions of Fritz Lang's deterministic universe. It made me laugh because I knew he had to have gotten me confused with another critic: I never gave a flying fuck about Fritz Lang.'

'Which one of his personalities came closest to being the real Sy Spencer?'

'I haven't the foggiest.'

'What do you think drove him, Germy? Money? Sex? Power?'

'Well, he certainly seemed to have enjoyed all of those. But he didn't *seem* driven, even though he must have been. He could be pleasant – even charming. But some integral part of his circuitry – the part that reaches out and makes human connections – seemed . . . disconnected.'

'What do you know about his ex-wife Bonnie Spencer?' Germy shook his head: never heard of her. 'She wrote the screenplay for a movie called *Cowgirl*.'

'I remember that one. It was a nice movie.'

'What was it about?'

'A widow of a small-time rancher literally puts on her husband's boots. It deals with her relationships with the ranch hands, the neighbouring wives. Some moving dialogue about her passion for the land. Beautifully photographed.'

'A major motion picture?'

'No. But a really decent minor one.' He took off his glasses again and did some more gnawing. 'Her name wasn't Spencer when she wrote it. Something else.'

'Sy married her after it came out. But then none of her other screenplays ever got made.' I had this vivid image of Bonnie in her bicycle shorts and too-big T-shirt leaning against the sink in her kitchen. It was not an image of a person who could in any way be in the movie business. 'Ever hear anything about her?'

'No,' he said.

'It sounds like he cut her loose when he realized she wasn't the hot property he thought she was.'

'That sounds fairly typical. Of the industry and of Sy.'

'What about Lindsay Keefe? I've been hearing her acting wasn't very good this time around.'

'Well, now we move on to gossip. I've heard the same thing, and I don't doubt it. She's a very cerebral actress. Her characters tend to be focused women, intelligent, passionately devoted to whatever they're doing, sometimes capable of deep emotion: abused women who write poetry, missionaries who join obscure revolutionary movements. That sort of thing. The character in *Starry Night*, though . . . she's different. Soft, endearing, the poor little rich girl. My guess is, Lindsay may be enough of an actress to project endearingness. But she's mostly head, no heart. The role would be one hell of a stretch.'

'Will they stop making the movie now that Sy's dead?'

'Are you joking? Making movies is a *business*. For an actor, a director, they'd have to stop for a few days until they could get a replacement. For an executive producer . . . they won't even stop for a cup of coffee.'

'Did you hear anything else about what was happening on the set?'

'The usual malicious innuendos.'

'Good. What are they?'

'That Sy was dissatisfied, and he and Lindsay may have actually fought over her performance. Or, even if there was no confrontation, she sensed she was in trouble with him. In either case, she took a deep breath . . . and pointed her major artillery at the director, Victor Santana. Made him an ally.'

'How did she get him on her side?'

'Her side? Her side was the least of it.'

'No shit! Lindsay was making it with Santana?'

'Steve, when the executive producer leaves the set for the day and the director and the leading lady then proceed to hold a script conference in the director's trailer for forty-five minutes with the blinds drawn *and* they don't ask a production assistant for coffee *and* the trailer is observed rocking back and forth, what do you think?'

'Fuck City.'

The real question was, what did Sy think? What did he know? And what had he been planning to do about Lindsay Keefe?

We sat in his kitchen eating ice cream out of pint containers, the way we used to. Halfway through, we switched; I got Germy's cookies 'n' cream and he got my coffee Heath bar crunch. Neither of those flavors had been invented when we were kids.

He told me how his mother's cancer had metastasized and how excruciating her pain had been and how she'd finally ended it by OD'ing on the Seconal she'd accumulated over a month. I told him I always thought she'd go on forever with that funny old bonnet and the pruning shears and how truly sorry I was she wasn't around anymore to call me cutie-pie.

He put down his spoon. 'Steve, when we were kids, I never had the courage to ask you . . . Your father just walked? Your mother supported the family?'

'Yeah. After he sold the farm, he had a few different jobs, but he'd always get canned for coming to work drunk. I'm not talking a little slurring; I'm talking pissed out of his mind. When you're working over at Agway, it isn't a plus to puke all over the biggest farmer in Bridgehampton. Anyway, he took a hike when I was eight.'

'You never heard from him again?'

'No. For all I know, he could still be alive somewhere, although I wouldn't make book on it.'

My father was a lazy, disgusting, dirty drunk. He was also, in rare, semi-sober moments, a sweet man, talking sports to me, buying a buck's worth of bubble gum so I could have the baseball cards. And he'd sit beside Easton as he built his model ships and say 'Good work,' although he couldn't help, because his hands shook with perpetual DT's. And once in a while he'd come up to my mother and say, ' "Ah, love, let us be true to one another," ' or

' "Shall I compare thee to a summer's day?" ' – and for that second, you could see there had once been something between them.

'You never let me come into your house,' Germy said quietly, as we walked back onto the terrace. 'You always had an excuse. The painters. Your mother was expecting company.'

'We didn't have any money. I couldn't have even offered you a soda. And the place was falling apart. You lived here, in all this richness, and this was just your summer house.'

We fell silent for a minute because, although we had often discussed Roger Maris's troubles, we had never spoken about our own; we had no idea where to take the conversation next. I got up, walked to the edge of the terrace and, for a minute, watched the brilliant red-and-white sail of a Windsurfer skim across Mecox Bay. I turned back to Germy. 'Remember your Sunfish? You got it for your sixteenth birthday.' He nodded. 'You let me sail it, and I took it out so far I was sure I was going to die or get in deep shit with the coast guard. I remember I was more afraid of the coast guard than of death.'

'That was when you were starting to get pretty wild. I remember the next summer, before college. You were drinking too much, even for a rebellious kid. I started . . . not to feel comfortable with you.'

'I know.'

'You were bragging about breaking into houses over the winter, trashing them – for fun.' He looked straight at me. 'Were you just bullshitting?'

'No. And it wasn't just a little vandalism. I'd gone bad, Germ. I was stealing. Color TVs, stereos. Sold most of the stuff to a fence over in Central Islip. I pissed the money away. Booze. Records. A leather jacket. Except one time I went to Yankee Stadium. Got a terrific seat, right near first. This was going to be my perfect day. But we lost. A shitty game.'

'When was that?'

'July of '66.'

'A shitty year,' Germy recalled. 'We finished last.'

'I remember. The first of many shitty years. For me. The Yankees got better. I didn't. Not for a long time.' I separated my thumb and index finger by maybe an eighth of an inch. 'This much,' I explained. 'I missed being dead or in the slammer by this much.'

'That must be scary.'

'Yeah, it was.' I thought for a second. 'Still is.'

# *Chapter Five*

By the time I finished with Germy, it was after three o'clock. And it was a Saturday afternoon and the set of *Starry Night* was closed down. So I had the movie people come to me in our temporary headquarters in the Southampton Village PD. I'd gotten use of the Xerox/coffee machine room for interviews – with the understanding that I could be interrupted in the event of a catastrophic copying crisis.

The room was no more or less ugly than any other small, windowless, fluorescent-lighted, metal-and-green-leatherette-chaired government-bureaucracy utility room. Its stale air was perfumed with the aroma of prehistoric coffee grounds and the fumes of copier fluid, its floor decorated with the pink and white and blue confetti of torn-off ends of Sweet 'n' Lows, Equals and sugar packets, as well as with a dusting of white powder that was not a controlled substance but non-dairy coffee lightener. It was no different from any other room where cops work: a place that was habitable yet degrading to the human spirit at the same time.

Victor Santana, the short-haired, thickly mustached, spiffy dude of a director who sat across from me, was willing himself to rise above his surroundings. He was doing a damn good job. He did not seem to belong in the room. In fact, he did not seem to belong anywhere except in a three-star restaurant, a four-star movie or a five-star hotel. The guy was one suave package: a white shirt with a dark red tie, pale gray slacks and a charcoal sports jacket made of some priceless fabric so exclusive a guy like me would never have heard of it.

Santana's name was Hispanic, and he was a pretty intense beige, but his accept wasn't Spanish. He sounded as if he was trying to have been educated at Oxford. It didn't quite work; his diction, like his sideburns, was a little too clipped. My guess was he wouldn't deny his heritage, but neither would he cry '*Caramba*!' to an offer to be grand marshal of the Puerto Rican Day parade.

He came off as urbane, the sort of guy James Bond would banter with at a chemin de fer table, whatever the hell chemin de fer is. But despite his civil smiles and even his I'm-so-accommodating dark-eyed glints, I knew I was getting nowhere fast. He seemed to be spouting the same essential script as Lindsay: *Starry Night* was great; Lindsay was a great actress; Sy Spencer had been a great producer. 'Making a film,' he was explaining, veddy Britishly, each consonant a pearl, 'is a collaborative process. I cannot tell you what a joy it was – artistically *and* personally – to work with Sy and Lindsay.'

So I said: 'Mr Santana, please cut the shit. We know for a fact that you and Lindsay Keefe were having an affair.'

His torso twitched, as if I had, for an instant, electrified his chair. 'That is absolutely untrue!' he declared. He pronounced the word 'as-so-lyutely.'

'We have witnesses.' Of course, all we had was a secondhand report of a rocking trailer. But it was worth a shot. 'Witnesses who can testify to you and Ms Keefe – in your trailer.' Suddenly he appeared to be studying the veins in his hand. After a second, though, I realized he wasn't into veins; he was communing with his wedding ring. Santana was in his mid-thirties and had had a couple of successes. Maybe he was calculating how much each lurch of the trailer would cost him if his marriage blew up. Had Lindsay been worth a hundred thou per hump? Or maybe he just felt guilty. 'Why not tell me about it?'

'All right,' he sighed. Total mush: here was this cosmopolitan guy who didn't have the presence of mind to ask who the witnesses were and what they had witnessed. It was going to be a cinch, because Santana was dying to Tell All. He settled his perfectly tailored ass back in the chair but leaned the rest of himself forward. 'We were having an affair,' he confided, real whispery, as if to say: Swear to God you won't tell. 'Please understand, this is no superficial run-of-the-play liaison. It is . . . well, it is a love affair. I wouldn't want you to think . . .'

'No problem, Mr Santana. Listen, normally, what you do is your own business. Two people working together can fall for each other. Happens all the time. It's just that in this case, the lady's boyfriend, fiancé, whatever, was shot through the head and heart. So I have to ask a few questions.'

'Maybe . . . Do you think I should speak to an attorney?'

'You can speak to whoever you want. Hire a whole law firm. You're a sophisticated man. You know what your rights are. But why? You're not guilty of anything, are you?'

'Of course not.'

'So just answer a couple of questions. Now, to make my life easier. Or later, if you want, with your lawyer.' I really wasn't trying to trip him up. I just didn't feel like hanging around until the middle of the following week when some dork in a dark-blue three-piece pinstripe could manage to get here from Manhattan, hook his thumbs onto his vest pockets and give me a harangue on prosecutorial discretion. 'Did Sy know about you and Lindsay?'

'No. Of course not.'

'How do you know?'

'I asked. I was a bit nervous, but she said she was certain.'

'Everything seemed lovey-dovey between them?'

'I'm quite certain he thought so.'

'Which means what?'

'Which means he didn't know how Lindsay felt about me – and I about her.' You know those hearts-and-flowers stories you read where the hero's eyes shine? Well, Victor Santana's eyes started to shine. He glowed with the glory of love. You wouldn't think a grown-up guy with such an expensive sports jacket could be such a sap, but he was.

'Was Sy happy with her acting?' This clearly was not Santana's favorite question. His glow dimmed. He sat up straight, tense. He tried to calm himself by stroking his tie; it had lots of little shield designs that I guess were supposed to be club insignias, or family crests. 'Hey, Mr Santana, I've been talking to a lot of people. I have an idea of what's going on, so do us both a favor. Don't get creative. Was Sy happy with what Lindsay was doing?'

'He was not thrilled.'

'Objectively, how was she?'

'She was *wonderful*. I mean that sincerely.' He stopped whacking off his tie; he started rotating his wedding ring.

'So Sy Spencer was wrong?'

'Yes. Completely.'

'Why would a smart producer like him think an actress – someone who he's also supposed to be in love with – is crapping up his movie? Especially if she's not?'

'Sy wanted total control over every aspect of Lindsay's life. When she started showing the smallest signs of independence, he began to undermine her – so she would be more dependent on him.' Santana's script was a little different from Lindsay's, but it was pretty clear from his mechanical delivery who had written his lines. 'Sy was terrified of losing her. So he played on her vulnerability. Superficially, Lindsay seems strong. But she's a very vulnerable woman.'

'What did Sy say to you about her acting?'

'He indicated that he felt Lindsay was cold.' Santana shook his head as if unable to comprehend such insensitivity – except the gesture was way overdone, like an actor in a silent film.

'What did he want you to do?'

'He told me to warm her up.'

'Did you try to warm her up in the acting area?'

'No. Truly, it wasn't necessary. She was giving a smashing performance.' Come on, I wanted to say. Get real, Santana. Your old man was probably a building superintendent, and here you are saying 'troooly' and 'smahshing'. 'The warmth was there,' he was explaining. 'Not in words. But in a million tiny gestures. The camera really doesn't lie, you know.'

'You saw this warmth in the dailies they show?'

'Definitely.'

'Who else saw it? Besides you and Lindsay?' In his silence, I could feel Santana's embarrassment. So I changed the subject before he could start resenting me. 'What about your work? Was Sy happy with it?'

Santana let go of his wedding ring and glanced up. 'Other than our disagreement over Lindsay, I think he was pleased. This was only our third week of shooting.'

'Did he ever have it out with you over how you were directing Lindsay?' More silence. 'Come on. Why should I hear a lot of fancy stories from third parties when I should hear the plain truth from you?'

'He said . . .' He shook his head as if refusing to give words to the unspeakable.

'What?'

'He said if Lindsay didn't start showing some real warmth . . .'

'He'd do what?'

'He'd replace me with someone who would be able to . . .'

'Say it.'

'He was . . . crude. What do they say about men like Sy? You can take the boy out of Brooklyn, but you can't take the Brooklyn out of the boy. He said, and I quote: "Give her a kick in the clit and get her to act like a real woman." '

'End quote,' I said.

'Oh, yes indeed,' he agreed. 'End quote.'

I wasn't really sure why Nicholas Monteleone was such a famous actor. It's not that he was bad-looking. Dark-brown hair, matching eyes. Big lips that critics probably called sensuous. And for a slim guy, lots of muscles, even in unnecessary places, like his forearms, as though he moonlighted as a blacksmith. If he'd worked in Homicide, he'd be second or third best-looking. But that someone was paying him – a million bucks a movie because he was such a hunk? I'd seen a couple of his pictures, and he'd never looked like a leading man to me. He had no intriguing dark corners; despite his sleepy, heavy-lidded eyes, he was all sunshine and light.

But he did look like his part in *Starry Night*: a playboy. His thick, almost shoulder-length hair was moussed back on the sides. He'd rolled up the cuffs of his pale-pink shirt just once, and miraculously, they stayed that way. But sitting in the Xerox/coffee room, Nick wasn't playing it smooth. More: Forget I'm a world-famous star. I'm a regular guy. Come on, let's be friends!

Temporary friendship was fine with me. He seemed genuinely good-natured, and what the hell, it's nice to have a movie star trying to grin his way into your heart. But for all his pleasantness, Nick Monteleone didn't seem to know anything worth knowing. Had he seen Sy angry? Hmmm. No, didn't think so. Had anyone been angry at Sy? Ummm, not that I know of. That type of thing for twenty minutes.

'Uhhh,' he finally said, 'I know this is a serious business, and I'm probably acting like a self-centered asshole, but I've gotta ask. By any chance did you happen to catch me in *Firing Range*? I played one of you guys.'

'Yeah,' I told him. It wasn't anything I'd go to the movies for; I'd caught it on cable, although I wasn't about to tell him that. 'You were very good.' In fact, he had gotten a lot of it right: the camaraderie of a homicide squad, the compulsive twenty-four workdays and, especially, the fatigue. But he'd worn a shoulder holster – which hardly anyone I know wears – and he'd been physically slow, almost clumsy. By the time he'd have drawn his gun, he would have been dead about forty seconds; he hadn't moved right. And now, watching him, I realized he couldn't even sit right. He was doing the relaxed, manly, lean-back-on-the-two-rear-legs-of-the-chair, when suddenly he lost his balance and almost crashed over backward. He saved himself, barely, but couldn't admit defeat by bringing the chair down on all four legs, so for a minute his feet did a hysterical cha-cha until he regained his balance. Forget his expensive muscles; I saw that Nick had the co-ordination of a Frankenstein windup toy. When he was a kid, the guys probably muttered, 'Not Monteleone!' when they were picking teams.

'Did you get what my character was about?' he asked. 'I mean, did *you* buy him?'

'Sure.'

Actually, thinking about it, I remembered shaking my head, wondering how come this white Chicago homicide lieutenant (in movies, homicide-cop heroes are always lieutenants) had a combo black-New York-Rambo accent: Yo, mothafucka, put that .38 (which came out like 'dirty-eight') on the table and get those hands up high. *Now*, putz.

'I mean, you probably think I'm just another narcissistic actor – and you're probably right – but I am just honestly curious: Could I have been someone you work with?'

What he wanted, I realized all of a sudden, was unconditional acceptance. Not just as my friend. As my colleague. I have to love him totally – and prove my love – or he wouldn't open up to me. So I gushed. 'You know, it was the goddamnedest thing! You really were one of us,' I told him. 'No shit, you could have had the desk next to mine at Headquarters.'

Nicholas's entire body eased. He let up on his macho chair routine. He stretched out his legs, crossed his feet at his ankles. He was wearing some kind of step-in shoes made from lots of thin strips of leather; they probably had some foreign name my brother would know.

'Tell me about dailies,' I asked him, now that we were practically best friends, to say nothing of partners. 'What are they exactly? The whole day's worth of film?'

'The film has to be processed, so what you're seeing is the footage shot the day before. All the takes. The director and the editor sit in the back and talk – whisper, actually – about which take is good, which isn't, what coverage they'll use, what kind of light and color corrections they'll want to order.'

'Who else goes to them?'

'Actors. Sometimes. Personally, I'm *super*analytical about my own work, and I like to see what everybody else is doing too. You know. Like how is my lighting? My costume? My makeup?'

'Did Lindsay go to dailies?'

Nicholas compressed his big lips. 'No. She always rushed back to Sy's house to work out. Swam laps in his pool. Had to keep those pecs toned.'

'How come she didn't want to see her acting? She's supposed to be smart. Isn't she analytical about her work the way you are?'

'The real truth? Lindsay is an egomaniac.' This said by a guy who went every night to watch his makeup. 'She's totally convinced she can gauge her performance as she gives it, so why bother to see herself? Besides' – Nicholas shook his head wearily – 'if she wants a reaction, all she has to do is look into Spanish Eyes after each take. You get what I'm saying? She can see her brilliance reflected.'

'She really got to Santana?'

'Got to him? She had him in a chain collar, on a leash. "Roll over, Victor. Good boy! Stay!" A *tragedy* for the rest of the company. The first week, Victor was very strong, full of ideas, energy, really exciting to work with. And actually giving Lindsay a rough time because from day one – well, day three or four – he was under the gun. Sy was not happy with Miss Keefe's work. Naturally, Lindsay being Lindsay, she *immediately* picked up that the balance of power had shifted – away from her. She needed a new ally. So she sniffed out Victor's weakness. *That's* her greatest gift, finding a guy's sensitive area.'

'What was Santana's?'

'Oh . . . being allowed to live in Movieland. I mean, Victor Santana was a damn good cinematographer and then moved to directing. He's directed two really well-received films, right? But beneath his "I'm *so* sophisticated" façade he's still wide-eyed about being in the business. Deep down, he can't even believe he made it out of East Harlem. And here's Lindsay, with her classical-theater background and her Commie Chic reputation and her half-naked *Vanity Fair*. Supremo nympho. The only guys who get into her are *major* lefties – or very heavy hitters with a net worth of at least fifty mil. So Victor thinks: If the same woman who screws the world's most interesting men – that Latvian novelist, Fidel Castro's minister of defense, Sy Spencer – well, if she wants to screw me, I must be in their league.'

'How did she get Sy? What was his weakness?'

'Oh, easy. Sy was the ultissimo intellectual snob. And even though she manages to take off most of her clothes in every movie she makes, Lindsay is still considered a very serious actor; she's convinced everybody she's getting naked as an *hommage* to the First Amendment. She gets brilliant reviews in all the right little magazines – the ones with French names and cheapo paper – and the big ones too. And she was politically correct on Nicaragua before anyone else knew you were even supposed to think about a Nicaragua. Also, she's a genuine beauty. No plastic surgery. And that for-real blonde hair.'

'No shit. The hair's real?'

'I've been told by highly placed sources that the bottom – it's a match.'

'Wow.' Then I said: 'Okay, we'd better get back to the dailies business. Did Sy see them all the time?'

'He had to. First of all, he genuinely cared. And also, they were the only way to monitor his investment.'

'Did he ever say anything about being dissatisfied?'

'No. I mean, it depends on the director, but usually it's not just the inner circle at dailies. There's the director of photography, the writer, cameramen, sound men, assistant directors, production assistants, hair and makeup, set designer. The whole cast and crew, if they feel like it. Usually about fifteen people show up, sit around, stuff their faces with trail mix and watch. So Sy – who prided himself on his classiness – wouldn't sit and bitch about Lindsay in front of an audience.' The skin around Nicholas's eyes glistened, almost raccoonlike, in the fluorescence. At first I'd thought it was some weird trick of the light. Then I realized it was face cream.

'So how did you know he wasn't happy with her?'

'Well, one day about a week ago, we'd been shooting *very* late. Hardly anyone came to dailies. Most people, Santana included, were wiped; they got the hell out the second after the lights came on. I was kind of hanging around, wanting to get a minute with Sy to talk about something – '

'What?'

'I forget. I'm sure it was nothing important. In any case, Sy starts letting loose to a few of his people. Not loud, and not even angry, which shows you how under control he was, because when you looked at Lindsay up on that screen it was like looking at Big-Tit Barbie. I mean, not one single spark of life. Anyway, Sy was supercool, just kidding about the scene and what a fortune it was going to cost to have an effects man add lightning, and did we really need lightning. Everybody started talking about lightning.

All of a sudden, Sy laughs and says how the best thing that could happen to this movie would be if lightning struck *Lindsay.* Then he said, "Just kidding." But naturally, everybody knew what he meant.'

'What did he mean?'

'If anything really happened to her? It's what the moneymen always say when one performer is crapping up a movie; if lightning struck, the completion guarantors – the insurers – would have to pay so they could begin production again with another actress. Sy was being lighthearted, but the subtext was: Forget the two-hearts-that-beat-as-one shit; he wished to hell he could be rid of her.' Nicholas paused. He was working up to something big. Inhale. Exhale. Inhale. Finally, he got it out: 'Can I call you Steve?'

I wasn't any actor, but I flashed my most engaging cop-friend smile. 'Yeah, sure.'

He smiled back. 'And you call me Nick. Now, Steve, just between us. About Sy's wanting to get rid of Lindsay. This last week, I think Sy *might* have been taking meetings off the set.' Nick had heavy eyebrows. He lifted them significantly. 'Do you get my drift.'

'He had someone else?'

'I'm not sure. But you could see Lindsay trying too hard to please him, and him not interested in getting pleased. I mean, she'd put an arm around him, and he'd put his arm around her. The movements were right, but hell, I'm an actor. Why do I get the big bucks? Because I'm intuitive. I *know* body language, and his was saying, "I have a headache tonight, dear." '

'Maybe he was just upset about her performance.'

'Maybe. But the first two weeks, he'd always be sniffing around her, hanging around the set most of the day. He knew then that she wasn't doing her best work, but he was so goddamn hot for her he couldn't be angry. I mean, you should have seen him: canned heat. But suddenly he's looking at his watch. He's leaving by eleven.'

'Did you hear any talk – vague rumors, even – about this from anyone?'

'No. It's just my theory.' Nicholas the Graceful stood up, stretching his arms, and – whammo – slammed his hand against the wall.

He sat down again and pretended his knuckles weren't throbbing. 'Listen, can I *really* trust you, Steve?'

'You bet.' I leaned forward and gave him a light, male-bonding arm punch. 'You know you can.'

'You know Katherine Pourelle?'

'The actress? Yeah, sure.'

'This is not for public consumption, but I used to have a thing with her, when we were both starting out. She was living with this guy from ICM. Her agent, in fact. Well, she was more than living with him. She was married to him. Anyhow, we had this big love, big breakup, big hate. But last winter we met in Vail. New husband – real estate developer. New agent. But you know what goes down. We stopped being silly and became . . . I guess you'd call it friends.' I assumed what he was trying to tell me was that he fucked Katherine Pourelle in Vail while her husband was out schussing. I gave him what I hoped was a knowing smile. 'Well, I got a call from her Tuesday night. From LA. She wanted to know what was with the production. At first I thought she'd heard about how lousy Lindsay was doing and just wanted to dish. Kat *hates* Lindsay and *loves* to dish. She did a play with her, years ago. Everybody who ever worked with Lindsay *loathes* her. Fine, I figured, so we talked about Lindsay and Santana, how he was her first non-Commie Hispanic. Oh, and about how Lindsay always closes her eyes when the director is talking, like she's concentrating on the voice of God, and how you wish you could smack her. Anyway, we had this long, really great talk, but there was something left unsaid. I could *sense* it. I mean, Steve, I earn my living by being open to feelings.'

'Right,' I said encouragingly.

'So I said to her: "Come on, Kat. Tell me what you heard." So she makes me swear not to tell a soul. She'd gotten a call from Sy that morning!'

'And?'

'He asked if she would give *Starry Night* an overnight read. *Super*secret. Do you get what I'm saying?'

'He wanted her to look at the part Lindsay was playing?'

'You got it!' Nick said. 'I think Sy knew that this was a potential twenty-million-dollar catastrophe. *And* I think he'd also found himself someone with blonder hair, or *plus grande* boobies. Lindsay had lost her hold on him. You know what, Steve? I think Sy was getting ready to pull the plug on Lindsay.'

When Lynne took me on, she knew we had a lot going for us. I wanted what she wanted: love, companionship, a family, plus – since she seemed to average one marriage proposal every two weeks – a chance to stick it to her stick-up-the-ass family. But in taking me on, she knowingly, willingly and of her own free will bought the whole package: recovering alcoholic (to say nothing of a guy with a former fondness for pot, hash, barbiturates and heroin), recovered fuck-arounder, about-to-be-old fart, compulsive runner, workaholic. Her acceptance of me was absolute, unquestioning.

Was she perfect? No. She was a pain in the ass about order, the type who in sixth grade would have won Neatest Three-Ring Binder. I was neat; she was nuts. She had to restrain herself from making the bed the minute I got up to go to the bathroom. She actually inspected her pencils every night to make sure they were all sharpened for the next day. Lynne's idea of wild spontaneity was going out for a nude moonlight swim – after she finished her lesson plan but before the eleven o'clock news. Still, as much as I bitched about it, deep down, her order comforted me. I needed a structured life filled with perfect pencil points and lights out immediately after Johnny Carson's monologue. Her imperfections turned out to be virtues.

So why was I less than wild with happiness? Why couldn't I accept Lynne without reservation, the way she'd accepted me? How come I couldn't say: Sure, she's a little serious, but who gives a shit with that hair, those legs? Why was I wasting time worrying that I wasn't one hundred percent ecstatic? Wasn't ninety-nine percent enough? What was wrong with me? She had five million sterling qualities. Why was I zeroing in on the one she lacked? Why the hell was I waiting for Fun?

It wasn't that Lynne didn't have a sense of humour. She did. But it was a sense of other people's humour. She'd smile whenever I'd say something even mildly clever. She'd laugh at Eddie Murphy and Woody Allen movies, at my friend Mary McCormack's stupid minister-rabbi-priest jokes (where the priest, naturally, always got the punch line) and at any attempt at comedy by any member of grades K through 6 at Holy Spirit Academy, especially her kids, the ones with learning disabilities.

What Lynne lacked was liveliness. I knew it wasn't fair to hold it against her. It was like saying to a woman, I want you to be five foot two and built like a brick shithouse, when she is, in fact, tall and willowy.

Still, I couldn't shake the low feeling that had come over me on the blanket in my backyard the day before. More then disappointment, less than dread. I didn't know what the hell it was. But there I was, taking a phone break, my feet up on the Xerox machine, making it worse – giving her an opening I knew she didn't have the capacity to fill. 'Okay, who do you think is sexier? Me or Nicholas Monteleone?'

And as Lynne, predictably, was responding, 'You,' I found myself ashamed of myself forwanting: 'Are you *kidding*? Nicholas Monteleone!'

She asked: 'Is he a nice person?'

'Yeah. Friendly; a good talker for somone who speaks other people's lines for a living. When I finished questioning him, I felt: Too damn bad he has to leave; he's great company. But he's so terrific that you start wondering whether it's him or it's an act. Like, if he thought that running around the room and imitating an aardvark would put him in a better light with Homicide, would he forget the congeniality bit and start licking up ants?'

'What do you think?'

'Ants,' Isaid. I looked at my watch. It was after five. 'Listen, honey, were you counting on lobster?'

'No, but that's what you told me you were counting on.'

'Did you melt the butter?'

'No, of course not. And you didn't buy the lobsters. I know you. I know you so well that right now I know I'm going to have a Lean Cuisine and then about ten you'll pop in – just to say hello.'

'I'm a very friendly guy.'

'Guess what? You won't be able to be too friendly. My roommates are home tonight.'

'Shit. All right, if I get finished by ten, ten-thirty, can I pick you up and take you over to my place?'

Just as Lynne was saying, 'Okay, but not too late a night, because I have a huge pile of test results for next year's kids I have to go through,' a Southampton Village cop appeared at the door with a surprise guest: Gregory J. Canfield.

Gregory gaped at the room, slack-jawed, trying to register everything, as if the decor – including the brown-stained hot plate of the Mr Coffee machine and me with my feet up – was going to be the subject of his final in Advance Set Design at NYU film school. Now that there was no corpse to upset his delicate balance, he was Mr Movie Man.

I said, 'People. Speak to you later,' to Lynne and 'Thanks' to the cop who'd shown Gregory in. Then I hung up, swung my feet off the Xerox machine and told Gregory to sit. But he barely got through the door when he stopped short. You could see his mind moving in for a close-up; he stood before the bulletin board, staring at a yellowing FBI Most Wanted list, at hand-printed signs offering Doberman-mix puppies, an '81 Datsun 280 ZX and a model 12 Winchester pump-action shotgun, probably wishing someone else from NYU was there to share this Moment of Authenticity.

'Okay, now you know what lower middle class looks like, Gregory. Time to sit down.' He did. 'You're here to help me. Right?'

He nodded. He looked slightly less repulsive than the day before, mainly because instead of baggy shorts, he was wearing baggy slacks. His skeletal white legs, with their bulbous kneecaps, were covered. 'I remembered what I couldn't remember last night.'

'Great,' I replied. I waited. He was staring at my holster, which was clipped onto my belt. 'You remembered something?'

'You asked me if there were any threats made to Sy Spencer.'

'And?'

'I don't know if you'd classify this as a threat. I mean, a genuine threat.' Gregory hesitated. Now he was gazing at me with the same passionate intensity he'd directed at the bulletin board. He'd obviously decided I was the star of this movie. He flushed. He fidgeted. He beamed at me. I was his True Detective.

'Listen, Gregory, anything you think is even remotely threatening – a dirty look – is something I want to hear about.'

'Did you know Sy had an ex-wife who lives in Bridgehampton?'

My heart gave a thump. I sat up, alert. Damn it, I'd been right. There was something about her. 'Bonnie Spencer,' I said. His face fell. 'Hey, if by this time I didn't know Sy had an ex in the neighborhood, what the hell kind of detective would I be?' Gregory still looked like he was debating whether or not to be clinically depressed. 'Now come on. You're my key man in this investigation. Okay, I gave you a name: Bonnie Spencer. But now it's your job to fill me in.'

'Well, Sy married her right at the beginning of his career as producer. She'd written the scenario . . . That's another term for screenplay. It's more common in Britain. In any case, she'd written a movie called *Cowgirl* in the late seventies. Unpretentious film. Her credit was Bonnie Bernstein.'

That big Utah jockette didn't strike me as a Bernstein. 'Had she ever been married before Sy?' I asked.

'I don't know.'

'Okay, go on.'

It's funny; as he was talking, I realized that Bonnie had been on my mind since I'd left her that morning. I couldn't shake the images I had of her. One was the real Bonnie as I'd seen her. The other one was even more vivid, and unconnected with reality; she was in some sort of sleeveless thing, a dress or a tank top, that bared part of her broad shoulders. I could see her arms and shoulders: strong, smooth, with the sheen of a deep tan. Incredibly silky skin. It was really, well, an exciting image – and a strange one, bacause the bare-shouldered Bonnie in my mind's eye was so incredibly desirable, and really had nothing to do with the big girl in the big T-shirt I'd interviewed.

'The marriage broke up,' Gregory reported, 'and she went into total eclipse as a writer.'

'How come?'

'I don't know.'

Maybe, I thought, Bonnie Spencer reminded me of someone else, some large, bewitching girl out of my past. That made sense. But my house was no more than four miles from hers; I could have passed her one summer evening on one of my runs and focused in on her best few square inches. Or maybe I'd give her a half second of consideration in my bar-hopping days, before moving on to someone better. Who the hell knew? In all those years of drinking – especially toward the end – there were black holes in my memory. We could have met at a cocktail lounge and discussed Truth and Beauty all night, and it would be a total blank.

'From what I've heard,' Gregory went on, 'Bonnie is pretty much of a zero. Her only real significance is that she used to be married to Sy. But even then, I probably wouldn't have heard about her if she hadn't come to the set.'

Right. Bonnie had mentioned she'd dropped in to see Sy. 'What happened?'

Gregory rubbed his palms together as though he was heating them up for a passionate prayer. 'One of the other PAs came running over to me, saying Sy's ex-wife was there and what should he do. But he couldn't do *anything*, because she was right there behind him. She'd *followed* him. To see her, she's this very plain Jane type, but you could understand how she must have learned a thing or two from Sy, because before I could say a word or go get one of the assistant directors, she walked right past me and knocked on the trailer door. I said, "Excuse me, miss, but that trailer is *private*. I'll have to ask you to please wait over by the craft services table." Well, that *second* Sy opened the trailer door. He took one look at her and . . . you would not believe his face!'

'Tell me.'

'Beet red, and I mean b-e-e-t. She said something like "Hiya, Sy!" as if she expected him to give her this major warm welcome, which, of course, he didn't.' Gregory drew in his sunken cheeks. he seemed to be waiting for applause.

I didn't clap. 'Gregory, you came in to tell me about a threat.'

'Oh. Right. Yes, well, Sy gave her this *withering* look and said, "This is not a Bonnie Bernstein production. You know you do not come onto a set unless you are invited." And believe me, the way he said it was not exactly *sotto voce*. I mean, Sy could be *heard*.'

Shit. Even though I knew there was something wrong about Bonnie, I felt lousy for her. 'How did she react?' I asked.

'Jolted. Absolutely jolted. I mean, for whatever reason, she had been expecting a red carpet. She must have thought he'd welcome her with open arms and—'

I cut him off. 'The threat, Gregory.'

'Right. Well, she stood there for a minute, paralyzed. I mean, you can *imagine* the humiliation. For a second, I thought she might cry. But she didn't. No. Quietly, and I mean *quietly*, like probably I was the only one close enough to hear, do you know what she said to him? She said, "Sy, you've just been a rotten bastard for the *last time*!" That's what she said. *Days* before he was murdered. And then she just turned her back on him – and walked away!'

# *Chapter Six*

Jesus, what a day! Trying to dope out what was under Lindsay's sheet of ice, behind Nicholas Monteleone's cloud of congeniality. Feeling upset that my brother was so upset, wondering if he'd be able to find another job. Seeing Germy again, seeing my past. Lynne.

And Bonnie Spencer. The hardest part of the whole day. Ever since the morning, I'd been fighting her off – the desirable, bare-armed fantasy Bonnie and the real Bonnie, big, plain. Okay, so with fantastic, gold-medal thighs. But Iwanted her out of my mind, and she wasn't cooperating.

After Gregory had gone – although not before he'd announced, in front of about ten guys in the squad room, that I was a 'fascinating combination' of Scott Glenn and Keith Carradine – I lifted the phone to call Marty McCormack, at home. I wanted to fill him in, ask him if he thought I should bring Bonnie in for questioning, scare her a little. Actually, I just wanted to talk to a friend.

But all of a sudden, I'd started feeling . . . It's hard to describe, but every drunk knows the sensation: a slight tightening in the throat, a fluttering of the heart, and then weariness, edginess. It all happens in that micro-second before your brain says, Hey, I *really* would love a drink. I hung up the phone and drove over to Westhampton Beach.

And at five o'clock, I was sitting on a brown metal folding chair in the basement of the Methodist church in the usual repulsive fog of cigarette smoke at an AA meeting. But I seemed to be doing everything I could to avoid making the old searching and fearless inventory of myself. Instead, I found myself easing into a real hot reverie – reliving my morning meeting with Bonnie, then improving on it. I was in her kitchen again, moving in on her. Her back was pressed against the sink, but now I was rubbing up against her. I kissed her, and she let out a cry of relief and desire and put her arms around me. Her arms felt so incredibly wonderful.

I became aware that I was breathing a little too deeply, crossing, uncrossing my legs. I forced my attention straight ahead.

The smoky basement haze softened the too-lipsticked dark-red mouth of the speaker. Her name was Jennifer. She had wide maroon makeup stripes on her cheeks and dark-brown eye shadow that went up to her eyebrows. But although she looked hard, she didn't sound it; she had that high, silly, sweet voice of a girl who asks you to make a muscle and then squeals 'Oooh!' She couldn't have been much older than Lynne.

'See, I used to empty out the saline solution for my contact lenses and put vodka in the bottles!' Jennifer explained. We all laughed, applauded; that was one we hadn't heard. 'Anyhow, I kept three bottles in a drawer at work. Two or three times a day I'd start blinking like crazy and rubbing my eye.'

Usually I hated meetings in the summer. Somehow, when I wasn't looking (or was too drunk to notice), AA had become a nonalcoholic version of a singles bar. Dingy church basements were packed with yuppies exchanging degradation stories and slipping each other business cards. Despite all warnings, pickups were common. 'Hi, babe. Need a sponsor?' AA had turned into the new Hamptons scene, and locals like me felt like . . . well, locals. Jennifer giggled. 'I'd grab a bottle of saline solution, toddle down to the bathroom and chug the vodka! And after work, I'd sneak the bottles into my purse, take them home and refill them for the next day!' This meeting wasn't all that bad; along with most of the others, I nodded with recognition at Jennifer's desperation and – despite her lack of anything resembling intelligence – her enormous ingenuity. I thought: We're all so cunning when we're desperate to fuck ourselves over.

I stretched out my legs and leaned back in the chair, forcing myself to relax, to listen, understand, learn. But just as I was thinking an enlightening thought – about how so many drunks have this almost religious beleif in the superiority of vodka, its odorless innocence, its purity – Bonnie pushed her way into my head again.

Beneath that straight-shooter veneer, behind the savvy, self-effacing humor, what the hell was she? A *Fatal Attraction* psychopath pursuing Sy, hounding him to produce some hunk of junk she thought was a screenplay – or to get him to love her again? Or was she simply a no-talent loser who had barreled onto the set after pumping up her courage with cocaine or booze or some dopey assertiveness training book?

And what about the threat Gregory had overheard? Look, telling someone it's the last time he's going to be a rotten bastard is, to a homicide cop, somewhat less significant than a vague 'I'm gonna get you' or a specific 'I'm going to hack your balls off and make them into cuff links.' Still, when I'd interviewed her, Bonnie had tossed off her visit to the set in a couple of words, giving the impression that dear old Sy had asked her to drop by just to be friendly: a little cheek-to-cheek air kiss, a little 'Oh, Bon, you must meet Johnny, our key grip,' a little chat about some dangling participle in her screenplay.

And what about her story about being invited to Sy's house, getting the fifty-cent tour? Why would a smart operator like Sy Spencer risk the Wrath of Lindsay by bringing home his tall-in-the-saddle ex-wife to have a look around the master bedroom suite with its king-size closets, its emperor-size bed? Why would he offer Bonnie a tour of a house that had to have pointed out to her: Sweetheart, did you get fucked over on alimony! Was he that insensitive? That much of a prick? Or had Bonnie pushed her way in there too? And why had she told me about it? Good old honesty? Or had anyone seen her, maybe making an unseemly fuss? rifling through drawers? taking something that didn't belong to her? Had she been smart enough to know we'd be dusting everything – from the doorknobs to the blade of Marian Robertson's Cuisinart – for prints and knew hers were there?

Goddamn Bonnie. It ticked me off that all day long I hadn't been able to get her out of my mind. When I thought about it, she was the one who'd ruined Lindsay Keefe for me. Here I'd been expecting at least a cheap thrill, and what happened? I'd actually gotten turned off because Lindsay, posturing in front of the window, had seemed so false after Bonnie's 'naturalness'.

Big deal. She was in great shape and she'd . . . I don't know. She'd amused me. But I knew, as I sat there, tuning out the AA meeting, that I was acting nuts, fixating on Bonnie. By any rational standard, I'd never had it so good. Lynne was great-looking, sweet, young. But there I was, eyes closed, imagining running my hands over the flawless satin of Bonnie's arms – even though, for all I knew, she could have clammy, fish-belly flesh or rough lizard skin, or her entire body could be dotted with dime-size brown freckles.

I wasn't sure what was going on. Had Bonnie Spencer gotten to me? Or had I gotten to me? Gregory, after all, had been right on target about her: a plain Jane. Barely nice eyes – okay, an interesting color. An ordinary nose. A forgettable mouth, most likely with chalky, premenopausal lips; I really hadn't noticed. So what the hell was I doing wanting to . . . I can't even say wanting to see her again. Just wanting her.

Forget reality. I wanted my fantasy too much to open my eyes: I had dropped my jacket onto her kitchen floor. My tie was unknotted, my shirt was open, and I was tearing off Bonnie's bra so I could hold her against me, skin to skin. Applause startled me. I looked up. Jennifer, smiling with lipsticked teeth, was stepping down.

Engaged-guy nerves. That was my problem. Definitely. After more than half a lifetime of drinking – and womanizing – of being a master self-deceiver ('Only three beers tonight') and a consummate liar ('Oh, sweetheart, oh, you're so beautiful, oh, I love you'), it was so hard to keep it simple.

Willie, the leader, a big local guy in a plaid shirt who was a motorcycle mechanic, stepped to the front. Years before, he'd gotten his teeth knocked out in a fight; his dentures looked as if they'd been molded for a giant; they made him lisp. 'Thith hath been a great meeting!' he boomed. 'Time to clothe now. Would all thothe who feel like it join me in the Therenity Prayer?'

Was it only that I was having the normal alcoholic's touble of keeping it simple? Or was I in deeper shit, really looking to self-destruct? To throw over Lynne, which equaled throwing ove happiness, stability, a chance to be a human being? Was I still drawn to oblivion?

Forty-five of us stood and held hands. I squeezed tight. I felt warm I'm-with-you squeezes back, even from the yuppie jerk in tennis whites on my right. I thought: *This* is what I'm here for. Support. I can't do it myself. I need these people. I need God. I need . . .

I couldn't fight Bonnie. Something is wrong about her, I thought. Plus, objectively, there is absolutely nothing about her to turn me on. And yet now I was imagining kissing her soft, warm skin.

'God grant me the serenity . . .' My voice was embarrassingly loud.

Maybe I couldn't keep it simple: Just admit she was one of those women who, despite the most commonplace looks, had always been an erotic genius, even now, even as she was getting too old for anyone to want. A not-homely, not-pretty woman you'd overlook on the street but who, in close quarters, knows exactly how to get to you. Or maybe she wasn't devious. Maybe she did it unconsciously: she gave off primitive, subliminal signals or secreted some subtle female animal smell. Whatever it was, I wasn't going to let it affect me.

'. . . To accept the things I cannot change,' I prayed. 'Courage to change the things I can; / And wisdom to know the difference.'

Amen.

On the basis of its architecture, my mother's house, an old place with weathered cedar siding and a deep front porch, should have been charming or quaint or inviting. But it wasn't. There were too many trees too close: overpowering oaks, dark, drippy maples, grim spruces; their humid shadows spooked the house. And inside . . . well, it was always dark, especially in the living room, with its never-quite-dry upholstery; sit there long enough and your pubic areas felt about to mildew. No wonder I'd gone off to Vietnam, come home for three days and then never gone back. But my brother had never moved out.

Oh, right, you could say, hearing that: He still lives with Mommy. But it really wasn't like that. Easton was no mama's boy. Sure, with his navy-blue blazers and golden color, he might look like some harebrained heir to a Southampton fortune. But in truth, he was very unindulged. My father had given him almost nothing, except an occasional unbankable belch, and in any case had cleared out soon after Easton's sixth birthday. My mother, although she clearly preferred him to me, spent every cent she had on upping her own Quality Quotient, not his; she would never pass up buying a hundred-dollar ticket to a benefit for hyperkinetic Maori Anglicans held on some rich socialite's lawn (with shrimp in sculpted-ice swan boats) in order to do somethig nice for her son. Still, Easton had inherited my mother's grand dreams, although unlike her, he had never lost touch with the truth. He was not the typical Bridgehampton local who falls in with the summer crowd; he did not get dizzy drinking rich people's champagne. No matter how much time he spent in their perfect houses, he knew he wasn't one of them, that he was, especially, poor and, in addition, not blessed with that mysterious personl magnetism that attracts money.

So forget Easton buying his own place, or even renting an apartment. Both assumed a steady income, and my brother understood that long-term job retention – unlike cutting lemon peels into translucent twists – was not one of his fortes. I'm sure he never actually sat down with my mother and said: Listen, I can play golf, tennis and croquet, sail a boat. I know the correct dress shoes to wear from Memorial Day to Labour Day. But for some reason I keep getting canned after six or eight months. So if you don't mind, I'm going to stay put here. Why go through the embarrassment of setting up housekeeping somewhere and then getting evicted? Right, Mom?

Actually, Easton's living at home suited them both. No rent for him, just whatever he could contribute, whenever. And living in the big house set far back from the road, he could pass himself off as a Bridgehampton blueblood. Who among his city slicker acquaintances would get out of their Porsches to inspect the house – and discover we did not own the adjoining farmland? Who, over the course of a lazy summer, would bother to check his credentials, to find out that his father had been not a gentleman farmer but a drunk given to pissing on the floor of the local tavern?

(I call Easton's friends acquaintances. Just like my mother, he lived for the summer people. From the time he got his driver's license, he ignored the kids at high school and hung out with a semi-social Southampton crew: the Daddy-is-on-Wall-Street-and-by-gosh-so-am-I fraternity. It didn't seem to matter who they were individually; they all had boats to invite him on, golf clubs to take him to, wives' college roommates to fix him up with. They were interchangeable: extremely tan, mildly wealthy and slightly stupid.)

Anyway, the domestic arrangement suited Easton. And I guess my mother liked having him around because he could do all the man jobs; mow the lawn, put up the storm windows, check the mousetraps in the cellar. She'd never been much of a farm wife, even when she'd had a farmer.

Living with Easton gave my mother an audience for her compulsive monologue no one else would be willing to listen to. She'd sit at the table, push her food around her plate, light up a cigarette and – puff, puff – talk about the French five-thousand-dollar dress Mrs Preston Cortwright had tried to return the Monday after her big party; the rumor that Mr Edward Dudley, husband of size-three Mrs Edward – puff, puff – had taken up with their Experiment in International Living seventeen-year-old fatso fräulein from Munich. Or – my mother would tap off the ash – how she herself had made all the right diplomatic moves and had *finally* been named deputy associate chairlady of the Southampton-Peconic Museum of Art's annual cocktail party.

My mother's pretentiousness, her coldness – her absolute nothingness – never got to my brother. Unlike me, he could listen to her expound on Quality without wishing she'd choke to death on one of her goddamn Protestant watercress sandwiches.

Not that they spent a lot of time together. My mother used the big back bedroom on the first floor, and Easton took over the second floor. I don't think either of them longed for more companionship. Okay, compared to me, Easton was my mother's pride and joy, but compared to what she had expected of him – the presidency of a major brokerage firm, senior partner of a Wall Street law firm – he was a loser.

But a well-dressed one.

Robby Kurz did a major double take after we rang the doorbell. 'Easton Brady,' my brother said to Robby, and shook his hand.

Robby stared at Easton. Then he blinked a couple of times, as if expecting his vision to clear. He had probably been imagining me minus two years, and that was sort of true. But he was also face-to-face with a gent in gray flannel slacks, a pale-blue Oxford shirt and a sapphire-blue V-neck sweater, a rich-looking Waspy guy who was combing back his hair off his forehead with his fingers – hair that was just slightly too long. Not hippy or scruffy hair, but hair that seemed to be saying: Forgive the length, but I just got back from sailing home from Bermuda.

Half an hour later, Robby was still sneaking fast, disbelieving glances from Easton to me. He sat at a folding card table across from Easton in my brother's sitting room; it had once been my bedroom. As a kid, Easton had used the table to build his model ships; now it was covered with a huge, square fringed gold cloth, like one of those scarves you see on pianos in old movies. It almost hid the table's skinny metal legs. I sat directly behind my brother, on a nice old cracked leather couch he must have picked up at some yard sale; the shrink at South Oaks had had one like it, the same dark brown.

My deal with Ray Carbone was that I could be at Easton's interview without being there. But every now and then my brother would turn his head and glance at me for reassurance as Robby questioned him about the cast and crew. What the hell: I'd nod, letting him know he was doing fine. Well, he was.

'What exactly were you doing in New York yesterday?' Robby was asking.

'I was meeting with our casting director. Going over deal memos and negotiating a price on some extra work we wanted done. Sy and Santana felt we had to cast the Colombian drug kingpin as threatening, but quietly threatening.

'You mean all the parts weren't filled yet, even after they'd started making the movie?' Robby asked.

'That's right.' Easton sounded casual, like someone who'd been in the business for twenty years instead of a few months. 'It happens fairly often. We knew we could always sign an actor we'd already read, but we were hoping for someone special. The problem was where to look.' I rested my head on the back of the couch's cool leather, crossed my arms over my chest and checked out my brother. Iwas impressed: no more of his sweaty, eager, fast-talking bullshit, like when he was selling houses or Jaguars or hand-knitted boat-neck sweaters. Easton had become a genuine movie guy. 'We'd seen just about every over-fifty swarthy actor in New York and California. No luck, but we weren't ready to give up. Well, not yet.' He really seemed to know what he was talking about. I was proud all of a sudden.

He kept plucking at the neck of his sweater, probably to realign the V in front. 'The casting director wanted to start looking at actors in Chicago, to farm the work out to her associate there. But the price she quoted us seemed out of line. Sy thought it would be better to negotiate with her in person than over the phone, but he couldn't do it. He was busy on the set and getting ready to go to LA, so he asked me to.'

'How long did that meeting last?'

'From before two until – I'm guessing now – three-thirty, four, I'm not sure. You could check with her.'

'Di you speak to Sy on the phone at all during that time?'

'No. I was going to drive over to his house after dinner, around nine, and tie up whatever loose ends there were.'

'Was he expecting any company for dinner?' I interjected.

'No,' Easton said. 'Just Lindsay.'

'Did you come straight back here after your meeting?' Robby asked.

'No. I went to Sy's shirtmaker to give him a swatch of Egyptian cotton Sy wanted to use and to pick up some other shirts that were ready.' I couldn't see my brother's face from the couch, but Easton must have smiled at Robby because, suddenly, Robby had on his super-toothy grin. 'Assistant poducer,' Easton continued, 'and swatch-carrier. My whole job was to smooth things out for Sy. I went to meetings, made phone calls, wheeled and dealed in a minor way. And even played errand boy.' He fell silent for a minute, then added solemnly: 'It was the best job I ever had.'

Outside my old bedroom window, the leaves on the oak tree were almost black against the blue-gray twilight. It's usually a down time for ex-drunks, but there I was, all of a sudden, feeling pretty up – about Easton.

My brother, obviously, had always had some inner aberration that had screwed up his chances at a career. But outwardly he'd been Mr Moderate. Balanced, temperate, neat, controlled. No fires burning in his soul. You couldn't believe he wasn't able to get a grip on his life, because he *seemed* so balanced. He did nothing to excess; when he drank, it was a watered-down Scotch or a couple of glasses of wine. When he drugged, it was one puff of a joint. Even the women he went out with were understated – to the point of invisibility; well-bred, well-dressed, with boobs barely bigger than their tiny noses.

But strangely, the movie business, famous for its bullshit, had managed to make Easton more real. He was much less pompous. Okay, still not the kind of guy you'd ask over for *Monday Night Football*, but friendlier, looser. A decent man instead of Charlotte Easton Brady's finely featured, immaculately groomed, elegantly dressed prig of a son. Maybe, I started thinking, after all these years, we could really be brothers. Lynne would say, Let's have Easton to dinner, and I'd say, Great.

'Why was Mr Spencer going to Los Angeles?' Robby asked.

'He had four or five different projects he was interested in. He had a lot of meetings lined up.'

I broke in. 'Isn't it a little unusual for a producer to leave town while his movie is being made?'

Easton turned around, giving me the profile that demonstrated who'd gotten the best of the genes. 'Not necessarily. Sy was executive producer. He had what's called a line producer to supervise the whole production, take care of the day-to-day problems. And he had me to put out smaller fires. So he could afford to get away for a couple of days.'

'Except things were pretty lousy here.'

'What do you mean?'

'The business with Lindsay.'

'Lindsay.' Easton seemed a little ill at ease, as if by confirming trouble he'd be letting Sy down. 'I see you've heard the rumours.'

'We heard about the lousy dailies,' I told him. 'Were they that bad?'

He shrugged. 'I can't be a hundred percent sure, Steve. I haven't been in the business long enough to really know. I mean, when Sy asked, I pretended to have an opinion and crossed my fingers and hoped I didn't sound like a complete fool. But whatever reactions I have, they're still pretty much the same as the man who buys a ticket and sits in a multiplex with a box of popcorn: either bored or enjoying himself. As far as I could see, Lindsay was doing all right. And she looked – there's no other word – breathtaking.' Robby started his compulsive Lindsay nodding. 'But I *think* I understood what Sy was talking about. Whenever Lindsay was on the screen, I wasn't riveted – except by her beauty. I looked, but I didn't really listen. My attention wandered. And to be honest, it probably would have wandered more if I hadn't been involved in the movie.'

'But she wasn't a disaster?' I inquired.

'Not her acting *per se*. But I think from Sy's point of view the movie itself was a disaster-in-progress, because the audience *had* to love this woman. And even I could see you did not love Lindsay in those dailies. Actually, you didn't even like her all that much. You just didn't care.'

Robby took over. 'Was Sy going to Los Angeles to speak to Katherine Pourelle about taking over Lindsay's part?'

Just before Easton whipped his head around to face Robby, I saw his reaction: absolutely stunned at how far we'd come so fast. 'Jesus, who told you that?' Neither of us responded. Finally, Easton spoke. 'Well, congratulations! Whoever your source was knew what he was talking about.' He turned back to me, really curious. 'Who told you?'

'I can't, East.'

'Oh, right,' he said. 'Sorry. I didn't mean to be pushy . . .' He smiled. 'Well, not too pushy. In any case, Sy *was* going to see Katherine Pourelle. But as far as I was concerned, it was just a typical Sy maneuver. You see, he would let word leak out that he was speaking to Pourelle and her agent. That would put the fear of God into Lindsay, make her wake up and start – well, start acting. But I swear to you Sy *never* would have fired her.'

'He told you that?' Robby asked, then cleared his throat. He was getting hoarse. It had been a long day, and he looked like one exhausted Howdy Doody. Even the perky points of the yellow handkerchief in his breast pocket had gone limp.

'No. But you see, I'd gotten to know Sy. He could be objective, tough, even callous about Lindsay the actress. But he was completely vulnerable to Lindsay the woman. She had an enormous hold over him.'

'Sex?' I asked.

'Yes,' Easton responded.

'Was it just a sex thing, or did love enter into it too?' Robby inquired.

'It must have been both.' Easton lowered his head. His shoulders rose and fell with each of his sighs. And all of a sudden it hit me. Easton, like Sy, was being objective about Lindsay's performance – but not about Lindsay herself. He couldn't hide it. He'd actually fallen for her.

'It's not just that she's beautiful, or talented or intelligent,' he was explaining, trying to sound detached, 'although she's all those things. She has a way of getting to a man.' Robby was bobbing his head again: Yes! Yes! Yes! 'Sy . . . Sy needed Lindsay too much to fire her.' I heard Easton swallow. He seemed to have needed her too. He had one hell of a lump in his throat.

'He needed her even if it cost him twenty million dollars?' Robby asked.

'*Yes.*'

But what about Nick Monteleone's theory that Sy had chilled on the fair Lindsay and was, in fact, getting his toes curled elsewhere after he left the set every morning at eleven? I though about those long, unblond hairs caught in the headboard in the guest room.

'Were you there for that conversation about if lightning struck Lindsay?' I asked.

Easton's posture went ramrod straight. Once again, he seemed amazed that we actually had been doing what we were supposed to be doing: being detectives. Finally, he said: 'God, you two are thorough! And . . . well, yes. I heard Sy say that. But that wishing Lindsay were out of the picture – literally – was just Sy's way of blowing off steam.'

'What do you mean?'

'She was a big disappointment, but he wouldn't have fired her. Trust me, Steve. There was no way he would have been able to cut her loose.' Easton's tongue came out to moisten his lips. 'He was helpless when it came to Lindsay.'

Normally, I would have gone after him, half kidding, half zinging it to him, saying: *Him* helpless? What about you, sucker? I'd have given him a lot of shit about falling for a movie star. But I wasn't going to embarrass my brother in front of Robby. Also, I realized that even if this was a hopeless crush, it was important; this was the first time in Easton's life where he was showing some passion. It was not something to laugh about.

'What about the other investors?' Robby asked. 'It wasn't just Sy's money, was it? What about Mikey LoTriglio?'

'Mikey!' Easton said. 'Yes, of course. He'd slipped my mind. God, you should see him. What a tough act. Makes Marlon Brando in *The Godfather* look like a pussycat.' He stopped and considered what he'd been saying. 'But maybe that's not fair. He has a thick New York accent. And he looks like such a . . . hood. Maybe that makes him seem tougher than he is.'

'Was Sy afraid of him in any way?'

Silence. Easton must have been chewing his lip over that. I peered around. There was a script on the coffee table in front of the couch. I picked it up. My brother turned at the sound of paper. He saw what I was holding. His body sagged; his poise deserted him. He seemed to have forgotten about Robby. 'See that script, Steve?' He sounded like a kid a few seconds from tears. 'Sy gave it to me Thursday, the day before . . . He handed it to me and said, "Our next movie, Easton. It just might make history." '

'I'm really sorry,' I said. 'Things were going great with him, weren't they?'

'I finally – ' He cut himself off, realizing Robby was there. 'My life was tied to his,' he said quietly. He took a deep breath, and when he spoke again he was the old Easton, aggressively cheerful. 'Well, I guess I'll have to beat the bushes, find something else.' He shook his head. 'I'd hate like hell to have to move to California, but I may have to. Be closer to the action, to people in the business.'

Oh, shit, I thought. Easton had lucked out with Sy. He'd found a patron who liked his Southampton style and who had the rare good instinct to trust Easton, to allow him to rise to all sorts of occasions, to prove himself. But Sy couldn't give a reference. And what the hell kind of résumé could my brother hand out in Hollywood? Failed car salesman? For years Easton hadn't even been able to sell madras Bermudas to congenital preppies. He lacked something – conviction, balls. What would he do in Los Angeles? How would he maneuver in a city of sharks?

'Uh, where were we?' Robby wondered. He was massaging the bridge of his nose as if it were some newly discovered acupuncture point that would induce bright eyes and a clear mind. Except it didn't work. Christ, he was wiped. I thought: Thirty years old is too young to get that tired that fast. Maybe that was why he was always trying to jump the gun, pushing for an arrest. The guy had no stamina. He couldn't keep it up for a long investigation.

'We were on Mikey,' I reminded him.

'Right. Mikey.'

'Sy did get . . . one edge when Mikey called,' Easton admitted to Robby. 'But "on edge" for you or me might mean losing our temper, biting our nails. For Sy, it was just a slight tightness in his voice. You'd have to know him quite well to pick it up.'

'Did he seem afraid?' Robby asked.

'I don't know. There was just that hint of tension. Although that in itself was a bit unusual. I mean, Sy never *got* anxiety. He gave it – to everybody. But every time Mikey would call, Sy would shake his head and mouth: "I'm out." '

While my brother talked, I opened the script. It said: 'Night of the Matador' and 'An original screenplay by Milton J. Mishkin.' I turned the page and read a little:

LOW-ANGLE SHOT of MATADOR, huge, commanding, menacing against black BG.

I am Roderigo Diaz de Bivar – El Cid. And I am Francisco Romero, seven hundred years later, piercing the bull with my sword.

SFX: Thunderous animal breathing. Is it the matador? Or the bull?

And I am Manolete, gored to death. And the young El Cordobes.

CAMERA RISES. BG brightens and WE SEE Matador in the center of the bullring, surrounded by PICADORS on horseback and BANDERILLEROS. He brandishes his red muleta.

I am Spain.

CAMERA MOVES IN to Matador's muleta for ECU and as we WE HEAR flamenco music:

I am man.

BEGIN OPENING CREDITS against red.

I thought: They couldn't pay me to read this shit, much less see it – which probably means it's a true work of art.

'Did Mikey LoTriglio call Sy a lot?' Robby was asking.

'The last week or so, yes. About two or three times a day.'

Robby began playing with the fringe on the scarf that covered the table, running his fingers through it. 'What were Mikey's calls about?'

'I gather he'd been hearing rumors that the movie was having problems. Sy kept denying it, of course.'

'Do you think Mikey made any threats?'

'I never heard his part of the conversation,' Easton said. 'But whatever his message was, Sy found it . . . disturbing.' He paused. 'Sy's upper lip would get those little beads of sweat. You can't imagine what that was like. Sy was *not* a man to sweat.'

Inducing perspiration is not, in the State of New York, grounds for arrest, but you couldn't tell that from Robby's face. Suddenly he was awake, alert. Mikey was his guy. You could see the gleam of handcuffs shining in Robby's eyes.

'Hey, easy, Robby,' I said.

'Steve, this is a good lead,' Robby responded, ignoring Easton, as if he were another cop – or a member of the family. 'Mikey's bad.'

'Sure, but he's no moron. Would he shoot Sy over a bad investment?'

'Come on. He's Mafia.'

'Yeah,' I acknowledged, 'but this doesn't look like their kind of hit. They tend to be more personal, more close-up than a couple of long-distance bullets from a .22.'

But Sy might have had other enemies, I thought: a pissed-off poet from his old magazine; an old show-biz connection with a grudge; some South Fork local he'd insulted – a gas station attendant, an electrician, a swimming pool contractor – some guy with a snootful of sauce and a pocketful of ammo. And what about Lindsay? Calculating, egotistical, arrogant, maybe ruthless, maybe about to be bounded in her dual role as star and concubine. Could she fire a rifle?

And, damn it: Bonnie. How much research had she done for *Cowgirl*?

'What about the ex-wife?' I asked Easton. 'There's some talk that Sy was developing her screenplay.'

Easton shook his head. 'No. Sy gave me her script fairly soon after I started working for him, before we were in production. Asked me to find some nice things to say about it. My guess is that when he told her no, he wanted to be able to say: "Oh, but the dialogue was so fresh, so honest." '

'How was the dialogue?'

'I don't know. Not horrible. But Sy said she was born forty-some-odd years too late, that she wrote 1942 women's B movies.'

'Did she ever call him?' Robby asked.

'Yes. A couple of times a week, as a matter of fact. And she dropped in on him on the set, which did *not* amuse him. I know; I was in the trailer with him. You know how cool Sy always was? Well, I thought he was going to have a fit.' Easton stopped. He turned around in his chair to face me.

'What are you thinking?' I asked my brother. 'Woman scorned?'

'I don't know,' Easton said thoughtfully. 'I'm not a cop. I don't know how to weigh these things. But, Steve, I have to tell you: I didn't like the look on Sy's face when he saw her. I had a feeling something was going on.'

# *Chapter Seven*

If I want to be on time, I had two minutes to make the ten-minute drive to Lynne's. So what did I do? I drove right to Bonnie Spencer's; parked around the corner and then stood diagonally across the road.

Her house was plain in that no-nonsense, almost severe colonial style – not much more than a large two-story box with a roof and chimney. But a big, soft willow stood in front, and, in the moonlight, the old gray shingles shone silver against the dark sky.

The curtains were drawn, although not so tightly that I couldn't see the blue flicker of a black-and-white TV. Jesus, what had I promised Lynne when I'd called from Southampton PD? That I'd be at her house by ten, ten-thirty? It was ten twenty-eight. I walked across the road and up the stone path toward Bonnie's house.

That Moose was some watchdog! There wasn't even a mild grrr until I rang the bell; then, through the long, skinny windows that framed the front door, I could see her tail going so fast it made her rear end shimmy.

The outside light went on. I stuck my hands in my pockets. I took them out. Finally, Bonnie walked into the front hallway. For a second I thought maybe I'd interrupted something that she and a guy had been doing with the TV on. But as she got nearer to the door I could see there was no guy. She had on baggy cotton sweats and a red sweater. No makeup, but then maybe she never wore makeup. Her hair was loose, down to her shoulders, but it stood up on the back of her head, as though she'd been lying on a couch for a couple of hours.

I tried to read her expression when she saw it was me. Relief that I wasn't some night-crawling creep, maybe mixed with some apprehension about what was I doing there again, and maybe – although it's a lot to read through a skinny window – anticipation. it could be that moving in on her that morning had worked.

Except, I thought, as the door opened, who needed it? I felt like such a jerk. I couldn't believe I had wasted a whole day fantasizing about this woman. 'I know it's late,' I said, before she could say anything, 'but this is a homicide investigation.'

'Uh, would you like to come in?' The corners of her mouth wiggled for a second, deciding whether or not to smile; she opted for not. Then she turned and led me toward the right, into the living room. She switched on a couple of lamps, turned off some old movie she'd been watching on her VCR.

I could see the indentation her head had made on a pillow on the couch. I sat down next to it; the cushion was warm. Moose stood by my legs, stretching her thick, hairy black neck, clearly contemplating the possibility of leaping up beside me. Finally, realistically, she lowered her big butt onto the floor, threw me the doggy equivalent of a come-hither look and, once again, lay down over my shoes. The girl may have turned out to be mediocre, I mused, but the dog was as fantastic as I'd remembered. I swiveled my foot back and forth, rubbing her belly.

Bonnie sat across the room from me, on a rocking chair. The room was nice – yellow and peachy pink and white – but not what I would have expected from her. Sure, it was comfortable, but it was a Manhattan interior decorator farmhouse. A room like this should be plain, nice at best, not charming. But it was all there: braided rag rugs on the pegged oak floor, old quilts, pillows made from more old quilts, samplers in frames and a lineup of old white water pitchers on the mantel. Plus, off to the left of the fireplace, a painted bellows big enough to inflate the fucking Goodyear blimp. She saw me eyeing it.

'When we bought the house, Sy got interested in American folk art.' To illustrate, she pointed out some shelves: books interspersed with wood decoys. 'If it looked like it could quack, he bought it. He even put in a bid on an 1813 hand-carved loom. What did he think he was going to do? Spend his weekends weaving? Anyway, then we had our first party out here. This famous book editor walked into the room, looked around and said, "*Very* cute!" The man was so mean! Why did he have to say that? But from that minute on, Sy hated the house.' I didn't respond; she filled in the silence, fast: 'So here I am – with a lot of ducks. Um, can I get you something? Coffee? A drink?'

'Why did you go to see Sy on the movie set?'

She took an instant too long to answer. 'Just being friendly. And I guess I felt some nostalgia for the good old days.'

'Between you and him?'

'No. Between me and the movies. Sometimes . . .' Her voice got a little scratchy. '. . . I miss it so much. The writing – writing something better than 'A yummy cloud of almost-silk." And I miss the people and – '

I cut her off before she could get into an 'I'm So Alone Blues' number. I didn't want to hear it. 'You went onto the *Starry Night* set. What happened? Was Sy happy to see you?'

'I guess you must already have the answer to that.' The lamplight made a patch of brightness on her dark hair, just where it grazed her shoulder.

'I want your answer.' I pulled my feet out from under Moose; the dog peered up at me, surprised at the sudden withdrawal of intimacy. 'What's the problem? Was he happy to see you or not? This shouldn't be something you have to think about.'

'He seemed upset that I came uninvited,' she said at last. 'Not furious, like he'd want to beat me to a bloody pulp and stomp on my head and – ' Suddenly her eyes grew wide with embarrassment. 'Oh, God, for a minute I forgot what you did for a living. I'm really sorry. I didn't mean to make fun of . . .'

'It's okay. You were saying he wasn't about to do you permanent damage.'

'Right. But he wasn't about to be polite and say: "Tsk-tsk, you might have called first, Bonnie, dear." '

'What was his attitude?'

'Something between – let's see – nonchalance and rage.'

'Do you want to be a little more specific?'

'He didn't yell.' I did a speed-of-light survey; her red sweater was just tight enough to show she had standard, conventional tits. If you took the entire female adult population of the world, Bonnie Spencer's tits would mark the median. 'But maybe that's because he was trying so hard not to spit.'

'If you were such great friends, why would he act that way?'

'I don't know. Maybe he was in the middle of a tantrum about something else and I just showed up at the wrong time.'

'Maybe.' I wanted to give myself a swift kick in the ass: to think that over the day I'd built up this Marlboro Man's sister to be an embodiment of sensuality.

And then Bonnie reached up and smoothed back her hair. For just a second, she held it up in a ponytail. The undersides of her forearms were pearly, flawless. I pictured her stretched out on the couch beside me, her head on the pillow, her arms lifted, showing off that soft skin. I'd bend over and kiss it. Run my tongue over it.

I coughed to clear my throat. 'Did you drop in on him to ask about your screenplay?'

'No.' She let her hair drop. The action was beautiful, graceful, like a slow-mo replay of a perfect catch. 'We'd gone over all his notes. I was working on the revisions.'

'And you say he liked it?'

'Yes.'

'Did you ever think he might be saying nice things about your work to lead you on?'

'Why would he do that?'

'The truth?'

'Go ahead.'

'Maybe he found you more interesting than your screenplay. Maybe deep down you sensed that and – '

Her face turned a hot pink. 'Let me clue you in to something. I am not one of those typical New York neurotic dames, just dying to believe the worst about herself. And Sy wasn't some sleazo who'd say, "Ooh, baby, love your montage." My work was good, and Sy liked it. I knew he did.'

'Hey, I'm not trying to hurt your feelings. It's just my job to probe. Okay?'

She calmed down. 'The fact is, Sy and I were friends. Look, I wasn't his type, not even when he married me, and ten more years didn't do much for me in the lusciousness department. I know what he went for. A Lindsay, someone breathtaking. Or someone wispy and intellectual and twenty-two from Yale. Or a jet-setty type with a French accent who could quote Racine – with hair under her arms and a château. I was his ex-wife; he had no reason to hand me a line. He knew better than anyone what I had to offer – and he'd already said no thank you.'

'What about for old times' sake?' She shook her head hard. Her hair swung softly. 'Bonnie, were you sleeping with Sy? Is that why you felt so free to drop by? Maybe just a nice, spontaneous gesture?'

'No!'

'Or maybe to let the world know you were back on the map?'

'No!'

'Because if you were, that wouldn't bring you under any suspicion.' Bullshit, of course. 'Here you were, two adults who knew each other very well, who liked each other . . .'

'Nothing personal, but that's a lot of bull.'

'Okay, no more questions,' I said, getting up and walking over to her. Moose, the town slut, stayed by my side. 'For now.' The I laid it on thick. Smile. Wink. Charm, charm. 'I'm sorry if I offended you.'

'It's all right,' she said, her voice softening. Charm, charm was working. She looked up at me; her eyes actually became a little misty, almost as she expected to be kissed.

'Good,' I said. 'Glad you understand.' I reached over and ruffled her hair. Too bad: the button on the sleeve of my sports jacket got caught in her hair. 'Sorry,' I said, really sincerely, and tried to get the button free. Her hair smelled of some spring flower I couldn't identify: lilac, maybe, or hyacinth. I grasped the button and got it away, but unfortunately it yanked on her hair. 'Listen, this doesn't count as police brutality.'

She smiled. A great, wide-open, western smile. 'I know.'

'See you around, Bonnie.'

When I got back to my car, I slipped four strands of Bonnie Spencer's hair into a small plastic envelope. Three had roots. Enough for a DNA comparison analysis.

I always hated making it with women who couldn't shut up. Listen, no guy minds an encouraging word here and there, a helpful suggestion, a sincere scream of enthusiasm. But for the longest time before Lynne came into my life, nearly every woman I picked up was a Gray Line tour guide of sex.

They'd all memorized the same script. About how the trip was going: Oh, it feels so wonderful. Oh, don't stop . . . Directions to the driver: A little harder. No, easy, slow. No, up higher, higher . . . And what tourist treat was just around the corner: I'm going to take you/it in my mouth (an offer I never sneezed at, since it embraced the twin joys of gratification and silence) . . . And of course, they'd always let you know when the tour was over: Oh, it's happening. Oh, yes. Wait, just a second. Oh, this is too much. Please, no. God, Jesus.

Lynne, though, was quiet. What a relief. Of course, she had the self-confidence of the young and the lovely: she knew she didn't have to keep up a monologue to hold a guy's attention. And she was quiet, also, because somewhere – maybe at Manhattanville College – she'd learned that nice young ladies do not shriek 'Fuck me harder!' when in the arms of gentlemen.

But that night, her quiet had some measure of the silent treatment. She was angry at me for ringing her doorbell at eleven-fifteen, saying, 'Oh, shit, I'm sorry,' when I saw she'd given up hope of seeing me that night and had gotten undressed. Plus she was pissed at herself for letting me go to her closet, grab her raincoat, put it over her nightgown and lead her out her door with a tired line like 'Please, I just want to be with you tonight.' She hadn't said a word in the car.

But she wasn't only getting back at me by being uncommunicative. As I unbelted her raincoat and eased it off, she reached over and turned out the bedroom light. She was denying me the pleasure of seeing her.

'You're really mad,' I said. I took my gun off my belt and laid it down on my chest of drawers gently, so she wouldn't be further put off by its offensive clunk. 'Why don't you say it?'

'All right. I'm angry.'

'Tell my why.'

'Because you just assume I'm always available to you, any hour, day or night. I understand that you work crazy hours. But you don't seem to understand that I have to make a life – a structure – for myself. No. You want sex, you want to talk, so you expect me to drop whatever I'm doing. That's not fair.'

'I'm sorry.' I came up beside her and slid my hands under the feathery cotton of her nightgown, easing it up and off. I pulled her to me. She was softening, but she wasn't yet at the point of offering assistance. I held her with one hand and took off my clothes with the other. 'I love you.' I waited. There was no 'I love you too' response.

Okay, a romantic sweep-her-off-her-feet gesture was called for. I was so goddamn tired. But I lifted her up, carried her to the bed and laid her down. A little risky in the dark, what with guys my age slipping disks, developing hernias. But Lynne was light, I was desperate and, hey, it worked. She didn't say 'All is forgiven.' She didn't say anything. But she reached up from the bed, felt for me and pulled me down beside her.

So in the blackness we started making love. Lynne's silent treatment wasn't so bad, I thought. Better, in a way, than her usual quiet, where she might say a couple of words; it enhanced the pleasure. I could concentrate on everything – the sound of her body against the sheet as she started to squirm, her breathing as it grew deeper.

This had potential; it might be more than a routine roll. But just as I was about to call out, 'Lynne,' I lost all sense of her.

I was no longer making love with my fiancée. I was screwing the way I used to: It didn't matter at all who it was beside me, on top of me, beneath me, just so long as it had all the stock parts. I just wanted to get it in and over with. And then . . .

Big surprise. Well, it was to me.

The faceless female disappeared. Bonnie Spencer was in bed with me. She was wild. The soft, stroking hands may have been Lynne's but the Bonnie in my mind had her legs wrapped tight around me and was clawing at my back. Then she groaned with pleasure, letting out the same animal sounds I was making. Louder. Her dark hair was spread out all over the pillow; the flower scent was intoxicating. As I entered Bonnie, she let out a sob. Oh, God, I thought, this is the best. I called out, 'I love you. Oh, God, how I love you!' and I heard Bonnie cry out, 'Help me!' as she started to come, and then, 'I love you so much.'

It was perfect.

It was over.

Lynne finally spoke. 'That was nice.'

'Yeah, it was.'

'Wake me at six. Okay? I want to get home early. I have a ton of reading I have to do.'

'Okay,' I said. Then I closed my eyes against the darkness.

I spent Sunday going over the lab and autopsy reports and doing my paperwork. Then, first thing Monday morning, I pushed open the heavy glass-and-brass door at five after nine and strolled right over to Rochelle Schnell, first vice-president of South Fork Bank and Trust, Bridgehampton branch.

'I respect your mind,' I told her, and sat on the edge of her desk.

'You gave me that line about twenty-five years ago.'

'Did it work?'

'No. Of course not. But I liked it that you tried.'

Rochelle was forty years old. I knew that because we'd started Sagaponack Elementary School together, in kindergarten, and since we'd been born two days apart, we'd had to share our class birthday party. (Her mother, Mrs Maziejka, was supposed to bring the cupcakes and mine the Kool-Aid, but since my mother worked, Mrs Maziejka had always brought both. She'd never bitched about it; in fact, she even wrote 'Rochelle!' in pink icing on half the cupcakes and 'Steve!' on the other half in blue).

Rochelle sat behind her immense wood desk in a dark-gray dress-for-success suit. But then – as she strode over to kiss me and say 'I haven't seen you around in months. You look fantastic!' – I noticed her skirt was one of those stretchy, midthigh things that look like an overgrown support bandage.

'Yeah? Well, so do you, Ro-chelle, except you've got a real

problem. No one is going to hand out their life savings to a banker whose skirt's so tight you can practically see her pudenda.'

'Don't bet on it. Now, what can I do for you? Or did you just drop in to check out my skirt?'

I put my hand on her back and guided her to her chair, then sat down across the desk from her. 'Off the record. I want to know if you have a depositor named Bonnie Spencer—'

Rochelle cut me off. 'Big no-no. You know I'm an honest woman. I can't even give you a name. I'll verify it with our lawyers, but I'm sure you have to give me a subpoena. Then, if she does have an account, I'll have to call—'

'All I want to know is if she has an account here. No details. Please. A personal favor, Rochelle. It's not like I'm some jerk you don't know.;

'No, you're a jerk I do know.' She exhaled slowly. Then she swiveled around in her chair, faced the computer terminal on her desk and put her hands on the keyboard. Her giant diamond ring, courtesy of Mr Schnell, who'd bought the bank to get her attention. sparkled; her long red nails clicked as she typed. 'Yes, she's a depositor.'

'Thank you.'

'You're welcome.'

'Tell me how much is in her account.'

'No. You're a cop. Comply with the law. And don't think you're going to charm it out of me. I've already told you more than I should. Not one more thing. Just go to the DA and get a subpoena.'

'But, Rochelle, with all that Bank Privacy Act shit, that means you're going to have to notify her that there's been an inquiry by a law enforcement agency.'

'Is that *so* terrible?'

'Yeah. Just hear me out. It's terrible because Bonnie Spencer is a genuinely nice lady and I don't want her to get hurt in this investigation. Her ex-husband—'

'Oh, *that* Spencer!'

'Yeah, well, the powers that be are getting a little antsy, and it would help if I could just find out – fast, without waiting for a subpoena and notification – that she really is as okay as she seems to be, that no big money was going in or out of her account. I'd like to see her name out of this. You know what I mean? This woman's a real sweetheart. She had nothing to do with a homicide. She had nothing to do with *him*. All I need are some numbers to back me up, so we can cross off her name. Time's a factor here. I don't want to risk some gung-ho first-year detective calling her employer and saying, "I'm from Suffolk County Homicide and I'm checking up on Bonnie Spencer." Please, Rochelle. Help me help her.'

Rochelle's nails went click-click again. 'She has a hundred and five in her checking account. There's regular activity, so I guess we're her banker.' Click. 'Six hundred thirty-four in a savings account, that last month had a balance of a little over seven hundred.' Click-click. 'And her Visa card . . . she hardly ever uses it.'

I pointed to the computer screen. 'What does all that tell you?'

'That her ex-husband was *very* behind on his alimony payments.'

'She wasn't getting alimony.'

'In that case, she's just plain poor.'

The only thing appealing about Bonnie's next-door neighbor, Wendy Morrell, was her name; it conjured up a dewy virgin gamboling in a field of clover. In fact, in the morning light, Wendy looked less like Snow White and more like the witchy stepmother – in an olive-green jumpsuit. She had a face full of those air bubble things that grow under the skin. There was one large one on her left cheek, and I found my finger reaching up toward my own cheek, maybe trying to perform a symbolic bubblectomy; I put my hand down at my side.

'I mean, naturally I've been reading everything there is to read about the murder,' she said, 'but in a million years it would never have occurred to me that *Bonnie* Spencer had any connection with *Sy* Spencer.'

Wendy Morrell was probably in her early thirties. Manhattan thin, a body that if seen in the Third World would evoke pity but that probably commanded admiration in the city. Under the wide gold bracelet on her forearm, you could see the outline of her radius and ulna. Wendy's hair was cut in that chopped-off style that only guys just out of basic training (or very, very beautiful women) should wear.

We stood by the front door of her modern house. She had not invited me in. Maybe she was an elitist bitch. Maybe she was embarrassed; houses like hers, million-dollar exercises in solid geometry, had, over-night, become Out on the South Fork. They'd been replaced by postmodern whiz-bangs, country houses so enormous that they seemed to have been built for a race of giants instead of the periodontists and pocketbook designers who lived in them. Wendy had planted herself smack in the middle of her doorway, as though afraid I'd elbow her aside in an attempt to see how rich people lived – or, if I was hip, to get a look at her hopelessly outdated high-tech kitchen and snicker at it.

'That those two Spencers lived on the same planet was a miracle,' she went on. 'I mean, I don't mean to denigrate her, but it's such a contradiction of style: elegance versus gaucheness. You know? Look, she goes running. I'm the last person in the world to be a spokesperson for jogging suits. Am I going to make a case for pastel sweatpants and matching zip-ups? I know this may not mean a lot to you, but if she's got a house in the Hamptons, not Kalamazoo or wherever she comes from, she should manage to have a little pride in her appearance, not wear clothes that look like she raided the boys' locker room at the end of the school year. I mean, *some* sense of appropriateness must have rubbed off from Sy.'

'You knew him?'

'Well, we were never formally introduced. But you know what they say: there are basically three hundred people in the world.' She suddenly realized she was talking to a member of the four billion minus three hundred, because she explained: 'That's a New York–Hamptons concept: You know there are certain places in SoHo or East Hampton and you'll walk in and there'll be Calvin Klein or Kurt Vonnegut or Sy Spencer. Sy happened to be a friend of a very dear friend. Teddy Unger. Commercial real estate. You know who he is? Well, he owns half of New York. The better half.

So even though we never got to meet formally, Sy and my ex-husband and I were all of the same world.'

Even if you stretched the definition of the Beautiful People beyond any rational limits, Wendy Morell would not have fit in.

'So what's with the ex-wife?' she demanded. 'Is she under suspicion?'

'No. This is strictly a background check. I'm just trying to get a sense of the sort of person Bonnie Spencer is.'

'I can't help you. I am not a neighbor type.' Wendy glanced over at Bonnie's, then at her own driveway, where I'd pulled my Jag all the way up, almost to her garage, so Bonnie couldn't see it from her house. She gave my car a suspicious look, as if it represented something nasty, sexual and, above all, unforgivably pushy, since it was not a car a cop should be driving.

'But maybe you might have picked up something, just out of the corner of your eye.' I suggested. 'Did she entertain guests with any frequency?'

'I wish I could give you a full report, but my days are *very* full. Believe me, I don't spend my time watching Bonnie Spencer.' She touched the gold pin that, thank God, held her jumpsuit closed. It was at that point of her body that, on a woman who hadn't starved herself, would have been called a cleavage. 'I have a business to run.' She said 'a business' as if she meant General Motors.

'What do you do?'

'Wendy's Soups. I'm president and CEO.' As in: Everyone knows Wendys' Soups. Well, everyone who's anyone, as I clearly wasn't. 'There have been major articles about me. *New York Times, Vogue*, et cetera. *Elle* . . . You know *Elle*? The piece was called "Superb Soups!" '

'Do you cook them here?'

She smiled. Big mistake. God had given Wendy Morrell the gift of gums. 'No. The plant is in a cute little ethnic neighborhood in Queens. I employ forty-six people.'

'So you don't live here all year round?'

'No. East End and Eighty-first. Just long weekends here. It used to be all August too, but then there was that cover story in *New York Woman*.' With, I assumed, a photo of a bowl of split pea superimposed over her ugly puss. 'We went through the roof. You can imagine!'

'Look, Ms Morrell, obviously you're a very busy person, but busy people tend to be the most efficient.' She obviously agreed. 'You're not the nosy neighbor type, but . . .'

'I don't know anything about her. We nod hello. That is all. When I'm out here I'm still plagued. The phone, the fax. My office cannot leave me alone. The pressure *never* stops. I have to *force* myself to relax. I do not do coffee klatches.'

'Does Bonnie Spencer have coffee klatches?'

'Not that I've ever seen.'

'What I'm getting at is, are there any frequent visitors?' She glanced at my Jag again. 'Men in sports cars?'

'Men in sports cars. Men in sedans. Men in all *kinds* of vehicles. Is that news to you?' She paused. 'Once . . . I saw a pickup truck. I happened to notice it because it was late at night. Well, let's be generous. Maybe she needed some emergency construction done by a kid who couldn't have been more than twenty-two, in tight jeans and work boots.'

'I'm going to be direct, Ms Morrell, but I feel I can be direct with someone who's a CEO.' She acknowledged the tribute with a brief flash of gums. 'Is it your impression that Ms Spencer is promiscuous?'

'Maybe she's just interviewing half the men in Bridgehampton for that happy-news column she writes. She came over once, asked if she could interview me! I was very pleasant. I told her I was horrendously tied up, but I'd love to. Some other time.' She stopped. 'Are you sure you're with the police?'

I handed her my shield. She brought it up close to her nose, breathing what was probably disgusting humid, lentil-dill breath on the plastic, and studied it. Then she handed it back.

'Have you seen any one car at Bonnie Spencer's recently? A black sports car?'

'Detective Whatever' – she smiled – 'I *know* what a Maserati is. My ex-husband drove a Ferrari 250 GT, '62. Believe me, I had sports cars burned into my brain during *that* marriage.' She looked over at mine. 'I know an E-type Jaguar roadster when I see one.

The English don't say "convertible", you know.' I hated it that this witch had any sort of intimacy with great cars. 'And the answer to your question is yes.'

'Yes, what, Ms Morrell?'

'There was a Maserati in her driveway. Last week. Every morning that I was here. A quarter to twelve. Like clockwork. And a *fabulously* dressed man got out of it. I realize now that it must have been Sy Spencer. But I'm sure there's an innocent explanation. Maybe she just served an early lunch.'

'Maybe. When did he leave?'

'Two, three, four.'

'Any sounds of fighting?'

She shook her head. 'I cannot believe it! He was so fine – and *re*fined. I mean, this man could have any woman he wanted. Why would someone like him waste his time on a nothing like her?'

'Maybe she's nice.'

Wendy Morrell cocked her head, drew her eyebrows together, as if she were hearing about a sensational new trend for the first time. '*Nice?*'

# *Chapter Eight*

Nice Bonnie Spencer.

Well, fuck her and the horse she rode in on. All along I'd known something was wrong. All along I'd known she was lying to me about Sy. Still, somewhere I'd kept a candle burning, a flicker of hope that she was a good person, that whatever ties she had to her ex-husband had to do strictly with making movies. Because if I ever was going to be friends with a woman, Bonnie would have been exactly the kind of woman I would have picked. She seemed so straight that in spite of all my doubts, when Wendy Morrell opened her gummy mouth, I truly believed she was going to say: A black sports car? No! The only car *I* ever saw in her driveway was the Lilco meter reader's – and he was never there for more than ninety seconds.

To hell with Bonnie, I shifted into third.

The trip from Bridgehampton to Headquarters in Yaphank was thirty-nine miles, most of it along straight-arrow, four-lane Route 27. Once it had been my own personal test track. Since sobriety, though, I'd become an old fart and never pushed much beyond seventy-five mph.

But now, going west against beach traffic, I decided I needed speed. I couldn't believe how badly I'd misjudged her. Moose wasn't the town slut; the animal wasn't the animal. The stupid bitch, Bonnie, couldn't keep her legs together. I shifted into fourth, heard the deep, throaty hum of the exhaust, watched the tachometer go into redline. I eased up when I got to a hundred and five. Fuck Bonnie Spencer! This was fantastic! In most sports cars, when you're in last gear, you feel like you're skyrocketing, leaving the pull of earth's gravity. But the XKE kind of squats, fuses with the road. It's the ultimate down-to-earth experience.

There just isn't anything like speed to take you away, especially sober. (Driving drunk, you known in your gut that Death, carrying a scythe, in that hooded bathrobe – sort of like Sy's, although not as good-quality terry cloth – is standing over the next rise.)

So fuck Bonnie. And fuck this case. The minute it was over, I'd say to Lynne: Come on. No waiting till Thanksgiving weekend. Let's find some priest whose dance card isn't filled up the way your guy's is. We'll get married right away. And forget Saint John. We'll go to London. I'll go to museums with you. To Shakespeare. I'll visit English schools and stand by your side and learn all about the newest methods for combating dyscalculia. I swear to God, I'll even go to the opera.

Sergeant Alvin Miller of the Ogden, Utah, Police Department talked re-e-e-al sl-o-o-ow, as if each word had to mosey down a long dirt road before it could come out. 'Well, now, Detective Brady. One of the boys passed on your message last night. 'Bout ten. I'm not with the department anymore. Re-tired, you know. Have been for eleven years.' I transferred the phone to my other ear. 'But seeing as you said it wasn't urgent, I wasn't going to call you up there in Noooo Yorrrk, where it was midnight.' He said 'New York' in the resentful way guys in my company in Vietnam did, as if ordinary people and ordinary places – suburbs, farms, beaches and forests – were just camouflage for a state whose sole business was mocking the rest of America. 'Hope my not calling back right away didn't hold you up.'

'No problem.' Across the room, Charlie Sanchez sat at his desk holding aloft a cheese Danish from the daily love-me bag of bakery goodies Robby had brought in. Charlie was sticking out his tongue, licking the yellow cheese in the center. The crime-scene photographs on my desk, showing Sy with his two small, neat little wounds, were less revolting than watching Charlie tongue a pastry. 'I appreciate your calling back,' I said to Sergeant Miller.

'You bet. Now, you wanted to know something about the Bernstein girl. Don't tell me she's in trouble?'

'No, she's okay. Her ex-husband—'

'She got a divorce?'

'Yeah. A few years ago.'

'No kiddin'. What was her first name, now?'

'Bonnie.'

'That's it, all right Bonnie Bernstein. She living in New York?'

'No. In Bridgehampton. It's a little town on the East End of Long Island.'

'Oh. I heard she went to Hollywood. She made a picture, you know. I forget what they called it, but I saw it. Not bad.'

'The detective I spoke to said you might know the family.'

'Yup. Knew them. Pretty well, at one time.' I wanted to grab this fucker by his string tie and shake him, make the words come out faster.

'Can you tell me about them?'

'Sure.' I licked my fingertip and erased a coffee ring while I hung round and waited for his next word. 'If memory serves me, the Bernsteins – that would be Bonnie's grandparents – opened the store.'

'Uh-huh,' I muttered encouragingly.

'Called it Bernstein's.'

'Did her parents keep it up?'

'Kept it up real nice.'

Out in the anteroom, Ray Carbone was handing one of Homicide's two secretaries a piece of paper. From the pained look in his eyes, it was probably a draft of the next press release, which would say, essentially, that we knew nothing. The secretary glanced around for her glasses, didn't find them, and so stretched out her arm and pulled back her head to read. Hanging above her head was the giant banner that no one could miss when they walked into Suffolk County Homicide: THOU SHALT NOT KILL.

'What kind of a store was Bernstein's?'

'A sporting goods store.'

'Bats, balls?'

'Nope. More like guns, fishing gear.'

'Handguns?'

'Sure, handguns. This is Utah.'

'Rifles?'

'Yup.'

'Is the store still around?'

'No. Mrs Bernstein – that would be Bonnie's mother – died. Dan – that's her father – sold the place and retired. I believe to Arizona, but I won't swear to it. Maybe New Mexico. And the boys – three or four of them – didn't stay in Ogden. One of them is a college professor at UU, and I don't know what the others did.'

'Bonnie was the only girl.'

'So far as I can remember, and I remember her because she was friends with the boys and girls in my Eddie's Mutual. I guess you don't know what that is.'

'No.'

'It's a group for Mormon junior high and high school kids.'

'Were the Bernstein's Mormons?'

'Of course not. You're from New York. You should know that.'

'Right. Okay, now, let me be straight with you, Sergeant Miller.'

'Best way to be.'

'The incident I'm investigating—'

'I know what kind of an incident. They told me you were on the Homicide Squad. You need a whole department out there on Long Island just for homicide, huh?'

'Yeah. The victim was Bonnie's ex-husband. He was shot with a .22. The perpetrator was a good shot. I'd like to rule out Bonnie.'

'What are you asking me?'

'I'm asking you whether you have any idea if she could shoot a .22.'

'I don't know.'

'Your best guess.'

'My best guess is, a girl like Bonnie – a tomboy kind of girl – whose family owned a sporting goods store and whose dad was probably the damn finest shot in Ogden . . . I used to go up to Wyoming with him and a couple of other fellas, hunting elk. Well, she was the apple of her father's eye. Possible he or one of her brothers taught her to shoot a .22.'

'Thank you.'

'Well now, you expect me to say she couldn't have done it, don't you?'

'I wouldn't be surprised if you did.'

'Well, I won't say it. She left Ogden. Went to Hollywood, then New York. Can't issue any guarantees under those conditions, right?'

'Right.'

'But just between you and me, Detective Brady? You may be from Noooo Yorrrk and think you're pretty wily, saying you're trying to rule out Bonnie Bernstein. Sounds to me like you've got it in your head that she shot her former husband. With malice aforethought. Maybe.' He took a long and very slow breath. 'But if the girl you suspect is anything like the nice, smiley girl in my boy Eddie's Mutual, you know what I think? I think you got yourself one lousy theory. You get me? I think you're pissing into the wind.'

Robby Kurz placed his bet: 'Fat Mikey LoTriglio. Okay, never convicted of anything, but his name has been linked with two mob hits. All he has to do is raise his fat finger, and someone dies.'

'No way,' I said. 'Bonnie Spencer. Motive. Opportunity.'

Ray Carbone added his twenty to ours. 'Who's left? Lindsay Keefe? All right. She may have felt concerned, her job, her reputation on the line. And she probably has a lacuna of the superego. It would be too much like a movie if she did it, but I'll go with her anyway.'

Charlie Sanchez was about to retire and didn't care enough anymore to join the pool. He wrote down our bets, folded the money and slipped it into the pocket of his beloved suede vest.

The interrogation room we were in at Headquarters was better than a naked light bulb and a chair, but it wouldn't win any awards for design excellence. Headquarters itself had originally been a county social services agency, and in the heart of the soft green and brown fields of Yaphank, the building rose up, uncompromisingly ugly. Inside, it was full of gray asphalt tile and orange plastic furniture – just to remind the meek that while they might be in line to inherit the earth, their actual lives were shit and likely to remain that way.

Four of us sat around the fake-wood table. Charlie who'd been with the department for twenty years and was within weeks of becoming head of security for a shopping center in Bay Shore, stroked the vest his girlfriend had given him for his forty-second birthday. He wore it inside and outside, even in ninety-five-degree heat. He loved the vest almost as much as he loved his girlfriend. (His wife had given him a snow-blower for his birthday, probably in response to the electric pencil sharpener he'd given her for hers.)

'We got a missing-one-thousand-bucks situation,' Charlie began. He'd been doing background on Sy. 'Here's what I found out. At fourteen minutes past eight on Friday morning, Sy was at the cash machine at the Marine Midland Bank over in Southampton.'

'His secretary in New York said he told her he'd be getting cash for his trip to LA,' Ray added.

Charlie went on: 'Sy had one of those preferred-customer cards, so he could withdraw up to a thou. Well, that's what he withdrew. Did any of you guys come across a thousand bucks?'

Robby shook his head. 'No. There was' – Robby checked his notebook – 'a hundred and forty-seven bucks in his wallet.'

I closed my eyes, concentrated. Then I said: 'Hey! Hold on! Listen to this timetable. Sy went to the bank at eight-fourteen. He got to the set in East Hampton eight thirty-five, eight-forty, which is about what it takes from Southampton to East Hampton if you don't make any stops. When he got there, he stayed pretty much in his trailer, talking to people. Right? That Gregory kid was around a lot, and we talked to everyone else who talked to Sy. Did anyone say anything about any cash changing hands? No. The people he was seeing were mainly technical – a special effects guy who was doing a fire and some gunshots, Nick Monteleone and his makeup lady. Spent a few minutes with Lindsay, but she was being fitted for a dress, so a seamstress and the costume design lady were there the whole time. He wasn't talking to union guys or local cops or politicians – people he might pay off. You with me?' Robby and Ray nodded. Charlie caressed his vest some more. 'Okay, assuming he didn't slip anyone a wad of cash, he leaves the set about eleven-fifteen with a thousand bucks in his pocket. Doesn't stop at Bonnie's this time. Instead he seems to have gone straight home; he was there at ten of twelve. We have the cook's word on that, because he asked for a green salad and bread for lunch, ASAP.'

'That's lunch?' Charlie shook his head. 'Can you believe it? A guy has a cook all to himself and he says, "Give me a salad." New York faggots, I swear to Christ. Makes me sick.'

'What does all this add up to, Steve?' Ray demanded.

'It adds up to that after he got home, Sy saw only one person besides the cook: the person he as a practicing nonfaggot seems to have humped in the guest room. Now, there was Bonnie Spencer-type hair on the pillow in the guest room – okay, we have to wait till Lifecodes finishes the DNA analysis, but I'll bet you anything it's hers.'

'Why are you fixating on her?' Ray asked.

'Because this is an intelligent murder, and she's very intelligent. Because he used her – twice – and I don't think this is a broad who allows three strikes. I think she's got a tough streak in her. And because she's been hiding something from me from the minute she opened the door Saturday morning. And because she was *there* Friday, at his house. Motive and opportunity, Ray.'

'You know what I can't figure out? He was cheating on Lindsay Keefe with his ex-wife,' Charlie said. 'What was he? Nuts?'

'Keep your eye on the missing thousand bucks,' I reminded them. 'Ask yourselves: Where was the wallet we found that *did* have some money in it?'

'In the inside pocket of his blazer,' Ray said.

'Where?'

'In his and Lindsay's bedroom, on a hanger outside the closet door. Stuff for his trip was all set out – a packed carry-on, a leather envelope with a couple of scripts.'

'Right,' I said. 'But the pockets of the pants he was wearing that day were empty except for some change and his car keys, and those pants were in the guest room. My guess is, he packs, then has an hour or so, decides he wants to get laid and calls Bonnie to get over. He sneaks her past the cook, upstairs, into the guest room. He throws his pants over a chair, fucks her, then . . .'

'Then what?' Ray asked. 'This is the first serious speculation I'm hearing about this person – other than the fact that she was his ex who lived nearby. What do you think went on?'

'My best guess? They had words. He tells her to get dressed and get out. Or he doesn't have to say it; she figures it out for herself. Whatever. But he grabs a robe and leaves her there while he goes for a fast swim before the plane ride. In any case, she feels she's been had. She goes through his pants, takes the thou.'

'And then she goes outside, finds a .22 and shoots him?' Charlie asked. 'A lady writer is able to score two bull's-eyes from fifty feet?'

'Could you do it, Charlie, if you had the rifle?'

'From fifty feet? Why not?'

'Yeah, well, why not her too?' I said. I told him what I'd learned about Bernstein's inventory from Ogden's finest.

'Well, *I* can't buy Bonnie as a serious suspect,' Robby said. He shifted, and his rayon pants rubbed against the plastic of the chair and gave off a squeaky fart sound. 'Even if she has long dark hair, even if she was sleeping with him, even if she can shoot that well, which I seriously doubt, why would she kill him?'

'Lots of reasons.' I was starting to like this, the explaining, the persuading, the idea that things were coming together. But most of all, I was liking the realization that I had no trouble making a case against Bonnie, that finally, where she was concerned, my head was harder than my dick. 'First of all, she's living hand-to-mouth,' I explained. 'She got shafted in the divorce. She's gotten a look at Sy's way of life, sees how he's given up the humble Farmer Spencer bit he was doing when he was married to her, the denim overalls and butter-churn crap. Now he's living like an out-and-out multi-millionaire, which he is. She sees the richness of his life, compares it to the poorness of hers. Probably has already told him how rough things are, asked him for help. And expects it too, what with her probably giving him a blow job and soup and sandwiches every goddamn day that last week. Except he says no.'

'Why didn't she just keep at it?' Ray asked. 'Play on his sympathy? Or make him feel guilty?'

'Maybe she's already given it everything she has – which isn't that much. She fucks and she's nice. What else does someone like her have to offer? And anyway, it wasn't just money. She could have been in love with him and really believed she could get him back. But no matter what she wanted from him, Sy said, No way.'

'He just turned off on her, so she kills him?' Robby asked. He didn't sound convinced, but then again, he had his twenty on Mikey Lo Triglio.

I pushed harder. 'All she's been doing is covering up, lying to us. Why? So we don't think she's a fast girl who lets a man put his thing into her you-know-what? No. Because she has something important to hide. A murder.'

Robby turned that over for a minute. Then he asked: 'But *why* would she shoot him? Revenge?'

'Revenge. Plus desperation, plus greed.'

'Where would she get the .22?' Charlie asked.

'She lives alone. Probably had it for years, a present from Daddy Bernstein. Could be she sensed this was the final fuck and brought it along in her car. Or maybe she left, went home, got it and came back. Come on, guys. Sy was wearing his pants at the movie set, so no one took the thousand off him there. Then he gets home, sticks it to the as-yet-unknown brunette we *know* has to be Bonnie, goes for a swim and bang. He's gonzo – and so is the money.'

'Even if she was there, it could have been someone else who shot him,' Carbone said.

'It could have been. But who? Why? We already know about Bonnie.'

'So she killed him for a thousand bucks?' Robby asked. 'I've got to tell you, Steve, that still doesn't compute. Not with the way you described her. She doesn't sound like a really bad person. Except for the screwing around, and what the hell, she's lonely.'

'But *why* is she lonely?' Naturally, I didn't look at Ray Carbone, even though I was playing to him, trying to get the psychology vote. 'Ask yourselves, what kind of a normal single woman stays in a town she has no roots in, a town that's deserted three quarters of the year except for locals like me and some antique-dealer types who talk about stuff like the bleak beauty of the winter seascape and shit like that. How come she didn't sell the house, which could bring her big bucks even with real estate being what it is, and move to Manhattan, get a decent job?' Charlie rubbed his chin, Robby looked mildly intrigued and Ray leaned forward. 'I'll tell you why not. She's a loser, and she knows it. She had one minute of success that might have been a fluke, and in that minute she lands Sy. You know what that marriage said to her? It said: "Bonnie, babe, you're terrific." But then he gets bored and takes a walk. She stays in that isolated house because she knows if she moved to the city, she'd have no excuse for being a loser. This way, she lives hand-to-mouth – but she can keep up her illusions. That Sy will come back. That one of her shitty screenplays will get made into a move. That she's worth something. And then what happens?'

Despite the fact that Mikey LoTriglio was due any second with his lawyer, Robby was getting hooked. 'What happens?' he said, as if waiting for the end of a bedtime story.

I gave it everything I had; I knew it would be a major asset to have Robby on my side, not off after the Mafia. 'Sy starts sleeping with Bonnie again, gives her hope. Suddenly she's thinking: I *am* terrific. I can have a life. I'll have my husband back and live in New York, on Fifth Avenue, and in a seven-million-dollar mansion on the beach. And she must have started sharing her dream with Sy, because all of a sudden he blows her off. Maybe nicely. Or maybe he just tells her the truth: "Bonnie, baby, I was PO'd at Lindsay and felt like a grudge fuck, and you were available. It didn't mean anything." '

Ray was breaking his empty Styrofoam coffee cup into white chips. 'All right. His rejection might hurt her. Destroy her. But would it push her over the edge?'

'Yeah, because this time he didn't leave her with any illusions. He didn't want her. He didn't want her screenplay. Don't forget: He humiliated her, treated her like a two-bit whore when she came to visit him on the set. And he didn't value old times' sake enough to help her out of a crappy financial situation. Look, two strikes: he'd used her once, to get a foot in the door of the movie business, and he'd used her again, to get his rocks of when he got mad at Lindsay. And now it was kiss-kiss, sweetie, I'm off to LA. I'm telling you, he walked out of that guest room leaving her with *nothing.*'

'It's just a theory,' Robby murmured. But he sounded on the verge of being convinced.

So did Ray. 'Okay, Steve and Robby,' he said, 'keep your other options open, but follow up on this Bonnie. It sounds like she needs a little extra attention.'

Fat Mikey LoTriglio looked like a Sicilian version of Humpty-Dumpty. He had no visible neck; his silk tie, a dark blue dangerously close to purple, seemed suspended from one of the chins that rested on his chest. 'I grew up wit' Sy,' he was explaining to me and Robby. 'He was like a brother to me. Let me tell you, you find the guy who took him out, you call me. You tell me, "Hey, Mikey, we found the guy who blasted Sy," and I swear to God, I'll—'

'At the time Mr Spencer was murdered,' Fat Mikey's lawyer interrupted, 'Mr LoTriglio was having cocktails with several business associates, who, naturally, can vouch for his whereabouts.' The lawyer, a guy around my age, wore round little glasses with wire frames, as though hoping someone would assure him that he didn't look like the sleazy mob lawyer he'd become, that he still looked like John Lennon.

'Hey,' Mikey turned to the lawyer. 'I don't have cocktails, okay? I have drinks.' He looked back at us and explained: 'This is a new lawyer. My old one, Terry Connelly. Ever deal with him? Massive stroke. They got him in some hospital in Rhode Island, poor vegetable. Sad, sad. And now this fuckin' murder . . .' He shook his head in disbelief. 'It's a knife in my heart, Sy gone.'

'What's going to happen to your investment in *Starry Night*?' I asked.

'Mr LoTriglio's participation in that venture has not been established,' the lawyer said.

'We know Mikey invested four hundred thousand in the move

and got his brother-in-law and an uncle to put up another six hundred thousand,' Robby said, but reasonably, not with his usual I'm-gonna-see-you-fry vengefulness. At some moment between the time Ray and Charlie left the interrogation room and the time Mikey and his lawyer walked in, Robby had switched to Bonnie Spencer. I smiled to myself. I was really happy. I'd won Robby over. I could stand back; she was his girl now, and he would do anything to get her.

'How was your investment going, Mikey?' I asked.

Mikey fluttered his eyes, a single flutter: his naive expression. 'What do I know about producin' movies?'

'You must know something if you put up a million bucks.'

'Hey, my friend Sy asks me to put up some money, I do it.'

'Mr LoTriglio's accountants were impressed by Mr Spencer's track record,' the lawyer said softly. 'They felt *Starry Night* was an excellent investment – albeit any investment in filmmaking entails a certain degree of risk, of which they were fully cognizant.'

'Did Sy let you know how the movie was coming along?' I asked. Fat Mikey shook his head; his chins jiggled. 'A million bucks, Mikey. Weren't you curious?'

'Nah. What do I care? Sy says this is gonna be an Oscar-winner. He says, "Mikey, get your tuxedo cleaned for a year from March." That's all I needed to know.'

'You didn't hear anything about any problems with the movie?'

Mikey smiled. Well, the corners of his lips moved upward. He crossed his arms and rested them on his belly. 'What problems?'

'Problems like the movie was looking like a piece of shit.'

'Fuck you. I didn't hear *nothin'* like that.'

'Problems like the only way to save it was to get rid of Lindsay Keefe, which would have put the producers – that's you – a few million deeper into the hole before they even began again.'

'Bullshit,' Mikey said.

'You were on the phone a lot with Sy Spencer last week. What were you talking about?' Robby inquired.

Mikey looked at his lawyer, who seemed to be lost in wonder, beholding his shoelace. 'You from Harvard!' he bellowed. 'Look alive. My memory isn't so good. I need a reminder. Maybe I happened to mention it to you. What was I talkin' to Sy about last week? I think Sy and I *might* have been on the phone a couple of times, but for the life of me I can't remember what we said.'

'I think you did mention that you had the most general conversation with Mr Spencer. Hello, how are you, how are things going – and he assured you all was well.'

'That's right,' Mikey said. He rotated his head and looked Robby right in the eye. 'All was well. And then – a fuckin' bullet. *Two* fuckin' bullets. I gotta tell you, a piece of me died when Sy went. We were like flesh and blood. When we were kids we'd follow his old man and my old man around through one of the processing plants, and while they talked about all the cheap shit they could stuff into one salami, Sy and me talked about . . . Life.'

*Life*?' I repeated.

'Yeah. Life. Like philosophy. *Now* I remember. We were talkin' about philosophy last week, on the phone.' His lawyer put a restraining hand on Mikey's huge sausagelike thigh, but Mikey either didn't feel it or was ignoring it. 'There we were, two businessmen, but we're such good friends we don't talk business. We talk . . . Plato!'

'Where were you last Friday night, Mikey?' Robby asked.

'You mean what's my alibi?'

'Mr LoTriglio was at Rosie's, a bar in the meat district,' the lawyer said. 'He is widely known there. A good many people saw him, and several engaged him in conversation.

'Talking Plato?' I asked.

'No, you stupid asshole,' Mikey answered. 'Talkin' fuckin' liverwurst.'

One of the guys I sometimes ran with, TJ, a marathoner, owned a couple of video stores on the South Fork. He was in love with my Jag, so I made a deal with him. Whenever I wanted to be inconspicuous, I could take one of his married-man cars – his Honda Accord or Plymouth Voyager – and leave my car in his garage. At a little after four in the afternoon, I parked the Voyager across from Bonnie's house and waited.

Surveillance had always been a snap for me. I'd bring along a bottle of club soda, a Thermos of coffee, and a jar to pee in, sit back and enter into some kind of twilight state. It was like being asleep with my eyes open; I could keep watch, but my mind was someplace else, and I'd be totally unaware of the passage of time. I'd know that I'd sat through a whole night when the sky turned red at sunrise.

But now I was itchy, looking at my watch every couple of minutes, as if to encourage it, wishing that I'd stopped at the luncheonette on the way over for a sundae because I felt like I needed a hit of chocolate. I was annoyed with myself that I hadn't sent off one of the younger guys to do this job. Finally, though, it wasn't that long a wait.

She came out at five o'clock, dressed for a run. The weird thing was, she was dressed exactly the way I would dress for running. Shorts and a T-shirt, wool crew socks, with a light sweatshirt tied around her waist, in case it got cool down by the ocean. She was carrying a red ball; Moose was barking with joy at her side. I slid down in the seat. She braced herself against her mailbox, stretched her calf muscles and then her quads. What a pair of legs! They looked like she'd been captain of the girls' soccer team since nursery school. She and Moose started out at a nice clip, picking up more speed as they rounded the corner and headed down toward the beach.

Jesus, I thought, as they disappeared, I really am in love with that dog. Maybe because it was black, it reminded me of a Labrador we'd had at the farm when I was little, Inky, a dumb, sweet-natured bitch who treated me and Easton as if we were her puppies, watching us play, barking if we wandered off too far, growling at anybody who drove up to the house and approached us.

I pulled on a pair of the thin rubber gloves we used for crime-scene work, turned off my beeper and checked out the area. Clear. I crossed the street, studying the house. I could probably sneak in through a basement window; even if I had to break a pane, she might not notice for days. Or I might be able to jimmy open the back door. But, as I suspected, neither was necessary. Bonnie had left the front door unlocked.

Even if she ran like hell and just threw the ball once down at the beach, I had a clear twenty minutes. But I worked the upstairs first, in case I heard her and had to get out the back door.

Bingo! She used one of the bedrooms as an office, and there, under a big framed poster from the movie *Cowgirl*, beside a computer half-covered with stickum notes, in a messy, overstuffed folder marked 'Pending,' was a Xeroxed real estate listing for her house. It was dated August 4, so she'd decided to put it on the market while there were still summer people around to come, look and oooh: 'Oh, Ian, the exposed beams!' Had she taken up with Sy yet? Was she selling it because she was already having dreams of a grand house by the ocean, a screening room, charge accounts, a wedding ring? Or was the real estate listing pre-Sy? Had she been at the end of her rope? I jotted down the broker's number.

I had to work fast – and neat. Neat wasn't too much of a problem since Bonnie's papers were just this side of chaotic. Still, this was not exactly what you could call a legal search, so I couldn't risk leaving any trace.

I went through her bedroom too, finding, mainly, that she kept the local library in business, that although her tangle of bras were what you'd expect from a female jock, utilitarian and uninspiring, her panties weren't: little string bikinis, black, red. I was starting to imagine her, but I cut myself off. Time. Also, there was something about being in her bedroom, its peacefulness, with its tied-back white lace curtains, plain four-poster bed and old-fashioned dresser with a white doilylike thing on top of it, that made me uneasy. I wanted out of there. I was half out the door, on my way downstairs, when I turned back to check out her closet.

Bingo again! Inside the toe of a red pair of boots – one of those places women inevitably hide their valuable stuff – I found it: a wad of cash rolled up in a rubber band. Eight hundred and eighty dollars. More than she had in her savings account. Big bucks for a poor girl like Bonnie.

Change from a thousand.

# *Chapter Nine*

What was so terrible? Sex, even with someone as fabulous as Lynne, can become routine. So big deal: you superimpose another woman over your dearly beloved and suddenly a predictable quickie becomes the Fuck That Shook the World. It can happen, especially if a guy's pattern has always been to step out a lot. Is that so bad? There is no betrayal. Nobody gets hurt.

But it wasn't just that one brief late-night fantasy. My whole life – not just the case – was starting to focus on Bonnie. Like when I'd gone to the bank to speak to Rochelle, I stopped at the cashier's for a couple of rolls of quarters. More than a couple: enough to hit every pay phone in the South Fork. And so once or twice – all right, three or four times – a day I'd drop in a quarter just to hear Bonnie say 'Hello.' Once, when I heard the tightness in her throat (she must have known it would be another hang-up, because who the hell else would call her?), I stood by the phone outside the East Hampton post office and got this terrible lump in my own throat; I wanted to cry for her.

Maybe I was so overcome with pity because an hour earlier I'd been looking over all the records we'd pulled on her, and discovered on the printout from Motor Vehicles that besides being five foot nine inches, which was not exactly a feminine asset, she was forty-five years old. Forty fucking five! I did the math three times. I couldn't believe it. But what kind of sense did it make for me to be getting all choked up with pity for a put-upon, middle-aged loser if I was the schmuck standing out in the rain, praying she'd give me another 'hello' before she slammed down the phone?

Listen, I told myself, this is definitely one of those sexual obsession things. But instead of ignoring it, or figuring it out, I kept borrowing TJ's cars, so Bonnie wouldn't spot my Jag. I drove by her house on the way to work and on the way home. Sometimes in between. All I had to do was spot a shadow passing by an upstairs window, or catch the flutter of a white curtain, and I would feel God's grace upon me. One time, Moose was lying on the front lawn, giving her front paw a manicure with her big pink tongue, and I had this dizzying, blood-to-the-head flush of joy.

And when I'd searched her house, I'd looked in her garage right before I left and saw an old Jeep Wrangler. It made me so incredibly, stupidly happy that Bonnie drove a four-wheel-drive recreational vehicle.

But I felt the same degree of happiness when I found the wad of cash in her boot. I thought: Fantastic! I've really nailed the bitch.

So when Carbone and the lieutenant, a guy named Jack Byrne, who was so shy or weird that he whispered instead of talked, called me in and said, Listen, here are a couple of people to see in the city. The first wife and Sy's divorce lawyer. You'll have to go, not Robby. We need someone with a little finesse . . . Well, I should have been relieved. Here it was: a chance to get the hell off the South Fork, shake off the fixation, stop the Bonnie mania, cut the shit.

Except as I drove west on the Long Island Expressway, all I could think about was her dark, shiny, sweet-smelling hair. I wanted to stroke it back off her forehead, play with it, wrap it around my finger after we finished making love. But also, I wanted to see it inside a small plastic envelope: Government Exhibit D.

Goddamn, I wanted to take TJ's minivan, park it down the street and watch her house all day, catch a glimpse of her. I didn't want to work. And I definitely didn't want to go to Manhattan.

Imagine a cartoon of snooty, stick-up-the-ass rich WASP. That's what Felice Tompkins Spencer Vanderventer looked like, except in 3-D. Yes, she'd heard her first husband had been murdered. Sorry.

Not really sorry or terribly sorry; she didn't gush. Everything about Felice was austere, from her face (which was very long and rectangular, like a gift box for a bottle of booze, except instead of a ribbon on top she had a thin figure eight of gray-brown hair tacked down by a couple of bobby pins) to her dress, which looked as if it were made out of a humongous brown Kleenex held together by a narrow brown belt.

She was Sy's age, fifty-three. Maybe when they were twenty-one they'd looked like a couple, but now, had he been alive and had they stayed married, she would have had to handle embarrassing references to her son; they had separated not only into different worlds but into different generations.

Like Felice, her Park Avenue living room was out-moded. But it wasn't austere. First of all, it was so big you could play basketball in there, except you'd break your neck because it was so chockfull of stuff. The place looked as though someone had bought out the entire inventory of a store specializing in dark, ugly antiques. There was no faded, restful old-money homeyness like at Germy's, just a lot of very high, overstuffed, heavy furniture with claw feet. It would have taken five moving men just to lift one of her hideous black carved-wood chairs. The pictures were heavy too, fancy gold-framed oil paintings of fruit and pitchers and dead rabbits.

'When was the last time you spoke with Mr Spencer?' My left shoe squeaked every time I shifted my weight. She hadn't asked me to sit.

'About ten years ago.' Even in the early-afternoon glare, the room was so shadowy it was hard to make out her features – except for her teeth. They were double normal human size; it looked as if she'd had a transplant from a thoroughbred mare. Felice was so aggressively unattractive that, considering her surroundings, you knew it was her, and not Mr Spencer or Mr Vanderventer, who owned the sixteen-foot-high ceilings and everything under them.

'Did you ever meet or speak to his second wife, Bonnie Spencer?'

'I saw them together briefly, once in front of Carnegie Hall. Sy introduced us.' Outside Felice's window, the only bright spot in the room, Park Avenue stretched out like a parade ground for the rich. The island in the middle of the street had huge tubs of bright-gold flowers; they gleamed like piles of money. Past the traffic, over at the curb, elderly doormen opened limousine doors and helped out the rich and able-bodied.

'During the time you knew him, did Sy ever mention a man named Mikey LoTriglio?'

'I believe so.'

'What did he say about him?'

'I don't know. Something about their fathers having been in the meat business.' She said 'meat business' with distaste, as if Sy had been in wholesale carrion. 'I never paid attention to that aspect of his life.'

I gave it another five minutes, but all I could get was that Felice had married Sy because he could quote all of Wordsworth's 'Intimations of Immortality from Recollections of Early Childhood.' She'd divorced him because she finally found out he was more interested in 'social advancement' than in poetry. And all right, yes, since I'd asked (her upper lip curled, covering about half of her giant teeth), because she caught him cheating. Who with? With her first cousin Claudia Giddings, a trustee of the New York Philharmonic. He told her he'd fallen in love with Claudia, that he wanted to marry her, but of course he never did.

The trip to Manhattan looked like a waste. What had I gotten? Corroboration that Sy couldn't keep his pants on, especially when there was someone screwable who could boost either his status or his career. And that Germy had been right on the money: Sy was a chameleon. A refined poetry-spouter to Felice. An 'I care' Down-to-Earth Human Being to Bonnie. A cool, masterful mogul to Lindsay. And not just to women: somehow, he became whatever anyone wanted him to be. A remote God of Cinema to Gregory J. Canfield. A congenial producer-pal to Nicholas Monteleone. A blood brother to Mikey. A savior to Easton.

I walked down Park Avenue to stretch my legs and let my shoe desqueak, twenty-five blocks from Felice's brown fortress of an apartment house to a silvery glass-and-granite office building. Nature had given up on this part of Manhattan and was hiding out in Central Park. On Park Avenue, there were only too-flawless horticulturists' gold flowers, and a thin, bleached-out strip of sky. Jesus, I hated New York.

Well, maybe not hated. When I was a kid I'd gone on a class trip to the top of the Empire State Building and to see the Christmas tree in Rockefeller Center, and I'd let out an 'Oooh!' of honest delight. But after that, I could never figure out what to do with myself in the city, except that I always felt I should do *something* – like take advantage of Culture. Once I'd been down at NYPD Headquarters on a case and then had taken a couple of subways uptown and wound up at the Metropolitan Museum of Art. But it was so big. And I'd had to check my gun with security. The guy there had treated me with a combination of suspicion and contempt, like I was some Bible Belt anti-smut loony who was going to shoot the dicks off the Greek statues. Finally, I had found myself in a room full of Egyptian mummies, and when I'd asked where the pictures were, a guard, who I'd actually smiled at because he looked like an older Dave Winfield, had said, ' "Pictures"? Do you mean "paintings"?' That had been it for Culture.

And just walking through the streets, either I'd see nothing but the homeless, and sick whores, and drug deals going down, or – today, as I pushed open the heavy door of the office building – swanky, Sy-like people saying, throatily, 'Hiiii' to each other. I always felt like a rube. All dressed up with no place to go. And no matter what jacket I put on in Bridgehampton, when I got to Manhattan my shirt cuffs were too short.

Jonathan Tullius Esq's cuffs were, of course, just the right length. He'd been Sy's divorce lawyer, both times. It looked like business was good. His office, filled with soft-looking leather furniture, smelled like the inside of an expensive loafer. 'Sit down, Detective Brady.' He had a deep, melodic voice and the barrel chest of an opera singer. He said: 'I called your offices immediately after I heard about the murder, and spoke with a Sergeant Carbone. And I see now I was right to do so. You people must have some interest in Bonnie Spencer, since you are, in fact, responding to my call.' He was crazy about the sound of his own voice. 'To get to the point, Detective Brady: Sergeant Carbone agreed this conversation would be strictly off the record and disclosed *only* on a need-to-know basis.'

'Right.'

'You see, on one hand the attorney-client privilege survives death.'

'Yeah.'

'Therefore, I should not be talking to you.' He swiveled around in his throne of a leather chair and then rested his elbows on his desk. 'On the other hand, Sy was a dear friend as well as a client. He called me last Thursday. The day before he was killed. He was quite, quite concerned.' Tullius had one of those soft, pampered, self-satisfied faces you see at Republican National Conventions.

'What was he concerned about, Mr Tullius?'

'Money.' I waited. 'And his former wife. Bonnie Spencer.'

I thought: Oh, fuck it! 'Was she holding him up for money?'

'No. But Sy was concerned that she might. You see, he'd run into her out in the Hamptons. She lives there full-time. Got their old summer house. He had nothing to do with her after the divorce, but then she'd dropped him a note about some screenplay she'd written . . .' He paused. 'You do know that she had been a screenwriter at one time.'

'Yeah,' I told him. 'I'm the squad's Bonnie Spencer expert.'

'They had one or two telephone conversations about it. He was trying to be nice, encourage her. And then he was out there almost the entire summer, filming *Starry Night*. Well, just on a whim, he dropped by her house. One thing led to another.' The lawyer cleared his throat.

'Sexual congress,' I suggested.

'Yes. He called me about it. Apparently, she's in a bad way financially, and Sy – *post hoc ergo propter hoc* – was worried that she might attempt to make some sort of a case for alimony because they had resumed sexual intimacy. I assured him she could not. The marriage was over, as was his responsibility toward her.'

'He said they openly slept together once?'

'Oh, yes. Absolutely. You see, he was living with Lindsay Keefe. Why, under that circumstance, he chose a dalliance with Bonnie is one of those conundrums only the Higher Powers can unravel, but there you have it.'

'Did Bonnie make any threats?'

'No, but Sy seemed unduly concerned over her. Disquieted,

guilty. And over a single lapse. It didn't "play", as they say in the film world. That's why I decided to phone your office. There was *something* about Bonnie. I met her during the divorce proceedings and, quite frankly, did not care for her. That rampant good nature; there was something so false. I simply did not trust her. My guess is, Sy finally smelled something fishy too. he might have been worrying about the possibility of extortion: Pay me or I'll tell Lindsay. Or he might have been thinking she would seek revenge against him, against his property. You see, he was quite taken aback by Bonnie's poverty. He said he'd seen holes in one of her pillow-cases. Just a symbol, naturally, but he *did* say about his little tryst with her, his little one-afternoon stand: "I wonder what this is going to cost me?" What's been bothering me ever since his murder is . . . did he have any intimation that the cost would be his life?'

What a toad-load, I thought, as I walked up Park Avenue again, back to my car. I couldn't believe Carbone and Byrne had insisted I piss away a day on these two fuckheads. The entire bureaucracy of the County of Suffolk was losing its grip, peeing in its collective pants over the media exposure the case was getting. CBS, NBC, CNN and ABC were showing helicopter shots of Sandy Court, and some photographer in a boat had taken long-distance shots of Lindsay walking on the beach. Plus there seemed to be thousands of close-ups of Captain Shea in front of a bouquet of microphones, saying, 'We are at the present time investigating a variety of possi-bilities.' Neither Peter Jennings nor Bryant Gumbel sounded hope-ful of an immediate solution. The *New York Times* came right out and said that the Suffolk County PD 'appeared stymied'. And *Newsweek* agreed: 'The police seem not to have a clue . . .' The department only wanted to look good and to protect itself, and that meant following up every single lead, even the most idiotic. So a whole day shot to shit. A hundred miles to New York and a hundred miles back, to find out that Sy Spencer liked to fuck rich and/or famous women and that some supercilious lawyer was sure Sy had foreseen his doom in a threadbare pillowcase.

I turned up a side street, went into a drugstore, got out a couple of bucks' worth of quarters. I stared at the colossal condom display, wondered what kind of a moron would buy blue, ribbed rubbers and dialed 1–516, the area code for Long Island. But instead of dialing Headquarters, I dialed Bonnie's house. She answered. 'Hello.' Her tone was cautious, weary, as though she expected another hang-up. I didn't say anything. '*Hello?*' she repeated. I hung up and called Robby. No DNA report yet. No nothing. To kill time, so I wouldn't have to drive back during rush hour, I had Robby give me the names, addresses and phone numbers for Mikey LoTriglio's known associates that he'd forgotten from the FBI and the NYPD.

Three of Robby's names were the guys who had sworn and deposed that Fat Mikey had sat with them in a booth at Rosie's Bar in the meat district on Friday, August 18, from approximately three in the afternoon to – at least – six or seven. A couple of the other known associates were unavailable, currently residing in Allenwood federal correctional facility in Pennsylvania. Mrs Fat, Loretto LoTriglio, had checked into Mount Sinai Hospital two days before the murder and was still there, recovering from a new silicon breast implant because the old one had slipped and her tit had wound up in her armpit or something.

So for lack of anything better to do, I decided to check out Mikey's girlfriend, Terri Noonan, a part-time receptionist for an optician, who lived ten minutes from the Triborough Bridge in Jackson Heights, Queens.

I had an image of a gun moll with blonde, teased hair and a wad of chewing gum. Terri Noonan had plain curly brown hair and no makeup. She wore a starched white blouse with a little round collar and a pale-blue cardigan sweater buttoned at the top. No jewelry. She looked like she belonged to an order of nuns that had given up the habit but not the vows. Except when you looked twice – and you had to because she didn't show it off – you could see she had an absolutely spectacular, long-legged, big-boobed showgirl body. My guess was that Mikey had gotten it mixed up: he'd married the bimbo and kept the sweetie pie on the side.

Terri tried a whispery 'Mikey Who?' but gave up after I said 'Come on, Terri.' She asked me in and made me a cup of tea. The apartment, like the woman, was comfortable, simple, although as I'd passed the bedroom, I'd spotted a round bed with a quilted violet cover. But the living room had a green-and-white striped plaid couch, green tweedy club chairs, a couple of trees in giant pots and green wall-to-wall carpet. Nice, comfortable. The kind of stuff a cop's wife who had good taste would buy. She poured the tea from a pot with flowers, then went back to the kitchen and returned with a plate of bakery cookies; she probably bought them fresh every day in case Mikey dropped by. I couldn't help staring; instead of the nun cardigan and the plain navy skirt, she should be wearing tassels and a G-string. She said, 'God, Mikey was so upset about Sy. No kidding.' She pointed to a Linzer torte. 'Raspberry jelly inside that one.'

'You mean Mikey was upset because they were fighting about the way the movie was going?' I didn't think Terri was trying to look dumb; Mikey probably hadn't told her a thing. 'You know,' I said. 'The movie Sy was making, *Starry Night*. The movie Mikey invested in.'

'I swear to God, Officer, he never said anything about any movie or any investment.'

'And he never said he and Sy had words?'

She crossed her heart, held her hand up and said, 'Cross my heart, my mother's life to die. Not a word. I mean, I knew about Sy because he was kind of famous, and one time when Loretta – Mikey's wife – was out at La Costa we went to a premiere and a big party after for one of Sy's movies. But they was friends from the old days, and Mikey didn't talk about him all that much, except, like, to reminisce. But when he died, Mikey came right over.' Terri blinked. 'He was in tears, and Mikey's not one of these phony guys who cries all the time. I never, ever saw him like that before.'

'When was that, Terri?'

'Uh, let me think. Saturday morning. That's when I make him my cheese omelet.'

'You know Sy was killed late Friday afternoon. About four-twenty.'

'I didn't know the exact time,' she said, and broke off a tiny end of a chocolate chip cookie and put it in her mouth.

I put down the teacup and looked straight at her. 'Terri, this is important. Where was Mikey at the time of the murder?'

'Friday?'

'Friday.'

'Why is it important?'

'Do I have to draw you a picture?'

Terri readjusted the stiff little collar of her blouse so it lay flat over the cardigan. 'Mikey was here. In this apartment.'

'With you?'

'Yes.'

'What was he doing?'

She glanced down at her flat-heeled shoes. 'It was personal.'

'You and Mikey were having relations at or about four p.m. last Friday?'

She raised her right hand. 'From three till six,' she swore.

'Mikey must be quite a guy.'

'He's a little on the large side, but he's in very good health.'

'Will you sign a statement to the effect that he was here with you?'

'In blood,' she said. Instead, I handed her my Bic and watched as she began writing, 'I, Theresa Kathleen Noonan, do swear . . .' 'See,' she said, after she signed her name, 'Mikey couldn't have been out in the Hamptons when Sy was killed, because he was here with me!'

But now Mikey had two alibis – which was as good as none at all.

So I should have felt better about Bonnie, right? It ought to be comforting to know that your sicko obsession may in fact be a nice, nonhomicidal girl.

Driving home on the Northern State, somewhere around the middle of Nassau County, I started having this fantasy about knocking at Bonnie's door and saying, Thank me. She says why, and I say, Because I blew Mikey LoTriglio's alibi out of the water. And then, We put a tap on his phone and guess what? He got a call from some two-bit, piece-of-shit wise guy who, it turns out, pulled the trigger of the .22 – on Mikey's orders. You're home free, Bonnie.

Then I had an alternate fantasy where she's back from a hard run, her face rosy, her breath coming in gulps, and I pull up, get out of the car and tell her, Listen, everything's okay. We did a routine check, and it turns out that Victor Santana, the director, was renting a house that had a gun rack – and the owner confirmed a .22 was missing! Oh, no – not Santana. Lindsay! She knew Sy was going to California to replace her, and she just snapped. Can you believe, she went to a sporting goods store five minutes from the *Starry Night* set and bought ammo. She was wearing dark sunglasses – like the guy at the store had never seen a movie and wouldn't recognize her! Listen, I tell Bonnie, I know it's been hell for you. I'm sorry. And Bonnie says, Thank God, and she's so grateful she puts her arms around me and I say, It's okay, but then I rub my face against the softness of her skin and one thing leads to another and we're inside in her bedroom, having incredible, sweaty sex that lasts the whole night.

The daydream lasted all the way to Southampton, to the point where I was crying out Bonnie, baby! and about to come for the fourth time, when, out of the corner of my eye, I spotted the turnoff to Lynne's. That's when I cooled down enough for my brain to start functioning again.

And it told me that no matter how many phony alibis he had, it wasn't Mikey or Lindsay who killed Sy Spencer. In my heart I knew it was Bonnie.

It was confirmed. It was confirmed by Bonnie's real estate agent that Bonnie had been expecting big things from Sy. I finally reached the agent at home. She answered her phone with a hearty 'Hi! Regina!' She sounded like one of those fervently friendly divorcées, women abandoned by rich men, stuck on the South Fork, who con other women with rich husbands into houses so expensive that the husbands will feel fucked over and so, after an exorbitant season or two, leave, thus creating still more real estate agents.

She was saying: 'I told Bonnie, "Hon, this is *not* a seller's market. Hold on to your house. Wait." ' It was after nine at night, but the agent's voice was still horribly hearty, although a little mushy around the edges, probably from two or three gimlets. 'But she said she really needed the money and to try.'

'Did she say what she was going to do if she sold it?' I asked.

'Let me think.' I waited. 'Something about going back to wherever it was she came from, even though I told her, "Bonnie, you can't go home again." Right?'

'Any interest in the house?'

'One or two offers, but very low-ball, and she was holding out for the asking price, which was very unrealistic, and believe me, I told her so.'

'And then?'

'I called to ask if I could come over and show the house to people, and all of a sudden she was saying, Sorry I have guests. This happened two or three times. Well, finally I said, Bonnie, they're not beating down the door to buy an upper-midrange listing, because you literally have hundreds of them from Quogue to Montauk, so the next time I call maybe you can take your guests to the beach or into town for a half hour. And then she laughed – she's got a sense of humor – and said it wasn't guests, it was a man. And the next day she called me to put the deal on hold, because things were really looking up. I asked her if that was French for man, and she said yes. Like, he was a very high-powered type, but he was still managing to see her *every single day* for the last few days, and so she wasn't about to have people looking at the house with that kind of interest. So I said, Marriage-type interest? And she said she'd settle for someone's hand to hold on New Year's Eve. Sweet. Right? But the thing of it was, she was staying put. To me, that meant she was thinking about more than a New Year's Eve date; it had a certain ring of seriousness. You know? I remember, I kidded her and asked if her man had a friend and we had a good laugh about two old dames like us – not really *old*, we're in our forties – having a double wedding.'

So Bonnie had expected something from Sy. Well, why not? She was putting out plenty. That, too, confirmed: the DNA report was on Carbone's desk first thing the next morning. The hair I had gotten off Bonnie's head was a genetic match to the hair on the headboard in Sy's guest room. She had been in the house with Sy the afternoon of his murder.

Motive? Yeah. And now, definitively, opportunity.

# *Chapter Ten*

I'd gotten Bonnie out of the tub. She was wearing a blue-and-white striped bathrobe, and the bottom of her ponytail was wet. Her wrists glowed from too-hot water. I guess she'd been trying to soak out the tension. Maybe she'd succeeded, although her eyes were puffy, probably from sleeplessness, possibly from crying. She had to know she was on our Hit Parade. Maybe she even knew she was Number One.

But she wasn't doing any wounded-petunia number. She crossed her arms and stood up straight, an I'm-not-taking-any-shit stance. 'I'd be grateful if you would come by during normal business hours,' she said. Her crossed arms pushed her breasts up. She saw me staring and, slowly, trying to look casual, lowered her arms and slipped her hands into her pockets. I pictured myself standing behind her, kissing her sweet-smelling hair, the nape of her neck, then slipping my hands into her pockets and feeling her.

It was one of those she-knows-that-I-know-that-she-knows moments. We both knew she wasn't wearing anything under the robe. We both knew I was aware of it. And we both knew if I tugged at the sash, the robe would open. We'd do it standing up in that front hallway of her house because we were so wild for each other we couldn't wait.

I said: 'I understand you don't like being disturbed this late. But these are my normal business hours.'

She said: 'All right. Excuse me for a minute. I'll put something on.' She walked upstairs. I closed my eyes, leaned against the wall and began to imagine I had pulled the sash. The robe opens and I pull her up against me – she's still hot from the bath – but before

I can ease the robe off, she goes for my pants, unzips them, takes it out, holds it in her hands and . . .

I heard her on the landing and opened my eyes fast, in time to watch her walk downstairs. She'd put on jeans and a white T-shirt, a man's V-neck undershirt of washed-out cotton, only hers was tucked in tight, so you could see every stitch of the white lace of her bra. I hadn't seen this one on my illegal search; it was one of those tiny bras women wear not for support but for men. I thought: Over-the-hill bitch. Except she looked fantastic. I caught myself rubbing the pads of my fingers together, in anticipation.

'Uh,' I said. Oh, was I one cool cop.

'Beg your pardon?'

'Where's your dog?' That was the only thing I could think of to say.

'My *dog*?' She started to relax. Even to get playful. 'Why?' Do you want to question her?'

'Yeah. I want to know about her relationship with the deceased.'

'I got her at Bide-A-Wee about two years ago, so I don't think she ever really got to know Sy. I mean, beyond the usual social superficialities. "Hi, angel. *Fabulous* haircut." '

I started to smile. 'I just asked where you dog was.'

Bonnie's tone stayed teasing, light. 'I shot her.'

'Stop it.

'Ha!' she exclaimed, like a TV lawyer who's just elicited a damaging admission in front of a jury that will help his client. 'See? Deep down, you don't think I'm capable of murder.'

'No. I don't think you're capable of murdering your dog.' Bonnie laughed a little too hard. She took a step back; this was too real, and suddenly she was comprehending how terrified she was. But she made herself take a deep, deliberate breath. Easy, she was telling herself. Relax. She stuck her thumbs into the belt loops on her jeans, cowgirl style, as in, Get off my ranch, mister. 'Where is she?' I hated to keep asking the same stupid question, but having made a fool of myself asking about the dog, I now had to treat it like it was a key to the investigation.

'She likes to go out at night.' A cool, matter-of-fact response. No, cold. 'Sometimes around ten I open the back door and yell for her. She's back inside in two minutes.' Bonnie turned away from me, probably to hide her fear. Despite her laid-back, home-on-the-range posture, it was stealing over her face – jaw a little rigid, eyes too wide. She strode into the kitchen, opened the door and yelled: 'Moose! Milk-Bone!' While we waited, she went to the refrigerator and took out an Amstel Light. She did not offer me one, so I wasn't able to say 'No, thanks.' By the time she popped off the cap, Moose came barreling up to the screen door. I opened it. She let out a blissful bark and started licking my hand.

But Bonnie was hardly blissed out. She was busy being tough. She pulled the dog away from me, patted its head, then took a doggy bone out of a cookie jar and put it in Moose's mouth. For that instant, Bonnie forgot herself and was tender, a mother offering her child a lollipop. Moose, meanwhile, glanced up. She may have been nuts about me, but I wasn't part of her nightly ritual; she decided I might want to grab her treasure, so she hightailed it out of the kitchen, bone in mouth. I grinned. Bonnie didn't.

'What do you want to know?' she demanded. She tilted back her head and took a swig of beer. I stared at the arch of her throat, the rise of her breasts. I wanted her so much. 'Well?'

All right. She wanted it, I'd give it to her. 'Can you shoot a .22 rifle?'

In a movie, Bonnie would have shown her shock by spritzing out the beer. Real life lacks grand gestures, or even spectacularly messy ones. She just swallowed a little harder than normal. 'That's not funny.'

'I'm not being funny. You're the funny one. I'm the cop. And I'm very, very serious. I want to know whether you can shoot a .22.'

'I don't have to answer that.'

'You already have. You didn't say no.'

'I didn't say yes, either.' Suddenly her fear turned to anger. she slammed the beer bottle down on the counter. 'Just let me tell you something. I've been watching detective movies since I've been eight or nine years old. I know hard-boiled and soft-boiled. I know you're supposed to frighten me so much that I spill whatever beans there are to be spilled. Or you're supposed to charm me, so I'll get giddy and babble all my girlish secrets. Well, guess what, buster? You're no Humphrey Bogart. And guess what again? I didn't do anything wrong. I have nothing to confess. You're wasting your time.'

'Yeah?' I shouldered an invisible rifle. I sighted. I pulled the trigger. 'Bonnie Bernstein-Spencer. Her family owned Bernstein's Sporting Goods in Ogden, Utah, a store which did not sell junior lacrosse sticks. No: rifles, handguns. Ms Bernstein-Spencer grew up with several older brothers and was reputed to be a tomboy. Her father was known as a fine shot; he even used to go up to Wyoming to shoot elk. Tell me, Bonnie, is Ogden a nice place to visit? Because if you don't answer my question now, I'll be on the next plane out, spend half a day in town, and I guarantee you, I'll come home with whatever's left of the rabbit you shot between the eyes in 1965, plus affidavits from ten witnesses who saw you shoot it.'

She started to cry, those round, silent tears that drift down cheeks and leave trails. 'Please,' she whispered, 'don't do this to me.'

'I just have to get to the truth.' I realized I was whispering too. 'Bonnie, can you shoot?'

'Yes.' I could barely hear her. 'But I swear to God, I didn't kill Sy.'

Jesus, I thought, I almost have her. Almost. 'You have to understand,' I told her gently, 'people swear to God all the time. "I swear to God, I'm innocent." '

'But I am.'

'Prove it to me.'

'How?'

All I had to do was pull her in very slowly, lovingly, as though seducing the most reluctant of women. 'We can rule you out with a simple little test. Come with me. I'll drive you down to Headquarters, stay with you the whole time. You just give a small sample of saliva and blood – a pinprick, nothing more. And then you're in the clear.'

For a long moment there was silence. I heard the deep hum of the refrigerator and then the click of Moos's paws as she toddled back into the kitchen, across the tile, to look up at us. She didn't understand why we weren't having fun.

'Come on, Bonnie.'

I imagined her beside me in the Jag on the way to Headquarters, our arms and shoulders touching when I took a curve; I thought about the heat that instant of friction would give off. Shit, I don't want this fantasy.

But then, at Headquarters, my bewitchment would finally be over. In that hard fluorescent light, I'd see Bonnie Spencer for what she was: a killer. Of course, she hadn't meant to do it. Of course, if she could live the moment all over again, Sy would still be alive. And of course, she was, without a doubt, honestly and profoundly sorry. But still, a killer. And seeing her in that merciless light, I would no longer be able to desire the thing I most hated. Murderer.

I would no longer spend every goddam obsessed minute creating different scenarios of kissing her, caressing her, fucking her: in beds, in chairs, on tables, in showers, on floors, in cars, on the beach, in the ocean, in the woods. I would be relieved of my madness. I would save thousands staying away from pay phones. I would go to my wedding with a peaceful mind and a loving heart.

All of a sudden, I felt sick, awful – the opposite of dizzy: heavy-headed. Despair settled on me. In that terrible moment, I wondered, How the hell am I going to live out the rest of my life without this woman? For a minute I truly could not speak. Then, I don't know how, I got it together: 'Let's go, Bonnie.'

'No.'

'Come on. You've got everything to gain, nothing to lose. Let it be over.'

'I want you out of here.'

'Bonnie – '

'Don't come back. I won't speak to you again.'

'Honey, I'm sorry, but you'll have to.'

'No. And I'm not your honey. Not by a long shot, you son of a bitch. If you have any more questions, you can speak to my lawyer. Now *out*.'

Robby Kurz came swishing over to my desk, licked his pinkie and ran it over his eyebrow. I told him: 'Hey, you're not telling me anything about yourself I don't already know.'

'Gideon is outside,' Robby simpered, in an exaggeratedly faggy way. Well, what do you expect from a cop? A gay rights button? 'He's simply *dying* to see you.'

'Gideon who?'

'Are you ready for this?' He waved a business card. 'Gideon Isaiah Friedman, Esquire. Of East Hampton, sweetie. Attorney for Bonnie Spencer.'

Gideon Friedman walked toward me. He didn't take little mincing steps. And he didn't lisp or wave a limp wrist. Still, you knew what he was. Maybe it was that his getup was impeccable country lawyer, English style: awesomely casual, perfectly cut brown tweed suit with a tattersall shirt, green knit tie and shoes that looked like wing tips, except that they were brown suede. Or maybe it was the flawless haircut, where every single strand of brown hair lay smooth against his head, as if his skull were magnetized. Or maybe it was that he was too boyishly handsome for a guy in his late thirties, with that innocent, round-eyed, ultra upper-class queer look male models have, the ones who always have very long scarves tossed around their necks in interesting ways. Forget his name; he had the look of one of those guys with a wood racquet who leap over the net at the Meadow Club.

Or maybe it was just the way he checked me out when I stood up to shake his hand. 'Hi,' he said.

'Hi,' I responded.

'I'm here representing Bonnie Spencer.' He had a breathy voice, like a waiter in one of those trendy, expensive seafood restaurants, Fish Hampton or whatever, that open and close every summer because nobody, not even the most pretentious schmuck from New York, would voluntarily eat rare scallops more than once. I looked at him and thought: Oh Christ, Bonnie's going to sit in Bedford for twenty-five to life.

'Why don't you sit down?' I suggested. He sat in the plastic chair next to my desk and glanced around the squad room. I figured he'd murmur, Oooh, how butch! or at least cross his legs at the knees. 'Well, Mr Friedman, what can I do for you?'

'Well . . .' And suddenly he stopped being a homo. He became a lawyer 'Why not start by telling me what this bullshit is about Bonnie coming in and taking blood and saliva tests to "rule her out" as a suspect.'

'I meant that. Sincerely.'

'Give me a break. You were referring to that DNA testing, right?' I shrugged. 'What's the story here? Sy Spencer was shot from a distance. Are we talking about some perspiration that dripped onto the murder weapon? A little saliva? Did the perpetrator drool?' It was weird, the hard-edge-lawyer sarcasm presented in that whispery waiter's voice. 'Or was there some kind of a fight, and you have blood – or skin cells from under Sy's nails?' For a lawyer with no leverage, who had no idea what we had or where we were going, he was pretty good.

'I'm not prepared to discuss the evidence at this time.'

'Why not?'

'You should know why not. There's no percentage in it.'

'Okay,' he said. 'Then I suppose there's no percentage in anyone taking any blood tests.' He stood, regretfully, as if he hadn't been able to save me from making the most grievous misjudgment of my career. 'I'm going to have to advise my client to stand on her Fifth Amendment privilege against self-incrimination and not take the test.'

It was only then that it hit me that Gideon probably represented dress designers. 'You're not a criminal lawyer, are you?' I asked.

I waited for him to get pissed or, minimally, petulant, but to his credit he stayed composed, serene, even. He sat back down and examined the nap of the suede on his English shoe. 'Why do you ask?'

'Because a criminal lawyer would know that a suspect in a murder case can't refuse a blood test.'

'Why not?'

'Because blood tests and other medical tests are fact, not testimony. They aren't covered by the Fifth Amendment.'

'Says who?'

'Says the US Supreme Court.'

'Really? Recently?'

'Within the last five or ten years.'

'It must have happened after law school. I'll check it out.'

All right, so maybe he represented a hairdressers' lobbying group. But he wasn't that bad a guy. Not full of shit. And not full of himself. Except what the hell would he do when he got to court? Go fancy dress, show up in a black robe and white wig? And what would he do when the chief of the Homicide Bureau of the DA's office cross-examined Bonnie? Take smelling salts?

'What kind of lawyer are you?' I asked.

He smiled. Perfect, even white teeth, like Chiclets. 'I specialize in real estate.'

'Real estate,' I repeated. 'Must be busy, over in East Hampton.'

'Let me tell you what you're thinking,' Gideon said. 'Okay?' I shrugged. 'You're thinking: Oh, goody! I can send Bonnie Spencer up the river for life and that land-use faggot lawyer who represents her won't be able to do a thing except wave bye-bye as she goes.' I sat back in my seat, trying to look astounded at such a ridiculous – no, prejudiced – notion. It was not all that easy since, basically, that was what had been going through my mind. 'Well, that's not the way it's going to be, Brady. Let me tell you how it's going to be. If you're just toying with her, I would hope you'd be smart enough to stop right now. Before I make a scene in front of your superiors.'

'You think I give a shit? Go ahead. Make a scene. The captain's in that office off the reception area.'

'You should give a shit, don't you think?'

'No.'

He paused for a second. 'All right. If you sincerely think you have any kind of a case, I'd appreciate it if you'd let me know. Because then I'd have to step out – and bring in Bill Paterno.' I picked up a pen and twirled it between my palms; Paterno was the best criminal lawyer in Suffolk County.

'Do you think Bonnie Spencer can afford Bill Paterno?' I asked, trying to sound casual, as though I didn't know how broke she was.

'No. But I can.' Gideon put on a little-old-man Jewish accent.

'I make a very nice living, tanks God, and have some vonderful inwestments.' Then he added: Bonnie is one of my dearest friends.'

Well, it figured. I could see them. Giddie and Bonnie. He'd have her over to his place in East Hampton for Mexican beer and guacamole or whatever nouvelle hors d'oeuvre had replaced it, and they'd giggle and gossip and talk about James Stewart and Henry Fonda – or Share Deep Feelings.

'You can hire Paterno, Mr Friedman. You can resurrect Clarence fucking Darrow. Bonnie's still going to have to take the tests. And then we've got her.'

'Why? Because she told you she could shoot? *Please.* Girls in Utah do that sort of thing.'

'They hand out a .22 with every box of Kotex?'

'Where's the rifle?' he inquired. I said nothing. 'Bonnie doesn't own a rifle. She doesn't have access to one.' Gideon waited. 'You don't have the murder weapon, do you?' I kept silent. 'Why Bonnie? Why not Lindsay?'

'Lindsay?'

'Lindsay can shoot. You don't believe me? Go rent *Transvaal.* Bombastic dreck, but you'll see her with a rifle.'

'She's an actress. Holding a rifle doesn't mean she can shoot it.'

'Why not find out?'

'Mr Friedman, we know where Lindsay Keefe was at the time of the murder.

'And?' he asked, lifting a nonexistent speck of lint off his tweedy sleeve. 'Are you implying my client was anywhere *near* Sy Spencer's house?'

'Possibly.'

'I don't believe you.' I shrugged again. 'Stop that shrugging!' he said. 'It's very irritating. Now let's get serious. You don't want to torment this woman, do you? You just want to get her a little agitated. Well, you've done it. She is agitated to the extreme. Now why don't you let me know *why* you want the tests. Be big about it. Maybe I can recommend taking them – if it's not unreasonable, or damaging to her interests.'

I thought about it. The only reason to let a suspect know what evidence you have is when you decide to short-circuit an investigation and go for a confession. I wasn't in that much of a rush; I could wait another twenty-four hours. I sensed there were still more leads to follow. And I had to cover my ass on the illegal search of Bonnie's house by getting a warrant and then 'finding' the real estate listing and the money in her boot. Those two items would give the DA's office more rope to hang her.

'You know,' I said to Gideon, 'the perpetrator was a very intelligent person. But not that intelligent. He or she' – Gideon made a sour face – 'left so many loose ends we're still tripping all over them. The evidence box on this one is going to be so heavy the court clerk will need a goddamned moving van to bring it in. So what's the point of telling you what we have, when by this afternoon we'd have to give you a major update.'

'You're playing poker,' Gideon commented.

'Do me a favor, Mr Friedman. Give your client a message for me. Tell her that if she did it, she should come in now. Maybe we can bring the matter to a conclusion that's mutually advantageous.'

'Why won't you be decent? She's a truly good person. Why won't you give her the benefit of the doubt?'

'Let me continue. If she lets this thing play out, if she doesn't come forward with a confession, it's going to be harder for her.'

'Tell me something,' Gideon said. 'Do you honestly think you can be objective about my client?' I didn't like the way he was eyeing me; I got a quick, bad, pukey feeling. Had he picked up something from me? Had Bonnie told him anything? But what could she tell him? that once I stood a little too close to her? That a couple of times she'd sensed a bulge under my clothes that wasn't my gun?

'Yeah, I can be objective. She's a lovely lady. Good sense of humor. Friendly. Personally, I think she's a sweetheart.' Gideon listened, alert. 'But she's a sweetheart with a mean streak.'

'You're wrong.'

'Hate to say it, but I'm right. You see, I think Bonnie got – what's the word – piqued at Sy. She was lonely, divorced, poor, unsuccessful. And along came her ex. He winked, then fucked her a few times . . . Hey, we know about that, even though she swears she didn't. She lies all the time. Anyhow, he fucked her. And then he told her goodbye. No companionship, no marriage, no money. Oh, and no movie. No nothing. So she blew him away.'

'You don't really believe that.'

'I do.'

'You have no evidence.'

'We've got plenty of evidence.' I put my feet up on the desk. 'I've got to tell you, I find homicidal behavior not worthy of a sweetheart. But what I think isn't important. The lady's going away. So be prepared. Maybe make her a nice bon voyage party.'

Marian Robertson, Sy's cook, was being paid by the movie production company to remain on her job until Lindsay finished *Starry Night*. 'Cook?' she sneered. 'Lindsay Keefe needs a cook? Do you know what she eats? Fruit. All right, an occasional nut. No wonder she looks like a glass of milk. I sit here all day so that maybe, when she gets home, I can make her seven Crenshaw melon balls. What kind of person can live on melon balls?'

For a second I couldn't answer because my mouth was full. She'd insisted on making me bacon and eggs, to say nothing of a tower of English muffins and coffee. 'You don't like her,' I managed to say.

'There are worse.'

'Who?'

'Oh, the pushy ones. The braggarts. And the ones who come in two minutes before a dinner party for twenty and tell me they're on Pritikin. The ones who have to explain to a colored woman what *mille feuilles* is.'

The marmalade was in a tiny white crock, like a soufflé dish for midgets. I spooned some onto another muffin. 'What about someone like Bonnie Spencer?' I asked. Marian Robertson started to gnaw on the inside of her cheek. 'Remember Bonnie? Sy's ex-wife.'

'Oh, of course! Nice girl.'

'Mrs Robertson, this is very difficult for me. I've known you since I was a kid. I look up to you. I would hate to see you in trouble.'

'Me?'

'Yes. We have physical evidence that Bonnie Spencer was in the house the afternoon of Sy's murder. Now, you can tell me you didn't know she was here, but sooner or later we're going to confront Bonnie with our evidence. And she may say something like: ". . . and that nice Mrs Robertson, who knew me so well when I was married to Sy. She always made me my favorite . . . whatever. Kumquat pudding. Well, Mrs Robertson and I had a nice chat that afternoon." And then you'd have a legal problem, because in your statement you said no one was here.'

'More coffee?'

'Mrs Robertson, withholding evidence, lying to the police – it's a crime.'

Finally, she said: 'You're barking up the wrong tree, Steve. Bonnie's as good as they come.'

'If she's that good, why did you lie to protect her? Don't you think it would be better to let her goodness shine through?'

'If she wanted to tell you she was here, it was her business, not mine.' She cleared the cream and the marmalade off the table. I was no longer a welcome guest.

'Was she here last Friday afternoon?' She took away the sugar bowl.

'Yes.' Clipped. No, Steve, you're looking fine. No, you were the best shortstop the Bridgies ever had.

'Did you speak with her?'

'Just hello, how are you, and just a couple of minutes of catching up.'

'Was it friendly? Did she kiss you hello? Did you make a fuss? "Good to see you, Mrs Spencer!" '

'I call her Bonnie. And I was glad to see her and she was glad to see me. I gave her a big hug. What are you going to do about that? Put me in the electric chair?'

'Mrs Robertson, I'm just trying to get the feeling of the afternoon.

'The feeling was, Mr Spencer must have gotten tired of Madame Melon Balls, because he actually brought Bonnie into the house. And he was smiling, happy to be with her – like the old days. And they didn't stay in the kitchen to chat. My guess is they had other fish to fry upstairs. But that was all right, because I got the feeling

Bonnie would be back. Then we would catch up. I know her; Mr Spencer would get busy on the phone, and she'd wander down to the kitchen and we'd have ourselves a good gabfest.'

'I'd like the truth now. Were there any sounds of fighting coming from upstairs?'

'No.'

'Any sounds of anything?'

'No. Listen to me. He wouldn't have gone out to the pool to relax and make his last-minute phone calls if Bonnie was still upstairs. Say what you will about him, his manners were perfect. It wasn't in his nature not to drive a lady home, or if she'd come on her own, escort her to her car. Believe me, after Bonnie and before Lindsay, there was quite a parade of women going upstairs to see his ocean view or whatever. He *always* said a proper goodbye.'

'Then how come you didn't hear him escort her out?'

'I don't know. Maybe I was beating egg whites. Maybe I was powdering my nose.'

'Did you hear Mr Spencer come down and go out to the pool?' She did a cheek chew before she nodded. 'And what about Bonnie? Did you hear her leave after he went outside?' She didn't answer. 'Okay, between the time Bonnie went upstairs with Sy and the time you heard the shot, what precisely did you hear? Her voice? Her footsteps? The sound of her car?'

'She didn't kill him.'

'What did you hear, Mrs Robertson?'

'I didn't hear anything.' She took away the muffins and my plate. 'Does that make you happy, Steve?'

I knew the old saying was true: You don't remember pain. Physical pain, like in Vietnam, when some new kid from North Carolina heard enemy fire, aimed his M–60, and blasted me through the shoulder. The medic shot me up with a ton of shit, but they had to stuff a gag into my mouth so I wouldn't scream and give away our position when they cut open my shirt. Me, who'd always looked at wounded, screaming guys and thought: Sure, it must hurt like hell, but can't he just bite the bullet, control himself? I kept moaning so loud that they kept the gag in, and they took it out only when I puked and almost choked to death on my own vomit.

I can recall thinking, when they joggled my shoulder as they put me on the stretcher to get me to the helicopter: I will not live through this flight because the pain will kill me. I truly cannot take it. I kept howling, 'I want a priest!' Me, whose last confession pretty much coincided with my first communion. But I don't remember the pain itself.

And you don't remember emotional pain either.

Like being a seven-year-old kid playing ball and my father drives onto the field in some farmer's tractor he's doing day work for, and he cuts the engine, stopping between the pitcher's mound and first base, practically breaks his neck getting down and then grabs a bat out of the hands of one of my friends and insists on hitting a few.

More pain? Being a thirty-five-year-old and seeing my pal, my confidant, the only person I ever really spoke to outside work, the one person I thought to buy a Christmas card for – the guy who owned the liquor store – flash his wife a look of revulsion when I walked through the door.

You know all that pain and more occurred. Recalling it, you might feel sad or even cringe. But you do not remember the pain itself.

So when I rang Bonnie's bell and got no answer, and then ran to her garage to see if her car was missing, and then, finally, spotted her in her chicken-wired garden, picking vegetables, I almost laughed at the panic I'd felt, the horror, the stab in the gut – the pain – when I thought she'd gone. So what if she had? you do get over these things.

And when Moose barked a welcome and Bonnie looked up and saw me and shuddered – a violent, uncontrollable shiver of fear – I wanted to disappear, or die, it hurt so much. But I said to myself: I'll get over it.

She was squatting over a basket of eggplants. 'What are you going to do with all those things?' I asked.

'Get out of here.' Her voice was a hoarse whisper. She braced her hands on her knees and slowly, as if it were too much of an effort, pushed herself up. All her energy, all her fire, all her humor was gone.

'Look, I just wanted you to understand . . .' What was I going to say? Nothing personal. 'You lied, Bonnie.'

She walked out of the garden, leaving the eggplants, a plastic bucket full of tomatoes, Moose – everything – behind. She headed toward the house, awkwardly, without any of her great jock grace, as if she'd lost her center of gravity. I followed her. 'We have a neighbor who can not only identify Sy's car as being here every day the week he died, but who can identify Sy himself. I mean, we can place you with him enough times . . . Why did you lie about a thing like that?'

She didn't answer me, didn't acknowledge that I'd grabbed onto her arm, trying to steady her or just hold on to her. 'And why did you lie about your screenplay? Didn't you bother to think that he'd tell the people he worked with that it was a piece of shit?'

She tripped over a tree root. I lost my grip on her, and she fell on her hands and knees. 'Are you okay?' I asked. She couldn't get up. She sat back on the ground, breathless, and looked down at the pebbles and grass embedded in her hands, at the little rivulet of blood that ran toward her wrist, but she didn't wince or weep. 'Bonnie,' I said. Her spirit was gone.

Moose wandered over, wagged her tail and licked Bonnie's hand, but Bonnie didn't acknowledge her. 'Please,' I said. I pulled her up. She didn't stop me. When she was on her feet again, she continued her unsteady journey toward the house. 'Listen, your lawyer friend . . . He's going to pay for the best criminal lawyer around.'

I felt sick. Empty. But I'd lived through too much. I knew. part of me understood that in two weeks, I'd be hoisting an alcohol-free beer, eating potato chips, and Lynne would be saying: 'Forget that you're going to get the fattest gut in Bridgehampton. Do you *know* what those chips look like on your insides?'

You forget pain. You really do.

Bonnie opened the screen door to her kitchen. 'Congratulations,' she said softly.

'I don't want congratulations. Believe me, I'm sorry.'

'No. You did what you set out to do. You got me. That's it. My life is over. What you did isn't homicide, but the effect is pretty much the same: a dead person.'

'It has to be,' I said.

'Why?'

'Because you killed someone.' She walked inside and closed the screen door. I looked at her, blurred, distant, through the mesh. 'Don't try and leave. There'll be a twenty-four-hour watch – '

'Where could I go that you wouldn't find me?'

'That's right.'

'It's so sad.'

'It is,' I agreed.

'No. It's sad because I didn't do it. You know I didn't.' It was about sixty-five degrees. I began to shake. I knew: This would be pain I would never forget. 'Don't worry,' Bonnie said, just before she closed the kitchen door. 'You'll get over it.'

## *Chapter Eleven*

We got to Bonnie's house before eight the next morning. Less than thirty seconds later, she looked up from the fine print on the search warrant, swallowed and said: 'I'll have to call my lawyer.'

'Feel free,' Robby said magnanimously, a second before he and the other detective, a short bodybuilder type in his late twenties, tried to push past her, into the house. The kid's thighs were so overdeveloped that he couldn't get his legs together. He walked like a chimpanzee.

'You can't do this!' Bonnie shouted trying to block us. I was the one who finally shoved her aside.

'Reasonable force,' I said. 'Call your Civil Liberties Union.'

At first I'd expected hysteria. Then – especially when I noticed she was wearing those tight turquoise bicycle shorts and a T-shirt – I did a fast fantasy number. She'd faint. I'd grab her, lead her over to her couch and mumble something calming, like 'Easy, Bonnie,' as, slowly, I let her out of my arms. Easy, Bonnie: I liked the idea of saying her name out loud.

But she'd just stood near the staircase, completely still. She was there, but she wasn't there. The world she was living in was so awful that she withdrew and entered some other, kinder universe. At last, she drifted past me, into the kitchen to call Gideon. I could have been a ghost, just air and vapor. Moose picked up Bonnie's mood, staying right beside her, concerned, not giving me so much a wag of the tail.

I followed them into the kitchen and started going through her cabinets as if assuming I'd find a cupful of .22 bullets behind the Down Home Gourmet barbecue sauce. For someone who was close to broke, Bonnie was spending too much money on mustard: honey mustard, tarragon mustard, green peppercorn mustard. I looked over at her. Maybe I'd try a little mustard humor, clear the air. But her back was toward me, and she was speaking quietly into the phone.

I shook a jar of popcorn hard and loud, like some maracas-playing fool in a Latin American band. I wanted attention. Maybe if she acknowledged I was alive I would be able to feel alive. I was so goddamn down.

Fuck this sadness shit, I told myself. Your obsession's dead. Be glad. But I couldn't let it rest in peace. And I couldn't stop trying to get a rise out of Bonnie.

I made a big production out of going through her pocketbook. Obnoxious. Intrusive. A deliberate invasion of privacy. I examined each key, flattened out a couple of linty tissues, studied a supermarket cash register tape. In slow motion, I took apart her wallet, laying out her seventeen bucks in bills, her forty-four cents in change, her driver's license, her Visa card, her library card, her video store membership card. And the pictures: father in a plaid shirt holding up a prizewinner of a trout. Father and mother – tall and broad-shouldered like Bonnie – all dressed up, like for a wedding, smiling, but starched, stiff. You just knew they'd rather be in their plaid shirts. Brothers and sisters-in-law on skis. Nieces with horses. Nephews with dogs. All the Bernstein pictures had mountains in the background.

I waited for her to show some spirit: run, try and punch me, scream out something like 'I hate you!' Nothing. So I made a big deal of opening a purple plastic case that held a couple of Tampax. I held each one – Super – up to the light, as if anticipating a fuse instead of a string. Zero response. Should I taunt her? Say, No shit. You still have a period? and then deny it if her lawyer bitched about my being insulting? But I kept quiet. Thighs, the kid detective, was around; I didn't want him to think I was anything other than neutral.

Bonnie hung up the phone. I went back to the pocketbook. There was some powder on the bottom of her purse, red, obviously the blushing stuff women put on with those big fluff brushes. But

I did a major number, sifting it into a plastic envelope, like it was a new, killer form of cocaine that made crack look like aspirin. She made no snide remarks. Clutching the warrant in her hand, she simply walked out on me. I stood there, a complete jerk, helpless, yearning, watching her turquoise ass until it disappeared into the hall.

I was like a husband whose wife has just walked out on him. I sank into the same chair where I'd sat that first day, having coffee. I was still holding her pocketbook.

About ten minutes later, when I finished the kitchen and found absolute squat, I went looking for her. She was sitting on the brick ledge in front of her fireplace, the search warrant beside her. She was hugging herself, as if waiting for logs to blaze up and thaw her out. Of course, there was no fire. Outside, it was already over seventy. The sky was too bright, an almost painful blue, the brilliant morning light of the end of August. The sun poured through Bonnie's living room window, making shining squares on a dozing Moose and on the dark wood floor beneath her.

Bonnie's head was down, so she didn't notice. Thighs rush over and hand me a heavy shopping bag. Since all he'd turned up so far was one of Moose's half-chewed rawhide bones under the couch, he was clearly longing for some significant sign of Bonnie's guilt.

I emptied the shopping bag onto the coffee table. Bonnie glanced over. There were two unopened boxes: a coffee grinder and one of those expensive espresso-cappuccino machines. In the bottom of the bag was an American Express receipt: Sy Spencer, card member since 1960, had paid for them.

I walked over to her, sat down on the other side of the search warrant and fluttered the receipt in front of her. 'Sy like a cup of espresso afterwards?' I inquired. 'Or before? Some guys need a little stimulant.' She didn't answer, but then I hadn't expected her to. I didn't exist. Plus Gideon had obviously warned her not to say anything, and she was taking him literally. 'Is your lawyer coming over?' I asked. She picked up the warrant. She looked for a pocket for it, but since she was wearing the shorts and T-shirt, she didn't have any. She just held on to it. I shifted so I could at least look at her. Her T-shirt was from some film festival, probably a feminist thing. Across her breasts it said WOMEN MAKE MOVIES in red and green and yellow and blue.

I rested the receipt on the top of the warrant she was holding and pointed to Sy's name. 'Three hundred and fifty-five bucks for a cup of coffee,' I said. Across the room, Thighs sniggered; he probably thought the sound was a manly detective laugh. Bonnie brushed away the receipt with the back of her hand. It floated onto the floor.

It was so quiet. The only sound was the dog's snoring and then the clunk, clunk of Robby walking around upstairs. I'd wanted him to be the one to find the money in her boot, the real estate listing. I told him: I'll stay downstairs, keep an eye on her.'

But she wasn't going anywhere, and I couldn't move anymore. I just sat there beside her. We could have been a heartbroken couple waiting for some sad appointment together, cancer specialist, marriage counselor. I kept sneaking glances at her; instead of wearing her hair loose, tucked behind her ears, or in a ponytail, she'd put it into a braid. I had the urge to reach over and, with the tip of my index finger, stroke each one of the shiny intertwinings. I'd say, It'll be all right.

What I actually said was: 'Where'd you hide the rifle?' She didn't move. 'Bonnie, your window of opportunity is closing, You make it tough on us, we'll make it tough on you.'

Just then, Gideon Friedman came striding in. Ninja Lawyer: baggy, rolled-at-the-cuff black, cotton slacks, a black sweater, hair combed back with slickum I stood up. 'Hey, Counselor Friedman,' I said. 'Good to see you.'

He walked past me and hunkered down in front of Bonnie. 'Did you say anything to him?' he asked her. 'Anything at all?' She shook her head. 'Good girl.' He picked up the search warrant, stood, and read it over. He saw it was okay. He wanted it out of sight, but since he didn't have any pockets either, he held on to it and, with his other hand, pulled Bonnie up and steered her into the kitchen.

They must have been talking softly in there. I couldn't hear anything, not even the hum of muted conversation. I walked over to her bookshelves. Most of them were paperbacks: hundreds of mysteries and novels. There were books about movies – biographies of actors and directors, *Cinematographer's Handbook*, *Farce in Film* – and about nature stuff. *Flowering Plants of Beach and Dune. Hiking Long Island*. There were no sex books tucked behind *Birds of North America*, no *Memoirs of a Victorian Serving Wench*, and no *Stop Being a Compliant Cunt and Get Him to Marry You*, one of those books single women always seem to have.

Just then Robby clomped down the stairs. His beige loafers had thick black heels with what sounded like metal taps. He was grinning, brandishing a plastic evidence bag with the wad of bills that had been in Bonnie's boot. I walked over to him, 'Eight hundred eighty!' he announced.

'In tens or twenties?' I tried to look amazed, thrilled. 'Like from a cash machine?'

'You got it.'

'Anything else?'

'Not really.' Robby seemed a little disappointed. He'd probably been hoping for a smoking rifle.

'No vibrator in the night table?' Robby shook his head. 'No interesting papers?'

'Nothing.' Shit, I'd have to go up to have a casual look-through and then find the real estate listing. Unless she'd thrown it out. 'Just a lot of movie script stuff in her office,' he said. 'Rejection letters in a file. But listen, we have enough! This money is the stake in her heart. And once we get her blood samples, it's all over.'

'Any rejection letters from Sy?'

'No, but we don't need any. Where is she?'

'In the kitchen with her lawyer.'

'Think we should stick it to her now?' He was like a leashed, drooling Doberman; he couldn't wait.

'Yeah,' I said. 'Might as well get it over with.'

My throat felt swollen. My chest rose, but I couldn't get enough air.

We walked into the kitchen. Robby waved the bag of money in front of Bonnie's face. 'Eight hundred eighty dollars in twenties,' he said to her.

'If you have any comments, please address them to me,' Gideon responded.

'Oh, *sorry*,' Robby said, giving him a big, shit-eating grin. 'We found this hidden in your client's boot. All I want to know is where this money came from. Maybe she could tell us.'

'Oh,' Bonnie began, 'its – '

'Quiet,' Gideon snapped at her.

'But, Gideon, it doesn't have anything to do with Sy.'

Gideon did not look thrilled with her. 'Would you please leave us alone for a minute?' he asked. We walked into the hall outside the kitchen, heard whispers. I took deep breaths, but I just made myself dizzy. Then Gideon called, 'All right. You can come back in.' When we did, he nodded at Bonnie.

She spoke to Robby, as if there was only one cop in the room. 'The money you found is what's left of twenty-five hundred dollars I got last December. I do a lot of work for a catalog company, and the owner pays me once a year. In cash.' Then she added, 'Off the books.'

'So there's no record of your having received the payment,' I said. Bonnie made herself look at me, except her eyes did not meet mine.

'That's the point of being paid off the books,' she explained, too patiently, as if talking to someone with an IQ in the minus column. 'There isn't supposed to be any record.'

'So we just have your word that that's where the money came from?'

'Where else would I get eight hundred and eighty dollars?'

'On the morning of his death, Sy Spencer withdrew a thousand bucks from a cash machine. It was gone when we found him.'

Gideon broke in. 'Do you call this police work? You don't investigate. You just drop whatever you can't explain at Bonnie Spencer's front door. Obviously Sy gave it to someone. Or he bought something.'

'No,' Robby said.

'Don't say no. I knew the man. He had a great eye, and he loved to indulge himself. If he saw a hundred-dollar tie he liked, he'd buy one in every color.'

'Believe me, we checked,' Robby continued. 'There was no time for him to buy anything. And he didn't give anything to anyone. Whoever was with Sy Spencer last took the money. And we know that person was Mrs Spencer here.

'You *know* that? How do you *know*?' Gideon asked, as if he couldn't believe our stupidity. But I could tell; he knew too.

'Because they were in bed together in the guest room of his house that afternoon.'

'Really?' There's nothing like watching a desperate lawyer trying to do an amused act.

'Yeah, really,' I broke in. 'There was some hair in the bed that wasn't Sy's. We're betting that when we get a sample of Ms Spencer's blood, it'll be a perfect DNA match.'

Bonnie's hand flew up to touch the top of her head. She remembered. She understood. She looked at me with a terrible mixture of fury and grief.

'Now, you want to know what happened the afternoon Sy was killed?' I could only talk to Gideon. I didn't have the courage to look at Bonnie anymore. 'Your client had relations with Sy Spencer. They had a disagreement. He left the bedroom. She took the thousand bucks from his pants pocket. When he went for a swim, she put on a pair of rubber thongs – '

'I don't have rubber thongs,' she said to Gideon.

' – and went downstairs. At some point, she walked to a spot right by the back porch where she – '

I could feel Bonnie staring straight at me. Her eyes were huge. '*No.* I did not do it. That money . . . I got it – '

'Okay,' I cut her off. 'Give me the number of the guy at the catalog company.'

Bonnie looked over at Gideon but didn't wait for a signal. Just as he started to shake his head no, she said, 'The man's name is Vincent Kelleher. He lives in Flagstaff, Arizona. I do three catalogs for him. *Country Cookin'*, *Juno* – that's for heavy women – and . . . God, I'm going blank on the other one right now. Oh, *Handy Dandy.* Hardware, gadgets.'

Before I could say anything, she hurried out of the kitchen

upstairs, to her office. I followed. Her hands were shaking as she leafed through her address book. 'Here.'

I dialed the number. The place wasn't open yet. Gideon came upstairs, into the office, followed by Robby. Finally, I got Kelleher's home phone from Information and woke him up. Yes, he was Vincent Kelleher. Thighs must have sensed something going on, because he came upstairs too, but the small office was too crowded for him to fit in; he stood outside the door staring at Bonnie's *Cowgirl* poster. Yes, Vincent Kelleher affirmed, he owned several mail-order catalog companies. Yes, Detective Brady, a Bonnie Spencer had done some work for him. Off the books? I demanded. In cash? No! Did you pay Ms Spencer two thousand five hundred dollars in cash last December? No! At any other time? No! She'd done work for him a couple of years ago, and he'd paid her . . . by check. Was she in some sort of trouble, Detective Brady?

I hung up the phone. I turned to Robby. 'He never made a cash payment to her.'

'That's what I figured,' he said.

Bonnie grabbed onto the lapel of my jacket. 'I swear to you – ' It was the first time she'd touched me. I pushed her hand away.

'Out of curiosity,' I continued, 'Mr Keller wants to know if the lady's in some sort of trouble.'

'I'll say she is,' Robby said. 'Big trouble.' He looked at Gideon and smiled. 'In fact, by tomorrow, I think the lady could find herself under arrest.'

'I think you and I should talk,' Gideon said to me.

'I think it's too late,' I said.

'The man's right,' Robby told Gideon. 'It's too late. Deal time is over.'

'There are not going to be any deals,' Gideon said.

'You're right,' Robby told him. 'No deals. You know why? because your client is dead meat – and all of us know it.'

Oh, right. Vietnam vet with Purple heart and Bronze star. Big, brave cop with brass balls so big they clang. Except when the cars lined up in front of Bonnie's house like a cortège – Bonnie and Gideon in Gideon's BMW 735i, Robby and Thighs in Robby's silver Old Cutlass, which was actually gray, and me – to take Bonnie to Headquarters for a blood test. I couldn't force myself to go along for the ride; I didn't have the guts to watch Bonnie being driven to her own funeral. As soon as we passed the two-block-long run of stores that was downtown Bridgehampton, I cut north off the main street and tore along the back roads until I got to the highway. Then I floored it. A hundred and ten.

Big stud in a Jaguar. When I got to Headquarters, way ahead of them, I couldn't even make myself go into Homicide. I went into a stall in the men's room and sat down on the can.

I was afraid to face Bonnie.

No, I was afraid to face what I had done. I sat there, heart hammering, realizing I was the butt of some Almighty joke: This woman who somehow had come to mean a lot – no, everything – to me, this woman who I couldn't imagine living without, was, due to my sharp investigatory skills, my crafty persuasiveness, my flawless logic, going to go to jail and would come out an old lady. I would never see this woman, this enchantress again.

Whatever the hell her magic was, this woman was able to do what no one else had ever done before: bring me to life. But before I could solve the mystery of what her power was, I solved the mystery of Sy Spencer's murder. Oh, I was one shrewd dude. I'd broken her spell.

So now I was totally, wholly and entirely without her, without any hope of touching her or talking to her, for the rest of what will be, at best, thirty or forty years of my lifeless life. I would move through marriage, kids, more homicides, grandchildren, retirement, as though moving through a thick and dirty fog.

There I was, a real man. A homicide detective, sitting on a toilet because I was afraid to face some killer with a shining braid who makes good coffee and has a wonderful dog.

But I got myself under control, except for one or two trembling breaths. Still, I couldn't leave for another five minutes because some guy from Sex Crimes or Robbery could come in to take a leak and when I passed him, I might suddenly get the shakes, or even burst into tears. He would realize then that, somehow, I was not the tough guy he and I and everybody else were so convinced I was.

So I just hid out in the toilet until I could become a man again.

Bonnie and Gideon, while not true locals, had probably lived on the South Fork long enough to know how to get to the Long Island Expressway without having to wait in the summer traffic caused by Yorkers, who, while normally the world's pushiest people, were totally feeble when it came to driving: sitting passively in their overheating cars, moving at the speed of a slug, on their way to buy a bottle of balsamic vinegar for thirty dollars. Their city brains could not comprehend the concept of turning off main roads. Naturally, all this would change the second *New York* magazine published an 'Insiders Tell Their Secret Hamptons Shortcuts' article.

But Bonnie and Gideon wouldn't take a shortcut. What was waiting for them that would make them want to rush over to Headquarters? And Robby and Thighs weren't going to push them; they knew just enough about the South Fork of Suffolk to know that a road on a map did not necessarily mean a road in reality. Why risk a wrong turn, wind up in the middle of a field of cauliflower and have Gideon reconsider and decide to spend a few days fighting the blood test, litigating the unlitigable? So they'd creep along with all the other cars. They could be another thirty, forty minutes. An hour even.

I left the men's room and dragged myself into Homicide. Since we work on shifts, two or three guys share a desk. Hugo the Sour Kraut was at mine. I waved at him to stay out and sat down at Robby's. Two minutes later, Ray Carbone stuck his head into the room. He was wearing his congenial expression, like he wanted to talk about the exit wound in Sy's skull, or the Jungian theory of personality, so I picked up the phone, dialed the number for time and made a show of holding on, expectant, like I was waiting to speak to some Ultimate Witness. 'Eastern Daylight Time, Ten-fourteen . . . and twenty seconds,' the computer voice said. Carbone saluted goodbye and left. I was too exhausted to even hang up the phone, so I just sat there, listening to time passing. 'Eastern Daylight Time, ten-sixteen . . . and thirty seconds.'

I opened Robby's drawer, searching for a pen so I could look like I was taking notes. No pens, but there were a couple of near-empty bottles of breath freshener drops, a business card from Mikey LoTriglio's lawyer and, toward the back, Robby's file on Mikey. I took it out. Michael Francis LoTriglio, aka Mikey LoTriglio, aka Fat Mickey, aka Mickey Lopkowitch, aka Mr Piggy, aka Michael Trillingham. Faxed forms and computer printouts from NYPD and the FBI showing his arrest record: extortion, loan-sharking, conspiracy to sell stolen securities, tax evasion. And homicide, twice. Richie Garmendia of the Retail Butchers Union had been found floating under a West Side pier with his skull battered in. And Al Jacobson an accountant for a carting company, was missing and presumed dead, death reportedly caused by being dropped in a cement mixer and thereby becoming part of Battery Park City in Lower Manhattan.

With all his arrests, Mikey had been brought to trial only once, on tax evasion. Well, twice. Two hung juries, and the government had severed him from their case.

'Eastern Daylight Time, ten-eighteen . . . and ten seconds.' I closed my eyes and pictured Bonnie as I'd last seen her; she had changed clothes to come to Headquarters. I'd watched her walk downstairs in a black cotton sweater tucked into a straight white skirt, and black-and-white high heels. She must have put on some makeup, because her eyelids had turned bronze and her lips looked like she'd been eating raspberries. It wasn't Bonnie; it was a tall and very tasteful tragic figure. She wore long gold earrings and looked heart-sick.

I opened my eyes but couldn't shake the vision of her, so I made myself look down at the file again. Robby had made lots of notes in his rounded fourth-grade penmanship: about Mikey's mob associations, including known hit men, about his use of his family's business as a front for Family business, about his friendship with Sy and his investment in *Starry Night*. Details notes, pages and pages. I could see how he'd prepared for Monday's Homicide meeting, for making his case that Mikey was our guy.

But at the meeting I'd convinced him our guy was Bonnie. And starting after the meeting, the pages had become paragraphs, the paragraphs, phrases. '8/22. 4:10.' That was about a half hour after Mikey and his lawyer had been in, not that Robby or I had cared all that much. We both knew by then who'd killed Sy. 'Spoke to Nancy Mikey, bookkeeper for Starry Night Productions, Inc,' he'd written. 'Finally admitted Mikey tried bribe for info re movie $$.'

I turned to the next page, but it wasn't there. I hung up on 'Daylight . . .' Something wasn't sitting right. No more notes? Even if Robby had a videotape of Bonnie pulling the trigger, he should have asked some more questions. Like what did 'Finally admitted' mean? Like how much was the bribe? Like how had it been offered to the bookkeeper? On the phone? In person? Like had this bookkeeper known what a bad guy Mikey was? How had she said no? Or hadn't she? I put the file back in the drawer, leaned back and closed my eyes. Relax. Not my problem.

But then I opened my eyes, leaned forward and called Nancy Hales in the *Starry Night* production office at a film studio in Astoria, Queens. I gave her a song and dance about Robby being assigned to another case; I was just checking up on his notes.

'How many times did you speak with Detective Kurz?' I asked casually.

'That once in person.'

'In your office?'

'Yes. And two times on the phone.' Her voice was husky and overly slow. She was dull-witted or southern, or maybe she was into phone sex.

'Tell me about Mikey LoTriglio.'

'I told – '

'I know, but I want to hear it in your own words, not rely on his notes.' Then I added: 'Believe me, it'll be better for you.'

'He said . . .' She was nervous. 'The detective said I wouldn't be in any trouble if I cooperated.'

'You won't be. Now tell me what happened.'

'Mr LoTriglio came up to the office one day looking for Mr Spencer, but I think he knew Mr Spencer wouldn't be there. Do you know what I mean?'

'Yeah.'

'He asked for the bookkeeper, and someone brought him over to my desk. He pulled over a chair and asked if anything funny was going on. I said, "Funny?" '

'What did he say?'

'He said, "Don't shit me." So I told him I couldn't discuss business with him and he told me he was a major investor and I said I knew that but he'd still have to get Mr Spencer's okay.' She paused. 'He was . . . I kind of knew he was a gangster. Not like *Scarface*, but still, I was scared. That's why I did it.'

'Took his money?' I asked.

'Uh-huh.'

'How did he give it to you?'

'He sort of slipped it under my telephone.'

'I mean, in what denominations?'

'Fifties.'

'How many fifties?'

'Didn't the other detective tell you how much it was?'

'I thought you were cooperating,' I said.

'Ten fifties.'

'And what did he get for his five hundred dollars?'

'The Lindsay Keefe business.'

'Do me a favor, Nancy. I'm making my own notes. Let's start fresh. Spell out the Lindsay business for me.'

'That the extra location scout and the two extra trailers and Teamster drivers and Nicholas Monteleone's bonus on signing and four interior sets we built . . . well, all that didn't exist. Sy just had me put in some invoices and . . . kind of move some money around.'

'Move some money to Lindsay?'

'Yes.'

'How much did it come to?'

She whispered: 'Half.'

'Half a million?'

'Uh-huh.'

'Why did Lindsay Keefe get an extra half million?'

Her whisper became even softer. 'I don't know. I guess she was threatening to quit.'

I didn't get it. Sy had wanted to get rid of her. 'When was this?'

'Three days before the start of principal photography.'

'I took a deep breath. 'Nancy, why would he give her a half million more? She had a contract, didn't she?'

'Yes.'

'So?'

'So he was crazy about her. I mean *crazy.* Like he would have done *anything* to keep her happy.'

Or, at that point, to keep her in his bed. No big deal. He was Sy Spencer. He could get creative with the budget, and when *Starry Night* made ninety mil, who'd miss a few hundred thousand? And so, for a million plus another half million, Sy had bought himself a truly superior lay – and a lemon of an actress who was killing his movie. That must have been some kick in his arrogant ass. 'Did you get the sense that Mikey LoTriglio had heard any of the negative talk about Lindsay's acting that was going around?'

'I think . . . There *were* a lot of rumors. I'm pretty sure he heard about them.'

'How?'

'Probably by paying off someone in the crew.'

'Like who?'

'I don't know.'

'And then he found out from you that Sy had diddled the books to give Lindsay a five-hundred-thousand-dollar bonus.'

'Yes.'

'And how did Mikey react?' Silence. 'Didn't Detective Kurz talk to you about this?'

'No. I would have told him, but he didn't ask.'

'And you didn't volunteer.'

'No. I was scared.'

'Tell me what Mr LoTriglio said.'

'He said . . . when he heard the exact figure on what Lindsay had gotten, he said, "My friend Sy is goin' to get his nuts chopped for this." And then he walked out.'

# *Chapter Twelve*

What the hell was wrong with Robby? Jesus, if I'd been the one assigned to Mikey LoTriglio, I'd have been kicking chairs, screaming at the cop who kept insisting the perpetrator was the ex-wife. So what if Bonnie slept with Sy, I'd yell. There's a law against that? She humped him, kissed him goodbye, told him to call when he got back from LA, and then went home. Period. Oh, your she-can-shoot theory? Is that your problem, jerk? Well, what about Mikey – or one of his boys? And what about Lindsay? Turn on your VCR and watch her toting a rifle, in loving color.

And even if the ex-wife had, in fact, slept with a .22 between her legs all the years when she was a kid in Utah, could she still bag Sy? Could such a nice, warm lady plan such a mean, cold killing? This is life we're talking about here, not goddamn Agatha Christie, where Lord Smedley-Bedley's black-sheep cousin gets murdered after crumpets with the vicar on a rainy afternoon.

And listen, jerk, I'd bellow, and maybe jab my pen toward him, like it was a dart, *listen*! What about the criminal personality? Who is more likely to shoot when betrayed? A kissed-off screenwriter who's slept with every other guy on the South Fork, who's so used to hearing guys tell her goodbye that she could write their rejection speeches for them? Or a Known Bad Guy who's just discovered his alleged good friend is screwing him out of half a million bucks?

If I were Robby I'd have fought. I'd have built up a terrific case against Fat Mikey. Against Lindsay, come to think of it. She was a movie star, a professional egomaniac, and Sy was about to blow her out of the water.

So what the hell was wrong? When I'd sat at the meeting,

stacking up the cards against Bonnie, why hadn't Robby knocked down a few of them? It would have been so easy.

I had a fast thought: Oh, Jesus, could I have destroyed an innocent life?

But then I told myself: Asshole, look what she's done to you! Miss All-Natural is a brilliant con artist. First she looks up from the warrant, gives you that look of pain, then that disbelieving how-can-you-hurt-me? stare. And then the cold shoulder. She's got great ESP, that Bonnie. You thought you were so cool, but she's known all along you've had a major thing for her. So she sits and shivers by the fireplace on a hot day. Lets her mouth quiver. Swears she didn't do it. Why shouldn't she swear? She knows how the conned want so desperately to keep being conned. But then she sees she can't get to you . . . Well then, okay, too bad; she gave it her best shot. So she goes upstairs and puts on a sexy skirt and gold earrings.

But what if she's telling the truth?

Then why did she lie so much?

Well, what if she lied through her teeth . . . but still didn't kill him?

Didn't kill him? Take Bonnie Spencer, Mikey LoTriglio and Lindsay Keefe. Which one of the three is most likely –

Robby came in just then and hurried over. He didn't like my feet up on his desk, near his pen set, but he was too excited to waste time in a protest. 'Bonnie's in the lab!' Only his nervousness that the side of my shoe would smear the 'Detective Robert Leo Kurz' brass plate kept him from positively gurgling with delight. 'She's down there now. With the lawyer.' I didn't budge. 'What's wrong? Don't you want to go?'

'What about Mikey's payoff?' I asked him. He gave me a village idiot look that was so completely moronic I knew it was fake. 'His payoff to the bookkeeper at the *Starry Night* office.'

'Who cares?'

'I care. We know Mikey's alibi sucks shit. So he had opportunity. And now, from what the bookkeeper says, motive. Why the hell didn't you pursue that line of questioning and – '

Robby held up his hand, swift, full-palm. Stop! Aggressive,

angry, like one of the neo-Nazi cretins in the police academy who demonstrate how to direct traffic. 'Wait just one second here, Steve.' Huffy. Definitely huffy. 'We *have* our perpetrator, who we all agree is our perpetrator, over in the lab, as we speak.' He did an about-face, marched out of Homicide, down toward the lab.

I kept up with him. What a born dork Robby was, with his white Tums crust at the edges of his mouth. He radiated hairspray scent. His suit matched his pale-beige loafers. A fucking dork suit: the fabric was supposed to look luxurious, like nubby linen, but instead it looked as if it was cut from a bolt of cloth that was having an allergic reaction to its own ugliness. You could see its unhealthy sheen; it was covered with minuscule bumps.

'Hey, I want to talk to you for a second,' I called out. He didn't stop.

We got to the door of the lab just as Bonnie and Gideon were leaving. She was pressing a gauze pad against the bend in her arm where they'd drawn blood, so she didn't see me until I said 'How'd it go?' She glanced up, startled, terrified, the nice girl in a horror movie who had just seen the monster.

I might as well have been one. She tried to get away so fast that she wound up stepping on her own high-heel shoe and would have fallen if Gideon hadn't grabbed her arm. She slumped against him for just a second, until she regained her balance.

For that one second, though, Bonnie's eyes were on my face. Finally, there it was: absolute fear. Eyes floating in the whites, unfocused, in terror of the monster who was stalking her. And then she was rushing away, down the hall. Her long, fast strides were restrained only by the knee-hobbling hem of her skirt, so Gideon was able to keep up.

After they disappeared around a corner, Robby said: 'I'll go over to court, get the arrest warrant.' He started to go.

I grabbed the sleeve of his repulsive suit. 'Not yet.'

'What do you mean, not yet?'

'I mean, we'd be making a mistake to push it.'

'No, we wouldn't.'

'Yes, we would.'

'No!'

'Robby, how many man-hours have you put in looking for that .22? Not enough. We've got to give it a better shot.'

His upper lip drew up, so he was almost snarling. His bared teeth were the same color as his beige suit and shoes. 'What the hell's the matter with you?' he demanded. 'You going soft? You going to risk letting her run?'

'Where is she going to run to?'

'Anyplace. Listen, I was in her closet. She has hiking boots! A backpack!'

'For crissakes, she's a Jewish broad. What the hell is she going to do? Go to ground in the wetlands?' I didn't tell him that was precisely it: the waking nightmare that had stolen five hours off my sleep the night before. Bonnie *could* get away. I'd almost choked myself with my sweaty, twisted rope of a sheet as I tossed around. She could disappear, live off the land, gradually make her way north, steal a boat, get off Long Island. 'Or you think the fag lawyer's going to hide her in his wine cellar?'

'She could go back to Utah!'

'And do what? We've got the addresses of all her brothers, and her old man in Arizona. There's no place for her to hide.'

'If we bring her in now, before the weekend, we're heroes. Damn it, don't you care about your career?'

'Blow it out your ass, Robby.'

Robby banged the wall with his fist. It made a dull, undramatic thud. But his voice made up for it, blaring, amplified by the narrow corridor so the whole floor could hear him. 'You're gonna fuck up this case!'

'No! I'm going to do my job, follow up *all* the leads. I'm not going to be some ass-kisser who cuts corners because he can't wait to pucker up.' I made a wet, kissy sound in the air. ' "Yoo-hoo, Captain Shea. Here is the solution to the heinous murder that has so captured the attention of the national media. Please, *you* take all the credit. I only want the satisfaction of a job well done – " ' Robby brought up his fists and bounced on the balls of his feet. His keys jingled in his pants pocket. 'Holy shit! Don't hit me, Robby!'

'Shut your fucking mouth, Brady.'

'Don't hurt me! I'm forty years old.'

'Listen, you loser, son-of-a-bitch drunk, I'm going to court to get a warrant. Now.'

'Good. Get the hell out of her. And while you're on your way, I'm going in to Shea and telling him what a lazy bastard you've been, and how you're jumping the gun and handing him a case that could fall apart five seconds after it gets to the grand jury.'

It was more like a movie than life, almost a freeze-frame. I didn't move. Robby kept his fists up, but finally, slowly, opened them. His fingers spread out; it looked as though he'd decided to throttle me. Finally, I said: 'Calm down.'

'Fuck you, you dipso.'

'Listen to me. Don't rush this. You're gonna push Shea, and then the DA will find fifty loose ends – like Mikey LoTriglio. Like Lindsay.'

'Lindsay,' he sneered.

'Don't you get it? Some rag newspaper in the supermarket is going to print a picture of her from *Transvaal* holding a rifle. "Is Lindsay Keefe Trained to Kill?" Don't you get that the *Daily News* is going to do a big piece on Sy's mob connections? And don't you get that unless we can respond to every single question that could come up with one single answer – Bonnie Spencer – the department could be made to look like it's trying to pin it on some poverty-stricken sweetie-pie of an ex-wife, and you and I are the ones who'll get creamed for it?'

Robby didn't answer. And he didn't choke me. He just lowered his hands, turned and, in his clunk-heeled beige loafers, stomped back to Homicide.

'Don't ask me about the case, Germy,' I said into the phone.

'I am not asking you about the case,' he honked in his hundred-thousand-dollars'-worth-of-New-England-schools voice. 'I am a film critic, not a gossip columnist. And I didn't ask what was wrong with your case. I asked what was wrong with you. You sound – it's hard to describe – flat. Tired.'

'I'm too old for this shit.' Having bounced the Sour Kraut from our mutual desk, I had my files fanned out in front of me, all unopened. 'Tell me about Lindsay Keefe.'

'I love it. Classic film noir. The uncouth cop falls for the ice-blonde sophisticate.'

He did it; he made me smile for a second. 'I just want to know about *Transvaal*.'

'Why?'

I hesitated, but then I said: 'I know you long enough to know you'll keep your mouth shut, Jeremy.'

'That's right, Steve.'

I saw I'd been doodling on the cover of Bonnie's file. Shaded 3-D boxes. Her initials: I realized they were mine, backwards. 'Okay, I heard Lindsay was shown shooting a rifle in the movie.' Germy made that upper-class exhaling sound that comes out between Ah! and Oh! 'What I'm asking is if – without raising bi-coastal eyebrows – you can get me the name of someone who knows what went on while they were making that movie.'

'Someone who knows whether Lindsay could actually shoot or if she just pulled the trigger and the sound editor went "Bang!" '

'Yeah.'

'Call me back in an hour.' He paused. 'And listen, from an old friend . . . You sound something less than yourself. Take it easy. All right?'

'Sure,' I said. 'I'll be fine.'

I called Lynne, hoping I'd get her machine. But she picked up. 'Hello!' Cheery, welcoming. I had nothing to say to her. I hung up the phone and dialed my brother.

'Easton, come on. *Listen*. Remember you told me Sy would never have fired Lindsay?' I asked.

'Um, he would have let her think it, but he never would have.' Easton sounded thick-tongued, slightly dopey.

I'd obviously woken him from one of his ritual marathon sleeps: striped pajamas on, phone on a pillow on the floor to muffle the ring, curtains safety-pinned to ensure unending darkness. His sleeps were escapes that would last for weeks, except for shuffling excursions in flapping leather slippers down to the kitchen, where he'd spoon soft food – ice cream, canned fruit cocktail – into his mouth listlessly, as though feeding a baby who wasn't hungry. Occasionally, he'd offer a thin excuse: The doctor says it's probably mono, and then give a feeble cough. Easton's sleeps came whenever he realized he wasn't going to be a superstar insurance agent, or hero of men's wear. He'd start going in to work late, coming home early – sometimes after lunch. A boss would call, first to lecture, finally to fire him, and Easton would simply mumble, If that's how you want it, and hang up the phone and go back to sleep.

Well, what did he have to stay awake for now that Sy was dead? 'East, come on. Focus for a second.'

Irritable. 'I *am* focused.'

'Do you think there was any chance Lindsay knew that Katherine Pourelle had been sent the *Starry Night* script, or that Sy was going to see her out in LA?'

Easton tried to rise to the occasion. You could almost see him shaking his head, clearing out the fog. 'Did she know?' he repeated. Suddenly he sounded alert, interested, protective. 'Why do you want to know about Lindsay?'

'Look, I know you're – you know – kind of attracted to her, but try to be objective, East. This is a homicide.'

'And you think if Lindsay had found out somehow . . . Steve, that's idiotic.'

'Probably. But I can't leave any loose ends untied.'

'Give me a second,' he said. 'I must have dozed off for a couple of minutes. I'm still a little groggy.' I reached into my drawer and retrieved a combo key ring–nail clipper I'd gotten at a grand opening of a car wash and gave myself something resembling a manicure. It seemed I'd have time to take off my shoes and socks and do my toes, but finally Easton spoke, although hesitantly. 'Lindsay had . . . a certain curiosity about Sy's business.'

'What does that mean in real life? She was nosy?'

'If you want to look at it superficially.'

'Give me a for-instance.' He didn't reply. 'Stop the chivalry shit. I'm not looking to arrest her. I'm just looking to finish the paperwork on this case.'

'Is Lindsay a real suspect?'

'No.'

'Who is?'

'Not for public consumption, okay?'

'Of course not.'

'The ex-wife, Bonnie. But Lindsay shot a rifle in a movie called *Transvaal*, so I've got to check her out some more. Now, how was she nosy?'

'The word I used was "curious". You see, Sy usually swam his laps after she did hers. So when she came back into the house, supposedly to take a shower, she'd actually go into his study.'

'And?'

'And pretend to be looking for a stamp or a paper clip, but actually go through whatever papers were lying on the desk. Oh, I just remembered. Sy had one of those pocket computer calendars. One time, I saw her pressing some buttons on it. My guess was she was reading of all his entries. I know this makes her sound like a sneak. She really wasn't. Sy was more than her lover; he was her employer. She knew as well as anyone how brutal he could be with anyone he wasn't pleased with, and he definitely wasn't pleased with her. So she was protecting her own interests, so to speak.'

'Bottom line, Easton. Do you think she knew why he was going to LA?'

'Bottom line?' He gave it real thought. I waited. 'She *was* getting curiouser and curiouser. Extra visits to his study. Checking out the fax machine early in the morning, before Sy was up, before she went to the set.'

'How do you know what went on so early?'

'I liked to get in early. This is . . . embarrassing.'

'Listen, do you think you're the first guy in human history to get stupid over a girl? I'm your brother. You can tell me. You went in early because you wanted to see her?'

'Yes. But she never really tried to hide her curiosity from me. Either she thought I was so much a part of the household that I was like wallpaper – there, no threat – or she sensed how I felt about her, and felt safe.' Easton sighed. 'I think that must have been it. But in any case, what you want to know is if I think

Lindsay knew Sy was going to take some action. And the answer is yes. I do.'

Germy called back a half hour later. He'd spoken to the producer of *Transvaal*. They had hired some South African game warden as a technical adviser, and he'd given Lindsay a couple of hours of lessons with a rifle. The producer had no idea what kind of a shot she was, but he'd added she'd had a quickie affair with a game warden but then switched over to a black actor who was playing an anti-apartheid activist.

Gideon called around noon. He was back in his office. He'd hired Bill Paterno for Bonnie, but wanted one last talk with me. In person. Man to man. He said that without self-consciousness. Could he come back to my office? I glanced over at Robby. He was hunched over his desk, going over all the DNA and lab reports, index finger inching down the pages, lips moving, calling on the God of Science to bless his crusade against Bonnie Spencer. He looked pasty and intense and a little nuts, so I gave Gideon quick directions to the nearest diner, told him to meet me there at one thirty, that he could have as long as it took me to finish a chicken salad and bacon sandwich and a vanilla malted – which, when I was minding my manners, took approximately four minutes.

The Blue Sky had once been a regular greasy spoon, but the Greek guy who'd bought it had done it over, so now the spoon was hardly greasy at all. The walls were paneled in fake oak, the ceilings dripped with fat-globed chandeliers and hanging plastic plants. The menu, a listing of every food product capable of being microwaved, was almost as thick as the Bible. The owner hovered over us, pad open, ready to transcribe whatever we happened to say.

I looked at Gideon. 'The cook usually washes his hands after he takes a dump, so you can have the chicken salad or tuna fish and not die. The hamburgers taste like snow tires. They nuke everything else.'

'Don' listen to him,' said the owner. 'He's a stupid cop. All my food's good. Today the special is nice flounder on a bed of spinach wit' feta cheese.'

Gideon said no thank you, he'd already eaten. Just an iced coffee. I ordered, and the owner strolled off, toward the kitchen.

'Go ahead,' I said. 'Make your pitch.'

Gideon adjusted his knife, fork and spoon and took a minute to make sure the edge of his napkin was absolutely parallel with the edge of the table. Once that was accomplished, he immediately opened the napkin and put it on his lap. I noticed that for all his clean-cut, square-jawed handsomeness, the bridge of his nose appeared to have gotten squished in the birth canal or in a fight and never popped back into place. 'I was hoping this conversation wouldn't be necessary,' he said quietly.

'It's not. You could have saved yourself the trip – and acid indigestion from the iced coffee. All we're doing now is neatening up a few loose ends. Probably by tomorrow we'll be arresting your client.'

'Her name is Bonnie.'

'I know that.' My cheeks began to ache; I could feel the pressure of tears someplace way behind my eyes. I wasn't going to lose it, but if I was, it wouldn't be in front of this guy. 'Let's get on with it.'

'Why are you out to get her?'

'Mr Friedman, with all due respect, you're her friend. And this is not your field. You're personalizing a criminal investigation. And you're wasting my time and not doing your client any good. Do everybody a favor: wait till tomorrow. Let Paterno handle it. He's used to dealing with us and the DA.'

The owner came back with the iced coffee and a little bowl of teaspoon-size containers of half-and-half. Gideon waited until he was gone. 'You're the one who's been personalizing it,' he said.

'What are you getting at?'

'I'm getting at that it is morally and ethically wrong to investigate someone you've – '

Put up the umbrella, I thought, because here it comes: a shower of shit. 'I've *what*?'

'Slept with.'

Heat rises. Blood rushed up to my forehead, my ears. I was so fucking furious. Disappointed too: I couldn't believe she'd resort to something that cheesy – which shows the state I was in. I'd had no trouble believing that, with evil intent, she could plan and execute a homicide. But tell a tacky lie? Not my Bonnie! 'That's total and complete crap,' I said.

'No, it's not crap.' He was calm, at peace. Whatever shit he was dropping on me, it was shit the bitch Bonnie had made him believe.

'Your friend has a little problem in the truth department, counselor. I never laid a hand on her. I never made a suggestive remark. Nothing.'

'Now, *that's* crap.'

'Look, you don't really want that iced coffee. Go back to East Hampton, practice some real estate law, forget this conversation.' He stayed put. 'Okay, the head of Homicide's a guy named Shea. Go ahead. Talk to him. Or file a formal complaint with the department.'

'What happened between the two of you that makes you want to get her so badly?'

I looked up and saw the guy coming back with my sandwich and the malted. The food looked pale, puffed-up, dead – like something pulled out of the water, something that, before you can stop yourself, makes you gag. 'Look,' I said to Gideon, 'obviously she has you believing something went on. I'm not going to try and talk you out of it.' A piece of bacon hung out of the roll, dark, curled, wormy. 'But I'm not going to ruin my lunch and sit here listening to you tell me I copped a feel when I was questioning her, or showed her my shield and said, "Fuck me or go to jail." Okay? So take a walk, Mr Friedman.'

I could hardly hear him. 'I'm not talking about the investigation. I'm talking about what went on five years ago.'

'What?'

'Five years ago. You . . . I wouldn't call it an affair. But it wasn't just a typical one-night stand.'

'Wrong guy,' I snapped.

'She called me about it the next day. I remember. She sounded elated. She said, "Gideon, I met this wonderful man!" '

'She's lying. Or maybe she's just . . . Maybe this whole experience has made her a little crazy, if she wasn't that way to begin with.'

'Bonnie's as uncrazy as they come.'

'So maybe it's an honest mistake, and she just thought she saw me under her covers. Look, I'm sure you know it isn't any secret that a lot of guys have rolled around in that bed.'

Gideon had put a lightweight olive-green blazer over his ninja outfit. Silk probably. He rolled down a sleeve, then recuffed it. 'Bonnie told me, "He grew up here in Bridgehampton. On a farm. About two minutes from here." ' I didn't say anything. I shook my head. 'I remember this conversation, Mr Brady. I'd never heard her so high. She said, "He's a cop, of all things. A detective. Very bright. And a wonderful sense of humor. I had *fun*." '

'Not with me she didn't.' He started working on his other sleeve. 'I'm sorry. I know you believe what you're saying, but it wasn't me.'

Gideon peeled the top off a little container and dumped cream into his glass. 'She said – '

'Please. There's really no point to this.'

'Let me finish. She said, "His name is Stephen Brady." ' I sat across from him in the booth, still shaking my head no. 'I remember your name, because we had this long . . . well, amusing discussion about whether Brady is a WASP or an Irish name and about the . . . sexual proclivities of each group. Bonnie said she'd ask you what you were the next time she saw you.' Gideon took a packet of Equal and sprinkled a dusting of the powder into his coffee. 'She had no doubt that she'd see you again. That was the funny part: her absolute certainty that the night had been special. She'd been around a long time, knew the ropes. She was never given to self-deception. She knew what happens when you ask someone to meet in a bar – '

'What bar?'

'The Gin Mill. Over on – '

'I know where it is. Go on.'

'What else is there to say? Bonnie knew that when you invite a man you meet in a bar to come back to your house, you don't expect him to send flowers the next day.'

'She said I sent flowers?'

'No. A metaphor for romance. But she felt something had happened between the two of you. Something out of the ordinary.' I rested my forehead in the palm of my hand and rubbed, back and forth. 'You can't have forgotten. Or even if she had been just another pickup to you, seeing her, seeing the house – '

'I'm telling you, I have no memory.'

Gideon's young, handsome, squished-nosed face looked more uncomprehending than angry. 'Why the vendetta if you have no memory?'

'There's no vendetta. She's guilty.'

His spoon clanged against the glass as he stirred, but his voice was very gentle. 'Why didn't you ask one of your colleagues to take over the Bonnie aspect of the investigation?'

'There was no reason to have someone else step in. I never met her before.'

'But you did. It happened.'

It took a very long time, but at last I said: 'Look, I'm an alcoholic. I've been sober for almost four years. But there are blanks in my life. Days, maybe weeks I'll never be able to recall. Maybe . . . There were a lot of women. For all I know, she might have been one of them. I had this feeling almost from the beginning that she looked familiar. I figured I'd seen her around town.'

'You don't deny it, then.'

'No. But I don't admit it either. Maybe I spent the night with her. Maybe I told her she was a terrific person. It was one of the things I always said: "It's not just the sex, babe. It's *you*. You're a terrific person.' But if I did spend some time with her, I'll never know what I did or what I said.'

'For the record, you told her you loved her.'

'But I never saw her again, did I?'

Gideon sat back in the booth and crossed his arms over his chest. Relaxed, conversational. 'She said you were heavier then.' I'd dropped twenty pounds after I'd stopped drinking and started running. 'And you had a mustache. Thick, droopy.' Yes. 'That's why it took her a minute to realize it was you at her door. And do you know what went through her mind then? She thought: Who cares why he never called? He's back!'

'Mr Friedman, don't you get it? Either she did a little research on me in town and made this whole thing up – or it actually happened. But it doesn't matter. They can take me off the case, put someone else in my place, and the outcome will still be the same. Bonnie Spencer will be brought to trial on – yeah, sure – circumstantial evidence. But *strong* circumstantial evidence. Most likely she will be found guilty. And she will go to jail. And whether I slept with her or gave her a line about loving her or never met her before I rang her front doorbell won't matter one goddamn bit.'

'Bonnie was right. You are very, very bright.'

'Thanks.'

'Hear me out. You've constructed an intelligent, imaginative theory about how Sy was killed. All I ask now is that you look back at your data, put that same creativity to work again.'

I shook my head.

'Try it. Build another case. A real one this time, not a myth.'

'I can't.'

'You have to.'

# *Chapter Thirteen*

I left the diner, my lunch untouched. The afternoon had turned from plain August hot to sweltering. I thought about finding an AA meeting but instead drove north, aimlessly, farther from Headquarters. I pulled into the parking lot of a shopping center. Suburban heaven, with its open-twenty-four-hours Grand Union, its nail salon, its frozen-yogurt store and its card shop featuring Charlie Brown paper tableclothes, plates, cups and guest towels.

I put the top up, locked away my gun and changed into the shorts and sneakers I kept behind the two front seats, on the parcel shelf of the car – my gym locker on wheels. I hooked my pager onto the elastic waistband of the shorts. I had used my running shirt with the Clorox-eaten sleeve to clean the dipstick, so I had to run shirtless.

The humidity was suffocating. I would gladly have taken one of those blue bandannas I'd been laughing at all summer, the kind New York runners were twirling and wrapping around their foreheads, trying to look like construction workers instead of rich idiots. And I'd even take one of their ass packs too, with its plastic bottle of mineral water.

For the first couple of miles through central Suffolk – past tract houses sided with cheap, already-pitted aluminum, where nobody, apparently, had enough home-owning pride to stick a mailbox with a painted 'The McCarthy's' up on a post, or plant a crab apple or a rosebush or anything beyond the token scraggly juniper the builder had stuck in the front lawn, past about ten acres of open grassland with a For Sale sign – I didn't think about Bonnie at all. I didn't think about anything.

I ran past a small farm, just like any on the South Fork, although here there was no sweet ocean tang in the air to obscure the harsh perfume of fertilizer and pesticides. Pretty, though: a brown field of russet potatoes, almost ready for harvest. It was edged by a border of dark-pink clover and white trumpet vines. The potatoes look good, I was thinking. A lot of Long Island farmers don't like russets because they can get all knobbly, but there'd been just enough rain –

Bonnie! Not a fantasy this time. A true recollection.

Labor Day, about four in the afternoon. Inside the bar – yeah, Gideon, the Gin Mill – it was murky, and packed, like the Friday night of Memorial Day weekend. But the season was over, and the too-old-to-be-yuppies were no longer cruising loose, happy, expectant. The same hot-shit Yorkers now jammed against the bar, pushing each other. They were overtanned and overdesperate, with stiff, extended, sun-dried arms, hands grasping for their margaritas ('No salt!'), drinking too hard to hide their despair that another summer had passed without their falling in love, or at least finding someone who wouldn't humiliate them by guffawing – Har! Har! Har! – in a movie on the Upper East Side, or by being fat in TriBeCa, or by wearing brown suede Hush Puppies on Central Park South.

It was the perfect time for a local like me, bored with a June, July and August of receptionists and nurses, who wanted (for one night) a grown-up, dressed-for-success lay. Easy pickings. By that first Monday in September, I knew the thirty-five-year-old lady corporate vice-presidents would have stopped playing the Geography Game, with an automatic You're Out for Hamptons hicks. I also knew all those frosted-haired, lip-glossed, scrawny-necked financiers would no longer be muttering 'Really?' and then two seconds later going to the ladies' room when they heard I was a cop. These women at the Gin Mill hadn't caught themselves a banker or a doctor or even an accountant without his CPA. So now it would be: 'I envy you, living here year round' and 'A *homicide* detective! Tell me, how can you stand looking at . . . what's the best way to express it? Looking at the dark side of the human condition day after day?'

Except instead of hitting on one of those, I spotted Bonnie. If I had to say why I chose her, it could have been because it was the Summer of the Perm, and she was the only woman without cascades of frizzles. Or because she wasn't wearing an outfit, one of those things with plaids and stripes and flowers, where nothing matches on purpose.

Bonnie leaned against the bar, foot up on the rail, standing tall among the other women. She was working her way through tissues and keys in the side pocket of a short red-and-yellow-plaid skirt, on her way to money to pay for a beer. She wore a red tank top. As I maneuvered toward her, I could see the sheen of her broad, tanned shoulders. Silky skin, I thought, not leathery. I put my hand on her shoulder. It was silky. I said: 'I'll buy,' and gave the bartender three bucks for her beer. She smiled. 'Thanks.'

But that was all that would come: an image. I kept on running, sweat dripping down onto the blacktop, for another two miles, all around the farm, then back past the grassland, into that pathetic stretch of aluminum-sided Long Island. I'd been hoping to clear my head. But all I could recollect in that killing heat was Bonnie Spencer in the crisp, conditioned air of the Gin Mill, holding her beer in front of her with two hands, the way a bride would hold her bouquet. Her hair was short then, a little choppy; maybe she'd tried to give herself a sophisticated haircut, but she'd wound up looking like a wood nymph's older sister instead. The recessed lights over the bar made her arms and shoulders gleam.

I walked around the parking lot a few times to cool down, except the air was so thick and humid all I was able to do was stop wheezing. I hung around for another five minutes, hoping for a breeze, but none came, so I got into the car and used the oil-streaked T-shirt as a towel. The pager had rubbed against my skin, and there was a dark-red bruised spot on my right side.

I got into the Jag, sprayed a little Right Guard under my arms and then contorted myself to get back into my shirt, tie and suit fast, before some housewife could peer down and catch me humping the steering wheel as I pulled up my zipper. I kept replaying the scene in my mind.

'I'll buy.' Putting down my drink – vodka with a wedge of lime – and handing three folded singles to the bartender.

Bonnie's smile, so radiant that for a second I felt light-headed. 'Thanks.'

I went into the supermarket and bought a big bottle of club soda. My face must have been close to purple, because the express-line cashier said, 'Y'oughta watch it, hon. This heat and all.'

'I'll buy,' I said to Bonnie.

'Thanks.'

I sat in the car again, glugging down the soda, trying to recreate what happened next. Logically I would have said 'Steve Brady' and she would have said 'Bonnie Spencer,' and a couple of minutes later maybe we would have chuckled about two Bridgehampton rubes having to meet in East Hampton, in a phony 'genuine' gin joint with a bullshit ceiling fan and bartenders who deliberately didn't shave because scruffy was a Great Look, surrounded by city slickers in two-hundred-dollar sandals.

Except I couldn't remember anything more. Maybe nothing more had happened. Maybe, for some reason, she had just recalled what turned out to be an aborted pickup attempt. Being a screenwriter, she'd whipped up a little love story around it and, casting herself in the leading role, said to her lawyer: Here, maybe you can use this. Except Gideon had remembered her euphoria, remembered hearing my name. Whatever else he was, he was a smart man, and a savvy, probably even an ethical lawyer. I didn't think he would lie to a cop during a homicide investigation, not even to help a friend.

Well, whatever had happened with Bonnie, it was lost to me. Too bad. I would have liked to know what it had been like, screwing her. I drove back toward the farm, put the top down again, took a leak by the side of the road and got back into the car to drive to Headquarters. I put my hand on the stick.

God almighty, it began to come back.

We took a sip of our drinks and then exchanged names and discovered we both lived in Bridgehampton, although on different sides of the tracks. 'You weren't born here,' I said.

'Which means you must have been.'

'Right. Where are you from?'

She must have said the West, or Utah, because somehow – and this came back so vividly – we got to talking about trout fishing. It turned out that she could tie her own flies. I said, I'm not much of a fisherman. I've only gone for fluke and blues a couple of times, but maybe we could go together one day. And she said, Night's better for trout, and smiled and added, Tell you what. Give me a call when you can tie at least three leader knots as easy as you tie your shoelaces, and I'll take you to the perfect mountain stream. I said, Can't I give you a call before that? and she flashed me a beautiful smile.

Just as I was thinking to myself, This is one incredible woman, somebody pushed to get closer to the bar, knocking me into Bonnie. Oh my God!

Electricity. Magnetism. Whatever the hell it was, I couldn't believe it was happening. We stood there, body against body, unable to pull apart, like victims of an uncontrollable mob, crushed together. Except we could have parted, without too much trouble. We were just being jostled by a crowd of ordinary, pushy New Yorkers. But I was so aroused, and the pressure felt so good.

And clean-cut Bonnie – courteous ('Nice of you to pay for my beer'), amiable, humorous, lover of mountains and fisher for golden trout – was as hot and irrational as I was. Her hand slide between my legs. Jesus! In the dim, smoky light of the bar, in the press of bodies, in the dehumidified, perfume- and aftershave- and mouth-wash-scented air, in the noise of raised voices and clanking glasses, she was tuning out everything – and going for it. Not just to provoke me, but for her own pleasure, which, of course, became my pleasure. She let out a small, low sound. She was going to be a noisy one, a wild one.

'Let's get out of here,' we both said at the exact same time. Normally, when that happens, you laugh, but we had crossed some boundary and gone where there was no kidding around.

What happened next? We took my car to her house. I must have been in a white heat, because I couldn't remember any conversation or anything about her street, or the downstairs of her house – only following her ass up to the bedroom and pulling off her clothes the minute we passed through the doorway.

We were just starting, but both of us were so inflamed we tore at each other, groaning, the way people do in that moment before the end. We parted for a second; Bonnie's hands were trembling, and she couldn't manage my buttons, so I undressed myself. She watched me, spellbound, and I became so excited by her intensity I couldn't finish the slow strip I'd begun. I threw off my khakis, my undershorts, my shoes.

Bonnie moved close to me and touched me for a second, to verify that what I had wasn't going to go away. Then she moved in even closer. She raised her hips, straddled me. No teasing, no foreplay; we were way past that. I pushed in right away and we stood, her back against the bedpost, screwing our brains out.

She came first. I lowered her onto the bed. I wanted to finish on top. Her arms and legs wrapped around me, and we became the two halves of a greater person.

I'd never had sex like that before. It wasn't that I was voluntarily letting go; it was that I had no control. Just when I thought that I'd ridden out the last wave, that I could catch my breath, slow things down, speed them up, subdue her, another, bigger wave knocked me senseless.

At last, her whimpers and moans turned to shrieks of pleasure. I joined her. I heard myself screaming so loud it scared me.

We lay there on top of the white popcorn bedspread, not knowing what to say to one another. It was that moment where my foot or my hand would inevitably begin to drift along the floor, searching for a sock or my shorts. Except I couldn't move. And I didn't want to go. Finally, Bonnie said: 'Think of a way we can get over the awkward silence.'

'Tell me more about fly-fishing.'

'You need an eight-foot glass rod,' she murmured. 'Don't let them talk you into bamboo.'

I held her lightly, running my hand up and down her back. Her skin was like velvet. A breeze that had a hint of autumn in it fluttered the white lace curtains.

'This is wonderful,' I said.

'I know.'

'I meant the breeze.'

Suddenly she noticed the window was open. She sat up. 'Oh, God.'

'What?'

'We were kind of loud. Just watch. One of my neighbors will think I was being murdered and call the police – after she serves the carpaccio.' I started to laugh. I hadn't told her what I did for a living. 'You won't think it's so funny when you hear the sirens.'

'Want to bet?' I pulled her back down, so she was lying facing me. 'I'm a cop. A detective on the Homicide Squad.'

'No. That would be too interesting. You're not.'

'Of course I am.' She shook her head. 'Okay, what am I?'

'I don't know. You sort of have a macho style, but you probably do something adorable. Sell children's shoes. Teeny size-two Mary Janes, with a free balloon.' She bit her lip. 'God, I'm going to die if that's what you really do.'

I forced myself out of bed and retrieved my pants from where I'd tossed them, between a little stool and one of those old-fashioned makeup tables with a skirt. Bonnie looked bewildered, then hurt; she combed her short hair with her fingers, as if preparing for a dignified goodbye. But I tossed her my shield. She caught it, too, and it had been a lousy throw. Her left hand shot out.

'Good reflexes,' I said.

'I need them. You're not exactly Sandy Koufax.'

We stared at each other across the room, she amazed that I was a cop; me, that she knew baseball. For some crazy reason, after all that had transpired, this was too intimate. Real fast, we began to talk over each other, she saying something pointless about loving whodunits, me asking if she had anything to drink. She offered iced tea or Diet Coke, but then I said '*drink* drink.' All she had was light beer and a bottle of one-step-up-from-rotgut red wine she'd bought to use for sangria, for a picnic, but it had rained. I settled for the wine. She threw on a bathrobe and went downstairs.

The minute she was gone, I got claustrophobic; I wanted out. It wasn't the room. I knew that much. It was sizable, appealing, all white except for the old wood beams and the painted blue-green chair rail. It definitely wasn't overstuffed; there was a four-poster bed with plain wood nightstands on either side, the little stool and vanity table with its ladylike yellow-and-white-striped skirt, and a clumsy, cozy-looking club chair, covered in a shiny cotton – big yellow flowers with blue-green leaves – a stand-up lamp beside it.

But even though there was that cool breath of air coming through the open windows, I wanted to get outside. Go home, have a couple of drinks, maybe drive up to the bay afterwards, watch the sunset. I put on my shorts.

I heard her coming upstairs, so I picked up the phone. I'd say 'Damn. Yeah. Right away' when she walked in, and then tell her a fast-but-grisly homicide story: maybe a stabbing followed by arson. Something nice and graphic, full of gaping tracheas, mutilated genitals. Run while she was still gagging.

Except she came in carrying a can of Diet Coke, a wineglass, the bottle, and holding a corkscrew between her teeth. She looked so goofy. I hung up the phone and took the corkscrew. 'Calling your office?' she asked, and handed me the wine.

'Yeah. No emergencies that can't wait.' I opened the bottle, poured, drank. The pressure to escape eased a little. I'm sure we must have talked for a while, because if I had taken her in my arms again, I would have been lost. I remember stretching out on my side, letting my fingers graze over her fabulous skin, but not getting too close. It was perfection, lying there like that, feeling the warmth of her, the coolness of the breeze. The sky had lost its daytime glare and had become softer, finer: blue tinged with pink and gold.

I whispered, not to disturb the beauty: 'I love this time of day.'

Bonnie glanced at the window. 'Magic hour.' She kissed me on the mouth, but sweetly, almost daintily. 'It's a term in cinematography. The time after dawn or before dusk. Enough light for shooting, but there's a fineness, a tranquillity to it – magical light. You have to work fast, because before you know it, the enchantment is over, but while it's there . . . you can get something beautiful.'

I drank some more wine. I must have fallen asleep for a couple of minutes. When I woke up I caught Bonnie studying my face. She averted her eyes and said too fast: 'I was just wondering how you'd look without the mustache.'

'No. You were thinking: This is one hell of a man.'

'Yes.'

I let my fingers glide down, over her throat and breasts. I caressed her stomach and felt her muscles contract. Two or three good, deep kisses. And then we were at it again, this time with a lust that made the last go-round seem a lighthearted tease. We were biting and clawing at each other. I heard myself growl.

Bonnie pulled back. The wildness disturbed her. She wanted to be civilized again, a sexy woman, not an animal. She got cool and urbane on me, did a couple of cute maneuvers with the tip of her tongue. Then she got to her knees to climb on top. I knew what would happen: She'd arch her back, toss her head, let her breasts bounce. Then she'd bend over and do some more tongue tricks. She wanted what I wanted: mastery.

But I didn't want well-bred sex games. I pushed her down, onto her back. We were animals, and I was the male. I wanted her to know that. I pinned down her arms, pried open her legs with my knee and started giving it to her. She was strong, and she struggled to get free, but at the same time, she was sobbing one word over and over: More.

After it was over she turned away from me. She wasn't making any noise, but I could feel her back shaking as she cried. I was kind of shaky too. I hadn't been in control at all. What if she hadn't cried for more? What if she'd wanted me to stop? Would I have?

I rested my cheek against the nape of her neck. 'Bonnie, it's okay.' She didn't say anything. 'Too rough?'

'No.'

'Too what?'

'Too much.'

'Too much what?'

'I don't know.'

I rolled her over onto her back and kissed her. Her cheeks were wet. 'Next time I'll be real suave. Okay? You'll think: Jesus, what technique!' Bonnie's face softened as she smiled; I knew she wasn't pretty, but for that second, she was so beautiful. 'I'll come up with some position where I'm all twisted up, with my head coming out of my ass and my dick pointing east. You'll have to slide on sideways.'

She wiped away the last tear with the tip of her index finger, a lovely ethereal gesture from such a big, hearty girl. 'When you were holding me down . . .'

'Tell me.'

'What if you'd been a bad person?'

'But I'm not. I'm a great person. Now let's talk about something else. Are your eyes blue-gray or gray-blue?'

'Please, I'm serious.'

I turned the pillow over to the cool side. 'Well, if you are serious, maybe you should think twice before inviting guys you've just met to come into your house.' Until I said it, I hadn't realized how much it bothered me. Angered me. Goddamn it, she had been so easy. I hadn't wanted her to reach out and touch me, a stranger. Play with me. In a public place, for crissakes. Here she was, tall and clean and fine, and she tied her own flies: a wonderful woman. But instead of a light kiss, a smile to turn down the thermostat after we'd been pushed together, she'd cupped my balls, stroked my dick; her hand was still cold from holding the beer. 'You knew absolutely zilch about me, and you said, "Let's get out of here." '

Bonnie didn't get that guilty, You-think-I'm-a-whore look I'd expected, maybe wanted. 'I thought you were better than this.'

'Hey, I'm not talking about morals. I'm talking as a cop who's seen some nice girls get hurt when things got out of hand.'

'I can take care of myself.'

'You're strong. Mountain woman, right? If someone you meet at a bar gets out of hand, you'll just use some self-defense shit you read in *Ms.* magazine. Let me tell you something, sister. Before you can stick your finger into his eyeball or crash down on his instep or knee him in the nuts, you could be raped – or dead.'

'I'm a good judge of character.'

'You think all those nice, dead girls said to themselves: "This guy's a psychopath, but he's got cute dimples"? No, they said: "I'm a good judge of character." '

For a minute she didn't say anything. Then she propped herself up on her elbow and said: 'Aren't you *starved*?'

'Yeah, come to think of it.'

'Scrambled eggs? An omelet and toast?'

I took a fast shower while she went downstairs to make supper. I put my clothes back on but went downstairs barefoot. Sitting in the kitchen and watching her in her bathrobe, flipping an omelet, I felt snug; I thought: This is what husbands must feel like. But it was strange: the homebody with the spatula didn't seem to have any connection with the wild woman I'd been fucking upstairs. Then she turned around, and I saw her mouth was swollen from all the kissing.

Bonnie handed me a blue-and-white plate with the omelet and the toast, buttered and cut in triangles. I went to the refrigerator and took out a couple of her crappy light beers. I remember we sat there in the kitchen talking for an hour or more, but I don't remember what we said.

Later, I remember thinking, as I followed her back upstairs, that Bonnie had grace. Physical grace that born athletes have. The surefooted walk, the upright, easy posture. And commonsense grace. When to kid around and when to be serious, when to talk, when to shut up.

And sexual grace. She loved having sex – and having it with me – and every kiss, every touch, every thrust was something she wanted. She didn't posture: didn't stick her ass out for admiration, even though it was admirable, didn't offer her tits up like they were twin trophies in some erotic contest. It was all natural. Graceful. No strings attached.

We must have been too exhausted to fuck, so we made love. Afterwards, I lay on my back, stared at the beams in the ceiling and thought: I did more than satisfy her. I'm important to her.

'Can I go to sleep now?' she asked.

'Sure.'

'I hope you'll stay till morning.'

'Of course I will.' I got mad, though. Did she think I was some goddamn one-night stand who was going to tiptoe out at three a.m.?

'Don't be angry,' she said. 'It's not you. It's me. I needed a little reassurance.'

'Be reassured,' I whispered.

At about three a.m. I woke up for a minute. She was sound asleep. 'Bonnie.'

Her head was resting on my arm. I could feel the flutter of her lashes as she opened her eyes. 'Hi.'

'Hi. Listen,' I said. 'I want to tell you something.'

'What?'

'I love you.'

'I love you too.' Then she asked me: 'Aren't we too old for this?'

'No. Go back to sleep.'

I got up about six-thirty. She made me coffee. I said it again: I love you. I promised I'd call her from work or, if things got crazy, the second I got off.

I got into the Jag. It had been out all night, and the leather seats were wet with dew. I drove home, wet, limp, but filled with what I suppose was joy.

I got home. Yawned. Wished I was back in bed, wrapped in Bonnie's arms. Really tired. Needed a pick-me-up. Made a double screwdriver. Drank it, then another. Called work and coughed. Said I had some lousy virus. A hundred and three. Ray Carbone said, You sound terrible. Yeah, I said. I feel like hell.

I went on a five-day bender. By the end of it, Bonnie was just a vague, irritating memory.

By the end of the following year, when I was forced to check into South Oaks for treatment for alcohol abuse – plus pancreatic insufficiency and malnutrition caused by my drinking – I had managed to wipe out her memory completely.

Bonnie Spencer never existed.

# *Chapter Fourteen*

I got back to Headquarters a little before four o'clock. Even before I saw Ray Carbone, flushed an ominous crimson, I saw Julie, the receptionist, pick up a pen and draw it across her throat. So I knew I was about to be declared dead. But since noncompliance with official department guidelines was standard operating procedure with me, I had no idea what I was going to get killed for this time. Then Carbone jerked his thumb toward the captain's office; I knew it had to do with the Spencer case – and I knew it was not going to be a routine reprimand.

And seeing Frank Shea, Captain Shea, tie knotted tight, jacket buttoned, jabbing his index finger toward a chair was not exactly reassuring. Despite the American and Suffolk County flags in back of him, Shea usually looked more like a lounge singer than a cop: a lock of Brylcreemed hair trailing over his forehead, his tie hanging unknotted, his shirt half unbuttoned, displaying a huge gold Saint Michael's medal, a crucifix, a long, curvy tooth from what must have been some large, pissed-off animal, plus three chest hairs. He put on his jacket only to see the commissioner and for funerals.

Carbone took a chair and put it beside Shea's desk, so they were both arrayed against me. 'What's up?' I asked.

'I warned you, Brady,' Shea responded.

'About what?'

'You know! Look at you!' Okay, I'd been running, then sitting in the car with the top down, thinking about Bonnie. So maybe I was on the verge of sunstroke; I'd glanced in the rearview mirror just a couple of minutes before, in the parking lot outside Headquarters, and noticed that under the sunburn, my skin was gray.

And I had a headache and couldn't stop sweating. But I didn't look *that* bad. 'Look at you!' Shea bellowed.

'What? The department has some new good-grooming directive?'

'Fuck you and die, Brady!'

I peered over at Carbone. 'Do you want to tell me what's going on?'

'Steve.' Now that Shea was playing bad cop, Carbone could get compassionate. He sounded like a cross between shrink and priest. 'Robby told us.'

'Told you what?'

Shea picked up a paperweight and slammed it down on his desk. 'That you wouldn't get a warrant!'

'Yeah? Well, goddamn right. I'm not ready to arrest yet.'

'Who the hell do you think you are?' Shea demanded. 'We've got enough evidence to send her away for life. She knows it! She's gonna flee!'

'Where?'

'Shut up! She's gonna flee while you're babbling theories about Lindsay Keefe!'

'Listen, we've been . . . a little hasty. My fault, probably more than anybody else's. But we've got to think about Lindsay. And Fat Mikey too. Shea, just cool it a second and – '

'You bastard, I listened to you once.'

'What are you talking about?'

'Remember? You told me how you were going to stay sober.'

'Well, fuck you. I am sober.'

'Robby Kurz says you're not.'

'I'm drinking? Bullshit.'

'Robby was genuinely upset. It killed him to tell me.' Shea paused for a second. 'He *swore* it was true! Robby saw how I kept shaking my head, not wanting to believe it, and he swore. Vodka. Drunks think there's no odor, but believe me, there's an odor. I've smelled it on people, and he said the smell was rising off your skin.'

'Robby can take a goddamn fifth of Smirnoff 's and shove it up his lying ass. Listen, we had a few words. Maybe I flew off the handle. But to say I was drinking is such slander – '

'He *smelled* it. You were weaving when you walked, and – '

'No!'

'He realized it two days ago. His only mistake was holding out, trying to protect you.'

I really thought I was going to be sick. I felt the acid burn of vomit in my throat. I got very quiet. 'You think I'm drunk now?'

Carbone looked sad for me. Shea said, 'Stinko.'

'I want one of you to walk over to the lab with me. I want a Breathalyzer test.' They shot a glance at each other; they knew you could only get accurate readings for about two hours after drinking. So I added: 'Blood, urine too. Right now. I want you both to understand: I've been sober for almost four years.'

'You're all red!' Shea accused. 'You're sweating like a pig.'

'Why the hell didn't you ask me how come? Don't you think you owe me that? You want to know why I look like I'm going to get sick?' I thought fast. 'I've been out at Old Town Pond in Southampton – less than a quarter of a mile from Sy's house – walking over every goddamn inch of marshland. You know and I know that we need the weapon, and that rat-ass Robby Kurz – who's been in charge of finding it – has been sitting on his behind, shoving Danish into his mouth, writing his acceptance speech for his commendation, instead of looking for the goddamn .22. Excuse me: writing his speech and making up lies.'

'You're accusing *him* of lying?' Shea asked, with a nasty, unamused chuckle.

'Yeah.'

'Why would he lie, Brady?'

'Because he's a fanatical, ambitious, self-righteous turd. You *know* what he's like when he goes after somebody. He wears blinders; he refuses to see reality. And he's lying because he knows if he can put the lid on this fast, he can make sergeant by next month – and be first on line for your chair when you retire. Plus he's a sneaky ass-kisser who doesn't like the way I operate and wants me out of the way. He wants me out of the way so I won't stop him from arresting her. Because I've got to tell you, Frank, I might stop him. I have real doubts, and if we false-arrest her, she can make trouble. She has a big mouth.' Shea and Carbone glanced at each other. I went on: 'And Robby wants me out of the way because Bonnie was my idea to begin with – as Ray can attest – and he doesn't want me to get any credit.' All Shea did was sneer. Carbone hung his head. He really liked me. He wanted to believe me. But he'd had too much Psychology 205; he knew alcoholics are infantile, egocentric, that they lie as naturally as most people tell the truth. 'Come on, Ray. Walk me down to the lab.'

'Brady,' Shea said, 'you know what this bravado shit – "Take me to the lab!" – is gonna get you?'

'Yeah. Exonerated.'

'No. Because I am going to call your bluff, you son of a bitch. I want you in the lab *now*. You hear me? You built a great case, and all of a sudden, when the commissioner, the country exec, the goddamn national media is at my throat, you're sabotaging it. What are we gonna look like when the press finds out we had her and we let her slip through our fingers?'

'Frank, ask yourself: Why would I let a thing like that happen?'

'Because you've been on a binge and you've lost all sense of judgment, of decency . . .' His voice got louder, more theatrical. He grabbed the paperweight, held it in his fist and shook it at me. '. . . of obligation to the department. And to me! I stuck my neck out for you.'

I stood and turned to Ray. 'You're the psychology genius. Why would I . . . Even if I'd fallen off the wagon and went on the biggest bender of my life, what motive would I have for screwing up a case? If I thought Bonnie Spencer killed Sy, why wouldn't I drink four or five toasts to justice and arrest the bitch?'

Shea didn't give Carbone time to answer. 'Because Robby saw you with her in her house when you went in with the search warrant. He saw how you go rid of him, sent him upstairs. And he saw you nosing around after her, following her from room to room. And then, when you asked her about where she got the money in the boot, you put on kid gloves. *So* gentlemanly. Wimping out: You called that catalog guy like it was killing you. Like the *truth* was killing you.'

'Shea, this is nuts.'

'And then all of a sudden, you're onto Lindsay theories, Mikey theories. Onto *anything* that will keep Robby off Bonnie Spencer. So to answer your question: Why wouldn't you arrest the bitch? Because for some stupid, drunken reason, you've fallen for her.'

I passed the Breathalyzer test, of course. Then I walked a painted line, from heel to toe, picked up a nickel, a dime and a quarter without fumbling, recited the alphabet. It took a couple of minutes more to pee into a cup and get blood drawn. Ray stood by while the tech stuck the needle in. He said, 'Shea will be glad to hear about the breath test, and if the others come out all right – '

'You believe that feeling in love shit?'

'I don't know.'

'You know Lynne, Ray. I'm asking you, do you think when I have someone like her I'd go for an old broad that every guy in town has had a piece of?'

'I saw her when she came in for the test. She's not bad.'

'She's no Lynne.'

'Look, all I know is you have a beautiful, well-constructed case against her – I heard you present it – and suddenly you're throwing it away. *Why?*'

'Because I don't think she did it.'

Carbone shook his head. 'I can't buy that, Steve.'

'Where's Robby?'

'Why?'

'Because I want to know why he didn't have the balls to face me.'

'He would have.'

'Except?'

'Except he's down at Southampton Town Court getting a warrant. And then he's going to arrest Bonnie Spencer.'

Bonnie opened the back door a crack. 'Do you have a warrant?'

'No. Listen, Bonnie – '

She shut the door hard, just short of a slam. I rang the bell. Nothing, except Moose right by the door, barking, trying to sound like a watchdog but giving away the game by the ecstatic wagging of her tail. I squinted, trying to see past the lace kitchen curtains. Bonnie had disappeared into the house.

I love the way cops in movies whip out a credit card, diddle a cylinder and the door springs open. I wasted about five minutes with a card, my Swiss Army knife and every key I had on my key ring. It was a bitch, because I had to do it quietly, so she wouldn't call Headquarters and claim I was harassing her. Finally, the lock clicked open and I was in.

I didn't have to do a room-to-room; Moose led me to an open door, then downstairs, to the basement. Bonnie stood by the dryer, folding a dish towel. When she looked up to greet Moose, she saw me. Jesus, did she scream!

'Bonnie, please, listen to me. I'm not here to hurt you.' Her head swiveled in a frantic search for something to protect herself with, but you can't fight off an armed and dangerous psychopathic cop with a plastic bottle of Downy. I took a step toward her, I suppose wanting to touch her, reassure her I was there to help, but she drew back, as if trying to disappear into the narrow gap between the washer and the dryer. So I kept my distance. 'I know you think I'm insane or something, but just listen, because there's not much time.' Shit. 'Not much time' was the wrong thing to say. Bonnie's eyes clouded, as if she comprehended she had only a few minutes more to live. 'Bonnie, pay attention. The guy I'm working with on this case, Kurz, the asshole with the hairspray. He left Headquarters before I did. He's going to court to get a warrant for your arrest. So time is a factor here. If he knocks on your door in the next couple of minutes, I can't . . . I can't help you. Understand?' She didn't say anything, but she was listening. She looked straight into my eyes. It was such a probing gaze I felt she could absorb all my thoughts, understand precisely what I was there for. But she just waited for me to go on. 'I have doubts. I mean, I don't think you should be arrested yet. There are still too many questions about Sy's death for us to be saying, The case is closed. I want those questions answered. I want the case to stay open. But it's your call. You can stay here, go with Kurz when he comes here for you.'

'Or?'

'Get the hell out of here. With me. Now.'

Smart girl. She thought to toss all the folded laundry back into the dryer, so it wouldn't look as if she'd run on a moment's notice. We raced out her back door, and I led her through her yard, across an open field to a small wooded area where I'd hidden the Jag, in case Robby showed. Moose sprinted after us, if something with that big a butt can be said to sprint. Bonnie got into the car, and while the door was still open, the dog leapt in, over her lap and into the driver's seat.

'Get her *out*,' I said, at the same moment as I opened the driver's door and grabbed her collar.

'When will I get back?'

'How the hell should I know. Two minutes, if you don't convince me.'

'What if I do?'

'I don't know.'

Suddenly she brightened. 'If you put the top down, I could hold her in my lap and there'd be room for the three of us'

'If I put the top down, you idiot, there'd be a hundred witnesses who could say, "Oh, I saw Bonnie and her dog. They were tooling over to Steve Brady's, in his car." A hundred witnesses to my hindering prosecution. A Class D felony.'

'You mean this isn't legal?' But before she'd finished the question, she knew the answer. 'I can't let you do this.'

She put her hand on the door handle. 'Don't move,' I ordered.

She shook her head. 'No, I'm getting out of here.'

I drew my gun. 'You move, Bonnie, and I'll shoot you between the fucking eyes.'

'Oh, stop it.'

Jesus Christ. My head was pounding, I was nauseous from dehydration, I was standing there holding a gun on a murder suspect I was helping escape, and there was a hundred-pound black, hairy mongrel with its tongue hanging out sitting upright, its claws gripped nice and tight into the leather, gazing out the front window, as if waiting for a traffic light to change. 'I'm not going to talk about this now! Your goddamn life is on the line, so get that mutt out of here and let's move.'

Bonnie's voice was so low I could hardly hear her. 'The back door is closed. She can't get to her water, and if I'm not there . . .'

I stuck my gun back in my holster, hauled Moose out of the car and climbed into the driver's seat. Which of course was the cue for Bonnie to open her door and get out. 'Get back in!' I shouted. She shook her head. I started the engine. 'Goodbye.' Bonnie whistled, two high, quick notes. Moose raced around to her side and Bonnie pushed her in.

And that's how we came to drive to my house with Bonnie in the passenger seat, me in the driver's seat, and fatso Moose stretched over both our laps, barking with pleasure at this wonderful game.

Migrant workers' shacks not being known for expansive rooms or cathedral ceilings, the architect-entrepreneur-loser I'd bought my house from hadn't had much space to work with, so he'd made most of the place into a 'family area,' one main room that served as kitchen, den, dining and living room. Then he hacked off a little at each end, so that when he was taking potential buyers around, he could make one of those *Voilà!* gestures with his hand and say, 'To sleep . . . ,' then wait for the Yorkers to say, '. . . perchance to dream,' and they could all be good friends and bask in the radiance of each other's culture, plus make a nice, civilized deal. Except I'd rather have gotten strung up by the nuts than say '. . . perchance to dream', and the architect had gotten real nervous because he knew I was a cop and therefore I might think the 'To sleep . . .' meant he was making a pass, because he wore a ponytail, and this could queer the deal in every sense. So he'd just added, 'The bedroom,' real fast and left it at that.

The master bedroom, like the rest of the house, had come furnished – since this was to be the model for the hundreds of migrant-worker shacks he had dreamed of renovating. But the bed he'd put in was just large enough for midgets to do it in the missionary position, so I'd gotten rid of it and put in a king-size bed. Once I did that, there was just enough space to get to the closets and the bathroom.

On the opposite side of the house, he'd taken the same amount of square footage and stuck in two guest rooms, connected by a bathroom. I led Bonnie into the first, which wasn't much different from the second, except instead of scallops and conch shells stenciled on the floors and around the top of the walls, it had pineapples. Since I hardly ever went near this part of the house, I'd forgotten about them, and about the hideous lamp with a green shade and a base of some fat sticks tied together with rawhide the architect had told me was a rustic touch I might conceivably wish to change. The poor guy was such a basket case because he couldn't sell his house; I wound up putting in a bid that same day.

I pulled down the shades. 'Don't get the wrong idea,' I said, my back to Bonnie. 'This is to make sure you're not seen.'

'I won't get the wrong idea.' Her voice had a tremor. That was the only sign she was as terrified as I sensed she was.

'Not that I get a lot of company, but just in case.' When I turned back to her, she was sitting, primly, on a small ladder-back chair. I sat on the edge of the bed, but because the room was so small, our knees were about four inches apart. 'Now, I want to hear what actually happened, right from the beginning. Every detail, from the minute you first spoke to Sy or laid eyes on him again. Unless you'd been in touch with him all the years since the divorce.'

'No.'

'Okay, but first, I want to clear up something.'

'You mean about – '

'No.'

But she couldn't let it be. 'Gideon called. He told me you have no recollection that you and I . . . that you and I had met.'

'Look, I don't have time for that now.' I was detached. Professional. 'What I want to clear up is your last lie.'

'You make it sound like it's the last of a hundred thousand.'

'It is, give or take a few.'

'If I'm such a liar, why would I tell the truth now, when the police are closing in on me?'

'Because you're desperate.'

'Well,' she said, in that trembling voice, 'I guess I am.' She dropped her head and stared down at her hands, folded on her lap. She had beautiful, long-fingered hands, with nice, no-polish oval nails, hands you would see in commercials for hand lotion.

'Okay, why did you make up the story about the eight hundred eighty bucks we found in your boot?'

'That *was* the truth.'

'Bonnie, understand one thing. You shit me, you're out of here.'

'Please, call him again.' I shook my head. 'Try to understand,' she pleaded. 'Vincent Kelleher is a very nervous, not-too-successful businessman who sells pot holders that look like armadillos, and size fifty-four sweatsuits in pink, aqua or lilac with appliqués. All of a sudden, this nebbish gets a long-distance phone call from a detective asking him about money he slipped me off the books. An illegal payment. He was always nervous about doing it, and when you called, he must have been convinced Eliot Ness and the tax squad would swoop down and arrest him.'

'You're good, Bonnie. Really good.'

'No. If I were that good, you would have believed the lies I did tell. I wouldn't be in this mess now. Please, call Vincent Kelleher.'

But just then my pager squeaked: 'Brady call Carbone ASAP.' I told her not to move, and I hurried across the house, into my bedroom, and closed the door.

Carbone asked where I was, and I told him I'd gone home after sixty hours of being on, because I was wiped, and sick of the shit he and Shea had handed me, but did he want me in for another Breathalyzer test, to make sure I wasn't sitting around with a bottle of Canadian Club and a straw? He said, Look, maybe we were too hasty, and Robby, not being a drinking man, might have misread some of the signs and . . . And *what?* I demanded. There's no sign of Bonnie Spencer, he said. Is Robby hysterical? I asked. Yes, and so is Shea, and if you think the commissioner isn't shitting a brick, then you're not thinking. Hey, Ray, everybody should calm down. It's six-thirty. The cool of the evening is upon us. Maybe she's down at the beach. Maybe she's having dinner with a friend. Tell everybody to relax. Have a drink – on me. Look, you want me to check around? He said, Maybe that would be a good idea. Okay, I said, I'll surveil her place until you can get someone else over there, then I'll check around, make a few calls. Just do me a favor. Page Robby. Get him the hell away from her house, because if I see him, I swear to God I'll kill him. Carbone said all right. He was about to hang up when I inquired: They finish my pee and blood workup yet? You're okay, Steve. Thanks. Be reasonable, he said. We've got an anxiety-provoking situation here. A lot of pressure. Sometimes people make errors in judgment. I asked him if Shea realized he had made an error in judgment, or would I have to piss into a Dixie cup every day? Carbone, being patient, said, Shea knows the results of the tests, and he's not a stupid man. But let's face it: the two of you don't have a natural affinity. He let you back on the squad because he needed you, not because he liked you or trusted you, which I guess isn't news. Not by a long shot, I said. Carbone said, So do yourself a favor, Detective Brady. Earn a gold star. Bring in Bonnie Spencer.

The engine on Robby's car was running as I drove up to Bonnie's, and when I pulled over beside him, he flung the arrest warrant into my car and peeled out – as fast as an Olds Cutlass can peel – before he had to look me in the eye or hear what I had to say. He knew what it was, though: I was going to get him. And I knew what his response would be: Not if I get you first.

A few minutes later, two Southampton Town PD squad cars pulled up. They were supposed to hang around until someone from Suffolk County Homicide came to relieve them, so I handed them the warrant to pass along and told them I was just going to check out the house one more time. I slipped on a pair of rubber gloves carefully, ostentatiously, as if getting ready to perform neurosurgery, and went in. Five minutes later I came out with some of Bonnie's underwear and a T-shirt folded flat in one pocket, along with her toothbrush, and a Ziploc with Purina Dog Chow in the other. I swung two evidence bags with a pair of sneakers and a hairbrush as I walked down the front path, then gave a mock salute to the Southampton cops before I drove off.

Some blithe spirit. My hands were clammy, my stomach churning. Not for any rational reason, like I knew I was destroying my entire professional and personal life, to say nothing of risking two years in the can for hindering prosecution by rendering criminal assistance to a person who has committed a Class A felony – like second-degree murder. I was actually very clear about the consequences of the devastation I was bringing on myself. I remember I contemplated what a felony conviction could do to my pension rights, wondered whether they had AA meetings at the Green Haven Correctional Facility and decided that because I had a couple of good friends in the Suffolk County DA's, maybe they'd only go for a misdemeanor. But the drippy palms, the twisting gut, had nothing to do with these objective considerations.

No, I drove back to my house with an unswallowable lump in my throat because I was afraid Bonnie would be gone. She'd think fast, as she had the week before, at Sy's, when she'd killed him, and do what she thought she had to do: run. *No.* She hadn't killed him. I did believe her. But she'd have visions of the jury nodding, convinced, as the People summed up its circumstantial case against Spencer, and she'd run. Or just be frightened, and want someone to hold her, comfort her, kiss the top of her head, like her friend Gideon, and she'd run. Or knowing Bonnie, be a good, chin-up American, face the music, trust in God and the Constitution, and she'd run, find a phone, call Homicide and ask, Is Detective Kurz in?

Oh, Jesus. What would I do if she wasn't there?

It was Thursday night, but weekenders were already pouring in. Traffic had gotten even heavier than when I'd left for Bonnie's a half hour earlier; it was like one endless, metallic reptile snaking its way east. And every person in those thousands of cars was an important person, with important things to do. They *had* to hear what last-minute truly fun invitations were on their answering machines so they could break the dates they'd already made. They *had* to change into the three-hundred-dollar black gauze shirt. They *had* to refresh their potpourri before their houseguests arrived. There was fresh mozzarella oozing in the shopping bag on the back seat, wetting their baguettes, an intolerable situation that *had* to be stopped.

Not a single car would defer and let me cross Montauk Highway. I honked and flicked my brights at a new 560SL, made eye contact with the driver and then didn't look back at the road; I kept staring at him – and driving. It unnerved him enough that at the last possible second, he slammed on his brakes. Hatred disfigures his jowly face, but he knew I looked demented enough to actually hit a Mercedes.

Then I floored it back to my house. Except I had to stop when the guardrail went down at the train tracks. It was the longest fucking train in the history of the Long Island Rail Road.

I rushed into the house and tripped over Moose, who was running to greet me. I said, 'Get out of my way, you goddamn bag of shit.' She wagged her tail. I patted her head. Okay, I thought, Bonnie left the dog. Clever: she knew I'd take care of it. The house was absolutely silent. I trudged toward the pineapple room and called out 'Hi' against the emptiness. Still a little hope. 'Hello?' Not a sound. 'Bonnie!' I yelled.

'Hi,' Bonnie called back. Did I jump! 'It's you! I heard you say "Hi", and I thought it was your voice, but I couldn't be sure. I thought: What if it's one of his friends, or a burglar?'

My whole body was flooded with relief, and it left me so empty, that sudden decrease in tension, that I had to lean against the wall for a minute to get my equilibrium back. Then I went into the pineapple room.

She was curled up on the bed reading *This Date in New York Yankees History*, the only book that had been in there. She put it down on the floor, then sat up on the bed, Indian style. 'Who is the all-time leader for career grand slams?' she asked.

'Gehrig,' I mumbled.

'It said Henry Gehrig. Is that the same as Lou?'

I nodded and said, 'Here.' I handed her the sneakers and hairbrush and took the underwear and toothbrush out of my pocket. I was still too emotional. I couldn't make conversation.

'Thanks.'

I jiggled the bag with the dog chow. She smiled and waited for me to say something, so I told her I'd give it to Moose, take a quick shower and be back. I was amazed; I sounded so matter-of-fact. Like a normal person. Did she want something? I had a bunch of TV dinners. She said, No, thanks, she wasn't hungry.

I shoved two Hungry Man dinners in the oven, figuring when push came to shove she wouldn't be able to resist an aluminum-foil tray of greasy, breaded chicken, or worst case, I'd eat it. I got into the shower. Water, a lot of soap, the nice pine smell of shampoo. This was better. A cool, clean man instead of a sweaty, feverish, overwroght wreck. I reached out for the towel, a little disappointed Bonnie hadn't sneaked in to hand it to me; in the back of my mind, I'd been imagining getting out of the shower and having her there. I'd say, Get the hell out of here, and she'd say, Let me do your back. But then, resting her body against me, she'd reach around to the front, stroke me, murmur, Oh, Stephen.

I got dressed, took out my notebook and called Vincent Kelleher, the catalog king. 'Detective Brady again.'

'Yes, sir?'

'Mr Kelleher, I don't know you, but somehow I get the feeling that you weren't being straight with me, and that makes me very upset.' Silence. 'Now listen, I'm not interested in your tax situation. You want to pay off the books, on the books, I don't give a damn. But I do give a damn if you lie in response to a simple question.'

'Why do you think I lied?' he whispered in Flagstaff, Arizona.

'Because I'm a cop. I *know*. You want to tell me about your financial arrangements with Bonnie Spencer?' Silence. 'If you're straightforward with me, we'll both hang up and that will be the end of it. If you dick me around. I'll pass on my suspicions to a buddy of mine in the IRS in Washington.'

'I paid her . . .' His voice faded. This guy had an Irish name; I couldn't believe he could be such a wimp. Fucking assimilation.

'How did you pay her?'

'In cash.'

'How much?'

'Twenty-five hundred dollars. She was the one who asked to be paid in cash. I swear to you, I never offered it.'

'How did you get it to her?'

'Her father lives outside of Scottsdale. She visits him once a year, then drives over, sees the mock-ups for new catalogs. We talk and . . .' If this guy went through a red light, he'd probably handcuff himself, turn himself in and beg the judge for the max.

'You talk and what? You hand her the money?'

'Yes, in an envelope. But I promise you, it won't happen again.'

All right! I thought, as I hung up. Score one for the good guys.

I searched around and finally found a couple of paperbacks, Stephen King and Clancy, and brought them into her room. I didn't want her to hate it, being stuck in there, and I didn't want her to think I was a semiliterate jerk who, when he read at all, read statistics – although that was more true than not. She was a writer; she had full bookshelves. What was I going to say? Hey, Bonnie, I may not read books much, but I read three papers a day and watch all the historical documentaries on cable. You want to know about the Battle of Midway? Metternich's life story? Just ask me.

'These are for later,' I said. 'Now it's time to talk.' I pulled back the shade and looked outside. The last of the soft, magic daylight was fading.

'Okay, but . . . I'm not telling you how to do your job . . . maybe you could give Vincent Kelleher a call.'

'Why?'

'Because he wasn't telling you the truth. And *I'm* going to tell you the truth. I know how badly I've messed things up for myself, and now you're giving me another chance. Well, I want to be worthy of your confidence. And I want you to believe me about everything.'

This time, the cop beat out the man. She shouldn't think she had me on her side; she should convince me. I said: 'Maybe I'll call him later. For now, tell me how you hooked up with Sy again.'

# *Chapter Fifteen*

'When you and Sy split, was there a lot of bad feeling?'

'No.' Bonnie leaned back against the headboard, one of those cheapo woven wood jobs that squeak every time you inhale. She was wearing what she'd worn when I found her folding laundry: red nylon running shorts and a black tank top. The white socks she'd had on had gotten filthy on the run through the field, so she'd taken them off. She hadn't been wearing shoes.

She drew her knees up together, folded her arms over them, then rested her head on the arms. Jesus, was she flexible; it was the kind of position that normally only an eight-year-old can be comfortable in. 'The day I signed the separation agreement, he took me out to lunch. Le Cirque. Soft lights, soft linen napkins. Soft food, so you wouldn't crunch when you chew. We were sitting on the same side of the banquette. He held my hand under the table and said, "It's my fault that I wasn't able to love you enough. But I'll always be there for you, Bonnie." '

So, obviously, would Moose. The dog rested her face on the blanket until Bonnie patted her. Then she lay down on my feet.

'Did you throw up when he said that?'

'No, it was before the appetizer. But see, in his own way, Sy was sincere. He truly believed what he was saying, even though twenty seconds after he dropped me off at Penn Station so I could get the train back to Bridgehampton, I ceased to exist. But since I hadn't given him a hard time about splitting up . . . I mean, I cried a lot and asked him to go to a marriage counselor, but that was all. I didn't want alimony. So he felt kindly toward me. If someone had asked, "Sy, what was your second wife like?" he'd have said,

"Hmmm, second wife. Oh, yes. Bonnie. So *sweet*. Down-to-earth." It was funny: If you crossed him, he'd never forget you, but niceness made no impression on him.'

'Why didn't you fight harder to stay together?'

'Because . . .' She put her hands together, prayer fashion, and touched her forefingers to her lips. Finally, she said: 'Because I knew he didn't love me anymore – if he ever had. Sy could fall in love, but it was like an actor immersing himself in a character. The week I met him, in LA, he must have just come back from a John Ford retrospective – so I became his cowgirl. He walked around wearing a denim jacket, squinting, smoking; this was before his decaffeinated days. He broke off the filters and lit his cigarettes with those matches you'd strike on the bottom of your boot; he actually took to wearing an old pair of shit-kickers, which wasn't so terrible because he was three inches shorter than me. God knows where he got them – probably in some Madison Avenue antique-boot boutique. We'd go riding a lot. Western saddle. He said, "The English saddle is so effete." But after three weeks back in New York – six weeks into our marriage – he got tired of being Hopalong Cassidy. And he got tired of loving me. I knew it.' She turned away from me for a minute and got busy folding over the pillow, so it made a better support for the small of her back. 'There was no percentage in fighting him on the divorce. He'd tried to be a decent husband, and it got to be too much of a burden.'

'How was he a decent husband? I thought you said he cheated on you – with some socialite.'

'Decent for Sy. He held doors open. He remembered birthdays, anniversaries. He had great style; one Valentine's Day he bought me a new tackle box, and when I opened it, there was a beautiful long strand of fourteen-millimeter pearls.'

'What are fourteen-millimeter pearls?'

'*Big* pearls.' Her hands described a sphere that was about the size of the average classroom globe. It annoyed me that she liked such an expensive gift. I wanted her to say, I told Sy to take back the pearls; I only wanted the tackle box. But she didn't. 'You have to understand Sy,' she went on. 'He couldn't be faithful. He couldn't be straight. He *had* to be . . . I don't know if "crooked" is the word. He had to manipulate every situation. Some of it was money. He was always afraid someone was cheating him, so he played one stockbroker, one lawyer, one accountant, against another. But *he* cheated people all the time. He hid personal expenses in movie budgets. I'm not just talking about a sweatsuit and a set of barbells; his second movie paid for a gym and a hot tub in our apartment in the city. And you couldn't use words like "illegal" or "immoral" with him, because in a weird way, he took them as compliments. He saw his finagling as an adventure and himself as a kind of swanky Robin Hood. But all he was doing was robbing from the rich to give to the rich.'

'You didn't see any of this when you agreed to marry him?'

'No. I just saw this charming, cultured man with crinkles around his eyes who was crazy about *Cowgirl* and who knew all about westerns. Not just a superficial knowledge: I remember him describing one of Tom Mix's silent movies – *Cactus Jim's Shop Girl.* Actually, he seemed to know about everything: Cambodian architecture, the Big Bang theory, the linguistic connection between Finnish and Hungarian. But I think what got me most about Sy was that he *appreciated* me. My work. My eyes. My hair. My . . . All the usual stuff. This man was such a connoisseur, I thought: Lord, am I something!'

She concentrated on massaging her knee, a slow back-and-forth motion, the way you do to ease an old injury. Suddenly she glanced up at me, then, quickly, back down to her knee. I knew what she was thinking: despite our very different résumés, I was like Sy. Oh, how I appreciated her that night: I swear to God, I've never met anyone like you, Bonnie. Bonnie, your skin is like warm velvet. You know what, Bonnie? Your eyes are the color of the ocean. Not a summer ocean. Like on a bright winter day – so beautiful. I could talk to you for hours, Bonnie. Bonnie, I love you.

'But Sy's enthusiasms never lasted. He had a closet with equipment from sports he'd tried a few times and given up: golf, racquetball, scuba diving, polo, cross-country skiing. And if he could have put women in a closet, he would have; he was on to other enthusiasms by our two-month anniversary.'

'I'm sorry.'

'Don't be. Actually, it got to be amusing.' She lifted her chin and gave a little closed-lipped smile, a superior city-slicker expression that overflowed with *savoir-faire*. It was fake as hell. 'I could tell who he was having an affair with by the way he dressed. One day he put away his nipped-in waist Italian suit and took out a torn T-shirt and bleached jeans, and I knew he'd stopped with the production designer with the surrealist jewelry and taken up with the third-string *Village Voice* movie critic, this girl with a lot of hair who was about ten minutes past her Sweet Sixteen. You couldn't help but laugh.'

'Don't bullshit me.'

The blanket on the bed, which the architect had probably decided was a grand bucolic design statement, was a pukey green plaid. Bonnie traced a thin, dark-green line with her finger. 'All right,' she said quietly, 'what he did to me stank. More than that. It broke my heart. I'm not the kind of woman men fall for. Then, finally, one did. I was so happy. But before I could even finish the love poem I was writing to him, a sonnet – fourteen lousy lines – he stopped loving me.'

'So the marriage was over before it was officially over.'

She nodded. 'We still had sex, but there was no love, and not much companionship. On the nights he was home, he'd hole up in his study and read scripts or make phone calls. After the separation, I went on with my life. It wasn't hard to do; we hadn't really been a couple.'

'But your economic situation, your social status, changed. What was your life like?'

'What do you mean?' She got very engrossed in following another, thicker line in the plaid.

'Happy, sad, wonderful, terrible?'

'It was okay.' She didn't look up at me.

'Come on, Bonnie.'

'Why is this necessary?'

'Because I want to know the circumstances surrounding your taking up with Sy again.'

'The circumstances were that I was – am – an independent woman. No ties. My mom died when I was seventeen: a brain tumor. My dad remarried – to a woman from Salt Lake who gets pedicures. He sold his store and they moved to Arizona, to a retirement community; they play bridge. My brothers are all married, with families of their own.'

She got quiet, thoughtful. She stopped with the blanket and reached back and played with the end of her braid. Absentmindedly, she unwound the rubber band. She unplaited her hair, and, as she began to talk again, stroked it, as if comforting herself. In the light of the green-shaded lamp, it gave off soft copper glints.

'My life. I live in a lovely town by the ocean in a part of the country I don't belong in. I have Gideon and his lover, two women friends, and a lot of pleasant acquaintances. Summers are a little better; I kept a couple of friends from my Sy days – a film editor, a *Wall Street Journal* entertainment industry reporter – and they have houses around here. We have some good times. I do volunteer work with illiterate adults and for every environmental cause that comes down the pike. That's how I met Gideon. He was representing a land rapist, and we started out screaming at each other because roseate terns have become an endangered species, but we wound up great friends. You want more? I make eighteen thousand dollars a year writing pap for catalogs and the local paper and industrial publications like *Auto Glass News*. What else do you want to know? Sex? Until AIDS, I slept with any man who appealed to me. Now I read and watch two movies a night and run five miles a day. I had an abortion when I was married to Sy because he said he wasn't ready to have children. I wanted to have a baby more than anything. From the time I was thirty-eight, when it dawned on me that I'd never get married again because no one would ever ask, I stopped using birth control. I was never able to conceive; I found out my fallopian tubes were scarred closed from a dose of gonorrhea I'd gotten from my husband about six months after the abortion. Well, that's it.' Bonnie clasped her hands on her knees. 'I guess you expected something a little more upbeat.'

'A little.' I had to be professional. What was the alternative? Taking her in my arms, hugging her, whispering tender words of condolence? I asked: 'We found two condom wrappers in a wastebasket in Sy's guest room. If you couldn't get pregnant – '

'AIDS, chlamydia, gonorrhea again. If I could have found a way of slipping a Trojan over his head before I kissed him, I would have, but it would have lacked a certain subtlety.'

'Tell me more about your life.'

'What's there to tell? I had such a happy childhood. And then my screenplay became a movie and got wonderful reviews, and then Sy came along and married me. Sure, I knew there'd be bumps. Tragedy even, like losing my mom. But it didn't occur to me that life wouldn't basically be wonderful. Well, it's not. It isn't terrible, but I never thought I would be so lonely.'

'But now you have to deal with something a little more serious than personal happiness,' I reminded her.

'I know.'

'Like the possibility of a murder conviction.' My voice was grim, deep and low, like a 45 record playing at 33. The small bedroom suddenly felt tight, airless, like a cell.

Bonnie seemed determined not to succumb to the gloom. She flashed one of her great grins. 'So worse comes to worse, I get convicted for murder. After twenty, thirty years in jail, think of the script I could write. None of those *Blondes in Chains* clichés for me. You know: the dyke matron, the ripped uniforms so breasts peekaboo out. No, I'll write a socially significant screenplay and maybe get on *Entertainment Tonight*.'

'Tell me about the screenplay you were working on with Sy.'

'Oh, right. *A Sea Change*. It's based on a real incident during World War Two. A German submarine surfaced off the coast of Long Island, and a couple of saboteurs slipped in. In my story, two women spot them down by the beach: a middle-class housewife and a bargirl who turns tricks on weekends. Anyway, it's about their helping catch the Nazis, and about the friendship that develops.'

'You sent it to Sy when you got finished with it?'

'I called him.'

'What happened?'

'Well, first I spoke to his secretary, asked that he call me back, which he did a couple of days later. Kind of wary, to tell you the truth: I guess he was nervous I might be asking for money. But when I told him what it was, he was nice: You sound fan*tas*tic. Send it Fed Ex. Can't *wait* to read it.'

It wasn't only that she didn't wear makeup, or that she did have incredible calf muscles; Bonnie was simply like no other woman I'd ever met. She seemed to be incapable of womanly wiles in any form. I looked her straight in the eye and she made no defensive feminine gestures. Her hand didn't fly up to touch her nose to check if it was oily, or up to her head to smooth down or fluff up her hair. She didn't make cow eyes or wounded-doe eyes, spread her legs an intriguing inch, thrust out her pelvis. No, she just looked straight back at me. I thought: Maybe it came from growing up with all those older brothers and that elk-shooting father and that rangy, broad-shouldered mother. Maybe she'd even tried batting her eyelashes or giggling, and nobody noticed. Maybe she'd acted wide-eyed and inept around all those Brownings and Remingtons and Winchesters in the store, or gazed upon the engine of the family Buick and said, 'Oooh, what's all that?' and got a swift kick in the butt, real or symbolic. She wasn't feminine. She was female.

'You say Sy liked your screenplay?'

'Yup.'

I thought about what Easton had said about it. 'Then why would he have told one of his people to find something nice to say about it, so he could get you off his back? And why would he have told Lindsay . . .' I tried to think of a way to say Sy thought the script was a piece of crap without actually having to say it.

'I can't say for sure. With Lindsay, I think it was natural he'd try and cover up any relationship with me.' Bonnie rotated her ankles, making circles with her feet. 'I mean, Lindsay has perpetually twitching, super-sensitive antennae that can pick up any other woman within a fifty-mile radius. Sy was so careful; he did everything except wear sunglasses and a false nose when he came over.' She stopped twirling her feet and started to do toe touches, flexing her calves as she bent over. She could have been stretching for a marathon; she was ready to run. She was not someone who could tolerate being confined.

'Why would he ask his assistant to find something nice to say?'

'Busywork, maybe.'

'No.'

'When did he ask his assistant to read it?'

'A couple of months ago.'

'I'd just handed in my second draft then. Sy *said* he liked it a lot but that he wouldn't have time to really go over it until *Starry Night* wrapped.'

'This was the rewriting you did based on his suggestions?'

'Yes.'

'Knowing Sy, was it possible he didn't like it, even though he told you he did?'

She considered the question. 'Knowing Sy, yes. Maybe he – I don't know – wanted me back in his life for a while.' She looked disheartened, as if she'd just gotten a brusque rejection letter in the mail. 'But he did write me this nice note. Something like: "Skimmed it. Adore it. Can't wait to *really* read it." '

This could be another one for the good guys; if Sy had liked the screenplay, and if she had written proof, she'd have every motive for wanting him alive; a dead executive producer can't make a movie. 'He wrote you a note?' I demanded.

'Yes. He has little three-by-five note cards with his name. He used one of them.'

'Typed or in his own handwriting?'

'I think he wrote it.'

'Did you save it?'

'It should be in my *Sea Change* file. In my office.' She stopped cold. 'Oh, wait a second. You want proof that he liked it originally too. Right? Fine. Look in that same file. There's his original memo, the one he wrote after he read the first draft. Typical Sy. Eight pages, single-spaced, multisyllabic. Talking about everything from character arc to how I misused the subjunctive mood. But filled with "brilliant" and "trenchant" and "poignant".'

'What does "trenchant" mean?'

She chewed her lip for a second. 'I don't know, to tell you the truth. It's one of those words that nobody in human history has ever said out loud, and you don't see it written that often. He also wrote it was "au courant". *That* must have been a shock to him. Sy had always told me I was born too late, that I belonged under contract to RKO – if there still was an RKO – because my writing talent was for great 1941 movies. He couldn't get over that I'd finally written a screenplay that would appeal to someone besides my Aunt Shirley, and a perverse USC film professor. An eastern, not a western.' She got off the bed and began to pace, which isn't easy when you can only pace three steps forward and three steps back. 'You know, you had a search warrant. How come you didn't read that file?'

'Robby Kurz probably looked at it and decided it wasn't important.' I took out my notebook and jotted down: 'Bon's Sea file.'

'Not important? You're hearing from people that Sy hated my work, that he rejected me – which would give me a motive to kill him if I was a homicidal maniac, which I'm not. And you say it's not important?'

'It's not our job to dig up exculpatory evidence.'

'No. It's your job to railroad people.'

'Sit down.'

'I don't want to sit down,' she snapped. 'God, I feel so cooped up in here.'

I was pissed. I wanted her to like being with me. 'Want to try a jail cell?'

'Do you? Maybe you can have the one next door. You know, when you go up the river for your Class D felony.' Bonnie's pacing got faster, more desperate. Suddenly she stopped short. Smiled. That phony, movie-biz smile, falsely warm, fraudulently agreeable. 'Listen, I have a great idea. We can share a cell! Have a hot affair after lights-out. Not just your conventional hot affair. I mean, a *love* affair. We'll actually talk! Tell each other our life stories. The true ones, even when they hurt. Not the slick ones we make up to entertain people. And sex! We'll do it standing up, sitting down, frontways, sideways – '

'Bonnie, stop it!'

'Why? I'm telling you, it could be magic. Like we were creating something the world had never known before. And then the next day – '

'I asked you to stop it.'

' – the next day you'd be free. You could forget it happened.

You could forget it meant something.' She hoisted an imaginary glass. 'Hey, I'll drink to that!'

'I'm sorry if I hurt you,' I began. 'That time of my life, I was a mess.'

I got up and walked into the bathroom. Moose followed. No tissues, so I brought her a wad of toilet paper, knowing she was going to cry. I came back and put my arm around her shoulders, ready to absorb her sobs. But she pulled away and turned from me; she wasn't crying, and she didn't want me comforting her.

'Bonnie,' I said to her back, 'in AA, one of the things we do is to make a list of all the people we've harmed. Then we've got to be willing to make amends. I know I harmed you. I'm not going to make excuses – '

'Gideon said you didn't remember what happened.'

'I didn't. But later, after he left . . . I remembered some of it. I know I'll never be able to know what really went on between us – what we talked about. But let me just say how sorry – '

She turned back and gazed at me so straight I looked away. 'No amends, okay? I don't want any magnanimous Twelve Step gestures that will make you Feel Good About Yourself. Yes, you hurt me. But I let myself get hurt. I was playing a raunchy sex scene, and I tried to score it with violins. Well, I was the dope.'

'You know it wasn't any scene.'

'I know it's history.' She sat down on the bed again, feet on the floor this time, hands in her lap. Mormon schoolmarm posture, not Bonnie posture. There was a long silence. It was broken by the screech of a gull flying toward the water. Bonnie finally said: 'I apologize for the outburst.'

'No problem.'

'I don't want to be a bitter person. I lost control for a second. I'm exhausted. I haven't been sleeping, not since Sy was killed. Not since you rang my bell. I'm scared. I wake up and the sun is shining and I yawn and stretch – and suddenly I'm overwhelmed with terror. I'm trapped inside a nightmare, and the sunshine doesn't give me any light. And you: I can't resolve my memory of you and my fear of you. It's very hard being here in your house.'

'I understand, and I just want to say how sorry – '

'Let's drop it now.'

'Can't I – '

'Please, don't.'

It was getting dark. I knew I had to call Lynne. I walked into the kitchen, but instead of picking up the phone, I put Moose's dog chow in a bowl and got her some water. Then I took the dinners out of the oven and brought them back into Bonnie's room on plates, with forks and napkins. I thought she'd say, No, thanks, I'm much too upset to eat, but by the time I got back again with Cokes, she'd woofed down a drumstick and half the mashed potatoes and corn.

I sat there holding a wing, like I couldn't figure out what to do about it, thinking that there were approximately a million subjects I wanted to talk to this woman about: what teams she liked, although I had a dread suspicion she would be a Mets fan; what Mormons were all about; whether she read about stuff like Eastern Europe and the national debt in the paper or just articles about movies and saving marsh grasses; what was her favorite running route; how had she hurt her knee; did she only like the John Wayne and Katharine Hepburn stuff or did she ever watch a good horror movie; did she believe in God and did she feel guilty or only regretful about her abortion; had it simply been the sex – amazing, all-star sex – or had she fallen in love with me in the course of that night.

What I asked her was: 'When did you begin sleeping with Sy again?'

'That last week.'

'Why?'

' "Why?" '

'What was it, a casting couch kind of thing? You thought if you slept with him, he'd make your movie?'

'You know,' she said, and reached for another napkin, 'there's an old show-business joke: A gorgeous, talented actress walks into a producer's office and says, "I want that part. I'll do anything, and I mean *anything*, for that part." She gets down on her knees and says, "I'm going to give you the world's most incredible blow job." And the producer looks down at her and says, "Yeah, but what's in it for me?" ' Bonnie wiped the bread crumbs from the chicken off her hands. 'So what was in it for Sy? Nothing. There was nothing I could do for him that would entice him into doing anything he didn't want to do.'

'But how could you sleep with such a bastard? Okay, he let you have the house, but other than that, he left you broke. He made you get an abortion – '

She cut me off. 'No one held a gun to my head.'

'Maybe he didn't, but he gave you the clap, didn't he? Forget that it's proof positive of adultery. It took away the chance for you to have the one thing you wanted more than anything in the world.'

I'd just hit her most painful spot. She didn't wince; she just stood, holding out her plate. 'Why don't I bring this into the kitchen?' Her voice was artificially high, as if she were being stretched too tight.

'No. I don't have curtains or anything on the windows. I can't risk having you seen. I'll take it in later.' I took the plate from her and put it down on the floor. 'You're going stir-crazy, aren't you?'

'And this isn't even stir,' she said softly.

'Put on your sneakers.' When she did, I turned off the lamp, took her arm and steered her out of the bedroom, through the dark main room and out the back door. It was nearly night; the sky, already dotted with stars, was a uniform blue. Dark, indigo, like my Jag. I sat her down on the back step and murmured, 'Keep your voice down.'

'You're worried about nocturnal farmers, plowing out there, right past those bushes, listening in?'

'I always worry about nocturnal farmers. Or a friend could drop over. So what do you want? To sit out here or go back inside?' In response, she leaned against the doorframe and took a deep breath. Whatever she'd had in mountains, this had to be better. The bracing salt of the sea, the fragrance of pine, the deep, musky smell of the earth. 'More questions, Bonnie.'

'Okay.'

'Why did you sleep with Sy after what he did to you?' She didn't answer; I think she was still with that lost baby. 'Come on,' I pushed her. 'You don't strike me as one of those masochistic broads who lets herself be used. You seem to play more by men's rules than women's rules. You have a good time, you say thank you and that's it. You don't wake up the next morning feeling like a piece of shit; you wake up and say to yourself, "Hey, I got laid. It was good. Cleared my sinuses." And that's that.'

'That is never that.'

'But it's not that far from the truth, is it? You're not saying, "Sweet Jesus, help me. I hate myself." '

'People of my persuasion generally don't say "Sweet Jesus." '

'You know what I mean.'

'Am I one of those women who sleeps around to degrade herself? No. I sleep around – or slept around – for sex. Sometimes to be held.'

'So answer my question.'

'I slept with Sy because he was there, a real, live person who *knew* me. He came to the house to go over his memo on my screenplay, and we wound up talking about my brother Jim's wife, who Sy had always had a little crush on, and about his Uncle Charlie's bypass surgery, and about all the movies he wanted to make after *Starry Night*.'

Talk about stars. The night was so clear that the stars were not cold, distant lights but twinkling points of warmth: Hi! Welcome! Nice universe we've got here!

Bonnie went on: 'When Sy saw the pitchers on the mantel, he reminisced about the trip we'd taken to Maine, where we bought a couple of them. It was so nice – a shared memory. What else? He said my script looked like hell and he couldn't believe I was still using a typewriter, and he picked up the phone and called his assistant and had him order a computer and printer for me.' I made a mental note to ask Easton about that. 'Let's see. He brought me flowers. So I guess you're wondering, was I had for an IBM-compatible and a bunch of day lilies? Partly. Sy swoops into your life, takes over everything. Let me tell you, it's very seductive, having someone come and care for you: buy you electronic toys, brush your hair, ask you how your day was. So that was part of it. And the other part was, I slept with him because I was so unloved. I couldn't stand it anymore.' Before I could say anything, she added:

'And don't ask if I really think he loved me, because we both know what the answer to that one is.'

'Why you? Look, I'm not putting you down, but he was living with Lindsay Keefe.'

'I'm sexier than Lindsay Keefe.' She wasn't being falsely immodest. She was being matter-of-fact. She meant it. Then she stretched out her legs and got busy doing toe touches again. She couldn't sit still; she had too much energy. I wondered how she sat for two hours to see a movie. It was such a dark, sedentary passion for someone who seemed all daylight and outdoors. 'It wasn't just sex for Sy,' she was explaining. 'He was screwing me literally to screw Lindsay figuratively. He was always so much happier when he was cheating. Somehow, his women always suspected, and he liked their scrambling to hold on to him. He liked their anguish too. And he *loved* the logistics of sneaking around. But with Lindsay, it was more than his usual infidelity. He was *furious* at her.'

'Why? Because she wasn't good in the movie?'

'Because she wasn't good – and she wasn't trying. See, Sy had his own money, the bank's money and some of his friends' money invested. It was a real risk. He knew this kind of sophisticated adventure-romance doesn't do fabulous business unless there's something very special about it. But he felt he had that in the *Starry Night* script. For all Sy's baloney, he truly believed in what he did.'

I remembered that Germy had liked the screenplay. 'Did you read it?'

'Yes. It was terrific. But Sy needed box office clout *and* ecstatic reviews: "An American classic! See it!" And Lindsay Keefe was his ticket. She's a star. Men, especially, love her. But more important, she's made quality movies. The critics take her seriously. Also, Sy knew that with the wrong stars, actors with a limited emotional range, *Starry Night* would be just another one of those 1950s Eastman Color-style rich-adventurers-on-the-Riviera movies, except set in the Hamptons and New York. But with actors who could show innocence, sweetness, under elegance, who could really deliver lines – because the dialogue is *so* good – he'd have a major commercial and critical hit. He was on his way; from what he said,

Nick Monteleone was born to play this role. He was debonair without being too Cary Grant; he was manly, exciting. But Lindsay just ruined it. She walked through the part as though it was beneath her, and that was showing contempt for Sy's judgment, and for Sy. You didn't do that to him, not if you had any brains. It was a major no-no.'

'Why didn't he kick her out of his house? Fire her?'

'Well, he wasn't going to fire her until he had a replacement, which was going to be terribly expensive. Lindsay had a pay-or-play contract: she got paid in full whether she made the movie or not. But he was looking for someone else. That's why he was going to LA. As far as kicking her out of his house, he was first and foremost a smart operator. If for any reason he couldn't make a deal with another actress, he'd be stuck with Lindsay, and while she was living with him and having sex with him and getting little ten-thousand-dollar trinkets from him, she'd at least be semi-manageable. If he gave her the heave-ho, she'd be blatantly hostile.'

'Do you think Lindsay knew Sy was seeing you?'

'Me specifically? No. Seeing someone? Definitely. Not that Sy told me, but he'd call her trailer from my house; they have those portable phones. She'd come to the phone and obviously ask where he was, and he'd take a long beat and then say, "Oh, I'm uh, having lunch with an old friend from college, uh, Bob, just ran into him. We're at this little hole-in-the-wall." And she asked him where, and he took another beat and said, "Uh, uh, Water Mill." He was lying but letting her know he was lying.'

'Did you get any sense from Sy that Lindsay might have someone on the side?' Bonnie smiled and shook her head, as if the possibility was too ridiculous to even consider. 'Why not? Was he that terrific in the sack that she wouldn't want anyone else?' I confess: this was not strictly a police question. I wanted to know.

Maybe she knew I wanted to know. But she didn't want to tell me. 'That's really not relevant.'

'Yes, it is. I've got to know everything about him. I've got to know how he behaved toward people, toward women. It's important that I know what kind of number he was doing with Lindsay Keefe. Why are you so sure she wasn't stepping out?'

'Because Sy could satisfy anyone.' She sat up, eyes right on me, trying to act detached, trying for a clinical look, like a woman in a white coat on TV selling April Showers douche. If she'd worn glasses she would have taken them off and looked sincere. 'Sy was extremely adaptable with women. He could be whatever they wanted. Well, he couldn't be six three, with a thing that went from here to Philadelphia. But he could talk dirty or romantically. He could be an animal, or he could be Fred Astaire to your Ginger Rogers. Forget real passion, or real warmth – he wasn't capable of either. But he could be a sensational animal, a fantastic Fred Astaire. Or whatever it was you wanted.'

Moose came to the door and started barking. She wanted to join the conversation. I couldn't risk letting her run out and setting off my neighbors' dogs in the dark. So we went back inside, back to the pineapple room. I switched on the lamp, and we took up our previously staked-out positions. But since we were getting along better, I decided it was safe to put my feet up on the bed. 'What if I told you Lindsay was having a go at Victor Santana?' I inquired.

'No!'

'Well?'

'I'd say . . .' Bonnie gave it about five seconds' thought. The fresh air had brightened her eyes, cleared her head. 'She probably could have gotten away with it. You know why? Sy would never believe it.' She pulled up her legs, hugged her knees. 'But if he did, that would have been it for her. He was *so* vindictive. If anyone – an agent, a studio executive – crossed him, he'd go on Sy's list. Seriously, he had this mental list, including a top ten, that kept changing. Whenever he could zing it to someone on his list, no matter what number, he would. And once you were on, you never dropped off.'

I kept thinking Sy's vengefulness had to mean something. Maybe he'd confronted Lindsay, worked her over about her crummy acting. Or he'd found out about Santana. Maybe she sensed he was about to do damage to her: not just fire her but try and destroy her career, let everyone know she'd lost it as an actress. Would she have gone after him then? It added up, I thought. No. But almost.

Bonnie said: 'I honesty don't think Sy knew. He wasn't in one of his I'll-rip-out-her-heart-with-my-teeth moods. He was very optimistic about his trip to LA. Very relaxed too. He'd planned on taking the ten-fifteen morning flight, but instead he decided to go over to the set, to make nice to everybody because he knew morale wasn't all that high. Then he called me to meet him at his place. I'd never seen it before. He gave me the grand tour. Wanted to hear me say "Gosh! Gee! My God!" '

'Did you?'

'Sure. If you're going to make a fuss over a house, this was the one to do it with.'

'He was relatively relaxed?'

'He wasn't tense. He said he'd done everything but wave pom-poms and cheer on the set, and when he'd left, he could feel the change in atmosphere. Much more positive. And as far as the LA trip, he'd gotten copies of the screenplay to three different actresses, and he was going to take the seven o'clock evening flight, get a decent night's sleep, and the next day he was going to have breakfast, lunch and dinner with them. He was going to make one of them an offer that same night. He told me, "I'm a little in the hole right now with *Starry*, but watch. I'm going to pull it out. It's going to be my biggest. My best." '

I put my feet down and pulled the chair closer to the bed: straight talk time. I didn't like being so charmed by her. 'Tell me why you threatened Sy.'

'What are you talking about?'

'Bonnie, come on. You went to see him at the *Starry Night* set. We have witnesses. You said: "Sy, you've just been a rotten bastard for the last time." '

'You call this an interrogation?' Too cute. Like a snotty Upper East Side bitch.

'Fuck off, Bonnie.'

'No, you eff off. Don't you know *anything* about people? Here's Sy Spencer, my former husband who's been coming to my house every day, having sex with me, telling me how he's missed me, how wonderfully *human* I am, how there's been an emptiness in his life since I've been gone despite all the other women and he's beginning to think he made a ghastly mistake. "Ghastly" was his word. Sure,

I knew it was almost all bull, but he said, I want you to come down to the set one day soon; I want you to see what I'm doing firsthand. So I went. Okay, it might have been better to wait for an engraved invitation: big deal. But when I got there, he told me to leave – so everyone could hear. I wasn't hurt. I was furious. And that *was* going to be the last time he was a rotten bastard. He came over to my house later and I wouldn't let him in. Over. Goodbye.'

'Except it wasn't over.'

'He called about two seconds later from his car phone. He said he felt *terrible*. He explained that if he had invited me on the set, it would look like we had something going, because he never took anyone to the set except big banker types. And he couldn't afford to have Lindsay focus on me; it would give the game away, and he wasn't ready for that yet. So he had to disavow me publicly. Naturally, he apologized all over himself and swore he was getting rid of her. As soon as she was gone, I'd have *carte blanche* to visit anytime I wanted. He said he was proud of me. I'd created *Cowgirl*. He wanted to parade me around, show me off to the crew.' I didn't say anything. I didn't have to. She acknowledged: 'Even if you were dying to believe him, you couldn't. For a sophisticated man, he could be such an ass.'

The day's heat was finally rising off the land. The first night breeze blew through the window. The shade flapped, and Bonnie shivered. 'Let me get you a sweatshirt or something.'

'No, thanks. I'm fine.'

Okay, I would like to see her in my old SUNY Albany sweatshirt. I would have liked to take her hands between my hands and rub them. The fact was, I liked having Bonnie in my house. Despite the insane circumstances, despite the occasional angry sparks that flared up between us, it was so comfortable. So much about her pleased me, from her not making cholesterol remarks when I handed her the TV dinner to her courage to her wonderful, glossy hair. But the great thing was, I realized, that in spite of the pleasure of her company, I had recovered from my obsession with her.

Maybe by allowing myself to remember what had gone on between us, I had broken her hold over me. Here I was, able to sit in a box of a room, inches away from her, question her, behave like a real cop. Her power was gone. I could relax, not fantasize about kissing her. Or about licking her lips, putting my tongue in her mouth. I was past that hump of desire. Hey, I thought, about time.

In that instant of self-congratulation, I glanced away from her mouth. If the shade hadn't been pulled down, I might have looked out the window, leaned back and watched the moon on the rise. But since there was no night sky to admire, no stars, I looked elsewhere and noticed the tautness of the nylon shorts stretched between her legs.

If we'd been characters in some porno cartoon, the God of Passion would, at that moment, have hurled down a bolt of lightning; it would have slashed across the sky, forked into two jagged spears and, at the exact same moment, zapped each of us, right in the pubes.

Just as my breathing deepened, Bonnie reached behind her, took the pillow and placed it in her lap. It was one of those unconscious gestures of self-defense. But without realizing it, she began fondling the edge of the pillow, rubbing the protruding corner with her thumb. Oh, God, I thought, she could be doing that to me. I got more and more excited. I could almost feel the soft pressure of her thumb.

I tried to picture Lynne, use her as a magic charm against what was happening: auburn hair, I said to myself, and big brown eyes, peaches-and-cream complexion. The waist, the gorgeous long legs. But I couldn't get the parts to add up to anything. I couldn't break Bonnie's spell.

But she could. Either she suddenly realized what she was doing or she simply sensed the change of climate in the room, because she tucked the pillow behind her again. 'What else would you like to know?' she asked, all perky, cheerleadery, like she was going for the Miss Teenage Ogden title.

'Why did you lie to me?'

'You mean, when you first came to my house?'

'I came in, asked a simple question: When was the last time you saw Sy? You said you weren't sure, but you thought a few days before, at the set. I asked when you'd seen him before that, and you were kind of vague, but you thought it was about a week before, when he gave you the fifty-cent tour of his house. You said you hadn't spent much time with him.'

'For someone who can't remember, you have a great memory.'

If I looked at her, I'd see her crotch, or her breasts, or the hollow of her collarbone where the neck of her stretched-out T-shirt drooped. So I looked right past her and concentrated on the weave of the crappy wood headboard. 'I asked if Sy had visited you at your house. Again, vague, but then you said maybe he had dropped by. Real casual. Just two old pals working on a movie script together. So what I want to know is, did you construct an alibi before I showed up? Or were you winging it?'

'Aren't you going to give me one of your warnings? You know: "If you don't tell me the truth, I'll bust your head open." '

'No. It's "I'll bust your fucking head open." Now, can we get on with it?'

'What's wrong?'

Just because I was making major eye contact with a headboard, she thought something was wrong? 'Nothing's wrong. I asked you a question. I'm waiting for an answer.'

'I had an alibi, but I was winging it too.' She took a deep breath. 'After Sy called, I drove over. He showed me the house, and – big surprise – we ended up in bed.'

'Yeah, big surprise.' I could picture him, his arm around her, leading her from room to beautiful room, the 'This could be yours again' unspoken. I could see his hand on her ass, guiding her into the guest room, closing the door. 'When did you start screwing and when did you finish?'

She snapped: 'Why don't you just come right out and ask me exactly what we did and how it was?'

'Why don't you shut your mouth? Understand something: you're here to work. I didn't bring you over for the pleasure of your company or to get off on hearing about your sex life.' Thwarted desire is great for the disposition. 'Now, from when to when?'

'From about one until two-thirty. Do you want to know if it was good for me?'

'I'm sure it's always good for you, sweetheart. Otherwise you wouldn't do it so often.'

Well, I'd said it to hurt her. And it worked. Nothing like a deep, wounding insult to snap a woman out of enticing you, put her on the verge of tears. Works like magic. 'It wasn't necessary to say that.' Her voice quavered; it was costing her to fight back.

'Did anyone see you while you were at Sy's?'

'Mrs Robertson. She's the cook.' She spoke to the green blanket.

'Did you have any conversation with her?'

'Yes. Sy went to call California for a minute, to make sure all his meetings were in place. She and I talked.'

'What about?'

'About our families, Sy's family. She'd begun working for us the second summer we were married. I hadn't seen her since the divorce.'

'Was that before or after you got laid?'

'Don't talk to me like that.'

'Before or after? Hurry up, Bonnie. There's a time bomb ticking. Robby Kurz is out there looking for you.'

'Before.'

'So you talked with Mrs Robertson, went upstairs, had sexual intercourse . . . Is that better?' She didn't answer. Just then I got another picture of Sy, with his tight cap of short gray hair, climbing all over her, petting, fondling, squeezing, feeling her skin. 'And then what? Come *on*. Any conversation?'

'Only about the three actresses he was seeing. Who I thought would be best for the part, and why. He said he'd call me from LA and give me a report.'

'That's it?'

'Pretty near.'

'What else?'

'He said he loved me.'

'Did you believe him?'

'I believed he believed it for that second.'

'Did you believe him?'

'No.'

'Any signs he was under pressure?'

'Not really.'

'So you kissed goodbye, and what?'

'He went to shower and pack, I guess. I went down to say goodbye to Mrs Robertson, but she wasn't in the kitchen. So I went home.'

'Did you speak to Sy again?'

'No. Never again. The next thing I know, I was out in the backyard, cutting some dahlias. The phone rang and it was Mrs Robertson, telling me what had happened, that the police were there. I was just . . . I don't know what I was. What she was saying wasn't making any impact: it was like dialogue that doesn't ring true. Then Mrs Robertson said, "They asked me if he had anyone with him, and I told them no. What they don't know won't hurt them, so keep your lip zipped." And I thanked her.'

'That was some favor.'

'She meant it to be. Please, don't hold it against her.'

Like I'd really arrest Mark Robertson's mom, impound her rolling pin, throw her into a cage with a bunch of hookers and crack dealers. But I just said to Bonnie: 'Go on.'

'I was too upset to cry. I put on the news. And then I began to think: What if the cops question me? I read police procedurals. I'm a natural: the ex-wife. I didn't sit down and plan anything, but during the night – I couldn't sleep – I realized my fingerprints would be in his house and his in mine, so I shouldn't lie about that. And also to say I'd been to the set – although I didn't realize anyone had heard me mouth off to him.'

'So you decided to tell the truth and just fudge a little on the details.'

'Yes. That's right. I thought I'd be smart, not mention that I'd been sleeping with him, avoid a lot of embarrassing questions. But I wasn't sure about saying I hadn't been in his house that afternoon. There was no reason *not* to admit it: I certainly had no motive to kill him; I wouldn't be a suspect. But Marian Robertson had already said I wasn't there, so I thought: Well, if worst comes to worst, I'll tell the truth, but if not, I'll keep quiet – for her sake and mine.'

'But worst came to worst, and you didn't tell the truth.'

Bonnie stood, pulled the shade back about an inch so she could see out into the night. 'I opened the door the next morning and . . .' She turned, leaned against the wall, faced me. 'Please don't interrupt now. It's going to be hard for me to say what I have to say.' I nodded. 'I only spent that one night with you, but it was significant. Well, significant is an understatement. I fell in love with you. When you didn't call, I tried to call you. Your home phone is unlisted. And at your office, I left my name four times. I assumed the Homicide Squad is geared up so that its detectives get phone messages and either they answer them or . . . they don't.

'I was in pain beyond anything I want to talk about. And so ashamed. It took me a long time to get over it. But I did.

'And then there you were, five years later, on my doorstep. I didn't recognize you for a second, or maybe I just couldn't believe it, and then . . . I was so happy! I mean, Sy had been murdered the night before, a shocking, horrible thing. I'd lost a good friend, or at least an ex-husband, a lover, a producer. But all I could think was: Stephen is back! But instead of showing any . . . affection, you showed me your badge. It suddenly hit me why you were there. And you were so correct. So I got myself together. I figured this must be as awkward for you as it was for me. But the odd thing was, you didn't *seem* awkward. You were businesslike but nice. Every once in a while I saw a flash of the man I'd known that night. You have a wonderful smile, which you use to great effect. And I . . .'

Again she turned to the window. I kept quiet, because she'd asked me to and because I didn't know what to say. 'I wanted you to want me again. I wanted your good opinion; I didn't want to be a tramp.'

'You're not.' I wished she would turn back again, but she just stood there, facing the drawn shade.

'It's my turn. You agreed. Fact: You picked me up in a bar. I came on to you; to put it mildly, I wasn't subtle. Fact: I brought you back to my house and, to use your terminology, got laid before I knew what you did for a living. Fact: I didn't even know what your last name was. I didn't know that until later, when you showed me your police ID. But all that didn't matter. I *knew* you were right. This was a miracle – and it was happening to me. So I just let go. I gave everything I had. Why hold back? It never occurred to me that you wouldn't understand completely, approve of me, rejoice in what we were doing, because we had this magic. You understood that.

'But five years after the fact, I was just some woman who felt you up in a bar, who couldn't wait to get you home. Then you asked me when was the last time I saw Sy. I wasn't going to say, Oh, yesterday afternoon, in his bed. Because I didn't want you to know I was still easy, that I'd dropped my drawers less than twenty-four hours before, for a man who was living with another woman: Lindsay Keefe, a world-famous beauty. You'd think that all I could possibly be was a quickie; I knew you'd assume that I had about as much value to Sy as I had to you, to any man: zero.

'I guess I wanted retroactive chastity. I wanted your respect. I wanted you to appreciate that my openness with you was exceptional, that you brought it out, that I wasn't a bimbo who'd do it for anybody. I never was like that. Well, maybe I'm not being totally honest. I don't know how many men I've been with: thirty, forty, maybe more.' I remember telling the shrink at South Oaks that the women I'd had were into triple digits, but I didn't know whether it was two hundred or five hundred. Summers in the seventies and most of the eighties, I'd fucked my way from Hampton Bay to Montauk. Bonnie said: 'You knew I was easy, promiscuous, whatever. You knew I had a past. But I thought: I have another chance now. Maybe he can come to understand that what happened between us was unique.'

At last, she turned back. She was so tired; her face was puffy with fatigue. I thought: She's old and now she looks it. Lynne is so young.

'You know,' Bonnie went on, 'you never asked me what I did. The morning you came to question me and it came out that I was working with Sy, I was so glad. Because I wanted you to be impressed. I wanted you to think, Gee, she's a screenwriter. She's not a slut; she's an interesting woman. A good woman. She has worth.' Bonnie stood tall and straight. 'I wanted to be a woman you would be able to love. And that's why I lied to you.'

A sharp breeze billowed the shade. It banged it against the windowsill. Bonnie jumped as if it had been the crack of a gun. I stood up and told her: 'I know I've contributed to your unhappiness. I'm sorry.'

She moved away from the window, until she was standing near the wood cube of a nightstand with its lamp, just inches from me. 'How about this?' she proposed. 'Instead of apologizing, why don't you just act with a little more decency? Stop talking about my fucking and screwing and getting laid as if I'm the Whore of Bridgehampton and you're a dumb, pig redneck in line for a gang bang. I'm a human being, and I'm in terrible trouble. If you're going to help me, why not be generous? Do it with a little kindness.'

'All right,' I said. The breeze was changing to a chilly late-August wind. I felt cold. 'Sorry.'

'Thank you.'

Bonnie had goose bumps on her arms and legs. I went into my bedroom to get a sweater and some stuff for her. Moose trotted beside me. I tried to put a pair of socks in her mouth so she could bring them in to Bonnie, like a retriever. It would be funny. But Moose didn't get it; she let the socks drop out of her mouth and threw me an injured look, like I'd been leading her on to think she was getting a Big Mac.

When I turned out the light to leave, I noticed the red light flashing on the answering machine. Two messages. Loud ones: I lowered the volume. One was Germy, saying he had a good source for Yankee tickets. They were on the road, playing Detroit, but did I want to go when they got back? And Lynne: 'Hi. I love you and I'm thinking about you. Honey, I *know* how busy you are, but could you call for just a second? I have to tell my mother if we want breast of chicken stuffed with wild rice or roast beef for the reception. You'll say it's up to me, but please, I want you to feel a part of this.'

I called Headquarters and got Carbone. No trace of Bonnie yet, he reported. I haven't found her either, I said. But I'd checked her house and it didn't look as though she'd left in a hurry or taken stuff with her. My guess was she'd gone out for the evening and would be back later. Meanwhile, I had my list of her friends and acquaintances and was going house to house, checking them all out. So far, no luck. I asked if Robby had gone home, and Carbone said no, he was still in the office, reading over the files.

I went back inside and gave Bonnie a set of sweats and some socks. Women usually look adorable when they put on your clothes, with the sleeves all floppy, but she just looked normal in mine; they fit. She tucked the socks into the elastic of the pants. I said: 'There were a couple of calls on my answering machine. Did they come in when I was over at your house?'

She reached for the sneakers I'd brought from her house. 'One did.'

'Were you able to hear it?' She nodded. I recalled Lynne's sunny 'Hi, I love you . . .' I felt blue, for Bonnie's sake. 'So you know I have someone.'

'Yes.'

'I'm getting married.'

'Congratulations.' Direct. No bitchiness.

'Thanks. She's really a find. Teaches learning-disabled kids. Wants all the things I want, you know? Stability. A family. And she's Catholic. That's important to me.' Bonnie double-knotted her sneakers. 'Lately – I guess since AA – I've been feeling this need to return to the Church. To have a place to pray. And for the ritual too, I suppose.'

I was really going on. But I wanted to tell her that the last time I'd been to church, I was eight, and the Mass had been in Latin. I was wondering what it would be like if you understood it, whether you'd wonder, This is what the big deal was all about? and lose your faith. I was a little worried about that.

And I wanted to tell her about how when my mother had married my father, she'd agreed to raise any children Catholic. She knew her obligations. She dropped me off once a week for confraternity class, but after I made my First Communion, she'd said: Steve, dear, you're a big boy. If you want to go to Queen of Whatever, you'll have to go on your bike. I would take you, but I'm on my feet all week. Sunday is *my* day of rest. I'd gone every single Sunday from that May until right after Christmas, when it began to snow. It was such a cold winter; the roads became a solid sheet of ice. After the spring thaw I never went back.

I started to smile then; I'd gotten to know Bonnie so well I could almost hear her: You're forty years old. Stop blaming your mother.

But I wanted to tell her how my mother hadn't sent Easton at all. She'd protected him from the killer Roman virus. Years later, when he was hanging out with the Southampton summer crowd, I'd heard him on the phone, going on about how his great-great-grandfather had been the Episcopal bishop of Long Island. I had no idea if my mother had told him that or if he'd made it up, but I knew it was a lie. What kind of person would lie about a God thing?

I was jabbering again. 'Listen, I know I'm going to feel ridiculous when I go in and say, "Bless me, Father, for I have sinned. It's been thirty-two years since my last confession." But it's something I want to do, and Lynne's so supportive. Okay, I don't need someone to hold my hand and drag me over to the priest. But it's nice that the Church will be part of our life together.'

Bonnie turned away from me, braced herself against the wall with both hands and leaned forward to stretch out her calf muscles. I felt so dumb. I was babbling like a silly woman trying to make an impression on a man fast, before he could bolt, and I couldn't stop. 'Lynne's young for me. Twenty-four. But she's a really solid person. And great-looking. Long dark-red hair – '

'Calm down,' Bonnie said, taking one last stretch. 'I'm not going to make a pass at you.'

'I am calm,' I said, trying to sound it. 'I just thought it wouldn't hurt if you knew what the score was.'

'The score was, and is, that you're not looking for a sterile forty-five-year-old Jew. Believe me, I know I'm not a hot ticket. But since you're going back in the prayer biz, which is admirable, you might want to check out your conscience with your Big Three. Would you have told me the score if you hadn't thought there was a good chance I'd heard your machine?'

'I don't know the answer to that.'

'If I hadn't found out the score, would you have made a pass?'

'I don't know that either. I think there's still a certain attraction between us.'

'It's more than a certain attraction.'

'Okay, it is more. A lot more. All I can say is I hope I would have had the strength to fight it. But now that it's out in the open about Lynne, I feel a lot better. A lot safer, to tell you the truth. Don't you?'

Bonnie laughed, a delighted, spirited laugh. I would have loved it, except it was at my expense. She said: 'Well, I wasn't worrying about my safety. But I'm glad it's out in the open. I'm glad for you. I wish you well. And I wish myself well too,' she added. 'I want to try to get out of this mess, if that's possible. I want a future.'

'I hope you have one.'

'Well, you're the detective. What's the next step?'

'I want to check Lindsay's alibi. It sounds as if she was over in East Hampton, glued to the camera, the whole time, but I want to make sure. There's supposed to be a lot of dead time making a movie, right?' She nodded. 'Tell me how that works.'

'Whenever they change the setup to get another angle, they have to move the lights, the tracks, the camera. It depends on how complicated the shot is: If the crew hustles, it can take twenty minutes, especially if all they're doing is moving in a little for a close-up. But if they're turning around, reversing the angle completely, all the lights that were in the background need to get put into the foreground. And crew members had been standing behind where the lights and camera had been, so the grips and prop men have to get in and hang pictures, put back furniture, that sort of thing. Then the script supervisor has to check the continuity; if a chair had an afghan draped over the left arm in the last scene, it has to have the afghan draped in the exact same way again. It can take an hour. Sometimes more.'

'I want to find out if there was about forty minutes of dead time. Twenty minutes between the set and Sandy Court, twenty minutes back. Now, who would be most likely to know her whereabouts? Her agent? Ever hear of a guy named Eddie Pomerantz?'

Bonnie knew the name. 'He's probably been around since D. W. Griffith. I doubt if he'd be on the set with her. He's a businessman, a deal-maker, not a hand-holder. More likely it would be a manager, or a personal assistant, if she had one of her own people.'

'No. I don't think so.'

'She might have spent time with other actors.'

'No. From what I saw and from what Monteleone told me, no one could stand her. She's cold. Nasty. Like someone told her: Okay, Lindsay, you're absolved from all the normal rules of behaviour that everybody else has to live by.'

'But she *is* absolved. When you're a big success in the movie business, you have license to behave badly. You know that. But even though Lindsay is a perfectly awful human being, and she can act – when she wants to. She's beautiful, and she has the best breasts in the world. And the most important thing – people feel compelled to watch her. They can't take their eyes off her. She is a true star. So it makes sense that she wasn't hanging out with anyone from the cast. They're just plain actors, not stars. And Santana: even if he is her boyfriend, by late afternoon he'd be too involved in problems on the set to take care of her.'

I thought back to the reports I'd read and all the interviews I'd done. 'From what I can remember, Santana was doing whatever it is directors do the whole afternoon. There's not even an indication he took time out to go to the john; he was out there the whole time. So who else could have been with her?'

'A lot of stars get close with their makeup and hair people. Like regular ladies do with their hairdressers; it's a natural, easy intimacy. They might have been working on her.'

'The idea is to break down Lindsay's alibi, not reinforce it.'

'The idea is to find the truth. Anyway, the makeup person would at least know if Lindsay had any good friends on the set. As for off the set, if she went anywhere or needed an errand, there'd be a Teamster driver. But I can't imagine her saying, "Jack, drive me over to Sandy Court so I can knock off Sy." '

'How can I get the names of all these different crew people, fast?'

'Everybody gets a crew list. There should be one at Sy's house.'

'When Sy was killed, he was on his portable phone with Eddie Pomerantz. Do you think there's a chance that word had gotten back to Pomerantz that Sy was going to see other actresses in LA?'

'Sure.'

'How?'

'Because this is a gossipy business. More than that: a public business. *Everything* – contracts, food, cars, sex, lawsuits, flatulence – is talked about. My guess is, if Lindsay hadn't figured it out for herself, Eddie Pomerantz would know what was going on, probably from two or three different sources, and was trying to convince Sy to call off his trip.'

'He claims they were arguing about some photo approval problems.'

'To quote you,' Bonnie said, ' "bullshit".'

'Okay. I'm going out to see if I can dig anything up. I want you to stay right where you are.'

Bonnie shook her head. 'No, I have to get back.'

'You're in a hurry to get arrested?'

'No. But I can't let you ruin your career by harboring a known fugitive. I mean that.' She did.

'You may read mysteries, but you don't know shit about the law. You're not a fugitive. Not yet. You're just my houseguest. Relax. Read a book. Go to sleep.'

'I can't sleep.'

'So write a screenplay about a producer who gets killed, and figure out whodunit.' She glanced past me, out into the house, toward the front door. 'You're thinking of taking a nice little run after I go. Right, Bonnie? Maybe a nice ten-mile sprint over to Gideon's? Ask yourself: Do you want to put your best friend in the position of either protecting you or turning you in?'

'No.'

'Then stay here. Promise me. I don't want my gut in a knot, wondering where you are, what you're doing, when I'm out there.'

She reached out and took my hand. 'Will you promise me that if you decide you can't help me, you won't arrest me?'

'Jesus, give me a little credit.' She squeezed my hand, then let it go. 'If I can't help you, I'll let you know. And you'll be on your own.'

She said, 'On my word of honor: No matter how it turns out, I'll never tell anyone you did this.'

'I know.' We stood together for a minute. Finally, I said: 'I have to go now.' But then I couldn't leave. 'Bonnie?'

'What?'

'Want to kiss me goodbye?'

'I tried that once. It didn't work out so well.'

'Yes, it did.'

'No, it didn't. Anyway, you have bigger things to do besides kissing.'

'Like what?'

'Like going inside and calling your fiancée and telling her chicken breasts or roast beef. And then going out to try to save my life.'

# *Chapter Sixteen*

Easton had taken to his bed and hadn't gotten out, but at least he wasn't sleeping with his blankie pulled over his head anymore; he was lying on his side, his cheek propped up by his hand, and he was absorbed in a script. I was mature, big-brotherly. I yelled 'Boo!'

He screamed, but he was so startled it sounded more like the squawk of an oversize bird. 'Don't ever do that again!' he roared. 'Don't you dare!' Two seconds later, he calmed down enough to ask, 'What did you do, you dimwit? Sneak up the stairs so you wouldn't have to say hello to Mother?'

'Yeah. You know, I remember when you used to call her "Mom" – before you decided to be born upper-class.'

'At least I can get away with it. If you tried it . . .'

I liked it. Easton appeared to be coming out of his big sleep. Not exactly tear-assing around town – he was still in his striped pajamas – but to be fair, where did he have to go that needed a pair of pants? 'You sound a lot better. When I spoke to you on the phone, it was like listening to a Quaalude commercial.'

'I feel better. I've had some good news!'

'What?'

'I'd been planning on making a few calls, to see if I could find something resembling work. Never got around to it. Too upset. Well, a friend of Sy's whom I'd met, Philip Scholes, the director . . . He'd been renting over in Quogue in July and needed some Xeroxing done fast and called Sy to find out where to go. Sy wasn't in, but I offered to help and got it done for him in less than an hour. Well, he called me today! He's been needing an aide-de-camp, and when he heard about Sy, he started thinking about me. Bottom line is, he's paying for a round-trip ticket so I can go out to California and discuss the job with him!'

'Hey, terrific!' Easton smoothed down the top of his pajamas as if about to begin the job interview. 'I'm really glad for you. It was such a rotten break with Sy. You'd come into your own, working for him; I'd never seen you so happy.' My brother gave a fast, sad nod of assent, but I could see his allegiance was already transferring to Philip Scholes. 'You can do something for me.'

'What?'

'Get me a copy of the crew list. You have one?'

Easton got out of bed, slipped into his backless leather slippers and padded into the next room, the study, the slippers flapping against his heels. 'Why do you need it?' he asked.

'Checking out if certain people were where they claimed they were last Friday.'

'Like who?'

'Like everyone who gave a statement. Routine shit.'

But Easton shook his head, stubborn, not buying it. 'Lindsay?'

'Lindsay.'

'Steve, believe me, you're way off base.'

'East, believe me, you've got such a hard-on for her you can't see straight.'

'Well, maybe I do. But so did Sy. He never would have gotten rid of her.' He got a little petulant. 'I *told* you that.' He opened a drawer of his desk, drew out a manila folder with an orange tab, leafed through the neat stack of papers. He knew precisely what he was looking for and where. It was amazing; we were so alike in that regard. Everything had to have a place, be under control. For most of my drinking days, when I'd come off a bender, I'd find bottles and cans neatly lined up against the splashboard of the sink; in that last year before sobriety, when I started finding beer cans on the floor by my TV chair and, once, an empty bottle of wine cooler on the bathroom sink, I began to understood how lost I was.

Easton handed me the crew list. 'I know what you told me about Lindsay, but we've got a lot of evidence that says you're wrong, that Sy was getting ready to bounce her.' Easton looked unconvinced, and a little shaken by the threat to Lindsay. I tried to cheer him up. 'Look, I'm sure she was in her trailer from four to seven, with a dozen unimpeachable witnesses. It's just that we found out that there was bad blood between her and Sy. Plus she was screwing around with' – my brother drew back his head, as though somehow he could avoid hearing – 'Victor Santana.' No expression, not even surprise, crossed his face. 'And it turns out she may have known how to shoot a rifle. She had some firearms instruction for a movie she did. *Transvaal.*'

Easton smacked the folder onto the desk hard, as if swatting a big, obnoxious insect. 'But what about Sy's ex-wife? Damn it all. I thought you had her dead to rights.'

'We're having doubts. Oh, by the way, did Sy ask you to buy a computer and printer for her?'

Easton looked blank for a second. Then he stared up at the ceiling, as if searching out the answer there. I was getting a little scared. What if she was still lying? Finally, he said: 'Right. I remember now. A bargain-basement computer and printer. Sy said forget IBM; too expensive. He'd heard the Korean ones were all right, and not to go above a thousand for the whole package.'

'Did he say why he was sending it to her?'

'No. I assumed it was a consolation prize for rejecting her screenplay.'

'Do you have a copy of the screenplay? *A Sea Change.*'

'No.' He paused. 'Steve, I'm not telling you your business, but she had every reason to kill him.'

'Why?'

'He passed on her script.'

'Did you read any memos, any letters he sent her, that said "I pass"?'

'No. That sort of thing he'd dictate to his secretary in the New York office over the phone; unless she faxed it back for him to proofread, she'd have signed his name. It wouldn't have come back to the house.'

'So you don't actually know that he turned down her script.'

'He couldn't have been trying to cement a relationship, for God's sake. He ordered her off the set. Very harshly. She must have been humiliated.'

'Even if she was, it may not be motive for murder – unless she's crazy, and she just doesn't seem crazy.'

'So you need a suspect, and now you're going to pick on Lindsay?' My brother, Mr Moderate, wasn't acting so moderate. His neck and ears were flushed bright red. He was really working himself up, defending his damsel in distress. '*Why*? Give me one good reason why Homicide would go after her. The publicity?'

'Don't be a jerk.'

'I think what you're doing is out-and-out disgraceful!' I shrugged. Easton stomped over to the leather couch and plopped down on it. He put his face in his hands and shook his head back and forth. I was about to break in, when he looked up.

Easton's mood had changed. He was quiet, thoughtful, no longer outraged; he seemed like a man beginning to acknowledge doubt. 'I don't know; maybe I can't see straight when it comes to Lindsay – my adolescent crush. Maybe you're right.'

'Right about what?'

'About Lindsay being less than the loving . . . well, not wife. Less than the loving lover. It's possible she *could* have been stepping out. I can't swear to it. You see, no one would talk in front of me because I was Sy's boy, so to speak. But I did hear a few whispers about her and Santana.'

'Was there any chance Sy knew about the two of them?' Easton gave it a lot of thought. Too much; it was getting late. I glanced at the crew list, then at my watch. Most of the *Starry Night* company was staying at a motel in the Three Mile Harbor section in East Hampton. Maybe I could catch them; some of them might have left town for a long weekend, but I didn't think many would voluntarily walk away from what was probably the most renowned vacation spot in America for three days on West Ninety-fifth Street or in Hoboken. 'East, I've got to go.'

'Sy played it very close to the vest,' he said thoughtfully, not hearing me. 'But I remember one thing. Maybe it's significant. Every Saturday, the week before, and the first two weeks of shooting, he gave Lindsay a present. Left it at her place at the table so when she came down for coffee, she'd find it. I don't mean a box of chocolates, I mean Art Deco diamond ear clips. Five-hundred-dollar cashmere shawls in a rainbow of colors: I think he gave her seven or eight of them at once. They were spilling over her chair; it was an incredible sight. A Piaget watch. Nothing he gave her cost less than two or three thousand, and the average was closer to five. But that last Saturday he was alive, all he left was a note: "In tennis tournament. See you tonight." '

'You saw the note?'

'Yes. It was just lying there. Not in an envelope, or even folded. And all right, maybe I'm not the gentleman I pretend to be. I guess you know that better than anyone. I have no qualms about reading other people's mail, especially not a note to Lindsay.'

'Was he actually playing in a tennis tournament?'

'I would seriously doubt it. He wasn't a particularly good player. Limp forehand; he would have been eliminated long before lunch. And, Steve, this is the thing: I was in the house when Lindsay came down. I saw her. She looked at her place setting. Nothing there. At her chair, under the table. Nothing. Then she read the note. And she *stormed* out of the room.'

The only time I went into a bar anymore was when I was on a case; otherwise it was a risk I figured I didn't need to take. Still, even though it was business, the first thing I did when I walked into the Harbor Room at the Summerview Motel was to grab a class of club soda, grip it hard and sip like crazy.

The Teamster drivers, a group of six, were big-bellied and Irish, beardless Santa Clauses who could hold their liquor. They were guys who had brothers or sons who were cops and who respected the shield. We got to be pals fast. Lindsay's driver was a two-hundred-fifty-pound apple-cheeked guy named Pete Dooley.

'She doesn't get a chauffeured limo?' I asked.

'Uh-uh.' Classic Brooklyn. 'Maybe, you know, Stallone, somebody like that. Lindsay gets me and a station wagon.' He glanced at my glass. 'Want something stronger?'

'Can't.' He understood. 'What's she like, Pete?'

'I've had worse. She's a bitch. Big deal. Doesn't feel she has to say things like hello or please or thank you. But on the other hand, she don't snort coke, or mess herself, or cry and ask me to hook up a hose to the tail pipe.'

'She ever talk to you?'

'Uh-uh. Just to say where she wants to go, what she wants.'

'What did she want on the day Sy Spencer was shot?'

'Nothing much. I picked her up at six in the morning. Didn't drive her home. Her agent came to break the bad news, and he took her back.'

'Did you see her at all during that day?'

'Just, you know, around. Before lunch, she sent a PA over to me with a note. I should pick up a package at an underwear store on Hill Street back in Southampton. Pay them, get a receipt – and make sure to count the change. What a bitch! So I waited till after lunch, did it, came back.'

'The package was already wrapped?' He nodded. 'Did it feel light like underwear, or could it have been something heavier?'

'Underwear. Four hundred sixty-three bucks and eighteen cents' worth of underwear, and this is for someone who lets 'em bounce all the time. Never wears a bra. What the hell could cost over four hundred bucks?'

'Beats me. Fancy lace shit, maybe. She gave you the money in cash, Pete?'

'Yeah. Twenties.'

I got another club soda. He and the other drivers went over the crew list with me. They said Barbara, her makeup lady, had gone back to the city for the weekend, but to try the hair guy and the costume lady. The pointed out their names and said they were probably somewhere around the motel.

Except for the fact that he had four or five super-blonde, Lindsay-color wigs in his room, on faceless Styrofoam heads, the hair guy could have passed for a cabdriver, or a steamfitter. He was about as stylish as the pizza sauce, cheese and pepperoni that had plopped down onto his shirt. He and a couple of other guys – he said they were grips – were watching one of those soft-core horny-airline-stewardess movies that motels pipe into rooms. All he could tell me was that in the party scene they'd been shooting, Lindsay trying to show how wild and carefree she was even though she was hurting inside, ran into the ocean, fully dressed. On the TV, a stewardess with no underwear in a tiny skirt was bending over to serve a passenger a drink, and the hairstylist kept turning back to watch her, like he'd never seen a bare ass before and couldn't get over how wondrous it was. Lindsay, I reminded him. We're talking about Lindsay. Right, he said.

Lindsay's own hair had been under a wig cap, and they'd put on dry wigs for when she ran and a wet wig for when she came up out of the water; he'd stood there in the surf, styling it for her. When they'd called her for a scene, she'd always been ready. Where was she when she wasn't acting? In wardrobe or her trailer. Yes, it was possible for her to have gone out and come back. Sometime late afternoon, there had been a turnaround that took over an hour. There was no big deal with the lights, but the Steadicam operator was having trouble with his harness. No one saw her during that time; she always liked her privacy. Nobody knew what she did: probably read magazines, because the trailer was filled with every magazine ever printed – she was probably looking for her name or her picture; they all did that. But maybe she slept, or meditated. Who knew? Who cared?

I thought that Lindsay would have been taking a big chance if she'd tried to slip away unnoticed, because of the time factor. Besides, as the hair guy explained, there could always be a wardrobe or script crisis that required her presence. Also, she was just too noticeable.

I asked if there were any other wigs around. Not white-blond ones. He said there were a couple of dark-brown ones in the makeup trailer, but they were for Nick Monteleone.

On the TV, one of the airline stewardesses was starting to play with another one's nipples; they were standing in the galley with their blouses off. I yawned. I was so wiped out. The grips gazed at the screen, nudged each other. I lost the hair guy's attention. I was too tired to care. I left the room.

The Summerview was standard motel, an elongated two-story rectangle with a balcony running the length of the upper floor. It was not for the socially ambitious visitor to East Hampton: no famous newspaper columists or politicians or fashion designers would be found rubbing shoulders over the toaster waffles in the King of the Sea Coffee Shop. It was a place for normal people who wanted to sit on a perfect beach by day and get a little glamour by night: browse in shops they couldn't afford, or squint into passing Rolls-Royces to see if Steven Spielberg was inside.

The *Starry Night* production company had taken over the whole second floor of the Summerview. I walked along the balcony. From the sounds coming from room 237, either that TV was on, too, and one of the stewardesses had found a guy – or a couple was making it in a major way. I yawned again and waited about thirty seconds for them to come, but they didn't sound like that was on the agenda for a while, so I knocked, hard. About a minute later, the costume designer, Myrna Fisher, opened the chained door abut two inches and peered out at me. She was a woman in her fifties, in an inside-out negligee. I showed her my shield and said I was sorry if I'd woken her, but I had some questions, and could I come in. She said she had a . . . a guest. I said I wouldn't keep them long. Just a few questions.

She unchained the door and let me in. In the bed, with the sheet pulled up to the top of his neck so just his skeleton head showed, was Gregory J. Canfield, Sy's production assistant – all one hundred and ten pounds and twenty years of him. 'Hi, Gregory,' I said.

'Hi,' he peeped.

I wanted to tell him it was okay, I wouldn't call his mother, but instead I motioned to Myrna to take a seat at the round Formica table that stood in front of the tightly closed drapes. I sat on the chair across from her. 'Tell me about Lindsay Keefe last Friday. How was she behaving? Did she see Sy Spencer when he came to the set? Anything you can think of.'

For a minute, Myrna kept feeling for the buttons of her negligee, but since it was inside out, she finally settled for holding it closed. I couldn't believe she was a costume designer; with her dumpy figure, gray hair and blotchy skin, she looked like a Suffolk County payroll clerk. 'It's the big party scene under a tent. Originally I was going to put her in a canary-yellow Scaasi – halter top, pouffy skirt – but then they changed the script and she had to run into the ocean, so she was in a saffron silk pants and blouse. Cheapies: we had six of them. Elizabeth Gage jewelry. Charles Jourdan mules, but she loses them in the sand.'

Gregory chimed in from the bed. 'Mules are shoes. Backless, with heels.' I nodded thanks. Myrna beamed at him before she turned back to me.

'Sy came into the wardrobe trailer sometime about eleven. We'd just gotten Lindsay out of her wet clothes, wrapped her in a bath sheet. They said hello.'

'Did they kiss or show any signs of affection?'

Myrna considered the question. 'I think – I won't swear to it – he kissed her on the neck or shoulder. But I didn't believe it. They'd lost it.'

'Lost what?'

'Their thing for each other. Well, his thing. It was always his. I've worked on three films with her, and I don't think she *really* . . .' She gave me a Know-what-I-mean? look; I gave her a Gotcha nod. 'But Sy Spencer was crazy for her.'

'What was the attraction, other than her looks?' I liked Myrna. She was a shrewdie. 'That she was such an intellectual?'

'Sleeping with brainy men doesn't make you an intellectual. Lindsay's not really all that smart. But Sy was wild for her – and not for her mind. He was wild because she was so cold. I'd never worked on one of his projects before, but my guess is that women fell all over themselves trying to impress him. Lindsay couldn't have cared less. He wasn't one of her left-wing passion pots. He was just a rich sucker who could buy her things. She didn't care what he thought, or what he had to say. It made him *crazy* about her.'

'But that stopped.'

'Yes.'

'Why?'

'Well, I don't know what went on in their bedroom.' She snatched a quick, happy eyeful of Gregory. 'But you must have heard there was a problem with her performance. I'm sure that didn't sit well with him. And also, she's very boring. She talks about her approach to a character – for hours. Or she gives you a speech on racism or on world hunger. She acts like she's the only person in the whole world with a conscience – except her boyfriends with *Viva Zapata!* mustaches. That's ridiculous. Most of us care. Some of us are charitable. But that's not how real people talk when they're getting a seam pinned. Lindsay does, though. She can't talk about normal things, real life, because she's dead inside. And in the long run, Sy Spencer was no necrophiliac.'

'That means—' Gregory began.

'I know what it means, Gregory.' I turned back to Myrna. She was smiling, charmed by Gregory's earnestness. 'What happened after Sy kissed her?'

'Not much. He said he was off to LA, that he hated to go and he'd miss her terribly. I didn't believe a word of it.'

'Anything else?' Then I added: 'Anything about money?'

'Yes. Right. She said she needed some cash, and he said all he had was the money he needed for the trip, but by that time she was going through his pockets – patting them, like police do – and took out a wad of bills.'

'What did he say?'

'Nothing. He let her have it. My guess is, it had happened before.'

'And then?'

'They both said, "I love you, darling," "I'll miss you, angel," and he left.'

'Did she seem sad? Upset?'

'Actually? Angry. She held that wad of cash like it was his balls. She squeezed as hard as she could.'

I sat in the office of the Summerview. The night manager had been more than cooperative. She'd stopped just short of curtsying when I'd asked to use the phone, and she'd begged to be allowed to bring me coffee. Either she was a cop groupie or she was running numbers out of there. Probably numbers.

I called Carbone at home and told him that since I'd been in East Hampton anyway, checking out Bonnie's friends, I'd dropped over at the Summerview on a hunch; I explained how I'd gotten the catalog creep to admit he'd paid Bonnie off the books, and now I had a witness who'd seen Lindsay dredging in Sy's pocket and coming up with a bundle of cash, and another who'd taken five hundreds' worth of twenties she gave him to pay for underwear.

'The case against Bonnie is starting to look feeble,' I remarked. He didn't respond, which I took as agreement.

I asked if he'd left Robby at the office, still reading files. Carbone said no, that he'd gone into the squad room right before he'd left and Robby hadn't been there. One of the other guys had told him Robby had rushed out as if something was up. Like what, I wanted to know. Carbone hadn't a clue, but knowing how Robby lacked stamina, maybe he'd just had to hurry and get home and hit the sack.

I hung up feeling edgy. Robby was on a rampage; he'd been enraged enough to lie about my drinking. A guy that crazed doesn't just go to sleep.

I drove west, toward Bridgehampton, then dipped south of the highway, past Bonnie's house. No sign of Robby: Thighs had just come on duty and was parked across the street from her place. He was devouring a bologna-and-American-cheese hero; the mayonnaise on his chin glistened in the moonlight. I asked, She turn up yet? He shook his head.

I had him come inside with me, up to her office. Bonnie had loads of files, but I couldn't believe it. For a writer, she had no sense of letters; it looked as though she'd never figured how to alphabetize. Most of her papers were in folders or manila envelopes, but these were stuffed, randomly, into drawers or piled on an old-fashioned wooden in/out box. Eventually I found her *Sea Change* file. My heart started to hammer. I opened the folder as if half expecting it would blow up in my face. But there were Sy's memo and his note: 'Adore it!'

I had Thighs read over my shoulder. I told him the case against Bonnie was falling apart, and he might as well pick up a few points by helping it collapse, bringing in the file showing that although Sly hadn't written, Sure I'll make your movie, he hadn't rejected her screenplay either, not by a long shot. You're sure you don't want the points? Thighs asked. You found this. Hey, I told him, it's okay, buddy. You'll be doing me a favor. I don't need points anymore; I've gone as high as I can go in the squad. And all I've been doing lately is sabotaging the case against Bonnie. Carbone and Shea already think I'm on some crazy crusade to clear her, and since she's going to get cleared anyway, you might as well be the hero. I sensed Thighs was no great fan of Robby's, so I added: I guess you've heard Kurz is nipping at my ass on this one. He wants to nail her. I'd appreciate it if you could help me out. Thighs said, My pleasure.

Good: I wanted a witness that the memo and Sy's note really existed. I couldn't believe that if Robby came back he would actually destroy them. But I wouldn't have put it past him to lose them for a few days.

I figured any guy who could eat bologna, American cheese and mayo was my kind of guy, a human septic tank, so after I left, I stopped at the deli, got a six-pack of Yoo-Hoo and some Ring-Dings and Devil Dogs, and brought them back to Thighs. That sealed off the deal, Jeez, he said, Steve, thanks a hell of a lot. Let me pay you for all this. You sure? Oh, hey.

He was mine.

Moose began to bark as I pulled into my driveway, and I had such a surge of gladness that I forgot I was stupid with fatigue. I pictured walking into the dog's delirious tail-wagging, hand-licking greeting, then rushing into the pineapple room, sitting on the edge of the bed and having Bonnie put her arms around me, draw me close, press her cheek against mine and whisper, Please, just hold me. The homeyness of it made it such an enticing vision.

I squared my shoulders, stood up straight and braced myself. I knew from AA how fatigue can make you vulnerable; you cannot stand firm when all you want is comfort. The mood I was in, it wouldn't be the consolation of booze that would seduce me. It wouldn't be wild sex. It would be sweetness, and soft conversation.

I strolled inside, gave Moose an indifferent, platonic pat and checked my answering machine. Just Lynne: 'I guess you must be *very* busy. Good night, Steve I love you and I'm thinking about you. Speak to you tomorrow.'

I was wiped; maybe that was why Lynne's understanding irritated the hell out of me. Why, for once, couldn't she say, You self-centred fuck, why can't you take two minutes and pick up the phone? But then I thought: No. You had to appreciate how serene she was, how adult, how truly superior. Only then, fortified, did I got in to see Bonnie.

She put the Stephen King book she'd been reading on the nightstand. She'd taken a shower, washed her hair; it was shiny and wet, pulled back tight, braided. She'd changed into the clean pink T-shirt I'd brought from her house. The plaid blanket was pulled up high, prim, almost to her neck, as if she'd decided to become the definitive old maid. Except she gave me her wonderful, welcoming beacon of a smile.

'Hi!'

'How's it going?' Hey, forewarned is forearmed. I was on alert. I could afford to be slightly friendly.

'It's going okay,' Bonnie said. 'I had a couple of minutes of panic. I mean, I've been making jail jokes, but when I actually think about it—'

'Then take it easy on yourself. It's been a rough time. Don't think about it.'

Hearing Lynne's message had really cleared my head. Bonnie was the next couple of days; Lynne was the rest of my life. The only thing that made me edgy was sleeping in the same house as her. I'd be okay. I was so knocked out I'd probably be asleep as soon as I took off my shoes. But I was troubled by a picture of Bonnie tiptoeing through the dark house and slipping into my bed and murmuring, Please, just hold me. Any touch – her fingers grazing my chest, her legs brushing against mine – might make me lose all sense. I couldn't afford to be faced with that. My palms started to sweat. I pretended to be kneading sore muscles and wiped them on my pants. I decided I would just lock the door of my bedroom.

Then I sat, but I maneuvered the chair so it was farther from her bed. Okay, this was better. The situation was under control. 'Let me give you the Lindsay Keefe story,' I said. I told her, in detail, everything I'd learned in the course of the investigation.

She sat with her arms hugging her knees, like a kid at a campfire listening to a riveting ghost story. I waited for her to say, Wow! Good work!

Except she just shook her head and said: 'Get a good night's sleep. You need it.'

'What do you mean?'

'I mean, you'll think better in the morning.'

'Stop that patronizing crap. It irritates the hell out of me.'

'You call this a case against Lindsay?' Bonnie demanded.

'She had a motive. He was going to fire her.'

'So she'd hire a lawyer and fight it. Or hire a publicist and leak word about what a disaster *Starry Night* is and how she couldn't compromise her standards of excellence by working on such a consummate piece of schlock.'

'Come on. Word was around the movie business about what a disaster she was. If Sy fired her, it could ruin her.' Bonnie gave me a fast roll of the eyes, a supercilious you're-not-an-insider look. 'I want you to stop being so fucking condescending, Bonnie.

'Who do you think Sy was? A 1939 mogul with a big cigar, a Louis B. Mayer who could say, "You'll never work in this town again"? No. Sy was a first-class producer, which is a good thing to be. But Lindsay's a star. One crummy performance wouldn't do her in.'

'You're the one who said her agent was probably begging Sy not to fire her.'

'That's his job. But what if Sy *had* told him to stuff it and did fire her? Lindsay would survive. Listen, she's as cold and calculating as they come. I'm sure she knew getting the ax wasn't going to help her career, but she also knew it wouldn't hurt it, not that much. Certainly not enough to kill for.'

'You're assuming she's rational,' I said.

'Do you have any evidence that she's not?'

I edged forward in the chair. I wanted to convince her, get her over to my side. 'I have to trust my gut in this business, and I'm telling you, she's flawed. Beautiful, yeah, but something major is missing. A realization that she's human. And when Sy withdrew from her, first as her number one fan, then as her boyfriend or fiancé or whatever the hell he was, it was a sign she wasn't perfect. And she couldn't take it.'

'I hate to say it, but you have a better case against me.'

'You know, you can read all the stupid mysteries you want, but you're still a total ignoramus when it comes to homicide.'

'How did she get from the set in East Hampton – without being seen – to Sandy Court?'

'I'll figure it out.'

'How?'

'What are you, her goddamn defense lawyer?'

'And even assuming she knows something about a rifle, beyond holding it right so she looks like she knows how to shoot, where would she have gotten the weapon?'

'In a gun store, you jerk.'

'You have to register in New York State, don't you?'

'They have to record the sale of rifles. But she'd give a false name.'

'And the gun store owner wouldn't recognize her and be overjoyed that Lindsay Keefe had bought a .22 from him? He wouldn't tell the world? Tell the police?'

'She's an actress,' I insisted. 'Do you think she'd walk in with blonde hair and tits, or would she disguise herself – maybe in one of Nick Monteleone's wigs?'

'Where would she have hidden a rifle? Under the bed she was sharing with Sy? In Mrs Robertson's cookie jar?'

I got up. 'Anything else?'

'Don't get angry just because I don't agree with you. Listen: I used to be a pretty good shot. My dad gave me a Marlin for my twelfth birthday, and I went hunting with him and my brothers on and off for the next six years. If I had to shoot someone through the head from what . . . fifty feet?'

'Yeah.'

'Okay, if I decided on the spur of the moment to blast Sy, could I get him in the first round? Maybe. If I'd planned a murder, took target practice, I'd say I'd have had a good chance. But to think someone like Lindsay – who had a couple of hours of instruction with some sex-crazed white hunter she'd been sleeping with – is going to be able to fire two bullets into Sy and score bull's-eyes both times, then you should hang up that gut you trust and go into another business.'

I didn't say good night. I didn't say anything. I just stalked out of the room.

# *Chapter Seventeen*

This is why I knew I wouldn't be able to sleep:

The gallon of coffee I'd drunk during the day.

My fears about Bonnie. Fear one: The case against her was unraveling, but the sideburnless, crew-cut, pink-faced assistant DA, who looked like a cross between a pig and a Ku Klux Klan grand kleagle, might still be able to get an indictment and then a conviction. Fear two: Bonnie, knowing her own innocence (or her own guilt), would steal out of the house during the night, and none of us would ever see her again. Fear three: She'd slip into my bedroom, and I'd have to reject her. Fear four: Knowing I'd never be able to reject her, Bonnie would slip into my bedroom, keep me at it the whole night, then use her hold over me, get me to build a case against someone – anyone – else. Fear five: Bonnie Bernstein-Spencer was a killer, whose rage was surpassed only by her coolheadedness and coldbloodedness. The girl with the great smile was a criminal genius, who would always be one step ahead of the smartest cop. Fear six: Bonnie was what she seemed to be, a good and smart and thoroughly decent human being. If I did manage to prove her innocent, she would spend the rest of her life alone, without ever having had someone to love her.

Also, I couldn't sleep because of the dry tickle in the back of my throat, and I couldn't shake the memory of how an icy, malty beer could soothe it.

And I couldn't sleep because I sensed this case was crucial, a turning point in my life. Was it that the crime had been perpetrated on home ground, the South Fork? Was it the coincidence that the victim and I, two men of the world, had used (or been used by) the same woman? Was it some cockeyed sense of Brady family honor, that this case couldn't wind up in an Open Investigation file drawer; I had to come through for Sy because he had come through for my brother? Or was I wide awake simply because this would be my last homicide investigation as a free man, unencumbered by husbandly obligations? Soon I would have to be someplace at five-thirty. To choose among swatches for our upholstery. To install our energy-efficient room air conditioner – dehumidifier. To set up the barbecue for the swordfish steaks we'd serve when Sister Marie, the principal of Lynne's school, came to dinner. To umpire our Little Leaguer's Little League game.

Forget sleep. I couldn't even rest. The coffee sloshed around in my stomach, and I felt sick, disoriented, frightened, the way a kid feels in a small boat on a rough sea when he loses sight of land. I lay in bed, worrying whether I should leave my bedroom door the way it was, half open, so I could hear if Bonnie made a move to escape, or whether to close it, lock out the possibility of a silhouetted figure whispering 'Are you asleep?'

I kept flipping from my side to my back around to my other side, trying to get my stomach to calm down. But all that happened was I wound up so mummified in the sheet I had to get up and unwrap myself. Then I lay back down and stared at the dark rectangle of ceiling. I couldn't get my motor to stop racing.

Another reason for insomnia: Somewhere along the way, as I'd been following the Spencer case, had there been a signal I'd missed, a sign I should have read?'

In the stillness, I heard my breathing, shallow, rapid. God, did I feel lousy. My neck and left shoulder were horribly sore, as though I had been punched again and again. The left side of my head began to throb. I tried to recall the relaxation technique they'd taught us at South Oaks, but I forgot whether you inhaled through your nose and exhaled through your mouth, or vice versa.

A stab of pain shot down my arm. My heart raced. I put my hand against my chest; my skin was clammy. The nausea wouldn't go away. A coronary? No, exhaustion.

No, a stroke. I kneaded my upper arm. The pain was receding, but the triceps felt almost numb. God, could this actually be a stroke? I thought: By the time I get up the courage to cry out for Bonnie, it'll be too late. All I'll be able to do is dribble and make mewing-kitten noises.

Just then, instead of falling into a coma, I fell sound asleep. It was such a deep, dreamless sleep that when I woke up and it was still dark, I thought: Holy shit, I slept the clock around. But then I propped myself up on my elbow and looked at the green gleam of the clock: three forty-six.

I performed my customary back-to-sleep ritual. I turned my pillow over and puffed it up into a mountain, fluffed out the sheet, turned the clock facedown to hide its garish, Emerald City glow. No good. I was wide awake.

I knew what had woken me. I wanted Bonnie.

Moonlight slipped past the curled edges of the shades, and the white walls of the pineapple room gleamed. I heard a rhythmic thumping, but it was only Moose's big tail slapping against the wood floor, applauding the prospect of unexpected fellowship. Bonnie stirred for a second, but the happy tail thump was obviously a familiar, comforting night sound. She curled back up, fast asleep.

I could have walked away right then. It would have been easy. Nothing to tempt me: no languorous arm draped across the narrow single bed, no naked leg or bare hip to tantalize. The only part of her not covered by the plaid blanket was her head.

But on the chair were the sweats I'd lent her, neatly folded, and dropped on the floor near the bed, less neatly, her own T-shirt. And the thin band of sheer white that was her underpants. That did it.

I sat on the edge of the bed, kissed her hair, whispered her name. She raised her head, opened her eyes. No fluttery eyelashes and pseudo-dopey where-am-I? looks. Bonnie knew.

'What do you want?'

'To visit.' I flashed what I hoped was a devil-may-care smile. Charm wasn't doing it, thought. There was no smile back. I drew aside the blanket. She was naked. 'See? You knew I was coming. You got all dressed up for me.' I lay down on the bed beside her. In the moonlight, the slender strips of white where a two-piece bathing suit had prevented a tan shone with a pearly luster, like the inside of a seashell. 'A host has an obligation to entertain his guest.' I kissed her cheek, her mouth, the demarcation line between her dark chest and white breasts. I was soft and gentle, demonstrating: I'm not just out for nooky. See? I've got finesse. Style. Technique.

Bonnie didn't arch her neck, or murmur a sophisticated That feels marvelous. No, she smoothed my hair off my forehead, away from my temples. It was such a loving gesture, and so soothing, that it caught me off guard. I stopped the casual kissing. I reached for her hand, but she kept it to herself.

'Tell me,' she whispered. 'Does this visit mean something?' Direct words, forthright gaze. Give me the truth, they said. Total bullshit: I knew I could tell her whatever I wanted to tell her. She was so goddamn gullible. 'Or are you here . . . is it just for tonight?'

She made it so much harder on herself. Why couldn't she simply pretend it didn't matter to her? She all but walked through life wearing a sandwich board that said BIG MOUTH BUT COMPLETELY VULNERABLE in huge red letters. What can you say to someone like that?

'Just for tonight, Bonnie.' We lay side by side, barely apart. If either of us had taken a deep breath, skin would have grazed skin.

'Another one-night stand? That's all you want for us?'

I closed my eyes because I felt tears. 'Yeah.'

'Can't offer me anything better?'

'No.'

'Does it make any difference that I love you?'

'No, it doesn't.' Before I could tell her how sorry I was, she pressed her fingers against my lips.

'Let me cut you off at the pass,' she said. 'Don't say "I'm sorry." Not that you would. Apologizing for not being able to love me . . . Well, that would be cheap, and you're not cheap.'

'Neither are you.'

'I know.'

She shifted that fraction of an inch so we were touching. I ran my hands over the whole length of her body. She was silky, sleep-warmed. I couldn't believe the softness of her.

'Wait. Listen to me,' she said. 'Here are my one-night-stand rules. You can't say "You're beautiful." You can't say "You're a truly fine person." ' She paused. 'And you can't say "I love you." Other than that, anything goes.'

She put her arms around me and guided me on top of her. Slowly, as if we had weeks, years, all the time in the world, she let her fingers drift down my back, over my ass, and then between my legs. I was so overwhelmed by finally being able to touch her again, kiss her, that I felt I was going to lose it.

I did. Suddenly tears were drenching my face.

'Stephen, are you okay?'

'Yeah. Just over-something. Overtired. Over-stimulated.' Bonnie wiped my cheeks with the sheet. It didn't help that she was so tender. I patted her hand, then pushed it away. 'I'm okay. And listen, nobody calls me Stephen.'

'You don't have to have sex with me if you don't want to, Stephen.'

'Does it feel like I don't want to?'

'No, it feels downright enthusiastic. But it and you may be two distinct entities.'

'Well, it and I want to make love to you.'

So we did.

Afterwards, I brought her into my bedroom, and before we slept, we made love again. My memory of our other night, five summers before, did not begin to do her justice. I had remembered the passion; I had forgotten the sweetness.

Except this time there were rules: Bonnie's Rules of Play for the One-Night Stand. No You're beautiful. No You're a truly fine person. No I love you. The whole time we were making love, and after, just lying there, talking softly about nothing much, I wanted more than moans, cries, animal grunts, sighs, inane sweet nothings. But all I could think of to say were the no-nos, words of love and admiration. I thought: Well, she's certainly mastered the fine points of the game; only an ace at one-night stands could anticipate the need for such rules.

I had to play fair. I didn't want her to think I was cheap. So I didn't call out, I love you. But I tried to show her.

When we finally fell asleep, my head was resting against hers on the pillow. I held both her hands tight in mine, close against my heart.

Magic hour.

Bonnie had made the bed while I took Moose for a run, but she'd folded the sheet over the top of the blanket, and there was too much sheet showing, so when she went into the shower, I fixed it. She spotted it right away. 'You remade the bed.'

'It wasn't right.'

'You're not supposed to care about order. It's not masculine.' She was sitting on the bed in her shorts and one of my undershirts. She gripped the mug of coffee the way a guy does; she didn't use the handle the way a woman is supposed to. 'Order is feminine,' she announced. 'Chaos is masculine.'

'After last night you're telling me I'm not masculine?'

'Don't you ever go to movies?' She held up her hands and positioned her thumbs at right angles to her outstretched fingers, like a director framing a shot. ' "CAMERA TRACKS INTO COP'S BEDROOM Total chaos. Suspiciously gray sheet half-off mattress. CLOSE ON night table, where WE SEE gun, empty whiskey bottle, crumpled papers, remains of last week's Chinese takeout and overflowing ashtray." So how come you're neat?'

'Good cops are organized. I like things under control. The real question is: Why are you such a slob?'

'What are you talking about? I'm not a slob.'

I laughed. 'Give me a break, Bonnie. I executed a search warrant. You don't pair your socks. You just throw them into a drawer, along with your bras, which look like a pile of spaghetti. Your teaspoons and tablespoons are all mixed up. Oh, and your papers aren't in alphabetical order; they don't make any sense.'

'Neatness doesn't count. Cleanness counts.'

'You haven't thrown out a magazine or a paperback in ten years. What kind of person keeps a *TV Guide* from 1982?'

'Obviously not your kind of person.'

Well, there it was. Ever since we'd woken up, a little before six, Bonnie had been withdrawing from me. Not the injured-female bit, with cold, clipped responses to my questions. No, Bonnie was all thumbs-in-the-belt-loops, howdy-partner friendly: Gee, OJ and raisin bran would be terrific. Thanks. Of course she understood she had to stay in the bedroom once I went out, that the windows in the main room weren't covered and on the off chance someone dropped by . . . And sure she'd be glad to tell me anything more I wanted to know about Sy. Discuss the whole case? You bet!

She could have been anyone I'd put up for the night – a visiting cop, someone grateful for bed and breakfast, a cheerful, outgoing kind of guy. When she'd finished the last spoonful of milk and put the cereal bowl back on the storm window I'd used as a tray because I didn't have a tray, she'd smiled and said, real chipper: You know what's good about you? Your cereal is crisp. I can never keep things from sogging up out here. Back in Ogden, you can keep Cheerios for *decades*.

'Bonnie, let's clear the air.'

She smiled a TV weathergirl smile: much too many teeth. 'The air's clear.' She reached over and picked up my clock; it was still facedown. 'Look, it's almost seven. The night's over. The sun's shining.' Her smile faded. Her lips pursed together, serious, prim. 'It's time to work.'

But I kept at it. 'I'm not much of a bargain, you know.'

'I know.'

'Something's missing. I'm defective.' No argument, no agreement. She sat silently, with too-perfect posture. 'The thing is, with Lynne I have a chance of coming closer to having a normal life than I ever thought I could.' I waited for Bonnie to cry out: But do you love her? What about me? She said: 'Let's talk about motive.'

'It's not that I don't care about you. You know I do.'

'I'm sure every single person in the *Starry Night* crew had some grudge against Sy.'

'Bonnie, if we talk, it'll make it easier for you.'

'Sy cheated people on money, he lied to them about opening credits, he humiliated them in front of fifty people. So there are seventy, eighty people right there in East Hampton who you'd think had a motive to kill him. And another five or six hundred people he'd hurt or insulted over the years. What do you do in a case like this, where the murder victim is an SOB?'

I'd only been trying to help her. But if she wanted to work, I'd work. 'You look for real injury,' I explained. 'Was there anyone Sy really harmed, or was about to harm? Not just hurt feelings, where someone might say, 'I hope Sy Spencer dies.' I'm talking damage that could destroy someone's life. So that's the main thing; you look for serious grievances. You rule out people who are just pissed. Pissed doesn't count. With one exception. Nut jobs. Maybe Sy promised some actor star billing three movies ago and the guy wound up with his name at the tail end of the movie, next to something like best boy. A normal guy would forget it. A nut job could have spent two, three years plotting revenge.'

'How often does that happen?'

'Not often. Even nuts get bored. They find new villains. So unless we get bogged down – I'm talking completely, totally stumped – we wouldn't do anything more than a routine check on a victim's distant past. See, nuts usually don't suffer in silence. They send hate mail, make threatening phone calls. And a guy like Sy would be smart; he's seen too many celebrities hit by psychos to ignore those kind of threats. Right?'

'Definitely. If Sy had thought someone crazy was out to get him, he'd have probably gone the whole route. Hired bodyguards, even. Sy had no physical courage.'

That surprised me. He was so smooth. 'Give me a for-instance.'

Bonnie thought, rubbing her forehead to help herself along. 'Like one time we were riding, up in the Grand Tetons. Sy got thrown. Nothing happened; he wound up with a sore behind. You couldn't blame the horse; it saw a bear and got spooked. But he wouldn't get back on that horse for anything, even when I kidded him about being a scaredy-cat – which, okay, I admit might have not been my most sensitive moment in my career as wife.

'But it didn't take an actual event to frighten him. Sy could get scared by nothing. We'd be walking in the theater district and if a couple of black guys who didn't look like they were headed for an NAACP fund-raiser at the Pierre walked by, he'd stiffen. Just a little, but you knew in the back of his mind he was seeing headlines:

'Producer Castrated by Rampaging Youth Gang.' What I'm getting at is, if someone from his past had been gunning for Sy, he'd have gotten protection. You'd have heard about it.'

'Good.' I went into the kitchen for another cup of coffee. When I came back I started telling her: 'You know, talk about riding, my family had a farm when I was little. We kept a horse. Prancer. I haven't ridden for years, but – '

'What do you want from me?' Bonnie asked softly.

'I don't know,' I answered, just as softly.

'Whatever we had ended an hour and a half ago. Just remember that. And no matter what happens today, what you find or don't find, I'm out of here by five o'clock. So I don't want to know that you rode horsies when you were a little boy. I don't want to hear about your first Yankee game. I don't want you to tell me how you got the monkey off your back after Vietnam.'

'I told you about that? My drug problem?'

'Your heroin problem. You told me. I don't care about it. And I don't care about your alcoholism – which obviously made you forget you told me about your heroin addiction.'

'What did I say about heroin?'

'Not much. It was when you were telling me about Vietnam.

'I told you about Vietnam?'

Bonnie said coldly: 'It must have been one heck of a night for you, that you remember so much of it.'

'I remember enough to know it was one hell of a night.'

'Do you remember talking about why you became a cop?'

'No. I didn't think I ever really gave it much thought, much less talked about it.'

'You told me how terrified you'd been after you got back from the war. Walking down a street, if there was a crumpled-up Burger King bag on the sidewalk, you'd stop short, almost panic. Remember telling me that?' I didn't say anything, but I couldn't believe I'd told anyone about that time; my heart would bang in my chest and I'd want to scream out, Clear the area! Clear out! Watch that crumpled Burger King bag! We can all get killed! 'We were talking about how come you chose something potentially dangerous like being a cop instead of something safe, and you said, "This will show you how irrational I was – I thought of being a cop as safe, maybe because I'd be armed. I was so goddamn frightened all the time." "

'I didn't realize how I opened up to you, how I – '

Bonnie cut me off. 'Well, it doesn't matter now. I want you to understand: I don't give a damn about what you did in Vietnam, or what Vietnam did to you. I don't give a damn about your drugs or your alcohol or your recurring nightmares. I don't give a damn about *you*. And while we're at it, I don't give a damn about your fiancée's long auburn tresses or her commitment to the learning disabled. In another ten hours – unless, God forbid, I happen to wind up in court and you're a witness for the prosecution – we'll never see each other again.'

I got up and walked out of the room. I remember nothing about what I thought or felt. I do remember rinsing the breakfast dishes and sticking them in the dishwasher and pouring what was left of the milk into the container. Then I went back in. Bonnie was the same; maybe even more remote.

If she had been in a movie, they'd have had some lens that would make her look as if she was moving back, farther and farther. Eventually she would become just a point of light. And then she'd vanish.

'Tell me who had a real motive to kill Sy,' she said.

'You.'

'Who else?'

'Lindsay.'

'You know what I think of that theory.'

'I don't give a flying fuck what you think,' I said. 'She's on the list.'

'Anyone else?'

'Some guy who invested in *Starry Night*, a guy from Sy's days in the meat industry.'

'Who?'

'Mikey LoTriglio.'

'Fat Mikey?' Bonnie's face got all pink and glowy; just hearing his name seemed to make her happy. She forgot to be remote. 'I love Fat Mikey!'

'You love him? He's a bad guy. Mafia.'

'I know. But for a bad guy, he was *so* wonderful. Well, wonderful to me.'

'What do you mean?'

'He knew I was a writer, so he was convinced I didn't have the foggiest notion about how the real world worked. He became very protective. Asking, "Sy treatin' you good?" I was always taking these ten-mile-long hikes through the city, and he didn't like it. Not one bit. He told Sy a husband shouldn't let a wife do things like that. But when he decided Sy couldn't stop me, he bought me a map. He marked all the neighborhoods he thought were dangerous in red. Oh, he called me Bonita. For some reason, he'd decided I was a classy dame, and he couldn't accept that I didn't have a more dignified name. When he heard we were splitting, that I wasn't asking for alimony, he called me up and gave me advice. I was so surprised to hear from him.'

'What did he say?'

'He told me he admired what I was doing but that this wasn't a movie. It was real life, "and in real life, Bonita, ladies whose husbands take a walk got to get lawyers." See, Mikey was Sy's friend. His loyalty should have been to Sy. That's the way people in his world operate. But he went out on a limb for me, tried to get me to go to a matrimonial lawyer he recommended. And the reason he did it was because he liked me a lot. And I liked him. I mean, he was a *man*. The men I met in New York, Sy's friends . . . they could get destroyed by a four-foot-two maître d' with bad breath and nose hair who sat them at a wrong table. Not Mikey. He was bad, but he was real.'

'Have you seen him or spoken to him since the divorce?'

'No.'

'Did Sy tell you he'd invested in *Starry Night*?'

'Yup.' Casual, relaxed, as if I'd asked if she wanted ketchup on her hamburger.

Except I'd asked her about Sy's investors before, and she'd given me some crap about his being edgy about 'the boys'. But she'd denied any knowledge of who they were. I blew up. 'I asked you about Sy's meat buddies before, goddamn it, and you told me – '

'Stop yelling.'

'I'm not yelling!' I banged my fist on the dresser. I hit my loose-change dish, and a dime jumped onto the floor. 'I'm talking loud.' I stopped, until I could regulate my voice. 'Tell me, Bonita, is there anything you don't lie about?'

'I didn't tell you about Mikey because he'd had a lot of trouble with the police in the past.'

'Do you think there may have been a reason for the trouble?'

'Oh, stuff it. Of course there was a reason for the trouble. He's a criminal. Just because he wears zoot suits and sounds like Sheldon Leonard in *Guys and Dolls* doesn't mean I don't know what he is. He's morally reprehensible – but he's not guilty of Sy's murder. If I'd told you about his investment it could have meant big trouble for him, and I *know* he didn't kill Sy.'

'Why? Because you did?'

'Yup.'

'Listen, honey, why don't you do Mikey a favor? Confess. Say: "Sy made me get rid of my baby, cheated on me, gave me the clap, burned out my tubes . . ."' No reaction. I could have been reciting my multiplication tables. ' " . . . and dropped me like a hot potato. Then he came back into my life and turned it upside down. He didn't love me, never has. He just *used* me. Over and over. And here I am: not getting any younger, lonely, broke. So I got out my .22 I brought back East from Daddy's store and shot the bastard." That would give Mikey a real alibi.'

'Stop babbling,' she ordered. 'Start thinking. Does Sy's murder sound like any kind of Mafia hit you've ever heard of?' It didn't, but all I did was shrug. 'It *couldn't* have been Mikey LoTriglio. There was no way Sy would have let things get to the point of offending Il Tubbo; he was afraid of him.'

'I thought he and Mikey were friends.'

'They were. Sort of. See, part of Sy, the cosmopolitan part, loved knowing someone who was connected, who could tell stories about how Jimmy the Nunz put Tony Tomato and his Lincoln Continental in the East River to see if they would float. And the ruthless part of Sy . . . well, having a boyhood friend like Fat Mikey was a potential business asset. But Sy's New York nervous-Nellie part was afraid of being with a man who carried a gun, someone who could order men hurt or killed. Sy was as afraid of potential violence as of real violence. He was the ultimate urban neurotic; he couldn't distinguish between a threat and an act. So no matter what it was, Sy *always* deferred to Mikey. I mean, we'd go out to dinner with Mikey and his wife or Mikey and his girlfriend, and Sy, who was the world's biggest, pickiest pain in a restaurant, would let Mikey order for him. He'd wind up eating what must have been fried goldfish or lard in marinara sauce because Mikey said, "You'll love this, Sy." So trust me on this one: If Mikey was upset that his investment was going sour, Sy would have taken out his wallet and paid Mikey back right then and there. Double.'

'We're talking a million-buck investment.'

'That wouldn't be a problem for Sy. He was probably worth ten or fifteen million.'

I shook my head. 'Forty-five big ones.' Bonnie looked astonished. 'You could have had a nice chunk.'

But she didn't seem interested in history. 'Who inherits his money?' she asked. 'His parents both died.'

'No one. He has some sort of charitable foundation set up. For the arts.'

Bonnie got up off the bed and lay facedown on the floor. She started doing push-ups, counting softly to herself. 'I don't like your list of suspects,' she said after forty-five. She wasn't at all winded.

'Why should you? You're on it.'

Maybe she and I were doing business, but I still wanted to keep my business private. Plus she'd passed sixty push-ups, which was more than I could do, and showed no signs of stopping; I figured I didn't have to be around to watch her hit a hundred.

I went into the kitchen and called Thighs, told him to track down Mikey; I had a couple more questions.

Then I woke up Germy on Beekman Place and asked him to get me the names of the cast and crew of Lindsay's rifle-toting African movie, *Transvaal*, ASAP. He told me I sounded better. I told him I was. He said he was driving out to Bridgehampton around noon, and to drop by over the weekend if I could. Bring my girl. I said

I'd try. He'd just gotten a copy of a beautifully edited video about DiMaggio that hadn't been released yet. He'd bring it out.

I called Robby. According to Freckled Cleavage, he'd left for work *hours* ago. Which probably meant he'd just lifted the garage door. I called back Thighs; he said he'd been in since six-thirty and hadn't seen or heard from Robby.

Then I called Lindsay's agent, Eddie Pomerantz, who had a house in East Hampton. I told him I'd be over in an hour. He said, Today isn't good, and in fact my whole weekend is booked solid, and I said, Have your attorney call me within the next ten minutes and he said, Awright, see you in an hour.

I called Lynne. She said she'd been thinking about me, and I said I'd been thinking about her. She was going to be home most of the day, going over the psychological evaluations of her kids for next year. I said I'd try and drop over, but not to hold her breath until I got there. She said she wouldn't, but it would be lovely if I could find a few minutes.

I thought, I'll have a wife and kids. I'll be happy. And I'm going to spend the rest of my life longing for what Bonnie gave me.

When I went back into the bedroom, Bonnie was sitting on the bed again, cross-legged, seemingly communing with her feet. She didn't look up. 'Listen' I said, 'about before. I'm sorry when I was ribbing you about killing Sy that I brought up . . .'

'My sterility.'

'Yeah. You know I go for the jugular. It was in bad taste.'

'Actually, it was beyond bad taste. It was cruel.'

'I apologize.'

'Fine,' she said to her nicely arched soles. 'Okay, let's get back to work. Any other theories? Random thoughts?'

'Like what?'

'I've been thinking about Sy. I know I told you he didn't seem worried, upset, anything like that. But on the other hand: he wasn't a hundred percent himself.' She paused. 'I feel uncomfortable talking about sex, but the last time we did it . . . he wasn't there. I mean, he was okay in the performance department, although that in itself doesn't mean a lot; Sy's equipment wasn't wired to his brain. But he wasn't concentrating on me. And that was such a critical thing for him, tuning in on precisely what a woman wanted and fulfilling that want. It was much more important than the physical act itself. But all of a sudden, it was strictly mechanical. Like he had some extra time because he'd changed his plane reservation, so he called and had me come over. But when I got there, he was an actor walking through a part that didn't interest him. He did what he had to do, but his mind was someplace else.'

'He was never preoccupied like that before?'

She shook her head. 'No. But see, it's nothing concrete. It's just a sense that a wife – or an ex-wife – gets about a man. That he wasn't really with me.'

'I don't want to hurt your feelings, but could he have been cooling down on you?'

'No, because then he wouldn't have had me come over. If he'd just wanted sex and gorgeousness, he could have spent some time with Lindsay in her trailer. Or found someone else. Don't forget; Sy was an unmarried heterosexual multimillionaire movie producer. With a hundred forty IQ and a thirty-two-inch waist. Women tend to find that attractive. But he wanted me that afternoon.'

'What for? I'm not being a shit now. I know why I would want you. Why would he want you?'

'Comfort. He could be himself with me. Well, as close to himself as Sy could ever get. I can't say he wanted me for fun, because he took himself too seriously to really let loose and laugh. But he seemed to have a good time bird-watching, walking with me; it was such a change from the rest of his life. And he loved sitting out in back – he called it his ex-yard – drinking lemonade and gossiping. And the sex was good.' I waited for her to say, Not anything approaching the way it was with you, Stephen. Ah, Stephen: what a beautiful name. She said: 'Sy and I knew how to please each other.'

'It's nice that you had that.' Tramp, I thought. I was so steamed. I went to my closet and picked out a tie, one that Easton had gotten me four or five Christmases earlier. Naturally, it was tasteful: red and blue and pale-yellow stripes.

Bonnie didn't seem to notice. 'I know you have to get going, but just think for a minute. From your professional point of view: Did anyone say anything that would back up the feeling I got of Sy's being preoccupied? Was there any kind of change in him?'

I sat on the edge of the bed and started doing my collar buttons. She did not lean over to help. 'That's not an easy call to make,' I explained. 'Sy had a talent – a genius – for being what people wanted him to be. Not just what you've told me about, in the sack. He could be tough with a Mikey, be intellectual with a film critic, be Mr Chicken Soup with an old Jewish reporter. He didn't seem to have any center. You knew him better than anyone. Who was the real Sy Spencer?'

'I don't know if there was one.'

'Right. So it's almost impossible for me to find out if Sy wasn't himself, because no one can tell me who "himself" is. Except that he always kept the lid on; I mean, his normal behavior was not screaming and kicking the crap out of production assistants and spitting on actors. And there was nothing in his behavior before his murder to show anything different. He was acting like a reasonable, rational man. No sudden blowups, no fits of melancholy.'

'So you don't see anything.'

'Shut up and let me finish.'

'Don't tell me to shut up. Ask me to please be quiet.'

'Please be quiet and go fuck yourself.'

'That's better.'

'Good. Now, two things strike me, but they're so petty they may not mean anything. But like you have a wife's sense, I have a cop's sense.'

'What are they?' She caught me staring at the inner part of her thighs again. Taut, no baggy skin. Paler than the tanned tops of her legs. She pushed herself back, so she was leaning against the headboard, stretched her legs straight out and clasped her hands over that indefinite region south of her vulva and north of her thighs. 'Come on,' she urged. 'You said two things struck you. Tell me. Function.'

'I am functioning. Okay, Sy could definitely indulge himself with material things, indulge women if he was in the mood. But basically he was a real cheapo. Always trying to get a better deal, always afraid that people were trying to cheat him. And you told me one of the reasons you didn't ask for alimony is that you wanted to stay in his good graces, and you knew he had a bug up his ass about women wanting him for his money. Am I right?'

'Yup.'

'Okay, so knowing all that, how come he paid Lindsay Keefe a half-million bucks more than her contract called for?' Bonnie looked astounded. 'Does that sound like him?'

'No. Not at all. It sounds like a schnook who never made a movie before.'

'Right. Some guy who's letting a movie star lead him around by the dick. I mean, so thrilled she's letting him in her pants, so scared she'll change her mind, that he throws in another five hundred thou.'

Bonnie brought up her clasped hands and rested her chin on them. She was intrigued. 'You're on to something. I don't know what. But Sy wouldn't let go of a nickel without reason.'

'So what was the reason? Is it possible he made an off-the-books deal with her agent?'

She began to gnaw her knuckles while she considered the question. 'I doubt it,' she said finally. 'Lindsay and Nick were getting a million each. Normally, they're in the two-to-three-million range, but they were getting it on the back end.'

'A percentage of the profits?'

'Yup. The first-dollar gross. And Lindsay's agent . . . Why would he go for an off-the-books deal? He's not going to trust an actress. He, his agency, is going to want the protection of a written contract to collect his ten percent.'

'So if a deal was struck, it would have been a private one between Sy and Lindsay.'

'It would have been. I just can't see him doing it. Except . . .'

'Except what?'

'Except she *was* living with him, had been for months. Sy took women out, had sex with them, maybe had an occasional sleep-over in Southampton for a weekend. But nobody besides me and Lindsay ever kept a toothbrush in his house; he didn't operate that way. So maybe he had fallen in love with her. Maybe he *was* going to marry her.'

'But it went sour.'

'Well, you have to ask whose fault that was. If it was hers, she was in trouble. Sy was vengeful.'

'How would he get his vengeance?'

'Just for starters, he'd stop having sex with her – but not tell her why. And he did that.'

'You don't know that for a fact.'

'I do know that's what he told me: He'd stopped sleeping with her. And I know him well enough sexually to know that you could stand on your head and whistle "Dixie" stark naked, and he still wouldn't – couldn't, probably – do it more than once a day. God, I hate getting clinical.'

'Get clinical.'

'Well, he could keep going for what seemed like forever, but once he . . . you know . . .' She got all flustered.

'Bonnie, you're forty-five years old.'

'Thank you. Well, once he came, that was it. And so if he was keeping company with me every single day, he would have had to put on a splint to do anything for her.'

'He saw you every day?'

'Every day. And he was so *angry* at her. He always got hostile during production, that quiet, nasty seething; I mean, if a fly would land on a wall, he'd want five grips with bazookas to go after it. But with Lindsay it was more. He was venomous. He called her terrible things, and that was so out of character for him.'

'Like what?'

'Well, maybe you won't think it's so terrible, because you have a filthy mouth. But Sy liked to think of himself as the epitome of refinement. And also as a clearheaded man of enlightenment. That meant buying politically correct ice cream and being pro-environment, anti-fur and ultra-pro-feminist. All of a sudden, though, he was calling her "cunt". You have no idea how out of character that was for him. Sure, he could be a miserable, heartless, vindictive rat, but always a genteel rat. He'd eat your face and tell you how profoundly he valued your friendship. So my guess is, Sy did love her. But then he turned on her. And just from his language, I'd say he'd lost control. In his mind, she'd betrayed him in some fundamental way.'

'Well, she'd betrayed him by screwing up her acting,' I suggested.

'Right. But for the first week or so, that didn't seem to stop his attraction. I mean, dailies were horrible, but you said people saw him around her on the set with steam coming out of his ears.'

'Okay. So what do we have? He was upset with her, angry with her, but he was still hot for her despite her lousy performance. But then she seeks out Santana as an ally – and Lindsay's way of forming an alliance is to fuck somebody. Then, within a day or two, Sy is looking to replace her. With other actresses for *Starry Night*. And with you for sex. So I'm asking: What's your gut? Doesn't it look like Sy knew?'

'It sure looks like it. I can't say definitely, because he had an enormous ego, and it would have been hard for him to accept that a woman would prefer anyone else to him. But on the other hand, he was very, very astute. And he *had* crossed her off his list. Now, you could call it a business decision, maybe a smart one; I don't know enough about the economics of moviemaking to say. But it was personal too. This was Lindsay's first soft, romantic role, and he was letting it leak to everyone in the business that she – his lover, girlfriend, fiancée, whatever – didn't have the versatility, the charm, the comedic talent, to handle the light stuff. He knew what the gossip would be: "If Sy has to replace Lindsay, she must be doing a *horrendous* job." '

'Was he trying to ruin her?'

'If he could have, he probably would have. But I told you: no producer today has the power to ruin a star. Still, Sy was out to do Lindsay as much damage as he could.'

'At the dailies, a few people were talking about lightning special effects. Sy said if Lindsay got hit by lightning, it would be the answer to his prayers. Obviously he was kidding about the completion guarantee business, but the impression was that for all he cared, she could be dead, and in fact, if she *had* been dead he probably would have thrown a party.'

Bonnie was doing a great job chewing her knuckles. 'Okay, Sy had fallen in love and had been cuckolded and was out to get even.'

I nodded. 'Right. Now all we've got to figure out is whether his Lindsay passion was a temporary lapse for such a dispassionate man, or if he was starting to lose his marbles.' I went and unlocked the strongbox on the top of my closet, got out my service revolver, then got my suit jacket. 'I have this feeling he was really losing his marbles.'

'Why?' She watched me putting on the holster and the jacket. I could see she didn't want me to leave. I could also see that, unlike every other woman I'd ever slept with (except for girl cops), she didn't blink or recoil or raise eyebrows or in any way show discomfort in the presence of a .38.

'Sy had this assistant or associate producer,' I said. 'A new guy he hired for *Starry Night*. A guy from around here.'

'Super WASP?'

'My brother. His name's Easton.'

'He's your *brother*? Oh, Sy told me about him.'

'What did he say?' Bonnie didn't want to tell me. 'Go on. I know what he is.'

'Sy said he was very good-looking, personable, but a little . . .'

'A loser.'

'Someone who hadn't had much success in life. But he turned out to be terrific. Sy liked him a lot. It was a perfect match. Sy needed someone who'd be on call twenty-four hours a day, who'd jump to do anything he wanted done. It sounded as though your brother was thrilled to do that. And more important, it sounded like he didn't have – forgive me, but I'm just repeating what Sy said – much ambition. Sy saw him as someone for the long haul.'

'A glorified valet.'

'Why don't we just say a lifetime retainer?'

'That's my brother. Anyway, I was over at Easton's, with Robby Kurz. Department ethics: I couldn't question my own brother. So I'm sitting there, and I pick up a script. Easton says Sy told him it was their next movie.'

'Was it mine?'

'No. Okay, now; in all fairness, I just glanced at it. And I never read a screenplay before. But I'm telling you, Bonnie, what I read was such complete, unmitigated shit I couldn't believe it. He was losing his marbles.'

'Do you remember the title?'

'Yeah. *Night of the Matador*, by – '

'Mishkin! Milton or Murray.'

'You read it?'

'Years ago. Look, Sy wasn't going to make *Night of the Matador*. Not in a million years. It was a joke. Well, the writer hadn't written it as a joke, but Sy had gotten it about a year after we were married, and it was so terrible it was funny. It was one of his Hideous Scripts collection. He treasured it. He used to give readings from it: "I kill the beast to kill the beast in my heart, Carlotta." Now, I'll grant you, Sy did get a little goofy over Lindsay. But he *never* would have gotten goofy enough to make that movie.'

'Then why would he tell my brother that was the movie they were going to do together?'

'Kidding around.'

'I don't buy that.'

'Knowing Sy, maybe he wanted to see if your brother had the guts to stand up to him, tell him it was the worst hundred and twenty pages in the world. And God forbid if he said he liked it; Sy would torture him about it for the next twenty years.'

'Easton was positive this was Sy's next project.'

'Well, it could all be a mistake. Maybe you just looked at the wrong screenplay.'

'Maybe,' I said. 'I'll give my brother a call.' I walked to the door. 'We have a deal,' I reminded her. 'You won't leave till I get back.'

'I know.'

'I said five, but if it's six, just hang on. I know it's rough on you. What can I tell you?'

'Tell me, "Bonnie, you're beautiful. You're a truly fine person. And I love you." '

'Bye,' I said.

'See you around, big boy.'

# *Chapter Eighteen*

Bonnie had wanted to call Gideon to reassure him that she was all right, and I'd wanted to call him before he decided her absence had something to do with me. I could picture him gazing at his phone, wondering, Is it possible? Could this Brady be one of those congenial psychopaths, someone who smiles, chats and tortures? Slowly, he would lift the receiver, call homicide, demand Shea, tell him I'd once slept with Bonnie and I might be obsessed. Dangerous.

But I couldn't risk a call from my house. Someone on the squad – Robby – could already have put an illegal tap on Gideon's phone, hoping she'd call him. So before I went to Pomerantz's, I stopped at one of those self serve gas stations/snack food stores, called something like Thrif-T Gas, a place where only locals went, since to New Yorkers, concepts like fuel supplied by a company not traded on the New York Stock Exchange, thrift, and sour-cream-and-onion-flavoured corn chips were too degrading to the human spirit to even consider. The place was on one of the more obscure north roads. I used the pay phone.

Gideon's boyfriend answered. He had one of those powerful, honeyed, southern Do-you-believe-in-Jesus-Christ-as-yo'-Savior? voices. When I said I was calling about Bonnie Spencer, Gideon got on right away.

'Your friend Bonnie is fine,' I said, disguising my voice so it sounded like a cross between Casey Stengel and a frog. 'She just didn't think it was time to get arrested yet.'

Gideon didn't bother to ask who I was. He knew. 'I'm concerned about her,' he said slowly. 'I would feel better if it knew – '

' – that she's okay? She said to tell you Gary Cooper was at his most beautiful in *The Westerner.*' I couldn't believe that I'd agreed to deliver such a goddamn stupid message. 'End of conversation. She'll call you tonight.'

An orange shirt, with its itsy-bitsy polo player, stretched across Eddie Pomerantz's belly, while a pair of half-glasses dangled from a darker-orange cord. The shirt hung over a pair of khaki bermuda shorts.

We were standing in his living room; the entire back wall was glass. The house itself stood on top of a bluff overlooking the bright, white-capped water and bobbing sailboats of Northwest Harbor. It was an incredible, expensive view.

'I went through this whole thing with you the night Sy got killed,' he said. 'Remember? We'd been discussing a picture of Lindsay that turned up in *USA Today* that she hadn't approved.' To show me he was keeping his temper, he filled up to his cheeks with air and let it leak out. I was trying not to lose my cool, even though he was lying through his shiny false teeth. 'I had to cancel a breakfast meeting because of this,' he complained. 'I don't know what you want from me.' He looked down at the giant face of his gold-and-stainless-steel watch.

I took out my stainless-steel handcuffs and swung them before his eyes. 'I don't want anything from you, Mr Pomerantz. I'm here to arrest you. Section four ninety-two of the New York State Penal Code.' I made that up. 'Impeding a criminal investigation. And section eleven thirty-eight, Sub A: Aiding and abetting – '

I didn't have to finish. He tottered backward to a long couch and dropped onto it. He seemed mesmerized by the swinging cuffs. I put them back in my pocket. He wheezed: 'If I tell you something now that's different than what I told you last week . . .' His mouth kept working, but he couldn't finish his sentence.

I didn't want him to drop dead of a coronary. Seeing him in daylight, I realized he was well into his seventies. My guess was, if I'd caught him when he was younger, he would have been tough enough to give me a hard time. But he was old, tired, probably not in the best of health. I felt kind of bad for scaring him. 'If you cooperate, nothing will happen.'

'I'll cooperate.' The couch was covered in something like sail-cloth, broad red and white stripes; his orange shirt looked particularly hideous against it.

'Tell me about the phone call,' I said. 'Did you call Sy or did he call you?'

'I called him.'

'What about?'

'He was having trouble with some aspects of Lindsay's performance.'

'I'd appreciate it if you didn't jerk me off, Mr Pomerantz.'

'Sy was going to California to take meetings with other actresses to discuss Lindsay's role. He seemed to be willing to throw three weeks of film into the garbage and reshoot with a new star.'

'And what were you trying to do?'

'Trying to stop him.'

'Any success?'

'I don't know. He wanted Lindsay out. He seemed to have made up his mind.' Pomerantz fiddled with his eyeglass cord. 'I was working on getting him to at least agree to call me after he met with the others, for one last talk. That's when he was shot.'

'Two shots?'

'Yes.'

'You're positive?'

'Yes. I know what a gunshot sounds like. I was in the army. Battle of the Bulge.' I nodded, respectfully. 'Wounded. You should've seen me then. A skinny kid. Three quarters of an inch lower, it would have gone straight through my heart. So I know from guns. And I heard two shots.'

'You do a lot of your business on the phone?'

'Sure. Most of it.'

'You must have a good ear.'

'A great ear.'

'If someone was having an off day, or had a sudden change of mood, you could pick that up?'

Pomerantz understood what I was saying. 'Yes. And there was nothing that made me think Sy saw anyone – with or without a rifle. Or that he felt something was wrong. But wasn't he shot from behind?'

'Yeah, but if the killer was someone he knew, he might have spotted him out of the corner of his eye, acknowledged him in some way and then turned away. What I'm looking for is a "Hi, Joe" or "Hello, Mary" that you might have picked up early in the conversation.'

'Nothing like that,' Pomerantz said.

'No pause at any point? No sudden intake of breath right before?'

'Nothing. Bang, bang, and then absolute silence.' He lifted his shirtfront and used it to clean his glasses.

'Let's talk about Lindsay. Straight talk. Did she know how bad things were with Sy, that he was getting ready to pop her?'

'Yes.'

'Did she know she was sleeping with Victor Santana?'

'Yes.' Tight lips. 'Fifty-two years in the business, and you know what I finally realize? I hate the ones who make it. Even the smartest of them are stupid. Stupid and arrogant. They think they can do anything they want, no consequences.'

'You can't do anything you want with a guy like Sy Spencer, can you?' I observed.

'No.'

'Do you think Sy had a clue that she was cheating on him?'

'Yes.'

'What makes you think so?'

'He told me. I was making my big pitch to keep her on *Starry Night*, and he said, "I can't do it, Eddie. You've seen the dailies. She's not putting out." He gave that cold laugh of his. It's like being stabbed to death with an icicle. And then he said, "Excuse me. She is putting out – in Santana's trailer." '

'In your mind, if any of those actresses in LA would have fit the bill, would it have been all over for Lindsay?'

'Bottom line?'

'Bottom line.'

'Sure it would have been all over – except for the fact that it would have cost too much. Even if Sy could have hired a not-so-hot for less money, it still would have cost him almost three million in salary and reshooting to start from scratch. He couldn't have raised it outside; he'd already maxed out on financing. So unless it was worth it to him to ante up two-point-seven-five million of his own money to get rid of Linsday, she would have stayed.

'Would it have been worth it to him?'

'I think he was considering it. But I'd been doing deals with Sy for ten years. I knew him. I knew what a tightwad he was. Look, it would have gotten real ugly, but in the long run the names above the title would have been Nicholas Monteleone – and Lindsay Keefe.'

'Did Lindsay know that too?'

'I told her.'

'Did she believe you?'

'I don't know. She was scared.'

'Of what?'

'Of Sy Spencer.'

I can't say Lynne was overcome with ecstasy when she answered her door, but she did look pleased. She stood in the doorway. Her beautiful dark-red hair fell over her shoulders. She wore a crisp white blouse and a polka-dot miniskirt. It took me a minute to grasp that she was waiting for me to kiss her. I did. Then she led me inside.

The house had a Sunday hush. Judy and Maddy, her two roommates, were at work, and Lynne had spread her folders over the living room coffee table. Well, not spread. I marveled at how they were in flawlessly symmetrical piles. Her pens and colored highlighters were parallel and equidistant from each other and just the perfect distance from the curved edges of the light wood table so that, should one decide to roll, she could reach it before it fell to the floor. 'You're my kind of girl.' I smiled at her. 'In 2013, when I'm looking for my 1996 New York State tax return, you'll be able to find it in three seconds.'

'You don't think I'm compulsive?' Lynne asked. I sat down in a club chair. She squeezed in beside me. 'Judy is always saying I'm compulsive. Just because I always put away my shoes with the toes facing out. She says if I could just throw my shoes on my closet floor I'd be more creative.'

'Look at it this way. Neither of us will probably ever write *Hamlet*, but we'll never misplace a bank statement or a kid. That's reassuring.'

'It is.' She smiled. 'Tell me, how is your case going?'

'We're getting there,' I said.

'Good. There must be a lot of pressure, with all the publicity.'

'There is.' I glanced around the living room. Nothing really went with anything else. The leatherette chairs and the striped chairs, the 1950s Danish-modern coffee table, the massive brass floor lamp, the poster of a bowl of flowers from the Boston Museum of Fine Arts, were castoffs from the families of three pretty, marriageable girls in their mid-twenties, all of whom would have husbands – and nice furniture that coordinated with tasteful rugs – long before they were thirty. 'How is your class for September?'

'I think it's really going to be a challenge. I'm excited. Do you have time for me to go through the student list?'

'Can you do it in two minutes?'

Lynne snuggled against me. 'That's all you have?'

'Sorry.'

'Did you think about stuffed chicken breasts?'

I slipped my hand under the neckline of her blouse, around her bra. 'These aren't chicken breasts.'

'You know what I mean!'

I smiled, eased my hand out.

I had no desire for her.

'Going to the beach today?' I asked.

'Well, I'd like to, but I have to get my hair trimmed.' She seemed to think the news would upset me, so she added. 'Just a little bit off the ends.'

'The ends look all right to me.' I was so bored, and so ashamed of myself for being bored.

I thought. I could be having this same exchange with Bonnie, about chicken breasts and hair ends, and okay, it wouldn't be the world's most enthralling conversation, or the most amusing, but I'd hang on every word.

Even if I'd had two months' vacation, I wouldn't want to hear about Lynne's dyslexics and dysgraphics. And it wasn't that I couldn't get interested in that sort of stuff; it was that I couldn't get interested in Lynne.

How could someone have the perfect résumé and not be right for the job? She was precisely what I should want. Why didn't I want her? Other men did. We'd walk down the streets, and heads local guys, city guys – would turn. Turn? Spin. Half the time her phone was ringing with old boyfriends, or guys she barely knew, none of them willing to believe she could actually consider marrying someone else before she listened to their fantastic, incredible lifetime offer.

Lynne played with the veins in the back of my hand. I suddenly realized that no matter how hard I tried, I couldn't make myself love her. There was nothing more about Lynne I cared to know. Not about her job, her family, her pastimes, her feelings.

But I wanted to know every single course Bonnie had taken at the University of Utah. I wanted to know her brothers' names, who she'd voted for in 1980 and why, what her first sex-experience had been like. I wanted her to tell me how a bunch of Jews wound up in Ogden, Utah. I wanted to see *Cowgirl*. I wanted to read her new screenplay and her descriptions of bathing suits for the fat-lady catalog. I wanted to meet her old man, haul him away from the new wife and the bridge games and go hunting with him. I even wanted to bird-watch with Bonnie – or at least watch her watch birds. I wanted to go running with her. Camp out. Fish for trout. Take her on a whale watch off Montauk. I wanted to tell her all about my work, my entire life. Watch the Yankees and her 1940s movies with her. Make love to her.

'You're quiet,' Lynne said.

'Yeah. I've got a lot on my mind.' I thought: Maybe all this is camouflage, and what I really want is custody of Moose.

'What are you smiling about?' Lynne demanded.

'Nothing much.'

'Tell me what else is new.'

I shifted, trying to sit up straighter, but she was wedged in so close to me I couldn't move. 'Oh, Lynne, I'm so sorry.'

She knew, but she asked, as if expecting a passionate denial: 'Is something wrong?'

'I don't know where to begin. I don't know what to say.'

'Oh, God.' She got up out of the chair, stood before me. So fabulous-looking. Such a nice person. Responsible. Solid values. Hardworking. 'What is it?' It would make so much sense to marry her. 'Are you drinking again?'

'No.' I don't have to say anything at all, I thought. I can let it ride. Close the Spencer case, sort things out. It made sense to take my time. Lynne was so right for me; there must be a way it could work.

'Is there someone else?'

I should stand up, take her in my arms. Say, Someone else? With you around? Of course not! I sat, paralyzed. 'Yes,' I said at last.

'Who is she?'

'Someone I knew five years ago.'

'Have you been seeing her?'

'No. It's nothing like that. I just ran into her again recently and realized.'

Lynne started to cry. 'Realized what?'

'I don't know.'

'Realized *what*, Steve?'

'That I want to be with her all the time.'

At last, I was able to make myself move. I got up and put my arms around her. I wish I could say I was filled with grief. But I didn't feel anything except sadness that I was hurting her. She was such a decent person and she loved me, or at least loved the man she thought was me, and loved the idea of loving someone who needed her help in getting through life.

She pulled away and gazed up at me. Everything she did was so pretty, even her crying. Two lovely, parallel tears coursed down her cheeks. She swallowed and regained some control. 'You don't love me?' she asked.

I took her back into my arms. 'Lynne,' I said, into her glorious hair, 'you're a wonderful person. You're beautiful, kind, patient – '

'You don't love me.'

'I thought I did. I truly thought I did.'

'Are you going to marry her?'

'No. I don't know. I don't know a lot. I don't feel in control anymore, that I understand anything that's going on. It's all just happening. When I came here, I was only thinking I'd spend a few minutes with you, touch base. In my wildest dreams, it didn't occur to me that we'd be having this conversation. I wish I'd been better prepared . . .' She started to cry again. 'I wish I could have made it less painful for you.'

She pulled out of my embrace. 'My mother ordered the invitations.'

'I'm sorry.' What was I going to do? Tell her that her parents, Saint Babs and the Scourge of Godless Communism, would be breaking out the champagne, tearing the invitations into confetti, throwing it into the air in jubilation?

'Is she prettier than I am?' Lynne wiped her cheeks.

'No.'

'Younger?'

'No. Older.' Then I added: 'Older than me.' Her beautiful brown eyes grew big with disbelief, as though beholding a Medicare card in a liver-spotted hand. 'Not too much older,' I added.

'Does she have a good personality?'

'Yes.' It was gutless, but at the moment I wished more than anything that I hadn't told her there was someone else, only that it wasn't working out and the blame was all mine. I was a too-old sad case, simply not the marrying kind. But Lynne would be tolerant, compassionate, like a nurse with an invalid who has a long convalescence before him. She'd wait, helping me recuperate, helping me become a better person.

'What does she do?'

'She's a writer.'

'Is she from the city?'

'No.'

'Is she rich?'

'No.'

'What is it? Sex?' I didn't respond. 'Is that it?'

'It's a factor.'

'It was fine with us. It *was*.'

'Yes, it was.'

'You owe me an explanation, Steve.'

'I know. I know I do. Forgive me.' What the hell could I tell her? The truth. Not the whole truth, but at least no lies. 'You're everything I admire. When we first started going out, I couldn't believe you were for real, because I thought: No one can be this decent; it's some sort of an act. But it wasn't. I came to understand that you're everything any man could want in a woman.'

'Then why don't you want me?'

'Because you *are* so wonderful. because I'm a messed-up guy and I can't live up to your high standards.'

'But I'm not telling you to be anything except what you are.'

'But see, Lynne, what I am doesn't necessarily want what you want. I can't live the life that would be right for you. I thought I could. I thought: If I have a good and beautiful wife and nice kids and a comfortable house, I'll be at peace. That's all I ever wanted. But I've got too much damage, and too many needs. Putting a white picket fence around me won't make me into a whole person.'

'What will?'

'She will.'

'Why?' Lynne asked.

And I finally answered: 'Because . . . we have fun.'

Carbone had be beeped three times in two minutes. I pulled off at a too-cute lobster restaurant and used the pay phone. 'What's so urgent, Ray?'

'Robby's got her nailed.'

'Her?' Lindsay. He'd say Lindsay.

'Bonnie.'

I knew I couldn't sound the way I felt: crazy with terror. I had to sound solid, sensible, the tough, experienced cop weary of Kid Robby's asshole antics. 'Jesus, is he still pulling stupid shit? I've been killing myself. I've got great stuff on Lindsay. We've got to start concentrating out resources – '

'Steve, listen to me. He went back to Sy's house late yesterday. To that area underneath the porch where we found the footprints from the thongs.'

'And?'

'He found another dark hair.'

'Stop it!'

'Like the ones on the pillow, Steve. It was caught in one of those crisscrosses of the latticework that covers the crawl space under the porch. She must have leaned against it for a minute. He drove it up to the lab in Westchester personally this morning. He's waiting for the test results, but you know and I know: It's got to be Bonnie. Now we've got her in bed with him *and* at the exact location where the shot came from.'

She lied, I thought. I stared at the phone, at its idiot instruction card for placing phone calls. That I'd believed Bonnie's explanations wasn't the worst part. The worst part was that I could go back to the house, kick furniture, throw things, pound walls, roar to her, You goddamn lying bitch, and she'd touch my arm, look me straight in the eye and say, Stephen, I wasn't there. I *swear* to you I wasn't there. Then how did your hair get there? She'd say, Someone put it there. That detective who's after me. You *said* he was out to get me, and he is. I'd say, You expect me to believe that, bitch? And she'd say, Yes I do.

And against all reasons, I would.

'Ray,' I said, 'you're not having any trouble with this?'

'What do you mean?'

'You don't think there's a chance that Robby got a little too enthusiastic?'

'Come off it. He wouldn't go that far. You know he wouldn't plant evidence. Face facts. Face what she is.' For a second it got so quiet I could hear water bubbling in the lobster tanks. 'Steve? You there?'

'I'm here.'

'What are you going to do now?'

'What do you think I should do?' I asked.

'Go find her.'

I happened to glance down toward the shelf in that dingy corner by the pay phone, with its ancient American Express application forms curled from the humidity, and the ashtray with someone's fat, ugly cigar ash. And all of a sudden, in that stinky, dreary corner, I got a gift – a flash of memory from that night five years before.

We'd finished eating and moved into the living room. It was sunset, and Bonnie left the lights off so we could see the horizon, royal blue, deep orange. Then she lit a couple of candles and we sat back in the flickering light. She told me how she'd come to love the South Fork, the vast and beautiful sky, the ocean, the marshes, the birds – she said she was one of those creeps who clomped around with boots and binoculars – but that she missed the mountains. Not just for fishing, hiking, skiing. Growing up in Utah, she'd look out the window in school, bike to the store to pick up a quart of milk for her mother, lie in her bed staring at the stars – and the mountains were always there.

'You sound a little homesick,' I said.

'Yes.'

'You ever think of going back?'

'None of my family's there anymore. It would just be me and the mountains and the Mormons.'

'You didn't answer my question.'

'I wish I could go home,' she said, very quietly.

And I whispered: 'I'll teach you to love it here, Bonnie.'

I threw in another quarter and called my pal in the DA's office, Sally-Jo Watkins. From the name, you'd expect one of those exhausted Appalachian women with fourteen children you see on Malnutrition USA documentaries. But Sally-Jo was strictly Canarsie and unexhausted. She came from a very old but extremely undistinguished Brooklyn family. She always walked double-time and barked rather than talked. She was a career prosecutor, Chief Assistant DA for Suffolk County.

'What do you want? I'm busy. This about the Spencer case? Ralph's doing that. Talk to Ralph.'

'I have to talk to you'

'Why? We got channels here, same as you guys. I'm drowning in a sea of motions, Brady, you stupid, insensitive mick cop moron. Whatever you want, I can't do it. Call Ralph.'

'He's too inflexible. I can't talk to him.'

'Well, I can't talk to you.'

'Sally-Jo, I saved your ass at least three times when you were in the Homicide Bureau. You fucking owe me.'

'I bought you a steak dinner. Remember? When you got sprung from the bin? I had to wait till you dried out, otherwise it would have cost me a year's salary, the way you drank.'

'Yeah, well, I put at least twenty thousand calories of cheeseburgers into you over the years, so let's say you still owe me the equivalent of one more extremely large lunch.'

'Shoot, schmuck. And shoot fast.'

'Hypothetically, say I did everything right: preserved a crime scene till after the autopsy, had my men go over everything with a fine-tooth comb. No rain, no high winds. Nothing to dirty the samples we took, nothing to make our job difficult. Ideal conditions.'

'Keep going.'

'Not much stuff except some circumstantial evidence good for making a DNA case. Hair. The victim's lover's hair in the bed where they'd been making it. Okay. Then a week later, four days after we take down the tape, I find another hair. Looks like the lover's. Let's say the lab says it is.'

'Where do you find said strand of hair?'

'Caught between two crossing slats of wood. If the lover had been firing the murder weapon, that criss-cross would be exactly where this lover of unspecified sex's head would have been. Now, as a prosecutor, would you buy this suddenly appearing new piece of evidence? Would you use it?'

'Okay. Generally, all relevant evidence is admissible at a trial. But the circumstances under which the evidence was found are admissible too. In a case like this, the defense would argue that since you did such a bang-up job under ideal conditions the first time, it's passing strange that you didn't find that extra hair when you were so busy being meticulous.'

'They'd argue it was planted.'

'Right.'

'A lawyer like Paterno would argue that.'

'A lawyer like Paterno would cream us on that. We'd claim it was an oversight. Human error. Cops are human, and what in the world would be our motive for trying to frame this lover? Because we believe with all our hearts and souls that the lover is guilty? Ridiculous!'

'If you were prosecuting a case like this, what would you do?'

'I'd spend a couple of days scaring the shit out of the cop who says he found the hair, telling him that if he's not a hundred percent sure that one of his colleagues didn't plant it – I wouldn't accuse him directly – he should forget about it because it could jeopardize our case, give the defense something to fight about. Then I'd sit back and think about it. Chances are, I wouldn't risk introducing it unless the rest of our case was very, very flimsy – but then I'd question the whole proceeding. But if our case was semi-solid, I'd still avoid using it. Look, that one hair makes the DNA testing an issue, and that would put our good evidence – the hair from the bed – into question. And who needs a lawyer like Paterno making the jury wonder how come a miracle happened after a week? From the DNA's point of view, a wondering jury is a dangerous jury. Reasonable doubt is a terrible thing.'

'Thanks, Sally-Jo.'

'So, imbecile, is it your hypothesis that Bonnie Spencer shot Sy Spencer or not?'

'Not.'

'That isn't what I hear.'

It was touch and go whether Bonnie would let go of the phone or I'd break her wrist trying to get it out of her hand. She finally let go, but the next thing I knew, she was making a dash for the door, frantic to get to the cops, turn herself in.

'Stop it!' I shouted. I had her in an armlock, but it was like trying to restrain a powerful guy, and her natural strength was reinforced by hysteria. 'You didn't do it, so what the hell are you – ' She said something, but her words were swallowed up by huge, loud gasps and gulps of air. I held her, waiting for tears, followed by her fervent plea: Stephen, *please* believe me. Instead, I got an elbow to the solar plexus. It knocked the wind out of me so badly that I let her loose. I bent over, hugging myself, trying to catch my breath. Jesus, did it hurt.

At which point Bonnie asked,'Did I hurt you? I'm sorry.' Except I couldn't speak. 'Stephen? Are you okay? Where does it hurt? Oh, God.' Actually, the shock of sudden pain – and pain inflicted by the woman you've just declared to your now ex-fiancée is the woman you love – just lasted for a second. But I didn't reassure Bonnie. I let her lead me to my bed, step by compassionate step, and ease me down. 'Take it slow,' she warned. By the time I was flat on my back, she was under control again. 'Can you breathe all right?' She peered into my eyes, maybe checking to see if the pupils were dilating. 'Stephen?'

'No,' I muttered, 'it's over.' She had to bend down to catch my words. 'You broke my rib and there's a huge splinter of bone that's piercing my heart. I'm a dead man, Bonnie. Goodbye.' I reached out, grabbed her hand and pulled her so she was sitting beside me on the bed. 'One last kiss.' She threw me a dirty look. 'All right,' I told her. Get hysterical again. Run. I'm not going to fight you. You're too big.'

'Listen to me. I *have* to turn myself in. That Robby – I guess it's Robby – is out to get me. If I stay here, he'll pull something else.' Her voice started to rise again. 'Let me go in now, while my lawyer still has a chance to make some sort of a decent case.'

'Get a grip on it!' She took a deep but tremulous breath. 'You can do it. I need you a little while longer. Once you've arrested, there may be a problem with bail. Second-degree murder, and your roots in the community aren't all that deep. You'll probably wind up in jail. Understand that?'

'Yes.'

'It's not a nice place. It doesn't get a fun crowd, and they don't show Bette Davis movies. You won't like it. So if I can, I want to spare you that. But even more, selfishly, I need you a little while longer for consultation. Just till five. Five o'clock, you can call your friend Gideon, have him alert Bill Paterno, and you can set the whole process in motion. But let me just warn you, if you're in the slammer, I may not be able to contact you. Your lawyer is going to say, No cops.'

'But I could explain that you're helping.'

'Bonnie, do you think a criminal lawyer is going to believe that a detective on the Homicide Squad has a soft spot for his client and will act in her best interests?'

'He might.' It disturbed me how naive she was, how God Bless America. She wanted to turn herself in, put her faith in the System. She'd been walking into a hellhole. Jail to her was movies about exploited women with pitiful stories and one twisted prison matron. To her, ugliness was a set designer's vision. She didn't know the lunatic screams, the rage, the violence, the stink. Her crack addicts were on NBC News; she had no idea.

'Now, you told me you were going to be very busy today, solving the case. How far did you get?'

'I don't know. You tell me.'

I took her hand. She pulled it away. I'd forgotten I hadn't mentioned that I loved her, or that I wasn't marrying Lynne, so I reached out for her again. But she stood up and went over to my leather recliner. There was a pad and pen on the table next to it, and as she sat back, she picked up the pad, held it to her heart as if it were the ultimate mash note. 'I read too many mysteries, see too many detective movies,' she explained. 'When I thought about the whole case, everything you told me, I wound up suspecting Victor Santana and Mrs Robertson.'

'Why, for Christ's sake?'

'Because he was jealous of Sy and knew Sy thought he was weak – and if Lindsay was going to be fired, he'd be next.'

'And Marina Robertson?'

'Who knows? Because Sy went strolling into the kitchen once too often and lifted a lid off a pot and stuck his pinkie into her béarnaise sauce and sniffed it and put a dab on his tongue and suggested a soupçon more chervil.'

'Too bad you're over the hill. You'd be some great cop.'

'You're not impressed by my deductive powers?'

'No.'

'I didn't think you'd be. That's why I gave up looking at the big picture – because I keep trying to turn it into a movie. I decided to concentrate on Sy. Analyze my last few days with him, factor in everything you told me.'

'Go ahead.'

She pushed back so the recliner was practically horizontal. She glanced from me to the pad and back again. 'Think of Sy's behaviour. What was out of character for him?'

'Not concentrating when he was humping you.'

'Let's just call it distracted behavior,' she suggested.

'Distracted behavior. Third-rate fucking. Whatever you want.'

'It was second-rate,' she said. 'With you it was third-rate.'

'No. You never had it so good. You know it. Admit it.'

'Nope. Anyway, Sy was distracted. That could have meant something big was happening – or about to happen. Now, what else?' I thought she was going to answer her own questions, but she was waiting for me.

I thought about it. What in the last few days of Sy Spencer's life had in any way been atypical? Love. 'He'd fallen in love with Lindsay,' I began. 'And she hurt him. All of a sudden, the ultimate victimizer was a victim. It must have come as a real blow to him.'

'Right. And so what was going on? Under the best of circumstances, Sy was a vengeful man if someone crossed him. And here was the object of his affection or obsession, his love, cheating on him. He was going to get even.'

'But ultimately, he couldn't get even.' I told her what Eddie Pomerantz had said, that because of money, Sy would wind up keeping her on the picture.

Bonnie's eyes got huge. 'That's even better!' She jumped out of the recliner, came right over to me. 'Think!' She ordered.

'Think about what?'

'Vengeance is one thing. That's what I was concentrating on. But how could he get vengeance *and* money?'

I bolted up. 'Jesus! The completion insurance!'

Bonnie grabbed onto my jacket sleeve. 'If lightning struck Lindsay, he'd get his money, he'd get his new actress.'

'And he'd get his revenge,' I said slowly. 'Okay, but let's slow down. The theory's good, but the truth of the matter is, Lindsay *wasn't* struck by lightning. Sy was. How does that figure?'

'Stephen, ask yourself: Who was killed? Sy?

'Of course Sy.'

'Or someone in a white, hooded bathrobe who was standing at the edge of the pool, the way Lindsay Keefe did when she came home from the set and did her laps?'

'Someone small,' I said.

And Bonnie said: 'Yup. Small, just like Sy.'

# *Chapter Nineteen*

Bonnie was all juiced up, talking too fast, bopping in a U-shaped path around the bed, stopping each time at the shaded window to bounce on the balls of her bare feet and peek out. She was not at her best, excited in a confined space. 'Okay,' she said. 'We've got to figure out if this really is a possibility, and then – '

'Stop. I'm running this show, not you. I'm the lead detective. You're zero.'

'Be quiet. I know what I'm doing.' She perched on the dresser and swung her leg back and forth fast, like a pendulum running amok.

'With all due respect, you may be semi-smart, but when it comes to police procedure you don't know your ass from a hole in the ground, and we don't have time to debate hierarchy, so I'm in charge.' She put her fingers up to her mouth, as though hiding a yawn induced by being too, too bored by such childish jockeying for position. 'Don't give me that yawn crap, Bonnie.'

'I'm not giving you yawn crap.'

'Now think; don't just shoot off your mouth. In the time you knew him, did Sy ever make threats against anyone, or wish a person dead in a way that made you fear for their lives? Beyond the "I hope he dies" we talked about.'

She swung her leg some more and finally shook her head. 'But that's not to say he wasn't spiteful. He had his hate list. If thirty years after the fact he could hurt someone who called him Peewee in junior high school, he definitely would. But he didn't think of revenge in terms of death. He didn't want to cause physical pain;

he wanted to inflict maximum emotional pain on anyone who ever got in his way.'

I added another item to Bonnie's asset column, which now had about five million items: She didn't sway with each trendy breeze. The way things were looking, it would have been easy for her to portray Sy as a Man with Murderous Instincts, but she was too fair to do that.

'All right,' I said. 'So what it boils down to is that Sy was just your average, malicious guy.'

'Except his malice got more intense as he got older – or as he got more successful and powerful. Look, maybe the man I married was no cute little cuddle bunny, but the Sy I got to know again after I gave him the *Sea Change* script was much harder; he was so full of himself, so disdainful of other people. Anyone who crossed him was bad, selfish, stupid and ipso facto deserved whatever damage Sy decided to inflict. In his mind, when he got back at someone, he was only making sure justice was done.'

'All right, think about this 'Did he have any morals at all?'

Bonnie gave the question some serious, leg-swinging consideration. 'He took decent political positions: apartheid is bad, rain forests are good. But no, I never saw any evidence of morals, not in a personal sense.'

'So we could call him amoral.' She nodded. 'And we can say, *maybe*, that he'd have no reservations about murder; it just was unnecessary or dangerous.'

'Or unseemly. Dartmouth men don't kill.'

'But what if Sy had gotten past unseemly? Look, he was on a nine-year roll, making good movies, big money. He could do no wrong. Is it possible he got so conceited that he finally thought everything he did was by definition seemly?'

Bonnie wriggled farther back on the dresser and sat cross-legged. She grew reflective, staring past me into space. 'Sure. It's possible. He believed his own publicity; Sy Spencer was superior, creative, refined. He could never be crass like the West Coast producers he was always going on about, screeching into their car phones or building bowling alleys in their houses. And he was so exquisitely sensitive he couldn't possibly be cruel. But forget Sy's idealized vision of Sy. I think all we've been talking about, all of what was going on in his life – thwarted love, his need for revenge, his need for money – played a part in pushing him toward the edge. What finally made him jump was that he got scared.'

'Of what?'

'Failure. The studios hadn't gone for *Starry Night*, but he believed in it and so he went out and got the financing himself. Give Sy credit. He told me *Starry* would be the best kind of American movie, where characters grow and finally come to deserve each other. But Lindsay was ruining everything. Not only making a fool out of him with Santana, really wounding him, but destroying what he really cared about most: his movie, which was his reputation, his immortality.'

'So she was costing him an extra half mil, plus future profits. And cutting off his balls and breaking his heart with Santana.'

'More than that. She was making him lose status in the business. Sy told me this much: People were starting to say, See? We were right. *Starry Night* was a dog from day one. And the way Lindsay's performance was going – so lifeless – the critics and all his fancy friends would get into the elevator after a screening and say, Was that *thing* we just saw a Sy Spencer film?'

'But you know about those old guys out in Hollywood – those Goldwyn guys,' I countered. 'They made movies the critics said were lousy, and all their so-called friends laughed at them, and they just went on.'

'But they were tough. They could take it.'

'You're telling me Sy couldn't?'

'Stephen, remember how we were talking about Sy being different things to different people, that he didn't seem to have any core? Well, it wasn't just something he chose to do when it amused him. Sy always let himself be defined by whoever he was with, and if those people were laughing at him – for being cuckolded by a fancypants like Victor Santana, or for making an adventure-romance that wasn't adventurous or romantic – he would allow himself to be transformed into precisely what they were laughing at: a failure, a nothing, a jackass.'

'So he wanted her dead for making him a laughing-stock. But he wouldn't have killed her himself?'

'No. I can't see him inject strychnine into her melon balls. Sy was much too squeamish to commit a violent act. And he wouldn't have dirtied his hands in the metaphorical sense. He was a gentleman; he never did anything nasty himself.'

Somebody was there to do it for him.'

'Always.'

'So who did he know who would do that kind of dirty work?' I asked. She knew, but she didn't want to say it. 'How about Mike LoTriglio?'

'No.'

'Why not?'

'Because if Mikey or one of his boys did it, Lindsay Keefe would be on the cover of *People* this week, with a "1957–1989" over her bazooms, and Sy would be rolling with *Starry Night* starring Nicholas Monteleone and Katherine Pourelle.'

I told her she was wrong, that La Cosa Nostra boys' invincible reputation was a myth, and in fact, half the time they were such a bunch of screwups they made the FBI look good.

She said she'd read *Wiseguy* and knew all about sociopathic Mafia morons who couldn't make it in the legitimate world, but Mikey was as clever as they come, and with a different background, he could have been CEO of Merrill Lynch.

I told her she was a fucking dunce, and she smiled at me and said she wasn't.

I had to go into the kitchen to call Thighs at Headquarters, but I didn't feel like leaving Bonnie because I liked looking at her, especially in my undershirt, which was a washed-out cotton you could sort of see through. Also, if I left her alone she'd probably wind up lying on the floor, bench-pressing my stereo, so I picked up the phone on my nightstand. No word from Robby at the Life-codes lab up in Westchester. And no leads at all to Mikey's whereabouts: he wasn't at home in his fifteen-room Tudor in Glen Cove, in Nassau Country, or at Terri Noonan's apartment in Queens, or at the Sons of Palermo social club in Little Italy. I asked, What about that bar in the meat district where he hangs out, Rosie's? Thighs said, I asked the bartender if Mikey LoTriglio was there, and he said: Mikey *who*?

'Rosie's?' Bonnie repeated when I hung up. 'I remember hearing about Rosie's.' She picked up the phone, got Manhattan information and asked for the number of Rosie's Bar and Grill on Ninth Avenue. Then she dialed and asked for Michael LoTriglio. I shook my head sadly, as in Pathetic. She was clearly hearing the same "Mikey *who*?" that Thighs had got. But she cut the guy off. 'You may not know Mr LoTriglio,' she said into the phone, 'but he comes into Rosie's every now and then.' She sounded commanding, secure, the way a good cop has to sound. 'I'd like you to do your best to get a message to him. Tell him that Bonnie Spencer – S-p-e-n-c-e-r – called and said it's urgent that she speak with him.' She gave him my number and hung up.

'Good luck,' I said.

'Thanks.'

I told her I was going to go to the set in East Hampton to try and harass Lindsay into cooperating, and tie up a few other loose ends. I started to enumerate them when the phone rang. I recognized the voice, gravelly, tough. 'Get Mrs Spencer,' it ordered. I handed it over to Bonnie.

'Mike?' Pause. 'Fine.' Pause. 'I've missed you too.' I stood beside her, tilted the receiver and put my ear right next to hers. 'Actually,' she went on. 'I'm not so fine.'

'What's the matter, Bonita?'

'I'm the major suspect in Sy's murder.'

'*What*?'

'They issued an arrest warrant for me.'

Mikey laughed. Not amused. An incredulous snort. 'That is so stupid it makes regular stupid look smart.'

'I know. But, Mike, let me tell you what happened.'

'You don't need to give me no explanations.'

'I know. But see, I was sort of keeping company with Sy again. And the police found evidence of my being at his house right before he died – and we weren't downstairs having tea. So they have this physical evidence from a bedroom, and they have this theory that Sy rejected me or my new screenplay and that I shot him. And that's another problem. They know I can handle a rifle.'

'What can I do?' Mikey asked. 'You got a blank check with me. You know that. Want me to find a nice, quiet place for you where you can get noticed? Need money? Want me to . . . Listen, I would never talk to you this way, but what we have here is not your standard situation. So you want me to say abracadabra? Make some rabbit disappear? Name it. You're a sweet girl, a lady, and you were a good friend to my Terri.'

'Terri's a lovely woman,' Bonnie said. I couldn't believe this conversation. 'You're lucky to have each other.'

'Thanks,' Fat Mikey said. 'I tell her she's too good for me, but she don't believe it.'

'Mike, let me tell you what I'd like you to do, and please, feel free to say no. You know me. I don't live in a world where people call in IOUs.'

'I'm listenin'.'

'There's a detective on this case, Detective Brady.'

'I met him.'

'He's on my side. He's trying to help me.'

There was a long pause where Mikey contemplated the alternatives, including, if he had half the brains Bonnie credited him with, a setup. But he trusted Bonnie. He had to, because all he did was ask: 'What makes you think he's on your side?'

'He knows it's a weak case, and he thinks he can make a better one.' There was a silence. 'And he's in love with me.' I stepped away from the phone and stared at her. She just continued with the conversation, so I stepped back and kept listening.

'The cop's in love with you?'

'I think so. So this is what I'd like, Mike – if you can see your way to doing it. I'd like you to talk to him. Anyplace you say. He seems to feel you might remember something now that slipped your mind during your interview.' Mikey gave another one of his laugh-snorts. 'He's sworn to me this would be off the record.' I grabbed her shoulder, shook my head, but she just kept talking. 'If you feel this would compromise you in any way, please don't do it.

I know how it feels to have the police after you, and it's not something I'd want for you or Terri or your family. It's a horror.'

'Where are you now, Bonita? The truth.'

'He's hiding me, Mike. I can't tell you where.'

'Tell him to meet me at the Gold Coast restaurant on Northern Boulevard in Manhasset in an hour.' I shook my head, made a stretch-it-out signal with my hands.

'I think it will take him more than an hour to get there,' she said.

'An hour and a half, then. Tell him to meet me in the parking lot in the back. Get out of his car, walk away from it and just stand there. Got it?'

'Thank you,' Bonnie said. 'I won't say I owe you one, Mike. But I will say I appreciate this from the bottom of my heart.'

'I know you do, Bonita.'

'I *love* you?' I said.

'I had to say something.'

'Do you honestly think I love you?'

'Yes. Not that it means anything. You've decided you need a life with a Ford station wagon and kids with freckles and trim-a-tree parties and intercourse every Saturday, Sunday and Wednesday. It's preventive medicine, something you have to take to keep from self-destructing. I think you've convinced yourself that passion is a dark side that's too dangerous for you. Well, maybe you're right. Look at my life. Where has passion gotten me? What do I have to show for forty-five years of letting go? One movie nobody remembers and a warrant for my arrest for murder. Listen, you made the right choice. What could I offer you? Two dried-up fallopian tubes and a few laughs? So forget what I said about the love business. I get delusional under stress. Don't think twice: she's perfect. Grab her, marry her. *Mazel tov*'

The restaurant was a block away from one of those sumptuous suburban shopping centers that attract people who need to spend eighty-five dollars for a cotton T-shirt.

Another cloudless day. Heat shimmered off the hoods of the Mercedeses, BMWs and Porsches, distorting the air, making the lot look like a slightly out-of-focus downtown Stuttgart. No Mikey. I'd been waiting for ten minutes, away from the car. All I saw was an occasional woman who had exhausted every possibility in the way of hair, makeup, nails, jewelry and clothes; one of them should have been put in a glass case in the Smithsonian just to show what we had become after eight years of Reagan.

I unbuttoned my jacket; all that accomplished was to allow more hot, humid air to circulate around my sweat-drenched shirt. Five minutes later, as I was loosening my tie, the door of a little red Miata convertible, top up, opened, and Mikey, with all the grace of sausage meat oozing out of its casing, somehow managed to emerge. He waddled across the blacktop. He'd obviously been watching me since I arrived. We nodded at each other. He was wearing sports clothes that looked more maternity than Mafia: white pants and a huge red, blue and purple-flowered shirt.

'Nice car.' It was all I could think of to say.

'Not mine.' I wasn't sure if he meant stolen or just borrowed. 'Take off your jacket and open up your shirt.' He motioned me over to the far side of a garbage Dumpster and examined my chest and back for evidence of tape or wires. While I was buttoning my shirt back up, he checked out my holster and patted down my pants, taking out my wallet, shield and handcuffs to make sure they were what they felt like. After he finished, he rumbled: Wanna go inside?'

I shivered at the frigid blast of air-conditioning. Mikey chose a table and, without asking me, told the waitress to bring us two club sandwiches and two iced teas. 'You don't got to eat it. It's for looks,' he explained. He had one of those Roman noses that begin at the forehead, but his nose, like the rest of him, was fat; you wanted to squeeze it and hear it honk. 'So tell me about our mutual friend.'

'I don't think she did it.'

'No shit, Ajax.' Even his earlobes were fat.

'But unless I find out who did, there's a good chance she'll go for a long vacation.'

'What do they got?'

'Circumstantial crap: a couple of people who'll say Sy wasn't going to make a movie out of some screenplay she'd written; they have a witness that he visited her house every day and they were having an affair. Either way, the DA could make a case for a woman who's been thrown over and who wants to get even.' No wonder no one had ever been able to nail Mikey. He was too smart. He just sat there, a huge flower-shirted Buddha, but I could sense him analyzing, weighing alternatives, computing – and all the while not missing a word I was saying. 'The physical evidence is more of a problem,' I continued. 'Four of her hairs got caught in one of those wicker headboards where she was keeping Sy company no more than a half hour before he was killed. You know about the new DNA tests we do?'

'I know more than you know, Brady. Keep talking.'

'They just found another hair, right at the spot where we figure the killer stood when he fired.'

Mikey shook his head in disgust. His chins quivered. 'Who put it there?'

'It could be Bonnie's.'

'You wouldn't be here if you thought that.'

'It's not important who put it there. It's important that I get some help. She's going to have to turn herself in by five o'clock, or they're going to declare her a fugitive. That wouldn't be a plus if she has to go to trial.'

'Why are you doing this?'

'Look, I have until five o'clock. Either I sit here and talk philosophy with you – I know how you like to talk about Plato – or I try to save Bonnie Spencer's ass.'

'Don't talk about her like that. Show some respect.' A busboy came over to pour some water. Mikey waved him off. 'What do you want to know?'

'You know about Sy paying Lindsay an extra half million?'

'Sure. The bookkeeper told me, as I'm sure you know. It bothered me, seeing the investors fucked, so she confided in me.'

'You bribed her and probably threatened her.'

'You're tellin' me about the five o'clock deadline, so don't waste your time on cop chicken shit.'

'Did you threaten Sy when you found out about the extra

payment? I'm not chicken-shitting you now. I'm trying to figure out his state of mind.'

'I didn't threaten him. I just told him what a stupid, fucking dick he was. Okay, I told him in a loud voice, and he was scared of me. I won't deny that. But I never would have killed him or had him mussed up or nothing. We went back too far, and I'm a sentimental guy.'

The sandwiches came. Giant, first-generation-rich sandwiches, showy with frilly lettuce, wasteful, so high they were held together with toothpicks the size of small swords. I ate half of mine, Mikey ate all of his and then the other half of mine. I didn't touch the iced tea because I was too jacked up from all the coffee I'd been drinking. Mikey talked and chewed simultaneously. Bits of bacon got spewed, and tomato seeds sprayed out of his mouth, but fortunately his lunch stopped just short of my plate.

'Do you think Sy was fearful of you?'

'Nervous. You know. Ever since we was kids, Sy would pee in his pants if I even made a fist. But he wasn't terrified or nothin' like that.'

'Did he say why he was giving Lindsay the extra money?'

Mikey shook his head, rolled his eyes, as if unable to believe mankind's capacity for idiocy. 'You wanna shit a brick, Brady? You ain't gonna believe this one. When I was yellin' at him, he broke down. Not cryin', but sittin' in a chair, doin' a lot of cringin' shit. He finally stopped the crap about that Lindsay got a better movie offer and needed a added financial incentive. He told me he gave it to her because she said – you ready? – "Sy, I hate men who hold back. I need a man who can give of himself." '

'*What*?'

Mikey shoved some potato chips into his mouth and said: 'I swear to God. Is that pussy-whipped, or what?'

'That's pussy-whipped,' I agreed. 'So he was really in love with her?'

'Out of his mind nuts for her. I'd never seen him so hot for anybody.'

'Not even Bonnie or his other wife?'

'The first was a stringy, ugly sourpuss wit' no tits and these big, ugly yellow teeth from some old family he married so people would think he was high-class. And Bonnie . . . I could never figure out that marriage. It was like a snake marrying a puppy dog. Probably had something to do with Sy's being all hot to get into the movie business, and she was in it then. And maybe he was tired of being a pretend WASP and got on a Jew kick, and she was a Jew but not too Jewey.'

'Do you think he would have married Lindsay?'

'Sure.'

'Then how come he took up with Bonnie?'

'Beats the hell out of me. When she called and said she'd been seeing him again, my mouth dropped open ten feet. You want my guess? The Lindsay thing knocked the shit out of him, and he was running home to Mommy.' He paused. 'You gonna eat your potato chips?' I pushed my plate over to him. He woofed down the chips and the crinkle-cut pickle slice.

'You're telling me interesting stuff but not helpful stuff.'

'You sayin' I'm holdin' back?'

'I don't know, but what you've given me isn't going to help Bonnie. Do you want to help her?'

He wiped his chin with the back of his hand. 'Don't ask dumb-fuck questions. Okay?'

'Okay.'

'I found out about the extra half mil the second week of shooting. I confronted him. He wimped out right away, apologized, like I told you. Next day he messengered over a half mil in negotiable securities to me, and if you try to use that against me, you better hire somebody to start your car every morning.'

'Mike,' I said quietly, 'no threats. I want to help Bonnie. That's all.'

'You married?' he asked.

'No.'

'Anyways, that was that. Until the Tuesday before he died. He calls me up, says he can't leave the Hamptons 'cause of the movie, but he's *got* to talk to me. He'll arrange for a private plane, or send a car and driver. I told him I don't like aer-o-planes and I don't use drivers because they got ears and mouths, but I'd drive out there because I was his friend. So I get there to his house – Jesus, that was some beautiful house. He tells me Lindsay's acting is terrible, that the movie is in deep shit. I tell him I'd heard that from my sources and so what else was new, and that if I lost my investment, I was sure he'd make good.'

'That's a great way to invest.'

'The only way. So then he tells me Lindsay is cheatin' on him. I start to say some garbage like "Too bad," but he didn't want that.'

'What did he want?'

'He wanted her removed.'

'Killed?'

'What do you think, Brady?'

'He asked you to get rid of her?' Mikey nodded. His chins, dotted with potato chip crumbs, bobbed up and down. 'Did he suggest how?'

'No, because I stopped him right there. Oh, he did say it would be easy: There could be a letter to make people think it was some crazy fan who did it. But I just told him to shut his mouth and keep it shut and don't even think about anything like that. He was an amateur, and he didn't know what the fuck he was doin'.'

'Actually, it sounds like he did.'

'I got to admit, it wasn't a bad idea. But no way I was gonna tell him that. He wanted to kill her because she was bompin' the director and because he wanted to start his movie all over again and needed the bucks. You think I'd get anywhere near somethin' like that?'

'Did he offer to pay you?'

'We didn't get that far.'

'Did he say anything else?'

'No. I got up and before I walked out I told him he didn't have what it takes, that his plan was full of holes, that if he tried to arrange something stupid with some two-bit local hood, they'd grab him in less than twenty-four hours. And then I told him to be a man. If he had to take a fall on the movie, take the fuckin' fall. And then I got the hell out of there. I gotta tell you: you know how I scared Sy?'

'Yeah.'

'Well, he scared me. I got a chill down my spine. What the hell's happenin' to this world if guys like Sy Spencer want to kill people? Tell me. What have we become?'

# *Chapter Twenty*

The tennis court of the East Hampton waterfront mansion that was *Starry Night*'s main set had everything: white wood benches, a water fountain, piles of snowy towels on a white wrought-iron stand, blue spruce and cypresses to obscure the chain-link fence. Beautiful. Except no one in their right mind would have wanted to be there. It was at least a hundred in the shade, but there was no shade. Lindsay Keefe and Nick Monteleone were volleying – if you could call it that – in about a hundred-and-ten-degree heat. There wasn't even a hint of cool air. Beyond the court, the foam on the waves made the ocean look as if it were boiling.

Every time Nick swung his racquet, he missed the ball and Victor Santana called 'Cut!' Then a sweat-removal brigade would race over to the actors. Production assistants got there first. Some of them held umbrellas over the actors' heads, others held battery-operated fans. Then the makeup and hair people went to work, while still other attendants offered bottles of water with straws so Lindsay and Nick could sip without getting drinking-glass dents around their mouths.

'One more take,' Santana promised me. His dark skin was flushed almost maroon. The color looked great against his Outfit of the Day: green jungle fatigues. All Santana needed was a scruffier haircut, an M-16 and I couple of joints of skag, and he could have passed for one of my old buddies. He went on: 'I must get enough footage of Lindsay because Nick . . .' He sighed in weary resignation. 'This is going to cost an extra half day of long shots, with a tennis pro standing in for Nick. I simply cannot believe it; we gave him a full four weeks of tennis lessons preproduction.'

'Monteleone has zero hand-eye coordination,' I pointed out. 'He'd need an instruction manual if he wanted to scratch his balls. Now look, Mr Santana, I know making a movie is the most important thing in the world and it's not easy making a guy who doesn't know a tennis racquet from a pogo stick look like a jock. But I need more cooperation from you than I'm getting.'

'Please, just one more take for the master shot.' The brigade was walking off the court. 'I give you my word of honor.'

Lindsay was no natural athlete, but she could place a serve and look beautiful at the same time. Her dark eyes were shaded with a pink sun visor. Her pale hair, done up in some special curly ponytail, began to flutter as some guy in surfer trunks turned on a giant wind machine to the breezy setting. Santana called 'Action' one more time.

I watched the crew watching the actors. The guys were taking in the whole scene. But the women seemed to have eyes only for Lindsay. Were they contemplating what life could be like with those breasts, those legs, that perfect ponytail? Were they curious? Jealous? Raging, that such glorious gifts had not been bestowed upon them? I thought about Lindsay's competition – Bonnie.

If Mikey had, in fact, nixed killing Lindsay, could Sy have persuaded his Annie Oakley of an ex-wife to pick up a .22 I'm *aching* to make your movie next, he'd have sworn. But I need some help getting over this rough patch. Or maybe: I want to marry you, bring you to Sandy Court, back to Fifth Avenue. My life will be your life, my friends your friends, my charge cards your charge cards. Remember how it was? Bonnie, darling, it was such a ghastly mistake, our splitting, and I know how profoundly lonely you've been. Let me make it up to you. But first, help me.

Why the hell was I thinking these things? Did I believe Bonnie Spencer was capable of willfully taking the life of another human being?

No.

The compressors in the trailer air conditioners had died under the strain of the humidity, so after Santana gave everybody a twenty-minute break, Lindsay and Nick, accompanied by assistants who, probably by tradition and job description, were paid to grovel, trekked up to the mansion – a modern interpretation of the White House cross-pollinated with the Taj Mahal – and went into two upstairs bedrooms. Before he went into his, my pal Nick gave me a for-your-eyes-only, homicide-cop-to-homicide-cop one-finger salute.

I was about to walk into Lindsay's room, which seemed to be some sort of homage to mosquito netting, but one of her designated toadies tried to shut the door on me. 'She needs to recoup,' the girl whispered in hospital-corridor tones. I pushed past her, ordered everybody except Lindsay to get out and slammed the door.

Filmy stuff formed a canopy and curtains around the bed. It covered the windows from ceiling to floor. For some reason, odd pieces of it were draped over chairs. There were three chairs and one of those chaise-longues in the room, but naturally, given the choice, Lindsay stretched out on the bed. I pulled up a chair and pushed away some stuff, so I wouldn't have to interrogate her through gauze. Right away she started with the lascivious shit, running her hands slowly over her face and neck, arranging pillows so she was angled to achieve maximum tit power.

On the table next to the bed, there was a six-pack of foreign water in blue bottles. She put out a languid hand to take one but couldn't quite reach it. She waited for me to get up and hand her one. I didn't. She got one for herself and drank, not sexily, but with the loud glug-glug noises of a cartoon character.

'I feel sick from the heat,' she said. I don't think she was acting. Her whole body was red and covered in a cold sweat.

'It must be a bitch out there.'

I guessed she'd fulfilled her courtesy quotient by making a comment about the weather. She snapped: 'Well, what do you want?'

'I want you to stop lying. If you don't stop lying, you're going to find yourself under arrest.'

'You tried that tactic with my agent. He's old, losing his touch, so it worked. It won't work with me.'

'Want to bet? Fifty bucks says before I even bring you in for fingerprinting, you'll – '

'Do you honestly think you can scare me?'

'Beats me. But I do know I can interrupt your moviemaking. And when you come before the judge, I can arrange to have a lot of reporters at the courthouse. You can explain to them how I'm not scaring you – even though I've arrested you for withholding information in the matter of the death of Sy Spencer.'

'You are a low-class shit,' she said.

'Yeah, but a low-class shit with the power to arrest.'

There was a too-long moment of silence. I felt like closing my eyes, relaxing, but in the interests of projecting authority and macho intensity, I glared at her. At last, Lindsay propped herself on her elbow. 'Sometimes I like low-class shits,' she said, her voice lazy, husky. She extended her hand to me.

'Ms Keefe, let me be honest with you. As far as I can see, you're not in that much trouble that you have to fuck a cop.' She pulled away her hand.

'You just have to answer a few questions, and chances are, your answers won't get any further than me. All right?'

'Yes.' Brusque. The momentary fake desire was supplanted by her normal disdain.

'Did Sy confront you about your affair with Victor Santana?'

'Yes.'

'This isn't Twenty Questions. Tell me about it.'

She finished glugging the water and took a second bottle. 'He didn't raise his voice, not once, the whole time. He told me, very calmly, as if he were giving me the next day's weather forecast, that I was a whore. That I'd lost my ability as an actor.' She stopped. She didn't want to talk to me.

'Keep going,' I said.

Finally, reluctantly, she did. 'He wanted me off the film. He followed me around the house all that evening and the next morning, calling me Whore, as though that were my given name. 'Going up to bed so early, Whore?' He kept telling me I was ruining *Starry Night*. Always in that calm voice.'

'When did this start.'

'The week he was killed. Monday night.'

'Was he threatening to fire you?'

'No. He wanted me to quit.'

'Why?'

'*Why?*' she demanded. She gave a snort of contempt, as if I'd just asked the stupidest question of the twentieth century. 'So I'd be in violation of my contract, that's *why.* So he wouldn't have to pay me. So he could get the guarantors to pay the completion insurance and start all over again.'

'Is that possible?'

'Of course it's possible. And then the insurance company could sue me to recover their costs.

'So you wouldn't quit.'

'Of course not. It was an insane suggestion.'

'Why would he expect you to quit if the consequences to you would be so bad?'

'Because.'

'Because why?'

'Because he was trying to make me so upset, so frightened of him, that I'd do anything he wanted.'

'What was he doing?'

'Before he told me he knew about Victor, he'd already started being cold. Very cold.'

'He stopped sleeping with you?'

She gave me a look that showed her distaste; I was getting off on her sex life. 'He wouldn't touch me,' she said. 'Do you want to know more? Of course you do. When I tried to take his hand, he pulled it away – as though I had leprosy.'

'But he wouldn't say what was wrong?'

'Not at first. Just horrible coldness.'

'Was he cold in front of other people? On the set?'

'No. That threw me off. He was delightful to me on the set.'

'And how were you to him?'

'Oh, grow up. What do you think? That I was going to let everyone know I was having terrible problems with the executive producer? He was acting very loving to me, so I acted loving to him. I thought: Well, he hasn't made anything public; maybe we can work it out. I stopped seeing Victor – in a private sense – on Wednesday.'

'You told Santana it was over.'

'No. I never burn bridges. What if I couldn't fix things with Sy? I just told him I was having a messy, painful period. *Very* bloody.'

'That's nice.'

'I know men. It works. In any case, I did everything I could to heal the breach with Sy. If not personally, then professionally. But it was so strange. And even when things got really terrible, we were still playing loving in front of everybody else.'

'Like the day he was killed, taking a wad of cash from him? Loving like that?'

'Don't make it sound like I was picking his pocket! It was a homey, wifely gesture.'

'You said things got terrible. When?'

'Thursday morning. My car came a little before six, and when I left the bedroom to go downstairs, Sy was out there in the hall, waiting.' Her face, under the sweat and layers of makeup, went rigid. Her mouth began to move mechanically, like a marionette's. She was somewhere between unsettled and petrified. 'He told me – he sounded so detached – that he had all kinds of friends. I didn't know what he was talking about, but I wanted to get away from him. He was standing right up against me. His face was less than an inch from mine. I could see each whisker where he hadn't shaved. He said some of his friends weren't very nice people, but they'd invested in *Starry Night* and they'd heard that the dailies were terrible. They were very unhappy, and they wanted me to quit. If I didn't, Sy said he couldn't be held responsible for the repercussions.'

'Did you ask what the repercussions were?'

'Yes.' Her body gave a fast, powerful involuntary shudder, almost a convulsion.

'What did he say would happen?'

'Acid in the face.'

'Jesus! What did you do?'

'I told him I was calling the police. I marched back into the bedroom and picked up the phone, but he grabbed it from me. I let him take it. The whole scene was so predictable.'

'Did he make any more threats?'

'No, of course not. He backed down. I knew he would. He

actually lost his cool, the little bastard. Apologized all over himself. *begged* me to forgive him.'

'And what did you say?'

'I told him I'd consider it.' Lindsay's lips arched into something like a smile. 'I knew how to handle Sy. I'd let him go out to LA, have his little meetings with Kat Pourelle and the other losers, and by the time he got back on Sunday night, he'd want me again. In his movie. In his bed. On a permanent basis.'

'You think he wanted marriage?'

'Oh, he would have needed a week or two to cool down over Victor, but yes. Definitely.'

'You think so?'

'I know so.'

'Would you have married him?'

'What do you think?'

'I don't know. He was a guy who threatened to have you disfigured. Ruin your life, ruin your career.'

'He was a man eaten up inside by jealousy.'

'He was a producer who wanted you out of his life, out of his movie.'

'Only because I'd wounded him so deeply. I admit it: I made a mistake. A big one. But Sy would have come around. We were so well suited, and he knew it. I'm . . . well, what I am, and he was a brilliant, successful film producer. He cared about serious social issues. *And* he was my intellectual equal. To tell you the truth, as far as the jealousy, I *loved* it that he was finally displaying some real emotion.' Lindsay began to rub her bare legs together; she seemed to be getting aroused, not so much by her recollection of Sy's crazy behavior but by the remembrance of her power over him. 'Jealousy,' she said again, savoring the word. 'Sy was *consumed*.'

'You think he loved you?'

'Of course he loved me.'

I got up and stood behind the chair. 'The killer was fifty feet away from a small, white-robed figure about your size. At the moment the rifle was fired, Sy was supposed to have been flying somewhere over Kansas. And you were supposed to be getting ready to do your late-afternoon laps in the pool.'

'No!' The makeup didn't help. Her skin started to lose its color. It took on a waxen cast, like a corpse's.

'Yes.' I pushed aside a drooping piece of mosquito net and walked out of the room.

I called Carbone and told him I was at the *Starry Night* set on the off chance Bonnie Spencer had connected with any of the crew members, and also to check if she'd showed up again after Sy threw her off, maybe doing some kind of neurotic, obsessive number. He said that Thighs, Robby and Charlie Sanchez were all out trying to get a lead on her. Casually, as if I already knew what the answer would be, I asked if the DNA results had come in on the new hair sample. It's Bonnie's, Carbone said. Still think she didn't do it?

I told him if he had nothing better to do to check the evidence record files. Find out the number of hairs we'd picked up that first night, then go down and look in the envelope the lab had returned. He'd find a minus-one factor.

He told me I was losing my emotional equilibrium, that I was projecting something – I forget what – onto Robby Kutz, that I needed a vacation, and if I passed the fancy Italian store in East Hampton to pick him up two pounds of sausage with fennel.

I hung up. Robby *had* to have planted the hair. And for sure, he had spread the drinking rumor, the Steve luvs Bonnie 4-ever rumor. He was out to get her – and me. Sooner or later, he was going to realize that Bonnie had a protector and had gotten some help with her disappearing act. And then he would be at my house.

Gregory J. Canfield was supposed to be in a store in the village doing his job as production assistant, which, in this instance, meant picking up fresh figs, prosciutto, a semolina bread and a bottle of Dolcetto wine for Nick Monteleone since, according to a couple of people on the set, Nick had mumbled that what with the heat, he wanted a light bite, not a heavy supper, and since Lindsay's performance was still so inert, any hope of salvaging *Starry Night* seemed to rest on Nick's well-moussed head, so finally, after forty minutes of consultation between the line producer and the first assistant director (which included a call to Nick's agent in Beverly

Hills), a definition of the term 'light bite' was agreed upon, and Gregory was dispatched.

But I figured he might stop in to say goodbye to his woman, Myrna the costume lady, and sure enough, they were holding hands in the costume trailer, staring into each other's eyes, giving each other sweet, delicate, pursed-lip kisses of farewell. It didn't seem to bother them that one of Myrna's assistants was no more than a foot away from them, ironing a duplicate of the tennis outfit Lindsay was wearing. And it didn't seem to bother them when I called out 'Hey, Gregory!' He gave me a slightly dopey glance, then gazed back into the depths of Myrna's eyes.

The trailer was huge, like a wildly inflated walk-in closet, with rack after rack of clothes, shelves of shoes, and drawers with scarves and underwear and fake jewelry spilling out. I walked to the back and tapped Myrna on the shoulder. 'Hello!' she said. 'How are you?'

'Fine, thanks.' She looked as messy as when I'd caught her in her inside-out negligee. This time she was wearing a long sacklike thing with a parrot design; it looked as if she'd picked it up on Woolworth's in Honolulu in 1957 and had worn it frequently since. 'Myrna, I need Gregory for a minute.'

'Is anything wrong?' she asked.

'No. Everything's fine. A couple of minor points need clarification.' She nodded, released Gregory's hands and gave him a tender nudge toward me.

I took him away from her, outside to where they had a table set up with bagels and cookies and doughnuts with melting sugar and M&Ms and nuts and raisins. There was a bowl of red grapes, but they were hot. He gave me a Coke from a cooler beneath the table. 'How's it goin', man?' he asked. A few nights with Myrna had turned him from Ultra-Geek into Mr Cool.

'It's going all right,' I told him. It wasn't. It was ten minutes to five; I wanted to get back to Bonnie, but I had nothing worth bringing her. I held the icy soda can against my forehead. 'Remember that conversation you mentioned to me that took place in dailies? The "if lightning struck" conversation.'

Gregory nodded. 'Sure, sure.' He had a thoughtful look. He was probably recalling the graininess of the film and seemed, worse, about to describe it to me. I cut him off.

'Who was there? You said it was late. Most people had gone.'

'Ummm,' he began.

'Don't "ummm." Talk.'

'Sy.'

'Good. Keep going.'

'One of the assistant producers, Sy's gofer. His name's Easton.'

'Who else?'

'Me. I think Nick Monteleone. The DP. Director of photography. That's another term for cinematographer.'

'What's his name, Gregory?'

'Alain Duvivier.'

'Is he French?'

'*Mais oui, monsieur le detective*. He was there, and his girlfriend.'

'What's her name?'

'Monica, Monique. But she's gone.'

'How come?'

'He started with the set dresser, Rachel.'

'Who else?'

Gregory shut his eyes and, for once, his mouth. He seemed to be trying to re-create the scene. 'That was it.'

'You're sure?'

'Positive.'

'Did Sy hang back to talk to anyone afterwards?'

'I don't know. He sent me out to put pink pages in his leather folder in his car. Revised pages of script. You change color with every revision. First blue, then pink, and then yellow, green, goldenrod, then buff – '

'Go get me Alain.'

'I can't. I'm supposed to be in East Hampton, and he's – '

'Get him *now*.' Now took two minutes.

One thing about movie people: none of them dressed in a normal, businesslike way. Alain Duvivier looked like a cliché of a French creative type. He was in his mid-twenties with blond and brown hysterical hair that tumbled over his shoulders, matching heavy eyebrows and one hoop earring. He wore bubble-gum-color shorts and one of those wrestler-style undershirts that have practically no sides. He was more the size of a grizzly than a man; beside him, Gregory was almost invisible.

'Hello,' I said.

'Alo,' he said, then added, with fitting somberness: 'Sy. Very, very sad.' He sounded so French you half expected him to say Ooh-la-la, but he didn't.

'Mr Duvivier, I understand you were at dailies the night a certain conversation took place.' He was concentrating too hard, so I slowed down. 'There were some remarks about lightning and a discussion – a talk – about what would happen if lightning struck – hit – Lindsay Keefe. Do you recall any of that?'

'Lighting Lindsay?' he asked.

'No, *lightning*. It was a conversation about lightning.'

'Lightning?'

I turned to Gregory. 'What the hell's the word for lightning in French?'

'I took Spanish.'

I turned back to Duvivier. 'Lightning.' I pointed up to the sky and made a streaking gesture back and forth. He glanced over at Gregory a little nervously, and it didn't help when I made a thunder noise and followed it with another lightning imitation.

He blurted out: Rachel!'

'Rachel?' I inquired.

Gregory said: 'His girlfriends translate for him.'

'He doesn't understand English?'

'Well, technical terms. And he says "Alo, pretty girl" a lot.'

'*Au revoir*,' I said to Duvivier.

'Bye-bye,' he responded.

Smart. The sound on the TV was low enough so someone standing outside would never guess anyone was home. I found Bonnie sitting in my recliner, watching a movie. Before she zapped the remote control I saw that even though it was a black-and-white thing, it was something I would watch, with Kirk Douglas or Burt Lancaster; I always got them mixed up.

She pushed herself out of the chair. 'Ready? It's five-thirty.'

'Relax.'

'We have an agreement.' She was very subdued.

'Are you all right?'

'I'm fine.' She wasn't, but since she wasn't crying, or sullen or angry, I couldn't get a precise reading. 'How do you want to go about this? Should I call Gideon first, or do you want to drop me off – '

'Listen, do you trust me? Trust my judgement?'

'Isn't it a little late to be asking that?'

'We've got to get out of here fast, because I have a sickening feeling that fuckface Robby is going to wind up here, looking for you.'

'Why?'

'I don't have time now. Let's get out of here. I'll explain on the way.'

'On the way home?' She sounded so quiet, thoughtful. Well, she had a right to be. Leaving my house was like picking the Go-directly-to-jail card.

'You're not going home yet.'

'You promised me.'

'I know, but there's one more shot. Will you have faith in me, give me another half hour?'

'Yes.' So hushed, proper, ladylike, even. 'I will.'

'Then let's haul ass, Bonnie.'

She looked past the mud room into the kitchen. The stove and refrigerator were older than I was, and the white porcelain table had deep black craters where it had chipped.

'Where are we?' Her voice was barely a whisper. I realized she'd seen me lift up an unplanted flowerpot and take the key that was under it. She assumed we were breaking and entering, and having gotten to know me, she did not appear to be surprised.

'My family's house.' I guided her – almost pushed her, because she didn't want to come – through the kitchen, into a hallway that led to the stairs. 'My brother was there for that "lightning" conversation. And he was always around, doing things for Sy. I want to see if he remembers what happened after those dailies, that night or maybe the next day.' Bonnie stopped so suddenly I banged into her. 'Come on.' I gave her a light shove and kept talking. 'I want to find out who Sy saw – ' She wouldn't move. ' – and who he talked to.'

And then I saw what she was staring at. A gun cabinet. Plain pine. Familiar to someone who grew up on a farm.

Or to someone who grew up in a sporting goods store, whose old man was the best shot in Ogden.

No, I thought. No. She didn't do it.

# *Chapter Twenty-One*

Growing up in the house of what had once been Brady Farm, I'd pretty much been able to disregard the slight stink of degeneration. That odor of decay had always been there, but it was elusive, except when I sat on the living room couch long enough. There, at the heart of the house, it could not be ignored.

But if I was just passing through – which, during the years after my father left, was how I thought of myself, a low-class transient who happened to have the last name Brady – I'd smell, instead of underlying decay, the tangy carnation scent of the room spray my mother had boosted from Saks, the stuff they used to smog dressing rooms after ladies with gamy underarms tried on Better Dresses.

On the rare occasions I visited after I'd moved out, I must have made an unconscious shift and begun breathing through my mouth, because I stopped noticing the smell. But as I led Bonnie to the staircase, I got a killer whiff of Mildew Plus.

I was embarrassed. I hoped that someday I could really unload, tell her my history, but for now I hoped she'd think well of my background. I didn't want her to notice the stink of my family's house, or the dry, blackened edges of the rips in the gray stairway runner. I wanted her to believe we were poor but nice, not that we were poor and so bitter we couldn't bestow any kindness on our surroundings.

When we got to the second or third step, she finally turned and faced me. 'Maybe I'd better wait downstairs.' I didn't bother to answer. What the hell could I do? Offer her a seat on the Odorama couch? That way, when I heard my mother come home from work, I'd have to run downstairs in time to say, Mom, this is Bonnie

Spencer, the Jew whose ex-husband was murdered in Southampton, and my mother could say, Oh, yes, that was the old Munsey place. Paine Munsey. He's in sugar. They're up in Little Compton now. They couldn't bear the new element, so they sold.

I put my hand on the small of her back. 'It won't take long.' I propelled her a little harder, and she continued up the stairs. I loved the chance to touch her.

But it was more than wanting her with me. It made sense to let Bonnie hear what my brother had to say before I let her go. She was so smart; maybe she could pick up some small, free-floating fact that could be added to the equation and, finally, make it balance. Sure, Easton had been in the city the whole day of the murder, but there might be a snatch of a phone conversation, a note, a memo – some indication of hostility – he'd absorbed subliminally the day before.

Could he have picked up even a single word – like 'rifle,' 'shoot,' 'pool,' 'insurance' or 'Lindsay' – soon after the 'if lightning struck' conversation at dailies?

I thought: What if one of those words had something to do with Bonnie? All of a sudden, on the last of those shadowy steps, I felt what I'd always felt as a kid. Not a memory, or déjà vu. The feeling itself – empty, and so sad.

I knew she couldn't have done it.

But what if she had? Well, then I would be what I was before. Nothing. My life offered only two compensations: baseball and work. But neither the Yankees nor the Suffolk County Police Department was set up to do the big job, save lost souls. And all the drugs I had tried – beer, pot, peyote, hash, yellows, women, 'ludes, LSD, booze, heroin, more women, more booze, Lynne – in the end had given me no peace either; they'd just taken the edge off for a little while. Only Bonnie Spencer had made me believe that, truly, I might be redeemed.

What if I was wrong about her? What could my future be? I could drink again, and die. Or I could become one of those old retired cops, clutching a felt hat in my hands, keeping busy shuffling between daily Mass at Queen of the Most Holy Rosary and AA meetings, until death came.

But I knew she didn't do it.

When I guided Bonnie into Easton's room, he wasn't the only one who was surprised. Bonnie was. Surprised, angered. Easton had stolen Sy Spencer's ties! Her hands became fists; she could have decked him. There they were – blue ties with tiny stirrups, green with minuscule anchors, red with itty-bitty French flags – laid out on the bed, ready to be packed for Easton's trip to California to meet with Philip Scholes, the director, about his new job. There was no doubt that they were Sy's: Easton could never had afforded them, plus I'd seen dozens of them on special hooks on a section of Sy's giant remote-control revolving clothes rack the night of the murder, when I did a walk-through of the house. And – Bonnie's face was so grim – there were Sy's sweaters, too, on that bed! Cotton knits and cashmeres meant to be fashionably baggy on a little guy like Sy, sweaters that would just, barely, fit Easton. Her expression declared: Arrest this man!

And Easton's expression? Furious, sure, at another of my tiptoed intrusions. He stood legs apart, arms crossed over his chest, maintaining his dignity despite the fact that all he was wearing was one of those shortie shaving robes, and a particularly hideous one. But he was also confused: I know who this woman with Steve is, but I can't place her. And embarrassed too, as all three of us stared at over a thousand bucks' worth of accessories from the wardrobe of the ultra-suave (and ultra-dead) Seymour Ira Spencer.

I suppose my expression was something less than sunny, reflecting my disgust at my brother's penny-ante thievery. I could just see him, hanging around, waiting for us to take down the crime-scene tape and go home, so he could do a search-and-destroy through Sy's closets under the guise of Setting Things in Order. My guess was that if I looked through Easton's drawers, I'd find cuff links, or one of those mini-VCRs, a pocket telephone, or maybe one of those skinny, gold-coin watches on an alligator strap.

I was just about to lighten the atmosphere with some joke about taking Easton in, when he got petulant, affronted by my drop-in with a tall woman of unknown origin in athletic shorts and grungy running shoes. 'I'd like to know what all this is about, Steve.'

'You would?'

'Yes. I would.' Just at that instant, as he was carving out a new niche in supercilious schmuckdom, he recognized Bonnie. Obviously, hers was not a calming presence. Easton began to sidle back and forth alongside the bed, doing an agitated step-together-step, as if trying to keep out of her line of sight – or block her view of her ex-husband's wardrobe. 'What is *she* doing here?' he demanded. His gracious-living voice disappeared, replaced by a troubled squeal.

'She's with me. You do know that this is Bonnie Spencer?'

'Yes.'

I steered Bonnie over to a straight-backed chair. 'Stay put,' I told her. I turned back to my brother. He stopped his sideways skedaddling. 'You saw her that day at the set, when she knocked on the door of Sy's trailer?'

'Yes.' His yeses sounded more like yaps than complete syllables. I thought: He's fucking mortified about being caught red-handed. Steal billions, everybody knows, and you're invited to the best parties; steal ties, and you're a tacky little piece of shit.

'And Sy told her to get off the set, that she didn't belong?'

'Yes.'

'Stephen, listen – ' Bonnie started to say, in her direct, you're-not-approaching-this-right voice, as though we were husband-and-wife detective partners in some 1937 movie.

'Not now!' Then I asked my brother: 'Did you know Sy was having an affair with her?'

'What?' It wasn't an assertion of amazement, as in: I don't believe it! It wasn't even a question. It was more a 'Duh' of befuddlement. Easton was on overload; he couldn't seem to get what was going on.

'Answer me,' I snapped at him.

I had to know how finely tuned in he was to Sy's private life. How much did he know? What could he guess at? After dailies that night, had Sy made any secret phone calls? When they'd gotten back to the house and Easton was setting out Sy's papers or his pj's or pink pages for the next day, had he possibly picked up another reference to 'Lindsay'? 'Lightning'? An icy laugh? An intense 'I need your help' spoken behind a closed door? Would Easton the Refined actually eavesdrop? Would Easton *not* eavesdrop was more the question. My brother wouldn't recognize an ethic if it snuck up and bit him on the butt.

But still, as I looked at him, I knew he'd make a fantastic witness for the DA, all blue-suited and white-shirted, with one of his new ties. His fair hair would shine in the harsh light of the witness box, his low-key gentleman's voice would appeal, convince. I thought: Wouldn't it be wonderful if he actually could remember something important?

State your name, the assistant DA would command. Easton Brady. I ask you, Mr Brady, the ADA would say, did you overhear a telephone conversation between Sy Spencer and Michael LoTriglio? The defense lawyer – Fat Mikey's, maybe, although I felt a twinge of regret at the notion – would leap up and object on the grounds of no foundation. The ADA would rephrase the question and inquire, How did you know who was on the phone with Mr Spencer? Well, I answered the phone and the man said it was Mike LoTriglio and he wanted to talk to Sy *now*. I'd spoken to Mr LoTriglio before, and this sounded exactly like him, Easton would begin.

I glanced over at Bonnie. Her eyes were riveted on Easton.

I remembered her eyes in that moment when she'd stood before the gun cabinet downstairs. I thought I'd seen a fleeting shadow of pain in them, a recognition of what was behind those doors.

What was behind those doors?

My old man's twelve-gauge shotgun.

And his .22

And then I knew what Bonnie knew.

Easton seemed to understand that, at last, I knew. He stood quietly, thumbs hooked into his pockets, watching me.

I had to get ready for an interrogation. Oh, we Bradys were so neat. I lifted Sy's folded sweaters from the bed and placed them – one, two, three – gently on the dresser. I was so painstakingly careful you could hardly hear the rustle of the tissue paper between the folds. Then I took my brother by the hand, and, together, we sat side by side on the space I had cleared.

'East,' I said.

'Yes?'

'You have something you want to tell me.'

'No.'

'Come on.'

His neck and his ears got fiery red, but he said, 'No. Absolutely not.'

'I found the rifle.' He shook his head. It could be taken to mean: I don't understand. Or: No, you didn't. 'I found it, East.' I prayed – neat, always put things back where they belong – that he had returned it to the cabinet, that he hadn't done something like take a ride on the Shelter Island ferry to drop it into Long Island Sound. But then I saw I was okay; Easton angled his body away from mine and with the side of his hand was ironing out an imperceptible wrinkle in the blue tie right next to him. I said softly: 'It's just a question of time before we get back the results of the ballistics tests.' He wouldn't look at me. 'We fire the rifle and then compare the markings on the bullet with the two bullets we took from Sy.' I was afraid if I looked at Bonnie I'd lose my rhythm, but then she didn't seem to want my attention. There was no sound, no motion; if I hadn't known she was sitting in a chair five feet away, I would not have sensed she was in the room. 'The markings will match, East. You know that.'

Easton lifted his chin and breathed out sharply, giving his nostrils a scornful, Southampton flare, so Old Society. 'I can't believe you can even *think* something like this!'

'How can I *not* think it?'

'You're my brother!'

'I know. Maybe that's why it took me so long to understand.'

In the past, when a case finally came into focus, I always got a wild burst of energy, a hunger to *know*. But now I felt heavy, sluggish, incredibly weary. If Easton ran, I wouldn't have been able to go after him; I was on some other planet, with terrible gravity.

'I want both of you out of here!' he ordered. He scowled at Bonnie. 'There is nothing to discuss.'

'There's a lot to discuss,' I said.

'This is totally asinine.'

'No. This is very serious and important.'

'You have no proof of *anything*.'

'I have the murder weapon.'

'Oh, don't be melodramatic! Are there fingerprints on it? Are there?'

'There may be, even if you think you took care of that. We use laser technology now.'

He shook his head. Either he didn't believe me, he wasn't impressed or he wasn't afraid. 'And what if there aren't fingerprints?' he inquired.

'Who the hell else would take Dad's .22 and shoot Sy Spencer? Mom?'

'You *would* bring her into it.'

'Relax. Who do you think she's going to blame for all this? You or me?'

I got up and walked towards Easton's closet. A regular closet, not a mahogany-and-brass state-of-the-art architectural space like Sy's. But Easton aspired. Everything was in perfect order: suits, shirts, ties – more of Sy's – slacks, blazers, shoes. Shoes in their cardboard boxes, stacked on the top shelf. The front panels of the boxes had been cut off so you could see each pair. Years of shoes; penny loafers, tassel loafers and Oxfords; white bucks, golf shoes and rubber-soled boaters; tennis sneakers, running sneakers, sandals, slippers. And thongs. Ordinary rubber thongs for the beach, the kind you can pick up anywhere. A men's size eleven, my size, my brother's size.

I covered my left hand with my handkerchief. I took out my pen with my right hand and, carefully, eased the box off the shelf and caught it in my left.

I said, 'You hated to bet when we were kids. You know why? I always won. But I'll bet you right now these thongs will match the molds we made from impressions in the grass right near Sy's house, where the shots were fired. A fancy, hot-shit lawn, East. Turf, they call it. It's a special variety of Kentucky bluegrass called Adelphi. The guy at the State Agricultural Extension said it must have cost him a fucking fortune to cover all that ground. But what the hell. The right shade of green makes a statement.' I held up the box. 'I'll bet you we find a blade or two of Adelphi right in here.'

It took a while before Easton could get his eyes off the shoe box. Then, in an I've-got-a-secret boyish manner that my mother would have found enchanting, he gestured me over with his index finger. Without looking at Bonnie, he whispered: 'Why is she here?'

'She's been giving me some information on the case. Some insights into Sy.'

'Oh.' He seemed hesitant about what to do next. His mouth opened, but nothing came out.

'Why don't I tell her to take a hike?' He seemed so relieved. He inclined his head; it was almost a bow.

I walked over to Bonnie and spoke softly. 'Can you drive a stick shift? Okay, you know where the nature preserve is, that swamp place, about a minute and a half north of here? Go there. Watch birds or something for an hour and a half. Then take back toads to your friend Gideon's. Don't park too close to his house. Don't call him to tell him you're coming. And make your approach from one of the houses behind his in case they're surveilling his place. Got it so far?'

She was levelheaded, serious and terse. 'Yup.'

'Explain to Gideon what's happening. Under the circumstances, he won't want you to turn yourself in. So just sit tight.'

'Do you need any help? Want me to call anyone?'

'No.'

'Promise me – '

'Yeah, I'll be careful. Now look, if for any reason they find you and scoop you up – arrest you – don't make any statements of any kind.'

'Okay.'

Her eyes darted over to Easton. I knew what she was thinking: There was a good chance that if I didn't nail him, she'd be nailed. And maybe, in the final analysis, I couldn't nail him. Or I wouldn't be able to.

'I trust you.' That's what Bonnie said instead of goodbye. Then she held out her hand for my car keys and was gone.

'You killed Sy,' I told my brother.

'Please, Steve.'

'You killed him.'

He lowered himself on the chair Bonnie had vacated. 'I didn't mean to.' His voice had the emotional intensity of someone caught running a red light. 'I'm sorry.'

'You meant to kill Lindsay.'

'Yes. How did you figure it out? From that one conversation about lightning?'

'Just tell me what happened, Easton.'

'You know what's funny?' He kept tugging at the hem of his bathrobe like a woman with lousy legs in a too-short skirt. 'You always call me "East", and now you're saying "Easton".'

'What happened?'

My brother's bright-blue eyes filled with tears. 'I want you to know I really loved that man. There was only a sixteen-year age difference, but Sy was like a father to me.' He put his hands over his face and wept.

I sat on the edge of the bed and watched him. I wanted to be moved by his grief, but I had too many years in Homicide; I'd watched this movie, *The Crying Killer*, too many times.

People who commit murder are weird, and not just in their willingness to stick out their tongues at God, to steal His gift of life, to commit the one act that is unquestionably and universally wrong. No, what always got to me about murderers wasn't their evil, their distance from the rest of humanity, but their closeness to it. I'd watched mothers sob at the coffins of babies they'd clubbed to death; I'd heard boyfriends scream out in anguish at the funerals of the girlfriends they'd battered, strangled and, post-mortem, raped. They were so vulnerable, so wounded, these killers. And I knew what would be coming next from my brother because, for me, this was the hundredth return of that scene. His eyes would plead: Pity me, help me, go easy on me, because I, the survivor, am also a victim of this monstrous crime. What a loss I've suffered! Look at these tears!

I played it with Easton the way I always played it. I gave him exactly what he felt he deserved: sympathy and support. 'It must be such hell,' I said.

'It is. Complete hell.' I shook my head as if I couldn't bear his – our – sadness.

What the fuck right did he have to kill? To fly off, with a new wardrobe of ties, to California, leaving Bonnie to spend the next twenty-five years paying for what he did?

I felt no sadness for my brother's stupid, wasted, empty life, and no guilt, not a goddamn twinge, about not having been a better older brother so I could have given him some values or shit like that. No, I just felt cold and very tired. 'Tell me how it happened, East,' I urged. Oh did I sound full of compassion.

'You're calling me "East" again.'

I smiled. 'I know. Hey, you're my brother, aren't you? Come on. Let's talk. Tell me what went on. Was there any discussion about getting rid of Lindsay before that night at dailies?' Every now and then I slipped, but I knew to avoid the word 'kill' when questioning a killer.

'No. Nothing. I knew they were having troubles. Sy had turned off on her completely, went from hot to cold overnight. But I'm sure you know by now that he wasn't the confiding type.'

'But then there was that remark that if lightning struck Lindsay, if she died, the problems with *Starry Night* would be over. What happened after that?'

Easton didn't answer. He yanked at the hem of his bathrobe. It was one of those Saks uglies that my mother had bought on final, maximum markdown and saved for Christmas; it was some sort of strange, long-haired terry cloth, and grayish-brown, the color of a rag used for unpleasant chores.

'Who brought up getting Lindsay out of the picture? You or Sy?'

'I did, but it isn't the way it sounds. I just asked him some questions about the completion insurance. He said that if a star dies, the guarantors will pay to make another movie. If you're on a forty-day shooting schedule and she dies when you're fifteen days into it, the producers will get fifteen days of money. Well, minus a deductible of either a couple of hundred thousand or three days. But Sy said the coverage was quite fair.

'But there was no suggestion he wanted you to facilitate matters?'

'No. Not then.'

My brother's face reflected a little hurt, as in why hadn't Sy leapt at his unstated offer right away. I had absolutely no doubt that Easton's questions about insurance were openings to Sy. Maybe Sy hadn't even thought about offing Lindsay before. Who knows? But all of a sudden, there it was, out in the electrified air: if lightning struck.

But Sy was no fool. He knew lightning was dangerous; only an expert could handle it. Like Mikey. Not a jerk like my brother. So he'd bypassed Easton, who was, most likely, doing everything but jumping up and down, waving his arms, calling out: Just ask me, Sy. I'm your boy. I'm your assistant producer. I'll do whatever you think needs doing. Sy, though, had gone to a pro. But the pro had been smarter than both Sy and Easton put together. He just said no.

'When did the matter come up again?'

'Wednesday night.'

I sat back on the bed, as though I were getting comfortable, all ready and eager to hear about my kid brother's first day of junior high. 'Tell me, how did he bring it up?' I asked.

'That's what amazed me, Steve! He was so unbelievably direct. He said, "We've got to terminate Lindsay." He already had the plane reservations and the appointments in LA, so he wanted it done over the weekend, when he was out there.' Easton was talking fast, freely, so I didn't stop him to ask how come he'd done it the day before the weekend. 'He didn't say, "Will you do it?" or anything. He just assumed I would.'

'Goes with the territory, right?'

'You don't have to be sarcastic.'

'Hey, East, I'm not. But I want us to talk straight, matter-of-fact. No bullshit between us. We're brothers.'

'Don't condescend to me, Steve. That's all I ask.'

'I'm not. Now, did he plan it out, or did you?'

'He had it all mapped out. He invented this imaginary killer –

a crazy fan. He would make believe Lindsay had gotten a letter from the fan, telling her he loved her, threatening to kill her if she didn't write back to him.'

'But she'd never gotten any letter like that?'

'Well, she *had* gotten crazy letters. All actors do. That was the beauty of it. She'd talked about them, to her agent, to some of Sy's friends at a dinner party a few weeks ago. Sy said that this murder would just seem to be a horrible extension of those letters. He'd tell the police she'd seemed a little upset about some new threatening letter, but that he'd never seen it. He'd say he kept after her to have one of the private investigation agencies who handle things for public figures look into it, and she kept saying fine, but she was busy with the movie and never bothered. And then *I* was supposed to say – but *not* volunteer it, only if the police asked me – that I'd overheard Lindsay telling him about the letter.'

'Was he going to write one for the police to find?'

'No. He said he'd given it a lot of thought, and almost did it, but it was just too chancy. Who knows what kind of scientific tests the police have these days? He didn't want to risk having it traced.'

What I couldn't get over was how clever Sy was. In the course of just a couple of days, he'd come up with a brilliant, almost foolproof scheme forgetting rid of Lindsay. Except instead of convincing Mikey to carry out the plan, Sy had relied on a fool. So maybe, in the end, he wasn't such a brilliant mogul. He'd executive-produced his own death.

'Who decided on the rifle?' I asked.

'I did. He wanted me to stab her.'

'Wouldn't that be a mess?'

'Yes, but it would be very convincing,' Easton explained. 'Stab her once, to kill her, but then do it again and again, so it looked like the work of a mental case. Except I told him I didn't have the stomach for it.' I nodded with great seriousness, trying to show how much I cherished my brother's decency. 'But then I told him I'd been a pretty good shot as a kid. And he *loved* it that I already had the rifle, that we didn't have to go out and buy one. He was very edgy about leaving any kind of tracks.'

'I don't blame him. We've been checking gun dealers' records going back six months. He was a smart guy.'

'Yes, he was.' My brother got teary again. He sniffed.

'East, how did you have the balls to pick up a rifle that probably hadn't been touched for years? And then to rely on your being able to bag Lindsay with one or two shots?'

He gave me an I-thought-of-everything smile. 'Well, it did take some balls, as you say. But I did some fast planning. Although first I had to find the key to the padlock for the gun cabinet. That took me hours! You'll never guess where it was.'

'On top of the gun cabinet.'

'You *knew*?'

'Yeah. You should have given me a call. I could have saved you some time.' We both went chuckle-chuckle. 'So you just took it out, locked the cabinet and went ready, aim, fire?'

'No. I cleaned it.'

'Smart. Did you try it out?'

He inclined his head. 'I went to a range.'

'Which one?'

'The one up near Riverhead.'

'Right. I've been there. Where did you get the bullets?'

'At a hardware store right near there.'

'Took some target practice?'

'Yes. But I didn't need much. It's like riding a bike. You never really forget it.'

'No, you don't,' I agreed.

'And from fifty feet, it's so easy.'

'Did you and Sy plan where you'd stand?'

'Yes. It had a clear view of the whole pool, but the spot itself was sort of in shadows because of the porch. The only thing I had to worry about was to make sure no one else was around. Sy would be in LA, the cook would be off. Sy was worried Lindsay would invite some people over for drinks. Or Victor Santana for . . . you know.'

'What did he say to do if Santana was there?'

'To wait, see if he'd leave.'

'But if not? Get rid of him too?'

'Not on Saturday. If he was there, I should leave and come back on Sunday afternoon. There was a good chance he'd have left by then, to go over the next day's work. She'd be alone. But . . . You want me to be totally honest?'

'I really do, East.'

'Well, if not, get Santana too. It would look like the crazy fan saw them together and got jealous.'

I stood, walked on to the open window, lifted the screen and leaned out for a minute. I pulled a couple of leaves off an overhanging branch. Then I turned back to my brother. 'It was a terrific plan.'

'It really was.'

'So how come it didn't work?'

Easton got real earnest. He crossed his legs, rested his elbow on his knee, braced his chin on the heel of his hand. 'That's what's so maddening. It *should* have worked. You know how impossible the traffic is Friday afternoons? I mean, the Long Island Expressway: the world's longest parking lot.' This quip hadn't been funny even in 1958, when it had probably been invented, and hadn't improved with either age or repetition. But I laughed as though hearing one of Western Civilization's Great Witticisms. 'Well,' Easton continued, apparently satisfied with my appreciation of his ability as a raconteur, 'the casting director was so crazed – she was casting another movie and two plays – that when I left, I realized she wouldn't have any idea of the time. And then I got finished at Sy's shirtmaker in about two seconds. So instead of taking the Expressway or the Northern State, I took every obscure east-west road ever built on the Island. I mean, if I'd been in your car, one of those potholes I went over would have swallowed me and the Jag whole!'

I laughed again. Such cleverness! Such superb humor! Of course, I'd done that audience appreciation bit more times than I could count. It was part of the job, not only turning a suspect into your friend but also turning yourself into the one person most able to savor his comic or tragic art. It had never bothered me before, this playacting. But now, every smile, every goodnatured nod of understanding I offered, cost me too much.

A couple of times I had to fight down surges of insane vitality – like rushes of a mainlined drug – to go for him, hurt him, kick him off his chair, hold him down and smash his bland, handsome face against the floor. The killer was so civilized; the cop was so savage.

'So you pushed a little and got home earlier than you'd expected?'

'Yes, a little before four. I'd been in quite a state all day, as you can imagine. This was not going to be any ordinary weekend.'

'Doesn't sound like it,' I said.

'I said to myself: I can't wait. I have *got* to get this over with today. I cannot *stand* the tension. But I was smart. I knew I'd promised Sy to wait until Saturday or Sunday, to make sure he was safe in California. But I called MGM Grand and asked if the plane, the ten-fifteen morning flight, had taken off on time and they said yes, it had, and it had landed in LA a little after four New York time. That's how I knew' – he squared his shoulders; so proud – 'that he was there!'

'You didn't call him, just to make sure?'

The pride evaporated. Easton seemed to shrivel into a smaller, older man. 'I didn't want to seem overanxious, make Sy think I wasn't up to handling it. He said we should call each other, because that would be the normal thing to do, but not to go overboard.'

Easton was holding something back. I could tell. He had that insecure, twitchy-tentative Dan Quayle smile, the one he'd put on as a kid when my mother asked him how he was doing at school and he'd say 'Fine!' not mentioning that he'd gone through the mail, found the Failure Notice in geometry and torn it up before she got home from work. 'you're leaving something out, East,' I said good-naturedly. 'Come on. What is it?'

'Sy left a message on my machine.'

'What did it say?'

'That he was taking a helicopter and going to make the seven o'clock flight instead of the morning flight, and that he'd call when he got to the hotel. But you see, I didn't play back my message when I got back from the city. To tell you the truth, I didn't even look at the machine to see if I had any. I can't believe I could have missed something so obvious. That's so sloppy. It's not like me to be sloppy. But I just changed out of my suit – '

'Into the thongs?'

'Yes. And a good pair of shorts and a shirt, so I'd look like I belonged.'

'Where was the rifle?'

'Oh, once I took it from the cabinet, I kept it in the trunk of my car, in one of those canvas sports duffels. Sy told me to do that, and to fill the duffel up with a bunch of clothes, so if anyone saw me, it would look like I was carrying a full weekend bag, not a rifle. He said carrying a rifle alone might call attention to the bag, make it look funny, bottom-heavy.'

'Then what?'

'I did everything Sy told me to do. Drove up to the side of the house, near the garage, to that space where there's room for three or four cars. You can't see it from the front. I opened the window, turned off the engine and sat for five minutes, by my watch.'

'He wanted you to make sure you didn't hear anyone.'

'Right. Then I got out, took the duffel and walked to that place right under the porch.'

'What time was it?'

'Sometime after four. I knew the *Starry Night* crew was doing the scene where Lindsay runs into the ocean, but I was praying she'd be very tired and bitchy and they'd let her go the regular time. They'd done that the last two Fridays.'

'Because she was tired?'

'No. Because she was Sy's, and she was spoiled rotten.'

'Would they stop filming once she left?'

'No, they'd keep going till six or seven, but they were scheduled to do Nick Monteleone's reaction shots. Most actors want the actor they're playing a scene with to be there so they can have a true reaction, but believe me, Nick would have been *delighted* to have Lindsay go home. I was counting on that.'

'You weren't worried about Mrs Robertson?'

Eastern clapped his hand to his forehead. 'Oh my God. That's right. It was Friday!'

'Forget about her?'

'Totally. Did she see me?'

'Come on, East. You know I can't tell you that.' I tried to make it sound as though we were kids playing a hot game of Candyland and I couldn't break any of the rules. Before he could think: This is no fucking Candyland, I pushed him further. 'So you were at that spot just under the porch. What happened?'

'Well, she was there. Standing alongside the pool, talking on the portable phone. Except it wasn't her.'

'You couldn't hear the conversation, I guess.'

'How could I? There's always the sound of the ocean, and there was classical music playing through all those speakers.'

'And his back was toward you.'

'Yes, and he had on a white robe, like the one Lindsay always wears. Well, there are robes like that all over the house, for guests, but it looked like Lindsay. It *did*, Steve.'

'I'm sure it did. Short, small – and with the hood up.'

'He'd gone for a swim. His head was wet.'

'That was so dumb! If the hood had been down, I'd have known right away.'

'When did you know it was him?'

He swallowed hard. 'When I got home.'

'You shot him and then turned around and drove home?'

'Yes. That's what he told me to do. Drive right home, not too slow, not too fast. As if I could go fast, in that traffic! And then call him at the Bel-Air, and if he wasn't in, leave a message that I met with the casting director; that's if everything went okay. If there was any problem, I was supposed to leave a message that I was Fed Ex-ing another three copies of the script to him.' He uncrossed his legs and sat up straight. 'I can't tell you . . . those messages on my machine! First playing them back and hearing Sy's voice saying he was taking the seven o'clock flight. And then . . .' There was no doubt Easton was genuinely crying again, but overall his performance stank; he stood, walked over to the wall, rested his head against it and then pounded it with his fist, again and again. It was something Sy would have rejected in one of his movies. Overdone! Sy would have snapped at the director. Lose it! 'And then,' Easton went on, 'there was that kid, that PA saying that I "might want to know" that Sy was murdered at his house. God almighty!'

'I don't know what to say, East. What a trauma.'

He turned around and leaned against the wall for support. 'What do I do now, Steve?' He wiped his eyes with the lapel of his robe.

I ignored his question and asked one of my own. 'What about that screenplay you showed me? That *Night of the Matador* thing?'

'There were bookcases full of scripts in his house. I just grabbed one late Saturday, after the police left. You see, once I realized what I'd done, I wanted to emphasize that I had a wonderful, *continuing* relationship with Sy, that he was my mentor. I wanted all of you to think I could never kill him. Because what would I be without him?'

'Tell me about the Lindsay business,' I said. 'You were acting like you were crazy about her. You weren't, though, were you?'

'No. Of course not. I saw her for what she was.'

'But you pretended you were gone on her. Why?'

'I thought of that afterwards too,' he said, brightening a little at the recollection of his cleverness. 'If anyone remembered that talk at dailies about it being better if Lindsay was dead, and someone put two and two together . . . Well, they probably wouldn't have gotten four, but I thought if you – if the police – thought I was in love with her, I'd be counted out right away.'

'Actually, if we'd been adding and came up with Lindsay as the planned victim, you'd have been suspected right away.'

'Why?' He looked annoyed.

'Because you had an emotional tie to her.'

'That's stupid.'

'Well, that's cops for you. Stupid, unimaginative. The civil, service mentality. We do it by the book.'

A barely tolerant shake of the head. 'Some book.'

'Well,' I said, 'book or no book, we got you. Didn't we, Easton?'

'No!' He rushed over and grabbed the shoulders of my jacket. 'Steve, you're not going to do anything?' His mouth and eyes formed huge circles of astonishment. 'Steve! Are you crazy? I'm your brother.'

'I know.'

'How can you even think of doing something so terrible?'

'Get dressed,' I said. But he just stood there, right in front of me, still clutching the shoulder pads of my suit jacket. 'It's getting late. Come on.'

'*Think*. Think about what you want to do. What about Mother?'

'She's due home soon; you can explain to her what's happening. Or if she's stopping off someplace, I'll come back and sit down with her later. After I bring you in.'

He let his hands drop to his sides. He spoke softly, his voice full of gentleness and understanding. 'Steve, you have to understand. This will kill her.' The good son.

'I don't think so.'

'I know her much better than you do. She won't be able to survive a blow like this.'

'Yes, she will.'

'You think she's tough. She's not tough.'

'I know she's not. She's empty. She'll survive. Please, don't make me have to act any more like a cop than I'm already doing. Get dressed.'

Instead, he sat down in the straight-backed chair. 'What would it cost you to let me go?'

'Bonnie Spencer's life.'

'No, it wouldn't.'

'It would. There's a warrant out for her arrest.'

'Then how come she was here with you?'

'Because I was taking care of her. I didn't think she should be arrested.' I looked outside. The light was softening, the prelude to dusk.

'Do you want me arrested? Do you want to see me go to jail?' I was still holding the two leaves in my hand. I ran my finger over a stem, up the veins. 'Steve!' Easton cried out. 'Who the hell is she? How can you want to protect her and not want to protect me?'

'I'm protecting her because she's innocent.' I spoke more to the leaves than to Easton.

'But I'm your brother.'

'You're a killer.'

Easton got up and went over to the window. I inched forward, in case he made a move to jump, but he just stared out at the muted light. 'Nothing can bring Sy back now,' he said.

'I know.'

He turned to face me. 'I don't want that woman to go to jail for me.'

'Since when?'

'Listen to me. We can work something out. I can give her an alibi.' I didn't react. 'Wait. Hold on a second. Just listen.' Easton rubbed his hands together. 'Okay, first of all, I'll tell them that Sy was very fond of her, that things with Lindsay had soured, and that he really seemed to be happy with the ex-wife again – and made no bones about it. All right. I didn't say anything earlier because I had such a crush on Lindsay I couldn't bring myself to say anything that would make her look bad. I'll admit I was terribly wrong. I'll apologize all over myself. So they won't think the ex had any reason to kill him. And I'll say . . . I know! I stopped at a pay phone on my way home from the city and called her about something. Like about her screenplay, and she was there, at home. Answered the phone and – '

'No.'

'Why not?'

'Because it's so full of holes it's a joke. Because she's decent and honorable and this fake-alibi crap would make her sick. And because she doesn't have to lie. We have our perp, Easton.'

'Is it all so black and white to you? Don't you see any grays?'

'I wish this weren't happening,' I said slowly.

'It doesn't have to.'

'What choice do I have? I'm a cop. I know there are a million shades of gray in the world. I see them. But I can only act on black and white.'

Easton came over and put his arms around me. A real hug. Except for my old man when he was soused, I don't think, until that moment, I ever had an embrace from any member of my family. 'Steve,' he said, 'I need you so much. My life has been one mistake after another. One charade after another. And now this. I don't know who I thought I was, who I was hoping to be, but

I botched it. More than that. I did a terrible thing.' I stroked the back of his head. His hair was so much softer than mine. 'A wicked thing. I know that, but I'm so messed up, so weak, that I didn't have the courage to face up to it. Until now.' He let me out of his embrace and backed away. 'Just hear me out. Please?'

'Go ahead.'

'I know you think I'm useless, and you're right. I never, ever asked myself: What's really important? And even if I had, and came up with love or friendship or something like that, it probably wouldn't have mattered. You know that. I still would have gone for the razzle-dazzle. But now I really have to face the music. I can go to jail for the rest of my life. You *know* what jail is like.'

'Yes.'

'It's as bad as they say, isn't it?'

'Worse.'

'I swear to you, by all that's holy, that I'll spend the rest of my life making up for this terrible thing I've done.' He stood before me in that perfect gold and pink and blue light. 'I know we've never been close. But we are brothers. I'm not asking for special treatment, Steve, but I am asking – begging – that you give me a chance. Neither of us has ever had much of a shot at happiness, have we? I know I've lost that shot now, forever. But maybe I can have something, at least. Something from you.'

'What?'

'Forgiveness.'

I looked past him, out at the light. It was the magic hour. It comes and goes so fast. In movies, though, it returns just after dawn again, and then, once more, just before dusk. Twice a day, opportunities for wonder. But in real life, those moments that allow the possibility of grace hardly ever come at all.

If I brought my brother in, that would be the end of him. Forgiveness, he'd said. I could allow him the possibility of finding his own salvation. Because what he said was true: nothing could bring Sy back. And the beauty of it was, I wouldn't even have to stand in shamed silence and let Easton present his twisted, transparent alibi for Bonnie. I could just let him overpower me, escape, and disappear into a new life.

'Can't you forgive me, Steve? Haven't you ever done wrong?'

'Are you kidding? Most of my life has been wrong. That's no secret.'

'So? We're two of a kind.'

'No, East. Even when I was wrong, I knew there were laws. I knew there was a God.'

'But God forgives!'

'I know. And maybe God will forgive you, or has forgiven you. I can't know that. And maybe I, personally, can forgive you. But a life has been taken.'

'What are you saying?'

I let the leaves drop to the floor. 'I'm saying an apology won't do it.'

'You're going to send me to jail?'

'No; that's not my job. My job is much smaller. I'm just going to arrest you for the murder of Sy Spencer.'

'That's sending me to jail, damn it!'

'That's doing what I have to do.'

'I'll tell them you're setting me up to save that woman!'

'The rifle, East. The ballistics tests. Your rubber shoes with the Adelphi grass.'

'Someone else could have stolen that rifle. Or my thongs.'

'And put them back?'

'Try and prove it was me.'

'There was a man who bought bullets in a hardware store, who took target practice with an old Marlin .22 at a range near Riverhead the day before the murder. A nice-looking man in his late thirties. Don't you think witnesses will recognize his picture? Don't you think they'll be able to point him out in a lineup? In court?' I opened the door of his closet. 'Get ready, East. We have to go.'

He knew better than to try and fight me. He might have tried to run for it, but being what he was, he just scurried around the bedroom for a few hysterical seconds. Then he got dressed. What else could he do? Rush outside on a Friday night in the height of the season, in a short, ugly, grayish-brown shaving robe? No. My brother had too much class.

## *Chapter Twenty-Two*

In the end, I called Ray Carbone at home and asked him to please come over. I couldn't bring myself to handcuff Easton, lead him through the house and take him to Headquarters. Also, I realized that the fact the perpetrator had a brother on the Homicide Squad should be a single sentence in the last paragraph of the news story, not a nightmare headline – HOMICIDE COP ARRESTS KILLER BROTHER; MOTHER CRIES 'MY SON!'

My mother, of course, didn't cry anything of the sort. She came home around seven, a couple of minutes after Carbone arrived. She was a little tipsy from a martini or two with some rich lady with a dog name from her latest charity committee: Skip or Lolly or something. When she finally understood what was happening to Easton, she didn't scream or faint or have a heart attack.

All she did was collapse onto the couch. I got her some water. Right before he left, my brother bent down and kissed her goodbye. He aimed for her cheek but somehow missed and got her nose. He told her he was sorry, for her, not for himself. Carbone said he'd be at Headquarters all night if I needed him and then mumbled a few words to my mother about how bad he felt for her troubles.

I pulled up a footstool and sat in front of her. She was a fine-looking woman, with neat, even features, genuinely remarkable green-blue eyes, large and round, and a slender figure. After that momentary slump into the chair, her Emily Post spine straightened up. Her back was at a perfect ninety-degree angle to her lap. 'What should I do?' she asked me.

I told her Easton needed a lawyer. I went into the kitchen and looked up Bill Paterno's number in the phone book. She asked me if he was expensive, and I said yes, but he was very good, and when she called him, to tell him I'd speak to him tomorrow and work something out.

'Does that mean you'll pay for it?' she asked.

'Yeah.'

'Not "yeah".'

'Yes,' I said.

'Do you really think Easton did it?'

Yes, I told her, and explained the evidence we had against him. She asked if I thought a jury would find him guilty, and I said most likely Paterno would work out some sort of a deal with a guilty plea so there wouldn't have to be a trial, but that Easton would go to prison.

'I seem to have made a mess of things,' she said quietly.

'No. Easton did.'

Her excellent carriage became even more excellent. 'I can't understand it. He was never a troublemaker,' she said, not mentioning who had been. She looked so fine sitting there. Well, fine, but dated, like a 1952 Republican country club lady brought back in a time machine. Even now, stunned, probably anguished, all she was missing was a Rob Roy with a cherry and an Eisenhower button. 'He had no drive, but you can't fault someone for that.'

'No, you can't.'

'He didn't belong in the movie business,' she murmured. No one looked the way my mother did anymore. No one would take that amount of time to produce that strange, dated effect. She set her hair every night on fat wire rollers so it would fluff up and curl under in the chin-length pageboy she'd worn as long as I could remember. She tweezed away most of her eyebrows and redrew them into a thin, light-brown line. Her makeup was pale powder, red rouge and matching lipstick, a little smudged after her martinis. Her nails, filed short and oval, were red too. 'He should have gone into banking. Not that he could have been a bank president. I would never deceive myself. But he kept trying to be a salesman, and he couldn't sell anyone anything. And then movies, with all those people. They're so hard. He wasn't cut out to deal with them.'

'No, he wasn't.'

'I thought he liked that man, though. The one he killed.' I explained how Easton had been doing Sy's bidding, how he thought he was shooting at Lindsay. She asked: 'Why didn't he just say "I won't do it"?'

'I don't know Mom.'

'Well, neither do I.'

I asked her if she wanted me to makc her something to eat. No, she wasn't hungry, and she'd be all right. I knew that meant she wanted to be alone, but I asked if she wanted me to stay the night, or if she wanted to come over to my place. She said no thank you, and yes, she would call me if she needed me. I told her I'd be over first thing in the morning.

'It will be in all the newspapers,' she said. 'On the television too.'

'It will be a bad couple of days,' I said. 'Well, in terms of publicity. I know it will be bad for you for much longer than that.'

'Do you think they'll fire me?'

'No. You're too valuable to them. And I think most people will go out of their way to be understanding.'

'They won't understand, though. They'll just be polite. Deep down, they'll all think I did something wrong that made him turn out this way.' She stood. 'I'd like to be alone now.'

'I'm so sorry, Mom.'

And then she almost knocked me over. 'Why should you be sorry? It's not your fault. You didn't kill anyone. Your brother did.' But before I could work up a major case of filial sentiment and possibly reach for her hand, or gush, I'll always be there for you, Mom, no matter what, my mother added: 'I'd like you to leave.' So I said good night and so did she.

Ray Carbone and Thighs were getting Easton's confession on videotape, and it was being transmitted, live, in living but somewhat purplish color, on the TV monitor in Frank Shea's office. Carbone was asking, 'Did you pay cash for the bullets or charge them?' and my brother, showing how ingeniously he and Sy had planned

Lindsay's murder, replied: 'Cash. Don't leave tracks: that was our motto.'

Shea started to explain to me, 'You'll see the beginning of the tape, how we read him his rights. We gave him every chance – '

I cut him off. 'A guy wants to talk, you can't muzzle him.'

'How's your mother taking it?'

'She's numb.' I didn't mention that the condition was probably congenital. But then, because Shea and I had been at each other's throats over the case and there was so much bad blood, I decided I'd better show him I was a decent guy. 'I'd be with her now, but she asked me to leave. Really wanted to be alone. I think she probably was going to fall apart and wanted to spare me.' That image of my mother going out of control and wanting to protect me had nothing much to do with reality, but it did make us sound like a normal family. Well, until you looked at the talking head on the TV screen who was telling Carbone that yes he'd cleaned the .22 at home, but when he got to the range the lever was so stiff he could hardly move it, so one of the men there – a black man with a goatee – helped him. I said to Shea: 'Listen to him Jesus, I can't believe we're from the same gene pool.'

He got up and walked to the TV. His gold chains clanged. 'I'll catch this later,' he said. 'Unless you really want to watch, but between you and me' – he was using his Compassionate Leader voice – 'I think you should spare yourself.'

'You can turn it off,' I agreed.

He did and then came back, stood behind my chair and put his hand on my shoulder. 'You want to take some vacation time, Steve?'

'Probably.'

'You've got it. Ray thinks you ought to see Dr Nettles, the new department shrink, get some counselling. Preventive medicine. That's up to you. Ray says she's good. I met her. She's got a face like a bulldog.' He clanged his way back to his big leather chair and sat down. 'Now listen, you've got my apology. The drinking thing. The saying you're in love with that Spencer woman.' I started to worry. What if, finally, it had all been too much, even for Bonnie? What if, now that it was over, she wanted to leave it all behind, go back to her mountains? 'That fucking Robby Kurz,' he breathed.

'Robby's in the squad room,' I said.

'I know. Did you have it out with him?'

'No. I didn't even go in. I'm wiped. My fuse is so short I'd blow in two seconds, and I don't want to do that. There are more serious matters than him saying I'm a drunk. And they're your territory, not mine.'

'The Bonnie hair,' he said.

'Yeah, the Bonnie hair.'

He picked up his phone, pressed the intercom and said, 'I'd like to see you, Robby. No, now.' He hung up and looked me right in the eye. 'Listen, I'm sympathetic to what you're going through. A family tragedy. But I won't mince words. The Suffolk County Police Department is a paramilitary organization. You know what that means?'

'You're the captain and I'm not.'

'That's right. Sometimes you seem to have some trouble with that concept. Now, you have a personal beef against this guy, and we may have a departmental beef. Guess which gets priority tonight when he walks through – ' At that instant, Robby walked through the door. 'Sit down, Robby.' It was an order, not an invitation, and Robby, after nodding at me, sat. Sitting across from Frank Shea's black-Irish, lounge-lizard good looks, Robby looked even puffier and pastier than usual; he was starting to resemble one of his crullers. 'You almost ruined Brady's career,' Shea said.

'I didn't mean to.'

'So how come you call him a drunk?'

'Because I thought he was.'

'Why?'

'I thought he was acting in an erratic manner, and I thought I smelled liquor on him.'

'How was I erratic, you weasel son of a bitch fucker?'

'Shut up, Brady,' Shea said. Then, remembering I was in the middle of a Major Personal Crisis, he added, 'Please.' He turned back to Robby. 'I won't call you a liar. But I question your powers of observation.'

'I know the tests say I was wrong. So I apologize.'

No one seemed to expect me to accept or decline the apology, so I just sat back and shut my eyes for a second. I wanted to tell him my back door was open, so they could get Moose, who might need more water or a walk.

'Let's get to the Bonnie hair, Robby,' Shea was saying. 'We had *everyone* on this case. Our best people. We examine, reexamine, re-reexamine the area where the perp stood.' He paused, to indicate that out of deference to me he was not using the perp's name. 'We find zip in the hair department. And then the next week: A miracle! Crucial evidence! One of Bonnie Spencer's hairs – with a root, no less, so we can get a DNA reading on it.'

'Are you saying I planted it, Frank?' Robby asked.

'I'm saying Ray Carbone checked the plastic thing we got back from the lab and the seal looked a little funny and one hair seemed to be missing. Would you call it a plant?'

'No. Obviously the lab lost a hair. You of all people should know they're not perfect.'

I thought: What if Bonnie doesn't want me? What if she thinks I'm too unstable?

'Why would Bonnie Spencer's hair be at the exact spot the perp stood if Bonnie Spencer wasn't the perp?'

'Maybe she just passed by.' You could hardly hear Robby's voice anymore. And he was slipping lower and lower into his chair. The only part of him holding up was his sprayed hairdo.

'That's your explanation?' Shea boomed. 'She was just taking a stroll around the six acres of grounds and her hair caught on that one infinitesimal little spot?' Robby didn't reply. Shea leaned forward. 'Let me ask you something. Do you think you're any better than any of the shits we lock up?'

'I deserve a fair hearing.' It sounded like Robby had already talked to a lawyer.

'I'm sure the department will give you one.'

'Thank you.'

'But as far as Homicide goes, you know what?'

'Frank – '

'Pack up your pencils.'

As far as I know, Robby Kurz did not pack up his pencils. He certainly didn't say goodbye. He just left for good.

I took my brother's tinny excuse for a convertible, a Mustang, went back to my house and got Moose. She sat in the passenger seat, raised her snout and let the rush of air blow her hairy ears back. When we stopped at a light, she gave some Manhattan yuppies in a Volvo station wagon the patronizing glance of a glamours dame who only travels top-down.

I pulled into Bonnie's driveway. At last the bureaucratic wheels were turning: they had discontinued the surveillance. Her Jeep was in the garage. The house was dark, and the front and back doors were locked. I rang the bell a few times, but there as no answer. I knew she had to be at Gideon's, but I was scared. I kept thinking crazy things, like what if she'd gone home, tripped on one of her stupid scatter rugs and cracked her head and was lying inside, dead. No. Then my car would still be there. But what if she'd hit an oil patch and the Jag went out of control and she'd gone off a bridge, or gone up in flames? The only sound came from wild ducks, and from the forced laughter over cocktails on the back deck at her neighbor's, Wendy Bubbleface.

It took me about ten minutes to get Moose back in the car. She was home and saw no reason to leave. She took a dump, chased a rabbit, then lay down on the front lawn. I made an ass of myself, clapping my hands and calling, 'Here, girl! C'mon, Moose! Oooh, let's go for a ride!' and whistling. She wouldn't budge. At last, I hefted her, all hundred pounds of her, and carried her back to the car.

It was dark when I finally found Gideon's house, one of those renovated barns set back a couple of hundred feet from the road. There was a small sign on a strip of barn siding that said 'Friedman-Sterling,' but Friedman and Sterling had planted so much fucking English ivy tht I drove past it at least five times until I spotted it.

I opened the car door, but before I could get out, Moose leapt over me, then sat, waiting, tongue dangling, for me to join her. But I couldn't get out. I reknotted my tie, then loosened it, then took it off, took my jacket off, rolled up my shirt sleeves, then got dressed again.

Maybe she'd taken an overdose of sleeping pills, thinking I was going to marry Lynne and she'd never see me again.

I wanted to hold her in my arms. I wanted to take her over to Germy's to watch the DiMaggio video and tell him, This is my girl.

I thought, I shouldn't be driving my brother's damn car, since Easton had stowed the rifle in the trunk. Now it had my prints and dog hair. The lab guys would be pissed.

My heart began to pound. She'd be in there, but she'd refuse to see me, and Gideon's boyfriend would stand at the door, his hand on his hip, and sneer: 'Bonnie's flying to the Coast tomorrow to sell her story for a CBS Movie of the Week and she's on the phone with her new agent and cannot be disturbed. Ta-ta.'

Or she wouldn't be there. She'd be on her way to the airport, to go to Utah. She'd stay with one of her brothers for a while, until her house was sold, then buy a cabin ten thousand feet high in some mountain by a trout stream. She wouldn't answer my letters or phone calls. I'd finally go out there and track her down, but she'd run out the back door up the mountains and wouldn't come back until I'd gone. The next spring, after the thaw, they'd find her. Dead. She'd frozen in February. She'd forgotten how hard winters in the mountains could be. She hadn't chopped enough wood for the stove.

I was so upset by the thought of her decomposing body that I didn't see Gideon until he was right next to the car. 'Is Bonnie here?' I demanded. 'Is she all right?'

'She's fine,' Gideon said cautiously. I guess I looked a little nuts. 'She's sleeping.' Moose, the town slut, had already transferred her allegiance to Gideon and was licking his hand.

'I guess she must be pretty tired,' I mumbled.

'Do you want to come in for a minute?'

For a barn, it was a nice place, with a vaulted ceiling and a lot of beams going to interesting places. Gideon introduced me to his friend, Jeff, who looked like a bouncer in a very rough nightclub. He stayed just long enough to shake hands, say 'Pleased to make yo' 'quaintance' and give me a thorough once-over; my guess was he could hardly wait for me to leave, so he and Gideon could launch into an exhaustive analysis.

A giant black iron chandelier hung from the main beam; it had cut-out sheep and cows and pigs all over it. Upstairs, there were closed doors off a landing that had once been the hayloft. 'Bonnie's in the middle room,' Gideon said, when he saw me looking up. I thought he would tell me not to trifle with her affections or something, but he just said how sorry he was about it being my brother. I told him my mother was calling Paterno, but that my brother had already given a videotaped confession – probably less because he wanted to make a clean breast of things than that he wanted to be thought of as pleasant company. And I told him about Easton's sick pride, that he'd planned the whole thing with Sy Spencer, big shot. Just the two of them. Sy and Easton, partners. I said I couldn't believe my brother had been so willing to let Bonnie take the fall for him. Gideon said, Take it easy. It's over now. He added that Shea had called Paterno and said they were rescinding the warrant and to tell Mrs Spencer sorry for any inconvenience.

'Do you think she'll be all right?' I asked him.

'She's strong.'

'I know.'

'But it's going to take a long time.'

'Do you mind if I go up and see her?' I asked.

'Once we knew it was officially over, after Bill Paterno called . . .' Gideon hesitated. 'Bonnie said you might drop by. She asked me to thank you for all you've done for her, but that you and she had agreed earlier that it would be best if you didn't see each other again.'

'I want to see her.'

'And I want to protect her.' We tried to stare each other down. 'It seems we're at an impasse,' he said, 'and since it's an impasse on my territory, I'm going to have to ask you to leave.' He stood.

So did I. 'I just want to tell her something.'

'I don't think that would be advisable.'

'Fuck you, Friedman.'

'Fuck *you*, Brady.'

I tried to count up to ten, to think of something else to say, but I only made it to two. 'Look, I love her.'

'You love her?' Gideon repeated. 'You must be a very loving man. You love the other one too.'

'If it's any of your goddamned business, I don't love the other one, and as a matter of fact and of law, Counselor, the other one isn't the other one anymore and the position is vacant. Now can I go up and see Bonnie?'

'Be my guest,' he said.

I could sense her waking as I opened the door. I came in and sat on the edge of the bed. 'You're beautiful,' I said.

'Sure. It's pitch black in here.' Bonnie stuck her hand out and groped for a lamp. She turned it on and squeezed her eyes shut at the light. She looked like Mr Magoo. 'Now say it.'

'You're beautiful. I love you. What was the third thing?'

'I'm a truly fine person.' The base of the lamp was a big china chicken. She turned it off.

'You're a truly fine person,' I said.

'I told Gideon not to let you up here.'

'I told him I was going to tell you I loved you, so I became his pal. Anything I want. His house is my house. His chicken lamp is my chicken lamp.' I turned it on again and pulled down the sheet a little. She'd taken off my T-shirt.

She pulled the sheet all the way up. 'Listen, I guess you'll be hearing this a lot, but I'm sorry about your brother. I'm sure it's going to be very painful for your family, and it's too bad you can't be spared that.'

'Thank you. It's too bad you couldn't have been spared your pain.'

'Thank you,' she said. 'I don't want to seem insensitive, but I'd like you to leave now.'

'Why? Are you going to cry or something?'

Bonnie gave me an angry nudge. Some nudge. It practically knocked me off the bed. 'You want to hang around and watch?'

'Yeah.'

'Well, I don't want you to. I want you to go.'

'I can't. I promised Gideon I'd ask you to marry me.'

'Well, ask me and then get out.'

'All right. Will you marry me?' Somehow, all of sudden, she knew. She didn't make any wisecracks about my having a previous engagement. She didn't tell me to leave. She just said 'Yes,' but then she told me I couldn't kiss her because she had sleep breath. I kissed her anyway. It was a sweet and beautiful kiss. After it was over, she asked, 'Am I *really* beautiful? Objectively.'

'No.'

'Am I *really* a truly fine person?'

'You're not bad.'

I stood up, took of my clothes and got into bed.

'Do you *really* love me?'

'More than anything in the world, Bonnie.'

'I've known that for years, Stephen.'

And together we turned off the chicken lamp, and we began our life.